Catherine Cookson was born in Tyne Dock, the illegitimate daughter of a poverty-stricken woman, Kate, whom she believed to be her older sister. She began work in service but eventually moved south to Hastings where she met and married a local grammar-school master. At the age of forty she began writing about the lives of the working-class people with whom she had grown up, using the place of her birth as the background to many of her novels.

Although originally acclaimed as a regional writer – her novel *The Round Tower* won the Winifred Holtby award for the best regional novel of 1968 – her readership soon began to spread throughout the world. Her novels have been translated into more than a dozen languages and more than 50,000,000 copies of her books have been sold in Corgi alone. Thirteen of her novels have been made into successful television dramas, and more are planned.

Catherine Cookson's many bestselling novels have established her as one of the most popular of contemporary women novelists. After receiving an OBE in 1985, Catherine Cookson was created a Dame of the British Empire in 1993. She and her husband Tom now live near Newcastle-upon-Tyne.

'Catherine Cookson's novels are about hardship, the intractability of life and of individuals, the struggle first to survive and next to make sense of one's survival. Humour, toughness, resolution and generosity are Cookson virtues, in a world which she often depicts as cold and violent. Her novels are weighted and driven by her own early experiences of illegitimacy and poverty. this is what gives them power. In the specialised world of women's popular fiction, cookson has created her own territory'

Helen Dunmore, *The Times*

BOOKS BY CATHERINE COOKSON

NOVELS

Kate Hannigan
The Fifteen Streets
Colour Blind
Maggie Rowan
Rooney
The Menagerie
Slinky Jane
Fanny McBride
Fenwick Houses
Heritage of Folly
The Garment
The Fen Tiger
The Blind Miller
House of Men
Hannah Massey
The Long Corridor
The Unbaited Trap
Katie Mulholland
The Round Tower
The Nice Bloke
The Glass Virgin
The Invitation
The Dwelling Place
Feathers in the Fire
Pure as the Lily
The Mallen Streak
The Mallen Girl
The Mallen Litter
The Invisible Cord
The Gambling Man
The Tide of Life
The Slow Awakening
The Iron Façade
The Girl
The Cinder Path
Miss Martha Mary Crawford

The Man Who Cried
Tilly Trotter
Tilly Trotter Wed
Tilly Trotter Widowed
The Whip
Hamilton
The Black Velvet Gown
Goodbye Hamilton
A Dinner of Herbs
Harold
The Moth
Bill Bailey
The Parson's Daughter
Bill Bailey's Lot
The Cultured Handmaiden
Bill Bailey's Daughter
The Harrogate Secret
The Black Candle
The Wingless Bird
The Gillyvors
My Beloved Son
The Rag Nymph
The House of Women
The Maltese Angel
The Year ot the Virgins
The Golden Straw
Justice is a Woman
The Tinker's Girl
A Ruthless Need
The Obsession
The Upstart
The Branded Man
The Bonny Dawn
The Bondage of Love
The Desert Crop
The Lady on My Left

THE MARY ANN STORIES

A Grand Man
The Lord and Mary Ann
The Devil and Mary Ann
Love and Mary Ann

Life and Mary Ann
Marriage and Mary Ann
Mary Ann's Angels
Mary Ann and Bill

FOR CHILDREN

Matty Doolin
Joe and the Gladiator
The Nipper
Rory's Fortune
Our John Willie

Mrs Flannagan's Trumpet
Go Tell It To Mrs Golightly
Lanky Jones
Nancy Nutall and the Mongrel
Bill and the Mary Ann Shaughnessy

AUTOBIOGRAPHY

Our Kate
Catherine Cookson Country

Let Me Make Myself Plain
Plainer Still

The Bonny Dawn

Catherine Cookson

CORGI BOOKS

THE BONNY DAWN
A CORGI BOOK : 0 552 14531 9

Originally published in Great Britain by Bantam Press,
a division of Transworld Publishers Ltd

PRINTING HISTORY
Bantam Press edition published 1996
Corgi edition published 1997

Set in 11 on 14 pt Century Schoolbook by
Hewer Text Composition Services, Edinburgh

Corgi Books are published by Transworld Publishers Ltd,
61–63 Uxbridge Road, London W5 5SA,
in Australia by Transworld Publishers (Australia) Pty Ltd,
15–25 Helles Avenue, Moorebank, NSW 2170
and in New Zealand by Transworld Publishers (NZ) Ltd,
3 William Pickering Drive, Albany, Auckland.

Reproduced, printed and bound in Great Britain by
Cox & Wyman Ltd, Reading, Berks.

One

The alarm went off in the middle of her dream.
She was dreaming she was dancing, not the
twist or jiving – these were beginning to be
considered old-fashioned at the club – but
something more old-fashioned still: she was
gliding to music that seemed to come out of
the clouds, for there was no orchestra that
she could see and no roof to the ballroom.
She knew there was a clear glass floor and she
could see her legs reflected in it, but not those
of her partner. She knew she was dancing with
a man and that she liked him, but when she
looked at the floor she could see no partner.
It was as a feeling of keen disappointment
was penetrating her dream that the alarm

went off. It brought her spiralling up from the glass floor, through the roofless room and on to the bed, where she clutched wildly at the pillow. Pushing her hands underneath it, she swiftly switched off the muffled tinkling, then turned on her back and lay gasping, her eyes wide, staring upwards into the darkness while her ears strained towards the wall which divided her room from that of her parents. She listened; but when no sound could be heard through the wall, slowly, like a deflating tyre, she let herself sink back again into the hollow her body had made in the bed.

It was four o'clock. Eeh! durst she do it? Durst she get up, creep out of the house at this hour? What if she wakened them? Lord, there'd be a set-to if that were to happen. And what would she say? Yes, what would she say? She could never tell them the truth; they would want to lock her in. A little giggle stirred inside her and mounted into a laugh, and she pressed her finger to her lips. Then sitting up she stared towards the glimmer of light at the window. She was surprised to find that she wasn't tired, even though she had danced from eight till twenty to eleven. Had she been only a quarter of an hour alone with him? Had all this been arranged in a quarter of an hour? When they had left the club he hadn't believed it when she said she had to be in by eleven. She had known he thought she was spinning a yarn and just wanted to walk with him a bit longer. He had not tried to kiss her or do any necking, and somehow it was a relief. It was nice not to have to fight when somebody was taking you home, to slap their hands from the front of your dress, to stop their fingers working in your palms. If her dad knew what went on there he would never let her go near the club; although it didn't go on in the club, it was after. And in a way she was glad she had to be in by eleven for she knew she wasn't up to coping with them, as Nancy Leary was with her parents, or Janet Castleton with hers. They could enjoy themselves and go as far as they wanted and hold their own, but she knew she wouldn't be able to. She was always afraid of passing out and leaving herself at the mercy of one or other of them. When she used to go to church, that was before she left school, she would pass out on a Sunday morning, nearly always at the same time, and then her dad put his foot down and wouldn't let her go any more. But that was years ago, years and years and years, when she was fifteen. She laughed to herself again for thinking it was years since she was at school. It was only two years ago.

Well, if she was going to go she had better get up.

Bridget Stevens stood on the bedside mat for a moment, biting at her lip, still undecided; and then with quick jerky movements she was dragging her clothes on, the same clothes that she had taken off last night when she came back from the dance. She hadn't worn a dance frock; she had made that mistake only once, and had sat out all night and not one of the lads had asked her on to the floor. No, her dance dress consisted of a full skirt with a stiff buckram petticoat attached and a V-necked cotton jumper with half sleeves. Her coat lay where she had flung it over the bottom of the bed, and after putting it on she picked up, not the stiletto-heeled, long pointed-toed shoes in which she had danced, but a slipper-like pair that lay under the bed and, carrying these in her hand, she crept to the door.

On the landing, she had to pass her parents' door, and then their Willie's door, which was across the little landing and next to that of the bathroom. When she reached the top of the stairs she opened her mouth wide and silently drew in a long gulp of air. Then cautiously, step by step, she crept down the stairs. She did not attempt to leave the house by the front door opposite, but turned down a narrow hallway into the kitchen, and here, standing by the table, she again opened her mouth wide and gulped air, but not so silently this time. Then, after unbolting the back door she opened it and closed it softly after her. She had forgotten her watch but she heard the clock on St Nicholas's Church striking the quarter: a quarter past four. She would be back at a quarter past six and no one would be any the wiser, for they would still be sleeping; they would sleep till nine o'clock this morning, because it was Sunday. She had never known her mother or father or their Willie rise before the paper-boy came on a Sunday. At nine o'clock on any other morning of the week the house was empty, for they would all have gone to work, her mother included, but Sunday was a day of rest and they took this literally; until nine o'clock anyway.

South Scardyke was the new part of the town and was covered with council houses. The Stevenses had moved here three years ago from East Scardyke when they were pulling the houses down in that quarter. Brid Stevens liked living in South Scardyke, no matter how her dad went on about it, and he did go on about it, proclaiming that her mother had never had to go out to work when they lived at the east side. His money had been sufficient for them all then, but now, even though the four of them were working, it still wasn't sufficient. Brid liked the cleanliness of Cornford Terrace, she liked the cleanliness of the house, she liked having a bathroom, especially when she could get it to herself for an hour or even more. She liked the view from the back bedroom window, their Willie's window, for it looked right across the open ground to the hills, and she knew that if you could have sawn the top off Stockwell Hill you would have had a glimpse of the sea beyond. The sea, the beach and the cliffs were only two miles from South Scardyke, and she was on her way there now. Well, not actually to the sea but to gaze at it from the top of Stockwell Hill.

There was a grass verge along the edge of the pavement, with young trees studding it here and there, and she kept to the verge to dull her steps, in case some light sleeper, hearing footsteps in the street, might look out from behind the curtains. You never could tell, for some people couldn't sleep. She thought this was very strange although she knew it was true: she herself couldn't get enough sleep, yet here she was at a quarter past four on a Sunday morning off to see the dawn and to see the sun rise over the sea from the top of Stockwell Hill. It was daft, wasn't it? She laughed inside and her stomach contracted with excitement. When she reached the end of the street she cut through a gap between the railings of two houses, which brought her to the recreation ground. As she crossed this open space she felt a little fear: this was the place where men waylaid girls at night. But the night was past, the street lamps were out, and the dawn was coming. She felt the light beginning to creep around her.

When she saw the grey outline of Coster Road School looming ahead, she knew she must hurry still more or she'd miss him. Her hurrying came to an abrupt stop when, without seeing anyone, she heard the monotonous tread of steps coming towards her along the road. That was a policeman. Quickly she turned up the side cut by the infants' passage, skirted the railings around the playground, passed the old church of St Nicholas, and then abruptly she was in the country and walking between the high hedges, making for

Stockwell Hill. And she became more excited and at the same time frightened than at any time since the alarm had wakened her.

Joe Lloyd had been waiting on Stockwell Hill for more than half an hour now, sitting in the same spot he always occupied. The grass at this spot was worn away and the ground hollowed into a scoop where, years ago, his father had raked the earth away with his bare hands to make him cushy. He hadn't been four years old when his father had first brought him to the top of Stockwell Hill, and early in the morning at that; not at four o'clock, no, not as early as that, but around about seven. And it was something for a youngster to be got out of bed and dressed and walk all this way at that age. It had taken them a solid hour on that first walk, but on their last they made it in twenty-five minutes. The last time his father and he had climbed to this point of contact with God, as his father had once called it, the last time they had come up here was just three days before he was killed. Joe felt no pain now that his father was no longer with him; there was only an emptiness, and this was enclosed within some chamber deep in the private part of his mind. You could not go on feeling and suffering as he had done without something dreadful happening, such as going mad. At one time he had thought he *would* go mad. His mother had said, 'Come out of the pit; that will help.' But he had refused. Among other things, he had inherited certain principles from his father. His father had not been like some pit-men, yelling down the work that sustained him in life. So he had said to his mother, 'No; what was good enough for Dad is good enough for me.' It was strange, he knew, that he should say this, and he knew his mother, too, considered it strange.

It was usually said from the opposite direction: it was usually the father who said, 'What is good enough for me should be good enough for you.' He had nothing against the pit: he could leave the pit the morrow if he wanted to; but he didn't want to, and this was strange, too, because he loved the light, he loved the dawns and sunsets. He did not so much care for the high noons and the blaze of the day, but he liked the shadows when they were pale and fresh in the morning, and he liked them when they were tired at night.

They had sat side by side at this very spot that last day, and his father had talked to him about women. He had spoken to him gently about women. There were other ways to talk about women and Joe knew this already: he had learned a lot in the six months he had been at the pit-head. His father had said quietly, 'I'm not going into details now for I guess you know as much about that side of it as I do; you young 'uns do, the day. Aw, but I think they always did. Woman's the great curiosity shop of life. You wouldn't be a lad if you didn't start groping that way from early on, so we won't go over old ground. But I'd just like to say this, lad, and I'm saying it from experience an' things I've thought out, things that have always been difficult to put into words. Yet now, on a morning like this, they are clear in me mind, and this is one of them, lad. When you go looking for a wife – not just for a lass mind, that's different – when you go lookin' for a wife try to see her as she'll be, say . . . five years on. You'd do better still if you'd try for ten. Now this sounds easy, but it isn't, lad. It's a very difficult thing to do, because if you're looking for a wife you're half in love already and it's gumming up your eyeballs. One tip I'll give you. Never take a lass who says she can't stand a liar, for you can bet your life she doesn't know what the truth is. When they're emphatic about things like that, look out. Look for some gentle streak in her, but don't be misled if she goes all goofy over dogs. By! I've seen some bitches who love dogs.' At this, they had both laughed, they had fallen on their backs and laughed, and when they sat up the tears were running down their cheeks, and his father had pushed him with his thick squat hand and, light with his laughter, he had fallen over again, and there had ended the one and only session of talking about the facts of life.

His father had been a wonderful man. Wonderful was the only word that seemed to fit him. He had been a gentleman ... gentle, the kind that meant tender, yet he could be firm and indomitable about some things. He had been that about not letting his wife go out to work. She had suggested it only once, and Joe remembered his father saying, 'You've got a husband, a bairn and a house, and if these can't keep you goin', lass, then there's something wrong.' It was the quiet way his father had said this that closed the subject for good. His mother had adored his father. Had, was the word; she could obviously adore him no longer.

Joe moved his buttocks in the mould of earth. Only three years had passed and she was thinking of marrying again. He couldn't believe it. The thought still made him sick. A fortnight ago he had first guessed what she was at when he came up on her giving tea to Mr Bishop, the grocer from the high town, and he had wanted to push his fists in Mr Bishop's face. Yet, prior to this, he had always liked the man. After his father went, Mr Bishop had been very good to them. But to have him in the house in his father's place, that was a different kettle of fish. It was because this thought was still troubling him that he had come over from their village of Johnson's Cross into South Scardyke a week gone Saturday night and looked in at the club: he was wanting company, for his mother was no longer his company. If he had sat with her or taken her to the pictures her mind would have been on Mr Bishop. He knew that. So he had made for the club and there had met up again with Sandy Palmer and his lot. Sandy Palmer, Ronnie Fitzsimmons, Clarky Leach, Charlie Talbot, all the lads who had gone to school with him. He was the only one from his class who had taken to the pits and he knew that they thought he was soft on top for doing this.

At school, because of the difference in their

height, he had been a little afraid of Sandy Palmer, and now three years later, Sandy had put on another four or five inches. He was six-foot two if he was an inch, whereas he himself had remained practically static. He was five-foot four and a half, and he knew that, like his father before him, he would remain five-foot four and a half. But he was no longer afraid of Sandy Palmer. Yet that wasn't strictly true. He had a certain feeling about Sandy, a feeling that warned him that it was better if they didn't meet, if their paths didn't cross. And perhaps they wouldn't have crossed again if he hadn't seen young Brid Stevens. He remembered her just faintly from their school days, just faintly because she had altered so much. Her eyes were grey and her forehead wide, and her hair was long and thick and swung away from her back as she danced. It was brown when it lay still, but it was gold when it moved. Her thighs were firm and her breasts were high and her face was kind, and she was all of an inch taller than him.

He had been to few dances. When he was fourteen he had gone to the club and one of the women had given some of the lads lessons. She had shown them how to waltz and fox-trot, and he had rather liked her. The club was just beginning then, but soon others came and before long there was nothing but rock-'n'-roll. He had never liked rock-'n'-roll. He didn't like to see girls wriggling like worms on the one spot. He thought they looked like corkscrews that never went through the corks. So when he had asked Brid Stevens to dance and without a word she had stood in front of him and started to wriggle, he had looked at her, then put his arm about her waist and taken her off surprisingly into a clumsy one-step. But in this he had not been able to cover the length of the room before they were pushed and knocked and joggled by the writhing bodies of the jivers. It was jive now, and he had brought ridicule upon them both because he couldn't do it.

During last week he had been to George's Coffee Shop twice and met Brid there. Then, without any dating being done, they had met again last night at the club, and as he looked at her he had tried to visualise what she would look like in five years' time or, say, ten. But he couldn't see her then, he could only see her now, and he knew that he wanted her, wanted her as his father must have wanted his mother, and he said to himself, as his father would have done, 'Now, no nonsense, go slow and careful, and don't frighten her off.' It was odd that he should think this way about her, because she was a regular at the club. She was seventeen and she knew Sandy Palmer and his crowd, and yet he knew that if he put a foot wrong she would be gone. Not out of the club, or South Scardyke, but out of this world that they were both tentatively entering.

At this moment he thought of his father with great tenderness and he got to his feet and looked over the brow of the hill towards the main road, and as he did so he said to himself, 'God, let her come.' And it was as though God had heard him, for instantly he saw a dark shape running along the main road. It disappeared from the sight of his straining eyes for a second behind some shrubs, and when it appeared again he had the urge to run to her as would a little lad who had not yet reached the self-conscious state of knowing he was no longer a lad. He remained still, watching her shape bounding towards him through the gathering light. And then she was standing a short distance from him, so that he had only to put out his hand with his elbow bent to touch her. She was gasping, and he could feel her hot breath on his face; even the warmth of her body came to him, she stood so close. For a moment he reverted to the naturalness of a child and said, 'I thought you weren't coming. Yes, I did.'

'Oh, but I said I would.'

'Aye, I know you did.'

'Well,' – she was still panting – 'I'm here.'

She had moved back from him, and the distance returned the meeting to some normality.

'You're not too soon.'

'No?'

'No, it'll be up any minute.'

'Will it?'

She turned to look towards the sea, but she couldn't make it out. It was as if it wasn't there. But she knew she had only to run down this hill to reach the edge of the tide. Everything was grey and violet. The grey she knew to be the water, the violet the sky. She felt strange, a bit weird, elated. She had the silly desire to laugh.

'Come and sit down. You put a coat on; that was sensible. Look, there's an armchair ready-made.' He pointed to the place where he had been sitting. 'I've warmed it for you.'

When she sat in the hollow she made a sound, half laugh, half an exclamation of amazement at finding the earth so comfortable. She pressed her back into the shape.

'I've never been up so early in me life.'

'No?' He was now sitting on his hunkers by her side, and they were staring at each other full in the face.

'No. It was four o'clock when I got up. The alarm scared me to death. What time did you get up?'

'I've never been to bed.'

'What!' Her chin was drawn into the soft flesh of her neck.

'No; I missed the last bus and I walked.'

'Aw.'

'Aw, nothing. I think I missed it on purpose, just to give meself an excuse. I like walking.'

'But what is it? It must be three . . . four miles from our place to your place.'

'Four and a half. But I didn't go all that way, I came here.'

She screwed round in the earth. 'You mean you've been here all night?'

He nodded, his lips tight and his eyes bright.

'No!'

'There's a bit of a cave down yonder; it's as warm as toast at this time of the year. Me Dad and me spent many a night there.'

'Your Dad?'

'Yes.'

'What did your mother say?'

'Oh, she got used to it; she didn't mind. She used to laugh and say we were no more than a couple of bairns.' His face sobered. 'He's been dead three years now.'

'Your Dad?'

'Yes.'

'I'm sorry. But you still come and sleep out in the cave?'

'Now and again. Not very often, except like last night. It seemed silly to walk the rest of the way home and then come back.'

'Did you think I'd come then?' She was looking towards the sea.

'I hoped you would.' He too was now looking towards the sea; and he exclaimed excitedly, 'Look at the colour. See it spreading along like hot jam slipping over the edge of the table?'

'Yes; yes.' She could see the picture of his description more clearly than the deep blushed horizon, and yet she said, 'What an odd description for the rising sun.'

'Me mother spilt a basin of warm jam she was putting into tarts one day and it ran right along the edge of the kitchen table. I never see that streak of colour unless I see that jam spreading over the whole place.'

She cast her eyes swiftly at him. He was new, nice, delightful somehow. She hadn't known before that she wanted to hear someone talk in this fashion, and yet why else had she gone to the coffee bar on the Monday night following the first Saturday she had seen him? That was only a week ago, a week last night. She must have seen him before when they were at school because he had told her he remembered her, although she couldn't remember him. But from the moment he had asked her to dance and Sandy Palmer and Clarky Leach and the rest had bustled them because they weren't jiving, she had wanted to see him again. She had liked the sound of his voice right from the start. She was sorry that he wasn't as tall as she was, having always told herself she would never go out with a boy who wasn't as tall as herself. But he looked nice somehow, and the way he held himself brought his eyes on a level with her own. Perhaps, she thought, it was the way she did her hair that made her appear taller than him, but she really knew it wasn't. When she was dancing with him his head looked big, big enough to fit a man much

taller, and his shoulders looked as though they
belonged to a six-footer. He had a wave in his
hair that started at his brow and disappeared
over the crown of his head. His hair was fair
and one part where the wave caught the light
looked blond. His eyes were a hazel colour,
and they looked kind, soft and gentle. They
were different from Sandy Palmer's and he
used them differently. He did not keep them
looking down the front of your dress or on
your mouth until your hands sweated.

'Look,' he said; 'look. It's coming up.'

'Oh, it's bonny. Oh, it is.'

'An' you've never seen it afore?' His voice
sounded excited, as if he were displaying to
her something magical which he himself had
created.

'No.' She was looking to the horizon, now
entirely taken up with the blaze of colour
erupting over the line of the sea.

As the sun rose with seeming speed she kept
exclaiming, 'Oh! Oh!' She had for the moment
let the wonder of the dawn supplant the feeling
of being alone in the early morning with this
boy. She knew that she was experiencing
surprise, a beautiful surprise. She had not
wanted to see the dawn but she had wanted
to be here with this boy in the early morning.

24

But now the dawn was showing her its worth and she became still under the wonder of it. It was so beautiful it was in a way painful, and she wished for a moment that she needn't look at it. As the glow rolled the grey mist back from the sea, almost it seemed to her very feet, she felt filled with an odd choking feeling. She was different somehow . . . she felt clean, washed, like. The dirt of life with which she was daily surrounded, and to which she was forever closing her eyes and stopping her ears, was receding. This light was like a great wet flannel wiping her mind clean.

'I never get used to it, never. It's always new. You know something?'

'No.' Her voice was dreamy.

They were both staring ahead now, their eyes resting gently on the picture before them.

'I think doctors must be daft. They mustn't really be thinking straight.'

'Why? How d'you make that out?'

'Well, just look. If they were to put sick people, especially those sick in their minds, if they were to put them somewhere so they could see the dawn every morning, I can't see but that they wouldn't be cured in next to no time.'

'It might frighten them.'

'The dawn?'

'Yes. Yes, I think it might.' She moved her head slowly while continuing to stare towards the great spreading glow. 'I'm afraid of the moon.'

'You are?'

'Yes, I used to scream at it when I was little. So perhaps this wouldn't do everybody good, 'cos . . . well, it makes you think, like.'

'Yes; yes, it does.' He brought his eyes on to her. He knew he had been right about her, and the intensity of his gaze brought her head round to him.

She was pleased with herself. She was talking, and not about silly things, like Janet and Nancy did in the office. She was pleased to think she knew that the dawn would frighten some people, for she had never realised that she knew this. Yet she had always known there was a different kind of talk from that which she heard at home, and at the office. Nancy and Janet talked of nothing but dress and lads . . . and babies. It was the latter that made her feel the most awkward. She never wanted a baby, never. She had never wanted lads either – well, not until this last day or so – for when she thought of lads she thought

26

of Sandy Palmer or Ronnie Fitzsimmons, and then her thoughts would shift to her mother and father, or her Uncle John, who was Sandy's father and not really her uncle at all. She just called him uncle because they had lived near each other for so long. She said now, 'It would do Sandy Palmer good to come and see this,' and immediately her face lost its light. Why couldn't she leave Sandy Palmer out of this? She hadn't wanted to think of Sandy Palmer.

'Yes, it would that. You live near him, don't you?'

'Yes, three doors away. It's strange, but we used to live three doors away from them in the old town, too, afore we moved.'

'Do you like him?' He asked the question without looking at her and she answered it without looking at him.

'No.'

'He likes you.'

She did not answer, but she looked into the blaze of colour until it dazzled her. She too had thought Sandy Palmer had liked her, had wanted her for his girl. She had never wanted to be his girl and her mother had warned her: 'You keep away from Sandy, don't have any carry on. Mind, I'm tellin' you.' And she had replied, 'What! me and Sandy Palmer? I don't want Sandy Palmer ... Him!' only for her mother to say, 'All right, but mind, I'm tellin' you,' whatever she was implying by that ... mother's warning.

Sandy never came to the house, never called for her, but whenever she was at the club he was there and he would walk back with her, even when she left early. She had tried to push him off: she cheeked him, snapped at him, tried ridicule, but it was no good. If she went home with Nancy Leary he would walk behind them, talking at them. Sometimes he would be alone, and sometimes there would be Ronnie Fitzsimmons or Charlie Talbot with him. Charlie Talbot lived on the other side of the Palmers and was nothing but a little toad. He went around with Sandy Palmer because he was a sucker-up and wanted to be in with the motor-bike crowd. But quite abruptly, about three weeks ago, Sandy Palmer had let her go home alone. He had been in the club all one evening and never once asked her to dance, hadn't even spoken to her. But he had kept looking at her in an odd kind of way. If she hadn't known him she would have called it a frightened way, but she did not think of fear and Sandy Palmer together, for he was afraid of nothing and no-one. Perhaps it was just coincidence that the time he stopped speaking to her should be the day after her mother and dad had had a terrible row, and yet it wasn't so odd, because the Palmer family and hers were connected with a link that was a source of misery to her. No matter what joy she felt, it was impregnated with this misery; the connection between the Palmers and themselves. Life was horrible, dirty, dirty . . .

'Don't let it make you look so sad.'

'What? What! Oh no. No, I'm not sad. It's bonny. It's too bonny to make you sad. It's the bonniest dawn I've ever seen.' She laughed. 'That's silly, as it's the only one I've ever seen. But it won't be the last.' Her eyes were bright again, looking straight into his. 'I can hardly see your face; it's the colours, they've almost blinded me.'

'You shouldn't stare like that, you should keep blinking and not look at the sun directly. Look away to the side. You were staring as if you were looking beyond it, from where it comes.'

'From where it comes?' A soft smile touched her lips. 'You say the funniest things. I suppose it comes up from Australia.'

Now he laughed. 'It doesn't come up from anywhere. It's us that comes up. It's always there. You know I worried about it when I first learned it was us who did the moving.'

'Why did you worry?'

'Oh, well, when you accept a thing you don't think about it, but when you look at a thing and know that you're not seeing what you're looking at, or what you're looking at isn't really there, if you know what I mean, well then, one thing leads to another and then you start asking questions. It worries me a bit even now when I know I'm standing on the crust of the earth and it's going round. I know now that it's gravitation that keeps me put, but what is gravitation? That worried me for a long time. I don't even know the answer yet.' He laughed self-consciously.

She said, 'Do you write poetry?'

'What me? Poetry? No. What gave you that idea?'

'They said you would.'

'Who?'

'They: Nancy Leary and Janet Castleton, Clarky and . . .' there it was again, the name, 'Sandy Palmer.'

'Sandy Palmer? Was he talking about me?'

'They were all talking around the table at

George's. They were talking about the beats in London and the poetry sessions. They said it was cranky. And then they were asking who knew any poetry and they said that the only ones around the club who would be able to spout poetry were Leslie Baker and you.'

'Sandy Palmer said that?'

'Yes, and the others.'

'Well, I can't write poetry; I don't even like it. I don't write at all and I don't want to. Too many people are writing things they know nothing about. You've just got to pick up magazines or books. Half of them write about places they've never been to . . . they get it all from the library. I've seen them sittin' there. One of the journalists from the paper, the one that writes under the name of "Adventurer", he's never out of the reference library.'

'No?'

'No. And I've never written poetry or anything else.'

He sounded vehement all of a sudden and she wondered why. Perhaps because he wanted to write and couldn't. Yet he sounded to her clever enough to write.

Joe was pleased that she thought he could write, poetry or anything else, but at the same time he was vexed that the subject had been brought up solely because he couldn't do what Sandy Palmer and the rest gave him credit for; write poetry, or anything else. He wasn't really telling the truth when he said he didn't write anything. He *had* tried his hand at it, again and again. His head was full of things he wanted to write, but his spelling was awful, his style was worse, and when he attempted it he couldn't get the stuff on to the paper for thinking how awful his spelling was. He was more concerned about his spelling than his writing, for he spelt phonetically and he knew now that was something to be ashamed of. He wished he had paid more attention at school, he wished he could have another chance, and yet he knew if he could have another chance it would be the same all over again. He wasn't one who could learn from books or reading, he could only learn by looking and listening. He learned more from listening to a chap talking about a subject on the radio than he had ever done by reading books on the subject. And again, if the subject was to do with nature, he learned more by using his eyes on a long walk than listening to all the authorities on the radio. He wished he could write, he wished he could. But he'd never be able to. The things in his head would only come out through talking, and there were few people he had met to whom he really wanted to talk. But there were some, and Brid here was one of them. He felt the heat of happiness pass over him at the thought. It was wonderful that he had found a girl at last that he could talk to, that he wanted to talk to, and one who wanted to listen to him. He was nineteen and he had begun to give up hope that he would ever find a girl he could talk to, just sit like this and talk to. But he mustn't let her think he was stuffy and that all he could do was talk. He said quickly, 'You like to dance?'

'Yes. Yes, I love it.' The admission was given in a tone of apology.

'You're a good dancer.'

'You think so?'

'The best at the club, I'd say.'

'Oh no, I'm not; there are many better than me. But I like it.'

'I'm no good at this jive stuff, that's why I don't do it.' He was making amends for his attitude on the dance floor the previous evening when yet once again he refused to stand like a jolting puppet while she dizzied and whirled in front of him. He had thought privately that those that wanted to have St Vitus's dance could have it, but he wasn't going to. And

again, that the girls looked like cock birds
out to attract the hens. The positions had
been reversed and it wasn't nice. Modern
times or no modern times, man should do
what preening there was to be done.

'I don't mind what I dance so long as I
dance.'

They remained silent now as they looked at
each other, and then they laughed and looked
towards the sun again.

'See there! Isn't that wonderful? See there!
That line of rocks, they're all purple. You
would think they were lit up by headlights,
wouldn't you?' He pointed away to the far
right towards where the land sloped more
gently to beach level.

She nodded, then said, 'But they say there're
quicksands there.'

'Maybe; but people don't swim over there;
the rocks here are a protection, but yon side
of them is deeper and dangerous. This side,
I've bathed for years.'

'You have?'

'Yes.'

'But it's got a warning up that bathing is
forbidden, that it's dangerous.'

'Yes, it would be if you didn't know what
you were at. Well look, the tide's out now

34

and there's still some water this side of the
rocks, deep enough to swim in and it's as safe
as houses.'

'Have you ever been beyond?'

'No; I wouldn't want to. It's deeper, and the
undercurrent is strong. I went in once, and
by! it didn't half frighten me. That was a year
or two ago. But you needn't go as far as the
rocks, even. You can swim all you want just
off the sand. And there's this about it, you
don't get the crowds here. Many locals come.
That notice is just for the holidaymakers who
don't know what they're at. This afternoon
you won't be able to put a pin on this hill
if it's fine; everybody'll be picnicking. And
on the beach an' all.' He said again quickly,
ahead of her, as if he were leading the way
through passages of thought, 'I never want
to leave this place.'

'You mean here?' She flapped her hand
towards the ground.

'No ... Yes, but not just this spot. The
coastline. Oh, the coastline's grand up here.
Look at it. Where will you see a grander sight
than that?'

She followed his moving arm. She hadn't
thought about it before. In all the years she
had lived so near to the sea she had scarcely

35

paid it any attention. She had taken the train into Morpeth every morning for over two years now and her nights seemed to have been taken up with hurrying home and getting the tea ready for her mother and dad coming in from work. They got in a quarter-past six, but the tea and washing up were never over before half-past seven. Then they would look at the telly. Her father never left her mother on her own at night, except when her Uncle John called in, and if that happened he and her dad went along to the club.

On such occasions, when they were left alone together, her mother would talk to her. She was different altogether when they were alone. She would put her arm round her waist and pull her up beside her on the couch and they would laugh about things. She was jolly at heart, was her mother, and she would often say to her, 'Come on, come on; don't look so sad. Prepare to enjoy yourself;' and she would laugh and quote the advert, which said, 'Prepare to be a beautiful lady'. But sometimes, even right in the middle of her laughter, she would suddenly turn serious, almost fierce, and say things like, 'Enjoy yourself; you're only young once. My God! you are. But not with Sandy Palmer, mind;' and her eyes would widen as she gave this apparent warning. 'Keep clear of Sandy Palmer, he's no good for you.'

Then, later in the evening, even though there might be a serial or some other interesting programme on the television, her mother would assuredly hear the back gate click and then the dual footsteps on the cement path, and she would watch her mother lean her head against the back of the couch and laugh, but quietly to herself. Then she would close her eyes, and when the two men entered the room she would always say the same thing; without turning her head to look at them she would say, 'We . . . ell!' Just like that. 'We . . . ell!'

And so in the evenings, even in the summer, she had never gone for walks by the shore. Once or twice on a Sunday afternoon she had gone out with Janet and got as far even as this point, but they had never descended the hill to the shore. For one thing it would have spoiled their shoes, and for another it had always looked so grim and forbidding to her. But now she wondered why she had ever thought that. It was beautiful, made beautiful by the dawn, this bonny dawn. Oh, it was a bonny dawn. Even if she hadn't been here with Joe Lloyd she imagined she would still have thought it was a bonny dawn, she couldn't help but.

'Look, every place is alight now.' His roving gaze finished on her and he repeated, 'Every place.' For her face was warm and rosy as if she had just got out of a hot bath, and her eyes were reflecting the colours of the morning. He could see the streaks of dawn light going down into them. And yet they were all grey, a bright clear grey . . . and wise. Her mouth was open, just enough to show two large white front teeth, and her lips were like painted joy as they spread when she exclaimed with her finger pointing, 'Look! there's a boat, a little boat. It must have been there all night. Fishing?'

'Oh yes; fishing.'

'It looks yellow and dark blue to me. What colour does it look to you?'

He laughed: 'Yellow and dark blue,' although he couldn't see it.

She said again 'Oh!' and her hands hugged at her knees. It was as if she had never before seen a fishing boat or imagined that anyone could stay out in a boat all night; and this was silly, because their Willie often went fishing at night. He went with Harry Palmer. They were both saving up to buy a boat, rather than a car. They both said they'd had enough

of cars, driving their lorries. Their Willie and
Harry Palmer had been pals since they were
at school. In this, they merely followed the
pattern of their fathers, because her father
and her Uncle John had been pals when they
were young, too, and they still were. At this
point in her thinking, her head jerked and
her mind went back to her brother Willie,
and she thought, It's funny, he's never had
a girl. Harry Palmer never bothered with
girls, either. He used to, her mother said,
until he was about twenty, and then he
and Willie started to go fishing. They both
worked for the same contractor and drove
the long-distance lorries, sometimes as far
as London and back. They nearly always
managed to go on the same consignment.
But when they didn't manage it, their Willie
mooned about the house and didn't even go
near the boat. Over the years, the boat had
become as familiar as her own bike and yet she
had never seen it. They hired it from Crosby's
up at the Bay, and she understood they always
managed to get the same one. But when they
got their own they would likely take her out
in it. She rather liked their Willie and would
have liked to be closer to him, to talk to him,
but she had the feeling that he always pushed

her off, evaded her. Yet when there were any rows in the house he supported her.

As she looked at the boat bobbing up and down in her line of sight she visualised herself lying in bed, her head pressed into the pillow and her hands over her ears to shut out the murmur of her father's voice from the next room. Her flesh crept when her father talked in that low entreating tone, but there was the night when he had screamed at her mother, and then she had heard Willie's door open and his voice crying across the empty landing towards his parents' room: 'Give over! you two, will you? Don't you know there's somebody next door?'

She knew that Willie hadn't been referring to the Pratts, but to her. She remembered his last words before he went back into his room and banged the door, 'God Almighty! at your age.' It was then she heard her father bounce out of bed. He seemed to jump from the bed on to the landing, so quickly came his voice yelling to his son: 'My age! Who the hell do you think I am? Methuselah?' Her father had been forty-five at that time, and she fourteen. Then she thought she heard him mutter, 'The unnatural bugger.'

In other ways, too, Willie had tried to

protect her against her father, and she had been puzzled up until recently by the fact that she should need this protection, but she knew she did. She was afraid of her father, yet she knew she could have loved him if he had let her. But he too pushed her off, much more so than Willie did. Her mother didn't push her off, her mother drew her close, yet she had known right from a child that her mother was the cause of the trouble in the house. This on the face of it was strange, for her mother was bonny and laughing, and quite kind. Perhaps she laughed too much really, but it was often at herself. She laughed the day she got her hair bleached. It had been a mousey brown and was going grey, and she had had it bleached. Willie had laughed and she had laughed with him, but her father had nearly gone mad.

Her eyes still on the boat, she took a great gulp of air into her lungs and as she let it out she muttered on the fringe of audibility, 'Oh, if we only didn't live near the Palmers.'

'What d'you say?'

'Oh, nothing. Well, I was just looking at the boat. My brother goes fishing.'

'I didn't know you had a brother; I thought you were the only one.'

'No, he's much older than me, he's twenty-six. He and Harry Palmer go out and sometimes stay out all night, fishing. He's Sandy's brother.' She turned her head towards him now and her face was serious. 'He's not a bit like Sandy, he's nice. Harry's a year older than our Willie. Everybody says they're like twins, they're always together.'

'It's nice to have a pal like that. I've got a pal; he's what you call my marrer.' He laughed as he gave her this information. 'He's two years older than me; he had his twenty-first birthday last week. By! there was a do. He'll just be coming up now.' He lifted his eyes towards the sky as if he were with his friend and the cage had just stopped and they were taking their first fill of light. 'We've been on different shifts for the last three weeks; it's the cut of the draw.'

'Would he have been with you all night if you had been on the same shift?'

'Not him.' Again he laughed. 'He thinks I'm up the pole. But we go to cricket together, and in the winter I always watch him play football. He's a grand footballer; he should have been a professional. Ossie, short for Oswald. He hates his name.' Joe smiled sympathetically. 'And I don't blame him.'

She looked towards the beach. The last lap of the tide had gone completely down now and licked lazily at the sand. She could see it leaving a line of bubbles, shining, rainbow-hued bubbles. The whole stretch of coastline looked like one great mouth and the tide like a tongue, as though it were the mouth of a happy dog with saliva dripping from it. But the picture was not translated into thought in her mind – her thoughts were taken up with Ossie. She did not like the sound of this Ossie. She felt that if they had been on the same shift Joe wouldn't have been here, nor would he have come to the club in the first place. He had come down there because he was at a loose end. She felt suddenly frightened at the fact of so much depending on so little. If Joe hadn't been at a loose end, if his pal hadn't been on the other shift, if . . . if. A sense of insecurity enveloped her. She was here just by chance, just because Joe had found himself at a loose end. She was being forced to the fringe of the deep fundamental fact that life itself was but a chance thing. She said quickly, 'Eeh! I'll have to be getting back now,' and before he could look at her she had swung herself up in an easy movement that spoke of youth. In a second, he was standing in front of her.

'Have you minded comin'?'

'No; oh no. I've loved it. I've never seen anything like it in me life.'

'Will you come again?'

'Yes, yes.'

'Do you swim?'

'Yes. Oh, yes, I can swim.'

'Are you doing anything this afternoon?'

'No. No, I'm not.' They were looking at each other, unblinking.

'Will we go swimming over there?' He did not take his eyes from her but motioned towards the bay.

'Yes. Yes, if you like.'

'The tide should be right just about two.'

'Oh, I don't think I could manage it at that time. You see there's Sunday dinner and . . .'

'Oh, I know. Me mother's the same; you've got to have the lot on Sunday. I've always thought that's a bit funny. Me dad used to think it funny an' all. He used to say that they could stew the guts out of bones all the week and half starve, but on the Sunday they had the lot. Six veg, some of them had. Aye, you wouldn't believe it. Some in our street are still like that. But not me mother. Oh no; me mother's a grand cook.'

She was staring at him; she loved to hear

him talk. There was a lilt to his voice, a sort of hidden laughter, and yet it sounded sad. She thought it was what could be called a deep rich voice. It seemed bigger than his whole body; like his head and shoulders, it didn't seem to belong to the rest of him. She saw him look away towards the road where she thought she heard a car passing, but she didn't take her eyes off his face. The sun was playing on his hair, and now it looked all silver.

Joe had glanced towards the road to the lorry. It was too far away to make out whose lorry it was, but his attention had been drawn to it when he'd heard it stopping. If it had been racing past down the road it would have been gone in a flash from his view. But it must have been going slowly for a while. As he looked at it he could make out the shape of the driver in the cab. It actually stopped only for a second and went off again, and he brought his gaze and thoughts back to her. She was pretty. And not just pretty . . . there was something about her that required a name. He would have to think. It wasn't beautiful. No, she wasn't beautiful, not as girls are beautiful. Was it exquisite? Oh no; that meant something beyond beauty. No, it wasn't exquisite. Homely? No, man, no, he said to himself; that was the other extreme.

And yet she could be. Yes, she could be homely. He tried to see her in five, ten, fifteen years' time, but he couldn't. He could only see her now, and with sudden contradiction of his previous summing up, he thought: Yes, she is, she is beautiful.

'Well, I'd better be going. I want to get back before six.'

'You'll make it. I'll come part of the way.'

'No, no.' For some reason she didn't want him to walk back with her. She wanted to keep the feeling of him in the dawn; the morning was coming up rapidly now and she didn't want him to come into the morning. He was all light as he was now. She did not want him to become part of the grey tone of the morning ... all mornings.

'All right,' he said. 'But look.' He turned and pointed. 'I'll be along there. Don't mind what time you can come, the day's me own. Right at the end where the cliff levels out; just above that there's a bit of woodland. It's lovely up there. I'll show you. The blackberry blossom is comin' thick. It's a week since I saw it, so it should be like snow now.'

She had to tear herself away from his

talking, for she found that she was waiting, waiting for him to say something unusual, strange, nice.

'All right, bye-bye then.'

Two

She wasn't forewarned in any way. The curtains in the front room were still drawn across the window, there was no life outside the house, none in the street, none in the town as yet, except for the milkman's electric cart that had joggled past her as she came round by the school. She had so forgotten the unusualness of her morning jaunt that she did not prepare herself for secrecy until she had taken half a dozen steps up the path; and then she lifted her heels from the ground and made her way to the back door on tip-toe.

There was a smile on her face as she stealthily turned the lock back, and then her loud cry of 'Eeh! Oh!' swept it away as her eyebrows lifted the whole skin of her face in shocked, frightened surprise. There sat her mother at the small kitchen table: she had her hands joined tightly together and they looked a dirty grey in contrast with the pale pink plastic covered top of the table. She was wearing a red dressing gown and it was open in a V down between her breasts. She was staring at Brid and she made no move from the table.

Her father was standing near the sink. He was wearing only his trousers; the sparse hair at the back of his head was standing up as it did when he was agitated, for when he was agitated he would run his fingers through it. The hair on his chest was thicker than that on his head, and it was black and curly. He too stared at her, his mouth open as if it were jammed wide.

Willie, in a pair of mauve coloured pyjamas, was standing near the door. He looked big, even massive in his night attire and more attractive than he did during the day. His round face was pink-hued and sleep was still in his eyes, but his face was tight as if he was holding back an outburst. Next to him stood Harry Palmer. Harry was still in his working clothes; the three-quarter length jacket that he wore on long journeys remained buttoned up to his neck, although the morning was already warm. He was the only one not staring at Brid; he had his cap in his hands and his heavy masculine face was bent towards it.

'Well?' It was her mother speaking, but it was a different 'well' from that with which she greeted the men: there was no light scorn in it; her anger left no room for that. 'What have you been up to?'

Brid cast her eyes swiftly from one to the other, her mouth at the same time half open in protest. She was indignant at the implication in the 'Well?' and the attack in the last words. 'Why, Mother, I've—'

'You leave this to me.' It was her father speaking. He was moving from the sink towards her. 'Where've you been?'

Her head swung two or three times backwards and forwards in the automatic movement of a doll before she exclaimed, 'I've just been along—' her hand went out now and wagged towards the kitchen window, and she swallowed and finished, 'along the top of the cliff.'

Her father was standing in front of her, glaring at her as if he hated her. Ever since she was a child she had had the impression that he didn't like her. She had once said this to her mother and her mother had laughed and said, 'Don't be silly; your dad thinks the world of you.'

'Who was the fella?' he now demanded.

'You . . . you wouldn't know him, he's not from here. He's . . . he's . . .'

'Who was he?'

'His name is Joe Lloyd.'

'Joe Lloyd?'

'He . . . he lives over in Johnson's Cross.'

'Is he going to marry you?'

'Marry me?' Her voice was crawling up the back of her throat now. 'Marry me?' There was a frightened choking sensation in her chest and it jolted into her mouth and made her cough as her father exclaimed, 'I said, marry you, you dirty little bitch, you!'

'I've done nothing, nothing I tell you. I only went out—'

'We know what you did.' He was wagging his hand within an inch of her face, so close that she had to bend backwards away from him. 'You came in from the dance at eleven. Oh aye, I heard you, you dirty little sod, you. And then you slipped out, didn't you, when we were all snug asleep, an' he was waiting for you outside?'

'No, he wasn't. He wasn't ... Mother –' she looked past her father and appealed to her mother; and her mother staring back at her, pityingly now, said, 'It's no good, Brid; Harry saw you.'

'But he couldn't have; I didn't do anything. We didn't do anything. We were only sitting on the top of Stockwell Hill. We went to see the dawn.'

'My God! . . . be quiet, girl!' The words were groaned out. Her mother was looking at her joined hands again.

'I tell you we were. I don't care what you think you saw, Harry Palmer, that's all we were doing.' There were tears in her voice now, an indignant yet pitiful sound, as she glared at Harry Palmer.

Harry Palmer bowed his head again. He wished he was in hell, this minute. He had never meant it to take this turn. His headlights had picked out the shape of entwined couples at intervals during the night, some in cars too clagged together at that time in the morning to be married. One couple, so young they looked like lost children, were asleep near a rick. It had just got light when he saw that pair. Not long after that, he had been so startled that he had nearly swerved off the road, when, with

53

the sun on her face and her head back, he had seen young Brid standing close to a fella and gazing at him as if she were entranced. It had given him a gliff. What could he do? By the time he had reached the depot he was thinking that he must have been seeing things. Yet he had scampered home, gone straight into the Stevenses' garden and lifted the prop and tapped on Willie's window. This was the usual signal for getting him up without disturbing the house. He had beckoned him down and told him what he had seen. Willie had dived upstairs and, sure enough, he had returned to say her bed was empty. What could he do but rouse his parents? He was sorry, sorry to the heart that he had to be the one to give her away for, in spite of everything, she was a decent kid, was Brid . . . At least he had always thought so.

'You're a liar, Harry Palmer, whatever you say. It's lies, lies. We were just looking at the sun coming up.'

'Shut your silly trap.' Her father's hand was raised, the back towards her face ready to skelp it when her mother cried, harshly now, 'We'll have none of that! You leave her be.'

Her voice indicated that she was about to take charge of the household once more. But

Tom Stevens was not taking any of that this morning. His face blazing with anger, he turned on her: 'Leave her be, eh? Leave her be? Aye, you can say that. There's been too many in this house let be, that's the trouble. Leave her be? Aye, I'll leave her be after I've stripped the flesh off her bones. She's one I'll cure of her whoring.'

'Shut your mouth! you'll have the place raised.' Alice Stevens's voice was low as if it were coming from deep in her bowels. She and her husband were facing each other as if they were alone in the kitchen, enacting one of their usual rows. Then quite abruptly she turned to Harry Palmer and said quietly, 'Thanks for coming, Harry.'

It was a dismissal, and the young man shrugged his body from one side to the other heavily before moving away, and as he reached the door he looked at Brid for a second with a shame-faced look and muttered something below his breath, which sounded like, 'Sorry it had to be me, Brid. Sorry.'

When the door closed on Harry, Brid, her eyes stretched, her mouth trembling, watched her father glare at it and speak to it, saying, 'Aye, that'll give them something to chew over. We'll have the big fella along here in next to no time wanting the facts. And why not, eh? Why not?' He had, as it were, thrown these last words at his wife, and she said again deeply, 'Shut your mouth!'

Brid felt sick in her stomach. Her father had referred to his life-long friend and pal, the man she called her Uncle John, as if he were a stranger, or at best a neighbour whom he didn't like. He had referred to him as 'the big fella' and he had put hate into the name.

She went to move quietly across the room when her father's arm shot out and barred her way. 'No, you don't! We'll get to the bottom of this or I'll bloody well know the reason why.'

'There's nothing to get to the bottom of, I've told you.' Her head bounced at him, and he stormed on her now: 'Nothing to get to the bottom of?' he cried. 'You're another one who can treat it lightly. It comes of practice, eh? How many times have you done this afore? You little tart, you! Sneaked out on a Saturday night, eh? Come on, out with it.' He had gripped her shoulders and was pulling her back towards the table, when Willie, who so far hadn't spoken, said quietly, 'Enough of that. You can get to the bottom of it without any rough play.'

'You an' all stay out of this,' his father quickly warned him. Then changing his tone as if he were continuing a reasonable conversation, he said, 'You know what I'm gettin' at. You know what it's all about, don't you? so leave me to deal with this.'

'You're not the one to deal with it; you're too prejudiced.'

'Prejudiced!' Tom Stevens's tone had changed again, and he glared at his son as he cried, 'You call me prejudiced after what I've had to put up with; another man would have—'

'Yes, another man would have . . . another man would have . . .' Her mother's lips were curling right back from her top teeth, and the gesture exposed this man for what his wife and son and herself knew him to be: a man who was all talk. A fearful man. Fearful in the sense that he dreaded losing the one person who was nothing to him now but a form of torture, but without whom he couldn't hope to live.

Brid felt her father's exposure like a deep cut from broken glass. She closed her eyes against it. Then the next moment they were flung wide as, stung into retaliation, he cried, 'You've gone too far. I've told you you would go too far. I'll throw her out, I'll throw her along the road where she belongs, but, and bloody damn you! not afore I've left me mark on her.'

It happened so quickly that she could only instinctively shield her face against him. Pinto's lead always hung on the nail to the side of the kitchen door. It was half leather and half chain and it was the chain that caught her shoulder and lifted her screaming from the ground. She was cowering over the table, her face buried in her arms, as the struggle went on behind her. When her mother's arms came above her and lifted her, the room was quiet. She knew that her father and Willie were standing somewhere near, she could hear their deep shuddering breaths, but she did not look at them. Her mother led her towards the door into the hallway, and there she drew her to a momentary halt, and her sagging breasts were dragged upwards as she turned to look back at her husband. And when she spoke, her words were guttural and deep with threat: 'My God! I'll take it out of you for this, you see if I don't!'

There was a deep moan engulfing Brid's body. It was from a variety of pains. She was holding her hand over the place where the physical pain was most keen, the thick part of her neck at the top of her shoulder where the end of the chain had caught her; there was the pain from her mind where the thoughts, breaking the skin of years, were forcing their way through into the daylight; there was the pain of her spirit, humiliated, brought low, made to feel guilty; and there was the pain which came from she knew not where, the pain of the severed blood-tie. Above all the other pains, this was the worst. It had to do with her father's dislike of her, and her Uncle John's liking of her. Her father had put into words that which for years now she had dreaded to hear. Her father had never done anything in the whole of her life to make her like him, and he had just struck her. He had, she knew, always wanted to strike her, and now he had done it. Yet still she could not hate him, she could not even actively dislike him, because she still wished he *was* her father, her real father. She didn't want her Uncle John for a father, because her mother wasn't married to her Uncle John, she was married to Tom Stevens, the man who *should* be her father.

Her mother was gently taking off her dress; her hands were soft and warm. She should turn to her and fling herself on her gaping bosom and get the sympathy that she knew was waiting for her, but she didn't. If there was anybody she disliked at this moment it was her mother. Yet her mother had always been kind to her. Her mother was kind to everybody with the exception of her father. She was known as a good sort, her mother was. An intruding thought told Brid that life would have been different had her mother distributed her kindness a little more evenly, then her father wouldn't have been so bad. She still thought of the man downstairs as her father. She would always think of him as her father. Life would have been happy, even joyous, had her mother been faithful to him, for her father could have been a nice man. He still could be a nice man, and it all depended on her mother. But her mother would never give him again what would make him into a nice man. Time had done too much to them.

As her mother pressed her gently into the pillow she felt in an odd way that her father had not really hit her, he had hit her mother.

'Lie still. I'll go and get some of me cold cream and rub it on. The skin isn't broken, but you're likely to have a mark there. But never you mind, I'll take it out of the sod for this. I'll make the bugger squirm.'

'Mother.'

'Yes?'

'Don't do anything. He didn't mean it; I know he didn't mean it.'

'He meant it all right. He's a vindictive sod, always has been. Well, you're old enough now; we'll have to have a talk, and soon.'

Although the movement was painful Brid turned her entire body away from her mother and stared at the wall.

Looking down at her daughter, Alice Stevens sighed. Well, she had to start some time, she supposed, but she'd had the idea that Brid was a bit different, that she'd wait until she married. She herself had known all about it long afore she married Tom Stevens. And it was just as well she got her fun in first, for it would have been a poor lookout after. Why in the name of God had she to go and pick a fellow like Tom? One-woman man all right, he was. She could have stood it if he'd gone off the rails, even before she herself had started. But God almighty! this till death us do part business got on her tripe. And what had he expected her to do, with him away in the services? Do tattin'? It was himself who had said to John 'Look after her,' and John had looked after her ... and how! And he would have been looking after her still were it not for Olive. Duty, be damned! Why the hell must he keep yarping on about Olive and his duty. He should have left her and come away when Brid was born.

Silently she turned her head towards her daughter's stiff, still form. Then contracting the muscles of her stomach, she ground out under her breath, 'To hell!' then left the room.

Crossing the landing, she almost kicked open her bedroom door; but, on finding the room empty, she closed it quietly behind her and began to dress. She put on a sleeveless summer frock that displayed her thick fleshy arms. The flesh was in hard nodules like the ridges you see on wet sand. It was a sign of ageing flesh. Yet time that was ravishing her skin was having no effect on the burning, desiring life within her. She was so made that she would keep her vitality until her dying day, however far away that was. The life urge seemed to renew itself daily in her, churning up her whole body and troubling her. Yet it did not show in her movements, which were slow.

She left the bedroom, only to come face to face with Willie. He blocked her way to the stairs. Standing head and shoulders above her, he said, 'If this goes on I'm moving.'

'Now don't you start!'

'Well, it's getting past it. An' people talkin'.'

At this she deliberately widened her eyes and mouth at him in mock surprise, and then she laughed. 'Talkin', you say? People are talkin'? That's good, that is.'

She felt a sense of victory as she watched the hot colour sweep upwards over his face, and when he side-stepped from her and made for his room she turned and said to his back, 'You want to think afore you speak, me lad . . . Talkin'.'

She did not immediately descend the stairs but stood looking down them, saying to herself, 'Talkin'. Talkin'. That's good, that is.' And as she stood there a sadness crept over her, and she turned her head slowly and looked back towards her son's door. Why had this thing that was full and flush in her . . . yes, and in his father an' all, give him his due, to take a twist like it had done in their son . . . ? Oh God, life was hell.

In the kitchen, Tom was sitting at the table, his head resting on his hands. He did not move when she came in and she did not speak to him, but she clashed and banged around him as she set about getting the breakfast ready, and when, putting a tray on the table, she deliberately struck viciously at his elbows, he raised his head and said quietly, 'One of these days I'll forget meself and do you in.'

'Huh!' she almost spat. 'I'll be waitin' for you!'

Tom looked at her for some minutes before he pulled himself up from the table. His eyes were still on her as he hitched his trousers up and moved out of the room. Slowly he mounted the stairs, and as he crossed the landing his eyes flicked towards Brid's door, but he did not stop. When he entered the bedroom he sat down on the side of the tumbled bed and, lifting one hand, he covered his face. After a few moments he lowered his hand and placed his thumb across his mouth and bit hard on it. He would . . . he would. One of these times he would forget himself and go for her, and he would only have to start and he wouldn't be able to stop, he knew he wouldn't. Funny, but he had never hit her. He had been near it a hundred times, but he just couldn't, somehow. And she knew it, blast her. But the other one – he never thought of her as Brid – he felt he wanted to belt her till the blood ran, and he would. She wouldn't go the same road as her mother, he'd see to that. His teeth eased off his thumb and now he flicked them with his nail. What would Palmer's reaction be to the latest? He would have liked to see his face when Harry gave him the news. It would have been a sort of payment for all he had endured. Why had he put up with it all these years? Keeping pals with him knowing what he knew . . . Why? He shook his head. It was getting that way that he couldn't let him out of his sight in case Alice and he got together. And they laughed at him, at least she did, when his shift worked out and he was on late turn every three weeks . . . If he could only catch them at it. He put his elbow on the bed rail and lowered his head and rested it on his hand. It was as if he were turning from the sight of himself, his fear, his cowardice. He could have caught them time and again but that would have meant facing up to the situation, and he couldn't. Not now, for it had gone on too long. He couldn't live without Alice. Rather she should torture him than leave him. Of a sudden he had the horrifying sensation that he was going to cry. It brought him up on to his feet, and grabbing from here and there, he got into his clothes.

*   *   *

'There, come on, sit up and have this. I've brought me cup up so's I can have one with you. There . . . there now. Eat that up while it's hot: the bacon's nice and crisp, just as you like it.' Alice put the tray on Brid's knees.

'I couldn't eat anything.'

'Don't be silly, get it into you. It isn't the end of the world.'

Brid watched her mother pull a chair up to the foot of the bed and sit down. Through the window at her back the sun shone on her hair, giving to it the appearance of a large halo.

'I couldn't eat anything, I couldn't.'

'Are you sure?'

'Yes.'

'Well, have that bit of toast then and a cup of tea . . . Hand me the plate; there's no use in wasting it; it's no good when it's cold.'

Brid watched her mother. She was eating the bacon as if she were enjoying it, as if nothing had happened. And then she contradicted this by wiping her mouth on the pad of her thumb and saying quickly, 'Well now, let's get this straightened out. Come on, tell me all about it.'

Brid looked down into the cup she was holding between her hands. 'There's nothing to tell, nothing to straighten out. Nothing . . . Nothing,' and she laid deep quiet emphasis on the last two words.

'Well now' – her mother's tone was patient, and yet had a hopeless ring about it – 'you don't stay out all night and have nothing to tell. You know me; I wasn't born yesterday, girl. And look, I'm not goin' to get mad at you. I understand, good God! don't I? Let's face up to things: you're part of me, you're the same inside as I am, and I know how I am, so don't be afraid to speak.'

'I tell you, Mother—'

'All right, all right; you were out all night and nothing happened. Well, then, tell me why you stayed out all night with him.'

'I didn't. I tell you I didn't; I never left this room until four o'clock.'

'Why four o'clock?'

Brid bowed her head. How could she tell this woman who suggested that her flesh craved the same satisfactions as her own, who knew no other desires, how could she say to her, I went to see the dawn come up? But she would have to, she could only tell the truth. She was looking into her cup again when she said, 'I went to see the dawn come up.'

'Aw, lass.' Her mother's voice sounded more hopeless now, and when it added the usual 'Well!' the word, translating itself to Brid, said, Aw, stop it for God's sake. Come off it. Come clean. What does it matter, anyway? You'll sleep with somebody sooner or later, so come on, let's have it.

'Mother.' The room became quiet for a moment as their eyes held. 'I came in at five past eleven last night. I put me alarm on and I got up at four o'clock this morning because I had promised him I would go and see the dawn from the top of Stockwell Hill ... And I went ... And that's all that happened. Harry couldn't have seen anything for nothing happened. I'm tellin' you, Mother. Well, look at the alarm ... you can see it's set for four.' Her words had ended on a run.

Her mother did not look at the alarm but said, 'Did you see him ... Harry?'

'No.'

'What were you doin'?'

'Just sitting looking at the colours on the sea.'

Brid watched her mother's eyes drop away, and her teeth drew her lower lip tightly into her mouth as she listened to her saying, 'Harry said he passed numbers of them along the road on his journey. It was a warm night; I suppose that was it. But you were just sittin'?' Her eyes lifted again, and Brid said slowly and quietly, 'Yes, we were just sittin'.'

'And it was dark when you left the house?'

'Yes.'

'Was it dark when you got there?'

'Yes, it was ... No, not quite; it was lifting.'

Her chest felt tight. She felt she could choke. If her mother said just once more, 'And you were just sittin'?' she wouldn't be able to stand it. She would scream, louder than she had done downstairs when her father had brought the chain round her shoulders. Her mother repeating nearly everything she said was causing a muzzy dizziness in her head and she felt sick. She supposed it was the shock from the blow. She wanted to be alone, she wanted to be quiet and think. She knew she would have to think, for nothing would be the same again. The pretence was ended, at least for her. She didn't know if she could go on living in this house, even if he would let her. She didn't know whether the truth that had burst into her mind this morning would allow her to go on living here and look at them playing out their lives. She didn't think she could do it.

Her father's voice coming from the landing startled her. She knew he was in the bathroom and shouting at Willie in his bedroom. 'Dancin', clubs, jivin' . . . squares, beats and all the bloody rest of it and nobody in the house when they come home, nobody. There's things to be said on both sides. Is there any home life here? I ask you, is there? My wage is good enough to run this house, I've always said it. They come home from school and not a bloody soul in sight. They come home from the office and not a bloody soul in sight. An' the years roll on, an' where's the home life? Where is it, for anybody, I ask you? I've had it.'

Brid put her hands over her ears as her mother rushed to the door and tore it open, but she could not shut out her voice. 'Aye, and you'll have it again. You know the cure, don't you? Well, take it, but you're not stopping me goin' out. No, me lad. This is just an excuse to start again, isn't it? Well, you can save your breath. Stay in the house and wash and cook and sit and wait for you comin' in? That's what you want, isn't it? Sit in the house and sew a bloody fine seam at night while you're out at the club or some such. Oh no. You say you don't go out much. Not now, because you've got the tele—'

'Shall I open the windows?' It was Willie's voice low and sarcastic.

'Well, if you think I'm gonna take this lying down—' she was still yelling.

'You take more than that lying down.'

Their voices came, together now, Willie's and her mother's, Willie crying, 'Cut it out. Cut it out. What are you coming to, anyway?' and her mother screaming, 'You dirty swine! That's all you are, a dirty swine.'

As the bathroom door banged, her bedroom door opened again and Brid knew that her mother was standing with her back to it. Then she was standing over her whispering fiercely into her face, 'Look; whoever this man is, make sure he won't lead you hell. Do you hear? See what I've got? Make sure, I'm tellin' you, afore you take the step.'

Brid stared up into her mother's wild eyes. How silly she was, really. How silly. Why hadn't she made sure? Could anybody ever be sure? Oh, if she would only go away and leave her alone. The buzzing was loud in her head. It felt as if it would burst. She would never marry anybody. Never. Never. She would never let a man touch her . . .

'Even if you get yourself landed with something, don't take him as a loophole, but make sure.'

'Leave me alone. Please leave me alone; my neck's paining me and I want to go to sleep. Leave me alone.' If her mother didn't leave her alone she would scream at her. She would scream and shout like the rest of them. She had to restrain herself from pushing her mother's face away. She didn't like the look of it. The cheery, laughing expression was hard. The eyes and the mouth were just straight lines on a brittle surface. She shut her eyes.

Alice Stevens withdrew slowly from the bed and stood for a moment talking, as if to herself now, and about domestic things. 'I'll never be able to start the washing the day, and there's a pile there. But I just can't. And there's the dinner to see to an' all. Well, he can bloody well go hungry. That'll settle him. But all that washing.' . . .

The door closed and Brid lay still, looking into the pattern of colour upon her closed lids. Sunday. Sunday. Day of rest. She had always thought that there should be two Sundays in a week, one on which you didn't have to do the washing. The Pattersons across the road, the Crosbys and the Wrights, they never washed on a Sunday. Her Aunt Olive never washed on a Sunday. On the rare occasions when her mother referred to her Aunt Olive she would say she was damned lucky to be able to stay at home and do her washing during the week, that she was damned lucky in all ways in having a man like Uncle John who'd come home at night and do the washing up, as well as the ironing.

In spite of her effort to restrain it, her mind took her down the street and into the Palmers' house.

Her Aunt Olive was often off-colour. She had an ailment that had no name but which took her to bed for days at a time and gave her headaches and pains all over. When the ailment was bad her Uncle John would come home from work and help in the house; he was very good to her was her Uncle John. Over the last few years he had bought her a television, a fridge and a washing machine, and only recently he had added to the latter a spin dryer. The house was well furnished and bright, and Aunt Olive was always at home when her man came in. She was a home woman who doted on her family. She was proud of Harry and worried over Sandy, and she loved Uncle John and kept him tied to her by sympathy. But the house always seemed a happy one. Once, her dad, in a storm of abuse when fighting with her mother, had given a reason for this. He had said, 'Who wouldn't be happy with two women, one at home and one away, and not so far away at that?'

Perhaps it wouldn't have been so bad during the last few years, Brid thought, if her mother hadn't left her old job with the light industry and gone and got set on in the paper mills where Uncle John worked. Yet even after that, her Uncle John continued to drop into the house and her father continued to go out to the club with him. It wasn't understandable, it wasn't. One thing seemed to shout liar at the other. How could her father, knowing that her mother was going with his pal, talk to him, go out with him, remain in his company, evening after evening. The whole set-up made her feel sick in her stomach. Yet it was behind this supposedly tolerant façade that she had taken refuge for years. If there was anything going on her father simply wouldn't put up with it. Her father and her Uncle John would have rowed. But as far back as she could remember she knew it had been going on, and her father and Uncle John hadn't rowed, which made it more horrible still.

The pain in her neck was becoming worse. Her head was muddly. She again wanted to be sick. She turned on her side, and now, under the cover of the bedclothes, a face loomed up clear and close. It was Joe's face, and he said to her, 'You shouldn't stare like that, you should keep blinking and not look at the sun directly. Look away to the side. You were staring as if you were looking away beyond it, from where it comes.'

'From where it comes.' She said the words aloud, then burying her face in the pillow she gave way to a storm of weeping, muttering at intervals, 'I wish I was there . . . from where it comes. I wish I was dead. Oh, I do.'

Three

Long after Brid had disappeared down the road Joe continued to sit on the top of Stockwell Hill. He had never known such a dawn: everything was afloat in light; even the sea seemed wrenched from its bed and to be straining skywards. There was a lightness and floating quality about the whole earth, and as usual he began a commentary to himself with, 'By! it has been a bonny dawn.' But when his words were checked by reason of the added lustre to the morning, his commentary went on, 'Well, she *is* nice. I knew she was; I wasn't wrong.' From the moment he knew he was attracted to her, he began to take her to pieces. Look at the heels she wore; and she had admitted she would like to wear coloured stockings. Fancy anyone wanting to put on red woollen stockings as if they were back in the fourteenth century. Funny, when you came to think about it, with the lot of them thinking they were the last second's delivery in time, so bloomin' up-to-date they couldn't be beaten, and then wearing coloured wool stockings. And her skirt showed her knees, like all the rest of them; you would swear they were wearing sawn-off crinolines. And she plucked her eyebrows. He wasn't against make-up, but when they plucked their eyebrows it was going too far. Yet on the Monday he had gone to George's coffee shop to see if she was there, and after talking to her he dissected no more; he knew she was all right.

It was hunger now that drove him homewards. He didn't go by the road but ran down the hill towards the beach, slithering and stumbling when the hill became very steep in its descent towards the sand. The sand was soft and dry and made walking slow, and the rim of the water seemed much further away than it had done from his perch up above. He crossed over from the dry sand to the wet and watched his feet now imprinting swift dark patterns.

From the top of the hill the distance towards the warning notice had looked nothing, but it took him nearly ten minutes to reach it. He glanced at the notice as he passed. The pole to which it was attached was leaning sideways; the faded letters on the board were still readable: 'DANGERS. DO NOT BATHE BEYOND THIS POINT.' He smiled at it. His father had introduced him to bathing here and the notice had been lop-sided then. When he reached the bay, hemmed in by the half-circle of rocks, he stopped for a moment to gaze at it. On a morning such as this, if his father had been alive, they would both have been in there rolling and sporting like two lads, not like father and son at all. The sand leading into the water of the bay dipped swiftly away from his feet at this point. That was why even when the tide was out you could always have enough water to mess about in. The tide left no impression on the bay, for it was as if at one time a giant hand had scooped out a hollow in the sand where the water would remain against falling tides.

As he stood looking over the bay he sniffed, then turned his head to look back up the beach which here sloped upwards to a deep copse of trees, black now against the bright light.

He had smelt the wonderful aroma of bacon
frying. Someone was likely camping out in
the woods up there. Glory! Couldn't he eat
some of that.

He turned about and quickly made towards
the trees. The scramble up to them was
nothing compared with the scramble down
Stockwell Hill, for it was merely a gentle
rise from the beach. When he entered the
comparative darkness of the trees he stood
blinking and sniffing for a moment. Whoever
was there, he couldn't expect them to dish
out any of their bacon, but they might likely
be good for a cup of tea. If they offered him
one he wouldn't say no. By lad! he wouldn't.
He hadn't realised how hungry and thirsty
he was.

He followed the direction of the appetising
smell, and it led him to the middle of the
copse, then onward to its edge; and there,
disappointed at not having espied a tent and
campers, he stopped and looked towards the
dark shape of the car parked on the verge of
the trees. As he approached it he could see a
woman sitting on a low camping chair with a
plate on her lap, and a man sitting on the car
step balancing a plate on his knee. A spirit
stove, on which stood a tin kettle, was nearby,

and the place around them was littered with objects that gave the appearance of a house without walls.

'Good-morning.'

They both looked up at him and answered, 'Good-morning;' and the man added, 'And it's a grand one too, isn't it?'

His voice was high. He was evidently not from these parts. Joe passed on, thinking, if they had offered him a cup of tea he wouldn't have taken it. They looked slovenly, dirty, somehow.

He arrived home to find his mother up and the breakfast set, and as he threw his cap on to the sofa and looked towards the table he exclaimed, 'By lad! I'm ready for this.'

Mary Lloyd turned from the stove to look at her son and asked, 'Well! where have you been this time?' It was as if he had just been out for an hour's stroll. With practice she was able to hide the fears that these midnight jaunts of her son created in her. It had been all right when he had gone along with his father, but even then she hadn't cared much for them jaunting off in the middle of the night; yet she had made no adverse comment on the escapades; men were men and had oddities in them. If you were wise you respected the oddities, and it was made easier when you loved your man. But her husband and son jaunting off for walks in the middle of the night was a different thing altogether to the lad going alone. He had been at it for three years now, but she still could not get used to it and always experienced a sense of relief when he was home again. His going down the pit did not fill her with the same apprehension as did his midnight rambling; there were others down the pit, whereas on these ramblings he was alone.

After Joe had washed his hands and face he returned to the kitchen and sat down with a flop on the couch. Putting his hands behind his head he lay back and let out a long breath as he said, 'It's a grand morning.'

'Yes, it is a grand morning. It's going to be hot. It's hot already.'

'There's a breeze coming up; it'll turn to a wind this afternoon, you'll see. It'll still be hot, though.'

'Come on, sit up.'

He pulled himself up with a jerk and took his seat at the table, but before he attacked the two eggs and three rashers of bacon reposing on the dinner plate he glanced quickly over the table as if for the first time he was noticing its shining quality. Everything seemed to be brighter this morning, or was it just him? No. The table was shining, and he realised that his home was a shining place. Always clean and spotless. His mother was clean and spotless too. As he chewed on a mouthful of rich-flavoured bacon, causing his digestive juices to fill his mouth so full he had to keep his lips closed while he ate, he looked towards his mother where she was standing pouring out the tea, and it came to him with a jerk of surprise that she was young, still young. She was thirty-seven, but she was still young. She had a nice figure. Perhaps her hips were a bit too big, but that was with sitting doing the dressmaking. She was a wizard with her needle and had done dressmaking for people for years. It had stood her in good stead after his dad had died. She was wearing a pink patterned dress, and again he thought, from her back view she could have been taken for a young girl. Even full-faced she could have passed for a young woman, until you looked into her eyes. They were blue and clear, but they had an expression in them that denied youth. Joe had noticed this before, but never questioned it further than to think his mother's eyes were strained with the sewing and that she should give it up. But now he paused in his eating as she handed him a cup of tea. Although she was smiling at him, the look was still there and he could name it now: his mother was lonely. He hadn't thought about her being lonely, for she was always so busy. Fancy, it had never struck him before. He seemed to be noticing lots of things this morning. It was as if he had lost a skin and was more sensitive than ever to the atmosphere about him. His mother was lonely. Had she always been lonely? He could always remember that look in her eyes. But his dad had loved her, loved her dearly, passionately should be the word, but he didn't like to say that in connection with his parents. Yet she had always had that look about the eyes. Was it because his dad went roaming at night when his shift allowed? Maybe. He had never thought about it. Funny, he had just never thought about it. Had his dad thought about it, that his wife was lonely? He couldn't have or he wouldn't have left her. Not his dad. That was why she wanted to marry Mr Bishop, because she was lonely. To his own surprise he heard himself talking quickly, rapidly, leaning across the table to her as he did so. 'I've been thinking' – although he hadn't, but was merely releasing an emotional pressure – 'You go ahead and do what you want. Don't mind me. I'll be all right. Things'll work out. You just go ahead and make your own arrangements and I'll fit in.'

She had stopped eating and was staring at him, and he watched the blue of her eyes become paler behind a mist, and her voice had a break in it as she said, 'But . . . but you know it'll mean leaving this house?'

'Well, what about it? You've always hankered after a modern one. Now, you have.' He nodded at her and laughed, trying to bring the subject on to a lighter footing. 'Anyway—' he bent his head over the plate and, taking up a forkful of food, chewed on it vigorously for a few moments before adding, 'who knows, I might stay here meself.'

'What d'you mean? Joe, look at me. What d'you mean?'

He looked at her, his eyes twinkling. 'I've got a girl.'

'You've got a girl?' Her voice was soft.

'Yes.' He put his knife and fork down and pushed his plate to one side, and hitching his chair towards the corner of the table so that his outstretched hand could touch hers, he said, 'She's nice, Mam. You know something?

She's nothing like you yet, but she's goin' to be, she's goin' to be. I know she is.'

She smiled softly at him, the while shaking her head. 'Is that a recommendation?'

'Aw, go on; you're only fishin'.'

'How old is she?'

'Seventeen.'

'But you're only nineteen . . . Are you serious, Joe?'

'Me dad married you when he was eighteen, remember? And I'll be twenty in six weeks' time. And yes, I'm serious, Mam. You know me. I've kept away from them 'cos I didn't seem to be able to find the right one.'

'But don't you think you should go out with a number before . . .?'

'No. No, I don't. I don't believe in that theory at all. That's the theory of the high-fliers. I hear it down below every day. "Test and try, man," they say. "Test and try afore you buy." No, Mam; that's not for me. And I knew as soon as I saw her; at least, not long after.'

'What's her name?'

'Brid Stevens.'

'Brid?'

'Short for Bridget. She said her mother had to call her Bridget after her mother-in-law, Brid's grannie: her grannie was buying the pram, and unless the child was called after her, no pram. She can be funny, she can't tell a tale without laughing ... she can be funny.'

'Are you going to bring her along home?'

'I'd like to, Mam.'

'What about this afternoon?'

'Fine, I'm meeting her along at the bay. We're going to have a swim. We should be back here about fourish. All right?'

'All right with me.'

They smiled at each other, and now Joe pulled his plate back towards him and continued to eat the congealing remains of his breakfast.

As his mother stood up to pour out more tea she asked him, 'Did you walk far?'

'Quite a way.'

'You tired?'

'No; I'm as fresh as a daisy.'

'I was thinking about going to church this morning, would you like to come?'

'Oh lordy! Mam, I *am* tired.'

As he lay back in his chair laughing, her hand came out and gently boxed his ear, and they both laughed. Then he said quietly, 'No, Mam; count me out. I'll come some time. As I said afore, I'll go one of these mornings on the spur of the moment and I won't know why. But, thanks all the same, not this morning. Fact is, I *am* tired . . . it's true. Yes, honest. I'm done in. I'm going to bed and I'll sleep until dinner time. Will you wake me around twelve? I want to be out by half-past one. All right?'

'All right.' As she passed him she touched his head softly and he put his hand up swiftly and caught her fingers and tightly squeezed them for a moment. It was a gesture that his father had been wont to make, and after it the kitchen was filled with a sweet, full silence. He went and sat on the couch and put his head back and yawned and stretched his arms. He was filled with joy, a new kind of joy: it was like a promise, a golden promise. A ray of sun shining through the kitchen window fell across his face and he took it as a seal on that promise. Life was to be full of light and wonder. This was living. This was loving, he thought as he climbed the stairs to his bedroom.

His mother called him at twelve o'clock and he woke immediately to her touch.

'Ossie's been,' she said.

'Yes? . . . Oh, lord.'

'He said for you not to miss the quarter to two bus. I didn't say anything.'

'I'd forgotten; but I didn't promise him anything. I just said if I felt like it . . . And I don't feel like it. Not today.' He smiled shyly at his mother. 'You mentioned nothing?'

'No, not a word.' She pressed her lips together as she gave him a confederate's smile.

'By, I'm glad of that. He would have chaffed the lugs off me all week. He'll have to know some time, I suppose; though that can wait. But I didn't want him to know so soon, for things aren't settled yet. With me they are, but not with her . . . I haven't sort of spoken. You know what I mean?'

'Yes, I know what you mean.' She patted his shoulder and left the room, and immediately he got out of bed. There was no bathroom in the house, and after donning a pair of old trousers he went downstairs to wash in the scullery. When he returned to his room he selected his best suit, even though he knew he'd have it off before he saw her and that it would be lying on the rocks getting creased. But still, he would be fetching her home and the occasion demanded his best suit.

At dinner his mother said jokingly, 'If you're going in the water you'd better not eat so much,' and he replied on a laugh, 'Why? I've never sunk yet. And never left a dirty plate, either.'

Suddenly, as if her mind had never left the subject, she said, 'Is she serious? I mean . . . well, you know what I mean, don't you?'

'Well, she dances the modern stuff, jive and all that, and makes up, and wears them stiletto heels, but she's all right. I know she's all right, Mam. Something tells me.'

'Where did you meet her?'

'At the club in South Scardyke.'

'The club?' There was a slight raising of his mother's eyebrows and he put in quickly, 'Yes, I know what you're thinking; about the lot that goes there. She was among them but on the side, if you know what I mean?'

'Does she drink?'

'Yes, coffee, and she likes it strong . . . Aw Mam, don't worry, you'll see her for yourself in an hour or two.' He was detecting a change in his mother's attitude, as if she had done a lot of thinking during the time he had been in bed and now, and was a little worried. But he wasn't displeased with her attitude. It showed she wasn't so taken up with her own affairs that she could let his slide. He said now, 'Mind if I go?'

'No; get yourself away. And I'll have

the tea on the table at half-past four, mind.'

'Half-past four it'll be, on the doorstep. You have the word of a Lloyd, Madam.' He saluted her, and she laughed and pushed him away.

He took up his jacket from the back of the chair and put it on and adjusted his tie, then asked, preening himself, 'How do I look?'

'No different from usual that I can see.' She shook her head with mock primness, then added seriously, 'But why you want to put your good suit on to go down to the beach puzzles me.'

'Does it? Then, Mrs Lloyd, you're dim. Goodbye, Mrs Lloyd.'

'Oh, away with you!'

He bent swiftly to her and gave her a rare kiss, and she remained still, making no more remarks. And he went out, closing the door quietly behind him.

He strolled down the village street. It was quiet with a Sunday quiet that hits most places around noon: everyone was indoors eating. The houses in the centre of the village, the original part of Johnson's Cross, looked mellow. They were all built of rough quarry stone, the colour of which time had blended to a deep thick cream. He liked the village;

he wished he would never have to leave it. But then if . . . The 'if' presented the future to him, and he said to himself, 'Well, I'll just have to, won't I?' And the answer caused an excitement in his stomach and quickened his step, and as he took the short cuts across the fields to the beach, he almost skipped.

When he came to the outskirts of the copse to where he had seen the motorists breakfasting that morning, he stopped and looked at the ground, then exclaimed aloud, 'By lad! you would think they would have the sense and decency to clear up after them. I bet that pair's left their trademark across the country.' He went on and was just about to enter the copse when the glint of something bright lying in the long grass to the left of him brought him to a stop. The glint was from the handlebar of a motor-bike. He took a couple of steps out of his way and ascertained that, yes, there was not just one motor-bike, there were three, and he muttered, 'Bust it!' for the motor-bikes meant there were fellows already down in the bay. Well, whoever they were, they mightn't stay long; perhaps they were just passing through and had gone down for a dip. Very likely they knew of this place. Of course they would have to know of it, for no one passing this bit of woodland would think that just beyond lay the sea. People never thought of the sea until they saw it from the open ground. Well, he supposed, if the worst came to the worst the bay would be big enough for four people . . . five. Five, he reminded himself.

Where the copse became more of a thicket, he saw the bundles of clothing. They were in three separate piles, yet similar, two pairs of black sail-cloth trousers being identical. The sight of them brought a strange uneasiness to him.

The sound of yelling voices brought him clear of the thicket to the top of the bank leading down to the beach, and there, picking their way tentatively on bare feet over the rocks towards him, were two of the Palmer gang, as he thought of Ronnie Fitzsimmons and Clarky Leach, with Sandy Palmer himself trailing behind. So taken up were they by the rough ascent that they did not become aware of Joe until they were within a few yards of him; and then it was Clarky Leach who, lifting his head, saw him first. He had been negotiating the rough gulley on all fours when, pretending to be a dog, he lifted his head backwards and sniffed; and it was then he saw Joe; and he stopped in his crawling to exclaim on a high, reedy note, 'Coo! fellas. Look who's here!'

Ronnie Fitzsimmons was the next to see Joe and he said, 'It's Joe.' The reference could have indicated that he was welcoming a pal, but he then added, 'Lloyd' and it took away the seeming friendliness from his use of the Christian name.

Sandy Palmer was standing on one foot extracting a piece of dry seaweed from between his toes when he heard the name, and his head shot up so quickly that he almost overbalanced. He stood staring up the rocky incline towards the slight, neatly dressed figure of Joe Lloyd ... Joe Lloyd. All morning he had been thinking of Joe Lloyd. It was as if his thinking had conjured him up out of the air. His feelings remained stationary and numbed for a moment with surprise. Dinner time on a Sunday at the bay, and there he was all dressed up as if he were going into town. It seemed odd, very odd. It came into his mind that he might have been praying all the morning and his prayers had been answered. The surprise faded away, and the fury that had been raging in him, the fury that had driven him out of the house without his Sunday dinner returned, its force making him tremble. All morning he had wanted to smash into something, to hit out at something, to hurt something, to ease the gnawing ache inside him. He did not recognise it as an ache but as a desire to rend and tear. He had been in this state for three weeks, although the feeling had been nothing compared with what he had experienced today. He began to climb upwards towards the copse now, his body straight. His feet ignoring the sharpness of the rocks, he walked as straight as if he were lording it through the town with his hands in his narrow pockets.

When he stood before Joe his pals were already one on each side of him, and he stared at Joe through narrowed slits before he said, 'What are you after here?'

'After? Nothing.' There was a trace of nervousness in Joe's voice, and he looked to each side of him, then back to Sandy Palmer before adding, 'Nothing . . . well, that is, the same as you, I'm goin' to bathe.'

'Bathe? What, in them!' Ronnie Fitzsimmons flicked his forefinger up the sleeve of Joe's jacket.

'Where's your towel and things?' It was like an interrogation, and Joe, looking straight into Sandy Palmer's tight face, said, 'I've never used a towel, I let the water dry on me.'

'He lets the water dry on him.' Sandy Palmer was not looking at Joe now but at his pals, first at Ronnie Fitzsimmons, and then his eyes, leaping over the top of Joe's head, came to Clarky Leach, and he repeated, 'He lets the water dry on him.'

Joe began to tremble. It was just a small reaction at first in his thighs, not noticeable in his face and hands, but it told him he was afraid. One of them he could have managed. With two of them he would have stood a poor chance. With three of them and Sandy Palmer in the lead he knew his position was hopeless. So he tried diplomacy. Forcing a smile to his face and an airy tone to his voice, he asked, 'Is it cold?'

No-one answered him. The two satellites looked towards their leader, and when he did not speak they took their cue from him, and Ronnie Fitzsimmons repeated, with the irritating stupidity of the dull-witted, 'He says, is it cold? Sandy.'

Sandy's eyes were wide open now. They were brown, almost black-hued, and should have been bright and sparkling, if only because he had just come out of the sea, but there was no sparkle in them. They looked dull, opaque, as if light had never passed through them. They were eyes coloured with frustration. Whatever change took place in them was brought about by strong emotion only. The eyes darkened still further now as he said, 'You're a swab.'

Joe made no reply but the trembling in his thighs moved downwards towards his knees.

'D'you hear what Sandy says? You're a swab.' Ronnie Fitzsimmons accompanied this statement with a thrust of his elbow that, for a moment, knocked Joe off-balance and took him a couple of steps away from them. Immediately they brought the distance between them back to what it was before.

'What were you doing last night ... all night?'

'Last night?' Joe blinked up at the tall naked figure before him, and paused as if he was thinking, then said, 'I was walking.'

'He was walking.' Clarky Leach bounced his head towards his two pals and repeated, 'D'you hear that, Sandy? he was walkin' ... he was walkin' all night.'

'Shut up!' Sandy Palmer continued to stare at Joe. Walking; he said he had been walking. Does a fella walk when he's got Brid Stevens with him? The ache that had been in him for weeks now sharpened itself until he felt it like an actual stab under his ribs. The very thought of Brid caused an active boiling inside him, and he wanted to hit out with both his hands and his feet: he wanted to tear into shreds the smooth face confronting him. Brid had been with this fella all night . . . Ever since he had been at school he had wanted Brid Stevens. He had even played a game with himself, saying, 'Aw, let her wait. There's plenty of time, an' plenty of others.' And he had gone round with others. Susie Wright . . . he had gone round with her for six months solid, while all the time being conscious of Brid down the street. Then there came the actual moment when he realised he couldn't play games with himself any more. It was time to make a move, for Brid had something that was attracting others. She hadn't taken to his advances at all, but this only put an edge to his appetite. That time when, coming back from the club – yes he had even left the club early to see her back so that her old man wouldn't go on – he had made up to her and she had turned on him, hit out at him she had, and he had laughed at her. He hadn't minded that; it proved she wasn't easy. He was glad to find that she wasn't loose-legged.

That night, their Harry had passed them in the street, and after Brid had plunged into the house and he was going back to the club to get a dance in before twelve, their Harry had called from the garden, 'Here a minute!' and he had gone back.

'Walk down the road,' said Harry. And he had walked down the road in the opposite direction from the club.

'You mad!' said Harry.

'What d'you mean, me mad?'

'Brid Stevens.'

'What about Brid?'

'Are you plain bats?'

'What're you gettin' at?'

They had stopped at the far corner of tho street under a lamp-post, and Harry had peered at him, then whispered, 'You don't know?'

'Know what? What the hell is it I should know?'

'Good God!'

'What the hell you good-Godding for? What's up with you? What should I know?'

'Well, I thought you knew about the old man.'

'Which old man? Brid's old man or our old man?'

'Our old man.'

'Well, for Christ's sake! what's wrong with him? Spit it out.'

'Don't be such a dim bugger. He fathered Brid; she's our half-sister. That's what all this business has been about for years: me mother bein' bad all the time and old Stevens driving everybody daft ... Don't look like that; I thought you knew. And when I saw you with her, well, I –'

'Shut up! Shut your flaming mouth!'

He had turned and run until he was puffed. Then he had walked for a long time, all the while thinking, not of Brid, but of his father, and the desire to kill him was stronger than any feeling he'd had in his life before.

After that, he hadn't kept out of Brid's way but had tormented her every time he saw her, until he realised that, half-sister or no half-sister, it made no difference to his feelings, and he would have to do something about it ... Something. But what? He had been groping in his mind about the something when he came downstairs this morning and his mother, brighter than usual, had imparted the news to him: 'There was hell let loose in the Stevenses',' she said. 'That Brid has been out all night with a fella.' He had wanted to hit his mother. He had known without being told the name of the fella. It was Joe Lloyd. He had come to the club two Saturdays running and had been in George's a number of times during the last couple of weeks, and each time she had sat nattering to him. And now, right here, dead plonk in front of him, was Joe Lloyd, and he had been out all night with Brid.

Like a flash of lightning, his hands went out and grabbed a fistful of Joe's jacket lapel, tie and shirt. The impact was so sudden that Joe would have fallen over backwards had not the grip on his clothes steadied him, and he put his hands up to his collar and strained his neck as he cried, 'Give over! you're choking me. Give over!'

'You had Brid Stevens with you, hadn't you? Come on, hadn't you?'

'No . . . No, only this –' A vicious shake, which jerked his head backwards, cut off the remainder of his words and he choked, then coughed and gasped. When he was again steady he was breathing as hard as if he had run a fast mile across the fells, and he just heard the tail-end of Clarky Leach's remark coming from way back, high in his nose: 'With Brid Stevens?' And he knew that whatever knowledge Sandy Palmer possessed was not shared by his two mates, because Ronnie Fitzsimmons was now verifying it: 'Coo! You little stinker, you. Fancy that. Him and Brid out all night. Coo! you dirty little bastard.'

'I wasn't.' Joe gasped. 'We weren't. Not all night. We –'

'Just long enough to have some fun, eh?' He was being shaken again; but this time he did not suffer it. For a moment his fear fled and righteous anger took its place. With a sudden tug he freed himself from Sandy Palmer's grasp.

He had got his release through the element of surprise, and it was shown on the boys' faces as he confronted them. He was a couple of yards away from them now but bending towards them in a crouching movement, and his voice was no longer conciliatory.

'You lay your hands on me again and you'll see what you'll get. That goes for all of you. Now mind, I'm tellin' you. Don't think you can come your gang warfare on me. It's like you to go around in threes; you're frightened to tackle anyone single. I'll take you on any day of the week, Palmer, alone, if you've got that much spunk.'

'Listen to him! Listen to him!' In a sideward glance, Clarky's eyes came to rest on Sandy

Palmer, who was standing as still as if he had been frozen to the spot.

Clarky was waiting for a cue from his leader, and in the next second he got it.

'Get him!'

Like three wolves, the boys pounced on Joe, who was instantly borne to the ground, and quickly his struggles were checked by Sandy Palmer sitting on his legs and by the other two holding his arms spreadeagled on the ground. They were all panting, and Clarky gasped, 'What you going to do with him, Sandy?'

Sandy was staring down into the now blazing face of Joe and he said quietly, 'You'll see. Take his clothes off.'

Joe made an attempt to struggle again, but finding this useless, he used the only weapon left to him, his voice. With a bellow that even shook his attackers, he yelled, 'Help! Help!' and as his lips framed the word 'Police!' Ronnie Fitzsimmon's hand clapped across them. 'Where's something to stuff in his mouth?'

Sandy Palmer motioned to Clarky Leach, saying, 'Go and get our things.'

Within a minute the clothes were being dumped down to the side of Joe, and Sandy Palmer said, 'Pass me me hanky here.'

Joe bit ineffectively at the hand that rammed the handkerchief into his mouth. Then his trousers and his short underpants were torn off, and Ronnie Fitzsimmons exclaimed, 'Look! he's got his trunks on. He was going in all right.'

Suddenly, Joe became still; the fight went out of him, and the trembling now reached every pore of his body.

'He'll go in all right.'

The words brought to Joe the quality of danger attached to this part of the coast. He had never before sensed it so clearly. What would they do? Dump him over the rocks into the gut?

Suddenly, he began to pray, the prayers he had learned at Sunday school. God of mercy, God who gave to the world his only begotten Son, Have mercy on me . . . Jesus, Jesus, Jesus.

'Look out and see if there's anybody down below.' Sandy Palmer jerked his head in the direction of the beach, and Clarky Leach ran to the end of the copse, then came back again panting. 'You can't take him down there, Sandy. There's a man and woman lyin' just along on the sands, not far. They're picnickin' an' the fella's been in; he's sunbathing.'

Sandy Palmer stared into Joe's sweating face for a moment, then looked about him as if searching for an idea. And seemingly he found it. 'You got any string, Clarky?' he said.

'String, Sandy? No.'

'You, Ronnie?'

'Might be a bit in me bag on me saddle.'

'Skip an' see.'

'What? Like this? I'd better put me clothes on; the bike's near the road.'

'Put 'em on, then! Here, give him to me.' Sandy Palmer took over his pal's position and his grip was fiercer on Joe, so much so that Joe's face screwed up with the agony of his cramped muscles.

When Fitzsimmons was dressed in his scanty attire of tight trousers, tight singlet and anorak, he scuttled through the trees to his motor-bike, and within a few minutes returned with three pieces of cord of different lengths.

'These do, Sandy?'

After glancing at the cord, Sandy said, 'Hang on here again until I get me things on,' and again they changed over. But all the while he was dressing he kept his eyes on Joe. Next he gave the order to Clarky Leach to get into his things, and again, when his grip took over from Leach's, Joe's body writhed in agony.

There was an unrestrained terror in Joe now; he was whimpering inside, gabbling to himself in his fear: God! God! What would they do? Oh, Mam! If only somebody would come. He's a fiend, a fiend. Hellish! But what's he up to? He can't take me down to the bay.

His thoughts were jostled as he was dragged to his feet, and when he realised that they were going to tie him to a tree his eyes almost popped out of his head; and he made one final effort. Supported by his fear, he curved his back and heaved his stomach upwards in an effort to wrench himself free from them; but he succeeded only in straining himself. When they pulled him straight again he found he wasn't against the big tree but between two slender young ones. He struggled madly as the other two held him while Sandy Palmer tied one of his wrists and an ankle to one of the trunks; but his struggling ceased when Sandy Palmer, with an upward lift, wrenched his other leg toward the second tree, for the scream that tore through his body even penetrated the gag in his mouth, and for a moment he felt nothing and saw nothing.

'Coo! look, careful Sandy; he's passed out.'

A thrust from Sandy Palmer's fist under Joe's chin showed that he had not quite passed out, and when the long, thin fingers clamped his cheeks inwards, Joe opened his eyes and looked dazedly at his tormentor.

'What if somebody comes?' There was just a trace of apprehension in Clarky Leach's voice now.

Sandy Palmer took no notice of this question. He seemed deaf to the fear in his pal's voice and blind to everything but the youth in front of him. And now words squeezed themselves up through his neck and between his teeth: 'I'll larn you to take a young kid out all night. I'll larn you. You won't do it again, will you?' The hand shook viciously, and Joe's head with it. 'An' what were you doin' crawling along here with these on, eh?' He pulled out the elastic on Joe's bathing trunks with his forefinger and let it snap back viciously into Joe's stomach. 'Goin' to meet her, eh? An' goin' for a bathe together, eh? To wash out last night's business, eh?' The elastic band was pulled forward again, this time with such force that the woollen material of the leg was split, although the band remained. Then with a flick of his wrist

Sandy Palmer drew out a knife from his back pocket and the blade seemed to present itself of its own volition. And when it was thrust under the band to split the elastic, the point seered the skin just as it was meant to. Each pore in Joe's body screamed in response and the groan again came through the handkerchief.

'Eeh! Sandy, man, lay off; you'll split his guts. Look, he's bleedin'.'

Again the leader made no response, but he calmly took a cigarette packet from his hip pocket and, standing close to Joe, he extracted a cigarette and lit it. It was at this point that a screaming began in Joe's mind. He knew what this meant. The word Jesus, Jesus, Jesus, raced around inside his head, intermingled with, Help me! Save me! Oh God. God save me. Bring somebody. Oh, Mam!

He closed his eyes tightly as he waited, and when the warm smoke wafted over his face he did not think of Sandy Palmer and his intentions, but strangely he was reminded of the last time he was in church. It wasn't his own church, but a high church in Hexham. His mother was with him; they were on a trip; and it was only her presence that had kept him in his seat, for as he listened to the preacher prattling on about Christ crucified, he was saying to himself, What good is this going to do me? I'd get much more good out of a tramp across the fells. And when the censer was being swung he had felt faint and wanted air. Outside, his mother had remarked, 'It was a very good sermon,' and he had answered, 'How I'm making it out now is that there's been more than one man crucified. They seemed to do it every day during the last war. I've been reading about Belsen,' which had shocked his mother, and she had come back at him straightway with, 'It isn't the same. He was different.'

The smoke was hot now on his face, and behind the racing, screaming matter that was now his brain lay a quiet section, and it was still occupied with that Sunday he had been to church. His mother had said, 'He felt like a man, but He was God.' Now the screaming penetrated the quiet section and it hollered, 'Anybody who goes through this comes out qualified to be a god.' It might seem impossible to make sense out of anything he was thinking, and yet he understood: nobody going through this would be the same again, not to themselves or to anyone else; nobody afterwards would think the same of them because they would only have to look into their eyes to know they had qualified to be a . . . 'Go–d!'

The scream, denied full utterance through his mouth, poured itself out through his skin; when the cigarette touched his flesh his nerves screamed themselves into sweat.

'Eeh! Sandy. God! man. You'll maim him . . . Give over . . . Look; I'm off.'

'You stay where you are.'

The copse became quiet. The two boys stood away from the stretched figure and their leader. Their eyes were fixed on the quivering, seared flesh between the naked loins. They gazed in petrified fascination, yet their bodies were half turned as if for flight; and then Clarky's quick ear caught a sound. It was a scraping of a foot on the rocks and he jerked round and ran to the edge of the clearing. There he saw a bent figure scrambling up the bank and his mouth dropped into a wide gape. The next second he was with his pals again.

'Sandy, it's her! It's Brid! She's here.' Clarky flung his arm backwards as if to indicate Brid.

Sandy Palmer did not even glance towards Clarky, but, his eyes darting once more over Joe, he called quickly, 'Out of it!'

The other two needed no second warning; they were off and would have made for their motor-bikes but that Sandy's arm waved them down behind a clump of bushes, and there they waited.

And Joe waited. His whole body was crying with pain. His mind was screaming with a mixture of anger and fear and the tears were running down his face. As he waited he looked away sideways in the direction of the sea. In the dawn of this morning he had felt a man. He had sat on a hill and looked at the dawn, and at his side had sat the girl who not only his body but also his spirit had told him was for him. He had wanted her to see him as somebody different, not as the little meek chap Joe Lloyd, not the open-air chap Joe Lloyd, not the chap who talked poetry but couldn't write it. He wanted her to see him as the man, Joe Lloyd. The man who she would feel was for her. A man of strength despite his size, a man of beauty despite his size, for his limbs were smooth and compact, and his skin was warm and sunburned from his feet upwards to the top of his thighs and upwards again from his navel. But how would she see him now, trussed like a drying rabbit skin, stark naked and with his privates still quivering from the burning cigarette end? His spirit bowed itself down low under the humiliation. It too was crying.

And there she was, coming out of the full sun into the dappled shade of the copse. He did not droop his head when her horror-filled gaze brought her to a dead, gaping stop. Then her head, pushing itself back on her shoulders, looked for a moment as if it would topple her backwards.

The look in her eyes brought a groan from Joe, for in her gaze was reflected the dirt of life, the dirt from which he had always washed his hands. Even in thought he had tried to keep away from the dirt of life. He had wanted to think of life as fine, grand, beautiful. This complex dream desire, this God-given yet God-forbidden instinct which came into evidence from the moment the lips suckled the breast, this spring of interest and curiosity that disturbed the adolescent mind, this promise of the body for ecstatic wonder . . . this was the one thing he had tried to keep clean. So much had aimed to soil it. The talk of the lads at school. The lavatories, and Ernie Bowen pressing against him. Bill Chaters and Frankie Potter talking on the backshifts. And the TV: the girls wearing only tights, bending backwards and wriggling their thighs to the camera. He had wondered for a while about these cameramen focussing the light on them, but dismissed it with the thought, They won't see it like that, it's just a job. But now he knew his efforts were as nothing, for he was seeing himself reflected in Brid's horrified gaze.

When she screamed he screwed his eyes up, and he kept them screwed even when he heard her gasping breath near him.

'Joe. Oh Joe. Oh my God! Joe. Oh, I can't get it loose. Oh God in heaven! Oh, the devils! The beasts! The beasts!'

Slowly Joe opened his eyes and looked at her. She was struggling ineffectively with the cords at his wrists, hurting him more as she tried to release him. She had not thought to take the gag out of his mouth, and as he made a motion with his head to draw her attention to his face, his own attention was caught by the sight of a man now entering the copse. He too was naked but for bathing trunks. For a minute he stood still with his hands extended away from his sides; then seemingly in a couple of leaps he was standing beside Brid, and he too was using the name of God, but going further, crying, 'God Almighty! God Almighty!' And to this he added, 'The bastards!'

113

It was hardly a word that a schoolteacher should use, but Leonard Morley was in the habit of using it frequently. Hardly a day passed but he would exclaim to himself, 'The young bastards!' It hadn't always been like this. He could look back to the time when he had liked young lads, when he had said that Robson, or Wheatley, or Colleridge was a lad, a young devil, but still a lad. The term 'lad' in itself had indicated that the boy in question was a bit of a devil. And the devil had indicated that the lad was an outsize of a lad. He could remember going home to Phyllis when they were first married and saying, 'What d'you think happened to-day? Some devil took Sefton's bike to pieces, completely to pieces. It looked as if it was in a thousand bits. I thought he would have taken off, the explosion was so great.' The funny side of this had been that Sefton was the gym instructor and advocated walking. And then there was the day that one of the lads with a knack for it had swapped some wiring around. He must have got into the school on the Sunday, and what happened on the Monday morning, especially in the chemmy lab, wasn't forgotten for a long, long time. The lads then had been devils . . . but they weren't bastards.

114

He couldn't actually remember the time when they had changed to being bastards, although he knew it wasn't directly after the war, but in the early sixties, he would say.

He tore at the cords fastening the boy to the tree and as he worked he talked rapidly. 'Who did this? How long have you been here? If you can get them they'll do years for this. My God! I would like to see them on the receiving end of a birch.' He put his arms underneath Joe to support him and half carried him out beyond the copse to the grass. He seemed unaware of Brid, and yet, after he had laid Joe down he looked up at her and said with a note of command, 'Run to the bank and call my wife.'

From where she was standing, her eyes fixed on Joe's pale, averted face, Brid did not seem to hear his words, and the man, realising this, put his hand to his mouth and called, 'Phyllis! Phyllis!'

As the call died away there came a movement from away behind them in the direction of the road, but he could see nothing.

There now followed the sound of motor cycles starting up, and on hearing it Brid bit into her lower lip for she knew, as plainly as if she had seen them, who the riders were.

Joe did not hear the machines. He was conscious only of pain and his nakedness, and to remove this from Brid's eyes he turned with an effort on to his face. Although his legs were pressed tightly together and his arms were hugging his body, his limbs still had the feeling of being stretched, and added to this was the sensation of a hot wire being drawn through the marrow of his bones. He wanted to slip away into oblivion; it would have been easy, for he was faint and sick. His mouth, which also still retained that stretched feeling, moved about some words, and the man kneeling on the grass and bending his ears to him said, 'What is it?'

'Me clothes.'

'Where did you leave them?'

His jaws moved twice before he brought out, 'About . . . somewhere.'

The man looked back to where the torn trunks lay between the slender trees and he moved hastily forward and picked them up, then went behind the few bushes, looking here and there.

The fingers of Brid's left hand were pressing upwards across her mouth, and her thumb was dug in under her cheek bone. The fingers were aiming to press down the fear that was filling her and which was attempting to escape in a gabble of words, a gabble of names which, strangely enough, did not include Sandy Palmer's. It was her mother's name, her father's name, and the name of her Uncle John which raced about in her mind, and would escape if she did not prevent them.

Her eyes travelled down from the back of Joe's head to his buttocks. They were small and firm and pale compared with the skin of his back and that of his legs. The soles of his feet were turned upwards and in this moment she was surprised that she could register the fact that they were without corn or callus. They were broad-soled, flat yet shapely, the feet of a walker . . . But her mother, and her father, and her Uncle John. Her mother and her father and her Uncle John: the words were spiralling higher in her head, but the man stopped them from escaping by making his appearance once again with Joe's clothes across his arm, just as a woman pulled herself up over the top of the bank as Brid herself had done only a few minutes earlier on her hands and knees. And when she straightened up, the man called to her: 'Here! Phyllis; come and look at this. No wonder she screamed. They had him gagged and spreadeagled between these trees.' He pointed. 'You wouldn't believe it . . . or would you? It's what I've been saying all along, they're not human any more.' He approached the woman, talking as if Brid and Joe weren't there, and then he turned with her and came towards them again.

'They were fellows on motor-bikes, I heard them go off. Couldn't have been anybody but them. Look at this.' He bent down and his hands came gently on to Joe's shoulder, and his voice changed now as he said softly, 'Turn over, boy, let my wife see. Don't worry, she's been a nurse.'

Joe, after turning his head slowly to the side and glancing at the woman dressed in a short-skirted sunsuit, turned his head quickly into the grass again and pressed his body to the earth.

'It's all right, I tell you. She'll know if you should go to hospital or not.'

Joe's body made a movement of burrowing, then he said, 'Give me me clothes.'

'Don't be silly.' The voice was gentle but brisk, and the woman, kneeling down by him, turned him over, and he, still too shaken to resist, was once again on his back. Her hands did not touch him and a silence fell on them, and then she swallowed once before saying, 'Why did they do this? Do you know them?'

Joe's head moved once from side to side. He said again, 'Me clothes,' and this time added with a beseeching note, 'please.'

As the man and woman helped Joe to his feet Brid looked away, looked out towards the sea. She knew that Joe did not want her to look at him. She had a nice picture of the sea framed in between the boles of the trees. On the horizon right at the top of the picture was a speck she knew to be a ship. She wished she was on that ship, far away from this place. Far away from everybody in it. But not everybody . . . Joe. She didn't want to be far away from Joe. Her father had said to her, 'You move out of this house the day and I'll skin you alive.' That was when she had gone down to dinner. After dinner she had gone upstairs and got her bathing costume and put it in the fancy basket with a towel. She had not cared then whether or not her father came out of the front room, for she had suddenly stopped being afraid of him. Lying in bed that morning she had faced the fact that all the wanting in the world wouldn't make him her father. He wasn't her father, and she had always known he wasn't her father.

That's where the trouble had lain, and still lay; he wasn't her father. She had known that if she met him on the stairs, or in the kitchen, and he tried to carry out his threat she would fight him, tooth and nail; she would fight him to get out and go swimming with Joe Lloyd. He had been sulking in the front room when she came downstairs. Her mother had been in the kitchen when she passed through and she had said no word to detain her, and Brid knew that in defying the man she called father she was scoring one against him for her mother.

As she had hurried along the road towards the beach she had thought, I'm seventeen and if I wanted to marry, I could; he couldn't stop me. Joe likes me, he does, and I like him. I do, I do. I've never met anybody I like as I like him. He's different. Not nasty. He could never be nasty. Not even when . . . Her thoughts had skipped away from the subject and she had covered some distance before she had said to herself, 'What if he's only being nice and not serious?' And there had come a longing in her, a prayerful longing that Joe Lloyd would be serious, for she saw in his seriousness a means of escape. She would stay at home for ever and ever, as bad as it was, rather than marry *anybody*; yes, rather than marry anybody. Then she had scrambled down to the beach and up the bank towards the trees . . . and she had seen Joe.

He had looked terrible. Without being told, she had known who had done this thing. Yet her mind would persist in ignoring his name. She could not even think of the name 'Sandy Palmer'; it was as if he didn't exist. But there were those who did exist, and they were her mother and father and her Uncle John.

The woman's voice came to her now, saying, 'Come and sit down,' and she was surprised when she turned to see them all sitting down, the man and the woman one on each side of Joe. Slowly she went and sat down opposite Joe but did not look at him, nor he at her. The man was saying, 'Now take my advice and go to the police. If they can do this once they'll do it again. They've only to get a taste for this kind of business, for anything abnormal, and they are away. You say you know who they were. What's their names? Tell me; perhaps I know them.'

Joe lowered his head still further. If he were to say Sandy Palmer the man would say, 'But why did he do it?' And could he say to him, 'He did it because he thought I was out all night with her, with Brid, when we only met at four o'clock.' And then the man would say, 'Four o'clock! Four o'clock this morning? But why did you want to meet at four o'clock this morning?' To see the dawn. It sounded funny now, daft, even improper, to ask a girl out at four o'clock in the morning. They would reckon that things could happen at four o'clock in the morning the same as they did at ten o'clock at night. Sandy Palmer had thought that . . . Sandy Palmer. He would get Sandy Palmer, and by God he would leave his mark on Sandy Palmer. Not in the same place as Sandy Palmer had left it on him. No, he wasn't that putrid. He could never stoop to that, but, by God in heaven! he would give Sandy Palmer something he would carry to his dying day, he would that.

'It was Sandy Palmer.' Brid suddenly blurted out the name, her head and chest bouncing forward as if she were being prodded in the back.

Swiftly, Joe lifted his head to look straight into Brid's eyes: it was as if she had spoken his thoughts aloud. He saw that she was still terrified. This was a new side to Brid. He hadn't had much time to find the sides to her, but this one he judged was part of her make-up; this fear-filled side came over in the trembling of her voice as she mentioned the name Sandy Palmer, and before he could say anything the man took it up, his voice hard.

'Sandy Palmer? Well, one needn't be surprised any more. Sandy Palmer ... I know Sandy Palmer. How did you come foul of Sandy Palmer?' But without waiting for an answer the man went on, 'Was it at Telford Road School? He went there, didn't he? I had him before that.' Leonard Morley stopped abruptly. His mind having groped back, he actually knew now the first time he had thought of boys as bastards. Sandy Palmer could only have been about eleven at the time. He remembered Sandy Palmer. Oh yes, by God! he did. For Sandy Palmer had left his mark on him, in a way, as well as on this boy. He hadn't been long at the Bodden Moor School; it was his third move since the war and he was unsettled. He remembered realising very quickly that a number of the boys at this school were tough lads. Sandy Palmer was one of them. Each had the same habit of filling the classroom with the gases from his body. They did it purposely, methodically, orderly, in rotation. To them, it was a belly-aching laughter game. Their faces would be tight with unexploded laughter. Their eyes round and bright, their nostrils would quiver as they sniffed the polluted air, and they would all be looking at him fixedly, their eyes, saying, 'What now, chum?' He should have had more sense than talk to them about this sort of thing. He had had enough experience to know that he should have got the ringleader on one side without witnesses and boxed his blasted ears, given him a kick in the backside, or shaken him until his teeth rattled, all metaphorically speaking; but no, he had had to address the whole form; and it was no other than Sandy Palmer who had run across the playground, right past the common-room window, yelling, 'What d'you think? Old Morley gave us a lesson on fartin'.' That was the day he acquired the name of Farty Morley.

He hated the nickname, loathed it. It made him curl up inside. Sandy Palmer had left the school when he was twelve, but the nickname had stuck.

At this moment Leonard Morley was hating Sandy Palmer more than was Joe. Joe's mind was muzzy, but the man's, in the main, seemed to be clear with a hard clearness, polished with years of classroom restraint; but with a section cut off as if by a thick plate-glass window behind which his turbulent thoughts were allowed to boil. He had a longing for Sandy Palmer to return. He could see himself rolling on the ground, pounding his fists into Sandy Palmer's face, beating out of him not only the humiliation that the nickname had carried, but all the nerve-stretching, mind-explosive irritations of all the little bastards he had been forced to suffer.

The words 'Come on! Come on! snap out of it,' being briskly spoken by the woman to her husband, startled Brid somehow, for the action that had accompanied them, the tapping of the man imperiously on the arm, reminded her of a scene in the kitchen at home with her mother saying, 'Come on! Come on! snap out of it. Get going. Snap out of it.' This scene on top of the cliff had taken on a semblance of home. She didn't know this man and woman from Adam, yet it was as if she had been with them for years.

Now turning, first to Brid, then to Joe, the woman said, 'Look, we'll go down and get our things, we've got a little stove. We'll bring everything up here and make a cup of tea, eh?' And Brid looked to see Joe's reaction, and when he acknowledged the words with small jerks of his head, Brid followed suit.

'All right. Fine. That's a good idea.' The man was on his feet. He was smiling slightly and was looking somewhat boyish. He too looked from Brid to Joe and his voice took on a light note as he said, 'And then we'll all go in and have a dip. A dip won't do him any harm, will it?' He had turned to his wife, questioning, but quickly returned to Joe, saying, 'That's what you came for, isn't it, a dip?' With a swift body movement he was down on his hunkers, his face level with Joe's, and speaking low and earnestly now, with bitterness threading the words, he said, 'Go in and have your dip. Keep to your purpose; don't let them budge you an inch. If you came here to swim, swim. If you allow swine like Palmer and his gang to deviate you one inch, they've won. You've got to go on and do what you want to do in spite of them. Go right through them. D'you understand?'

Joe's head had been slightly drooped, but now he was looking at the man eye to eye. The fellow was right. If you let them frighten you, you were finished. If he remained frightened now he would never see Brid again. He could see himself avoiding this beach, avoiding the club and George's; in fact moving away altogether, just because of Sandy Palmer and what he would do next. No, the man was right. 'Go through them,' he had said, and that's what he would do. He could see his future actions clearly, he could see them reflected in the man's eyes. He would get Ossie to go with him. Yes, he would ask Ossie to go with him. He would go to the house, Sandy Palmer's house, and say, 'Look, I could have gone to the police. I could have had you locked up for what you did to me. But come on, we'll fight it out. You bring one of your chaps, I've got mine.' And they would go to some place on the fells. The light he was seeing in the man's eyes seemed to dim, and with it his heroic action of having it out with Sandy Palmer the clean way. No. It couldn't be like that; that was the way things were at one time, the way his dad would have done it, but you could not do it now. If he beat Sandy Palmer, Sandy Palmer would catch him one dark night and he'd have his pals with him. They would waylay him and beat him up. He knew the procedure; it had happened to other blokes. He had heard about them now and again in the club, and yet that club was supposed to be a good club where things like that didn't happen, because no louts or beats were allowed in.

The man said, 'What about it?'

Joe sighed, then looked at Brid. She still had
that frightened look on her face. He wanted
to put his hand out past the man and grip
hers and say, 'Don't worry. Just let them try
anything again, just let them.' He wanted to
say things to her that would take that look
off her face. It was an awful look. Perhaps the
man was right. If they went in and had a swim
it might make things normal again, it might
make her look less frightened. 'All right,' he
answered, 'as you say.'

'That's it.' The man got to his feet, and as
he was straightening up Joe's head came up
quickly and the words tumbled out of him:
'I can't. Well . . . you see . . . me trunks.' He
pointed to the ground where his trunks lay,
the elastic band still supporting the ripped
material. Then the woman, going and picking
them up, said, 'Oh, I'll soon fix these. I haven't
any needle and thread with me but I've a
packet of tiny safety pins in my bag. We'll
do a botching job. Wait till we come back;
we won't be a minute.' She turned and ran
towards the top of the clearing, and the man,
after one look which he divided again between
Brid and Joe, ran after her.

They were alone with a matter of three feet
separating them. They did not look at each

other but purposely watched the man and woman running. They watched them until they had dropped over the steep bank; and they both continued to look in that direction for quite some time after the couple had disappeared. Joe would have liked to lie back and just let his body relax. It was paining again. The pain had eased off a while ago but now it was back, the skin cut on his stomach was stinging and the burn seemed worse than ever. He wished he could look at it, examine it. What if it didn't heal and spread . . . He turned quickly towards Brid and said softly, 'I'm sorry for all this.'

'What?' The word sounded inane. She had looked slightly stupid as she spoke it; and she said again, 'What?' But now it didn't sound stupid to him, for it said, Why should he say he is sorry? Look what has happened to him.

'It's all because of me.'

'Don't take it like that. Don't look at it like that. He would have got at me for something else.'

'He'll not let up. I'll have to . . . I mean I won't have to—'

He didn't let her finish. The man had said, 'Go right through them, don't be diverted,'

129

and so he interrupted her with rather more conviction than he felt.

'You won't have to do anything of the sort,' he said. 'You mean that you'll stop seeing me, don't you? Well, that's what he wants, and he won't get that satisfaction. You're going to go on seeing me . . . aren't you?'

He really didn't want to be bothered talking like this, not at the moment; he wanted to lie down and rest, just rest. He felt sort of weak all over, shaken, like he'd never felt even during his worst moments in the pit. In this case, the shaking wasn't only in his body and his mind, it seemed to have gone deeper. He couldn't quite make it out. He told himself that his head was too muzzy to think, but he said to Brid, in a voice that he tried to make masterful, 'The man said we came here to bathe and we did, didn't we? And that's what we'll do. We'll act as if nothing had happened.'

He turned slightly away and leaned rather heavily on his elbow. My God, that was a daft thing to say, even in an effort to take that look off her face. Act as if nothing had happened. That was wishful thinking all right, for he knew that when this muzziness left his mind his thoughts would be like those that had filled him during the moments of his ordeal;

things would scream at him. Questions would scream at him; life would scream at him, life peopled with fellows like Sandy Palmer. And the main question would be: why were fellows like him allowed to get away with things? Short of murder, they got by.

By twisting round and leaning towards him, Brid brought his attention back to herself. She had one leg under her, and her hands flat on the ground supported her as she leaned forward. Her face looked even whiter than it had done before; she was looking scared beyond reason and she said, 'There's something I've got to tell you. There's something you should know. It's about . . . about what's happened, connected with it, like. It's about Sandy Palmer.'

He felt the pain of the burn lessen, he felt his whole body go cool, even take on a degree of coldness, as if he had been pushed momentarily into an ice-box. She wanted to tell him something about Sandy Palmer. Had she and Sandy Palmer . . .? Before he could stop himself he was saying in a low and agonised voice, 'You haven't been with him, have you . . . not Palmer?'

Her arms lifting quickly from the ground arched her body as if she were about to execute a backwards somersault. 'Me been with him! Me? No! No! Not that!'

He was out of the ice-box and his body began to burn again. Nothing mattered, nothing. If that wasn't the case, nothing mattered. He could stand anything but that, anything. He didn't think he could have stood that, he didn't. No, he didn't . . . Aw, well . . .

She was saying now, 'You see it's like this. His father—' Her head moved downwards, she couldn't say it.

He put out his hand towards her. 'What is it? I don't mind anything.' And he didn't. Nothing she could tell him would shake him so long as she hadn't been with Sandy Palmer. He said, 'You're frightened about something, not only this the day. What is it?' He remembered the odd way she had spoken of Palmer only a few hours ago, but now she was talking about Sandy Palmer's father.

She said in a whisper that he could only just hear, 'My mother and his father—' But she couldn't go on, she couldn't say, Sandy Palmer's father is my father, I'm his half-sister; she didn't want to admit that anything that was in Sandy Palmer was in her. At this moment, it was this thought that was terrifying her as much as anything else:

that in a way she was part of Sandy Palmer,
the same Sandy Palmer who had tied Joe in
that way to the trees, who had stripped him
naked and burnt him on . . . and burnt him
on the . . . She gulped on her thoughts again
and her head drooped further, and Joe's hands
squeezed hers as he said, 'Look, Brid; it doesn't
matter to me what your mother's done, or
Palmer's father. They are nothing. Look, it's
just us. Don't you realise that? It's just us.'
Things were galloping much faster than they
should have done. He knew where he stood in
relation to her, but nevertheless things should
have been taken in stages with a sort of . . .
well . . . wonder. But now the pace was being
forced and there was no wonder in it.

Her head was still down, and she muttered,
'It isn't only that. I . . . must tell you—'

'Well, here we are!' The woman's voice came
from the brow of the slope, and when she fell
forward on to the ground from a too forceful
push from her husband she laughed as the
things spilled out of her arms, and she called
across to Brid, 'Come and give me a hand,
will you?'

Brid rose slowly to her feet. She was feeling
stiff and tired and yet relieved, as if she had
been saved from disaster. Yet she knew the

relief to be only temporary, for Joe would have to know sooner or later.

'All this paraphernalia,' the man Morley said. 'We seem to move house every weekend. The car's like a covered wagon . . . There now!' He dumped his armful of utensils and clothes almost at Joe's feet and jocularly said to him, 'Take on a bet? How many minutes before you get a cup of tea, eh?'

Joe did not respond to the jauntiness; he could not, but just moved aside and the man said, 'Five minutes from now,' and then like an agitated ant he began darting here and there, picking out things, erecting this, discarding that, while his wife smiled tolerantly at his antics as if at a child showing off.

Phyllis Morley loved her husband because she understood him. Up to a point, she guided and ruled him . . . but only up to a point. Her mother had said to her the night before she married, 'If you remember that all men are little boys you'll get along all right.' After nursing men during the war she knew all about the little boy side of them, but it wasn't the same little boy side as her mother and those like her prattled on about. She knew that the juvenile side was really a handicap, something that put a spoke into

134

their maturity. The side that wanted to lash out with fists when their tongues would have been more effective, the little boy side that could shy away from responsibility. At one time, the teacher had taken the load, then the mother; only then came the turn of the wife. But what happened when the little boy became the teacher and the bulwark for other little boys? A war was bound to break out. Her Len was a good man, and a good teacher . . . A good teacher had to like boys, and he had liked them . . . up till then? She couldn't remember the exact date, but she could remember the name Sandy Palmer. It was from the time she first heard this name that Len's nights became restless, when he would shout out in his sleep. And she had never heard him use a really heavy word until then. She did not know all the ins and outs concerning the trouble Len had had with this boy, but she did know that he was never the same from then on. His temper became brittle, his nerves taut. It was because of this that she insisted they spend every available minute of his free time in the open, walking or swimming. When it was fine, like today, they would come down to the beach before breakfast and make a day of it. Len was always better afterwards, at least for a time. She wanted to feel resentful about the intrusion of this hated name Palmer into the day, but she couldn't, for in some peculiar way she felt that what that Palmer boy had done to this boy here had helped Len, sort of given him a form of release. Here was the little boy again. Another boy had suffered at the hands of the bully and he was no longer alone. Things weren't so bad when shared. Although her husband did not realise it, he was, in a way, glad of what had happened to this lad. She could gauge this from the boisterousness of his manner. She did not like being possessed of this knowledge.

She hastily picked up Joe's trunks and began effectively to pin a seam in them.

It was almost the same moment when the man with a cry of triumph said, 'There! Water boiling. Tea mashed. What d'you think of that for smartness?' that the woman, throwing the trunks into Joe's lap, added, 'And how's that for smartness too? They look as if they are decorated with gold thread, don't they?'

'Thanks.' Joe handled the trunks, and the woman said, 'Shall we have a cup of tea before you change, or after?'

'Oh, let's have it now,' said her husband.

'Well, give it time to draw,' she said.

'Oh, I've put enough tea in to hold a knife straight up. Come on, where are those cups. D'you mind the top of the flask?'

Brid shook her head.

'There! and with two teaspoons of sugar in it.' The man handed the cup to Joe, then added, 'Oh, I didn't ask you if you took sugar, but I suppose you do.'

Joe said, 'Thanks.' He did not mention the fact that he never took sugar. It didn't matter. He put his hands round the cup and held it to his mouth. It tasted good. Different from the tea he had at home, but good, and warm. Although his body was burning again, inside he felt the need of warmth, for, somehow he didn't feel over-good.

'Have another one?'

He handed his cup to the man, and received it from him again with another 'Thanks,' and they all sat drinking in silence for quite a while. Then with a sudden bound Len Morley was on his feet again. 'Well, now!' he said; 'we don't want to wait until it's low tide, although it doesn't matter so much down in the bay. Only it means you've got to go practically to the rocks before you get out of your depth. Well, what about it? Going to get changed?'

Brid rose slowly to her feet. She didn't want

to get changed, she didn't want to bathe, but as she stood undecided the woman said, 'There's a good place over here. Come on.' And she rose and walked away to the left towards a clump of bushes, and Brid followed her.

And now the man, looking down at Joe, said seriously, 'It'll do you good, you know. It's funny what the sea does to you; it seems to wash away all your troubles. At least while you're in it.' He put out a hand and patted Joe's shoulder. 'Which school did you go to?'

'Telford Road.'

'Where are you working now?'

'The pits.'

'You mustn't let what's happened affect you too much. We must have a talk. I'm a teacher. By the way, for your information, I once taught Sandy Palmer.' Their eyes met and held, and the man nodded. 'I know Sandy Palmer only too well. You must come and have tea with us one night. Bring your friend.' He looked towards where his wife and Brid had disappeared behind the bushes, and he added, 'She's nice. A nice girl, I should say. I'll give you our address before we leave. And now come on, come on up.' He helped Joe to his feet, then said, 'I'll leave you to find

138

your own dressing-room. Can you manage by yourself?'

'Yes; yes, I can manage.' Joe's steps were rather unsteady, not drunken, but were just as if he had indulged in a few pleasurable pints. When he stood up his head felt muzzy and he shook it vigorously as he walked in the opposite direction from Brid and also towards a clump of bushes.

The patch of bush he chose screened him effectively from the clearing but only partly from the rest of the copse. It was as he pulled his shirt over his head that he heard the sound of a motor-bike stopping. It arrested the movement of his arms and he pushed his head upwards through the neck again and looked out in the direction of the road, his body now stiff and erect and for a moment painless. It was a good many seconds later when he actually pulled his shirt off and his limbs relaxed and he felt the pain again, but as he dropped his trousers on to the ground he thought, If I saw one of them now, I'd kill him.

Four

Charlie Talbot had not been able to go swimming with the gang that morning because he had had to take a message to his granny in Morpeth. The ride to Morpeth and back was nothing, but once his granny opened her mouth she forgot to shut it again, and she always yapped and yapped to keep him till the last minute. He would have left right away and to hell with her, but she was always good for a few bob, even a pound or two when she was buttered up a bit, and he had done some buttering this morning. By! aye, he would say he had; he was in need of a few quid. He wanted to treat the gang to something special, Sandy and them. It was mostly Sandy he wanted to treat. He felt that if he had some money to splash about he might take the place of Ronnie or Clarky in Sandy's affections. Sandy, he knew, held him of no account, and Ronnie and Clarky followed his example. He was a member of the gang only on sufferance. Of this he was well aware. Perhaps this was because he didn't look tough. But he could be tough. He could make himself tough. He'd buy another knife, one of the latest, and he would bet his mother wouldn't get her hands on that one . . . His mother! He moved his head impatiently on the thought of his mother. He had given her some lip before leaving the house this morning, although he had had to run for it. 'And if you're not back in time for your dinner, I'm not keepin' it!' she had yelled. His dinner. She could keep her dinner, she knew what she could do with it. He laid the bike against the bank and moved into the trees. Perhaps they hadn't gone home yet; they might be still on the beach. Perhaps their bikes were further in the copse. Clarky had had his lamp pinched recently. There were sods who'd pinch your granny's upper plate when she was yawning. Coo! That was a good 'un. He'd have to tell Sandy that one. As he threaded his way forward his small eyes widened and brightened as he saw the slant of a bare arm above the bushes. Coo! he was lucky; they were still here. He put his hand to the hip pocket of his tight jeans to where his wallet was bulging. What would they say when he showed them this little lot? Ten quid he had now with the three pounds he had borrowed from his granny. He stretched his nose as he thought of the word borrowed. None of them had as much as this left after they paid the instalments on their bikes and this and that. He hadn't paid his instalment for a fortnight now. The thought of his mother came to him again, and he answered it with a movement of his shoulders as he went forward, saying almost aloud, 'Well, let her find out, she can only shout.' And it was as though the word was a prompt, for he shouted, 'Sandy! I've made it, Sandy. You—' He had caught sight of a naked figure through a screen of bushes to the right, and it wasn't Sandy's. Quickly he moved his head, endeavouring to get a better view; and then his mouth fell into a long wide gape . . . It was a lass with nowt on.

He was about to turn his gaze questioningly towards the bushes to the left of him where he had first thought Sandy Palmer was, when he received the shock of his short and useless life as somebody hurled himself at him, and before he could even gasp a bloke was lathering into him with his fists. As he automatically hit back in a vain effort to stave off the blows he shouted all kinds of things. 'Help! Help! Give over! What's up? Look . . . Look here a minute! Give over! will you?' And then he was rolling on the ground crying out in agony as a fist rammed into his eye. Maddened with the pain, he now tried to bring his knee up into the fella's stomach but all he could manage was to defend his face. Then, of a sudden, the fella was wrenched off him and he lay on the ground panting and looking up through narrowed vision into a face he knew. It was Joe Lloyd, the fella that had started coming to the club and George's and looked as if he was going soft on Brid Stevens. He was being held now by a man in a bathing costume.

A woman came and bent over him and helped him to his feet, and when he was upright, with his hand covering his damaged eye, he stood swaying.

Looking at Joe, who was standing taut within the man's grasp, he said between gasps, 'You'll get it for this. What's up with you? I've done nowt to you. But you'll get it for this. See if you don't.'

Joe Lloyd was struggling again in an effort to free himself from the man, who now shouted at him, 'Get yourself away and quick!' And when he didn't move, the man added, 'Unless you want some more.'

He backed a few steps, then stopped again. And looking from one to the other, he said, 'You'll get some more; the lot of you'll get some more. Don't think you'll get away with this.' But as he turned to go he looked towards the bushes, where he had seen the girl standing with nothing on; and then, in spite of the pain of his bruises and the shock that the attack had caused, he gaped again, for although he could see only a bit of her hair and face he knew he was seeing Brid Stevens. And it was revealed to him why he had been attacked. Dragging his eyes from the bushes back towards Joe again, he cried, 'You won't get off with this. Just you wait, you mad bugger!' and the words seemed to impel him to get away, and quickly, for it was obvious the man could hardly hold back Joe Lloyd.

He was trembling as he mounted the motor cycle. He could only see out of one eye. Half of his face seemed to be extending to the end of his shoulder. He touched his cheek-bone. It felt as if it were cracked, and as he opened the throttle he said, 'Wait until I tell them! Just wait!' And he glanced in the direction of the clearing before driving off . . .

Ten minutes later Mrs Talbot, looking at her son standing in the doorway, exclaimed, 'My God! You've come off. Well, I knew you would one of these days. What happened? What did you hit? Don't just stand there. My God! What a face!'

'I didn't hit nowt.'

'You didn't hit nowt? How did you get that, then? Bill!' She threw back her head and called to her husband: 'Come here and see this. This is what I've said would happen all along.'

'I tell you, Ma, I didn't hit nowt.'

When his father appeared in the doorway he said again, 'I didn't hit nowt, Dad. I went to me granny's, as you know, and I was comin' back. I got off me bike up above the bay, near the little wood, because Sandy and them—'

'Sandy and them?' His mother's head went back. 'That Sandy Palmer will lead you to no—'

'Oh, shut up! Ma, and let me tell you. And give me something for me eye. You won't shut your mouth. I haven't seen Sandy. I went to see him; I thought they were swimming. I thought I saw him behind the bushes and I went up

146

and I saw—' He stopped, and then said more slowly, 'There was a lass behind the bushes. She had nowt on.' He watched his mother's face shrink into primness. 'And then a fella came at me. I didn't know what hit me. He knocked me to the ground and pummelled me until another bloke pulled him off. It was a fella called Joe Lloyd, and the lass was Brid Stevens from along the road.'

'Brid Stevens? D'you mean to say she was the lass with nothing on?'

'Aye; yes, she was. She was behind some bushes and she had nowt on. Neither had he.'

'And because you caught them, the fella went for you, was that it?'

'Aye. He came at me from behind. He went mad. But he won't get off with it. When I tell Sandy—'

'You say it was Brid Stevens?'

'What've I been tellin' you . . .? Dad,' he appealed to his father who had remained silent all this time – 'haven't I been tellin' her, and she keeps on. It was Brid Stevens and this fella Joe Lloyd.' He turned back to his mother: 'Get me somethin' for me face, will you? Have you any steak? They say steak's good.'

'I've got no steak. How would I have steak

on a Sunday afternoon? The meat's cooked. My God! look at the mess you're in . . . and your suit. And that Brid Stevens. This is through her, the dirty little bitch. Goin' the same road as her mother . . . Well!'

'That's enough! That's enough!' It was the first time the man had spoken, and his wife turned on him angrily now, saying, 'Oh . . . that's enough. It's the likes of her who get sympathy. Disgrace she is, and the trouble she's caused. Look at poor Olive Palmer next door. Ruined her health and everything, the carry-on has, for years.'

'That's enough, I said. It's got nothin' to do with this. He butted in on the fella and the girl, and the fella turned on him . . . Were you looking for it?'

'No; no, I wasn't. I tell you I was just lookin' for Sandy and this fella came at me. And I wouldn't have been lookin' for it; you just have to go on the beach if you want to see that.'

'Keep your voice down.' The father looked at his son, whom he didn't like. The boy was a weak-kneed, dim, little ignoramus, and a sneaking, light-fingered liar into the bargain, whose one desire in life was to be like that lout of a Palmer next door. Bill Talbot wondered, and not for the first time, how children could be so different from their parents. He hadn't much time for John Palmer and his carrying on with Alice Stevens, but the man didn't seem to be of the type to breed a Sandy Palmer, nor did Olive Palmer seem the kind of woman to breed such a son. Funny things happened with offspring. He would have wished to have been able to say there was something of himself in his son, but look what he had been saddled with. His lad was eighteen and he was no good. No good whatsoever. He shuddered to think what he would be like at twenty-eight.

He said now, 'Well, a black eye won't kill you.' Then his attention was brought sharply from his son to his wife as she stood taking off her apron. He watched her smoothing down her hair with quick strokes of her fingers before he asked, 'Where d'you think you're goin'?'

'I'm going along to the Stevenses'.'

'What for?'

'What for? You've got to ask what for and his face like that! I don't know this Joe Lloyd, but I know Brid Stevens, and anyone with any sense knows why he got his face, 'cos he saw her when he shouldn't have seen her.'

'Now look here, you're not—'

'You can talk as much as you like. You've never done anything in your life for him but criticise him, and I don't expect you to defend him. Well, that may be your way of looking at things, but it isn't mine. I'm goin' along to the Stevenses'.'

Bill Talbot rested one hand on the table, the other he rubbed across his mouth. It was no good and he knew it. He could stop her going to the Stevenses'. Yes he could stop her by force: he could push her into the room and give her a clout, and it wouldn't be the first time. But when he was at work he couldn't stop her from doing what she wanted to do. If she didn't go to the Stevenses' now, she would go the minute he went out of the house . . . He turned and went back into the front room and took up the paper.

'Come on.'

'Aw! Ma.'

'Never mind aw Ma'ing me. Come on, I say.'

'Look Ma; I'll see Sandy—'

'You'll see Sandy when I'm finished with you. Come on.'

'What about somethin' on me eye?'

'I'll see about that later. Come on, it'll keep.'

She yanked him by the upper arm across the

kitchen and out of the back door and down the long back garden. As they reached the gate a voice from the next garden said, 'Anything wrong, Mrs Talbot?'

Olive Palmer had always addressed her neighbour as Mrs Talbot. She was of the opinion that her family were a cut above the Talbots, and she imagined she made this evident by never resorting to Christian names. Christian names made for familiarity. From her seat behind the glass porch adjoining the scullery she had heard the Talbots going at it, and now she rose from the deck-chair and looked down the garden towards where the mother and son waited.

'It's that Brid Stevens. Charlie here was going looking for your Sandy, when he was attacked by a fella, all because of Brid Stevens.' Mrs Talbot was well aware of Mrs Palmer's condescending attitude, and her own retribution took the form of pity and vindictiveness; what affected Brid Stevens affected John Palmer . . . and so on.

'Brid?' Mrs Palmer was slowly advancing down the garden, and she said again, 'Brid?' And now the two women were facing each other close over the fence, and Mrs Talbot gave the rest of her information in tones which were low and hushed, as the subject warranted. 'She was up there in the wood naked, so my Charlie says. He came on them, and this fella went for him. Just look at his face.'

Mrs Palmer looked at Charlie Talbot's face and her body began to quiver, though not noticeably. She said again, 'Brid?' and added, 'like that?' And Mrs Talbot made a slight obeisance with her head before pushing Charlie forward and moving away.

Olive Palmer returned up the garden path more quickly than she had come down it. Her walk was even spritely, and this was rather surprising, for she was a semi-invalid, carrying in her body aches and pains which were the symptoms of no known disease. Yet they were there and gave, from time to time, evidence of their presence by sending her heart into a panic of beats and her nerves to screaming pitch. When she reached the kitchen her husband was putting the last of the dinner dishes away. He had washed up as he always did on a Sunday, and every other day, for that matter. The dishes were always in the sink to greet him on his return from work, but this did not disturb him.

John Palmer's disposition was such that

he could take the chores of housework in his stride. He was at heart a kindly man, aiming to hurt no-one, but nevertheless hurting, through weakness, all those people who touched on his life.

He turned at the unusual sound of his wife's quick step. He had a side dish in one hand and a tea towel in the other, and with a not unusual feeling of apprehension he waited for her to speak. But she stared at him for a full minute before saying, 'There's trouble up there.'

The words were ordinary enough, and it wasn't the first time he had heard her utter similar ones, but he could see now she was excited about something, even pleased. He knew every phase of his wife's reactions to practically every situation and he knew that whatever the trouble was now, it was bad. He had never heard her walk so briskly or look so bright for a long time.

John Palmer never criticised his wife, even to himself; he knew that for whatever had happened to her he was to blame, and he remembered that she hadn't always been like this. At one time she had been lively and pleasant. If the war had not brought him and Tom Stevens together again and renewed their boyhood friendship, and if

Alice Stevens had been a different woman from what she was, things between them might have been different. If only Tom had attempted to prove, back at the beginning, that Brid was not his, things would have come to a head and been finished with. But apparently Tom couldn't bring himself to do it. He likely fooled himself that women were known to be a few weeks over their time. It was not unusual. And if only Alice had been a bit decent to him and not treated him like a mucky rag; after all, she lived in the same house and took his money.

The first time he had refused to leave Olive and the two youngsters and go off with her, Alice had threatened to go off on her own and leave both him and Tom high and dry. And since that day she had repeated the plea and the threat at least twice a year. But she had never been able to carry out the threat. She wanted him as much as he wanted her. That was the funny thing about this business, John Palmer thought: that he could have principles which tied him to his wife and children, yet he could still go on taking his pal's wife whenever he had the chance. It was this facet of his life that made a mockery of decency and troubled him not a little. Even now, when the desire for Alice nearly drove him up the wall and the solution would be to do as she had always wanted, go off with her – there were no young bairns to think about now – he just couldn't bring himself to do it. He had only to look at Olive and see what he had reduced her to, and that would be enough. He put down the side dish and said, 'What's the trouble? How d'you know?'

'It's Brid. Mrs Talbot's just dragged their Charlie along to them. His face is all knocked about. He said a fella hit him because he came upon them, this fella and Brid, in the copse above the bay near Stockwell Hill.' She now lowered her eyes demurely and delivered the barb: 'Brid had nothing on, he said.'

'What! nothing on? I don't believe it. Brid? I know what Charlie Talbot is, he's a little rat of a thing, is Charlie Talbot.'

Olive Palmer saw that her husband was angry, agitated and angry, and hurt, and she wanted him to be hurt. She watched him roll down his sleeves, then go to the back of the door and take down his old coat.

'Where are you going?'

'Where d'you think?' His tone was unusually sharp, to her, that is.

As he passed her, Olive Palmer warned

herself to say nothing: if he knew her reactions she also certainly knew his. With this knowledge she had kept him where she wanted him for years. She had experienced all she wanted of one side of married life long before Sandy was born. Her husband's affair with Alice Stevens had broken her up, but rather from the fear of losing the security that a nice home and a regular pay packet ensured than of losing the love of her man. She hated Alice Stevens, but more so did she hate her daughter Brid. Not only because she knew without a shadow of doubt that her husband was Brid's father, but because of the fear that had grown in her these last few years that their Sandy was getting sweet on her. The only thing that had stopped her from telling her son the truth was the fact that he would be nearly sure to turn on his father, and if things were dragged into the open there was no knowing what John might do. He might, even at this stage, walk out on her – there were no children to hold him now and Alice Stevens was always ready and waiting.

She picked up the tea towel that had dropped to the floor, and as she was about to hang it on the rack near the stove, Sandy appeared in the kitchen doorway. 'I'm off,' he said.

'Sandy!' She had her back to him.

'Aye?'

'There's trouble down below. Your Dad's just gone along.'

'Trouble? What kind of trouble?' Sandy was standing stiffly with his hands by his side, his eyes narrowed. He was staring at the back of his mother's head and she still didn't turn to him as she spoke.

'It's to do with Brid. Apparently she's been sportin' in the copse above the bay with some fella and Charlie Talbot saw them. He was looking for you.'

'Sportin'?' The sparse flesh on his face moved into furrows as he repeated the word. The questioning tone he had used made her reply defensive.

'Well, what else would you call it, her running around up there stark naked?'

'Brid? Nak—' He did not finish but stared at his mother as she turned towards him.

'Well, I don't know how far it's true. You know as much as me, but that's what Charlie Talbot came back and said, and he's brought his face to prove it. You should see it. He's along there now with his mother.'

She watched her son's eyes drop away from hers. She did not care if Brid Stevens ran around stark naked with the whole of South Scardyke so long as it wasn't with her son. She saw the fury behind the tightness of his face and it confirmed her opinion of his feelings for Brid Stevens. She felt sick. Pray God this business today would put the damper on it. She watched him spin about and run along the passage, and then she heard the front door bang, to be followed almost immediately by the faint click from the garden gate. He must have taken the path in a couple of leaps.

'All right, Mrs Talbot. All right.' Tom Stevens was speaking in a quiet way, a toneless quiet way. 'You've had your say and Charlie's had a beatin' up. Well, you're not going to hold me responsible for that, are you? And don't say again—' he held up his hand almost in front of her face— 'and don't say again that it's Brid's fault. When I see all you've said I'll believe it, and not until.'

'You think he's a liar then, you think she wouldn't do it?'

'I'm sayin' nowt until I see her.'

After the scene of the morning Tom Stevens seemed strangely calm. He moved now towards the back door and, opening it, indicated that he wished Mrs Talbot and her son to leave. And Mrs Talbot, pushing Charlie out in the same way as she had pushed him in, said, 'Of course, you won't want to believe it. That's natural, I grant you. But something's goin' to be done about this, an' I can tell you straight I'm goin' to report that fella to the police, and you won't be able to hush things up then.' She looked around the assembled company from Tom Stevens to Alice Stevens, and then to the corner of the triangle, as she thought of him, John Palmer, and said plainly, 'There's been too much hushin' up, if you ask me.'

'Aw, come on, Ma. Come on out of it.' Charlie's voice pulled her after him.

Tom Stevens closed the door quietly on the pair, and then with the knob in his hand he stood looking at it for a moment before turning to face his wife and his pal. It was a different Tom Stevens now, entirely different from the one who had just denied Brid's lapse to Mrs Talbot, for, after staring first at his wife and then at his pal, then back to his wife again, he brought out between stiffened jaws, 'Nice set up, isn't it, eh? Playin' games in the wood stark naked. That's for you, eh?'

'I don't believe it, Tom, and you shouldn't either.' John Palmer's voice was quiet, and he was startled at the bellow that answered him.

'No! you wouldn't believe it. No! of course you wouldn't, not you. But I do. I believe it all right, and I've got good reason to believe it.' His gaze swung to his wife, and his voice dropping slightly, he said again, 'Runnin' round naked in the wood. By God! I hope she's still naked when I get me hands on her; I'll take the skin from her ribs, you see if I don't.'

As he dived across the kitchen, pulling at his shirt collar to bring the ends together, Alice Stevens found her voice and in a high squeak demanded, 'Where're you goin'?'

'Where d'you think?' He had unfolded his collar and was dragging a tie round his neck now. 'Where d'you think? I said she hadn't to go out, didn't I? I said what I'd do if she did, didn't I? Well, I'm going up there to see the fun and games and add me quota to them. That's where I'm going . . . MRS STEVENS!'

'No, you're not. Oh, no you're not. By God! you're not.' She was standing in front of him. They seemed to have forgotten the presence of John Palmer.

'You try an' stop me. Just try and stop me. Try and stop me hammering her. If I don't do it the day I'll do it the morrow. She's been askin' for something big for a long time and by God she's going to get it. I'll let her see if she can shame me. Runnin' round naked. By God! I will. I'll let her see; you wait. You wait, just wait.'

'She wouldn't do that, not Brid. Have some sense you silly, dim bugger.'

'Silly, dim bugger, am I? Silly dim bugger.' His face had turned a pasty grey and his upper set of false teeth moved in unison as he ground his lower teeth against them. 'Aye, I'll have some sense. After all these years, I'll have some sense. You'll see what sense I'll have.'

He was nodding in emphasis at her when John Palmer spoke in a voice different from that which either of them had heard before: there was no laughter in it, no jocular tone, no placating, no quiet reasoning, but a definite quality of authority: it stated his right to have a say in what was to happen to Brid. He said, 'You won't touch her. You won't lay a hand on her.'

'I won't, eh?' Tom Stevens had turned and was eyeing his life-long pal, and he repeated again, 'I won't eh?' and John said, 'You won't, Tom. You won't now or at any time. We'll have this out later, but at this minute I'm

161

going to—' He was stopped by a knock on the back door and at the same time it was pushed open and his son entered, his whole attitude trigger-sprung for trouble. But he didn't give his son time to open his mouth; instead, he demanded in a voice of strange authority, 'You got your bike out back?'

Sandy nodded sharply before saying, 'What's this I hear—?'

'Never you mind what you've heard. Get the bike going and come on. Take me to Stockwell Hill.'

Sandy remained rigid. There was nothing more he wanted than to go to Stockwell Hill and see Brid caught red-handed at something or other. Yet he felt he'd be too late for that now, and his sharp wits told him that if he went to the hill and that bloke was there and he spilled the beans there might be trouble. But his Dad was acting different, not easy goin' and laughin' any more. When he was pushed through the door he wrenched his shoulder from his father's grasp and snapped, 'Give over! Who you pushin' about?'

'I'll let you know that an' all later. Meantime, get that bike goin', and quick.'

As he growled this order at his son, Tom Stevens's voice came yelling after him, 'We'll see who's goin' to deal with this. Who the hell d'you think you are? Don't forget I've still got me rights. Don't try to take them an' all off me or you'll be in for something, mind. Worms turn, you know, worms turn. You mind your own damn business; this is my business and I'll see to it, and her. You'll bloody well see I will, at that.'

When he heard the sound of the motor-bike starting up he was dragging his coat on, and he turned to Alice where she was standing near the window, her hand across her mouth, and he shouted at her, 'Nice thing this, isn't it, eh? Nice thing. One thing after the other over the years I've been stripped of, through you and him. Well, this is the showdown, Alice, me girl, this is the showdown. As he said, we'll talk later, and by God we will an' all. But he's not playing God Almighty in this business; I've brought her up and to all intents and purposes she's mine . . . mine!' He was now standing close behind Alice, and he dug his forefinger between her ribs so forcibly that her head jerked. But she didn't move, nor did she speak. 'I've brought her up, haven't I? To all intents and purposes I'm her father. Aren't I her father? Go on, tell me I'm her father.' He waited, and when she made no answer he went on, 'Well then, I'll act like her father.'

There came another dig between her ribs, and on this Alice Stevens turned and dashed to the table. She grabbed a knife by the handle, and gripping it in her fist and pointing the blade towards him, she growled, 'Get out! Get out while you're able or by God I'll ram this in you. You sod! I will, mind . . . I will.'

Slowly he backed a few steps from her. He was checked and evidently a little frightened, but he laughed and said, 'You would like to, wouldn't you? Go on then, why don't you do it?' For a moment longer he watched the knife trembling in her fist, then he turned on his heel and went out.

When the door closed on him she dropped the knife onto the table, then put her hands to her head for a while before running upstairs and pulling some shoes from the bottom of the cupboard and a coat from the wardrobe. She was pushing her arms into the coat as she ran down the stairs again. Once out of the house, she slowed her running to a quick walk down the road towards Furness's Garage. She couldn't wait for a bus, there wasn't time, and anyway they ran oddly on a Sunday. She would have to get a taxi out to Stockwell Hill before he got there.

'If he wasn't one of them, there wasn't much sense in it, was there? You shouldn't take it out on Peter for what Paul has done.'

The teacher knew that if he had been in Joe's place he would have done the same thing, but he couldn't get over the habit of moralising.

Joe was sitting on the ground again and he was panting, but he said in angry tones, 'He was one of them; I know him. He's always trailing after them. They likely sent him back to see what was going on. Or if I'd skedaddled or not. Or perhaps to see if you had gone' – he jerked his head at the teacher – 'so they could come back and try on some of their games.'

'No; no, I don't think he came for that. In fact, I think I heard him call out Sandy Palmer's name.'

'Yes, he called out all right, but that could be a blind. You don't know that lot.'

The teacher gave a twisted smile and said with a touch of authority in his voice, 'I know them. I knew them before you were born.'

Joe's head drooped, and he swung it slowly from side to side, biting on his lip as he did so, and when he stopped he asked quietly, 'Do you think he'll bring them back?'

'There's no knowing what he'll do, but I shouldn't worry. If they come back there's always the police to deal with them. You would have let them deal with the matter in the first place if you had taken my advice. But there, come on; are we going in the water or not?'

Joe looked from the man to the woman and then to Brid and back to the man again. The man, he thought, seemed to be running things and he didn't know now whether he liked it or not. He could recognise in him the teacher, ordering, organising, setting a kind of life pattern. He supposed the man had done this so often that he couldn't get out of it. If he hadn't felt so worked up and worried, and his body hadn't felt so painful and his head so muzzy, he thought that he might have answered, 'If you want to go in, go in. Leave us be, will you?' yet at the same time he felt that he owed this man and woman something, and it made him rise to his feet.

The woman now laughed and said, 'The pins held, anyway.' Then, in the manner of a young girl, which did not suit either her figure or her age, she ran with a leaping movement towards the bank top, and the man, after dividing a smile between Joe and Brid, followed her, but more slowly.

Joe now looked at Brid. Her face was even whiter than it had been, if that were possible. It was so white he was forced to say, 'Don't worry, they won't try anything on. As the man says, if they do we'll get the polis. Come on.' He half extended his hand towards her.

She didn't take it, or move, but she said, 'I'm frightened, Joe. Charlie Talbot's spiteful; he could bring them back, as you said.'

He moved closer to her and was about to deny the assumption, which he felt in his own mind was really inevitable, when his glance was caught by the discoloured mark on her neck. It was a disjointed mark, stopping and starting over a patch of about six inches, dark blue in the middle and red at the ends. The red spread down to the strap of her bathing costume. He brought his eyes up towards her face and he said quietly, 'That's fresh.'

'It's nothing.' She hitched the strap carelessly over the mark as if to demonstrate that it caused her no pain.

'Who did it?'

'I . . . I . . .' She jerked her head rapidly and brought out, 'I fell against the bed-post.'

'That's not good enough. Who did that?' He lifted his finger and pointed to her neck.

'Joe—' she was looking into his face, 'I've got to talk to you. I've got to talk to somebody. It's about me father. We'll talk after . . . Look, let's go and have that swim now. They'll only come back for us. They're trying to be kind. They're nice. Let's go.'

'All right, all right. Have it your own way.' His body, for the moment, seemed to reclaim its old strength. The fact that she was evidently frightened, that someone had hit her and that she wanted to talk about her father made him in some odd way feel old, and responsible; her need of him was like a salve on the humiliations of this past hour. He said, 'All right, but we won't stay in long, 'cos me mother's expecting us home to tea.'

'Me as well?'

'Of course . . . I've told her about you.'

Her lids drooped slowly, then she raised them quickly and her eyes held his with a searching look for a second. Then she turned from him and walked towards the edge of the clearing.

When they reached the bank top, the man and woman were already in the water; and when Brid waved a hand, the woman shouted, 'Hurry along! It feels grand.'

Joe helped Brid down the bank, and then they picked their way over the sand-strewn rocks to the edge of the tide.

The water felt wonderfully cool as it flowed round Joe's legs, and when it was above his knees he turned to Brid and actually smiled, saying 'It feels good, doesn't it?'

She nodded back at him, but did not answer his smile.

'How far can you swim?' he asked her.

'Not very far. The width of the baths . . . back and forth. I've never tried the length yet.'

'You can always swim further in the sea; it's the salt that keeps you up.'

He went under and when his head broke the surface again he stood up and squeezed the water from his hair. It was as the man had said, he felt better already. His body had stopped aching and the burn, after smarting unbearably for a moment, had ceased to pain him. It was as if the salt water had cauterised it; it felt healed.

Brid stood still in the water. She felt reluctant to go further and let it cover her. She looked towards the man and woman and a section of her mind wrenched itself from the

169

fears that were filling it and paused to deal
with them. She watched them diving up and
down like porpoises. They were laughing and
making a lot of noise, as young people did.
It was odd, she thought, them going on like
that; it wasn't right somehow, for they were
old. Well, they were over forty. And it was
odd an' all how they had tacked themselves
on to them. Yet she realised that if the man
hadn't come when he did Sandy Palmer and
the others would surely have come back right
away. She shivered as if from the coolness
of the water. Charlie Talbot would be home
now. Would he tell Sandy Palmer? And would
Sandy Palmer go and tell her father? No, she
didn't think he would, somehow, because if
there was any explaining to do there would
be trouble for him all right. She looked at
Joe now. He was swimming with jerky breast
strokes. Joe was nice. He was more than nice.
She wanted to think about Joe but her mind
would not stay on him; it was back on Sandy
Palmer again. Once she had started thinking
of Sandy Palmer she couldn't stop. Joe, her
mother and father and Uncle John were, for
the moment, blotted out. What more would he
have done if she hadn't come up the cliff at that
minute? Eeh! God. She would never be able to

get rid of the picture of Joe's stretched body. Sandy Palmer was rotten, filthy. If he came near her ever again she would scream, even if it was out in the street. She had a picture of herself clawing his face. She could see the flesh coming off in strips. Shocked at the ferocity of her thinking, her body responded and she plunged away into the water until it was almost up to her shoulders. Joe came swimming towards her, and as he straightened up and stood in front of her she noticed that his oxters weren't even covered with the water, yet their heads were on a level. They were practically of the same height. He had rather a large head, had Joe. It was a beautiful head. He had beautiful eyes too, and she liked his voice. She found she wanted to cry and her lips trembled.

'Come on. Come on.' His voice was very low and coaxing. 'Look, there's nothing to be frightened about any more. I tell you there isn't. They won't dare show up again.'

She shook her head and lowered her eyes to the miniature waves that were dancing between them.

'Is it something else that's worrying you?'

She jerked her chin to the side, almost on to her shoulder and she was looking towards the man and woman again. Side by side, they were swimming towards them, and with a deep note of irritation in her voice, she said, 'I wish they would go. I wish they would leave us alone.'

He had his back to the couple and he said, 'Aye yes, so do I. But look, we'll soon be on our way home. Come on, have a swim for a little. It'll make you feel good. It has me. You've no idea. I wouldn't have believed it.'

'Take the plunge!' It was the man shouting. He, too, was standing upright now and addressing Brid. 'If you don't go right under you'll catch cold. You shouldn't stand about even on a day like this, you should go under. Come on, we'll race you to the rocks. What d'you say? All of us. Let's see you do your stuff.' His voice was loud and jovial and seemed much larger than himself. His wife stood abreast of him. Her short hair and face were running with water. At this moment it resembled a boy's face, a boy's head. She too addressed herself to Brid. 'Come on,' she said; 'breast stroke. Can you do the breast stroke?'

For answer, Brid, moving to the side of Joe and not waiting for any signal, dropped passively into the water and began to swim. The three of them watched her for a moment.

Her movements were slow and her style was good. Then Joe was following her. Then the man and woman, and now they were all swimming towards the rocks that looked like a half circle of schoolboys' caps bobbing on the horizon.

Joe turned his head to look at Brid. She was swimming steadily, slowly. She had said she could do only the width of the baths, but from the sureness of her strokes he guessed she had been modest or had compared herself with some of the top-notch swimmers. She was a better swimmer than himself, that was sure, or the man and woman.

'We'll sit on the rocks.' It was the man calling.

When they reached the peaked black caps they hung on, one after the other. There had been no effort made to race by any of them. The man, last in grabbing at the slippery surface, shouted as if they were all miles away: 'It's going down fast. It'll show the flat ones shortly. We'll be able to lie here and sunbathe.'

Joe became irritated again. He wished the man would shut up. He always seemed to be talking. As he clung on to the rock he felt himself being forcibly swayed this way and

173

that by the pressure of the water dragging through the rocks. When the pressure pushed him up he could see right out to the far horizon, or where he guessed it to be, for now the whole surface of the sea was a shimmering sheet of light which hurt his eyes. He looked along at Brid. She was about three yards away from him, and she too was moving up and down, and she too was looking towards the horizon. He was thinking how nice it would have been, in spite of all that had passed, if they had been here alone together. And yet he knew he should be grateful to this couple. God knows what might have happened to him if the man hadn't come along. His thoughts at this point took on the same pattern as had Brid's. They would likely have come back and started on him again and made Brid watch. Oh, he knew Sandy Palmer was capable of anything. Anything. He had heard a lot about badness, real badness. He had only to listen to the men in the pit talking during the break time. If any of the old soldiers got together it was always about the war and the things the Germans did. And the things that some of the Russians did to the Germans. But – and he had thought of this before – they never talked about what the English did to the Germans.

No, they never talked about that. They talked
as if they, the English, were a race without
human frailties, without such reactions as
bitterness, hate, and wickedness. He knew
that they liked to think of themselves in that
light. Decent blokes, too. He had said as much
to his father once, and his father had said, 'Put
a gun into any man's hand and he's no longer a
human being. You've just got to see what they
do to animals. Nice fellas who say they love
birds and get all sentimental when they see
them flying against a dawn sky. Then bang –
bang! Down they come. But that's nothing to
wartime, 'cos then they've a licence for killing
men, and the more poor buggers on the other
side they blow to hell the more applause and
medals they get. In peacetime you would be
locked up and hung for the things you get
praise for in a war. You're a bad bugger if
you kill a man without a licence. War is a
funny thing, and you can take it from me, Joe,
that when Johnny Hertherington and Fred
Cooper start thinking back an' talkin', they
are likely shutting their eyes to the things
they did themselves. I was in the war and I
know ... I know. Even after the peace was
signed, the things that happened ... my God!
the things that happened. It's circumstances

and chance that bring out the rottenness in a man.'

Could you blame circumstances and chance for the things that were in Sandy Palmer? His dad had been wise, but could he have found an explanation for Sandy Palmer? He doubted it. Without war, without chance or circumstance, Sandy Palmer would be bad, really bad, vile. He'd make his chance. He'd make the circumstances. His mother would have said the devil was in Sandy Palmer, and my God, she could be right.

They were all quiet, all seemingly taken up with bobbing up and down and retaining their hold on the slippery cracks in the rocks. The water was making a different noise now, not just a lapping, slapping noise, but a sucking, swishing noise, deep and distant, yet near, under their feet, in fact. The tide had turned and already it was racing for freedom away from the enclosure of the bay, struggling to get between the barriers into the wider sea again.

The man felt the suction through his toes and was about to remark upon it, but as he looked along past his wife's face, her chin resting on the surface of the water, to the other two, he decided to remain quiet. He was worried a bit, more about the girl than the boy because, whereas the boy was trying to throw off his experience, she still retained that terrified expression, as if she were waiting for something similar to happen again. If she were his daughter he would be worried about her altogether. She looked all nerves, tightly strung. He was well aware that both the boy and the girl were wishing him and his wife were far away; they were not clever enough to be able to hide their feelings. Oh yes, they were civil, and even grateful that he had made his appearance when he did, but he knew that they wanted to be alone. He could leave them alone from now on, yet somehow he was reluctant to do so. He himself had had enough of the water. This was the third time he had been in in as many hours. Now he would like nothing better than to go and continue his sunbathing on the beach, but this couple seemed to have a call on him. He couldn't understand really why he felt as he did – teacher's training, he supposed. The emergency was over and he should leave them to themselves, but there was a subtle reason why he was reluctant to go. Phyllis would likely be able to put her finger on it. She was very good at being able to spot the whys and wherefors of one's actions and reactions, much better at it than he was, and yet it was he who always did the talking and explaining. He wished they could have a talk now. He would put the question whether or not what the girl saw today would have a lasting effect on her. Was she the sensitive type who wouldn't be able to forget in a hurry that slim figure stretched between the trees? He doubted it really. The modern girl was different. All the anatomical secrets of a boy were known to her even before she left school. By! yes. Her curiosity was like an acid eating through the outer covering, not resting until it laid bare the exciting stimulus beneath. She couldn't wait. There had been that case of Ridley, which must have been going on since he was ten and the girl twelve, and under everybody's nose at that. That was an odd thing about the present generation of girls. It was no new thought that women were the real hunters but they had, in other generations, covered their actions with a veil of decorum. But not the girls of today. They did the chasing openly, shamelessly. It had made him actually squirm to see an unresponsive male leaning up against a wall with a girl's stomach, breasts and thighs pressing hard at him while her hands sought to rouse him with widespread fingers stroking both sides of his face. And look at that young cow in the fifth form at the Barnes Road School, who had nearly driven Pat Bailey up the wall sitting with her legs apart whenever she got the opportunity and pulling her skirts up to show him a bit more, and never blinking when she looked at him, and saying, 'Ye . . . es, sir, Mis . . . ter Bailey.' They had laughed in the common-room, offering to change places with him, but it had been no laughing matter. It had been serious. So serious that Pat had moved. He had been sorry about that, for he had liked Pat.

But about this girl here. No, he didn't think it had been the sight of her boy-friend's naked body that had shocked her so much as . . . Well, what? He really didn't know. Was it this Palmer gang she was afraid of? She had looked ready to pass out when the young fellow had jumped on that interloper a few minutes back. And the look of fear hadn't eased from her face since then. He looked towards her now. She was moving from the rock to which she had been clinging to the next one, and he saw her twist herself about and up, and sit as it were on top of the water, and he called, 'Oh, you've

179

found the flat one, then. There's another just to the side; we'll all be able to get on it in a minute or so. She's running down fast now.'

Joe did not listen to the man; at least, he paid no heed. He moved along towards Brid's legs and, looking up at her, he said, 'How did you know it was a flat one?'

'I could see it through the water. I'm . . . I'm a bit tired, I think.' She made an attempt at lightness by saying, 'It's a bit wider than the baths.' She had been looking down at Joe as she spoke, and then he saw her eyes lift above his head as a voice came from the beach, and he registered immediately, with an answering tremor of fear in his stomach, the swift intensifying of the expression that had been on her face since he had first seen her this afternoon.

When he pulled his body round and trod water he could just make out the two figures on the beach, and if Sandy Palmer's outline had not been seared into his mind he would not have recognised him. For a moment, he felt sick, as if he had swallowed a mouthful of salt water, and his body began to ache again and the burn began to smart.

'Brid! . . . Brid! . . . Here a minute!' It wasn't Sandy Palmer's voice that came across the water but that of the man with him, and the teacher, now close to both Brid and Joe, said rapidly, 'That's Palmer, isn't it? Who's that with him?'

He too was treading water and he swung round to look up at Brid. She was staring towards the shore as she muttered, 'Me Uncle John . . . his father.'

'You're cousins, then?' The man's mouth remained open when he finished speaking.

'No. No.' She shook her head slowly, still looking towards the shore. 'I . . . I just call him that. They live near us.'

She looked down now and into Joe's face. She was drenched with an apprehensive fear that amounted to terror. She began gabbling to herself and it became almost audible. Oh, she wished that man and woman weren't here, then she could tell Joe.

'Brid! Brid! Come here a minute!'

'Don't go.' The man put out a hand as if she had been about to drop into the water, but she had made no motion whatever. She remained still. Rigidly still. The water was just lapping round her buttocks now and she had her hands flat on the rock on each side of her hips, pressing hard as if to support herself.

'You stay where you are. I'll go and talk to him.'

Joe wanted to put out his hand and say, 'No, you don't, this is my business. I'll deal with this. It's about Brid and me. It's our business, my business.' But he didn't, for he knew he was in no state to deal with Sandy Palmer and his father. His legs stopped their treading at the thought that if Sandy Palmer came into the water and went for him, there was no doubt but that he would get the better of him. Hold him under. He could well imagine him doing it. That business up on the cliff must have taken a lot out of him; he felt weak as if he hadn't eaten for days. Deep inside he knew that he was no match for Sandy Palmer or any of them. Yet he had lathered into Charlie Talbot. He was pleased at the memory. But that had been done on the spur of the moment, and Charlie Talbot was alone. If Sandy Palmer's father was anything like his son there would be little chance for anybody they decided to tackle. He stayed where he was and watched the teacher swimming towards the beach, and knew that the woman had moved past him and hauled herself onto the rock next to Brid. She did not touch her but just sat next to her in a similar position, with both her hands flat at her sides . . .

Sandy Palmer did not recognise the man swimming towards them; even when he stood up in the water and, with a swing of the hips, thrust his legs forward he still did not recognise him. But when he stood before them, running his hands over his head, he thought with a start, Why, it's old Farty Morley. What's he doin' with them? When the man looked at him he stared him straight back in the eye. He had taken old Farty Morley's measure at school: pap soft he was, always yapping. He had made up his mind to lead him one hell of a life but he had been moved away before he really got going. Lucky for him.

John Palmer did not know the man standing before him and he said gruffly, 'What d'you want?'

'I might ask you that.'

John screwed up his eyes and peered at the bloke. 'Who are you, anyway? I was calling to my . . . to young Brid Stevens. I want her here a minute.'

'She's not coming.'

'Not coming? Look here! Who the hell are you? What business is it of yours what she does? I've never clapped eyes on you in me life afore.'

'No, you haven't, but your son here has. We know each other, don't we, Sandy?'

Sandy Palmer remained silent; only his lower jaw moved, first one way and then the other, to be thrust forward as the man continued, 'I saw your handiwork this afternoon, Sandy. I would have recognised it anywhere.'

He was speaking as a teacher now, treating him to his sarcastic form of address, calling him Sandy as if he liked him.

Sandy Palmer said not a word, but his father put in briskly, 'Look here! I don't know what you're at.'

'No, I don't think you do, Mr Palmer. I'm referring to a little game your son played on another young fellow this afternoon, just over an hour ago. Do you know he thought he was in Rome, crucifying the Christians?'

John Palmer lowered his head and stared under drawn brows at the man before him. He sounded a little bats. What had he to do with this anyway? And talking about Sandy crucifying a Christian. He darted a quick glance at his son before saying, 'Look, I don't know who you are or what you're getting at, but to me you're just talking plain daft.'

'I happen to be a teacher.' The voice now was brisk. 'I once taught your son. I was on the beach this afternoon and heard a cry. It was from the girl you call Brid. She had just reached the top of that bank' – he flung his arm dramatically sideways, his finger pointing – 'and she saw there . . . D'you know what she saw there, Mr Palmer? Just what I said, a crucifixion, or an imitation one. Your son and his pals had strung up a boy, her boy, between two trees. They had stripped him naked. And you know something else?'

'Shut your big mouth, you're daft. He's up the pole, Dad.' Sandy had advanced one step towards the man, but before he could raise his hand, as was his intention, his father's arm came across him, and John Palmer said to the man quietly, 'Go on.'

The teacher looked into John Palmer's face, which was not more than a foot from his now, and he went on. 'They had not only stripped him and stretched his limbs between two trees, but—' he paused, 'he, your son, burnt him with a cigarette . . . here.' As the teacher pointed dramatically down to himself, John Palmer, after following the man's hand, turned and looked at his son. He had no need to ask if this were true, for in his heart he knew it *was* true. He knew there was something rotten in his son, and he had feared it. Of late, he'd had a number of worrying fears about him, the main one being that he was sweet on Brid. He had lain awake at nights in a sweat and an agony over this, and would get up in the morning determined to tell him; only, when he looked into his son's face across the breakfast table, the truth would freeze in his mouth because he was afraid of the boy's reaction to this knowledge. It had been different with Harry. Harry knew, but had never turned nasty. He had never told Harry, his mother had. His son's voice was now shot at him, crying. 'All right! All right! I did it. And I'd do it again. He was out with Brid all night, wasn't he? You're supposed to like Brid, aren't you?' He dared at this point to thumb his father in the chest, and when he added, 'Concerned about Brid, aren't you? very concerned about Brid.' John Palmer knew with a shock of surprise that his son had somehow become aware of the relationship between himself and Brid.

John Palmer did not now think of himself, or of the other one who was concerned in Brid's beginnings, or of those who had suffered from her existence; but he thought of that boy stretched between two trees, naked and waiting for the cigarette end to be pressed on his privates. Christ! and his son had done that! The sweat ran out of the pores of his face, and he rubbed the back of his hand up under his cap.

'Oh, for Christ's sake don't look so bloody pi! You're as bad as this bloke. He—'

'Shut up! Shut your mouth. I'll deal with you later.' There was in his father's voice a deep threat that Sandy had not heard before. To his mind his old man had always been easy going, even a bit soft. It wasn't until that night he had talked with their Harry that he knew why he had been easy going . . . soft. He was caught, caught in a cleft stick between two women and he had to go easy. He had never been afraid of his father, despising him somewhat even before he knew of his double life, and since this knowledge had come to him he had hated him, and when he was confronted with the placidity of him he wanted to spit in his gob. But now, looking at his father, he could see no placidity; his face was changed. He had turned into someone who would strike out even before speaking, hit out as quick as

187

look at you. He knew the type, he'd had to weigh them up. There were those who'd take it and those who wouldn't, and his old man had become one of the latter. They were staring at each other. Then his father's eyes lifted sharply towards Stockwell Hill, away above the beach, and he knew that the figure he saw slithering down the sand was his Uncle Tom. Then, almost the next moment, standing at the top of the rise leading into the copse, he saw Brid's mother. Funny, but he had never called her Aunty Alice. She shouted now, calling, 'John! Come and help me down, John.'

When his father hurried forward and began to climb the rise, Sandy turned back to the schoolteacher. This was one he could handle.

'Think you're clever, don't you?' His features converged to a point and seemed to pierce the teacher's face. 'You forget that people leave school. You want to mind your own bloody business.' There was a sing-song quality to his voice, and the teacher recognised it as a prelude. This was the way this type talked before an attack, but he knew that Sandy Palmer would not attack him at this moment. Yet he knew also that he wasn't finished with Sandy Palmer, or, more correctly, Sandy Palmer wasn't finished with him. He would likely suffer for defending the boy back there in the water. Well, let him start anything. The anger was strong in him now, strong as it had been when he first heard his nickname. Just let him start anything and he would have him along the line for as many years as it was possible for him to get. Just let him try anything on him. Just let him. He felt his heartbeats quickening, his stomach contracting, and the muscles of his shoulders hardening, and he thought, The dirty bastard. He had a desire to spring on this boy and pound his fists into the thin leering face, the face that was a portrait of evil in its essence if he had ever seen it, the face that nothing in this life would be able to alter for the better ... Redemption. The word presented itself to him and he literally almost spat it out of his mouth, and his mind answered it as if it had been voiced by another, saying, Who are you talking to? Redemption ... and this. I've been dealing with them for twenty-eight years, don't forget. If Christ Himself came and laid his hands on him he would be unable to make him clean. Here, he actually shook his head as if answering the voice, Aw! Don't talk to me.

He came to himself with a voice calling 'Brid!' and before turning his attention to the woman who was shouting, he thought for a moment, Let him try anything on, just let him. The woman was now standing at the edge of the water with the man Palmer and she was calling, 'Brid! Brid!' Sandy Palmer did not go near them and not one of the three seemed to bother about the man running along the sands.

When the man stumbled past the teacher he was gasping, and he spoke between great gulps of air to the woman's back, crying, 'Think you're clever, eh? Think you're clever.' He did not look at the teacher. He did not bring him into the focus of this family affair. He was looking at his wife and his pal, and now at his pal's son. Then going to the receding line of the tide and raising his hands to his mouth, he yelled, 'Come here you! Come here! Do you hear me?'

'Shut up!'

'What! What did you say?'

The two men were looking at each other straight in the eye for the first time in years, and John Palmer repeated, 'I said, shut up! I'm going to deal with this, I've told you. It's me that's going to deal with it.'

'Be God! you are. Be God! you are.'

'Yes, I am, Tom.' John Palmer's voice had dropped swiftly to a quiet, reasonable tone. 'And listen, there's something about this that I just don't get. Brid isn't in her bare skin, nor the lad. An' there's a woman out there with them.'

'That's my wife.'

They all turned towards the teacher and he, somewhat puzzled, went on, 'I don't know what you mean by bare skin; the girl has never been in her bare skin, not to my knowledge. I have told this man here how I came upon them.' He nodded towards John. 'And it's lucky I did, or else this one' – he indicated Sandy Palmer – 'might be in a police van at this minute. And my opinion is that's where he should be.'

Tom and Alice Stevens, their attention pulled from the water for the moment, stared at the man. To them he might have been talking German, but not so to John Palmer. And when Sandy advanced towards the teacher, muttering, 'Mind! I've told you. If you don't keep your tongue—' his father barked, 'Hold your hand! An' keep your tongue quiet and them fists down or else I'll deal with you an' all.'

'What's this? What's this, anyway?' Alice Stevens looked from one to the other in a bemused way. 'I thought we came here to fetch Brid. Look, whatever it is, we'll sort it out after.' She turned now and called with a beseeching note in her voice, 'Here! Brid. Come here, I tell you. I want you.'

The tide was no longer lapping over the top of the rocks. Brid was sitting stiff and straight as she looked across the bay towards her family. There seemed to be coming over the water from them a density of feeling: all the hate, subtlety, pretence, anxiety, frustration that had existed between the two families for years came at her. Her own share of these emotions had been pretence and anxiety. Anxiety had become a recognised part of her existence. The feeling was so strong now that she wanted to retch into the water.

Joe Lloyd swam up to her unnoticed, and when he put his hand on her knee she jumped as if his touch had burned her.

'Don't be frightened. What are you frightened about? You've done nothing. Come on. Come on back to them. I'll go with you.'

'No. No. I'm not going. Not now. I'm not going back, I'm not, I'm not.'

'Don't worry, don't agitate yourself.' It was

the woman speaking. She put her hand on Brid's shoulder and Brid turned to her swiftly as if to her mother and said, 'They can't make me, can they? They can't make me.'

'Nobody can make you do anything you don't want to.' She became concerned: the girl was terrified of something or someone, likely that Palmer individual. She looked towards the shore and she herself began to feel nervous. She wished Len would come back.

The group on the beach waited.

Alice Stevens said helplessly now, 'What can we do if she won't come?' She was speaking to John but it was her husband who answered. 'She can't stay out for ever, that's a certainty, and I can wait.'

At his words she drooped her head for a moment, then put her hand inside her coat and gripped at her breast. And then her attention was brought again to the strange man. The teacher was in the water up to his knees and was facing them. 'What do you want her for, what has she done?' he said. 'Why can't you leave her alone?'

'Look here, you! This is none of your business. I don't know who the hell you are, so keep out of it if you know what's good for you. I've stood enough.'

The teacher addressed himself solely to Tom as he answered, 'I'd say it was my business, I've been thrust into it. I've told you. And my advice to you is leave her alone. She's doing no harm. She's having a swim with her boy-friend. Is there anything wrong in that?'

The word boy-friend seemed to have an electrifying effect on Sandy Palmer, for it was at this point that he began stripping himself of his clothes, tearing them off, and his father, turning quickly and looking at him, said, 'What are you up to?'

Sandy was now stepping out of his trousers. He left on his short pants. His body was skinny yet appeared to be hard and wiry. He looked back at his father. 'You want her out, don't you? You came in a bus load to get her. Well, if she won't come on her own, she's got to be made to, hasn't she? That's all.'

'Look; you stay where you are.' John Palmer moved from the group and towards his son, and Sandy, backing from him, said fiercely, 'You try an' stop me—' then under his breath, he finished, 'you and her and him,' and on this, he swung about and plunged into the water.

At the first sight of Sandy Palmer stripping himself, the teacher had turned from the group and made rapidly for the rocks again. Alone, he was aware he would be no match for the Palmer hooligan, but with the lad out there, and his wife not a bad third, he would be able effectively to stop him scaring that girl to death.

John Palmer was now standing in the water seemingly unconscious of his shoes being flooded. Then without looking at his feet he lifted his knees and, having loosened one shoe after the other, threw them back on the beach. He would have followed his son whether or not Alice Stevens had beseeched him, 'Yes, you go, John. You go and fetch her. She won't come for Sandy.'

'Look here! If there's anybody goin' —' Tom Stevens moved towards the water's edge, but the water had only covered the rims of his shoes before his wife's scathing voice hit him and he knew that the situation had suddenly gone out of his control. Her voice even told him that he had never controlled any part of it.

'Don't be so bloody soft,' she said; 'you can't swim an inch; you know you can't.'

The truth bent his shoulders for a moment and made him shrivel up, and he stepped back into line with her and watched his friend swimming after his son . . .

Joe was still near Brid's knees. When he

stretched his toes down he could feel the bottom now; in a few minutes he would be able to stand up. With her and the woman he watched the teacher swimming towards them. He had heard the voices on the beach but could not make out what they were saying. But he saw clearly the figure of Sandy Palmer stripping off his clothes.

When the teacher was alongside them he stood up and turned round to ascertain the distance that Palmer had yet to make before reaching them, and he drew a great gulp of air into his lungs before saying, 'He means trouble. Now look.' He cast his eyes up and back at his wife: 'I don't like the idea of us being stuck up there. The tide's going down fast and if we can stand on our feet we'll be able to manage him better. Come on.' He held out his hand towards Brid. 'Don't be frightened. We won't let him get near you. I don't know what all this is about. Have you done something or other? Been up to something?'

She shook her head swiftly, and then said, 'Me? . . . Me? No. Nothing. I've done nothing.'

'Well, I don't know.' He sighed. 'Anyway, come down.'

As his wife was slipping down from the rock into the water, he put up his hand towards Brid's arm while Joe's hand went out to take her other arm; but she pulled back quickly from them, saying, 'No! I'm not going. I'm not going. I'm not going back while they're there. I tell you I'm not.'

'But you can't stay here all the time.' It was Joe speaking. He coaxed now, 'Look, Sandy Palmer can't touch us. There are other people there. He wouldn't dare. And anyway he's not got me alone now, the shoe's on the other foot. Just let him try anything. Come on, come on down before he gets here.'

She pulled her feet up from out of the water and under her, and edged further back on the flat piece of rock; and the teacher, speaking now with a touch of irritation and even anger in his voice, said, 'Look, don't be foolish. Come down off there.' He even made to clamber up on the rock, when the grip of his wife's hand on his arm turned him about and he followed the direction of her eyes to where Sandy Palmer was changing his course and was making for the rocks to the side of them. And as they watched him they knew his intention. Brid was on the rocks and that was where he was going. He had only to clamber up further along and if his feet could withstand the jagged edges he would presently be in an advantageous position. With this thought in both their minds, Joe and the school teacher immediately pulled themselves up beside Brid, although the woman remained in the water.

When Sandy Palmer stood balancing himself on the sloping surface of rocks, he addressed himself to Brid, shouting as if she were miles away, 'Well, are you coming back, or do I have to fetch you?' She did not answer, but, scrambling to her feet, she stood up between Joe and the teacher, and it was Joe who answered for her. 'Come and try and get her.' A pause followed this, and then Joe added, 'She doesn't want to come out and if she doesn't want to come out she's not comin'! You understand?' Joe was bending forward, his teeth bared. There was an overwhelming desire in him to bridge the distance with a leap, for he was feeling Palmer's breath on his face once again and seeing the cigarette sticking to the skin of his lower lip. The burn under his trunks began to smart furiously.

Sandy Palmer stared back at Joe and his words were carried on the dark gleam of his eyes. 'I'll deal with you after. In the meantime, shut your gob if you know what's good for you. Haven't you had enough?'

'Get down off there!'

The voice from the water startled them all except the woman, and they looked to where John Palmer was standing at the foot of the rocks, his feet on the sand and his head well above the water now.

'You keep out of this; it's none of your business. I've told you.' Sandy Palmer was bending towards his father, and they stared at each other for a moment before he added, 'Aye, but I suppose you would say it was your business. But you've left it a bit late, eh? What d'you think? You haven't had the guts to tell her . . . well, I'm goin' to tell her.'

'Come down out of that.' John Palmer's voice sounded steady, even untroubled, so untroubled that, under the circumstances, it was more frightening. For answer Sandy spat into the water, then moved towards Brid and the two men flanking her. So steady was his approach that he could have been walking on a flat surface, and his unhesitating advance caused a spasm of fear in both Joe and the teacher. Sandy Palmer was a bully, a coward at heart, and yet the teacher recognised in some inscrutable way that he was now being driven by a force of which bravery was the weakest element. Nothing could stop him from coming at them and getting his hands on this girl.

Sandy Palmer stopped when he was just over a yard from them, and his father's voice beat at him now as he made ready to spring. 'Sandy! D'you hear me? . . . Sandy!' As John Palmer pulled himself on to his knees on the rocks just to the side of the teacher he almost fell back into the water again, for Brid let rip a scream. The next moment she had jumped backwards. It was like a child doing hopscotch, and her legs meeting with John's head as he made to rise sent her sprawling. Within a split second and another scream she was in the frothing water on the ocean side of the rocks.

The tide all the time had been gushing, rushing and hissing through the crevices. The surface of the water behind the rocks was bubbling and churning and creating a froth. They knelt on the rocks and strained and reached out to her, but when she went whirling and dizzying from them Joe stood up, then dived. But there was no accountable period of time between his outstretched arms hitting the water and those of Sandy Palmer.

Joe had hold of Brid. One minute he was seeing the white faces capping the black rocks and the next minute the far horizon was bobbing before his eyes. They went twisting and turning time and again before his efforts brought them anywhere near the rocks. He wasn't conscious of Sandy Palmer being in the water until the hands came down from the rocks and grabbed at Brid. It was when he was relieved of her weight that the hand clutched his ribs, and he was spun round and down. For one terrifying moment all the churning, boiling water in the sea seemed to be racing down his throat, and when, spluttering and coughing, he slit the surface he could see nothing for the salt in his eyes. But he knew that Sandy Palmer was near him. He thrashed at the swirling water, and as his vision cleared and he saw the rocks before him he felt the grab again, at his leg this time. As he twirled and twisted and kicked out there was a fearsome screeching terror ripping through him in all directions. Sandy Palmer was trying to drown him. He came up again, and now he was quite near the rocks and there were hands outstretched to him, and he grabbed at them and caught them. But the hold was on his legs once more, like

201

being in the grip of a revolving steel hawser. His body was being stretched again. It was like torture, just as it had been when he was tied to the trees. This was his lot. This was the end. Palmer was going to make sure of him ... Oh! Christ ... An almost insufferable agony went through his brain as his hair was gripped and his scalp pulled upwards. There were nails digging into his shoulders; there were hands around his throat. His face was close to the rock and he was being torn in two. Then the steel girder snapped and he was free, and his body was catapulted up the face of the rock and he was lying gasping and panting and spluttering on top of the teacher and his wife.

John Palmer was still kneeling on the rocks. He was breathing hard as if he himself was actually battling with the current. When he saw his son's head appear amid the froth, the words, like a prayer, were wrenched from the depth of his bowels and he cried, 'Oh God, if only he would drown.' But it was a futile prayer, for his son could swim like a fish. What was more, he had always been able to stay under water for long periods. Hadn't they just witnessed what he could do under water? He had stayed down long enough to attempt to pull another lad to his death. No one would ever have any proof. Even this teacher fellow and his wife could not say that it was his son's hand that had held the lad down. They could think as much, and surmise as much, but only he would know. For was it not he himself who had first introduced him to this water game, diving under him and tweeking his toes? Sandy was about seven at the time. When he was ten he could turn the tables effectively and haul him under, as big as he was.

Sandy was yards out now from the rocks. Strong swimmer that he was, the submersion under such conditions had taken it out of him. He made for the rocks again, swimming hard against the pull of the water, and when he was within a couple of breast strokes from them he looked up to see his father staring down at him, and he twisted into a position of treading water. Even in this turbulent spray he had the control to do that. It was only for a flashing second that he saw the look in his father's eyes, but it was long enough to tell him there were no secrets of any kind between them any more.

The feeling that John Palmer had for his son at this moment went beyond hate and horror. It went beyond self-analysis. What this boy possessed was what he had put into him. Not in a moment of passion – he could in a way have understood it then – but in a duty-filled moment, a Friday-night habit. That fact at least should have bred some sort of ordinariness, should have bred a boy cut out to a decent pattern. Bred out of duty, and without passion, and brought up respectably. Nor had he known hardship or want, the two spurs that made men different, that created so many different urges. Sandy had known none of these things and yet he was different, frighteningly different. Scaringly different. Repulsively different. Hatefully different.

John Palmer was oblivious now to the turmoil on the rock. The commotion going on to the side of him seemed to be of no concern to him. He stared at his son, who was now making to swim with the current and towards his right, where the rocks were more easy of access. His gaze followed him. Without moving his body he kept his eyes on him. He knew what he was going to do once he had him up on top. He felt his fingers moving into a fist. He could already feel the shock going through his system with the contact of his knuckles between his son's eyes, and that would only be the beginning. Although he was aware that he could never knock out of his son what was in him, he knew he would have to make a show of trying. He saw that he was now about fifteen feet away to the side of him, and not more than two yards away from the rocks. One minute he was watching him swimming, the next he was watching him bobbing and splashing and thrashing with his arms. Then he saw him spin round. It was as if someone had got hold of him and was twisting his body into a corkscrew. He uttered a sound that was like the screech of a terrified animal. It was cut off abruptly, smothered in the twisting.

When John Palmer saw his son twist again in that odd way he sprang up from his knees and jumped along from the top of one rock to the other until he was opposite him. He saw him spin again, helplessly now, and he flung himself flat on the rock into a position from where he could stretch out his hands to him. There was a split second when his long arm could have reached the flailing arms of the boy, but it passed. His fingers seemed locked in the crevices of the rocks below his chest. He remained motionless, as he watched Sandy's body being whirled away over the gut to the quicksands beyond.

When he heard the groan to the side of him he knew it came from the teacher fellow, and he dropped his face forward until his chin touched the rock, and he did not lift it even when the man yelled at him, 'Can't you do something? Look, I'll go in, hang on to me.'

Then John Palmer's fingers were released from the rock and he grabbed at the region of the man's ribs, then worked them upwards to his arm and gripped it. And when he spoke there was froth around his mouth. 'It's no use, it's . . . it's the undercurrent; you'd only be sucked in.'

'God Almighty!' The teacher had had a final glimpse of the face of the boy who had given him the name of Farty Morley. It was a terrified face. White, bleached, horrible, already without flesh. It showed for one second longer and then was gone. There had been no shouting or crying. The fear that Sandy Palmer had instilled into others had turned on him and he had gone under, paralysed by his own weapon.

'Oh God. Oh God Almighty!' The teacher forgot that he hated Sandy Palmer; he could only think of him being sucked down by the undercurrent. And again he said, 'Oh God.

Oh God,' and the sound of his voice seemed to echo across the water. As he looked at the sun almost blinding him with its reflection on the waves, he thought. It can't be, it can't be. The whole thing, the whole day, had taken on an atmosphere of nightmare, and it wasn't until the man at his feet groaned that this feeling was dispelled.

John Palmer was standing now and looking into the frothing surface of the water. There was no hole left to show that his son had passed through that surface . . . And the sins of the fathers will be visited upon the children, even to the third and fourth generation. Well, there would be no chance of a third or fourth generation through Sandy, he had made sure of that. A thought hit him with the shock of a bullet in the chest: he could have saved him, he could, he could. But he had let him drown. The rising panic in him was quelled by a steadying voice which said, Better so, better so. He was no good. He would have done for her; one way or the other he would have done for her. I've always known that, he thought. He brought his head slowly round and looked along the jagged pinnacle of rocks. He could see the lad lying flat on his face and the woman next to him, and she had her arms about

Brid and Brid was yelling. His daughter was yelling and struggling. He brought his gaze back to the strange man who was looking at him, his face convulsed with pity, and as he was about to speak, John Palmer put out his hand and said, 'Say nothing . . . Not now. Say nothing.'

The teacher's wife now called, 'Len! here a minute! Help me,' and he scrambled over the rocks towards her with a slightly drunken gait. He too was feeling tired, and sick.

Brid was still struggling in the woman's arms and talking incoherently, and when Len tried to restrain her struggles, she screamed louder. It brought Joe into full consciousness again, and he turned on his elbow and raised himself a little. When, between the jerking movements of her head she saw him, her screaming dropped into a whimper, and her struggles ceased and she said with a semblance of rationality, 'Joe. Oh Joe. I thought you were . . . Oh Joe.' She fell towards him and put her arms around him as she might have done if they were alone.

Pulling himself up into a sitting position he held her, and Len knelt at his back and supported him. The woman stood up. She seemed thankful for a moment's respite from Brid's struggles and as she looked towards John Palmer he spoke to her quietly, his voice, again terrifyingly ordinary, saying, 'I'm going on out; will you bring her?' He did not wait for an answer, and she offered none, but she watched him slide into the water and wade towards the shore. The water now was below his chest. She looked at her husband and asked impatiently, 'Where's the other one?'

He swallowed and for once was lost for words. The voluble teacher was lost for words. With a trembling hand he thumbed the tumbling foam behind him, and his wife put her fingers across her mouth as she muttered, 'No! No!'

Joe put his head well back now to look up at the teacher, and his words sounded as thick as those of a drunken man as he said, 'You mean he's . . . that he's—?' The word ended on a high note, right up at the back of his throat. And when the man did not answer him he drooped his head and stared at Brid. But she was not looking at him; she had her face buried in her hands, and her hands were resting on his knees. He couldn't take it in. It couldn't be true that Palmer was dead. Dead

. . . Drowned. That's what he had tried to do to him, drown *him*. He began to shake, trembling from the crown of his head to the nails on his toes. The experience that had been dimmed for a moment in semi-consciousness was back. He could feel the grip on his ankle, he could feel the two hands clawing at his legs. He looked over Brid's head towards his feet. There'd be marks on his ankles. That grip would have surely left marks, but he couldn't see them because of Brid's head. He was shaking so violently now that his teeth began to chatter and a strange voice from behind him said, 'You've got to get them in.' When he was pulled to his feet Brid still clung to him and wouldn't let him go, and when they tried to get her off him she yelled, and he said like a stuttering man, 'Le–le–leave her b–be.'

And like this, they waded slowly towards the shore.

Meanwhile John Palmer was facing Tom and Alice Stevens, and, without any preamble, he said in a quiet, even deadly-sounding voice, 'Sandy's gone, caught in the undercurrent.'

'What!' The word came screeching out of Alice. 'What? Dead! My God! Olive'll go mad. He was all she had.'

'Yes; you saw to that.'

'What!' Again the screech. 'You're blamin' me for all this, when it's that damned lad, that maniac that got Brid out at four in the morning? My God! And poor Sandy dead . . . blaming me!'

'Well, there's one thing for sure. If he hadn't drowned, he would have been in prison before long, on a charge of torture.'

'Torture? What are you sayin'?'

'I'm sayin', this very afternoon he headed his pals and tortured that lad there.' He thumbed to where Len was supporting Joe's back against a rock. 'They stripped him naked, tied him, spreadeagled, to trees, and my son burned him with a blazing cigarette. I leave you to guess where. Only God knows what would have happened if Brid had not arrived on the scene and her screams hadn't brought that teacher and his wife up from the beach here, where they had been bathing. The wife, being a nurse, thought the best thing for them both was to get them into the water to calm them down, for they were both in a state.'

'Huh! He couldn't have been all that bad, when he could bash young Talbot as he did,' said Tom Stevens.

'Well, from what this man tells me, that happened later when young Talbot arrived, meaning to join the gang. What he saw was young Brid naked. She was with that woman behind a bush, getting into her bathing costume. And this lad saw him, and then went at him mad, like.'

'I don't believe it,' Alice said. 'Anyway, she's coming home,' and she thrust past John and made for her daughter, where she was kneeling beside Joe.

'Come away from there; you're coming home.'

Brid sprang to her feet, yelling, 'I'm not! I'm not! Never! Not to you three!'

The men were now lined alongside Alice, and Brid cried again, 'I'm not! Never! You're filthy . . . rotten, all of you!'

'Rotten we may be, but I brought you up.' This was a bark from Tom. 'I'm your father . . .' he was saying, only to be thrust back by John's arm, and his yelling, 'You're not her father, and she knows it. I'm her father, and from now on I'm acting like it, and if she says she doesn't want to come back among us rotten lot, she's not comin' back, she's goin' her own road.'

'By God! she's not.' Alice's arm was thrust out to make a grab at Brid, only for Len and his wife to react together to shield her, the while John, gripping Alice by the shoulder, thrust her well back.

The three stood staring at each other, and for what was next said, they could have been in the privacy of one or the other's house, for in that odd quiet voice John said, 'This is final. It's the finish; and not before time. We are movin'—' he was staring at Alice. 'I should have done it years ago. You, Alice, are like a disease that has to be hidden, and it gets worse with the years. You blackmailed me because of Brid; and you, Tom, like a worm, you took it. Oh! don't put your fists up at me. I could have floored you years ago; and I could do it this minute, not because I've detested your guts, but because of the weals that are showing up on my daughter's shoulder and neck. And they are not strap weals, they were caused by chains.'

'Yes, they're from chain,' Tom Stevens came back at him. 'I, too, should have done it earlier. I wish I had now.'

John Palmer remained quiet for a moment. His teeth were clenched; then he said, 'Try practising it on the one who deserves it. And good luck to you, for you'll have only each other now, for what you mightn't yet know is, the two lads are setting up on their own;

they've taken a flat. Yes, as Brid said, we're a mucky lot.'

Alice Stevens was standing now, her eyes wide, her lips stretched from her teeth, her whole body taut as if ready to spring. 'You swine, you!' She had brought out the words through tight lips. 'I could kill you meself, this very minute. You're a dirty, cowardly swine.'

'Yes; yes, perhaps I am. It seems I've always known that. But there was your laugh. Laugh everything off, that was your motto, wasn't it? while you drove your poor bugger of a husband mad. The only thing I'll say in my defence now is, I am not proud of that part of it.' He cast a rather pitying glance towards his one-time pal, before saying, 'You can take her home now because I'm goin' to see that Brid goes where she wants to, and that's with that lad.'

He was about to turn away when he paused and said, 'By the way, it'll be in the papers the morrer that my son was drowned while trying to save a fellow swimmer. That's, of course, if the lad agrees to it. If he doesn't, all the muck will come out, and you wouldn't like that, would you, Alice? So be careful what you say when you get back there.'

John now turned and addressed himself to Len, saying, 'Have you a car?'

Stiffly, Len replied, 'Yes, I have a car; it's behind Morgan's garage.'

'Well, I would get it, and get the lad home.'

For a moment, Len did not reply; but he turned to his wife and said, 'Bring their clothes down, and anything else you can carry. Then go and get the car.'

The woman nodded, but before obeying her husband, she ran towards a group of small rocks where she picked up a linen skirt, into which she stepped before pulling on a sleeveless blouse. And with this, John Palmer turned to Brid, where she was again kneeling by Joe's side, and he said quietly, 'You want to go with the lad, Brid?'

Her face had worn a grim, defiant look, almost of hate, as she looked at him, but his kindly tone softened her reply: 'Yes, I do, and . . .' she paused, 'for always.'

'Good enough. There's nobody goin' to stop you. I'll see to that.'

Then turning to the Stevenses, he said, 'I'd get away if I were you, because I'm not movin' until they're in that car.'

*   *   *

'Twenty-eight,' Joe called from the back seat of the car, where he and Brid were sitting close and supporting each other; and Mrs Morley, looking out of the car window, said, 'Yes; it should be the next one;' and straightway she said, 'Here! Len.'

When the car stopped opposite the green-painted door, Len and Phyllis got out quickly. While Len was helping Joe to alight, his wife was knocking on the house door.

When Mrs Lloyd opened the door and saw her son standing there, being supported, it would seem, by a strange man, and a tousled-haired girl being assisted by a woman, she exclaimed, 'Oh! Dear God, what's happened? What's happened to you?'

'It's all right, Mother. It's all right.'

As his mother banged the door closed behind them, Joe did not make for the kitchen door, but turned his shaking steps down the short passage and led them into the sitting-room and, staggering, he made his way to the chintz-covered couch and dropped on to it.

Lying back, he closed his eyes for a second, and said on a gasp, 'Brid ... rest. Sit down.'

As Phyllis helped Brid lower herself into an easy chair, Mary Lloyd kept repeating,

'What is it? What's happened?' And she bent over Joe now, saying, 'Where are you hurt?'

When Joe did not answer, Len put in, 'There's been a bit of trouble, Mrs Lloyd. I'll explain presently.'

'Mother' – Joe's voice was pleading – 'go and mash some tea. Take . . . take my friends with you.' He hadn't paused on the use of 'friends', but added, 'They'll explain.'

'But . . . but—'

'Mother; please! I'm all in at the moment. I'd . . . I'd like a cup of tea. Go on now . . . go on.' He gave a weak wave of his hand after pushing her off, and she backed slowly from him as if reluctant to go. She then looked at the two strangers and said weakly, 'Will you . . . will you come this way?'

When the click of the door came to Brid, where she was leaning her head in the corner of the high-back chair, she opened her eyes and looked across at Joe; then pulling herself up from the chair, she dropped on to her knees beside the couch, whispering now, 'Oh! Joe . . . Joe.'

'It's all right. It's all over,' and he put an arm around her shoulders, and she laid her head on his chest for a moment. But her tenderness did not quell the terror and shivering that

217

was in his body, and of which he imagined he would never be free, for he could still feel the snakelike grip of Sandy Palmer's hand on his ankle, dragging him down, round and round, dragging him deeper and deeper, never to rise again. He had thought he could never experience greater fear than when he had lain for seven hours behind a fall in the pit, and he'd had company there; three others were with him. But the terror of the time he had been in that maniac's hold was beyond anything he could explain in words.

As if Brid had picked up his thoughts, she now whimpered, 'I'm still terrified, Joe. I know he's dead, but I can't stop shaking inside. I'm frightened now that, in some way, she'll come and take me back.'

He made an effort and pulled himself further up the couch so that he could hold her with both arms; and his voice had the comfort of his old assurance: 'Oh no, she won't,' he said. 'That man . . . the other man who said he is your father, he won't let them. He's different. Anyway, I'll see that they don't come near you. You'll never need to be afraid any more. Here you are, and here you'll stay.'

'But . . . but your mother.'

'She knows all about you. I told her before I left the house this afternoon that you were for me.' And now he added, 'You are, aren't you?'

'Oh, yes, Joe. Yes, Joe.' She put a hand on his cheek. 'I . . . I love you. I seem to have known you for years. But where will I stay until—?'

'You'll stay here, my love . . . here, until we're married. And that can be soon.'

'Will your mother not mind?'

'No; she'll be glad. Now she can marry her grocer. She's been waiting to do so, but I've been the stumbling-block. She wouldn't leave me here on my own. Now she'll go to his house, and we'll live here.'

'Oh! Joe. Joe . . . I . . . I can't believe it.'

'You can believe it all right, my Brid.'

On these last words his mother came back in to the room. She had one hand tightly over her mouth; she had been crying. And when she came to the couch, he held out his hand to her, and she took it. Then she lifted her eyes from him to the kneeling girl, and put her other hand on Brid's head, and stroked the still damp hair.

They looked at each other, and in their gaze, they both saw the years ahead.

And now, looking at her son, Mary Lloyd said, 'I've mashed the tea. Your friends are staying for a cup. They are a nice couple. Do you think you can make it to the kitchen? Come along, lass.' She held out her hand.

THE END

An extract from THE DESERT CROP,
the magnificent new novel from Catherine Cookson.

1

Daniel stared up at his father and wondered why a man
so old could still retain boyish habits, for his father wasn't
sitting behind but on the edge of his study desk and was
swinging one leg the while he talked to Pattie. When
he had anything of importance to say he always talked
to Pattie, never to him, perhaps because she was four
years older, being thirteen now. Yet at the same time
he knew his father very often got angry with Pattie,
and he was showing signs of it now because his leg
was swinging more quickly than usual. She had just
said to him, 'Mother has only been dead for two years,
and the house goes on the same way, so why . . .?'

'I know your mother's been dead only two years, but
two years is a decent enough time to wait until one
marries again. As for the house, it isn't run as it was
before: Rosie is a lazy bitch; the meals get worse.'

Daniel now turned his gaze on his sister, awaiting her
reply, and she said, 'It's a big house. She has to clean the
place, besides cooking now. And there were two other
maids when Mother was alive.'

Daniel noticed his father's leg had become still; then he

slid off the end of the desk, stood straight for a moment, before bending towards his daughter and saying, 'There were lots of things different when your mother was alive; for instance, you were spoilt. If you are finding the house dirty then you should bestir yourself and get a duster in your hand, if not a pail and mop, Miss Stewart.'

The plain, fair-haired girl did not flinch from her father's stern gaze as she retaliated, saying, 'You sent me to school, the village one, but you could send Daniel, here, to a boarding school. Why?'

'Why, miss? Because he's a boy and needs special education, whereas you, all you've got to do is to prepare yourself for marriage.'

'I may not want to get married, Father. Not everybody gets married.'

'Those with sense do, child, so that they are enabled to run their own household. But if you've decided already that you're not going to be married then you will have to make yourself useful in my household. Now, have you anything more to say, daughter?'

The boy watched them staring at each other; then his sister said boldly, 'Yes, Father. Why are you marrying Moira Conelly? She's a relation, isn't she? Moreover, she's Irish.'

Hector Stewart drew in a long breath; then turning sharply to his son, he said, 'You have a sister, boy, who's going to find life very hard, for already she is proving to be a finicky, pestering female. But I shall answer her questions and enlighten you too. I am going to marry Moira Conelly because I happen to like her. As for being related to her, her father was my father's half-cousin. Now when you're doing your mathematics, work that out. As for her nationality, you both know' – he now jerked his head towards his daughter – 'that she is Irish, for she has spent two holidays here, hasn't she? That was when your mother was alive.'

Daniel spoke for the first time: a slight smile on his face now, he said, 'She lives in a castle, doesn't she, Father?'

Once more Hector Stewart drew in a long breath before returning his son's smile and saying, 'Yes, Daniel, in a way she lives in a castle, but it isn't as we think of a castle. Nevertheless it's called a castle.'

'She is old.'

Hector's head jerked back towards his daughter as he demanded, 'What do you mean, old?'

'She must be twenty-five.'

'Yes. Yes, she is all of twenty-five years. And you consider that old?'

Pattie did not seem to be able to find an answer to this, and her father, his expression softening now and his voice too, said, 'Wait till she comes: you will grow to love her; you won't be able to help yourself for she's such a happy soul. She will lighten this house.'

When again Pattie did not seem to be able to find anything to say, or perhaps she had considered it expedient to keep her opinion to herself, her father said, 'Well, now, time's getting on. This young gentleman is for the road to his school tomorrow. Go and help him pack.'

'I've already packed, Father,' Daniel said.

'Oh, you have, have you? Ah well.' He straightened his shoulders, buttoned the middle button of his collarless jacket, then looking from one to the other, his manner a little awkward now, he said, 'I have work to do. I'm away to the farm. And you, Pattie, I would suggest you go to the kitchen to see what mess Rosie has concocted to present us with at supper time. As for you, boy: as it is your last night at home for a while I'll leave you to your own devices.' And on this he unbuttoned the middle button of his coat again before marching out of the room.

Daniel turned to his sister. Her usually pale face was flushed, indicating she was in a temper, and his voice had a soothing note as he said, 'I remember her, Pattie. She was jolly, and she made me laugh. You might get to like her. And Father said she's bringing her maid with her, and she is a working maid, so you may not have to do any work at all.' He put out his hand and took hold of hers, and now her voice came strange, almost a whimper, as she said, 'You won't be here, Dan. You don't know what it's been like since Mother died. He never bothers with me, and there's nobody to talk to, that's why – ' she now paused and, lowering her head, shook it before going on, 'when I do get the chance I keep asking him questions, just to make him talk to me.'

'I shall write to you from school.' Daniel's tone was tender.

She looked at him, her eyelids now blinking rapidly. 'It isn't the same,' she said.

'Haven't you made friends at school yet?'

'Oh, that crowd. Betty McIntosh, Theresa Holmes, they're stupid, dull, and the boys are like clodhoppers. As for Miss Brooker, she doesn't know how to teach. I could teach *her*. Mother taught me my tables when I was four. As for being able to tell the time and count up to a hundred, and reading, I can't even remember learning those things. Mother was so advanced in her knowledge. But that school! Huh!'

She now threw off his hand as if getting rid of the whole school and its occupants. And when she turned away he had the urge to pull her back and put his arms about her and hold her close, to comfort her and at the same time be comforted himself.

He now followed her out of the room, down a passage and into a stone-flagged hall from which the shallow oak stairs rose. And he watched her hesitate at the foot of the stairs, then shrug her body about and make for the kitchen door at the far end of the hall.

Daniel walked to the front door and so out on to the flagged terrace that bordered the front of the house. He walked to one of the two small stone pillars that headed the six steps which led down to the gravel drive and, laying his forearms on the flat top, he gazed away over the expanse of his father's farmland.

The house was situated on a rise and this gave a view of the patchwork of fields straight ahead and also of those stretching away to the right. To the left there was a cluster of buildings obscuring the view, and behind which he knew there to be the five cottages. But away beyond the cottages the hills rose, as they did for some way behind the house, thus giving some protection against rain, sleet, and the north-east winds.

Daniel did not know why, loving this house and its surrounding land as he did, that it should make him feel lonely. He had been thinking of late that if, like his sister, he had a probing mind, he would have already been given the answer. All he could tell himself was that he needed something but he would never allow himself to go as far as to think that what he needed was to hold and be held.

He recalled the day they had buried his mother and the strange thought that had come into his head as he stood by her grave, for it was true she had never hugged him. His mother hadn't believed in hugging, and she had stopped Rosie from hugging him. His mother hadn't even believed in holding his hand.

He straightened up and sighed. He'd be glad to get back to school tomorrow. He liked Crawley House. The food wasn't very good but that didn't matter; the matron was very nice. He was very fond of her. In the spring, when he'd had a cough, she had given him linctus, and she had kept him in bed for a day and had stroked his hair. She was the first one he could remember ever stroking his hair. Rosie used to ruffle it. His father had, now and again, ruffled it, too, but no one had ever stroked it until matron did.

In the far distance over the gardens he could see Barney Dunlop, Rosie's husband, ploughing the barley field. It had been a good harvest but the ploughing pointed out that they would soon be in autumn. He thought he would go and say goodbye to Barney. He liked Barney.

He went down the steps, turned left, and walked to the end of the house and round the corner to where it opened out into the yard. There was no one in the yard. The four horse boxes were empty, the tack room door was closed, as were the outhouse doors; but when he approached the open barn two dogs which had been lying on the straw got up lazily and sauntered towards him. They gave him no barked greeting but, one at each side, they walked just a step behind him; and he turned and looked from one to the other, saying, 'Good boy, Laddie,' then 'Your ear better, Flo?' And for answer both dogs wagged their tails.

A doorway at the far end of the yard led into a walled vegetable garden. It was a large area of land, and prominent were rows of late beans and peas.

Keeping to a pathway that skirted one wall, he went through an archway and into a field that had at one time been a lawn. Walking through the long grass he was reminded of his surprise when he had returned from school last summer and realised how quickly grass grew when it was not kept cut, and also how quickly weeds spread among the flowers and obliterated them. This had been brought about, he knew, by his father's dismissal of Peter Kent and Will Brown. Peter had seen to the vegetables and the garden, and Will had helped him now and again when he wasn't attending the horses. But now the two hunters and the two carriage horses were kept down on the farm. This had all happened since his mother died.

Why? This was the question he had put to Pattie when he had first seen the long grass on the lawn, and her answer had been, 'Mother's money went with her.'

At the time, he had thought that very odd and he had had a mental picture of the money being spread round her as she lay in her coffin on the billiard table which had been draped in black.

Would things return to what they were before, after his father married Moira Conelly the Irish woman? Perhaps she had money.

Everything seemed to depend on money. His father had to pay money to keep him at this school, and he had pointed out to him that he was lucky. He supposed he was.

This thought set him running and the dogs bounded away from his side and chased each other in the long grass.

The field ended where a stretch of woodland began, and he ran zig-zagging through this, the dogs at his heels now barking with excitement. Once through the woods they were into ploughed land and skirting the neat furrows. In the distance he could see Barney Dunlop unharnessing the horses from the plough. When he reached them, the old man turned and spoke as if he hadn't been made aware of his approach by the barking dogs, saying, 'Why, there you are, Master Daniel. Where've you sprung from?'

'Granny Smith's Well.'

The old man and the boy now smiled knowingly at each other; for a long time this had been their usual greeting and answer. It was the answer Barney's wife always gave him when he asked her where she had been: 'Down Granny Smith's Well,' she would say.

Granny Smith's Well was the deepest in the district and it was known never to have run dry even in the season when no rain had fallen for weeks.

'All ready for the morrow mornin', eh?'

'Yes, all ready, Barney.'

'Want to lead Princess? although she needs no leading, stone blind she could be an' still find her way. But Daisy, her daughter here' – he thumped the other horse on the rump now – 'daft as a brush, she is, skittish she is, would be off to the market in Fellburn, she would, if I wasn't keepin' an eye on her.'

As Daniel walked by the head of the big shire horse and listened to the old man chattering away he experienced a feeling of contentment. He wasn't sure why he felt this way, but at this end of the estate life seemed to go on in a different pattern from the other end.

The farmyard was filled with noise and movement. Arthur Beaney was driving in the cows from the pasture; Alex Towney was carrying fodder for the horses, and at the far end of the long earth yard his father was talking to Bob Shearman, the shepherd, his hand waving as if he were angry.

He had reached the stable door and let go of Princess's

halter and was turning to ask Barney if he could help him water the horses, when he saw that he too was looking to where the shepherd was now coming across the yard towards them. As he passed to go into the stable Bob Shearman hissed, 'You know what now, Barney? he's bloody well telling me I've got to take Falcon into the market the 'morrow. I asked him why not one of the carriage horses. He told me to bloody-well mind me own business. But I told him I was a horse man afore he put me on shepherding and that Falcon isn't past it; he's still got a lot of jump in him yet and would burst a blood vessel to please him. But no, it's him that'll have to go; he must keep the carriage horses for his fancy piece that's comin'. I tell you, Barney, this place is goin' to hell quickly.'

'Be quiet! Be quiet!'

Bob Shearman glanced to where Barney was indicating the boy. And now he said, 'What odds? he'll learn how the land lies soon enough. And when he should come into his own there'll be nowt to come in to. You mark my words.'

Daniel did not ask Barney if he could help water the horses, but he said, 'I'll say goodbye, Barney; I've got to go now.'

'Goodbye, Master Daniel. It won't be long afore I'll be seein' you again. Christmas isn't all that far off. What's ten weeks or so?'

Without saying goodbye to Bob Shearman, Daniel turned away; but as he walked through the wood he thought of the man's words, 'When he should come into his own there'll be nowt to come in to.' Was this all because his mother's money had died with her, as Pattie had said? But what about the money his father got from selling the corn and the eggs and the vegetables and the milk, and of course the pigs and the sheep? That must come to a great deal, surely. What did he do with it? He couldn't ask him, so he supposed he'd never know.

Oh, well, he was glad he was going back to school tomorrow for there was so much to do there that you never had time to think about unpleasant things such as nothing to inherit when you grew up. He now called to the dogs and galloped with them through the wood.

2

Daniel didn't have to wait until the Christmas holidays to return home; he was granted three days' leave to attend his father's wedding. Over the past week he had become the centre of attraction in his house, after he had confided to Ray Melton, his friend, that his father was going to marry a lady from Ireland who lived in a castle and who was bringing her maid with her. Ray had, of course, passed this information on to the other boys in their dormitory, and consequently Daniel found himself bombarded with questions after lights out.

The lady would be his stepmother, wouldn't she?

Yes, she would.

Would he like that?

He didn't know yet.

Was she rich?

He wasn't sure.

Well, if she travelled with a maid she must be. You had to be really of the aristocracy to have a personal maid.

This last remark caused some controversy. Three of the boys claimed that they knew of friends of their parents who had personal maids.

This was topped by someone saying that his cousin visited a manor house in Northumberland where, with the butler and the footman, there were twelve indoor servants . . . how many would Daniel have?

Daniel was aware that were he to be truthful and say, 'One,' his prestige would sink drastically. So he did not consider that he was really lying, when counting in the farmhands and their wives, he said, 'Eight.'

There were one or two murmurs of 'Oh! Oh!' Eight seemed to be a satisfactory number on which to run a household to which an Irish lady was coming with her maid.

As Daniel settled down to sleep he told himself he must remember to explain to Ray how the eight servants were dispersed and that only one of them, Barney's wife, Rosie, worked in the house, because he had promised Ray he would invite him to tea during the coming holidays to see the farm, and, of course, the house. It was a very interesting house, one part of it being more than two hundred years old. But in the meantime that was nothing to worry about, for Ray lived miles away in a place called Corbridge.

He could feel the change in the house before he entered the door. As he jumped down from the trap, which had brought him from the station, and made for the front door, the laughter seemed to flow out of it on a wave, and it caught him up and he rode in on it to the middle of the hall, where, stepping off the stairs, he saw his future stepmother. She wasn't as he remembered her; she looked younger and prettier and more plump. And when she leant forward and held her arms out to him, crying, 'Why! Daniel, you are grown up. Come here. Come here,' he did not rush towards her and into her arms, but approached slowly, feeling that he should be polite and say, 'How do you do?' But when her hands caught him and drew him down to her breast he put his arms about her waist and looked up into her face and he laughed, and she laughed, and her laughter was almost in his ear, and it wasn't a tinkling laugh such as you would expect from a lady, but a jolly, rollicking one. And now, on loosening one arm from about him, she stretched it out and pointed to a fat, dark-haired woman now approaching from the kitchen, and said, 'This is Maggie Ann, Daniel. And I'm warning you: beware of her, she practises magic and she casts spells.'

The big woman laughed and seemed to swim all over him as her plump hand gripped his chin and lifted his face towards hers. 'So you're Daniel, are you?' she said, 'God! but you're thin, boy. You'll never brave the lions' den, not until we get some flesh on your bones.' She smiled now, and he noticed that a number of her teeth were crooked and that her hair was very dark, as were her eyes.

When she let go of his chin she patted his cheek, saying, 'You'll do. You'll do. You'll shape up nicely. What d'you say, me dear?' She had turned to her mistress, to whom Daniel, too, turned; and she, her head on one side, surveyed him as if she had not seen him before. 'He doesn't take after his father, not in looks anyway,' she said; 'but he'll do splendidly for himself.'

'Who doesn't take after his father?'

Hector had entered the hall from a side door, and Moira, now turning a laughing face towards him, said, 'Here's your son come home and never a greeting to him. Where have you been?'

Daniel watched his father come striding towards them and straight away put his arm around the waist of his future wife and hugged her close, before turning to him and rumpling his hair, saying, 'Well, here you are! and I declare you've grown another inch in the last few weeks.'

'He's too thin by half.' This was Maggie Ann speaking, and when Hector made to answer, it wasn't in the free and easy tone he had just used, for his voice was cold even as he smiled at the woman and said, 'Well, you'll have to see that your culinary process in the kitchen outdoes Rosie's, won't you?'

But Maggie Ann's manner or tone didn't change as she addressed her new master: 'Oh, begod!' she said on a loud laugh; 'don't expect miracles in that quarter. And look, I don't want to get up the good Rosie's back again, for it's taken me these three weeks to stroke down her ruffled feathers by each day asking her to show me the ropes, and begod! I'd like to see the ropes I couldn't untangle meself, given time of course.'

Daniel watched his father stare hard at the woman before, turning again to his future bride, and smiling now, he said, 'I must go and change because I smell of the farmyard, and then I'll take you for that promised jaunt around the countryside and introduce you here and there.' With that he hugged her to him once more, then made for the stairs, taking them two at a time as would a man half his age.

As if they had forgotten Daniel, the two women, talking in quick exchange, now walked to the door that opened into a corridor and what had once been the servants' quarters. At the end of it a sharp turning led to the back entrance to the kitchen. It was as Daniel entered the corridor to follow the women that he heard their voices coming from this passage. His future stepmother was saying and in a tone that held no laughter, 'Now I warned you, Maggie Ann, what it would be like . . . Do you want to go home?'

The answer came, 'Not without you. D'*you* want to go home?'

'Don't be silly, woman.'

'He's looking down his nose at me.'

'Well, to him you're a servant. I've explained it all to you.'

'Begod! I was a servant across the water and neither himself nor your ma ever tripped over themselves to tell me of me position. We worked together, we talked together, we ate together, the only thing we didn't do was sleep together, except for you, for you slept with me for years. So how d'you expect me to take this new situation, I ask you?'

'Maggie Ann. You've either got to take it or you go back across the water. Now I'm only repeating what I said to you before we came.'

'Aye, I know. But then, I hadn't had a taste of what it was goin' to be like. Even that Rosie, the ploughman's wife, looks at me as if I am the slush running out of the cow byre. And I have to lower meself and make believe I'm a numskull of the first water and know nothing about a kitchen or a kale pot.'

'I also told you, Maggie Ann, that they don't eat as we did, neither in food, nor ways.'

'Aw, you've made that evident enough an' all. It's in the kitchen I've got to sit. Look, Miss Moira, himself, your own father, was from one of the best families that ever trod Irish soil and if he could sit down with me and me like and eat his food, then who the hell in England should think themselves any better!'

There was a long pause and Daniel was making for the hall again when he heard Moira, as he was thinking of her now, say, 'It's not going to work, is it, Maggie Ann?'

This statement was followed by another silence before Maggie Ann, speaking quietly now, said, 'You know damn fine I won't leave you. You've been me life from you were born. So there's nothing for me but to stick it and make it work. I can tell you one thing, though, Miss Moira, you'll have to make it work an' all, because that young madam looks upon you almost in the same way as her father does on me.'

'That isn't news to me, Maggie Ann – I'm well aware of that – and so it will be up to me to make her change her attitude. By tomorrow I shall be her stepmother and mistress of this house. Thanks be to God. Yes, mistress of a house. And I say again, Maggie Ann, thanks be to God. Now together we could make it work, but only if you watch your tongue and fall in with the new ways and remember that the English gentry are a different breed altogether from our lot.'

'Ah!' Maggie Ann's voice came high now. 'What you talking about, Miss Moira, with one mouldy servant in the house, gentry? Huh! Even himself managed four, and he without a penny to his name. By the way, I'll ask you, do they know that?'

Moira's voice was low as she replied, 'They know only what I choose to tell them, and that there's money coming, which is true enough.'

'Yes; God speed the dead.'

'Go on with you, Maggie Ann. I don't wish anybody dead. But come on, give me a smile, give me a laugh. It's pulled us through so far. As Mama used to say, keep your pecker up.'

'Aye, and himself used to finish, "When the other hens are pinching your corn." '

236

Keep your pecker up while the other hens are pinching your corn. What a funny saying. But then they talked funny all the time.

When Daniel heard the rustle of their skirts he quickly went back into the hall and made for the main entrance to the kitchen.

Rosie Dunlop turned from the table where she was thumping a large mound of dough with her fist and said, 'Oh, hello, there, Master Daniel. So you've got back.'

'Yes, Rosie. You baking?'

'Bakin'? I've never stopped for the last four days. A quiet weddin', your father said, and we're having breakfast at the hotel in Fellburn, he said, only to add, there'll be a few friends dropping in for the evening: you can knock something up for that, can't you? And I've been knockin' something up, as I said, for the last four days now: he wanted hare pie, brawn, spare ribs, a leg of pork, and that was just for starters. Just push it on the table, he said, where they can help themselves. Have you met them?'

Daniel paused a moment before saying, 'Yes. Yes, Rosie, I've met them. I've been talking to them in the hall.'

'Well, what d'you think?'

He knew he would have to be what was called diplomatic and so he said, 'I don't know, Rosie, I've only just met them.'

'Well, she's been here afore. Did you like her then?'

'Yes, she appeared all right.'

'But what about the other one?'

He smiled as he said, 'She's very large.'

'Aye, and in the head an' all, I should say, for it appears full of water, like her body. And there's a squad of them due shortly.'

She now came towards him, and in a voice just above a whisper, said, 'Has she money? I mean, Miss Conelly; is she bringing money in?'

'Money?' he repeated, recalling the conversation he had just overheard; 'I don't know, Rosie; but I suppose she has money; perhaps when her people die.'

'Live horse an' you'll get grass . . . that! That's what that means.' Rosie flounced back to the table, and after pounding the dough for a few seconds she stopped and, motioning her head towards the bench in the corner of the long kitchen, she said, 'I've made some sly cakes, a couple will never be missed. Take one to Miss Pattie.'

'Pattie's in?'

'Oh, aye, she's in. Like you, she's off school for three days. Why, I don't know.'

He picked up the two pieces of pastry filled with currants, saying, 'Thank you, Rosie,' and putting them on a plate, he added, 'Where is she . . . Rosie?'

'Well, where she always is these days, up in her room or in the nursery.'

'Yes, yes.' He nodded at her before running out and across the hall and up the stairs.

On the landing he paused, undecided whether to make for Pattie's room at the far end or take the stairs that led to the nursery and school-room floor, and above them the attics. He decided on the latter and, without ceremony, burst into the old school-room to be greeted by Pattie saying, 'Why didn't you call?'

'Why should I? You knew it would be me.'

'How was I to know it would be you, silly? I didn't know you were back.'

'Well, you should have been downstairs, then you would have seen me. Here!' and he smiled as he handed her the sly cake. 'Rosie sent that for you.'

She took it from him without offering any thanks and bit into it, and she'd eaten the whole square before he was half-way through his.

'You hungry?'

'Yes, I'm hungry. I didn't have any breakfast.'

'Why?'

'Why? Well, because I didn't want to sit down with my laughing jackass-cum-stepmother, nor sit in the kitchen with her great sloppy maid. And Father said I had to do one or the other, so I did neither.'

'You can't do anything about it, you know,' Daniel said quietly, and as he watched Pattie lean against the table, the while gripping its edge, there came in him again that feeling for her that saddened him, and he didn't like it, so he looked from her to the table and the scraps of paper spread out and asked her, 'What are you doing?'

She straightened up and now asked *him* a question; her voice eager, she said, 'Can you recall any of Father's friends who have the nickname of Barbie?'

He thought for a moment, then said, 'Barbie? Sounds like a girl's name. Short for something? No: there are the Talbots, but Mrs Talbot's called Lilian, isn't she? And then there's Frances. Mrs Farringdon, she's called Tessa, and there's Janie. But why do you ask?'

'Look' – she pointed now to the table, and he leant over and looked at the pieces of torn and charred paper, and with a stabbing finger she pointed to the signature still evident on one piece, and saying, 'What does that read?' And he, looking closer, said, 'Barbie. But this is a letter. And why all these bits?'

'Yes' – she was nodding at him – 'why all these bits? Why all these letters? There were a number of them. I happened to go into the study one night this week and

239

Father was burning papers in the grate and he asked me what I wanted. I said I wanted a book. And he said, 'Well get it and go.' And I went. But I waited until he came out and had gone upstairs; then I went back, and there was all this charred paper, with here and there unburnt bits.' She now stabbed her finger at the pieces of what had evidently been a letter, and went on, 'They're not all of the same letter. But look, three times there's the same name, Barbie. There's only half the signature on that piece, it says, Bar, but look, it's the same kind of writing as this complete one, Barbie. And see, on that piece of paper it says, "You can't". And over there – ' she now pointed to a small piece of paper about an inch long and her fingers stabbed out the words, "Years and years". And look at this piece.' With her other hand now she turned over a strip of charred paper that showed an uneven white line where the tops of letters had been burnt off. And she said to him, 'What d'you make of that?'

He looked closely at the paper, and then he said, 'Oh, I think that word is time, but I can't make out the rest.' And she said, 'I can. That is "if".' And to this he nodded: 'Oh, yes it could be.'

'And the next word is, "ever".'

'You're just guessing,' he said.

'No. Look!' and now taking a pencil, she pulled a piece of clean paper towards her and wrote 'ever' on it.

He nodded, saying, 'Could be.'

'Well,' she said, 'it looks as though it reads, "if ever the time came." '

He scrutinised the charred scrap again and said, 'Perhaps you're right. But even so what does it mean? What do you make of it?'

She turned and leant against the side of the table and, looking straight at him, she said, 'Why should Father be burning those letters? Mother's name was Janice. The one downstairs, her name is Moira. Who, I ask you, is or was Barbie?'

He smiled now, saying, 'Don't ask me, Pattie. It's you who have set a puzzle, but I can't see you working it out.'

'I . . . I will some day.'

His face straight now and his voice low, he said, 'Why are you so bitter against Father? You said before that you talked at him because you want him to take notice of you. Well, if you do, why are you bitter?'

She shook her head twice before she said, 'I suppose it's because Mother was bitter against him.'

'Mother? Bitter against Father?'

'Yes' – she was bending down to him, her face now thrust into his – 'Mother was bitter against Father. You know nothing, you're a fathead.'

'I am not a fathead, and don't call me a fathead.'

That she was surprised at his retaliation was evident, for now she almost apologised, saying to him, 'Well, you know I didn't mean "fathead" really, but, you see, Daniel, you've been away to school for more than two years now. You were just turned seven when he packed you off, and you know nothing about what's happened in the meantime. I missed you when you went to school. Do you know that?'

When he didn't answer she said, 'You will be ten and I'll be fourteen in December, and you know what I'm going to do next year?'

'Leave school. You'll have to, won't you?'

'No, I'm not; and I won't. I'm . . . I'm going to pupil teach, starting with the infants. Miss Brooker said I can.'

'I thought you said Miss Brooker was a thickhead; that she didn't know anything.'

241

'Well' – Pattie hunched her shoulders – 'she knows I know as much as her, I suppose.'

'Does Father know?'

'Not yet.'

'Do you think he'll let you?'

'He'll have to.'

'Oh, Pattie.' He smiled sadly at her. 'You know you can't make Father do anything that he doesn't want to do.'

'No, perhaps not me, but his new wife will because she won't want me under her feet all day. I'll make myself felt right from the start, so she'll be glad to get rid of me. Oh, she'll back me up; I'll see to that.'

He laughed, saying, 'You know, Pattie, you're a terror. If you had been a man, you're the kind that would have caused riots.'

'Very likely.' She nodded at him. 'And I wish I had been a man, because then I wouldn't have to go and put linen on the four guest beds.'

'How many are coming?'

'Well, as far as I know, her mother and father, two brothers and their wives, and a great aunt.'

'Are they staying long?'

'No, thank the Lord, only tonight; then they're taking the late train to the boat after the wedding.'

'But why are they leaving it so late when Father's being married at eleven in the morning?'

'It's cheaper travelling that way, so Rosie says.'

'How did she know that?'

'Well, don't you know that Rosie's half Irish? Her mother was Irish. Oh.' She now turned to the table again and carefully gathered the pieces of charred paper together, adding, 'They are spattered all over the country, the Irish. Miss Broooker said that, when

242

I told her my father was marrying a lady from Ireland. What she actually said was, "More of them? They're already spattered all over the country." Come on, help me with the sheets. But mind' – she stopped abruptly on her way to the door – 'don't tell Father anything about this,' and she pointed to the envelope containing the remains of the letter. And his tone held indignation as he answered her, 'Now why should I do that? What reason would I have?'

'Well, you never know; things slip out.'

'You won't get it out of your head that I'm a dumb-bell, will you?'

She now pushed him and gave one of her rare laughs in which he now joined and they went out together.

Daniel sat on the deep window ledge of the third window in the long dining-room and his eyes darted from one to the other of his future stepmother's family, and the only words he could call to mind with which to describe them were odd and different.

There was Moira's father. He was tallish and thin, very thin and very dark-haired and, like his daughter, he laughed a lot, and he never seemed to stop talking. His wife seemed about half his size but her figure was dumpy. She too was dark, and her face was lined. She looked old. She smiled a lot but she didn't laugh and she spoke only now and again. Then there was a brother named Brian. He was as tall as his father and very like him, and he, too, talked a lot but he didn't laugh, nor did he even smile. Apparently, they called his wife Mary, because he alluded to her often, saying, Mary here said so and so. And Mary, too, talked a lot. Yet the younger son – Moira said he was younger, although he looked almost like a twin to his brother – this son

243

was called Rory, and his wife's name was Bertha, and they stood out because they rarely spoke. And then there was the great aunt. Now she was very odd and so old that he couldn't remember having seen anyone quite as old. Yet, she was what you would call spritely, for he had watched her previously walking around the room fingering the pieces of silver on the sideboard and opening the drawers of the old chest at the end of the room where the best dinner service was kept, together with the trays of cutlery. And what stood out was that everybody seemed to adhere to her wishes. They plied her with the eatables from the table and, as did all the others, she ate as if she hadn't seen food for days.

His father kept putting plates in Pattie's hands and directing her to offer their contents to the guests, but he felt he needn't have bothered because Maggie Ann, as everybody called her, was doing that all the time.

His father had seen to the drinks, too, but the company seemed to pick only two kinds, beer or whisky, and they drank a lot of each, seeming to wash the food down with it.

Although his father kept moving about the room from one guest to another, Daniel knew that he wasn't at ease.

They had been eating for more than an hour when Moira suggested they should move to the drawing-room. She did it, as he was finding out, as she seemingly did everything, on a laugh and with a funny quip; standing in the middle of the room, she called, 'Would the remnants of the Conelly family of ancient lineage follow their daughter over the battlements to rest their bones in the luxury of the drawing-room.'

At this and amid joined laughter she held out her hand to his father and he led her down the room, out into the hall and across it to the drawing-room door, where, relinquishing her hand, he pressed her forward into the room, then stood aside while Sean Conelly and his wife, with their aged aunt between them, passed him with a smile. Then followed the dour Brian with his wife, and lastly Rory and his wife. But when Maggie Ann came up in the rear and intent on joining the family, he put out an arm to block her way and, inclining his head towards her, he said, 'Would you please see to the coffee?'

The smile slid from her face and she replied briefly, 'They don't take coffee; tea's their drink when they can't get anything else.'

He brought his jaws together for a moment before allowing himself to speak: then under his breath he said, 'All right, it will be tea. But listen one moment: you and I must have a talk, you understand?'

She stared into his face. She understood, but she made no reply. Swinging her large body about, she made for the kitchen, pushing aside Daniel and Pattie who had been making their way towards the stairs but were stopped by their father's voice saying firmly, 'Come!'

Reluctantly, it seemed, they moved towards him, and as they went to pass him he stooped and quietly but firmly he said, 'Remember your manners and who you are. We have guests in the house. You understand?'

Neither of them answered nor indicated by a nod that they understood, but they went forward and into a buzz of laughter and chatter . . .

Daniel did not know how much later it was when the argument started, only that it was long after they had drunk tea and further glasses of whisky had been passed around. It started with the man called Brian, saying, 'When you used to come across to us, Hector, you gave us the impression that you lived like landed gentry, and her there, our Moira, she did the same. Well, you've got the house all right, an' the settings for it, but where's the staff? I thought we'd be greeted to a dinner tonight and be meeting all your friends.'

'Shut your mouth! Shut your mouth, Brian. It always gapes wide after the hard stuff. You should keep off it. Aye, you should that, unless it's under your own roof.'

'Aw, Dada, you said as much yourself.'

'I said no such thing, and I warn you, behave yourself. If you soil our name with your chatter I'll cut your throat, begod! I will. With me own hand I'll do it.'

'Huh! That'll be the day that you do anyt'ing with your own hand.'

All eyes were now turned on Brian's wife, for she too had imbibed of the hard stuff. 'And why shouldn't my Brian open his mouth and tell them a t'ing or two over here? 'Tisn't much opportunity we get. And as you know, neither my Brian nor me was for Moira making this match, as long in the tooth as she is.'

'How dare you! Mary Conelly.' It was Moira bristling: no smile on her face now; no laughter in her voice.

However, immediately the attention of everyone in the room was caught by the old lady saying to Hector, 'Did you meet Mr Palmerston, Hector?'

'No, Aunt Mattie.' Good Lord, how old did she think he was?

'A great man. A great man. If anyone could have saved Ireland, he was the one. And you didn't meet him?'

'No.' The word came sharp, definite.

'Oh, then you never heard him speak, which is a great pity. He was a great orator; he kept your men in London on their toes. Great many stupid men up there. And your Gladstone is a ditherer, a ditherer. You have nothing like the Land League here, have you?'

The answer to this came sharply: 'No, thank God, else they would be out to destroy us as they are destroying Ireland.'

'Destroying Ireland? Listen to him!' It was Brian shouting now. 'Just listen to him, destroying Ireland. You can't destroy a thing twice, man. You've already killed it, or nearly. You do know, don't you, that you did away with half a million? Starved them to death. Aye, starved them to death with your bloody corn laws.'

'Nonsense! Nonsense! Even the child knows it was the potato famine.'

'Aye, but what followed the potato famine? Migration to America. And what happened when they got there? They were so depleted they died by the hundreds.'

'Look, Brian, this is not a political meeting. It is a get-together prior to a wedding. Isn't that so, dear?' Hector had turned to Moira.

For once Moira did not make a laughing reply but she said somewhat quietly, 'Yes, that was the idea, Hector, and I must apologise for my lot.'

'Begod! you'll not apologise for me, our Moira. And what's come over you, anyway? there was nobody stauncher than yourself. It was you that boycotted Jimmy Bradley first, wasn't it, following Parnell's advice to every decent Catholic.' He now turned his gaze on Hector, saying, 'The bloody landlord turned Davey Sheenan and his family out of his farm, on to the road he put them. And there was Jimmy Bradley ready to go in. But we fixed him: the cattle got no water and he couldn't buy in the market, nor sell. He's going to emigrate now an' all, God's curse on him.'

'There was a law made, I understood, that eviction had to stop. I mean – ' said Hector stiffly, only to be interrupted by the old man letting out a great, 'Huh!' of

247

a laugh, saying, 'Ah, Hector, boy, there's one law for the English and one for the Irish, that is the Irish farmers and peasants. But there's another law for the Irish Protestants, always has been. But their time's running out: the door of Home Rule is ajar and one of these days it'll be thrust open, blown open in places, oh aye, blown open, literally I mean, if you get my meaning.'

'Dada! Dada! Be quiet. You know that's only talk. Been talk for a long time.'

'Talk, daughter? You haven't been here in this land but days, and you're telling your Dada to be quiet, and that it's only talk. And you whose belly has gone hungry like the rest of us. You live in a castle, people say. My God! I'd change it for a good cow byre any day.'

'That isn't true, Sean.'

'Perhaps not, Kathleen.' The old man's voice was soft now and he nodded at his wife, saying, 'We're all at sixes and sevens. I never wanted to come; you know that' – he turned from her and now looked straight at Hector who was standing stiffly before the fireplace – 'because this is a kind of wedding that's never been in our family. Not in my time or my father's or our fathers' before him, but, Protestant that you are, you're still of our line. Why wouldn't you talk to the priest?'

'Oh, we've been through all this over and over. And what difference would it make, anyway?'

'None to you, seemingly, but, to her – she knows she should be married in church.'

'Well, what was to stop her marrying me in a Protestant church? but you wouldn't have that, would you? So it's the registry office. Anyway – ' Hector shook his head vigorously now and his voice was loud as he said, 'We've been through all this. When I was with you last I told you what I had decided and I left it to her. It was up to her.'

'No good'll come of it.' It was Brian's wife speaking again in her thin high voice. 'And as I said, before we put foot on that boat . . .'

Her voice was cut by the old woman now turning on her and crying, 'If you said your prayers, woman, as often as you open your mouth, you'd be flying with the archangels at this minute; but even then your wings would be flapping faster than theirs.'

There was a titter now from both Rory and his wife. It was the first sound they had made since they had come into the room. It seemed to affect Moira and, with the exception of Brian, it was taken up by the others until the room was filled with laughter. Even Pattie and Daniel who were sitting on a small couch in the shadow of a French screen turned to each other and grinned. Then Pattie, putting her mouth close to Daniel's ear, said, 'I wish they were staying. There'd be some fun, wouldn't there?'

When he didn't answer she muttered under her breath, 'Well, don't you think so?'

'Father wouldn't think so; he's mad.'

After a moment she said, 'Yes. Yes, he is, isn't he. He's let himself in for something.'

Daniel lowered his head now and muttered, 'Did you know anything about this business of a priest and marrying in a Catholic church?'

'No. No. All that talk must have happened when he was over there . . . Anyway, it proves one thing.'

'What?'

'Well, she wanted to get married or get away from Ireland, one or the other.'

Still with bent head he said, 'Did the Irish people really starve to death?'

'Yes, I suppose so.' Then with an unusual flash of

249

humour she moved her head closer to his and almost spluttered as she muttered, 'But this lot's going to see that they themselves are not going to starve to death. They've eaten enough tonight to last them for six months. They'll be like the cows, they'll chew their cud.'

'*Daniel! Pattie!*' Their father's voice was stern. 'It's very bad manners not to share a joke. What were you laughing about? Come on' – his voice was aiming to be merry now – 'we're all dying to hear.'

Daniel looked at Pattie and Pattie looked at him and for once she hadn't a ready answer, and he realised this. So, he said, 'We were talking about cows, Father, re . . . regurgitating.'

'Cows regurgitating?' There was silence for a moment. Then Hector, looking around his guests and on a slight laugh, said, 'They were talking about cows chewing their cud.'

'Jesus in heaven! man, you don't need to translate the word. We might have just come over but our hair's dry. And I was at college in Dublin until I was eighteen. Regurgitating. Regurgitating.'

Brian swung round in his chair now and looked towards the children, saying in a quite pleasant voice, 'And why, may I ask, were you talking about cows regurgitating?'

Daniel rose to his feet and he looked across the room to the man with the dark thin face and deep set eyes who was staring at him. And he found himself speaking as he sometimes thought, 'No reason whatever, sir, not that could be explained; it just came up in the course of conversation about cows. Why were we talking about cows? Well, I couldn't rightly say. Thoughts jump, you know, from one thing to another. It's, I suppose, what you would call a lack of . . . of

250

concentration.' He knew he was talking like Mr Piers, who took history.

The room seemed quiet as if there were no one in it, and then his father said, 'Come along and say good night. It's about time you were both in bed. It's going to be a busy day tomorrow.'

As Daniel led the way down the room, to the women present he bowed slightly, saying, 'Good night, ma'am,' and to the men he said, 'Good night, sir.' And Pattie, seeming for once to follow his lead, did the same, with an added dip of the knee. Then they turned to their father and, looking up at him straight-faced, and as if rehearsed they spoke together, saying, 'Good night, Father.'

They watched his Adam's apple jerk twice before he said, 'Good night, children,' as he stepped aside so they could pass him.

They now walked sedately from the room, closing the door after them; they scrambled across the hall and up the stairs. And it was Pattie's room they made for, and once inside, and again as if of one mind, they threw themselves on the bed and buried their faces in the quilt in an effort to smother their laughter.

When they turned on their sides their faces were wet, and when Pattie said, 'Oh, Daniel, you did sound funny. However did you manage to come out with something like that?' he replied in a measured tone, 'Well, I seem to think like that, but usually I can never get it out.'

'You got it out then, didn't you? It shook that big-mouthed Irishman. In fact, it shook the lot, Father most of all. Oh' – she put out her hand and caught his now – 'I wish you weren't going back to school.' And he, feeling a great warmth pass over him, said, 'I wish I wasn't either, Pattie.'

*   *   *

251

In later years what he remembered most about that night was he and Pattie lying on the bed laughing until they cried, and then she had held his hand.

**Read the complete book – out now in
Bantam Press hardback.**

JUSTICE IS A WOMAN
by Catherine Cookson

The day Joe Remington brought his new bride to
Fell Rise, he had already sensed she might not
settle easily into the big house just outside the
Tyneside town of Fellburn. For Joe this had always
been his home, but for Elaine it was virtually
another country whose manners and customs she
was by no means eager to accept.

Making plain her disapproval of Joe's familiarity
with the servants, demanding to see accounts Joe
had always trusted to their care, questioning the
donation of food to striking miners' families – all
these objections and more soon rubbed Joe and
the local people up the wrong way, a problem he
could easily have done without, for this was 1926,
the year of the General Strike, the effects of which
would nowhere be felt more acutely than in this
heartland of the North-East.

Then when Elaine became pregnant, she saw it as a
disaster and only the willingness of her unmarried
sister Betty to come and see her through her
confinement made it bearable. But in the long
run, would Betty's presence only serve to widen
the rift between husband and wife, or would she
help to bring about a reconciliation?

0 552 13622 0

THE MALTESE ANGEL
by Catherine Cookson

Ward Gibson knew what was expected of him by the village folk, and especially by the Mason family, whose daughter Daisy he had known all his life. But then, in a single week, his whole world had been turned upside down by a dancer, Stephanie McQueen, who seemed to float across the stage of the Empire Music Hall where she was appearing as The Maltese Angel. To his amazement, the attraction was mutual, and after a whirlwind courtship she agreed to marry him.

But a scorpion had already begun to emerge from beneath the stone of the local community, who considered that Ward had betrayed their expectations, and had led on and cruelly deserted Daisy. There followed a series of reprisals on his family, one of them serious enough to cause him to exact a terrible revenge; and these events would twist and turn the course of many lives through Ward's own and succeeding generations.

0 552 13684 0

THE YEAR OF THE VIRGINS
by Catherine Cookson

It had never been the best of marriages and over recent years it had become effectively a marriage in name and outward appearance only. Yet, in the autumn of 1960, Winifred and Daniel Coulson presented an acceptable façade to the outside world, for Daniel had prospered sufficiently to allow them to live at Wearcill House, a mansion situated in the most favoured outskirt of the Tyneside town of Fellburn.

Of their children, it was Donald on whom Winifred doted to the point of obsession, and now he was to be married, Winifred's prime concern was whether Donald was entering wedlock with an unbesmirched purity of body and spirit, for amidst the strange workings of her mind much earlier conceptions of morality and the teachings of the church held sway.

There was something potentially explosive just below the surface of life at Wearcill House, but when that explosion came it was in a totally unforeseeable and devastating form, plunging the Coulsons into an excoriating series of crises out of which would come both good and evil, as well as the true significance of the year of the virgins.

'The power and mastery are astonishing'
Elizabeth Buchan, *Sunday Times*

0 552 13247 0

A SELECTION OF OTHER CATHERINE COOKSON TITLES AVAILABLE FROM CORGI BOOKS

THE PRICES SHOWN BELOW WERE CORRECT AT THE TIME OF GOING TO PRESS. HOWEVER TRANSWORLD PUBLISHERS RESERVE THE RIGHT TO SHOW NEW RETAIL PRICES ON COVERS WHICH MAY DIFFER FROM THOSE PREVIOUSLY ADVERTISED IN THE TEXT OR ELSEWHERE.

13576 3	THE BLACK CANDLE	£5.99
12473 7	THE BLACK VELVET GOWN	£5.99
14063 5	COLOUR BLIND	£4.99
12551 2	A DINNER OF HERBS	£5.99
14066 X	THE DWELLING PLACE	£5.99
14068 6	FEATHERS IN THE FIRE	£5.99
14089 9	THE FEN TIGER	£4.99
14069 4	FENWICK HOUSES	£4.99
10450 7	THE GAMBLING MAN	£4.99
13716 2	THE GARMENT	£5.99
13621 2	THE GILLYVORS	£5.99
10916 6	THE GIRL	£5.99
14071 6	THE GLASS VIRGIN	£4.99
13685 9	THE GOLDEN STRAW	£5.99
13300 0	THE HARROGATE SECRET	£5.99
14087 2	HERITAGE OF FOLLY	£4.99
13303 5	THE HOUSE OF WOMEN	£4.99
10780 8	THE IRON FAÇADE	£4.99
13622 0	JUSTICE IS A WOMAN	£5.99
14091 0	HATE HANNIGAN	£4.99
14092 9	HATIE MULHOLLAND	£5.99
14081 3	MAGGIE ROWAN	£4.99
13684 0	THE MALTESE ANGEL	£5.99
10321 7	MISS MARTHA MARY CRAWFORD	£5.99
12524 5	THE MOTH	£5.99
13302 7	MY BELOVED SON	£5.99
13088 5	THE PARSON'S DAUGHTER	£5.99
14073 2	PURE AS THE LILY	£5.99
13683 2	THE RAG NYMPH	£5.99
14075 9	THE ROUND TOWER	£5.99
13714 6	SLINKY JANE	£4.99
10541 4	THE SLOW AWAKENING	£4.99
10630 5	THE TIDE OF LIFE	£5.99
14038 4	THE TINKER'S GIRL	£4.99
12368 4	THE WHIP	£5.99
13577 1	THE WINGLESS BIRD	£5.99
13247 0	THE YEAR OF THE VIRGINS	£5.99

All Transworld titles are available by post from:

Book Service By Post, P.O. Box 29, Douglas, Isle of Man IM99 1BQ

Credit cards accepted. Please telephone 01624 675137,
fax 01624 670923 or Internet http://www.bookpost.co.uk
or e-mail: bookshop@enterprise.net for details.

Free postage and packing in the UK. Overseas customers: allow
£1 per book (paperbacks) and £3 per book (hardbacks).

LISTENING TO PROZAC

Peter Kramer is associate clinical professor of psychiatry at Brown University and has a private practice in Providence, Rhode Island. He studied at Harvard and at University College, London.

Also by Peter D. Kramer

Moments of Engagement:
Intimate Psychotherapy in a Technological Age

LISTENING TO PROZAC

PETER D. KRAMER

FOURTH ESTATE · London

First published in Great Britain in 1994 by
Fourth Estate Limited
6 Salem Road,
London W2 4BU

First published in Fourth Esate Paperbacks in 1994
10   9   8   7   6

Printed and bound in Great Britain by Cox & Wyman Ltd, Reading, Berkshire *for Eric and Lore*

CONTENTS

	Introduction	*ix*
1	*Makeover*	*1*
2	*Compulsion*	*22*
3	*Antidepressants*	*47*
4	*Sensitivity*	*67*
5	*Stress*	*108*
6	*Risk*	*144*
7	Formes Frustes: *Low Self-Esteem*	*197*
8	Formes Frustes: *Inhibition of Pleasure,*	
	Sluggishness of Thought	*223*
9	*The Message in the Capsule*	*250*
	Appendix: Violence	*301*
	Notes	*315*
	Acknowledgments	*379*
	Index	*383*

Introduction

Toward the end of 1988, less than a year after the antidepressant drug Prozac was introduced, I had occasion to treat an architect who was suffering from a prolonged bout of melancholy. Sam was a charming, quirky fellow, inclined to sarcasm, who prided himself on his independent style in sexual matters. He was of Austrian descent, cultivated a continental, nonconformist manner, and would not have been ashamed to be called a roué. A central conflict in his marriage was his interest in pornographic videos. He insisted his wife watch hard-core sex films with him despite her distaste, which he attributed to inhibition and narrow-mindedness.

As he neared forty, Sam fell into a brooding depression set off by a reversal in his business and the death of his parents. He consulted me, and we began to talk. Though he had fought with his parents, Sam had dreamed of reconciliation, of making their farm his crowning design project. But time overtook these plans. First his father, then his mother died, and the farm was sold. As we talked, Sam began to believe he understood his depression in terms of the events that preceded it, but his feelings of paralysis and deep sadness persisted. I prescribed an antidepressant; Sam responded only partially, able to function at work but left with a constant feeling of vulnerability.

In our meetings, Sam recalled having been a somewhat obsessional child, given to worrying about death and to spending hours rearranging his many collections, which ranged from stamps and coins to bottle caps, coasters, and whatever else came his way. This quality faded as he entered adulthood and focused on his career. When Sam's depression failed to respond to traditional treatments, I thought further about the hints in his history of something vaguely resembling obsessive-compulsive disorder. Prozac, then a new antidepressant with which few doctors had experience, was thought to have the potential to ameliorate compulsiveness. I shared my speculations with Sam, and he agreed to try Prozac.

The change, when it came, was remarkable: Sam not only recovered from his depression, he declared himself "better than well." He felt unencumbered, more vitally alive, less pessimistic. Now he could complete projects in one draft, whereas before he had sketched and sketched again. His memory was more reliable, his concentration keener. Every aspect of his work went more smoothly. He appeared more poised, more thoughtful, less distracted. He was able to speak at professional gatherings without notes.

I will explore later these aspects of Prozac, its ability to make certain people "better than well" and its effect on mental agility. Here I want to focus on a solitary detail that troubled Sam: though he enjoyed sex as much as ever, he no longer had any interest in pornography. In order to save face in the marriage, he continued to rent the videos that had once titillated him, but he found it a chore to watch them.

Altogether, Sam became less bristling, had fewer rough edges. He experienced this change as a loss. The style he had nurtured and defended for years now seemed not a part of him but an illness. What he had touted as independence of spirit was a biological tic. In particular, Sam was convinced that his interest in pornography had been mere physiological obsessionality. This conviction was based on a visceral sensation: on medication he felt less driven, freed of an addiction. Although he was grateful for the relief Prozac gave him from his mental anguish, this one aspect of his recovery was disconcerting, because the medication redefined what was essential and what contingent about his own personality—and the drug agreed with his wife when she was being critical.

Sam was under the influence of medication in more ways than one: he had allowed Prozac not only to cure the episode of depression but also to tell him how he was constituted. I might have been less struck by this response to Prozac had I not observed a parallel tendency in myself. Though I had never taken psychotherapeutic medication, I, too, seemed to be under its influence.

Shortly after Sam reported his loss of interest in pornography, I made two ordinary mistakes that caused me to wonder about the source of my own beliefs about people.

The first occurred in my care of a college student with a collection of problems not uncommon in young men who consult psychiatrists: He was angry at and mistrustful of authority, and at the same time he was uncertain of his identity, without goals or direction—at once asking for and resenting guidance. He was also depressed in a way that interfered with his ability to study or interact with classmates. As the situation deteriorated despite psychotherapy, I suggested he begin taking an antidepressant.

The young man accepted my prescription, and at the next session he appeared with a new collection of symptoms. Now his voice was tremulous, and when I questioned him he said his heart was racing and he was feeling markedly anxious. It is not unusual for a person beginning to take an antidepressant to experience an amphetaminelike effect on the third or fourth day—the feeling of having drunk too much coffee. Often this sensation disappears spontaneously. Sometimes it is necessary to lower the medication dose or to add a second, sedating medication at bedtime or to select a different antidepressant.

I considered these alternatives and began to discuss them with the young man when he interrupted to correct my misapprehension: He had not taken the antidepressant. He was anxious because he feared my response when I learned he had "disobeyed" me.

As my patient spoke, I was struck by the sudden change in my experience of his anxiety. One moment, the anxiety was a collection of meaningless physical symptoms, of interest only because they had to be suppressed, by other biological means, in order for the treatment to continue. At the next, the anxiety was rich in overtones. Hearing that the anxiety was not a medication side effect, I had an instantaneous sense of how I appeared to the student—demanding, judgmental, punitive, powerful in the face of his weakness—and how it must feel for him to go through life surrounded by similar figures. Here was emotion a psychoanalyst might call Oedipal, anxiety over retribution by the exigent father. The two anxieties were utterly different: the one a simple outpouring of brain chemicals, calling for a scientific response, however diplomatically communicated; the other worthy of empathic exploration of the most delicate sort.

Anxiety is at the heart of the psychological understanding of man. The "dynamic" in psychodynamic psychotherapy is anxiety; anxiety is the motor force behind psychoanalysis, a discipline replete with such phrases as "signal anxiety," "anxiety neurosis," and, of course, "castration anxiety." Beyond the profession, in the work of existential philosophers like Kierkegaard and Heidegger, the individual's struggle with anxiety is the preferred route to self-discovery. As a psychiatrist, I have spent most of my professional energy attending to psychological issues—to the significance of anxiety. Now, like Sam, I appeared changed in my perspective: I had caught myself assuming that a patient's anxiety was meaningless.

The weekend after my encounter with the depressed and anxious student, I was invited to the home of old friends I see only now and then. The husband in this couple is a fine finish carpenter; the wife, a funky graphic artist. The afternoon I was with them, I noticed about their children what one so often notices about children—

namely, how much they resemble their parents. The son was a boy mechanic, the type whose favorite toy is an old vacuum cleaner he can take apart and reassemble. The girl had her mother's ethereal manner and her fascination with ornamentation, shape, and color. I thought to myself, "Don't the genes breed true!"

I was about to say something of the sort when I remembered that these children were adopted and, beyond being human, had no genetic relationship to these parents. Evidently I had developed the habit of mistaking the psychological for the biological not just in the office but everywhere. And here, in my friends' home, the issue was not a symptom but the whole of who the children were: their style, their talents, their preferences. Since when had I—I, who make my living through the presumption that people are shaped by love and loss, and above all by their early family life—begun to assume that personality traits are genetically determined?

These three incidents occurring in conjunction—Sam's response to Prozac and my own to the college student and my friends' children —made me keenly aware of the effect of medication on my own and my patients' view of the self. This effect was not occurring in a vacuum. Our culture is caught in a frenzy of biological materialism. Newspaper columns, sit-coms, comic strips, talk shows—our public banter is replete with corollaries of the thesis that biology is destiny. When we laugh, if we do, at the claims that the genes for noticing dirty dishes, asking directions, and making commitments in relationships are absent on the Y chromosome, or that the gene for channel-surfing with the TV buzz box is present only there, it is because these beliefs are not distant from ones we actually hold.

I remember the days when you could be hounded off a college campus for suggesting that IQ is partly heritable. Recently I noticed in a *Newsweek* "Ideas" column an explanatory parenthesis—a bit of by-the-way information for those not *au courant*—containing the estimate that genes account for "half the difference in individuals' IQs and thirty percent of personality differences." What was only recently taboo is now the background assumption that sets the stage for discussion of human behavior.

My sense when I began my inquiries—and this is still my sense today—is that the new biological materialism is a cultural phenomenon that goes beyond the scientific evidence. There have always been observations favoring nature over nurture. What changes, in response to the spirit of the times, is the choice of evidence to which we attend.

It is instructive to follow the course of scientific opinion regarding the heritability of such disorders as manic-depressive illness and alcoholism. At least three times in recent years, the genes for these ailments have been discovered. In each instance, the studies proved impossible to replicate, and re-examination of the original data showed it to have been both flawed and incorrectly analyzed. My impression is that the result of each of these *failures* to demonstrate that a disorder is genetic has been a paradoxical *increase* in the conviction, both of scientists and of the informed public, that the disorder is and will soon be shown to be heritable in a simple, direct fashion.

Why have our beliefs changed faster than the evidence? The answer is probably in the province of sociology. Carl Degler, a Stanford professor who has charted the fall and rise of social Darwinism over the past century, has concluded that cultural needs influence the evidence scientists attend to. During the American civil-rights struggle, for example, the proposition that biology is destiny became unthinkable. Today, in a society filled with the material fruits of the new biology—PET and CAT and MRI scanners, genetically engineered plants and animals, recombinant-DNA probes, and so forth —the proposition may seem incontrovertible.

No doubt, in seeing my friends' children through genetic lenses I was influenced by this change in culturally permissible thought. But as a psychiatrist I was under a more particular influence—the influence of drugs.

I was used to seeing patients' personalities change slowly, through painfully acquired insight and hard practice in the world. But recently I had seen personalities altered almost instantly, by medication. This impressive, close-up view of the power of biology over an unexpectedly broad spectrum of human behavior—over a range of traits even hardened pharmacologists had thought impervious to simple physiological influence—had done a good deal to move my assumptions about how people are constituted in the direction of the contemporary zeitgeist.

Prozac—the new antidepressant—was the main agent of change. There has always been the occasional patient who seems remarkably restored by one medicine or another, but with Prozac I had seen patient after patient become, like Sam, "better than well." Prozac seemed to give social confidence to the habitually timid, to make the sensitive brash, to lend the introvert the social skills of a salesman. Prozac was transformative for patients in the way an inspirational minister or high-pressure group therapy can be—it made them want to talk about their experience. And what my patients generally said was that they had learned something about themselves from Prozac. Like Sam, they believed Prozac revealed what in them was biologically determined and what merely (experience being "mere" compared to cellular physiology) experiential.

I called this phenomenon "listening to Prozac." As I thought about it, I began to understand how far my own listening to Prozac extended. Spending time with patients who responded to Prozac had transformed my views about what makes people the way they are. I had come to see inborn, biologically determined temperament where before I had seen slowly acquired, history-laden character. I formed new beliefs about how self-esteem is maintained, how "sensitivity" functions in interpersonal relationships, and how social skills are employed. Seeing how poorly patients fared when they were cautious and inhibited, and how the same people flourished once medication had made them assertive and flexible, I developed a strong impression of how our culture favors one interpersonal style over another. I do not mean that I had thought these issues through, only that the experience of repeatedly seeing a medication catapult people into new ways of behaving had exercised a great influence on my habitual way of seeing the world.

I write a monthly column in a trade paper for psychiatrists, and in it I began musing aloud about Prozac. First I wrote about Sam and his sense that medication simultaneously transformed him and taught him how he was put together. Then I wrote about patients who became "better than well," patients who acquired extra energy and became socially attractive. My mnemonic for this effect was "cosmetic psychopharmacology."

That two-word phrase, as it happened, did for me what Prozac had done for certain of my patients: it made me instantly popular. By the time my second essay about Prozac appeared, in March 1990, the drug was hot. It had appeared on the cover of *New York* magazine and was about to hit the national media. I was the psychiatrist who had written about Prozac—I had said out loud what thousands of doctors had observed—and as a result, I was due my fifteen minutes in the limelight. I was quoted in a cover story in *Newsweek,* interviewed on talk radio, asked for opinions by any number of magazine and newspaper reporters, and finally referenced in the definitive contemporary article for physicians on the use of antidepressants, in *The New England Journal of Medicine.*

After that flurry of activity, I continued to track Prozac's fame. How extraordinary it was to see a green-and-off-white capsule on the cover of *Newsweek,* where we expect the falsely sincere phiz of a head of state, the curves of a starlet. Here was a phenomenon that required explaining. For forty years, pharmaceutical houses had been making antidepressants, a new one every three or four years on average, and where were they, Tofranil and Nardil and Wellbutrin? They were not in the rotogravure, not talked about at cocktail parties or in movie lines.

Prozac enjoyed the career of the true celebrity—renown, followed by rumors, then notoriety, scandal, and lawsuits, and finally a quiet rehabilitation. Prozac was Gary Hart, Jim Bakker, Donald Trump.

Prozac was on "Nightline" when you went to sleep and on the "Today" show when you woke up. How could a medicine preoccupy us, stimulate us so? The news stories, the sober ones that tried to describe what the drug does, told little. Prozac, they said, has fewer side effects than other antidepressants. But why did we care about side effects? Since when had we taken to reading day after day about the fine points of a medication for mental illness? No, the news was not side effects. The news was takeoff. Prozac enjoyed the fastest acceptance of any psychotherapeutic medicine ever—650,000 prescriptions per month by the time the *Newsweek* cover appeared, just over two years after Prozac was introduced.

And then the backlash began, in the great American tradition of tarnishing the idol's luster. The occasional column or feature story asked why we had jumped on the bandwagon. People were taking the drug for weight loss and for binge eating, for premenstrual tensions and postpartum blues. These were women mostly, and the question arose, was Prozac another Miltown or Librium, the "mother's little helper" from which we expect too much and about which we know too little?

Just before *Newsweek* made Prozac a star, an ominous report had appeared in a scholarly journal. Six depressed patients experienced urgent suicidal thoughts while on Prozac. Yes, some had considered suicide before. But when they took Prozac, their self-destructive drive was more persistent and more intense. Lawyers began to venture the Prozac defense in murder trials. Celebrities associating as they do, Prozac was implicated in the suicide of a celebrity, the rock star Del Shannon. Lawsuits sprouted like toadstools after rain.

Geraldo reappeared on the scene, with Donahue, Larry King, "Eye on America," "Prime Time Live," and *Time* magazine, eager to see bad where *Newsweek* had seen good, and finally *Newsweek* again, not contrite, just reporting the trends, with a cover story on violence, in which "Backlash Against Prozac" marched side by side with "Violence Goes Mainstream" (*The Silence of the Lambs, American Psycho*), and, yes, "Apocalypse in Iraq."

On the talk shows, there was word of Prozac Survivor Support Groups, as if the pill were an abuser—a molesting parent, perhaps. The Scientologists came whooping in, seeing in Prozac conspiracy, coercion, evil incarnate. Fear reigned: Macy's barred a man from a Santa Claus job because he was taking Prozac.

Time began the backlash to the backlash, with a cover exposé of the Scientologists, who were shown to be fomenting much of the anti-Prozac hysteria. Then "60 Minutes" weighed in with a balancing piece: Lesley Stahl confronted women who claimed not to have been suicidal before taking Prozac—leaders of the anti-Prozac movement—with a medical report and doctor's letter saying they had.

By now, new drugs had entered the market—Prozac wannabes. They were not Prozac, but perhaps Prozac was no longer what it had been. The craze was over. And we were free to wonder, what had the fuss been about?

My own sense was that the media, for all the attention they paid Prozac, had missed the main story. The transformative powers of the medicine—how it went beyond treating illness to changing personality, how it entered into our struggle to understand the self—were nowhere mentioned. Scientists who studied Prozac had for the most part worked to satisfy the Food and Drug Administration. They tested the medicine on seriously depressed people and reported their results: a reasonable main effect, diminished side effects. Then they spoke to the media about what had been strictly proved. These researchers were hardly likely to address questions of personality, self, transformation.

Meanwhile, clinician after clinician had written or stopped me at meetings to say he or she had seen Prozac change patients' outlook and self-image in quite fundamental ways. If researchers could not speak to the implications of this phenomenon—what it means that a medication can, even occasionally, transform personality—I thought I might be able to. I was also curious about what I call the dyer's-hand question—how I and others who see psychotherapeutic medication in action had been tainted by what we work in.

By now, not yet five years after it was introduced, eight million people have taken Prozac, over half in the United States. My concern has been with a subset of these millions: fairly healthy people who show dramatic good responses to Prozac, people who are not so much cured of illness as transformed.

I have focused on this phenomenon because I find it intriguing and because I believe it has power to influence the way we understand human nature. As a result, I have all but ignored certain issues. Side effects, for example, though they should play an important role in anyone's decision to take or forgo Prozac, have been of secondary interest to me; even if Prozac were shown to cause one or another serious physical illness, that reality would have little to say about this other question: how is it that taking a capsule for depression can so alter a person's sense of self? The controversy over Prozac and suicide or violence, stimulating though it is, I treat in an appendix. Nor do I address many of Prozac's positive results in treating major mental illnesses from psychotic depression to eating disorders to schizophrenia.

I have limited myself to exploring the impact of mood-altering drugs on the modern sense of self, a large topic and an absorbing one. My quest has led me deep into territories whose results inform my clinical work but whose culture and customs are foreign: cellular physiology, pharmacology, history of medicine, animal ethology, medical ethics, descriptive psychiatry. The research literature turns out to be compelling; theories from diverse fields overlap and mesh in tantalizing ways. But, finally, it has been my own patients' responses to medication that have shaped my conjectures. Those stories of people experiencing inner change will, I hope, take the reader with me to a frontier of contemporary thought, a point at which such concepts as mood, personality, and self become at once unstable and fascinating.

LISTENING TO PROZAC

1

Makeover

My first experience with Prozac involved a woman I worked with only around issues of medication. A psychologist with whom I collaborate had called to say she was treating a patient who had accomplished remarkable things in adult life despite an especially grim childhood; now, in her early thirties, the patient had become clinically depressed. Would I see her in consultation? My colleague summarized the woman's history, and I learned more when Tess arrived at my office.

Tess was the eldest of ten children born to a passive mother and an alcoholic father in the poorest public-housing project in our city. She was abused in childhood in the concrete physical and sexual senses which everyone understands as abuse. When Tess was twelve, her father died, and her mother entered a clinical depression from which she had never recovered. Tess—one of those inexplicably resilient children who flourish without any apparent source of sustenance— took over the family. She managed to remain in school herself and in time to steer all nine siblings into stable jobs and marriages.

Her own marriage was less successful. At seventeen, she married an older man, in part to provide a base outside the projects for her younger brothers and sisters, whom she immediately took in. She never went to the movies alone with her husband; the children came along. The weight of the family was always on her shoulders. The husband was alcoholic, and abusive when drunk. Tess struggled to help him stop drinking, but to no avail. The marriage soon became loveless. It collapsed once the children—Tess's siblings—were grown and one of its central purposes had disappeared.

Meanwhile, Tess had made a business career out of her skills at driving, inspiring, and nurturing others. She achieved a reputation as an administrator capable of turning around struggling companies by addressing issues of organization and employee morale, and she rose to a high level in a large corporation. She still cared for her mother, and she kept one foot in the projects, sitting on the school committee, working with the health clinics, investing personal effort in the lives of individuals who mostly would disappoint her.

It is hard to overstate how remarkable I found the story of Tess's success. I had an image of her beginnings. The concrete apartment in which she cared for her younger brothers and sisters was recently destroyed with great fanfare on local television. Years earlier, my work as head of a hospital clinic had led me to visit that building. From the start, it must have been a vertical prison, a place where to survive at all could be counted as high ambition. To succeed as Tess had—and without a stable family to guide or support her—was almost beyond imagining.

That her personal life was unhappy should not have been surprising. Tess stumbled from one prolonged affair with an abusive married man to another. As these degrading relationships ended, she would suffer severe demoralization. The current episode had lasted months, and, despite a psychotherapy in which Tess willingly faced the difficult aspects of her life, she was now becoming progressively less energetic and more unhappy. It was this condition I hoped to treat, in order to spare Tess the chronic and unremitting depression that had taken hold in her mother when she was Tess's age.

———

Though I had learned some of this story before my consultation with Tess, the woman, when I met her, surprised me. She was utterly charming.

I have so far recounted Tess's history as if it were extraordinary, and it is. At the same time, people like Tess are familiar figures in a psychiatrist's practice. Often it will be the most competent child in a chaotic family who will come for help—the field even has a name for people in Tess's role, "parental children," and a good deal is written about them. Nor is it uncommon for psychiatric patients to report having had a depressed mother and an absent father.

What I found unusual on meeting Tess was that the scars were so well hidden. Patients who have struggled, even successfully, through neglect and abuse can have an angry edge or a tone of aggressive sweetness. They may be seductive or provocative, rigid or overly compliant. A veneer of independence may belie a swamp of neediness. Not so with Tess.

She was a pleasure to be with, even depressed. I ran down the list of signs and symptoms, and she had them all: tears and sadness, absence of hope, inability to experience pleasure, feelings of worthlessness, loss of sleep and appetite, guilty ruminations, poor memory and concentration. Were it not for her many obligations, she would have preferred to end her life. And yet I felt comfortable in her presence. Though she looked infinitely weary, something about Tess reassured me. She maintained a hard-to-place hint of vitality—a glimmer of energy in the eyes, a sense of humor that was measured and not self-deprecating, a gracious mix of expectation of care and concern for the comfort of her listener.

It is said that depressed mothers' children, since they have to spend their formative years gauging mood states, develop a special sensitivity to small cues for emotion. In adult life, some maintain a compulsive need to please and are thought to have a knack for behaving just as friends (or therapists) prefer, at whatever cost to themselves. Perhaps it was this hypertrophied awareness of others that I saw in Tess. But I did not think so, not entirely. I thought what I was seeing was a remarkable and engaging survivor, suffering from a particular scourge, depression.

I had expected to ask how Tess had managed to do so well. But I found myself wondering how she had done so poorly.

Tess had indeed done poorly in her personal life. She considered herself unattractive to men and perhaps not even as interesting to women as she would have liked. For the past four years, her principal social contact had been with a married man—Jim—who came and went as he pleased and finally rejected Tess in favor of his wife. Tess had stuck with Jim in part, she told me, because no other men approached her. She believed she lacked whatever spark excited men; worse, she gave off signals that kept men at a distance.

Had I been working with Tess in psychotherapy, we might have begun to explore hypotheses regarding the source of her social failure: masochism grounded in low self-worth, the compulsion of those abused early in life to seek out further abuse. Instead, I was relegated to the surface, to what psychiatrists call the phenomena. I stored away for further consideration the contrast between Tess's charm and her social unhappiness. For the moment, my function was to treat my patient's depression with medication.

I began with imipramine, the oldest of the available antidepressants and still the standard by which others are judged. Imipramine takes about a month to work, and at the end of a month Tess said she was substantially more comfortable. She was sleeping and eating normally—in fact, she was gaining weight, probably as a side effect of the drug. "I am better," she told me. "I am myself again."

She did look less weary. And as we continued to meet, generally for fifteen minutes every month or two, all her overt symptoms remitted. Her memory and concentration improved. She regained the vital force and the willpower to go on with life. In short, Tess no longer met a doctor's criteria for depression. She even spread the good word to one of her brothers, also depressed, and the brother began taking imipramine.

But I was not satisfied.

It was the mother's illness that drove me forward. Tess had struggled too long for me to allow her, through any laxness of my own, to slide into the chronic depression that had engulfed her mother.

Depression is a relapsing and recurring illness. The key to treatment is thoroughness. If a patient can put together a substantial period of doing perfectly well—five months, some experts say; six or even twelve, say others—the odds are good for sustained remission. But to limp along just somewhat improved, "better but not well," is dangerous. The partly recovered patient will likely relapse as soon as you stop the therapy, as soon as you taper the drug. And the longer someone remains depressed, the more likely it is that depression will continue or return.

Tess said she was well, and she was free of the signs and symptoms of depression. But doctors are trained to doubt the report of the too-stoical patient, the patient so willing to bear pain she may unwittingly conceal illness. And, beyond signs and symptoms, the recognized abnormalities associated with a given syndrome, doctors occasionally consider what the neurologists call "soft signs," normal findings that, in the right context, make the clinical nose twitch.

I thought Tess might have a soft sign or two of depression.

She had begun to experience trouble at work—not major trouble, but something to pay attention to. The conglomerate she worked for had asked Tess to take over a company beset with labor problems. Tess always had some difficulty in situations that required meeting firmness with firmness, but she reported being more upset by negotiations with this union than by any in the past. She felt the union leaders were unreasonable, and she had begun to take their attacks on her personally. She understood conflict was inevitable; past mistakes had left labor-management relations too strained for either side to trust the other, and the coaxing and cajoling that characterized Tess's management style would need some time to work their magic. But, despite her understanding, Tess was rattled.

As a psychotherapist, I might have wondered whether Tess's difficulties had a symbolic meaning. Perhaps the hectoring union chief and his foot-dragging members resembled parents—the aggressive father, the passive mother—too much for Tess to be effective with them. In simpler terms, a new job, and this sort especially, constitutes a stressor. These viewpoints may be correct. But what level of stress was it appropriate for Tess to experience? To be rattled even by tough negotiations was unlike her.

And I found Tess vulnerable on another front. Toward the end of one of our fifteen-minute reviews of Tess's sleep, appetite, and energy level, I asked about Jim, and she burst into uncontrollable sobs. Thereafter, our meetings took on a predictable form. Tess would report that she was substantially better. Then I would ask her about Jim, and her eyes would brim over with tears, her shoulders shake. People do cry about failed romances, but sobbing seemed out of character for Tess.

These are weak reeds on which to support a therapy. Here was a highly competent, fully functional woman who no longer considered herself depressed and who had none of the standard overt indicators of depression. Had I found her less remarkable, considered her less capable as a businesswoman, been less surprised by her fragility in the face of romantic disappointment, I might have declared Tess cured. My conclusion that we should try for a better medication response may seem to be based on highly subjective data—and I think this perception is correct. Pharmacotherapy, when looked at closely, will appear to be as arbitrary—as much an art, not least in the derogatory sense of being impressionistic where ideally it should be objective—as psychotherapy. Like any other serious assessment of human emotional life, pharmacotherapy properly rests on fallible attempts at intimate understanding of another person.

———

When I laid out my reasoning, Tess agreed to press ahead. I tried raising the dose of imipramine, but Tess began to experience side effects—dry mouth, daytime tiredness, further weight gain—so we switched to similar medications in hopes of finding one that would allow her to tolerate a higher dose. Tess changed little.

And then Prozac was released by the Food and Drug Administration. I prescribed it for Tess, for entirely conventional reasons—to terminate her depression more thoroughly, to return her to her "premorbid self." My goal was not to transform Tess but to restore her.

But medications do not always behave as we expect them to.

Two weeks after starting Prozac, Tess appeared at the office to say she was no longer feeling weary. In retrospect, she said, she had been depleted of energy for as long as she could remember, had almost not known what it was to feel rested and hopeful. She had been depressed, it now seemed to her, her whole life. She was astonished at the sensation of being free of depression.

She looked different, at once more relaxed and energetic—more available—than I had seen her, as if the person hinted at in her eyes had taken over. She laughed more frequently, and the quality of her laughter was different, no longer measured but lively, even teasing.

With this new demeanor came a new social life, one that did not unfold slowly, as a result of a struggle to integrate disparate parts of the self, but seemed, rather, to appear instantly and full-blown.

"Three dates a weekend," Tess told me. "I must be wearing a sign on my forehead!"

Within weeks of starting Prozac, Tess settled into a satisfying dating routine with men. She had missed out on dating in her teens and twenties. Now she reveled in the attention she received. She seemed even to enjoy the trial-and-error process of learning contemporary courtship rituals, gauging norms for sexual involvement, weighing the import of men's professed infatuation with her.

I had never seen a patient's social life reshaped so rapidly and dramatically. Low self-worth, competitiveness, jealousy, poor inter-personal skills, shyness, fear of intimacy—the usual causes of social awkwardness—are so deeply ingrained and so difficult to influence that ordinarily change comes gradually if at all. But Tess blossomed all at once.

"People on the sidewalk ask me for directions!" she said. They never had before.

The circle of Tess's women friends changed. Some friends left, she said, because they had been able to relate to her only through her depression. Besides, she now had less tolerance for them. "Have you ever been to a party where other people are drunk or high and you are stone-sober? Their behavior annoys you, you can't understand it. It seems juvenile and self-centered. That's how I feel around some of my old friends. It is as if they are under the influence of a harmful chemical and I am all right—as if I had been in a drugged state all those years and now I am clearheaded."

The change went further: "I can no longer understand how they tolerate the men they are with." She could scarcely acknowledge that she had once thrown herself into the same sorts of self-destructive relationships. "I never think about Jim," she said. And in the consulting room his name no longer had the power to elicit tears.

This last change struck me as most remarkable of all. When a patient displays any sign of masochism, and I think it is fair to call Tess's relationship with Jim masochistic, psychiatrists anticipate a protracted psychotherapy. It is rarely easy to help a socially self-destructive patient abandon humiliating relationships and take on new ones that accord with a healthy sense of self-worth. But once Tess felt better, once the weariness lifted and optimism became possible, the masochism just withered away, and she seemed to have every social skill she needed.

Tess's work, too, became more satisfying. She responded without defensiveness in the face of adamant union leaders, felt stable enough inside herself to evaluate their complaints critically. She said the medication had lent her surety of judgment; she no longer tortured herself over whether she was being too demanding or too lenient. I found this remark noteworthy, because I had so recently entertained the possibility that unconscious inner conflicts were hampering Tess in her dealings with the labor union. Whether the conflicts were real or illusory, the problem disappeared when the medication took effect. "It makes me confident," Tess said, a claim I since have heard from dozens of patients, none of whom had been given a hint that this medication, or any medication, could do any such thing.

Tess's management style changed. She was less conciliatory, firmer, unafraid of confrontation. As the troubled company settled down, Tess was given a substantial pay raise, a sign that others noticed her new effectiveness.

Tess's relations to those she watched over also changed. She was no longer drawn to tragedy, nor did she feel heightened responsibility for the injured. Most tellingly, she moved to another nearby town, the farthest she had ever lived from her mother.

Whether these last changes are to be applauded depends on one's social values. Tess's guilty vigilance over a mother about whom she had strong ambivalent feelings can be seen as a virtue, one that medication helped to erode. Tess experienced her "loss of seriousness," as she put it, as a relief. She had been too devoted in the past, at too great a cost to her own enjoyment of life.

In time, Tess's mother was given an antidepressant, and she showed a modest response—she slept better, lost weight, had more energy, displayed a better sense of humor. Tess threw her a birthday party, a celebration of the mother's survival and the children's successes. In addition to the main present, each child brought a nostalgic gift. Tess's was a little red wagon, in memory of a time when the little ones were still in diapers, and the family lived in a coldwater flat, and Tess had organized the middle children to wheel the dirty linens past abandoned tenements to the laundromat many times a week. Were I Tess's psychotherapist, I might have asked whether the gift did not reveal an element of aggression, but on the surface at least the present was offered and received lovingly. In acknowledging with her mother how difficult the past had been, Tess opened a door that had been closed for years. Tess used her change in mood as a springboard for psychological change, converting pain into perspective and forgiveness.

There is no unhappy ending to this story. It is like one of those Elizabethan dramas—Marlowe's *Tamburlaine*—so foreign to modern audiences because the Wheel of Fortune takes only half a turn: the patient recovers and pays no price for the recovery. Tess did go off medication, after about nine months, and she continued to do well. She was, she reported, not quite so sharp of thought, so energetic, so free of care as she had been on the medication, but neither was she driven by guilt and obligation. She was altogether cooler, better controlled, less sensible of the weight of the world than she had been.

After about eight months off medication, Tess told me she was slipping. "I'm not myself," she said. New union negotiations were under way, and she felt she could use the sense of stability, the invulnerability to attack, that Prozac gave her. Here was a dilemma for me. Ought I to provide medication to someone who was not depressed? I could give myself reason enough—construe it that Tess was sliding into relapse, which perhaps she was. In truth, I assumed I would be medicating Tess's chronic condition, call it what you will: heightened awareness of the needs of others, sensitivity to conflict, residual damage to self-esteem—all odd indications for medication. I discussed the dilemma with her, but then I did not hesitate to write the prescription. Who was I to withhold from her the bounties of science? Tess responded again as she had hoped she would, with renewed confidence, self-assurance, and social comfort.

I believe Tess's story contains an unchronicled reason for Prozac's enormous popularity: its ability to alter personality. Here was a patient whose usual method of functioning changed dramatically. She became socially capable, no longer a wallflower but a social butterfly. Where once she had focused on obligations to others, now she was vivacious and fun-loving. Before, she had pined after men; now she dated them, enjoyed them, weighed their faults and virtues. Newly confident, Tess had no need to romanticize or indulge men's shortcomings.

Not all patients on Prozac respond this way. Some are unaffected by the medicine; some merely recover from depression, as they might on any antidepressant. But a few, a substantial minority, are transformed. Like Garrison Keillor's marvelous Powdermilk biscuits, Prozac gives these patients the courage to do what needs to be done.

What I saw in Tess—a quick alteration in ordinarily intractable problems of personality and social functioning—other psychiatrists saw in their patients as well. Moreover, Prozac had few immediate side effects. Patients on Prozac do not feel drugged up or medicated. Here is one place where the favorable side-effect profile of Prozac makes a difference: if a doctor thinks there is even a modest chance of quickly liberating a chronically stymied patient, and if the risk to the patient is slight, then the doctor will take the gamble repeatedly.

And of course Prozac had phenomenal word of mouth, as "good responders" like Tess told their friends about it. I saw this effect in the second patient I put on Prozac. She was a habitually withdrawn, reticent woman whose cautious behavior had handicapped her at work and in courtship. After a long interval between sessions, I ran into her at a local bookstore. I tend to hang back when I see a patient in a public place, out of uncertainty as to how the patient may want to be greeted, and I believe that, while her chronic depression persisted, this woman would have chosen to avoid me. Now she strode forward and gave me a bold "Hello." I responded, and she said, "I've changed my name, you know."

I did not know. Had she switched from depression to mania and then married impulsively? I wondered whether I should have met with her more frequently. She had, I saw, the bright and open manner that had brought Tess so much social success.

"Yes," she continued, "I call myself Ms. Prozac."

There is no Ms. Asendin, no Ms. Pamelor. Those medicines are quite wonderful—they free patients from the bondage of depression. But they have not inspired the sort of enthusiasm and loyalty patients have shown for Prozac.

No doubt doctors should be unreservedly pleased when their patients get better quickly. But I confess I was unsettled by Ms. Prozac's enthusiasm, and by Tess's as well. I was suspicious of Prozac, as if I had just taken on a cotherapist whose charismatic style left me wondering whether her magic was wholly trustworthy.

The more rational component to my discomfort had to do with Tess. It makes a psychiatrist uneasy to watch a medicated patient change her circle of friends, her demeanor at work, her relationship to her family. All psychiatrists have seen depressed patients turn manic and make decisions they later regret. But Tess never showed signs of mania. She did not manifest rapid speech or thought, her judgment remained sound, and, though she enjoyed life more than she had before, she was never euphoric or Pollyannaish. In mood and level of energy, she was "normal," but her place on the normal spectrum had changed, and that change, from "serious," as she put it, to vivacious, had profound consequences for her relationships to those around her.

As the stability of Tess's improvement became clear, my concern diminished, but it did not disappear. Just what did not sit right was hard to say. Might a severe critic find the new Tess a bit blander than the old? Perhaps her tortured intensity implied a complexity of personality that was now harder to locate. I wondered whether the medication had not ironed out too many character-giving wrinkles, like overly aggressive plastic surgery. I even asked myself whether Tess would now give up her work in the projects, as if I had administered her a pill to cure warmheartedness and progressive social beliefs. But in entertaining this thought I wondered whether I was clinging to an arbitrary valuation of temperament, as if the melancholy or saturnine humor were in some way morally superior to the sanguine. In the event, Tess did not forsake the projects, though she did make more time for herself.

Tess, too, found her transformation, marvelous though it was, somewhat unsettling. What was she to make of herself? Her past devotion to Jim, for instance—had it been a matter of biology, an addiction to which she was prone as her father had been to alcoholism? Was she, who defined herself in contrast to her father's fecklessness, in some uncomfortable way like him? What responsibility had she for those years of thralldom to degrading love? After a prolonged struggle to understand the self, to find the Gordian knot dissolved by medication is a mixed pleasure: we want some internal responsibility for our lives, want to find meaning in our errors. Tess was happy, but she talked of a mild, persistent sense of wonder and dislocation.

My discomfort with Tess's makeover had another component. It is all very well for drugs to do small things: to induce sleep, to allay anxiety, to ameliorate a well-recognized syndrome. But for a drug's effect to be so global—to extend to social popularity, business acumen, self-image, energy, flexibility, sexual appeal—touches too closely on fantasies about medication for the mind. Patients often have extreme fears about drugs, stemming from their apprehension that medication will take over in a way that cannot be reversed, that drugs will obliterate the self. For years, psychiatrists have reassured patients that medication merely combats illness: "If the pills work," I and others have said, "they will restore you to your former self. I expect you to walk in here in a few weeks and say, 'I'm myself again.' " Medication does not transform, it heals.

When faced with a medication that does transform, even in this friendly way, I became aware of my own irrational discomfort, my sense that for a drug to have such a pronounced effect is inherently unnatural, unsafe, uncanny.

I might have come to terms with this discomfort—the unexpected soon becomes routine in the world of pharmacology. But Tess's sense of dislocation did not disappear immediately, and her surprise at her altered self helped me to understand the more profound sources of my own concern. The changes in Tess, which I saw replicated in other patients given Prozac, raised unsettling issues.

Many of these were medical issues. How, for example, would Prozac affect the doctor's role? To ameliorate depression is all very well, but it was less clear how psychiatrists were to use a medication that could lend social ease, command, even brilliance. Nor was it entirely clear how the use of antidepressants for this purpose could be distinguished from, say, the street use of amphetamine as a way of overcoming inhibitions and inspiring zest.

Other questions seemed to transcend any profession, to bear directly on the way members of our culture see themselves and one another. How were we to reconcile what Prozac did for Tess with our notion of the continuous, autobiographical human self? And always there was the question of how society would be affected by our access to drugs that alter personality in desirable ways.

I wondered what I would have made of Tess had she been referred to me just before Jim broke up with her, before she had experienced acute depression. I might have recognized her as a woman with skills in many areas, one who had managed to make friends and sustain a career, and who had never suffered a mental illness; I might have seen her as a person who had examined her life with some thoroughness and made progress on many fronts but who remained frustrated socially. She and I might suspect the trouble stemmed from "who she is"—temperamentally serious or timid or cautious or pessimistic or emotionally unexpressive. If only she were a little livelier, a bit more carefree, we might conclude, everything else would fall into place.

Tess's family history—the depressed mother and alcoholic father—constitutes what psychiatrists call "affective loading." (Alcoholism in men seems genetically related to depression in women; or, put more cautiously, a family history of alcoholism is moderately predictive of depression in near relatives.) I might suspect that, in a socially stymied woman with a familial predisposition to depression, Prozac could prove peculiarly liberating. There I would sit, knowing I had in hand a drug that might give Tess just the disposition she needed to break out of her social paralysis.

Confronted with a patient who had never met criteria for any illness, what would I be free to do? If I did prescribe medication, how would we characterize this act?

For years, psychoanalysts were criticized for treating the "worried well," or for "enhancing growth" rather than curing illness. Who is not neurotic? Who is not a fit candidate for psychotherapy? This issue has been answered through an uneasy social consensus. We tolerate breadth in the scope of psychoanalysis, and of psychotherapy in general; few people today would remark on a patient's consulting a therapist over persistent problems with personality or social interactions, though some might object to seeing such treatments covered by insurance under the rubric of illness.

But I wondered whether we were ready for "cosmetic psychopharmacology." It was my musings about whether it would be kosher to medicate a patient like Tess in the absence of depression that led me to coin the phrase. Some people might prefer pharmacologic to psychologic self-actualization. Psychic steroids for mental gymnastics, medicinal attacks on the humors, antiwallflower compound—these might be hard to resist. Since you only live once, why not do it as a blonde? Why not as a peppy blonde? Now that questions of personality and social stance have entered the arena of medication, we as a society will have to decide how comfortable we are with using chemicals to modify personality in useful, attractive ways. We may mask the issue by defining less and less severe mood states as pathology, in effect saying, "If it responds to an antidepressant, it's depression." Already, it seems to me, psychiatric diagnosis had been subject to a sort of "diagnostic bracket creep"—the expansion of categories to match the scope of relevant medications.

How large a sphere of human problems we choose to define as

medical is an important social decision. But words like "choose" and "decision" perhaps misstate the process. It is easy to imagine that our role will be passive, that as a society we will in effect permit the material technology, medications, to define what is health and what is illness.

Tess's progress also seemed to blur the boundary between licit and illicit drug use. How does Prozac, in Tess's life, differ from amphetamine or cocaine or even alcohol? People take street drugs all the time in order to "feel normal." Certainly people use cocaine to enhance their energy and confidence. "I felt large. I mean, I felt huge," is how socially insecure people commonly explain why they abuse cocaine or amphetamine. Uppers make people socially attractive, obviously available. And when a gin drinker takes a risk, we are tempted to ask whether the newfound confidence is not mere "Dutch courage."

In fact, it is people from Tess's background—born poor to addicted and dependent parents, and then abused and neglected—who are most at risk to use street drugs. A cynic may wonder whether in Tess's case drug abuse has sneaked in through the back door, whether entering the middle class carries the privilege of access to socially sanctioned drugs that are safer and more specific in their effects than street drugs but are morally indistinguishable in terms of the reasons they are taken and the results they produce. I do not think it is possible to see transformations like Tess's without asking ourselves both whether street-drug abusers are self-medicating unrecognized illness and whether prescribed-drug users are, with their doctors' permission, stimulating and calming themselves in quite similar ways.

More unsettling to me than questions of definition—licit versus illicit—was an issue raised by Tess's renewed professional success: how might a substance like Prozac enter into the competitive world of American business? Psychiatrists have begun to recognize a normal or near-normal mental condition called "hyperthymia," which corresponds loosely to what the Greeks called the sanguine temperament.

Hyperthymia is distinct from mania and hypomania, the disorders in which people are grandiose, frenetic, distractible, and flawed in their judgment. Hyperthymics are merely optimistic, decisive, quick of thought, charismatic, energetic, and confident.

Hyperthymia can be an asset in business. Many top organizational and political leaders require little sleep, see crises as opportunities, let criticism roll off their backs, make decisions easily, exude confidence, and hurry through the day with energy to spare. These qualities help people succeed in complex social and work situations. They may be considered desirable or advantageous even by those who have quite normal levels of drive and optimism. How shall we respond to the complaint that a particular executive lacks decisiveness and vigor? By prescribing Prozac? In Tess's work, should the negotiators on the union side be offered Prozac, too? The effect of Prozac on Tess's style in her corporate work—and Sam's in his architectural practice—raises questions about how a drug that alters personality might be used in a competitive society.

Nor is it possible to witness Tess's transformation without fearing that a drug like Prozac might bolster other unfortunate tendencies in contemporary culture. Even Prozac's main effect in Tess's treatment—the relief it provided from social vulnerability—might, in societal terms, prove a mixed blessing. Tess had come for medication treatment only after a prolonged effort at self-understanding through psychotherapy. But I could imagine a less comfortable scenario: A woman much like Tess, abused and neglected in childhood, though not fully aware to what extent and to what effect, seeks treatment in a society that prefers to ignore victimization and that values economy over thoroughness in health care; the woman seems subdued and angry, is discontented for reasons she cannot easily put into words. By what means will her doctor attempt to help her? Would Prozac, alone, be enough?

But my central concern, as I watched Tess's story unfold, involved her personhood. Tess had every right, on the basis of both childhood

17

experience and unhappiness in adult life, to be socially vulnerable in adulthood. But once she had taken Prozac, she—and those who knew her—had to explain her newfound social success on medication. If her self-destructiveness with men and her fragility at work disappeared in response to a biological treatment, they must have been biologically encoded. Her biological constitution seems to have determined her social failures. But how does the belief that a woman who was abused as a child and later remains stuck in abusive relationships largely because of her biologically encoded temperament affect our notions of responsibility, of free will, of unique and socially determinative individual development? Are we willing to allow medications to tell us how we are constituted?

When one pill at breakfast makes you a new person, or makes your patient, or relative, or neighbor a new person, it is difficult to resist the suggestion, the visceral certainty, that who people are is largely biologically determined. I don't mean that it is impossible to escape simplistic biological materialism, but the drama, the rapidity, the thoroughness of drug-induced transformation make simplicity tempting. Drug responses provide hard-to-ignore evidence for certain beliefs—concerning the influence of biology on personality, intellectual performance, and social success—that heretofore we as a society have resisted. When I saw the impact of medication on patients' self-concept, I came to believe that even if we tried to understand these matters complexly, new medications would redraw our map of those parts of the self that are biologically responsive, so that we would arrive, as a culture, at a new consensus about the human condition.

An indication of the power of medication to reshape a person's identity is contained in the sentence Tess used when, eight months after first stopping Prozac, she telephoned me to ask whether she might resume the medication. She said, "I am not myself."

I found this statement remarkable. After all, Tess had existed in one mental state for twenty or thirty years; she then briefly felt different on medication. Now that the old mental state was threatening to re-emerge—the one she had experienced almost all her adult life—her response was "I am not myself." But who had she been all those years if not herself? Had medication somehow removed a false self and replaced it with a true one? Might Tess, absent the invention of the modern antidepressant, have lived her whole life—a successful life, perhaps, by external standards—and never been herself?

When I asked her to expand on what she meant, Tess said she no longer felt like herself when certain aspects of her ailment—lack of confidence, feelings of vulnerability—returned, even to a small degree. Ordinarily, if we ask a person why she holds back socially, she may say, "That's just who I am," meaning shy or hesitant or melancholy or overly cautious. These characteristics often persist throughout life, and they have a strong influence on career, friendships, marriage, self-image.

Suddenly those intimate and consistent traits are not-me, they are alien, they are defect, they are illness—so that a certain habit of mind and body that links a person to his relatives and ancestors from generation to generation is now "other." Tess had come to understand herself—the person she had been for so many years—to be mildly ill. She understood this newfound illness, as it were, in her marrow. She did not feel herself when the medicine wore off and she was rechallenged by an external stress.

On imipramine, no longer depressed but still inhibited and subdued, Tess felt "myself again." But while on Prozac, she underwent a redefinition of self. Off Prozac, when she again became inhibited and subdued—perhaps the identical sensations she had experienced while on imipramine—she now felt "not myself." Prozac redefined Tess's understanding of what was essential to her and what was intrusive and pathological.

This recasting of self left Tess in an unusual relationship to medication. Off medication, she was aware that, if she returned to the old inhibited state, she might need Prozac in order to "feel herself." In this sense, she might have a lifelong relationship to medication, whether or not she was currently taking it. Patients who undergo the sort of deep change Tess experienced generally say they never want to feel the old way again and would take quite substantial risks—in terms, for instance, of medication side effects—in order not to regress. This is not a question of addiction or hedonism, at least not in the ordinary sense of those words, but of having located a self that feels true, normal, and whole, and of understanding medication to be an occasionally necessary adjunct to the maintenance of that self.

Beyond the effect on individual patients, Tess's redefinition of self led me to fantasize about a culture in which this biologically driven sort of self-understanding becomes widespread. Certain dispositions now considered awkward or endearing, depending on taste, might be seen as ailments to be pitied and, where possible, corrected. Tastes and judgments regarding personality styles do change. The romantic, decadent stance of Goethe's young Werther and Chateaubriand's René we now see as merely immature, overly depressive, perhaps in need of treatment. Might we not, in a culture where overseriousness is a medically correctable flaw, lose our taste for the melancholic or brooding artists—Schubert, or even Mozart in many of his moods?

These were my concerns on witnessing Tess's recovery. I was torn simultaneously by a sense that the medication was too far-reaching in its effects and a sense that my discomfort was arbitrary and aesthetic rather than doctorly. I wondered how the drug might influence my profession's definition of illness and its understanding of ordinary suffering. I wondered how Prozac's success would interact with certain unfortunate tendencies of the broader culture. And I asked just how far we—doctors, patients, the society at large—were likely to go in the direction of permitting drug responses to shape our understanding of the authentic self.

My concerns were imprecisely formulated. But it was not only the concerns that were vague: I had as yet only a sketchy impression of the drug whose effects were so troubling. To whom were my patients and I listening? On that question depended the answers to the list of social and ethical concerns; and the exploration of that question would entail attending to accounts of other patients who responded to Prozac.

My first meeting with Prozac had been heightened for me by the uncommon qualities of the patient who responded to the drug. I found it astonishing that a pill could do in a matter of days what psychiatrists hope, and often fail, to accomplish by other means over a course of years: to restore to a person robbed of it in childhood the capacity to play. Yes, there remained a disquieting element to this restoration. Were I scripting the story, I might have made Tess's metamorphosis more gradual, more humanly comprehensible, more in sync with the ordinary rhythm of growth. I might even have preferred if her play as an adult had been, for continuity's sake, more suffused with the memory of melancholy. But medicines do not work just as we wish. The way neurochemicals tell stories is not the way psychotherapy tells them. If Tess's fairy tale does not have the plot we expect, its ending is nonetheless happy.

By the time Tess's story had played itself out, I had seen perhaps a dozen people respond with comparable success to Prozac. Hers was not an isolated case, and the issues it raised would not go away. Charisma, courage, character, social competency—Prozac seemed to say that these and other concepts would need to be re-examined, that our sense of what is constant in the self and what is mutable, what is necessary and what contingent, would need, like our sense of the fable of transformation, to be revised.

2

Compulsion

As I was becoming acquainted with Prozac, I was consulted by a woman who I thought needed no medication at all but who, from the start, knew better. Julia telephoned because she had read a magazine article I had written about psychopharmacology. A patient described there, a woman who responded to Prozac, reminded Julia of herself. Would I see her and put her on the drug? As Julia elaborated, I was less impressed with any sign of mood disorder than with her frustration at work and home. I suggested that, rather than consider medication, she might speak to a psychotherapist. I referred Julia to a woman social worker who is reliable and charges modest fees.

In the course of the first two therapy sessions, the social worker came to believe that Julia's problems arose from a perfectionistic style. The evaluation took place just as stories about Anafranil, the first medicine approved for the treatment of obsessive-compulsive disorder, were appearing in the news. The social worker thought it might make sense for me to have a look at Julia after all.

When I met her, I was impressed, as I had been on the phone, with how well put together Julia seemed. She was pleasant and well spoken and appeared comfortable with herself. Her life had definite form to it: she had completed training as a registered nurse, married, had children, and taken a short-day job at a nursing home, a position that allowed her to be back at the house to greet her children on their return from school.

But there were problems on every front. She demanded extraordinary control in the household. The beds had to be made just so. The children had to be scrubbed and organized before leaving for school. Julia's husband was uncomfortable with her inflexibility, and she found herself raising her voice to him and the children more than was right. Also, the nursing-home job was beneath the level of her abilities. Julia was not challenged, but she saw no way out. How could she manage her tasks in the house and at the same time tackle a more demanding job?

These were the sorts of problems I had hoped might respond to a reassessment of her own or the family's needs in therapy. I certainly did not want to prescribe a "mother's little helper," a pill that would allow Julia to feel less frazzled in a domestic setup that, ideally, required better negotiating between spouses or a clearer understanding on Julia's part of her own anxieties over her competency as nurse, wife, or mother. I wanted, in short, to avoid medicating Julia for what looked like marital dissatisfaction.

I began with the most prosaic questions. Did the housework, child care, and job duties fall on Julia's shoulders in unfair ways? Had Julia considered hiring someone to help with the cleaning? Might she find after-school programs for the children? Would she feel relief if her husband took on additional responsibilities in the house? If he came home earlier, would she be freer to find fulfillment in her career?

Julia said her problems could not be solved in these mundane, operational ways. Her husband had made these suggestions and others, but she could not let go. She needed to be home in any event, because she disliked disorder. If she were not home, the straightening up would not be done to her satisfaction, and the children would not be neat and scrubbed in the way that pleased her.

And it was, she said, very much a matter of pleasing her, of her comfort. She was not absolutely compelled to perform any particular task; if there were sufficient reason, she could leave the house with chores unfinished, although she felt better if everything was done, and done according to her standards. I asked about explicit obsessions. Julia did not fear contamination, was not anxious over germs. In fact, she did not have any formed worrisome ideas; she just disliked it when things were left messy. But her style, her preferences, her sense of propriety, her perfectionism were so pronounced that she was continually angry at her children and husband and, given the impossibility of instilling her standards in them, stalemated in her career.

There are many ways of understanding Julia's dilemma, but perhaps it is most instructive to see how the problem was understood in the period before Julia telephoned to request medication.

Four years into her marriage, and some six years before I saw her, Julia and her husband visited a psychologist for couples counseling. The psychologist, the director of a university program here, found that Julia was unhappy in her marriage. She was not depressed, but she found her husband unresponsive to her needs. Things had to be "just so" to please her, and not only matters of household organization. The husband had to take her out a certain number of nights a month for her to feel loved. If he fell one night shy, she would fault him—but she might not have said openly how many was enough. The psychologist worked with the couple on "communication skills," and he believed they profited. He had never considered a formal diagnosis of depression or of obsessive-compulsive disorder for Julia, although he said she certainly was discontented and had a perfectionistic style.

Julia's internist also found her anxious and unhappy on occasion, conditions he attributed to her perfectionism and her sense that she was not getting enough attention from her husband. The doctor prescribed antianxiety medication for what he called a "situational reaction associated with depressive overtones," a label for a problem that does not quite rise to the level of illness but that nonetheless seems to call for treatment. Julia's gynecologist understood the same intercurrent problems as premenstrual syndrome, a condition he tried at various times to alleviate with diuretics ("water pills") and oil of primrose (a plant extract intended to raise prostaglandin-hormone levels), and more antianxiety medication, without apparent effect.

Julia, in sum, was a patient without a diagnosis, or with bits and pieces of many diagnoses. As a psychiatrist, I was in no better position to categorize Julia's problem than her psychologist, internist, and gynecologist had been. My preference, as I have said, was not to call her ill at all, but to focus on some intimate aspect of the self or the marriage. I wondered about her self-esteem. Where did her need for control, her ineffectiveness in marital negotiations, and her heightened frustration with the children arise, if not from a disorder in self-image? Her perfectionism, if I had to guess, might be a defense against the terrible feelings she anticipated if her imagined inadequacies were laid bare.

I also considered family pathology. Could the husband be undermining his wife, playing on her anxiety in some way that guaranteed she would tend to home and hearth rather than throw herself into her career? Frequently when an otherwise competent patient becomes dysfunctional in one limited sphere, the greater pathology is in the apparently more flexible spouse.

But, in order to consider biological treatment, it seemed important to capture Julia's waxing and waning symptoms in a diagnosis. Julia's other doctors had all on occasion noticed a depressive tendency. The current diagnostic system contains a category—"dysthymia"—for patients who do not quite meet the standards of major depression. But dysthymia applies to people who suffer depressed mood "for most of the day more days than not" for two or more years running, and who when depressed have disturbances of sleep, appetite, energy, concentration, and the like. Julia did not have that sort of disturbance, and her depression was not at all constant. What was constant was her perfectionism.

Perfectionism makes a psychiatrist think of two diagnoses, obsessive-compulsive disorder (OCD) and compulsive personality disorder. Julia did not meet the criteria for these, either, and she said as much in describing herself. She had read about OCD in the newspaper. "I'm a neat freak," she said, "but I am not at all like that— not that extreme."

OCD is among the most terrible of psychiatric disturbances. Anyone who has seen a man or woman whose skin is macerated from repeated scrubbings, or who cannot leave a room for fear of germs, or who spends long hours repeating meaningless calculations, or who cannot stop demanding reassurance over an unlikely but paralyzing source of dread, will have a sense of how distinctive and relentless OCD is. Personable, accomplished, interactive with friends, able to do any particular thing she chose—Julia bore little resemblance to the patients a psychiatrist ordinarily labels as having OCD, and she did not fit the standard definition.

That definition rests on two concepts, the obsession and the compulsion. Obsessions are "recurrent, persistent ideas, thoughts, images, or impulses that are experienced, at least initially, as intrusive and senseless." The example given in the official manual is a parent's impulse to kill a loved child. Julia had no such thoughts. Compulsions are "repetitive, purposeful, and intentional behaviors that are performed in response to an obsession" or in a stereotyped fashion and which are designed to neutralize the dreaded obsession or to prevent discomfort. Here Julia's behavior came closer to the mark, though her actions were more flexible and less strictly compelled than those the definition is meant to indicate.

Perhaps Julia almost met the criteria: there were weeks when she did two loads of laundry every day; if the floors were dirty, she might stay up late to wash them. But these behaviors appeared as compulsions only when her routine was disrupted. Most days, she was organized enough to do what felt right to her on a schedule she found acceptable. Julia's condition fell, let us say, in the penumbra of OCD.

Certainly she had a compulsive style. Extremes of style are called, in the insulting language of psychiatry, "personality disorders." Personality disorders have traditionally been thought not to respond to medication. In the case of compulsive personality disorder, the key elements are "restricted ability to express warm and tender emotions," "perfectionism that interferes with the ability to grasp 'the big picture,' " "excessive devotion to work," and indecisiveness—none of which Julia had—as well as "insistence that others submit to her or her way of doing things," which, along with a good many other people, she had to a fair degree.

I had seen many patients with compulsive personality disorder —the kind who threaten to bore you to death by perseverating on small details of topics whose emotional import is never made clear —and I found Julia entirely unlike them. She was engaging and able to focus well. This having been said, if we had to give a name to what ailed Julia, it would be hard to avoid reference to compulsiveness.

In making a referral to the social worker, I had attempted to define Julia's problem as one of either marital or inner conflict. Julia, however, experienced her disorder as medical. If she were made well, the turmoil in the family would disappear. And that is what happened.

By the time I met with Julia, reports had emerged that, like Anafranil, Prozac was effective in treating OCD, and it seldom caused the weight gain common with Anafranil. Julia was concerned about her weight, and she identified with the patient I had written about who responded to Prozac. We discussed the risks and benefits of different approaches, but in the end I gave her what she had come for. I wrote a prescription for Prozac and told Julia what I tell every patient, that antidepressants take about four weeks to work—two weeks to build up a good level in the brain, and then, for unknown reasons, two weeks to affect the illness.

The first week on medicine, Julia reported, was "like night and day." The children behaved more obediently, and when Julia remarked on the change, they told her she was yelling less. Her husband became more cooperative as Julia became more pleasant with him. Then she noticed she had markedly more energy. "I could not have imagined this" was her comment, meaning she did not want me to think she was experiencing a placebo effect.

I suspected Julia might be experiencing the lift of an amphetaminelike effect, the burst of energy that can arise early in the course of antidepressant treatment. I wrote in her chart, "Good early response," and asked her to return in three weeks.

By then, the early euphoria had worn off. Julia missed the sense of vitality she had felt in the first days, but she remained moderately improved, on better terms with her family. Obsessive-compulsive disorder often requires higher doses of medication than does depression. Though Julia's was at best a "penumbral" case of OCD, I raised the dose and marked her progress. She reported steady, modest improvement in her mood and in her ability to tolerate messiness. Antidepressants do work this way for some patients—a progressive amelioration of symptoms that does not plateau for months.

There were ups and downs. Some weeks, Julia reported having been nervous with her children and having yelled excessively. These fluctuations often correlated with particular stressors. For instance, being home on weekends was harder than responding to the structure of work.

And that structure was changing. First Julia quit her part-time job. She chose instead to do hospital shift work on an on-call basis —a particularly disruptive way to live, but, she felt, the best way for her to re-enter the career path of hospital nursing. She began to specialize in pediatric nursing and found she could enjoy the unpredictability of young children in a way that had been impossible for her in earlier years. She believed that without medicine she could never have taken this step, accompanied as it was by complex caretaking arrangements for her own children and a need often to overlook a degree of chaos in the home.

Julia felt—much as Tess had—that her life had been transformed. Her relations with her children and her husband were more easygoing, and she was able to tolerate a certain messiness in the structure of her life. Whatever intermittent anxiety and depression she had suffered had disappeared.

Once a patient has done well on an antidepressant for five or six months, I generally try to discontinue it. Julia reached that point early in the spring. She came in then to report she was "doing great—could not be better." She had requested and received a promotion at work and been offered regular hours. In the past, she had applied only for jobs for which she was overqualified: as a registered nurse, she had sought positions advertised for practical nurses. Now she was doing work normally done by nurses with master's degrees.

She proudly listed the indicators of her improvement. "I left for the hospital even though the beds were unmade! And I was not upset when the children got grease on their new pants. I didn't punish them or make them feel guilty." Then she told me the biggest news—she was getting a dog.

Before, the messiness of a dog had been repugnant to her, not to mention the effect on her schedule. Now she was ready. "I can't wait," she said, "even though I'm allergic." She had researched breeds whose fur she could tolerate. The children were ecstatic.

We lowered the dose of medicine, and two weeks later Julia called to say the bottom had fallen out: "I'm a witch again." She felt lousy—pessimistic, angry, demanding. She was up half the night cleaning. And there was no way she could consider getting a dog. "It's not just my imagination," she insisted, and then she used the very words Tess had used: "I don't feel myself."

I suggested we wait a bit longer to see whether Julia might be experiencing an odd effect related to medication withdrawal, or perhaps—this happened to be the timing—a premenstrual phenomenon of some sort. But the next week she saw the social worker, who called me to ask what I had in mind. Julia was back to square one, and none of the external circumstances of her life had changed.

Julia resumed taking the higher dose of Prozac. Within two weeks, she felt somewhat better; after five weeks, she was "almost there again," with many more good days than bad. She said work had been torture on the lower dose of medicine: "The patients drove me crazy." She had been unable to block out distractions and had been so aware of time pressure that she could never pause and enjoy the children she was tending.

And, at home, she had been unable to ignore her own children's failings. On the higher dose of medicine, she was once more tolerant. She was again ready to get the dog, and keenly aware that she could not have let a dog into the house when on the lower dose of Prozac. Julia went out of her way to impress on me how much more confident she was, how much more engaged in every facet of her life, when on an adequate dose.

Her husband had nothing but good things to say about the effect of the drug. Sometimes when she behaved in this more relaxed way, he wondered whether she was buttering him up, trying to get on his good side for an ulterior purpose, so unused had he been over the years to having a wife who could sit with him of an evening without being jumpy and critical.

By this point, Julia had stopped seeing the social worker entirely, and the social worker contacted me to express concern—not about Julia's well-being but about her own adequacy. I asked the social worker how she would have understood the case if medication were not available. As she saw it, Julia's story, and her needs, were not difficult to encapsulate.

When Julia first came to the office, her distress related to frustration over her stalled career and certain personal issues—unresolved family-of-origin conflicts that had re-emerged in her marriage. Julia's father, a businessman, had been a high-strung perfectionist; the son of a depressed mother, he was the more nurturant of her parents. Julia saw her mother as passive and distant. Julia's older sister seemed to stumble from failure to failure, and as a result, Julia was moved to care for her and to identify with her competent father.

The conflict in Julia's own marriage, as the social worker formulated the case, involved gender-role conflict. Identifying with her father, Julia secretly, or even unconsciously, felt herself to be more competent than her spouse. At the same time, not least for her own sense of security, she wanted to maintain the illusion that her husband was like her father, strong and decisive. The social worker saw Julia's obsessionality—and her paralysis in career and home life—as an expression of inner conflict over control in the family; she was torn by a wish to let her husband take the lead, opposed by repeated urges to barge in and do things right. These same conflicts emerged in her handling of the children, whom she pushed hard while telling herself she was giving them their head.

The social worker saw Prozac as having had an interesting effect on these conflicts. It had tipped the balance in favor of assertiveness, allowing Julia to make it clear to her husband what she needed and why; at the same time, it made her less urgent, which allowed her husband to do things at his own pace, a condition under which he appeared quite competent. Before she began her Prozac treatment, Julia had obsessed over which bedspread to buy her daughter. All were imperfect, because the real problem was that Julia disliked the paint color in her daughter's room, a subject she had been reluctant to raise with her husband. On medication, Julia simply asked her husband to repaint the room and then waited patiently for him to complete the task. Once the painting was under way, Julia had no trouble selecting a bedspread. In this interaction, both husband and wife were able to exert control in their different ways.

I asked the social worker why she felt guilty. The medication had done what she would have wished to accomplish with her psychotherapy: it had facilitated an improvement in the family dynamics. The problem, for the social worker, was that this change came about without any increased self-knowledge on Julia's part. I said that evidently insight had not been necessary. This comment did not allay the social worker's concern. She believed that medication-induced change, unaccompanied by growth in self-understanding, was inferior to what psychotherapy has to offer.

To Julia, the story was entirely different. As so often happens, the pill reified the illness. If there was a chance in the world that Julia might see her difficulty in adjusting to married life as anything but a result of a "biological disorder characterized by compulsiveness and depression," her relapse and rescue by the increased dose of medicine ended it. Once the drug kicked in, she had visited the social worker only infrequently, and then with skepticism. "If I had been on Prozac," she said, "I would not have needed to see the marriage counselor either."

I found I had little desire to cling to my earlier hypothesis of family pathology—the competent wife secretly undermined by the threatened husband. Even my sense of her perfectionism as a defense against low self-esteem was shaken, although I was beginning to wonder whether medication could perhaps provide self-esteem. Certainly on medication Julia was able to make major adjustments in her life with no sign of inner conflict. Her husband was enthusiastic when she moved on with her career. If anything, the response of Julia and her family to the medicine made the various scenarios conjured up by psychotherapy seem hypercritical and ungenerous.

But what did Julia "have"? Since her condition responded to a medication that can treat OCD, do we want to say she had OCD?

This decision is consequential. Large numbers of patients who visit doctors with psychological complaints are not "diagnosable." To make them diagnosable would mean expanding the current schema, and thus calling many more people mentally ill. Whether we want to change our view of mental illness and whether we want to make medication response a deciding criterion are interesting questions, with humane arguments available both for and against expansion.

If we do say that Julia has, say, an incompletely expressed case of OCD, we will be recapitulating in biological psychiatry the history of psychoanalysis. Once reserved for the most obviously ill patients, "obsessional" and its contrasting counterpart, "hysterical," came as the period of psychoanalytic dominance progressed to be applied to people's social styles. The advent of biological psychiatry originally resulted in a severe restriction of the use of such terms; but, with the discovery of new biological treatments, the operational definition of OCD is expanding once again, in part because what responds like OCD comes to be called OCD.

"Obsessionality" and "compulsiveness" are now used by those who treat illness with medication to encompass what in earlier days would have seemed mere personal idiosyncrasy. Increasingly, what was once the penumbra of OCD is fully in its shadow. But the expanded disease has its own penumbra. Now there will arise questions about how patients slightly less compulsive than Julia should be categorized and treated.

To see how far this new penumbra extends, I want to return to Julia's decision to contact me for treatment. Julia called because she identified with a patient I had described in a magazine article. That patient was Tess. I had described Tess as "a hard-working executive so attentive to detail in her professional life that she found little time to socialize. . . ." Those few words struck a chord with Julia, convinced her that she and Tess—very different women—might have something biologically in common.

And it's true that I had treated Tess for something rather like perfectionism. When Tess responded to imipramine but remained stuck in love and work, I began to wonder whether what held her back might bear some relationship to OCD.

Tess had no compulsions. She was, to be sure, obsessed with a hurtful lover; otherwise, she was not obsessional even in the colloquial sense. But she was *driven* to an unusual degree. What distinguished Tess was her success under impossible conditions, her determination, and her insistent and effective nurturance of others. She was, one might say, almost too giving. I don't know at what point I began looking at that goodness from the odd perspective of the biological diagnostician; I can only say that there are in pharmacology, as in psychotherapy, important moments when the clinician suddenly sees the patient afresh. In one such moment, I began to re-examine, to recategorize, those traits that made Tess special.

I have characterized clinical psychopharmacology as an impressionistic art. The doctor listens to a patient and, on the basis of the patient's story and the empathic response it evokes—bizarre biological probes, so qualitatively different from the usual blood, urine, and spinal-fluid tests—the doctor attempts to make an assessment of the state of the patient's neurons. The pharmacologist assumes that the complex constellation of behaviors and feelings a patient reveals reflects a simple physiological state. On the basis of the extraordinary, unique shape of a patient's life, the pharmacologist asks such questions as "Is this a disorder that is likely to respond to a drug that treats OCD?"

What an odd thought this is—"dedication to others less fortunate" as a form of aberrance that can lead a doctor to choose one medication over another. But, in the inexact process of extrapolating back from symptom and behavior to chemistry, the psychiatrist takes every bit of help he can get. We are not beyond grasping at straws, and I grasped at this one: I wondered whether Tess had a touch of the obsessional about her.

I began to ask Tess about her strengths as one might ask other patients about their weaknesses. How had she managed to raise her siblings so effectively? She answered, "You don't understand. I had no choice. The only other possibility was to disappoint everyone who counted on me, and I could not bear that."

We are accustomed to thinking of compulsiveness as a disorder or an annoying style of relating to the world, and it can be. But some of the characteristics of compulsiveness—the deep sense of responsibility, the vigilance, and the attention to detail—are also virtues. Sociobiologists have speculated that compulsiveness survived in the human species because it was a competitive advantage for our ancestors' tribes to contain one or two members who were prudent and driven in the extreme. Certainly Tess's family survived because of her inability to tolerate failure.

I am morally certain that I would not have had these ruminations if Prozac did not exist. Because an antidepressant likely to be useful for compulsive patients was available, it made sense to ask whether Tess's strength of character could be a manifestation of the same biological constellation that in other people shows itself as compulsiveness. Equally, it was because her dedication might be, in physical terms, something like OCD that—with so many tried and true medications available—I turned to a new and relatively untested drug for Tess.

In clinical pharmacology, contemporary technology plays a dominant role in shaping ideology. What we look for in patients depends to a great degree on the available medications. That Tess's depression was accompanied by what could be construed as compulsiveness was of interest only because this trait might be an indicator of something we could now treat.

Who Julia is—whether she is a fully functional woman with marital troubles or a slightly handicapped woman adjusting uncomfortably to reasonable constraints—is largely a function of drug development. We may decide on similar grounds whether Tess's dedication is a moral or a psychopathological trait. How we, as observers of our fellow men and women, look and listen, how we categorize, how we understand the tensions between people and their predicaments, is in part a product of the available means of influence. The interaction between a drug and cultural norms does not require the use of medication by the people we are assessing but can result from the mere availability of a substance that colors our beliefs about deviance and how it is produced.

Tess's self-understanding revolved around a quality she identified as seriousness. Once on medication, she explained her newfound success with men in simple terms: "I am less serious."

Seriousness covers a lot of ground. For most of her life, Tess did not allow herself to seek out pleasure. She focused on duty, and heeded the warning of a strong "superego," or conscience, that always put work before play. On medicine, her ability to attract men owed something to her increased flexibility, to a more generous sense of permission to enjoy. The problem earlier may have been as much one of unwillingness to attract men as inability. These traits, which might loosely be termed compulsive, disappeared when Tess took Prozac. And of course we may attribute her new ability to forget her married ex-boyfriend Jim to a true anticompulsive effect of drug treatment.

We have earlier considered Tess's transformation in terms of the alleviation of chronic depression. Here is a somewhat different way of conceptualizing her responses to medication: the imipramine had handled her acute depression. The Prozac cured her of a masked form, or variant manifestation, of compulsiveness.

Tess's recovery parallels Julia's. In both instances, the very traits targeted as compulsive disappeared on the appropriate medication. The question then becomes just how far we are willing to "listen to drugs." Will we want to expand the definition of OCD or compulsive personality disorder to include someone like Tess, who has no compulsions whatsoever and who meets none of the explicit criteria of illness except, perhaps, exaggerated devotion to work? Though we may resist it, the temptation is there. Surely, in a colloquial sense, part of what happened to Tess when she took Prozac was that she became less compulsive.

Facing someone like Tess, I think we are drawn in two directions.

One is to stretch the scope of illness to encompass her character traits. Another is to say we have found a medication that can affect personality, perhaps even in the absence of illness—only now, instead of restricting our powers to the depressive-to-manic continuum, we are considering whether we may not also be able to influence what we might call the obsessional-to-hysteric continuum.

Either way, we are edging toward what might be called the "medicalization of personality." Or perhaps, once we say that traits on both the depressive-to-manic and the obsessional-to-hysteric continua respond to medication, we are over the edge. Those two spectra cover a good deal of what makes different people distinctive. It is not only Tess's "seriousness" whose biological underpinnings are likely linked to compulsion or depression. If seriousness is subject to chemical influence, we can imagine a large collection of pairs of opposed traits that will be as well: contemplative/action-oriented, rigid/flexible, cautious/impulsive, risk-averse/risk-prone, masochistic/assertive, by-the-book/by-the-seat-of-the-pants, deferential/demanding, and many others. The first element in any of these pairs might equally be associated with depressive or obsessional leanings and might equally be a candidate for drug treatment.

The extension of our reach beyond depressed/manic to obsessive/hysteric is significant. The obsessional-to-hysteric continuum was once a mainstay of psychiatry. Toward the middle of this century, most relatively healthy patients, those with what was then called "neurosis," were discussed for treatment purposes in terms of whether they were more obsessional or more hysterical. Every person can be understood as sitting somewhere on this spectrum.

We recognize the flavor of compulsiveness even in the absence of a single symptom. Think about Bert and Ernie on "Sesame Street." They represent extremes in the diverse styles of healthy children. Bert has a fixed, serious, even worried look, and he is decidedly more reliable and less spontaneously playful than Ernie. Children identify with Bert because they love order; they identify with Ernie because they love mischief. Every child has mixed affinities for discipline and innovation, noise and quiet, group activity and solitude. I am hardly suggesting treatment for Bert or Ernie. But I suspect we would be near the truth if, putting aside such formal labels as "obsessional" and "hysterical," we were to say that what Prozac did for Tess was to shift her from a personality like Bert's to one more like Ernie's. Only Ernie would make or enjoy three dates a weekend; only Ernie would venture the gift of the red wagon.

This broad view of obsessionality, in which any affinity for the Apollonian virtues as opposed to the Dionysian suffices to make the diagnosis, gives some sense of what it might mean to introduce a medicine that can affect minor degrees of a trait that exists along a broad continuum, extending from illness to health.

We may not be convinced that Tess was compulsive. But even extending the definition of OCD to include Julia (and I think, especially taking into account the way her symptoms returned when her medication dose was lowered, many psychiatrists today would consider her to suffer from something like OCD) raises interesting questions for me. I recall, in my own childhood, having been specially scrubbed and warned against messy play before visiting certain demanding older relatives. Those relatives had grown up in Germany, where extremes of neatness and order were the cultural norm. Their homes were, every day, more tidy than any homes I have seen since even on special occasions. Julia reminded me of the wives in those families; perhaps my comfort with them explains my reluctance initially to accept Julia's behavior as symptomatic of medical illness.

Those wives, if my childhood perceptions are accurate, were not conflicted about their perfectionism, nor did their husbands seriously challenge it, though it was a matter for teasing and banter. I doubt the wives would have gone to bed with the floor or clothes dirty, but neither would their schedule often have required them to do so. There was in those families, I suspect, a certain male comfort in being the better-acculturated, more flexible spouse—the cock of the walk—while the wife assiduously tended the homefires. This arrangement inevitably led to a certain amount of marital unhappiness, but I would say that for the most part the couples managed to make their way through life contentedly.

Once Julia responded to medication, I found myself wondering whether those more contented perfectionists of years past would have responded to Prozac similarly. There are reasons for thinking not. To be neat in a culture that prizes neatness may bespeak a very different, less aberrant biological state than maintenance of the same behavior in a culture that has adopted different values. And if those perfectionistic housewives could have been relieved with medication of some of their need for order, their lives might not have been improved so much as made complicated in interesting ways. To say something less speculative: whether a particular behavioral style like perfectionism is deviant is very much a matter of cultural expectations, and that culture can be as broad as a nation and as narrow as a twosome.

This particular contrast—the contented and discontented perfectionist—gives rise to further thoughts about the notion of the "mother's little helper." Mother's little helpers were pills—Miltown, amphetamine, barbiturates, Librium, and Valium were the most popular and widely available in the fifties and early sixties—that were used to keep women in their place, to make them comfortable in a setting that should have been uncomfortable, to encourage them to focus on tasks that did not matter. I cannot think of the phrase even today without hearing it in Mick Jagger's sneering tones.

In Julia's story, the mother's-helper role is most clearly played by the various antianxiety pills given her over the years. Those medicines allowed her to perform her housekeeping tasks with a diminished, but still substantial, level of anxiety. The failing of those medicines was not that they did not work well enough but that they worked the wrong way altogether. The point, in retrospect, was not to make Julia less anxious but more bold.

Prozac's status in Julia's treatment is more complex. At the most obvious level, it was the opposite of a mother's little helper: it got Julia out of the house and into the workplace, where she was able to grow in competence and confidence. I see this result often. There is a sense in which antidepressants are feminist drugs, liberating and empowering. In this scenario, it is the failure to prescribe medication that keeps the wife trapped, apparently by her own proclivities. We may even want to say that nonbiological therapies, like the couples counseling, though apparently aimed at change through understanding, are in fact palliative and likely to lead only to a slightly more tolerable form of inertia.

It is hard not to see Prozac in these stories as the opposite of a mother's little helper. But the memory of my fastidious relatives makes me want to include a small caveat, a reminder that we might want to maintain awareness of how culture-bound this reading of events is. After all, should a person with a personality style that might succeed in a different social setting have to change her personality (by means of drugs!) in order to find fulfillment?

Even Tess's success falls under a similar caveat. I have in mind a recent remark by John Updike: "Masochism is as unfashionable now as aggressiveness was twenty years ago. . . ." If we see Tess's transformation as a victory, it's because of a change in mores, because we value the assertive woman and shake our heads over the long-suffering self-sacrificer. Perhaps medication now risks playing a role that psychotherapy was accused of playing in the past: it allows a person to achieve happiness through conformity to contemporary norms. This accusation is the "mother's-little-helper" label in modern colors.

We may have difficulty entertaining such a point of view, because cultural expectations have shifted so decisively. We can hardly imagine wanting to do anything other than relieve Tess's suffering by freeing her from her addiction to sadistic men. We can hardly imagine wishing for Julia that she find more fulfillment in her well-kept home. But to say this much is to excuse us as a society for failing to find a satisfying, growth-enhancing niche for women with obvious strengths and two rather common forms of personality organization.

Certainly our valuation of compulsiveness in men has undergone a change. One has only to consider Phileas Fogg, "the most punctual man alive," who nonetheless had the spunk and resourcefulness to travel around the world in eighty days. For decades, the eccentric and fastidious Englishman was at once a figure of fun and of admiration—he ruled the Empire. It took the work of such writers as Edmund Gosse and the Bloomsbury group to begin to make tenderness a male virtue, overattentiveness to work a failing, and eccentricity an aspect of fatherly tyranny rather than masculine charm. (Indeed, from the 1930s through the 1960s, an influential critique of capitalist society held that it created and rewarded the "anal character"—compulsive, hoarding, and industrious—while repressing sensuality and spontaneity.)

In the everyday practice of medicine, and in the everyday valuation of human success and suffering, it is fruitless to try to maintain the viewpoint of cultural relativism. Here is the physician's compulsion, and perhaps society's as well: once we have seen Julia recover or Tess become "better than well," we inevitably assess their personality styles as handicapping forms of minor mood disorder. The operational definition of wellness must be in relation to the demands and goals of our society, here and now. Once we have seen the joy on patients' faces, we can only be grateful for the availability of more powerful and specific medication. But the awareness that what we are altering is a personal style that might have succeeded in a different, and not especially distant, culture may make us wonder whether we are using medication in the service of conformity to societal values. Indeed, experience with medication may make us aware of how exigent our culture is in its behavioral demands.

The reader may still be puzzling over a different question: whether Tess and Julia and Sam had something "really" like compulsiveness or "really" like depression. Not only do depression and OCD have penumbras and penumbras-of-penumbras, but these larger areas of shadow often overlap. People who are pessimistic tend to be cautious, and vice versa. Moreover, the effectiveness of Prozac for both conditions may lead us to wonder whether the conditions are related.

Here is another important aspect of listening to drugs: responsiveness to medication can influence our thoughts about which illnesses are distinct and which overlap. How doctors divide up mental illness may seem an issue merely internal to psychiatry, but for decades the debate over the continuity or separateness of mental illnesses has colored our understanding of the way human beings are related to one another.

The most basic diagnostic distinction in psychiatry is that between manic-depressive illness and schizophrenia, the disorders defined and declared to be separate by the father of modern diagnostic (or descriptive) psychiatry, Freud's contemporary Emil Kraepelin. At the turn of the century, Kraepelin showed that manic-depressives have a different course of illness from that of patients suffering from schizophrenia; he assumed that both diseases had a biological basis. By mid-century, many American psychiatrists were prepared to ignore Kraepelin's distinction and, indeed, to discard almost all diagnosis. As late as 1963, Karl Menninger wrote that "we tend today to think of all mental illness as being essentially the same in quality, although differing quantitatively and in external appearance."

This declaration was part of an egalitarian manifesto, the assertion that the well and the ill differ primarily in the degree of trauma they have suffered, and secondarily in the strength of their natural constitutions. This spectrum theory of mental illness arose from psychoanalysis. As Donald Klein, a formidable critic of the spectrum theory, put it, "The predominant American psychiatric theory was that all psychopathology was secondary to anxiety, which in turn was caused by intrapsychic conflict. Psychosis was considered the result of such an excess of anxiety that the ego crumbled and regressed, and neurosis, the result of a partially successful defense against anxiety that led to symptom formation." The well and the mentally ill differed only in the degree of anxiety they bore; and therefore the same treatment, the diminution of inner conflict via psychotherapy, was applicable to all ailments and all people. The spectrum theory was part of a broader psychology that emphasized the qualities people have in common.

Disregard for diagnosis was an American phenomenon. Though admirable in its demand that people be seen and treated similarly, it led to peculiar contrasts with observations in Europe. Considering diagnosis a mere administrative requirement, American psychiatrists had begun calling all seriously ill patients schizophrenic, a practice Menninger encouraged. The result was international data showing that New York had more schizophrenics and fewer manic-depressives than did London. This discrepancy was then treated as reflective of real phenomena, and theories were generated to explain it: perhaps urban violence in New York caused schizophrenia, whereas the calm and dull life of London was conducive to mood disorders. Racial theories were also advanced.

At last an epidemiological study was conducted, using uniform criteria (the British criteria, based on Kraepelin's distinction) to diagnose patients in the two cities. The landmark "U.S.-U.K. study," published in 1972, concluded that, "In spite of the gross differences in the diagnostic statistics produced by the hospitals of the two cities, in spite of the profound social and cultural differences between the cities themselves . . . when uniform diagnostic criteria are employed the diagnostic distributions of patients entering hospital in New York and London are to all intents and purposes identical." The apparent differences in proportions of illness were due entirely to differences in doctors' diagnostic practices. But which diagnostic system was superior? That question would be answered by a drug, lithium.

The story of lithium has the quality of legend. Lithium is an element of the periodic table, where it sits just below sodium. Like sodium, lithium readily forms salts. Early in the century, lithium bromide had been used as a sedating tranquilizer (hence our term "bromide" for a commonplace saying), but lithium fell out of favor in the 1940s, when it was used in an uncontrolled way as a sodium substitute for cardiac patients, some of whom died. At just this inauspicious time, in 1949, the Australian John F. J. Cade, "an unknown psychiatrist, working alone in a small chronic hospital with no research training, primitive techniques and negligible equipment," discovered that lithium salts were a remarkable specific treatment for manic depression.

Cade's discovery is often characterized as serendipitous. Cade had found that the urine of manic patients was especially toxic to guinea pigs, and he was looking for the responsible substances. He thought one might be uric acid, and he began experimenting with lithium urate, not because of any psychiatric properties of lithium, but because lithium urate was the most soluble salt of uric acid. To Cade's surprise, far from being toxic, the salt protected guinea pigs against the urine of manics, and it also sedated the animals, effects Cade found were due to the lithium. He immediately tried other lithium salts on himself and, when they proved safe, on ten hospitalized manic patients, all of whom recovered, some almost miraculously. The discovery of lithium as an antimanic agent resulted from one man's curiosity and powers of observation and deduction.

Because of the cardiac deaths, as well as Cade's lack of renown in the profession, the use of lithium for mania spread slowly. But by the late 1960s, doctors once more considered lithium to be a reasonably safe drug. It was also understood that lithium can treat and prevent recurrences of manic-depressive illness but is only rarely effective for schizophrenia. Once lithium's safety and specific efficacy for manic depression were accepted, diagnostic distinctions mattered in a way they had not before. At the same time, pharmacologic outcome could guide diagnosis.

This reasoning was precisely circular: since diagnosis was needed to predict medication response, medication response should determine diagnosis. It seemed, for the most part, that lithium treated all manic-depressive illness and nothing else; and no other medication treated manic depression. That is, lithium conformed to a one-drug/one-disease model of pharmacology, a model so aesthetically pleasing as to be irresistible. Lithium responsiveness confirmed the Kraepelinian model of manic depression and caused American psychiatrists to expand their use of the diagnosis. Lithium had performed an extraordinary "pharmacological dissection," defining for all the world the boundaries of a particular disorder.

The success of lithium set off an explosion of precise psychiatric diagnosis. In a few decades, American psychiatrists went from using only two diagnoses, neurosis and schizophrenia, to using hundreds.

Lithium and the one-drug/one-disease model had an enormous influence on the minds of physicians. Lithium made it look as if medications would be splitters—definers of illness. But, sadly, there has never been another lithium. Most subsequent medications have been lumpers, and none more so than Prozac. Within a couple of years of its introduction, Prozac was shown to be useful in depression, OCD, panic anxiety, eating disorders, premenstrual syndrome, substance abuse, attention-deficit disorder, and a number of other conditions.

The firm link between one drug and one diagnosis has become an ideal model which even lithium no longer fits. With an effective medication available, American psychiatrists became such enthusiastic diagnosers of manic depression that today only half of the patients who receive that diagnosis respond to lithium, and two or three other drugs are in common use for the illness. And lithium is now being used to treat other forms of disturbance.

Medications, it is increasingly understood, alter neurochemical systems. They do not treat specific illnesses. And the proliferation of illnesses has become so disturbing that the cutting edge of research involves attempts to elucidate links between them.

OCD and dysthymia, for example, are classified in contemporary psychiatry as discrete entities, one related to anxiety and the other to depression; but a countervailing movement, based in part on observations of drug effects, characterizes them as related disorders. Our confusion over just what the medication is working on in Sam, Tess, and Julia suggests that diagnostic specificity may have its limitations. Especially in mildly disturbed or near-normal patients, syndromes that should be distinct overlap. As a drug prescribed for these fairly healthy patients, Prozac casts a spotlight on the indeterminateness of diagnosis. This boundary-blurring constitutes an unanticipated— humanistic—effect of listening to drugs: like psychoanalysis, drug response can emphasize commonality, and the futility of attempts at mechanistic categorization. Tess and Julia and Sam share something very much like "neurosis," psychoanalysis's umbrella term for the mildly disturbed, the near-normal, and those with very little wrong at all.

What is especially noteworthy about the blurring of boundaries is its source. For decades, the thrust of biological psychiatry—not only because of lithium, but in response to evidence from brain scanners, genetic studies, and research on neurotransmitters—has been to bolster the discrete-disease model of mental deviance and to undermine the spectrum concept. Thoughtful people may have anticipated that the pendulum would some day swing the other way, but not, perhaps, that the new challenge to distinctions among illnesses, and between health and illness, would come from one of the fruits of biological psychiatry, the psychotherapeutic drug.

3

Antidepressants

Though the reception accorded Prozac is unique, it is not unprecedented. The first modern antidepressant, iproniazid, enjoyed its own meteoric career.

Iproniazid was developed as an antitubercular drug in the early 1950s and at first it appeared successful. Not only did it decrease the number of tubercule bacilli in the sputum, it also stimulated patients' appetites, gave them energy, and restored to them a general sense of well-being. Iproniazid was immortalized in an Associated Press photograph of 1953 that shows residents of the Sea View Sanatorium on Staten Island, attractive black women in ankle-length cotton print skirts and white blouses, smiling and clapping in a semicircle while two of their number do what looks like the Lindy Hop. "A few months ago," the caption read, "only the sound of TB victims coughing their lives away could be heard here."

Iproniazid did suppress the replication of bacteria, but the patients' inclination to dance did not derive entirely from the remission of their illness. Iproniazid was discovered to be a "psychic energizer," to use the phrase of Nathan Kline, the psychiatrist who investigated the drug's effects on the mind. Kline hoped an increase in a patient's vital energy would reverse depression. Using the language of psy-

47

choanalysis, then the dominant theory of mind, Kline wrote: "The plethora of id energy would make large amounts of energy easily available to the ego so that there would be more than enough energy available for all tasks. Such a situation would result in a sense of joyousness and optimism."

The drug's manufacturer was unenthusiastic. Iproniazid had been superseded by other antituberculars, and the company was ready to stop production. But in April 1957, *The New York Times* reported the contents of papers to be given at a research conference in Syracuse indicating preliminary successes in treating depression with iproniazid. Years later, Kline wrote: "Probably no drug in history was so widely used so soon after the announcement of its application in the treatment of a specific disease."

Approximately four hundred thousand depressed patients were treated in the first year. Unfortunately, 127 of these patients developed jaundice. Given the prevalence of viral hepatitis, this was probably a small number of cases for the population involved, but the manufacturer thought (wrongly) that it had a more potent antidepressant coming to market, so, rather than fight the bad publicity, it withdrew iproniazid. Iproniazid's reputation had been fatally tainted by the report of side effects, and it was never heard from again.

The extraordinary initial reception of iproniazid had been due to two factors. First, it had already been used in the treatment of tuberculosis. As a result, doctors were comfortable with it, and when the research results were announced, it was already on the market, ready for use. Second, the pent-up demand was enormous. Depression is an extraordinarily prevalent affliction, and there was at the time no acceptable way to treat it biologically. It was well understood among physicians that, though certain medications could alleviate one or another symptom of depression, short of such extreme interventions as inducing a seizure through administering high doses of insulin or through shocking the patient's brain electrically, there were no physical treatments that gave relief from the whole spectrum of symptoms and ended the episode of depression.

While Nathan Kline was on the lookout for energizing drugs, a leading researcher in Switzerland, Ronald Kuhn, was pursuing a different line of reasoning. At the time of the discovery of iproniazid, the most effective drug treatment for depression was opium. Opium was recognized as an odd substance. It caused some of the symptoms of melancholy in healthy subjects and alleviated symptoms in the depressed. Kuhn thought opium presented the proper model for a true antidepressant.

For unknown reasons, rare depressed patients even today will respond to no medicine except opiates, and a few researchers into depression have become newly interested in these substances. Fifty years ago, most patients who felt better on opium probably valued it for its ability to ameliorate scattered symptoms, such as sleeplessness, anxiety, and a general sense of malaise. Perhaps for mistaken reasons, Kuhn took the occasional success of opium to set the standard in the search for antidepressants. The hallmark of opium was that it restored energy in the depressed without being inherently energizing. Kuhn set out "to find a drug acting in some specific manner against melancholy that is better than opium"—that is, a nonstimulating antidepressant.

Iproniazid met only part of the standard. In some patients, it ameliorated all the symptoms. But it also seemed to have the ability to stimulate a variety of people—witness the dancing tubercular women—so it was not clear at first whether its effects came from reversing a basic process of depression.

In his search for a nonstimulating antidepressant, Kuhn began by looking at antihistamines. Antihistamines are the drugs, like Benadryl, used to treat allergies. Many antihistamines are sedating—indeed, the active ingredient in Sominex, the over-the-counter sleeping pill, is the same as the active ingredient in Benadryl. Kuhn was interested in sedation because opium is sedating, and he was interested in the antihistamines because the first modern psychotherapeutic medicine, chlorpromazine, was an antihistamine.

Chlorpromazine (Thorazine), introduced in 1952, constituted a breakthrough in the treatment of schizophrenia—it is known as the drug that emptied the state mental hospitals. Chlorpromazine had some efficacy in depression, calming agitated patients. Kuhn had already tested new antihistamines to see whether they were effective as sleeping pills. He now returned to the sedating antihistamines, especially those whose structure resembled that of chlorpromazine, to see how they affected depression.

In September 1957, less than half a year after the reports regarding iproniazid's initial success, Kuhn announced that he had found a substance that sedated normal people but relieved depression. As Kuhn put it: "We have achieved a specific treatment of depressive states, not ideal, but already going far in that direction. I emphasize 'specific' because the drug largely or completely restores what illness has impaired—namely the mental functions and capacity and what is of prime importance, the power to experience."

Kuhn's new drug was called imipramine. The theoretical importance of imipramine (Tofranil), the first nonstimulating antidepressant, is underscored in a memoir by Donald Klein, the pharmacologic researcher who so eloquently opposed the spectrum theory of mental illness. Klein worked with imipramine on an experimental basis in 1959. He later wrote:

> We knew that amphetamine was ineffective in the treatment of severe depressions, but we hoped this new agent would be much more stimulating and blow the patients out of their pit.
>
> Imagine our surprise when we found that giving imipramine to severe depressives first resulted in sedation, and shortly after that in an increase in appetite, hardly stimulant effects. Further, marked mood improvement was usually

not evident for several weeks. At that point many patients' moods returned to normal but they rarely became overstimulated. . . .

Therefore this drug was certainly not a stimulant. Further, when given to normals it did not cause stimulation or elevation of mood, but rather sedation. So, whatever the drug was doing was the result of an interaction between the medication and the pathophysiological dysregulation that produced the pathological state. In this sense the drug seemed a normalizer, not a stimulant.

In other words, imipramine was the grail—the true antidepressant, a substance of more conceptual importance even than iproniazid.

Despite the enthusiasm of isolated researchers, the announcement of the efficacy of imipramine was mostly met with skepticism. An entirely new medicine with no other indication than the treatment of depression, imipramine took some years to catch on. Though slower out of the blocks, imipramine was to enjoy a fate happier than that of iproniazid; but it turned out both drugs were antidepressants. The nearly simultaneous demonstration of the efficacy of imipramine and iproniazid signaled the opening of the modern era of research into human emotion. The two medications still set the terms for our contemporary understanding of the biology of mood.

In discussing patients' responses, and my own, to the success of psychotherapeutic medication, I have alluded to the tendency to "listen to drugs" as if they could tell us something about how human beings are constituted. (If Julia's fastidiousness diminishes in response to Prozac, then it "really" was a penumbral form of OCD; Sam's prurience, similarly, is revealed as a biological obsession. Tess has "really" been depressed all her life, and her social failures are a consequence of that depression.) Listening to drugs is not merely a popular phenomenon. For the last half-century, scientists have relied on medication response to infer the cause of disease.

"Pneumonia is not caused by a lack of penicillin" is the sort of statement used to ridicule such reasoning. But, in the absence of other easy approaches to the human brain, researchers have tended to use drugs as probes and to try to understand mental disorder in terms of the mechanism of action of effective medication. The great result, in terms of our theoretical understanding of mental functioning, has been the biogenic-amine theory of depression.

Stated simply, the theory holds that mood is determined in the brain by biogenic amines—complex chemicals a part of whose structure resembles that of ammonia. Even before the discovery of antidepressants, amines were known to be involved in the regulation of a variety of functions, from heart rate and gut motility to alertness and sleep. The discovery of iproniazid and imipramine led scientists to conclude that these amines also regulate mood.

Shortly after the drugs were introduced, it was shown that both iproniazid and imipramine influence the way nerve cells terminate messages. Nerves communicate by releasing "transmitter" substances—in this case amines—into the space, or synapse, between cells. The message is then ended by a two-stage process in which the amines are taken back up into the transmitting cell and inactivated by "janitorial" enzymes. Imipramine slows the reuptake of amines from the synapse into the transmitting cell, thus leaving the amines active in the synapse for a longer period of time. Iproniazid poisons the janitorial enzyme that digests the amines. Poisoning the enzyme makes more amine available for use in transmission. Thus, both known antidepressants (imipramine and iproniazid), by different mechanisms, made biogenic amines more available in relevant parts of the brain. This finding was taken as strong support for the hypothesis that depression is caused by a deficiency of amines.

If the amine theory held true, then (by somewhat circular reasoning) iproniazid and imipramine acted on the core biological problem in depression. They were increasing the efficacy of necessary, naturally occurring bodily substances. The amine theory was a very attractive model of mood regulation, because it made depression look like illnesses whose causes were well known. A person who has too little insulin suffers from diabetes; an excess of insulin causes low blood sugar (hypoglycemia). Thyroid hormone can be too high (hyperthyroidism, as in Graves' disease, suffered by President and Mrs. Bush); or it can be too low (causing hypothyroidism, or myxedema). Under the amine hypothesis, mood disorders now looked like those ordinary illnesses. An excess of amines was thought to cause mania (not least because an overdose of iproniazid could sometimes precipitate mania), and a deficiency, depression. For technical reasons, it was impossible to deliver biogenic amines directly to the relevant part of the brain. But the deficiency state could be ameliorated by slowing the breakdown or reuptake of the amines.

The amine hypothesis is perhaps false and at least incomplete. Like the evidence supporting the amine hypothesis of depression the evidence against it came from drug effects. For one thing, researchers identified antidepressants (not in use in this country) that have no direct effect on the amines. For another, there is a curious time lag in the onset of action of antidepressants. Imipramine can block the reuptake of neurotransmitters in a matter of minutes or hours. But it takes about four weeks for patients on imipramine to begin to feel less depressed. Why should a patient with effective levels of the relevant neurotransmitters not experience an immediate change in mood? Why do some depressed patients not respond at all? The amine hypothesis cannot answer these questions.

A particular line of evidence made it clear early on that the biogenic-amine hypothesis was imperfect. There are drugs that deplete the brain of complex amines, in effect doing the opposite of what antidepressants do. (One of these drugs, reserpine, has been used for many years to lower blood pressure.) Depleting the brain of amines should cause depression, and it does—but only in about 20 percent of patients. People who get depressed in response to amine depletion tend to be those who have already been depressed in the past or who are under stress in their lives. Depletion of amines is not enough in itself to cause depression.

From the time it was propounded, researchers understood that the amine hypothesis could not be the whole story. Indeed, the amine hypothesis is, in a sense, a self-deceptive form of listening to drugs. Most drug development takes place by homology. If one drug is effective, researchers will create physically similar substances, chemicals structured with what some cynics call the "least patentable difference" from the already successful medication. Scientists synthesized a host of substances similar in chemical structure to imipramine, and the success of these medications in treating depression strengthened the hold of the amine hypothesis. Almost all drugs on the market could be shown to affect amines—not surprising, given the modes for their development. The second popular way of developing drugs is through analogy: if one chemical that works as an antidepressant affects amines, then researchers will look for antidepressants among structurally different substances also known to affect amines. The potential for circular reasoning in this case is even more evident.

Only 5 percent of neurotransmission in the brain occurs via amines, but amines are the lighted streetlamps under which the secret of depression is most often searched for. The amine hypothesis may some day be superseded. In the meantime, its usefulness in predicting the effectiveness of compounds for the treatment of depression, and its heuristic power to explain their mechanism of action, have led it to dominate the scientific landscape. That these compounds were developed by analogy or homology with other compounds that affect amines is the irony embedded in the amine hypothesis.

Imipramine is a highly effective antidepressant. Perhaps 60 or 70 percent of classically depressed patients—those with insomnia, depressed appetite, low mood, and low energy—will improve on imipramine, as will certain patients with a variety of other disorders. But imipramine has serious limitations. One is side effects.

When Ronald Kuhn chose to look at antihistamines as a source for antidepressants, he created a complication the field did not overcome until the advent of Prozac. The antihistamines known in the 1950s, as well as most developed thereafter, tend pharmacologically to bring on the body's fight-or-flight response. They do this by interfering with a neurotransmitter called acetylcholine. When acetylcholine-related nerve transmission is diminished (as imipramine causes it to be), the body is ready for action. The heart beats rapidly, and energy is withdrawn from functions that can be postponed, like evacuation of bodily wastes. As a result, imipramine can cause a host of side effects—sweating, heart palpitations, dry mouth, constipation, and urinary retention among them.

Iproniazid and its relatives arouse the fight-or-flight response somewhat less often. This advantage alone might have made them popular. But an unexpected effect on blood pressure emerged in those drugs, a complication that pushed them to the sidelines, at least in the United States, and left the field to imipramine.

The drugs related to iproniazid are of particular interest because, although they are chemically quite distinct from Prozac, they can be seen, in terms of their effect on patients, as Prozac's predecessors. Like Prozac, they seem to reach aspects of depression that imipramine does not. In particular, it was recognized as early as the 1960s that they can be especially effective in patients who may not suffer classic depression but whose chronic vulnerability to depressed mood has a global effect on their personality

The relatives of iproniazid are called monoamine-oxidase inhibitors, or MAOIs. Monoamine oxidase is the janitorial enzyme that oxidizes (burns, or inactivates) certain amines. By inhibiting monoamine oxidase, MAOIs prolong the effective life of those amines in the brain. In the years before Prozac was available, a doctor might have considered putting a patient like Tess on an MAOI, especially after she experienced an incomplete response to imipramine; but the doctor likely would have hesitated, because of concern over what else an MAOI might do: in the 1960s, a rash of deaths from brain hemorrhage was reported among patients taking MAOIs; other patients, though they did not die, experienced severe headache on the basis of extremely high blood pressure, an odd occurrence because the MAOIs were used to *lower* blood pressure in people with hypertension.

The means by which MAOIs make blood pressure skyrocket was elucidated in an interesting way. A British pharmacist who read a description of patients' headaches wrote a seemingly naïve letter noting that they resembled those his wife suffered when she consumed cheese, but not butter or milk. He asked whether the reaction might not be related to an interaction between MAOIs and some substance in cheese. Barry Blackwell, the doctor to whom the pharmacist had written, at first dismissed the suggestion—no drugs were known to interact with food substances in this way. But then he began to observe a series of patients on MAOIs who suffered headache and even extremely high blood pressure upon eating cheese.

Convinced that the "cheese reaction" was real, Blackwell set out to identify the offending ingredient. It turned out to be a chemical, ordinarily broken down by MAO, that causes nerve cells to release complex amines. Aged cheeses contain large amounts of this substance—so much that, when the janitorial enzyme is poisoned, a cheese eater on MAOIs will be flooded with biologically active amines, including ones that raise blood pressure.

Once the problem had been explained, it was a simple matter to advise patients to avoid foods that interact dangerously with MAOIs. But sticking to a restricted diet is constraining—the list of proscribed foods has grown over the years, and includes such disparate items as Chianti wine, fava beans, and ripe figs—and the requirement is dangerous for impulsive patients who "don't care if they live or die." MAOIs remained in widespread use in England, where they have been mainstay antidepressants for over thirty years. But in America the drugs were withdrawn from use, and even though they were later reintroduced, American doctors remained wary of them. Imipramine and related compounds dominated the medical treatment of depression.

Imipramine, however, is a "dirty" drug—a drug that affects many systems at once. Not only are its side effects wide-ranging—the result of its action on nerves using such chemicals as histamine and acetylcholine—but imipramine's main effects are also nonspecific.

From the time antidepressants were developed, two different amines were understood to influence mood: *norepinephrine,* a substance that was familiar to pharmacologists because of its close relationship to adrenaline, and *serotonin,* another substance that is active throughout the body but about which less was known. Imipramine is "dirty" in its main effects and its side effects because it affects both norepinephrine and serotonin. Once imipramine's mechanism of action was understood, pharmacologists set out to synthesize a "clean" antidepressant—one as effective as imipramine but more specific in its action.

This goal proved unexpectedly elusive. In the three decades after imipramine's introduction, pharmacologists synthesized and tested many chemicals similar to it in form. Like imipramine, the better known among these drugs, such as the antidepressants Elavil (amitriptyline) and Norpramin (desipramine), had three carbon rings in their chemical structure, and thus the group came to be called "tricyclics." Each new tricyclic antidepressant, as it was introduced, was said to have fewer side effects than imipramine—to have less effect on the acetylcholine or histamine pathways—or to act faster on depression. Some of these claims held up marginally. But most of the purported advantages evaporated as the drugs came into general use. None of the tricyclics is more effective than imipramine, probably none has a different time course of action, and all are "dirty" in the sense of influencing pathways involving both histamine and acetylcholine.

The only increase in specificity was the development of drugs that affected norepinephrine (and histamine and acetylcholine) without affecting serotonin. Desipramine, for example, is perhaps fifteen hundred times more active on norepinephrine than on serotonin pathways, and as a result a good deal of modern research has been done using this drug. But two goals eluded researchers: finding an antidepressant without side effects related to histamine and acetylcholine, and finding an antidepressant that preferentially affects serotonin.

This last goal was especially enticing. As the years passed, it seemed a number of conditions, ranging from atypical forms of depression to OCD and eating disorders, might involve derangements of serotonin. Here the MAOIs sometimes played a role. The MAOIs were very dirty. They affected not only norepinephrine and serotonin but a third amine, dopamine, the substance implicated in schizophrenia and Parkinson's disease. But the MAOIs were often more effective than the tricyclics for the disorders thought to be related to a lack of serotonin. Pharmacologists came to believe that the MAOIs' distinct efficacy might have to do with a strong effect on serotonin pathways, and that the tricyclics' limitations related to their lack of potency in raising serotonin levels. The new grail, pursued throughout the 1960s and 1970s and well into the 1980s, was a drug that would be like imipramine but that would selectively influence serotonin.

In its search for a clean analogue of imipramine and for an analogue that would strongly alter serotonin levels, psychopharmacology treaded water for over thirty years. This stalemate was frustrating to clinical psychiatrists. I remember as a medical student, and then again as a psychiatry resident, struggling to memorize charts regarding the characteristics of the tricyclic antidepressants. Generally, these charts would have a list of drugs running down the left-hand side and a list of neurotransmitters across the top. In each cell where the drug and a neurotransmitter intersected would be a series of plus or minus marks. Thus, a given drug would be + + + + for norepinephrine, + + for serotonin, − − for histamine, and − − − for acetylcholine. Medical students and residents for the most part do not mind this sort of chart; it makes demands on familiar skills and helps psychiatry seem like the rest of medicine. But the charts for antidepressants had no reliable relation to patients' responses.

The embarrassing truth about clinical work with antidepressants was that it was all art and no science. Various combinations of symptoms were said to be more serotonin- or norepinephrine-related, and various strategies were advanced for trying medications in logical order for particular sorts of patients. But these strategies varied from year to year, and even from one part of the country to another. It was true that a given patient might respond to one antidepressant after having failed to respond to another, but the doctor would have to manufacture a reason to explain why.

Psychiatrists were reduced to the expedient of choosing antidepressants on the basis of side effects. A patient whose depression was characterized by restlessness would be given a sedating antidepressant to be taken at night; a similar patient who complained of lack of energy would be given a stimulating antidepressant to be taken in the morning. But these choices said nothing about how the medications acted on depression: in all probability, both drugs amplified the effect of norepinephrine. It was as if, after discovering penicillin, researchers had synthesized a series of antibiotics, some of which incidentally made patients weary and some hyperalert—and then, when treating pneumonias, clinicians chose between these antibiotics not according to the susceptibilities of the infecting bacteria but according to whether the patient was agitated or prostrated by the illness.

Hopes that a more specific agent would make a difference were dampened by the advent of Desyrel (trazodone) in the early 1980s. Desyrel worked via serotonin, but its effects were difficult to distinguish from those of earlier antidepressants. Much of the problem, again, was side effects. Desyrel was so sedating that it had been marketed first in Europe as an antianxiety drug. You could do with Desyrel what you had been able to do with the tricyclics—treat a fair percentage of seriously depressed patients—but patients would tend to become tired or dizzy before you could get them on doses that radically changed the functioning of nerves that use serotonin.

This was the stage onto which Prozac walked: thirty years of stasis. The tricyclic antidepressants were wonderful drugs, but in practical terms they were all more or less the same. And it was not clear whether a drug that was pharmacologically distinctive would be any different in clinical usage from the many antidepressants that were already available.

Prozac was made to be distinctive. In the history of therapeutics, the development of Prozac belongs in a different chapter from the stories of lithium, imipramine, and iproniazid. Prozac was not so much discovered as planfully created, through the efforts of a large pharmaceutical firm, using state-of-the-art animal and cellular models and drawing on the skills of scientists from diverse disciplines. And yet, as was true in the cases of lithium and iproniazid, the development of Prozac required serendipity.

The story begins in the 1960s, with Bryan Molloy, a Scots-born organic chemist who had been synthesizing cardiac drugs for the pharmaceutical firm Eli Lilly. Molloy was interested in acetylcholine as a regulator of heart action. In the 1960s, a pharmacologist, Ray Fuller, came to Lilly to test potential new antidepressants. Fuller had worked with a method, using rats as test animals, for measuring drugs' effects on serotonin pathways; he tried to convince Molloy that the availability of this method made the time ripe for research in brain chemistry. Fuller proposed that Molloy leave his heart research to look for a substance that could affect amines in the brain without acting on nerves that use acetylcholine.

Like prior researchers, Molloy thought the right place to start in looking for an antidepressant was the antihistamines. He did not know whether he could develop an antidepressant without antihistaminic properties, but he thought he might have a tool that would allow him to minimize the acetylcholine-related side effects—dry mouth, urine retention, and rapid heartbeat—that so limited the use of the tricyclics.

In his cardiac research, Molloy had hooked up with Robert Rathbun, a member of the group at Lilly called the "mouse-behavior team." Rathbun was working with a model in which mice were given an opium variant, apomorphine, which lowers the body temperature in mice. Antihistamines block this response—except for antihistamines that also affect acetylcholine. Using Rathbun's model, Molloy hoped to be able to distinguish drugs that work purely on the histamine pathways from ones that affect acetylcholine as well.

Molloy synthesized compounds to test. He began with Benadryl, the antihistamine in common use as a remedy for stuffy noses and allergic rashes. He played with the Benadryl molecule, substituting one or another chemical group at one or another spot in its structure. Molloy developed dozens of compounds, including several that were good at blocking the effect of apomorphine on body temperature in mice. He thought he might be on the path toward eliminating acetylcholine-related side effects.

Meanwhile, a fourth researcher at Lilly, David Wong, had become dissatisfied with his area of work. Wong had been looking at mechanisms within the cell that allow antibiotics to combat infection, but to date all his research had led to medications for agricultural uses. He wanted to make drugs for humans, not animals, and in 1971 he began moonlighting in the area of neurochemistry. A particular book had caught Wong's attention, a newly published summary of what was known about the chemistry of mental disorder. Whereas by 1970 most research in America was focused on norepinephrine as the key chemical in mood regulation, this book summarized findings, better appreciated in Europe, that pointed to a role for serotonin.

The paths of Wong and Molloy crossed at a lecture by Solomon Snyder of Johns Hopkins University. Snyder is one of the great minds in modern biological psychiatry, a man whose name is often mentioned for the Nobel Prize. Most major developments in American biological psychiatry rely to some degree on an element of Snyder's work. Snyder had been invited to Lilly's laboratories in 1971 to receive an award and deliver a lecture. As his topic, Snyder chose his research into neurotransmission.

Snyder had been trying to isolate the nerve endings that handle biogenic amines. He found that, by grinding up rat brains and using various techniques to divide the ground-up products, he could produce a collection of nerve endings that still functioned chemically. This preparation he called a "synaptosome."

The synaptosome promised to be immensely useful in neurobiological research. You might, for example, pretreat a rat with imipramine, allowing the drug time to bind to nerve endings. Then you could kill the rat, grind up its brain, centrifuge and separate out the nerve endings, and produce an extract that was still active —still worked like the terminals of living nerve cells. You could then expose this extract (the imipramine-treated synaptosomes) to a neurotransmitter, such as norepinephrine or serotonin, and see how much of the neurotransmitter was taken up. This procedure almost defied belief—you could more or less blenderize a brain and then divide out a portion that worked the way live nerve endings work— but in Snyder's hands the technique succeeded. Not only did Snyder lecture on synaptosomes, he also instructed the Lilly team on the fine points of what neurochemists call "binding and grinding."

Wong immediately set about applying the bind-and-grind technology to Molloy's series of promising antidepressants. It turned out that the compounds on which Molloy was focused, those that worked in Rathbun's apomorphine-mouse model, were, like drugs already on the market, potent blockers of norepinephrine uptake in rat synaptosomes. But Wong did not stop there. His research showed that the rat synaptosome, and presumably the human brain, treated very similar drugs differently. If one chemical blocked the uptake of norepinephrine, a structurally similar chemical might block the uptake of serotonin. So Wong decided to look also at chemicals in Molloy's series that had failed in the apomorphine test.

One of those compounds, labeled 82816, blocked the uptake of serotonin and very little else. In all, Wong quickly tested over 250 compounds, but none looked as selective in its effect on serotonin as did 82816. The chemical was then tested in Fuller's rat system, the one that had initially sparked Molloy's interest in brain chemistry. There and elsewhere, 82816 selectively blocked the reuptake of serotonin into transmitting cells. Compound 82816 was fluoxetine oxalate; it turned out to be easier to work with a related preparation, fluoxetine hydrochloride. Fluoxetine hydrochloride is Prozac.

In June 1974, David Wong's laboratory and Bryan Molloy publicly reported that fluoxetine is a selective inhibitor of serotonin uptake into synaptosomes of rat brain. Fluoxetine was two hundred times more active in inhibiting the uptake of serotonin than of norepinephrine—and it did not affect the histamine or acetylcholine systems either. Fluoxetine was a clean drug. Wong and Molloy understood they had a new powerful research tool with which to study the functioning of serotonin, as well as a potential new type of antidepressant. Later research showed that the drug was suitable for the treatment of depression in humans.

The research that produced Prozac succeeded despite a number of mistaken beliefs early on. At the time Molloy was developing his series of compounds, no one knew what Rathbun's apomorphine-mouse model really did. It turns out the model is a reasonable test of a drug's ability to block norepinephrine reuptake; that is why a substance that had no activity in Rathbun's model proved to be of such interest.

Molloy's series of compounds paid off for an unanticipated reason: the molecule in the nerve-cell membrane that transports norepinephrine (in the reuptake process) is similar to the molecule that transports serotonin; so drugs that block the transport of serotonin can be quite similar structurally to those that block the transport of norepinephrine. In a series of related drugs, many of which block norepinephrine reuptake, there may well be a few that block serotonin reuptake. In other words, Molloy played with antihistamines and tested them in a system that measured action on norepinephrine neurons—and he ended up producing a drug that is not an antihistamine and has minimal effect on norepinephrine activity.

Also, the model that signaled Molloy that the time was ripe to study neurotransmission, Fuller's rats, turned out to be tangential to drug development. Molloy and Fuller were right about timing because of an unrelated breakthrough, Snyder's work with synaptosomes. A key element in the story is Wong's appreciation of the potential of bind-and-grind methods and his persistence in testing compounds in Molloy's series of molecules that had failed to block the effects of apomorphine on mouse body temperature.

The Prozac story represents a typical sequence in modern drug development. The medication resulted from an expensive and profitable process, the collaborative efforts of scientists working at the limits of the technology of their time.

Prozac stands in marked contrast to lithium. Whereas lithium is the simplest of chemicals, an element, unpatentable, its usage discovered by a solitary practicing doctor with no eye toward profit, Prozac is a designed drug, sleek and high-tech. It comes from a world even most doctors do not understand. I sometimes wonder whether this "feel" of Prozac—so different from that of lithium—has had some subtle influence on its reception, as regards both the sense of wonder and the sense of discomfort at its (alien) power.

The story of Prozac is typical in another way as well. Chemists working today to develop drugs for the mind start not so much with diseased patients as with models of nerve transmission, and they tailor molecules to affect that basic process. The goal is clean drugs—drugs that are ever more potent and specific in their effects on nerve transmission. The likely result of this form of research is not medicines that correct particular illnesses but medicines that affect clusters of functions in the human brain, often both in well and ill persons.

When Prozac was released in December 1987, no one knew whether potency and specificity would make a practical difference. There was some reason to think not. Psychiatrists were aware that Anafranil (clomipramine), a relative of imipramine that had achieved wide usage in Europe and Canada, was about to be introduced in the United States. Though as dirty a drug as any—it alters serotonin transmission the most but, like its cousin compounds, also affects norepinephrine, histamine, and acetylcholine pathways—Anafranil seemed to have a special efficacy in a hard-to-treat, serotonin-related condition, OCD. Also, psychiatrists had become newly accustomed to admixing medications for difficult-to-treat depressions—for instance, adding lithium to imipramine—and thus making a dirty drug dirtier. Perhaps antidepressants worked best when a variety of pathways were affected. Now that a clean drug had been found, no one knew whether it would prove superior to the many dirty ones.

Professional complacency about what, on theoretical grounds, promised to be a breakthrough antidepressant had also to do with the way new drugs are tested for marketing. To get approval from the Food and Drug Administration, a drug company has to show that a new substance is safe and effective for a given indication. With antidepressants, this standard means, in effect, that a drug is shown to be as safe and effective as imipramine for major depression. So Prozac had been tested on patients with typical major depression, the kind in which decreased sleep and appetite lead the way in the whole picture of severe mental slowing. In these patients, Prozac was only barely as effective as imipramine. This testing—combined with the repeated failure of scientists since the middle of the century to produce a drug that remained distinctive once it entered the doctor's office or patients' lives—led to muted expectations.

What no one appreciated in advance of Prozac's widespread clinical use was how different from its predecessors it really was.

The relative lack of side effects allowed Prozac to be used freely. A psychoanalyst colleague told me he almost never prescribed antidepressants before Prozac. Merely listing the side effects of the tricyclics interfered too much with the analysis. Patients would accuse him of hostility, of unconsciously wanting to poison them. If they did take the medicine, patients would spend long sessions on the couch complaining about how the analyst had made them constipated. MAOIs, with their requirement of a restricted diet and risk of strokes and death, mixed even less well with psychoanalysis.

Prozac did not interfere with the psychotherapeutic relationship as other antidepressants had. Also, Prozac was safer in the hands of potentially suicidal patients who might attempt to overdose on the drug. Because of the reduced likelihood of effects on the heart, Prozac overdoses are relatively benign. The lack of effect on acetylcholine proved to be enormously important as well. Patients do not feel "drugged" on Prozac, as they do on tricyclics or MAOIs. Because both patients and doctors were comfortable with Prozac's side-effect profile, the medication came to be prescribed both for less ill patients—those heretofore treated with psychotherapy alone—and for more impulsive patients with depressive symptoms. These are people in the penumbra of major depression. In other words, the group for whom Prozac was prescribed was different from the group on whom it had been tested. Before Prozac, drugs were dirty, but the disorder for which they were indicated was clean; here was a drug that was clean, but its field of action was, if not dirty, then at least amorphous in shape.

Prozac turned out to be remarkably effective for certain "penumbral" patients. Indeed, it may be these patients, who are not densely depressed, for whom Prozac is most helpful, so that Prozac's side-effect profile led it to be prescribed for just those people it could benefit most.

Prozac's lack of side effects and its ability to ameliorate disorders in which tricyclics often fail have led to changes in the way psychiatrists see patients and the way patients see themselves. In particular, Prozac has occasioned a heightened awareness of a phenomenon that occurs commonly in people who have never had a mental illness— indeed, a phenomenon so ordinary that it may seem intrinsic to the human condition: sensitivity to rejection or loss.

Sensitivity

A young woman comes to the office complaining she is boy-crazy. Last week, she found herself walking through a dangerous part of town at two in the morning in the cold and dark. She had a crush on a certain young man, and she knew he liked a rock band that was playing a one-night stand at a small club. So she showed up at this club in a godforsaken neighborhood to hear music that did not even appeal to her. Heading home alone in the small hours, she thought, "I really ought to talk to someone about what I am doing."

She says her focus on this young man and others like him—they are all dismissive of her and a bit wild—is disconnected from the way she ordinarily sees herself. She is a quiet and self-effacing young woman, dressed in a way that plays down her femininity, devoid in her manner of any hint of seductiveness.

Her history is dominated by one event. When Lucy was ten and living in a third-world country where her father was stationed, she came home to find her mother dead, shot by a young manservant—a beloved and trusted member of the household—who had become crazed and violent. Lucy showed no immediate reaction to this ghastly occurrence. She remained a productive, well-liked girl. As the oldest child, she assumed additional responsibilities, helping her father raise the other children. For his part, the father, though concerned and loving, had always been focused on his work, and became even more so as he felt the family responsibilities on his shoulders alone. In supporting him, Lucy delayed meeting her own needs until she could leave home. Her father's attention to his work hurt her repeatedly; she often felt he was not there when she needed him.

How we see a person is a function of the categories we recognize—of our private diagnostic system. A psychotherapist may see Lucy, wandering through the darkened city, as suffering from father hunger, mother hunger, adolescent rebellion, repetition compulsion, or a delayed grief reaction. Each of these very different frames is historical: to "understand" Lucy's behavior is to place it in relation to her traumatic past.

She is a young woman with a damaged self-image, a tendency to place men first, and a willingness to put herself at risk. To the part of her that every moment remembers her mother's murder, the world is so fraught with danger that to exercise caution seems derisory self-delusion. Lucy is, in her tolerance for danger, re-enacting an aspect of her childhood, seeing whether in her young-adult life she can control fate. We may find there is some urgency to the matter, a need to save her from a compulsive association between men and violence. We may also wonder about the love object she has chosen—is he too much like the hard-to-reach father, too much like the murderous servant? Lucy herself, when asked to explain her boy-craziness, puts forth a theory related to deprivation: she had to postpone her adolescence, and she yearned for warmth and closeness, so now she is sacrificing everything to the quest for love.

Psychotherapy—talk—calms things down. Lucy, an Ivy League undergraduate, sublimates her morbid impulses to her studies, writing papers on abnormal psychology, the sociology of violence, and other topics obviously related to the central questions of her history. And she begins dating a classmate who has none of the openly frightening qualities of the young men she has tended to pursue.

But though the form is more subdued, the boy-craziness persists.

Lucy begins to notice a disturbing tendency in herself. She cannot bear it when her boyfriend looks away for a moment. If he turns his back on her to glance at the television screen, her heart sinks. She experiences terrible feelings of worthlessness if he shows up five minutes late for a date. If he says "I" instead of "we" in talking about something they have done together, or if he says goodbye in the wrong way, Lucy may experience pain for days. When she sees her boyfriend talking to another girl, Lucy becomes listless for the better part of a week, and no amount of reassurance can break the spell of demoralization. These moods are often deep and protracted. She is disorganized, paralyzed, hopelessly sad, overtaken by unfocused feelings of urgency.

Lucy understands this sensitivity, too, as originating in the apprehension that she will lose anyone she loves. But she cannot shake it—it has a life of its own. The smallest slight throws her into a tailspin. Although she may start the day optimistic and focused, she knows she may at any moment be swamped by despondency. She finds herself putting her boyfriend to little tests: If I set my book down, will he set his down as well? Will he notice the pin I am wearing? The day is full of these tests, some of them magical: He must look at me before the light turns green; he must place the keepsake I gave him at the front of the dresser. When her boyfriend fails to act as Lucy hopes, confusion or sadness sweeps over her. She does small things to get his attention—and at the same time she understands that the dependency she communicates may doom their relationship.

Lucy's craving for attention has deep roots. She remembers feelings of desperation on nights when her father came home late, tells of recurrent pain in response to his focus on work rather than on her. She remembers as a child playing sick—heating the thermometer under a light bulb—to elicit her father's concern. She would often do more than her father expected, would, even as a fairly young child, set the table at night for the following day's breakfast, in hopes of winning his approval. Sometimes she feels she is addicted to attention.

Lucy's neediness, like her sensitivity and her flirtations with violence, is rooted in her history. But her hunger for approval and the disorganizing pain she feels on rejection will bring to mind, for psychiatrists of a certain ilk, a particular understanding of what ails Lucy, one that all but divorces the present from the past.

This other approach entails taking Lucy's hunger for attention and her fear of rejection very much at face value, as discrete symptoms, in the way that insomnia and loss of appetite are symptoms. More broadly, this ahistorical viewpoint sees the combination of applause hunger and rejection-sensitivity as an autonomous syndrome, a category of human behavior that might respond to treatment with medication. If Lucy can be spared the pain that rejection causes her, she will not need to behave in a dependent or self-injurious way. Examination of history, even of so evocative a history as Lucy's, will be superfluous, an interesting enterprise in its own right, perhaps, but not crucial to the patient's healing.

●　●　●

We all react to disappointments, even minor ones. A date stands us up. A colleague makes a cutting remark. A bad grade or a critical review arrives unexpectedly. The business proposal, the grant submission, the application for promotion is rejected. A friend announces he is moving away. A phone call is not returned; an expected invitation fails to arrive. We are ridiculed, scorned, slighted, given the cold shoulder. Always there is a visceral response: the sinking in the stomach, a feeling of weakness, confusion of thought, a momentary sense of sadness and world-weariness. It will pass, we know, this leaden dullness, but for the moment we are deeply affected.

For some this pain is worse than for others—lasts longer, paralyzes more thoroughly. They are not depressed, but they are vulnerable. "Sensitive" is what we call such people, as in: "Oh, don't be so sensitive," or "She's just overly sensitive." It is not only what a person feels but also how he or she shows it that makes for sensitivity.

Someone who displays a slight wound too insistently, or who too assiduously avoids the risk of disappointment, is most liable to the charge. "Oversensitivity," in this use of the word, is a personality trait, sometimes annoying, sometimes endearing.

What lies behind oversensitivity? Is it a manipulative style, a form of self-pity, or one among many reasonable ways of addressing the complexities of the social world? For the most part, psychiatry has ignored sensitivity as unremarkable—not a category of analysis. In the standard diagnostic manual, there is no category labeled "sensitive."

But the standard manual is a mere matter of consensus. There are many unofficial ways of mapping human variation, charts highlighting colorful byways that, though they have never made it into the conventional guidebook, promise rewarding vistas. One such conceptual route, a diagnosis that under various names has intrigued biological researchers for decades, may be, with the help of Prozac, on its way to becoming a major thoroughfare. The idea underlying this diagnosis is that certain people are physiologically wired to be deeply sensitive to rejection. On experiencing a loss, these people feel more pain or come closer to depression than do most men and women. According to this theory, a variety of personality styles, typical behaviors, and even mental illnesses can be traced to the complex adaptations oversensitive people make to the abnormality in their emotional thermostat.

Rejection-sensitivity as a psychological category is a contribution of the psychopharmacologic pioneer Donald Klein, a conceptualizer of great originality. This is the same Donald Klein who was an early opponent of the spectrum theory of mental illness and an early proponent of imipramine. He is director of research at the New York Psychiatric Institute and a professor at Columbia University. Although he has long held positions of leadership in psychiatry, the field has always treated Klein as a maverick, a man whose thinking, even if difficult to refute, is almost too creative.

Klein started looking at antidepressants in the late 1950s. He began with an idiosyncratic approach to research, one shaped by the diagnostic sloppiness of American psychiatry in those years. In most pharmacologic studies, a researcher looks at patients with a single, strictly defined diagnosis and attempts to treat them with one or two particular medications. But when Klein was doing his early work, no one knew which diagnostic distinctions were relevant to medication choices, and, moreover, there were few medications to try. Klein worked at Hillside Hospital (now part of the Long Island Jewish Medical Center), a typical psychotherapy-oriented mental hospital of its day. His method was to take whatever inpatients he could get colleagues to refer him—generally patients not responsive to psychotherapy, most of whom were diagnosed as schizophrenic by the ward staff—and to medicate them with whatever was at hand, often matching medication to patient on the basis of one or another small clue. He then worked backward from drug response to diagnosis, sometimes creating a new diagnostic category to fit his observations. In other words, he took on all comers and tried to say something about them based on their response to the medication.

To Klein, a number of hospitalized patients labeled schizophrenic, borderline psychotic, or hysterical seemed at base to have not so much an abnormality of thought or personality as a nasty disorder of mood. To these hidden mood disorders, Klein gave a variety of names depending on the form of the affliction. Two such categories are of particular interest: atypical depression (in which patients increase rather than decrease their eating and sleeping when depressed) and hysteroid dysphoria. This latter category expressed Klein's notion of pathological vulnerability to loss.

To appreciate the originality of Klein's contribution, one has to understand the central place in psychotherapy of the hysterical patient. Freud's first psychoanalytic patients, those around whose treatment the new science of psychoanalysis developed, were hysterics. Hysterics in the nineteenth century had physical symptoms, such as seizures and paralyses, and were (incorrectly) understood to suffer from neurological illness. One of Freud's early, legendarily controversial contributions was the assertion that hysteria is a disease of the mind and that the seeming neurologic symptoms are actually a metaphorical, almost poetic expression of repressed psychological conflicts.

For half a century or more, when Freudian thinking dominated in America, hysteria was considered the easiest disorder to treat with psychoanalysis. Hysterics' symptoms bore exploration and interpretation, and the patients were responsive to the charm of the psychotherapeutic relationship. Training institutes saw to it that the first patient of almost every psychoanalytic candidate was a hysteric.

But in time there developed two problems with the diagnosis. First, the term "hysteric" spread far beyond those with unexplained neurological symptoms to cover almost any patient who was emotional, unresponsive to reason, or seductive, particularly if the sufferer was a woman. And, second, many hysterics proved refractory to psychotherapy. In the therapy, as in their lives outside the psychoanalyst's office, these hard-to-treat patients were emotionally volatile. They often seemed more intent on winning the therapist's attention than on recovery, and might become desperately seductive or otherwise self-destructive if the therapeutic relationship appeared to be coming to an end. Characterizing the hysteric's potential in the psychoanalytic setting, the renowned analyst Elizabeth Zetzel began a generative essay with the nursery rhyme lines "When she was good she was very, very good, but when she was bad she was horrid."

In considering how to medicate horrid hysterics, Klein took into account their eating and sleeping habits. Although they generally did not suffer true, protracted depressions, these flamboyant patients tended, when upset, to overeat and oversleep, just like atypical depressives. Privy to the work of British researchers who made the case that atypical depression responds better to MAOIs (relatives of iproniazid) than to tricyclic antidepressants like imipramine, Klein tried an MAOI on the difficult hysterics referred him by his psychotherapeutic colleagues. He found that it sometimes smoothed the course of the patients' lives. Klein tried to encompass these medication-responsive patients descriptively, thereby—and herein was the apostasy—carving out a group of hysterics whose disorder was after all not so much of the mind as of the brain. The patients looked hysterical, but the underlying disorder was a problem in biological regulation of mood. These were the patients Klein called "hysteroid dysphorics."

Klein tried to distinguish such antidepressant-responsive hysterics according to their behavior. They were not, for instance, hysterics with unexplained seizures or paralyses; nor were they the most irritable, impulsive ones. What distinguished the hysteroid dysphorics was an extreme appetite for attention and a marked fear of rejection, a desperate emotional state that resulted in a constellation of behaviors amounting to a caricature of femininity. Here is a typical, brutally clear description by Klein of hysteroid dysphorics:

These patients are usually females whose general psychopathological state is an extremely brittle and shallow mood ranging from giddy elation to desperate unhappiness. Their mood level is markedly responsive to external sources of admiration and approval. Such a patient may feel hopelessly bereft when a love affair terminates, then meet a new attentive man and feel perfectly fine and even slightly elated within a few days. Their emotionality markedly affects their judgment. When euphoric, they minimize and deny the shortcomings of a situation or personal relationship, idealizing all love objects. When they are at the opposite emotional pole, feelings of desperation are expressed very disproportionately to actual circumstances.

They are fickle, emotionally labile, irresponsible, shallow, love-intoxicated, giddy, and short-sighted. They tend to be egocentric, narcissistic, exhibitionistic, vain, and clothes-crazy. They are seductive, manipulative, exploitative, sexually provocative, and think emotionally and illogically. They are easy prey to flattery and compliments. Their general manner is histrionic and flamboyant. In their sexual relations they are possessive, grasping, demanding, romantic, and foreplay centered. When frustrated or disappointed, they become reproachful, tearful, abusive and vindictive, and often resort to alcohol.

Klein's second paragraph may sound less like a neutral syndromal description than a misogynist's picture of womankind. But it probably does not differ much from a psychoanalyst's behavioral characterization of what by mid-century had become the prototypical hysteric—a woman seeking desperately for the attentions of an idealized version of the father who in reality had disappointed her. Klein contended that these symptoms arose not from persisting inner conflict (such as emotional ambivalence about the father) but from the effects in her contemporary, adult life of the patient's recurrent, intense, abnormally painful experience of loss.

Klein did not at first enter the debate over whether hysterics had one or another sort of childhood experience; presumably a person might come to rejection-sensitivity through any number of genetic or environmental pathways. It hardly mattered what set the sensitivity in motion. For hysteroid dysphorics, the pain of rejection was so extreme, and the elation following approval so (fleetingly) intense, that it made sense for seduction to become a full-time imperative. The phrase Klein selected to deal with questions of causation was "functional autonomy." In Klein's words, "a cause engenders an adaptive response (function) that persists after the termination of the cause (autonomy)." Regardless of its origins, the vulnerability to loss had a life of its own in adulthood.

The concept of functional autonomy makes biological treatment attractive. The great claim of psychoanalysis is that it removes the causes of neurosis. To a psychoanalyst, every hysterical symptom has hidden within it, in secret code, its cause—both the historical cause (early emotional trauma) and the ongoing, active cause (unconscious conflict, resulting in the mind's attempt to repress the memory of that trauma and the mixed emotions it arouses). A similar assumption has long predominated in the popular consciousness as well, and it is this model that makes Lucy's boy-craziness so naturally understandable. For psychoanalysis, the route to recovery is bringing the unconscious struggle into consciousness. Psychoanalysis is often called a pessimistic discipline, but it revolves around an appealing, humane view of symptoms and the people who carry them: that the truth can set men free. Functional autonomy implies that symptoms become unmoored from their origins, so there is no longer any special reason to imagine that truth will have the power to heal.

Klein saw symptoms—in this case histrionic behavior—as being fully explained by patients' expectable reactions to instability of mood. Where the unstable mood came from was irrelevant. Such concepts as conflict, the unconscious, trauma, and truth were superfluous. Klein described his relationship to psychoanalytic hypotheses of causation in proudly agnostic terms: "It is hard to prove a negative—that is, that there is no case in which intrapsychic conflict plays a necessary role. . . . [But] like Laplace, I have no need for these hypotheses."

What Klein felt need of was a tool to reregulate hysteroid-dysphoric patients' emotional thermostats—to decrease the pain they felt when rejected. We have already noted that hysteroid-dysphoric patients were not, in the classical sense, depressed. Their mood, unlike that of people in a dense depression, tended to be quite responsive—too responsive—to external events. There was no *a priori* reason to believe that antidepressants would help these patients; as we have seen, one of the heuristically appealing aspects of antidepressants was that the medications did not, on the whole, help people unless they were in the midst of a depressive episode. But Klein found that MAOIs acted to prevent the brief terrible mood downturns of hysteroid dysphorics.

The medicine set a floor beneath patients; it prevented the bottom from falling out.

Klein wrote, "A crucial consequence of putting these patients on MAO inhibitors is that they do not become dysphoric upon loss of admiration. This affective modification makes it no longer necessary for them to fling themselves into self-destructive or unrewarding romantic involvements." At the heart of Klein's formulation is the notion of a simple psychobiological defect (heightened pain in response to loss) elaborated by the patient into a complex adaptive behavior (the caricature of femininity). The treatment for the disorder is to restabilize the affective regulator and then to help the patient learn that she no longer needs her self-injurious character style.

● ● ●

Klein's model of emotion and behavior—the elaboration of simple mood disregulation into complex symptoms and even personality traits—found widespread acceptance, not with regard to hysteroid dysphoria, which remained an obscure diagnosis, but in relation to a quite different condition, panic anxiety.

Panic anxiety is a commonplace, understood by everyone. It is the condition in which a person is subject to panic attacks, those awful moments in which the pulse races, each breath is hard to come by, nausea and dizziness threaten, and it feels as if death were imminent, although—so awful is the foreboding—death may seem almost preferable to the terror at hand. Panic anxiety has been shown in surveys to be among the most prevalent of psychiatric disorders. The term "panic attack" has transcended psychiatry and entered everyday speech. We find it unremarkable if in a shopping mall we hear one person say to another, "I was so shocked I almost had a panic attack."

It is hard to recall that fifteen or twenty years ago there was no such concept. Neither in medical school nor psychiatry residency, both in the 1970s, did I ever meet a patient with "panic anxiety." Only toward the end of residency did I hear of research into the panic attack. Although it is now among the most common diagnoses in psychiatrists' offices, in the recent past panic anxiety prevailed neither in the clinic nor in the popular consciousness.

That blindness to what is now a ubiquitous phenomenon may seem all the more remarkable when we learn that, unlike hysteroid dysphoria, panic anxiety is not a newly described entity. In 1895, when he stood on the cusp between neurology and the discipline he was to create, psychoanalysis, Sigmund Freud wrote a monograph about what we now call panic. Though it contains no case vignettes, the monograph is fascinating. It attempts to carve out of neurasthenia, the nineteenth century's broad category of mental weakness and distress, a particular entity, "anxiety neurosis."

As always, Freud was an exquisite observer. In characterizing anxiety neurosis, he listed every symptom we now ascribe to panic anxiety: rapid or irregular heartbeat, disturbances of breathing, perspiration and night sweats, tremor and shivering, vertigo, diarrhea, night terrors, and what he calls "anxious expectations." Freud also recognized incomplete forms of the disorder, which he called "rudimentary anxiety attacks," "equivalents of anxiety attacks," and "larval anxiety-states." He also understood anxiety neurosis sometimes to be associated with agoraphobia, the fear of leaving the home.

Freud considered anxiety neurosis to be entirely biological. Throughout the monograph, he insisted that the anxiety "does not originate in a repressed idea, but turns out to be *not further reducible by psychological analysis, nor amenable to psychotherapy.*" Anxiety neurosis was either congenital or caused, directly and physiologically, by the pressure of undischarged sexual excitation, as in virginity, abstinence, or, most notoriously, *coitus interruptus.* Women whose husbands were sexually inadequate or subject to premature ejaculation were at risk.

Freud's assertion that anxiety neurosis is biological sounds firm. But in his clinical reports he had begun undermining that position

78

even before he stated it. One of my favorite footnotes in Freud appears in the *Studies in Hysteria* (1893–95). It concerns a case that looks for all the world like anxiety neurosis—except that the symptoms arise from repressed conflict. Freud begins: "I was treating a woman of thirty-eight, suffering from anxiety neurosis (agoraphobia, attacks of fear of death, etc.)." Though at first the patient indicates the attacks are of recent onset, Freud finds they began in her teenage years as episodic "dizziness, anxiety, and feelings of faintness." He traces their onset to a particular moment, when she was shopping in preparation for a ball. The patient remembers little more, and Freud presses his hand on her head to make a recollection appear. She thinks of two girls who had just died—one a close friend—and remembers that with the dizziness she thought, "I am the third." What had been driven from consciousness was shame at preparing for a ball in the wake of a friend's death, and fear that the frivolity would result in divine punishment. Moreover, the attack occurred near the dead friend's house. And—deeply important, from Freud's point of view—the patient was having her first menstrual period (presumably a shameful event) just at the time, so that the attack, and all subsequent attacks, become understandable as the expression of ongoing conflictual feelings. Freud does not name the conflict explicitly; presumably, awakening sexuality and perhaps even satisfaction at a rival's death are counterbalanced by fear and shame.

This understanding of anxiety in terms of personal history and inner turmoil began as the exception but soon became the rule. During Freud's lifetime, the discrete category of anxiety neurosis—an irreducible somatic disorder—was swallowed by a broader category, "neurosis," a catchall term for minor mental disturbances rooted in the psyche. By the 1960s, "neurosis" even encompassed conditions in which the patient was unaware of feeling anxious. The specific diagnosis "anxiety neurosis" was applied loosely. Any fairly healthy psychotherapy patient typically had an anxiety neurosis, a usage that corresponds closely to the ordinary-language term "neurotic."

This declawing of anxiety neurosis resulted from the growth in importance of the concept of anxiety in Freud's work. As Freud focused on the unconscious, he relied increasingly on meaningful anxiety as a motive force. At first, he merely expanded his original formulation, so that the notion of undischarged sexual drive became ever more symbolic and less biological. But as the theory grew in scope, Freud, and especially his followers, came to see meaningful anxiety—the result of conflict between repressed drives and defenses (this is the "dynamic" in "psychodynamic psychotherapy")—as underlying a broad spectrum of illness. Such terms as "castration anxiety," a key element in the Oedipus complex and the Oedipal period in normal male development, moved into common speech. It was this reliance on anxiety as virtually the sole motive force in the development of mental illness that led Klein to make his remarks regarding the spectrum theory of mental illness: "The predominant American psychiatric theory was that all psychopathology was secondary to anxiety, which in turn was caused by intrapsychic conflict."

Klein began to focus on anxiety because of a discrepancy between the prevailing theory and the results of pharmacotherapy. By 1959, when Klein was studying imipramine, it had been established that Thorazine was helpful to many people suffering from schizophrenia, generally considered the most severe mental illness. If all mental illness lay on a spectrum—the major disorders differing from the minor ones merely in terms of the degree of anxiety involved—then a medicine that works for schizophrenics should work all the more powerfully for patients who merely suffer from overt anxiety but are not psychotic. Klein knew Thorazine did little for these less ill patients; indeed, it often made them worse. This result spoke against the spectrum theory of illness.

So Klein took on anxiety, a concept as central as hysteria to the theory of psychoanalysis. Just as he had asked whether there were forms of hysteria unrelated to intrapsychic conflict, Klein asked whether there were different varieties of anxiety. He was attempting to use pharmacology as an investigative tool to unearth flaws in psychoanalytic theory and practice.

Klein focused on the most insistently anxious patients on the hospital ward—the ones who constantly ran to the nurses for help. Because there was no other solution to their problems, Klein persuaded a group of these patients to try imipramine. For the first couple of weeks—and remember that imipramine takes a few weeks to work—patients and staff were in agreement that imipramine was of no help. But, as Klein recalls:

> By the third week, although both patients and psychotherapist insisted that no gains had been made, the ward staff had a different, more positive view. When pressed to stipulate exactly how the patients had improved, the staff was at a loss. Finally, some keen clinical observer pointed out that for the past 10 months the patients had been running to the nursing station three times a day, every day, proclaiming that they were about to die and needed instant succor. The nurses would hold the patients' hands, reassure them and sit with them for about 20 minutes. The patients would finally walk away, their acute, overwhelming distress somewhat alleviated. A few hours later, however, they would be back again. The nurses pointed out that for the past week or so the patients had not been doing this.
>
> When we suggested to the patients that they were feeling better, they vociferously denied any improvement and accused the staff of obtuseness concerning the degree of their distress. When I asked them, "Why have you stopped running to the nurses' station?" their answer was that they had finally learned that the nurses could not do anything for them.
>
> "You mean that after 10 months you learned that just this week?"
>
> "Well," said the patient, "you have to learn some time."

Klein came to a different conclusion. In taking patients' histories, he had found that they typically recalled a series of what are now called panic attacks that came out of the blue. Klein hypothesized that the patients' disorder began with these spontaneous instances of overwhelming terror. It is a terrible thing constantly to be liable to debilitating panic. Around the attacks, patients would elaborate secondary fears: they might fear driving over bridges because being enclosed in a car with no route of escape while suffering panic anxiety is worse than suffering anxiety when apparent escape is possible. But there was no special symbolic significance to the bridge, no meaning traceable to childhood trauma or current ambivalence; the only significance of the bridge was as an unpleasant place in which to suffer spontaneous panic. In general, Klein considered agoraphobia a secondary elaboration of spontaneous panic attacks.

The difference between what patients reported and what nurses observed was easily explained. The imipramine had cured the patients of their spontaneous attacks, but the patients did not yet know they had been cured. Since they still bore all the anticipatory anxiety— the fear of having panic attacks—they continued to feel anxious even in the absence of the underlying disease. The patients had to be taught over time that panic anxiety would not return, and the elaborated secondary or anticipatory anxiety would fade.

Klein published his results and hypotheses in 1962 and again in 1964. "These reports were received like the proverbial lead balloon," Klein recalls, and for a number of reasons. Imipramine was believed to be an antidepressant, and therefore it ought not to be effective in treating anxiety. According to the spectrum theory, it especially should not cure severe anxiety, since it was known to have no effect on mild anxiety. And, of course, Klein was striking at the heart of psychoanalysis, anxiety, without talking the language of psychoanalysis. Klein recalls that the simplest prevailing response was that he had misdiagnosed depression as anxiety.

As a side note, Klein did hypothesize about the origin of panic anxiety. From the early months of life, human infants—and ape and monkey infants, too—exhibit separation anxiety. In infants mature enough to have a mental schema of "mother," the mother's absence will elicit squalling, presumably in order to allow or even compel the mother to relocate her young. Separation anxiety later disappears, as primitive brain functions in the developing primate are suppressed by more complex ones. Klein thought spontaneous panic attacks might be a recrudescence of separation anxiety—an atavism or form of neurological disinhibition.

The separation-anxiety hypothesis goes a distance toward explaining anxious patients' greater comfort when at home or in the presence of relatives—the patients feel "separated" only when cut off from home or family. But the theory has problems, too, among them that separation anxiety and panic anxiety seem to involve different neurotransmitters.

Klein and others have put forth alternative models of panic, including a much-studied hypothesis called the "false-suffocation alarm." The healthy brain and body rely on a variety of mechanisms to prevent suffocation. If a person begins to asphyxiate, physiological monitors detect the problem and cause intense arousal, gasping for breath, and the urge to flee. The false-suffocation-alarm theory holds that, in a person with panic anxiety, defective monitors fire even when he or she has enough oxygen. Common to both the separation-anxiety theory and the false-suffocation-alarm theory is the absence of any need for causation rooted in the subtle psychological experiences of the anxious person. Faulty wiring is enough to elicit the panic; the complex psychological elaboration then evolves in response to the random bouts of anxiety.

By 1980, Klein (and the many other biological psychiatrists who researched this issue) had prevailed, at least in terms of the diagnostic manual. Panic anxiety became a recognized disorder, distinct from what was by then called "generalized anxiety." But what appeared in the manual was not yet universally accepted by practitioners. When

Klein presented his most fully elaborated discussion of panic anxiety, also in 1980, his paper was followed by a lecture by an eminent psychoanalyst who made the case for panic anxiety having a psycho-dynamic root. The analytic talk very much echoed the argument Freud had made in his footnote of the previous century.

Even among biological psychiatrists, there remained doubt as to whether imipramine in agoraphobic patients was acting directly on the syndrome or was making a nonspecific contribution through lessening coincident depression. In fact, it is anxious patients who are not simultaneously depressed on whom imipramine works best. But those in the field were for a long time uncomfortable with the idea that what had been called an "antidepressant" might also be an anxiolytic (as the antianxiety drugs are called). The most acceptable model for a medicine was still the use of one drug for one disease.

On the theoretical level, Klein had achieved a breakthrough—a "pharmacological dissection." That is, he had carved out panic anxiety from the sort of nonspecific anxiety that underlies "neurosis," using response to imipramine as the crucial test. (Pharmacologic dissection is a high-level form of "listening to drugs"—that is, of allowing drug response to inform or even dominate our sense of how human behavior is best categorized.) But, for various reasons, Klein's achievement did not have the overwhelming impact of the work John Cade, the Australian physician, had done with lithium in manic depression. Klein did not discover the therapeutic use of imipramine, as Cade had discovered that of lithium. Imipramine was already in use, though not for anxiety disorders. And whereas there was a clear pool of manic-depressive patients waiting to be treated, psychiatrists had by 1980 lost touch with panic anxiety—they had to be educated before they could see the problem. Also, imipramine was a confusing drug for this indication. It had many side effects; despite Klein's early success, the necessary dosage turned out to be difficult to determine; and the drug made some patients worse before it made them better, so in-experienced office psychiatrists had trouble convincing themselves that imipramine worked. The real explosion in diagnoses of panic anxiety awaited the marketing in 1981 of a new medicine—Xanax.

Xanax is an unusual compound. The molecule looks a great deal like a benzodiazepine—the class of medication that includes Librium, Valium, Dalmane, Halcion, and most of the other currently popular anxiolytics and sedatives—although part of the Xanax molecule looks like an antidepressant. The great benefit of Xanax is that it lowers anxiety without, for the most part, making people sleepy as Librium and Valium do. In other words, Xanax is more specific for anxiety than is Valium, and for certain indications, like panic anxiety, it may also be more potent. (Some pharmacologists believe Valium would be as good for panic anxiety as Xanax if you could give it in high enough doses, but at those doses most patients are asleep.)

Although the FDA did not make this use a specific "indication" for ten more years, it was recognized by the time Xanax was first released that the new drug was an extraordinary treatment for panic anxiety. Unlike imipramine, Xanax made patients with panic anxiety feel better from the first dose. And Xanax has very few side effects.

With a convenient, effective drug available, doctors saw panic anxiety everywhere. Patients told one another about the drug, and the mass media spread the news. Panic anxiety and panic attack became bywords.

The newly rediscovered panic anxiety looked pretty much the way Klein said it would. It was of no use to get patients a little better. You had to medicate them to the point where they got no more attacks at all, and then you had to use a crowbar to get them back out into the world to conquer their anticipatory anxiety.

Not only did the full syndrome of panic anxiety respond to Xanax; many of the partial syndromes Freud had observed responded, too. If a patient had bouts of unexplained diarrhea or dizziness, or feelings of dread without palpitations or perspiration, or even if he just seemed inexplicably timid about making forays from the home, doctors would press for a more complete story and might prescribe Xanax whether or not a full picture of panic emerged. The underlying dynamic for a broad range of symptoms and behaviors is now understood to be incompletely expressed panic anxiety rather than unconscious conflict.

The profession, and then the public, had listened to drugs in two stages: imipramine, through its success in Klein's studies, re-created panic anxiety in theoretical terms; Xanax made it ubiquitous. But then Xanax proved to be a fiercely addicting drug; it is also short-acting, so certain patients are constantly chasing their anxiety, and their withdrawal from Xanax, with another pill, around the clock. Probably imipramine, if patients can tolerate it, is a better long-term treatment for panic anxiety than is Xanax. But in terms of social impact—translating an esoteric theoretical concept into a new public understanding of how people's emotions work—Xanax will have had a lasting effect even if, as is likely, it is superseded by longer-acting, less addictive compounds.

• • •

Donald Klein's model of panic anxiety now prevails. When it comes to anxiety, clinicians accept the concept of a complex behavioral syndrome rooted in simple dysregulation of emotion.

That the same did not happen for rejection-sensitivity and its elaboration into hysterical personality is perhaps due, as much as anything, to the absence of the right drug to act as a popularizer, in the way that Xanax popularized panic anxiety. As long as MAOIs remained the drug of choice to "set the floor" under rejection-sensitive patients, the concept of hysteroid dysphoria was unlikely to take hold. Patients who eat or drink the wrong foods can have strokes or die on MAOIs. Few physicians were willing to take a flamboyant, self-absorbed woman prone to brief catastrophic depressions and put her on a pill that would allow her to commit suicide by drinking a glass or two of Chianti or eating a piece of Stilton. A similar line of thought inhibited the widespread use of medication in less disturbed "hysteroid" patients. It is difficult to justify putting a relatively healthy person at risk of stroke. Besides, healthier histrionic patients were still thought to be among the most responsive to psychotherapy. For forty years, Klein's formulation of hysteroid dysphoria remained a stimulating concept without widespread application.

Prozac may change all that. Regarding hysteroid dysphoria, Prozac may be to the MAOIs what, in the case of panic anxiety, Xanax was to imipramine.

This assertion may sound odd. MAOIs affect many transmitter systems, whereas Prozac affects mainly nerves that use serotonin. Nevertheless, converging evidence of diverse sorts suggests that Prozac has a good deal in common with the MAO inhibitors.

One experiment, performed recently by a group at Yale, is so simple and elegant that it is remarkable it was not done long ago on the early antidepressants. It is based on an old technology used by scientists studying human dietary requirements. Besides vitamins, we need amino acids—"the building blocks of protein"—in our diet. Some amino acids the body can manufacture, but others are "essential"; that is, we need to eat foods that already contain them. L-tryptophan is an essential amino acid, and it is the substance from which the body makes serotonin.

When testing amino-acid requirements on army recruits, researchers developed a low-tryptophan diet, one whose protein content is supplied by foods such as gelatin that do not contain L-tryptophan. The researchers could then stress the body by giving the recruits a drink made of amino acids but omitting L-tryptophan. The sudden supply of amino acids induces the body to manufacture proteins, thus depleting it of what little tryptophan remains. This tryptophan-starving amino-acid drink results in rapid serotonin depletion in the brain. In normal people, the results of this dietary stress are not dramatic, although certain subjects may become tired or irritable or blue.

The Yale researchers applied the old technology to patients who had been depressed, had recently recovered on antidepressants, and were still taking the medication. The results were striking. Patients who had recovered on a selective serotonin-reuptake inhibitor (similar to Prozac) became depressed *within hours* of taking the amino-acid drink, and in just the way they had been before taking the SSRI, with precisely the same constellation of symptoms coming on in the same order. Upon their return to a normal diet, the depression once more remitted, within a day. This result makes sense. If the SSRI is working through maintaining effective serotonin levels, serotonin depletion should result in a return of the depression, and refeeding should allow the drug once again to take effect.

The same dietary regimen was applied to patients who had recovered from depression on desipramine, a tricyclic antidepressant that affects norepinephrine (but not serotonin) pathways. These patients did not relapse when given the amino-acid drink.

In the same test situation, patients who had responded to MAOIs relapsed within hours, just as the SSRI-treated patients had, taking on all the aspects of the depressive syndrome from which they had recently recovered. Thus, even though MAOIs are known to act on a number of neurotransmitter pathways, it seems their effect in depressed patients depends on serotonin.

Research at the level of the cell supports this conclusion. The way in which serotonergic cells respond to MAOIs has a similar time course to the response of depression to the medication; cells that use norepinephrine respond also, but changes in norepinephrine levels do not seem to occur at the same time as changes in mood.

At the level of anatomy, the effects of Prozac and the MAOIs also look similar. Psychotherapeutic medications tend to be anatomically selective—to affect circuits only in certain parts of the brain. If you look at changes in receptors on nerve cells, you find that certain MAOIs and Prozac are active in similar parts of the brain, whereas medications like desipramine present a very different pattern of local action.

Cellular research, anatomical studies of brain function, and the dietary challenges all suggest that Prozac and the MAOIs share common sites and mechanisms of action on depression. There is also early work indicating that Prozac and MAOIs are effective in similar subgroups of depressed patients. Small studies first from England and more recently from the University of Michigan show that Prozac, like the MAOIs, may be especially effective in atypical depression, the kind characterized by weight gain and excessive sleep.

Such preliminary data, as well as experience with patients, have led practicing doctors to suspect that Prozac will turn out to be a clinically acceptable alternative to the MAO inhibitor. This speculation extends beyond atypical depression to the issue of sensitivity to rejection and loss. Prozac's relatively benign side-effect profile is especially important here: if you can "set a floor" under emotionally brittle patients—consistently spare them the terrible pain and disorganization that follow losses—without putting their health and safety at risk, then the concept of rejection-sensitivity becomes useful in practical terms. Because of experience with panic anxiety, psychiatrists are quite comfortable with the idea of using medication to head off affective crises in the hope of "breaking the back" of a more complex problem of behavior and self-image. Thus, within psychiatry, the availability of Prozac has reawakened interest in hysteroid dysphoria.

If hysteroid dysphoria were the whole story, Prozac's specificity and potency would be of limited interest: after all, to how many women does Klein's description apply? I don't see many hysteroid dysphorics. Nor, I suspect, do other psychiatrists. Partly this is due to a change in vision. Because of the derogatory implications of hysteria, we prefer to see patients' problems in other terms—depression, anxiety, post-traumatic stress syndromes, multiple personality, borderline personality disorder. The diagnosis that succeeded hysteria, "histrionic personality disorder," is used infrequently.

But I do see people who are highly sensitive to loss or rejection. A few have a flamboyant style; many more are controlled, self-effacing, focused, and driven. Lucy is a good example of a person whose interpersonal style is shaped by her extreme sensitivity to rejection but who is clearly different from the women Klein described. It seems rejection-sensitivity may be a much broader category than hysteroid dysphoria.

To understand how the broad category of rejection-sensitivity came to be represented by hysteroid dysphoria, we must return to Donald Klein's early work. Klein was not merely dissecting out diagnoses but also wielding his scalpel on the prevailing hidebound, pseudo-Freudian, antibiological form of psychoanalysis. Because Klein cured with drugs rather than with interpretations, it was harder to discern that he, like Freud, was as much invested in theory as in clinical results. Imipramine for panic and MAOIs for dysphoria were primarily test cases for the accounts of psychic causation inherent in the psychoanalytic concepts of anxiety and hysteria. This focus on theory helps explain why, among all possible forms of rejection-sensitivity, Klein focused on hysteroid dysphoria. The question is whether the concept needs to be so narrowly restricted. Why should all emotionally vulnerable women become *femmes fatales,* or *femmes fatales manquées?*

Klein tried to explain why rejection-sensitive women become "hysteroid." He believes, as do many theorists, that the appetite for social approval is a direct reinforcer, or a primary, innate drive, for humans. To satisfy that drive, both boys and girls learn early in life to use the interpersonal skills valued in them by their families and society at large. Because sex typing occurs early, and because certain forms of charm are valued in females, girls may be drawn to exhibitionistic and seductive social tactics to win admiration and approval. Most learn to use "feminine" social skills effectively and discreetly. But a girl with a wider range of moods—keener pleasure and pain in response to others' attention and inattention—may become over-trained, an "applause addict." This pattern will be particularly marked in the daughter of narcissistic parents who neglect the child unless she provides the sort of performance they require for their own stimulation and gratification.

Klein's account can be seen as a biological behaviorist's version of the Electra complex. The great difference is that in the psychoanalytic account the family trauma is primary—the competition for the father produces the emotional instability, and therefore merely treating moods will miss the mark—whereas in Klein's version "the interpersonal tactics and . . . relationships are secondary reverberations of the basic affective difficulty."

Working backward from instances of difficult-to-treat pathology, Klein explained plausibly how hysteria might be grounded in a mood disorder. But is hysteria the only possible outcome of rejection-sensitivity? Klein's metapsychology shows how rejection-sensitivity can cause hysteria, but it does not explain why hysteria should be the unique consequence of mood instability. Surely for every rejection-sensitive person who evolves into a caricature of femininity there must be a dozen who adapt and cope in other ways.

Once we focus on rejection-sensitivity apart from hysteria, all sorts of people come to mind to whom the label might apply. There are people who feed their applause addiction through competition at work, and people who respond to unmet needs with withdrawal, self-pity, and excessive caution. Klein, in his academic writings, never moved past the early battle with psychoanalysis. But, in response to his own discomfort with the widespread misuse of "hysteria," Klein did twice rename his syndrome, first as "chronic overreactive dysphoria" and then as "rejection-sensitive dysphoria." Implicitly, these new labels de-emphasize hysterical traits and focus on the underlying inner state—the disordered affective regulator. Indeed, Klein has written that his major contribution in this area has not been the identification of a group of hysterics who respond to medication but, rather, the highlighting of responsiveness to loss as a critical factor in shaping personality, self-image, habitual behaviors, and symptom complexes.

•   •   •

Rejection-sensitivity is a powerful concept. Looking once again at Tess and Julia, we may see the overly controlled quality of their lives as due in part to an apprehension that minor failure can bring catastrophic sensations of loss and inadequacy. Perhaps rejection-sensitivity looks different in risk-avoiders like Tess and Julia than in stimulus-seekers like Klein's hysteroid dysphorics.

As is true of compulsiveness, rejection-sensitivity occurs in quite healthy people, where its effect can nonetheless be pervasive. I am thinking of an accomplished woman who came to see me. Gail had had an uneventful childhood. She grew up in the 1940s, in a warm, supportive family, which she described in stereotypical, sit-com terms: the blustery, warmhearted father, and the driven and directed mother who ruled the roost. Gail attended a one-sex parochial school where girls naturally assumed positions of leadership. With her mother's encouragement, she went on to become a physician at a time when few women did so. She married her teenage sweetheart, Frank, also a doctor; they were two of only a handful of children who emerged as professionals from their working-class ethnic community.

Gail and Frank successfully raised twin daughters, but in time the marriage became unsatisfying, and when Frank was offered a job at a university some hours away, he took it, leaving Gail alone except on weekends. She preferred this arrangement, because it allowed her greater control at home. She had been reluctant to fight with her husband, fearing his sharp tongue—she could not stand mockery— and she felt she had let him dominate for years.

Frank was constantly angry because he could not control Gail's spending. To Gail, her professional status justified her shopping. She was always dressed in the latest fashions—not in a seductive way, but with the sort of "drop-dead" effect of perfectly matched outfits and exclusive accessories. I often had trouble scheduling a session with Gail, not because of her busy practice or academic obligations but because of her hair and nail appointments, which were frequent and inviolable. By her own, certainly conservative estimate, clothes purchases consumed 20 percent of her pretax income.

Gail consulted me because she realized she was "taking too many pills for a woman who has nothing wrong with her." She was more or less addicted to Fiorinal for headaches (Fiorinal is aspirin plus caffeine and a barbiturate), even though she was already taking another medication, Inderal, to prevent migraines. She took Restoril to sleep and BuSpar for anxiety and Xanax for the anxiety the BuSpar and Restoril did not handle.

As we talked, I formed the impression that, between shopping and medicating, Gail was almost constantly rushing to treat or head off a succession of ill-defined bad feelings. The fuller story took time to emerge, as is sometimes the case with people who have compensated for emotional shakiness with extraordinary social skill. Gail found little pleasure in life and was very vulnerable to attacks on her self-esteem. Minor insults or oversights would leave her feeling incapacitated for days and might even result in weeks of minor depression. She did not so much choose as need to be well dressed, perfectly dressed, for fear someone would find fault with her. When Frank decided to change jobs, Gail did not resist in part because she suffered so badly when he mocked or teased her—which he did often, in response to threats to his own sense of self-worth. Spending money made her feel valuable and independent, reassurance she craved because she so often felt worthless and needy.

Imipramine can sometimes prevent migraines, and I suggested that Gail try it; my hope was to be able to wean her off Fiorinal, which can be a fiercely addicting drug. It is always difficult to stop taking barbiturates, harder if you anticipate debilitating headaches as the price. Imipramine was fairly successful, not just as an anti-migraine drug but as an anxiolytic. On imipramine, Gail was able to stop taking Inderal, Restoril, BuSpar, Xanax, and most of the Fiorinal. But the success of imipramine had a paradoxical effect. Imipramine lifted her heretofore unrecognized depression enough for

Gail to feel half-treated—more aware of her vulnerable emotional state than she had been before taking medicine, or perhaps newly aware that the condition could be altered. After she had spent eight rather good months on imipramine, I switched her to Prozac.

Gail was a good responder. Like Tess, she felt newly confident on Prozac, able to make public presentations without notes, able to engage in confrontations without breaking down. Gail was one of the patients who made me understand that Prozac might have a role in the treatment of rejection-sensitivity. I had not given it to her precisely for that indication (although the emphasis on dress brought the diagnosis to mind), but as soon as the drug kicked in, she began to report an unusual change in attitude: her sensitivity to social slights had diminished. A friend had often remarked, "You never ask for anything." Gail said she had always dreaded being refused. Now she asked for more.

One thing she wanted was a hospital-department chairmanship that had opened up. Friends had urged her to apply for the post, but she had feared being turned down and had transformed that fear into a belief that the job was beyond her skills and status. On medication, she believed that she could do the job—that any sentiment on the part of others to the contrary was prejudice against women. But it was still hard for her to put her hat in the ring. She asked whether I could raise the dose of Prozac so she would feel comfortable applying for the post. I did not know whether a different dose would have a different effect, but I saw no reason not to try. She took extra Prozac, and she applied for the promotion. She was eventually turned down, but was able to take the rebuff in stride. She put her response in words of the sort I have heard from other patients: "I can stand disappointment. I feel confident. I don't tear myself down."

Perhaps the most interesting medication effects were those evident in the marriage. Gail now found her husband more affectionate and less hostile. I understood this change in perception as stemming from Gail's greater tolerance for teasing—that is, a diminished sense of vulnerability. Of course, her husband might have modified his behavior, but it seemed that the initial change was one in the way she experienced him—and a change in the way a wife experiences her husband can influence the way he responds to her, and vice versa. To the extent that this understanding of events is right, we can see medication as having broken a marital stalemate.

In time, both spouses were able to contemplate living together again. In Gail's case, this newfound tolerance was linked to an enhanced sense of independence. Before, she had felt the urge to turn to her husband during each episode of upset, and the resulting feeling of dependency had made her want to keep her distance. Now that she was less desperate, she could allow him back home.

On Prozac, Gail had little use for Fiorinal. It would be convenient to report that she also did without shopping sprees, but though Gail's need to dress perfectly may have diminished, she held on to her right to spend money on herself as a badge and an instrument of independence, and as a bargaining chip in the marriage. If anything, she enjoyed shopping more. "I don't feel guilty about spending," she said. "My husband can say what he wants."

•　　•　　•

Gail, a well-adjusted woman who sits more at the inhibited than the histrionic end of the behavioral spectrum, nonetheless suffered limitations in her life as a result of a heightened emotional responsiveness to disapproval. She was not totally without the symptoms Klein uses to characterize hysteroid dysphoria: she was focused on clothes, and she turned to medication for self-stabilization. But she otherwise had nothing in common with the impulsive, flamboyant, desperately self-centered women Klein studied. It can also be argued that Gail—a decisive physician, able to choose to live apart from her husband—had little in common with people we ordinarily call "sensitive." To understand Gail as suffering from rejection-sensitivity is to enlarge the scope of what we mean when we say someone is sensitive.

It is the effect of Prozac on patients like Gail that leads me to believe our understanding of sensitivity will undergo a sea change. Like panic, sensitivity will become reified, I suspect, so that when we call a person "sensitive" we will come to mean that the person we are discussing has a slight biological derangement, one that must be taken into account in assessing his behavior or opinions. Prozac's ability to decrease rejection-sensitivity suggests that how people respond to loss is a function of the state of their serotonergic neurons.

Once we think about it—and I believe that one of the effects of medication is to make us think about it—we will find reasons why the set point for sensitivity should be biologically regulated. We are an affiliative species. The idea that depression serves to maintain social stability is an old one: the threat of depression keeps primates bonded. But major depression is an infrequent event. It seems much more likely that pair-bonding is maintained through small experiences of loss—that is, through rejection-sensitivity.

The psychiatrist Ronald Winchel has even suggested that primates' affiliative needs are constantly spurred by what he calls the "aloneness affect," a dysphoric feeling that is present unless inhibited by association with others. Winchel suggests that people differ in the responsiveness of this system to successful bonding. In some people, bonding suffices to suppress the aloneness affect; others remain always hungry for more affiliation, and they run through many mates, scratching an itch that will not go away. Winchel suggests that the relevant neurotransmitter in this system is serotonin.

For the moment, it may be enough to say that one of the unanticipated benefits of Prozac's potency and specificity is its ability to act as an acceptable substitute for MAOIs. This function makes hysteroid dysphoria a workable diagnosis and, more broadly, makes rejection-sensitivity a distinct phenomenon worth looking for. The efficacy of medication for rejection-sensitivity makes interesting a whole body of speculative literature that emphasizes the physiological underpinnings of human nature. The medicine likewise draws attention away from the causes of sensitivity—whether inborn or acquired, a person's level of sensitivity is presumed to be encoded as a particular state of the neurons—and refocuses it on the effects of what is now presumed to be a functionally autonomous trait.

Rejection-sensitivity is not a diagnosis—neither an illness nor a personality disorder. It is a personality trait, one that plays differing roles even in the few patients we have met. Sometimes, as in Lucy's case or perhaps Tess's, it appears to be the result of trauma; at other times, as in Gail's case or Julia's, its cause is unclear. Rejection-sensitivity is both a manifestation of difficulties and a pathogen, causing further difficulties of its own.

Rejection-sensitivity is the sort of category we would expect to arise in a discussion of psychotherapy, like "narcissism" or "low self-worth." And this is exactly the point: it is now sometimes possible to use medication to do what once only psychotherapy did—to reach into a person and alter a particular element of personality. In deciding whether to do so, the psychopharmacologist must rely on skills we ordinarily associate with psychotherapy.

Treatment of rejection-sensitivity reveals a new wrinkle in "cosmetic psychopharmacology." It is one thing for a doctor to be able to transform a patient with medication, quite another for the doctor to be able to sculpt the patient's personality trait by trait. Psychotherapists have sometimes been demonized as Svengalis, but at least psychotherapy requires extensive collaboration on the part of the patient. How much more uneasy will we be if doctors can reshape patients' social behavior in detail, through chemicals?

• • •

Once you have reason to look for rejection-sensitivity, you see it everywhere.

For instance, I treated a case of homesickness with Prozac, on the grounds that at root it was an instance of rejection-sensitivity. The patient was a young man from a prominent European family. He had come to do graduate work in this country because the best training in his field of study was to be found here. After meeting an American colleague he might want to marry, he considered settling in the United States, but he felt a constant pull to return home to Europe. What tugged at him, he was aware, was the hope of hearing words of approval from a strong mother who was, by the son's account, stinting in her attention to her children. Though his girlfriend was somewhat warmer, her occasional failure to act empathically could send the young man into a severe tailspin. The patient understood his plan to return home as a way of resisting the urge to display undue dependency on his girlfriend, as well as an attempt to gain his mother's attention. On Prozac—along with focused psychotherapy—he settled in and made progress with both career and relationship.

A very different patient, a claims processor in a large insurance company, complained bitterly of social isolation. She pursued men but never enjoyed more than the briefest relationships with them; she said her hunger for approval frightened men off. She felt mired in her job but, because she had invested almost enough time to achieve a good pension, she saw no way out. Her rejection-sensitivity was most evident in the details of her life. For example, she said, "If I get a letter I think may contain criticism or anger at me, I put it aside for a year; even then, I may be afraid to open it, so sometimes I just throw letters out." Hearing statements of this sort made me ask further about her isolation and career paralysis. It turned out that she cut off social contact whenever she felt she might become close enough to be injured by loss or disappointment. She complained she was overlooked at work, but in fact she had never applied for a promotion, because she feared the pain she would suffer on being turned down. Prozac allowed her to date a variety of men calmly, and to settle into a long-term relationship with one. She also was able to tolerate applying for and accepting a promotion.

I perceived rejection-sensitivity in a private banker who, despite enjoying his marriage, needed a series of mistresses in order to feel emotional security. The problem, as he put it, was that he could not feel close to his wife because he was so much more affected by fear of her criticism than by the experience of her support. (Though both applause hunger and fear of humiliation may be present in rejection-sensitivity, the latter is generally far stronger than the former.) He suffered for days when he lost an account, even if the reason had nothing to do with his competency—for instance if a client moved out of state. Attainment of an equivalent new account would not restore his peace of mind. Tellingly, he said, "I cannot engage in banter. If I am strong with someone, he may be strong back, and I can't stand it."

One patient showed a sort of sensitivity that seemed periodic— and therefore all the more strongly biological. She was the daughter of parents both of whom had suffered recurrent depression as well as a degree of social isolation. Productive, considerate, socially mature, the young woman ordinarily liked to spar with her boyfriend, teasing and being teased. But there were also weeks when for no apparent reason she felt infinitely vulnerable, threatened, and often thrown into brief episodes of depression by jokes that involved barely perceptible threats of loss of love. These intervals appeared—came over her, so that she was aware she was "in a state"—in a way that seemed unrelated to external stressors.

Having seen Prozac in action, I now look for signs of rejection-sensitivity in any patient with marked social difficulties. Consider two quite common problems: first, the young man or woman, well into the usual age of courtship, who has never had an adult romantic relationship, and, second, the man or woman stuck in an abusive relationship. These patterns—on the one hand, social avoidance, inhibition, or phobia; on the other, social masochism or the sort of disregard for self associated with low self-worth—can be understood in a variety of ways. But socially isolated or injured patients will commonly describe themselves as exquisitely sensitive to slights, and often attending to that part of their makeup will afford them relief and allow some behavioral flexibility. In instances where I see a combination of rejection-sensitivity, lack of social flexibility, and continuous or recurrent minor depression—and this is by no means a rare grouping—I often find antidepressants to be helpful.

Rejection-sensitivity is not limited to people with social difficulties early in life. When a spouse dies, the remaining partner may reveal a long history of vulnerability, just barely buffered throughout adulthood by the constant attentions of a supportive mate. This lifelong rejection-sensitivity will sometimes respond to medication, resulting in a quite confident widow (or widower), surprised by a newfound competence.

The mitigation of rejection-sensitivity has, like some of the other uses of Prozac, both its welcome and its uncomfortable aspects, not least because the target of treatment has ill-defined boundaries. My own sense of discomfort in this regard is strongest in my work with college students. Late adolescence is a time in which it is normal for rapidly changing moods to accompany an unstable sense of self. Identity, which includes sensitivity to approval and rejection, is a central developmental issue. Still, some undergraduates seem more sensitive than others.

Some of these more vulnerable students have sustained a loss in childhood, perhaps the death of a parent or a divorce. Others have a history of temperamental sensitivity; they have always been "easy blushers," keenly aware of their appearance in social interchanges. In either case, these students' hunger for attention may have been gratified through the response of teachers in grammar and high school —I have in mind children who are bright, or artistically talented, or perhaps just "prematurely mature" and therefore especially charming to adults. Social challenges may have been delayed, particularly if the child went through school with an unchanging cohort of classmates, so that the task of making new friends arose rarely.

Arriving at college, such students may become suddenly unconfident. Meeting with an adult in an intimate setting such as the psychiatrist's consulting room, they appear composed and well spoken. But, though they may have friends on campus, these vulnerable students lack the social skills to elicit the high degree of attention and approval they require. They may respond to their inner sense of urgency by becoming withdrawn and studious or, on the contrary, wild and exhibitionistic. In either case, it is hard for them to act constructively or to feel comfortable unless their drive for approval is addressed.

One student I treated said she became disorganized as soon as she realized a boyfriend was sexually experienced: "If he has a past, he is more likely to leave me, and I feel terrible as soon as I have that thought, long before he has any chance to leave." Another said, "I can't stand to see anyone lose at tennis. I have too vivid an imagination." That is, he imagines people feel as devastated when they lose as he does. Most often, a student may say, "My lover can do nothing right with me, because when the least thing goes wrong I get too deeply hurt."

Shall we medicate these students? They are just the people for whom certain forms of short-term psychotherapy were developed. Probably we will go that route first. And then? For reasons that probably have less to do with objective clinical judgment than with a cultural mistrust of psychotherapeutic medication, I am reluctant to prescribe for patients this young. But if there is any additional reason to prescribe—if, for example, the student undergoes a depression of any duration, or if it is evident that, whatever the prospect for psychotherapy in the long run, the student's vulnerability is creating too much immediate damage to his or her sense of self-worth, social standing with peers, or ability to function—I may go ahead and try a course of medication, and often the student will do substantially better in all areas. An incidental consequence of this success is that it reinforces my tendency to see "functionally autonomous rejection-sensitivity" everywhere.

•   •   •

Lucy, the boy-crazy college student who as a child had discovered her mother's murder, continued to suffer emotional turmoil, despite psychotherapy. During a period of particularly disorganizing upset for Lucy, I started her on Prozac. Lucy never met Klein's criteria for hysteroid dysphoria: she was not "egocentric, narcissistic, exhibitionistic, vain, and clothes-crazy," nor was she "seductive, manipulative, exploitative, sexually provocative" or "histrionic and flamboyant." She was, to the contrary, quiet, cautious, self-protective, and self-effacing. But I thought she was nonetheless rejection-sensitive.

Lucy's initial response to Prozac was promising. The medication interrupted her downward spiral. She reported a newfound ability to "back off" in her relationship with her boyfriend. The medication may have allowed her to stay at school, and to preserve the romance. These effects were of some importance; they stabilized her life. Lucy's brief, strong response to Prozac allowed me to consider the possibility that a good deal of her behavior, despite its obvious roots in her reaction to the murder of her mother, was now grounded in a functionally autonomous emotional sensitivity whose biological encoding had something to do with serotonergic neurons.

It was not possible to keep Lucy on Prozac. She reported an increase in her sense of undirected urgency. Overcome with cravings, she did not know what she craved. She had to do something, yet she did not know what. Case reports had emerged of Prozac's causing patients to experience suicidal ruminations, and I thought that Lucy's agitation resembled aspects of incidents in those reports. I lowered the medication dose, but Lucy had one more episode of agitation, so I stopped the Prozac. I might have tried medicating her with another antidepressant, or perhaps even restarted the Prozac, if her sense of bleakness had deepened. But without any medication Lucy began gradually to feel better.

One factor was, I think, her heightened awareness of her response to subtle slights. The brief period, on medicine, of relative invulnerability to loss allowed Lucy to understand her social behavior as stemming from exaggerated apprehensiveness. (We might say the medication acted like an interpretation in psychotherapy: it gave Lucy a new perspective.) Or perhaps having been prescribed medication in itself gave Lucy a sort of dual vision—an ability to see how her behavior looked, say, to her boyfriend. She became more open to examining her responses to rejection. When she found herself too acquiescent in her relationship, she was able to ask herself whether she was holding back out of fear of a catastrophic emotional response. Merely labeling the problem allowed Lucy to act more assertively. She felt more in control, and her confidence elicited attentive behavior from her boyfriend.

There was a change in my psychotherapy, too. I remained interested in Lucy's memories of her childhood. But Lucy's hunger for attention and her pain in response to rejection were also at the forefront of my thinking, and this constant awareness, on both our parts, of her social behavior seemed to hasten her progress. Or perhaps a biological effect of Prozac—the calming of an overexcited system—had something to do with Lucy's ability to change.

Sigmund Freud's granddaughter, the social worker Sophie Lowenstein Freud, made a thoughtful comment at a hospital academic conference where I presented an aspect of Lucy's case. Sophie Freud suggested that all people are rejection-sensitive, in the sense that rejection hurts them, but that Lucy might be more skilled than most at *perceiving* rejection. That is, her boyfriend really is spurning her (perhaps even half-knowingly, sadistically) when he turns to the television, and Lucy differs from others only in being aware of that truth. It follows that a therapy based on treating rejection-sensitivity is asking Lucy to decrease her accurate perceptual acuity. The goal is to blind her partially.

The comment is a wise one. It recognizes two factors we have already discussed, the ubiquity of rejection-sensitivity and the enhanced perceptiveness of those who have had to contend with certain special childhood circumstances. But Sophie Freud's comment goes further. It is grounded in the belief that all people—if they perceive themselves to be rejected—feel the same pain internally. They differ only according to how small a cue they need to recognize rejection. This reading of sensitivity is very much in line with the traditional psychoanalytic belief that people differ mainly in the way their history has shaped the cognitive processes by which they integrate, interpret, distort, and screen out current experience. If all people are similar in how they translate loss into pain, then the instrument we are adjusting is not the internal amplifier but the external receiver—we are asking the person to create an artificial attentional deficit, to ignore loss. Sophie Freud, in her brief comment, went on to say that in some therapies we do have to teach people to be less sensitive—less perceptive.

The alternative view—one that seems more likely—is that sensitive people, when they perceive rejection, feel it more keenly. I take this to be Klein's position. The primary deficit is increased amplification, but a person who is vulnerable to extreme pain will become, secondarily, hypervigilant, and therefore more aware of hints of rejection. A medicine capable of treating major depression is probably, even in the realm of minor depression, altering an internal mechanism concerned with such things as mood stabilization and resilience in response to stress.

For the most part, I do not believe that either medicine or psychotherapy makes people less perceptive. But people come as wholes. You cannot tinker with one part and expect others to remain unchanged. Once we turn down the amplification, small slights, even if they are noticed for a moment, may pass without being registered into memory. If they are not remembered, it is as if they never happened. In this sense, a secondary effect of reduced amplification is reduced perception. If the recurrent pain can be muted, a sensitive person ought to become less apprehensive, and perhaps less apprehending as well. He or she might go on in time to ignore small cues that portend minor rejection. The slight blandness apparent in some cheerful, formerly sensitive patients may reflect this loss of subtlety.

Lucy did not become bland. But I think it is true that she moved from being confusingly perceptive—able to see people doing things to her that not even they knew they intended—to being perceptive in a way that allowed a less painful interaction with friends and strangers.

Off medicine, Lucy plateaued at a certain level—better but not well. I was aware of an irony in her treatment. Even though Lucy had been unable to tolerate Prozac, the concept of rejection-sensitivity continued to dominate the psychotherapy. She and I now saw rejection-sensitivity as a central problem for her, even though Prozac had failed to cure her. The persistence of our focus on rejection-sensitivity, in the absence of the drug response that would have justified it, underlined for me the remarkable imperialism of the biological.

In thinking about medication for Lucy, I had begun with evidence that a well-defined disorder, hysteroid dysphoria, responds to a given type of medication, the MAOI. From there, by a series of leaps, I devised the untested hypothesis of rejection-sensitivity in people who are by no means hysterical. Another chain of reasoning justified the use of a quite different type of medication, one that selectively blocks serotonin reuptake. I then applied this weakly supported model to a particular case, Lucy's, in which psychological causes of social discomfort were vividly apparent. The medication did little for Lucy. And still the medication had the power to shape my understanding of how Lucy functioned.

Now Lucy *had* a particular treatable thing, vulnerability to loss. I was continually amazed that I could look at a woman with such a distinct history—such clear psychological cause for suffering and self-injurious social behavior—and, even some of the time, see a quasi-biological quasi-entity, "sensitivity."

Even if medication fails, the patient and the therapist alike may tend to think not that the model is wrong but, rather, that the biological problem persists, untreated. In Lucy's case, I turned to medication a second time when, toward the end of a semester, she became irritable with her roommates. She felt constantly hurt by them and desperate about the self-isolation she created by her demands on their attention. She began to complain of panicky feelings as well as a lack of interest in her work, and she became afraid her mood state would damage her relationship with her boyfriend.

By this time, a new antidepressant was available that, like Prozac, inhibits serotonin reuptake without directly affecting other neuro-transmitter systems. Lucy began taking Zoloft, the new selective serotonin-reuptake inhibitor (SSRI), and after four weeks she reported a striking change. She no longer worried about whether her boyfriend called on time: "I don't freak out."

As weeks passed, this change only increased. Lucy began to prefer space and time to work alone. She reconciled with her roommates and expanded her circle of friends, no longer isolating herself with her boyfriend. She decided to take on junior teaching responsibilities in her department at school, and she found herself able to plan ahead. In general, she said, she was less fearful, better able to count on herself, more open to others' points of view, and at the same time more confident in her own responses. And in the therapy, Lucy found herself—this is after over two years of meeting at least once a week—newly able to discuss aspects of private feelings, in relation to both the past and the present. She was altogether less fragile and more available. These changes were of the sort that psychotherapy had produced, but with the medication there was a sense of a leap forward, of communication with aspects of the self that had been closed off for half of Lucy's young life.

After a few weeks on Zoloft, as on Prozac, Lucy experienced an intensification of her objectless cravings. These cravings ended in an interesting way. Lucy had occasion to visit with her boyfriend's mother, a woman who heretofore had seemed cool and judgmental. This weekend went much better, and Lucy felt her cravings disappear. They had been, she reported, a form of longing for her own mother, a feeling Lucy believed had enveloped her from time to time and that had always seemed too overwhelming to face. She decided in retrospect that the sense of urgency had not been a side effect of medication but, rather, part of its restorative function: on medication, her emotions and memories were more available to her. The medication seemed to have weakened inhibitory barriers to a visceral yearning stemming from the loss of her mother. It was impossible to know whether Lucy's understanding of the phenomenon was correct. But if it was, as a psychotherapist I had once more been misled by my attention to the biological. My focus on medication side effects had blinded me to the obvious psychological meaning of this young woman's sense of urgent intentionality.

I don't imagine Lucy would have done as well as she did without psychotherapy. At the same time, Lucy's response to the SSRI was decided and convincing. "I have the feeling if I fall I won't crack," she said. "Nothing can stop me now." And these declarations came only weeks after a period of marked fragility.

Lucy had harbored a kernel of vulnerability that the psychotherapy did not touch. It was as if psychological trauma—the mother's death, and then the years of struggle for Lucy and her father—had produced physiological consequences for which the most direct remedy was a physiological intervention. But how does psychic trauma become translated into a functionally autonomous, biologically encoded personality trait? How can a mother's death become a change in serotonergic pathways? Lucy's response to medication raises those questions. We are in a speculative realm, but there are answers to be had.

CHAPTER 5

Stress

The stories of transformation we have considered so far have involved people with mild degrees of impairment: minor depression, minor compulsiveness, sensitivity to loss, personality styles fallen from favor. In order to understand how painful experiences can lead to conditions that respond to medication, we must look further afield, because in psychiatry biological research is rarely done on healthy people. It is done on nerve cells, on rats and monkeys, and on patients with serious levels of illness.

What is probably the dominant theory regarding the influence of experience on mood is grounded in observations of the gravest mood disorder, "rapid cycling." In discussing rejection-sensitivity, we encountered the notion that the social style of certain people represents less a response to inner conflict than an attempt to cope with vulnerability to painful emotions. Now to take a further step: there are people in whom mood seems to have lost its attachment to any psychological stimulus whatsoever, in whom affect has become utterly dissociated from their experience of the everyday world.

These people may shift back and forth from deep depression to startling euphoria or to extreme irritability, sometimes in a matter of days or even hours. The radical swings may occur in response to very slight provocation, such as a minor disruption of sleep. Or the cycling may be entirely autonomous—that is, the shift from mania to depression or vice versa may occur out of the blue, or even at fixed time intervals.

These rapidly cycling patients are notoriously hard to treat, so they tend to collect at institutions of last resort. Robert Post, a psychiatrist who has devoted his professional life to the elucidation of manic-depressive illness (or "bipolar affective disorder," as it is now properly called), decided to study a series of rapid cyclers on the clinical wards of the National Institute of Mental Health in Bethesda, Maryland. Though a biologist trained to work at the level of chemical processes within the single neuron, Post has always remained interested in the experience of the patient. Since the start of his career, he has been curious about the time course of manic depression. Through painstaking interviews with patients and their families, Post compiled time-line charts of the onset, termination, and severity of manic and depressive episodes in the lives of bipolar patients. He found that rapid cycling was the end stage of a chronic recurrent illness. Sufferers would typically experience a single episode, usually of depression, in early life. Three to five years later, they might have a second episode. Two years later, an outbreak of depression would blend into subsequent mania. The later recurrences would typically include all the symptoms of earlier episodes, plus additional symptoms. The general pattern was a decrease in the interval between episodes and an increase in the severity and complexity of the episodes, until finally rapid cycling set in.

Post also tried to determine whether a given episode of mania or depression could be related to a trauma, such as loss or disappointment. In general, he found that, as time passed, it required ever smaller stimuli to trigger an episode. In a summary by Post of his own studies and those by other researchers, a psychosocial trauma could be found to precede 60 percent of first episodes of depression or mania, but only 30 percent of second episodes, and so on out to rapid cycling, where only 6 percent of episodes could be linked to discrete stressors.

Like Donald Klein in the case of panic anxiety, Post was redocumenting in the modern era a finding that had been noted at the turn of the century and then neglected. Emil Kraepelin, the contemporary of Freud who differentiated manic depression from schizophrenia, had noted that a severe mood disorder typically began with trauma, was later reactivated, and finally took an "independent course."

Post defined the progression of rapid-cycling bipolar affective disorder: decreasing intervals between episodes ("increasing cyclicity"); increasing complexity and severity of episodes; and an ever-diminishing requirement for external stimuli to set off overt illness. He then searched for a biological model. How do you create an illness characterized by increasing cyclicity and decreasing requirements for trauma? Most processes in biology look just the opposite. They operate according to a "negative feedback loop" in which a system requires ever-increasing stimulus to elicit a response. For example, an addict of street drugs may require progressively larger fixes to obtain the same "high."

But there are a few examples in biology of conditions in which the organism becomes sensitized to, instead of tolerant of, stimuli. One that attracted Post's interest was the "kindling" of seizures, a concept developed in the 1960s by neurosurgeons interested in an animal model for epilepsy. Seizures are "kindled" in an experimental animal—usually a rat or a monkey—by applying an electrode to a relevant part of the brain and passing current. If you pass a small amount of current, at first nothing observable will happen. After a series of intermittent small stimuli, the animal will have a limited seizure. If after an interval you again stimulate the sensitized site, less electricity will be required. With enough intermittent stimulation, the animal will exhibit more widespread seizures: first it will chew and nod its head, then one forepaw will go in and out of spasm, then both forepaws, and so on. In time, the animal will start to seize spontaneously, with no stimulus at all. Eventually, the interval between these seizures will decrease, with spontaneous seizures occurring in ever more rapid succession and with greater symptomatic complexity.

To Post, the kindling model of epilepsy looked highly analogous to what he was seeing in the life charts of rapid-cycling bipolar patients. The limitation to Post's model was that it was "nonhomologous." That is, although the progression over time of induced epilepsy in animals resembled that of manic depression in humans, no one was suggesting that bipolar patients had epilepsy. Kindling merely provided a way of thinking about possible biological mechanisms in recurrent affective illness.

If Post had restricted his work to theoretical modeling, it might have gained a following among laboratory researchers only. But Post was faced with a distressing clinical population, the rapid cyclers. Some of these patients responded to lithium, the standard medication for manic depression, but many did not. Post decided to try these patients on Tegretol, a medicine heretofore used mainly to control seizures in outright epilepsy but bearing a chemical resemblance to the antidepressants. (Among other things, as with the tubercular patients on iproniazid, Tegretol seemed a promising drug because of a sort of "experiment of nature": epileptics on Tegretol were observed to experience improvements in mood.) Psychiatrists were wary of Tegretol. Like MAOIs, it has a rare, severe side effect: Tegretol can cause an irreversible drop in the production of white blood cells, which are needed to fight infection. But Post was dealing with such terrible illnesses that he and his patients were willing to take a risk. Post had marked success. Tegretol turned out to be a better medication for rapid cycling than lithium; indeed, Tegretol has turned out to be useful in other types of manic depression that do not respond to lithium.

Nothing drives the interest of practicing doctors like success with medication. Here was a new treatment for a refractory disorder. And the fact that Tegretol is a neurologist's drug, an anticonvulsant (anti-epileptic), made it even more intriguing. If rapid cycling and epilepsy are connected, beyond analogy and their responsiveness to Tegretol, it is in a complex, still-undiscovered way. Both do often occur in the same part of the brain, and both probably involve a disorder in the transmission of signals, but there was still a good degree of serendipity involved in the discovery that two possibly "kindled" illnesses respond to the same medicine. The kindling model was not necessarily any more intellectually compelling after the application of Tegretol to rapid cycling than before. Nonetheless, once they began successfully treating bipolar patients with an anticonvulsant, clinicians found Post's nonhomologous model, kindling, hard to ignore.

Researchers soon turned from the time course of kindling to an examination of the physical processes that underlie it. Kindling has dramatic effects on nerve pathways. Applying current to relevant cells in the rat's brain causes "downstream" cells (those receiving signals from the electrically stimulated cells) to change *anatomically,* and these changes can occur early on, before the animal develops seizures. Cellular biologists are right now studying the process in detail, and they are already speculating about the general picture. It looks as if a series of chemical reactions in the downstream cell reach right to the nucleus and affect the way the cell's DNA and RNA produce complex chemical substances. These substances include hormones that determine whether the cell makes new connections with other neurons or allows old connections to wither. Some cells die; others "sprout," or change shape. Kindling rewires the brain.

Changes in "hard wiring" become apparent long before a kindled animal has its first seizure—the brain reshapes itself anatomically in response to small noxious stimuli. If kindled epilepsy is an accurate model for the development of mood disorders, then we would expect anatomical changes in the brains of traumatized people—perhaps children with the sorts of experiences Tess or Lucy suffered—even before any symptoms of depression appear. It is important to emphasize that we are reasoning by analogy: kindled rats suffer physical trauma, whereas the histories of most depressed people reveal psychological trauma. But the similarity in pattern of illness between depressed patients as they progress to rapid cycling and kindled rats as they progress to epilepsy allows researchers to speculate that, for certain brain cells, physical and psychological trauma may be quite similar in their effects.

Here, then, is a biological image of "functional autonomy": trauma is translated into anatomical changes in the brain, even before any major illness becomes evident. Under the kindling model, rats become sensitive to ever more subtle stimuli. This model reflects some of what we see in certain rejection-sensitive patients: Symptoms become "unmoored" from their historical antecedents, and people who have suffered serious trauma later find themselves vulnerable to what for others would be minor losses or threats of loss.

The kindled-epilepsy model also resembles models of how animals learn to see. At first, animals have to scan a visual field painstakingly; in time, they presumably make hard neural connections that allow certain complex shapes (or rules about perspective) to be processed simply and rapidly. In both cases, kindled epilepsy and perceptual learning, a repeated stimulus results in an anatomical change in the brain. Kindling appears to be a kind of learning, but a learning that can occur independent of cognition.

Researchers have used the kindling model to study treatment and prevention, as well as causation, of illness. They have given kindled rats various medications and discovered two interesting things: First, medication can normalize chemical production in the brain cells of kindled animals; that is, it can prevent the production of hormones that reshape the brain's wiring. And, second, different drugs are effective at different stages of the disorder.

Early in the development of kindled epilepsy, Valium will prevent seizures; but once the seizures become spontaneous—independent of external stimuli—Valium is ineffective. Dilantin (another anticonvulsant) is ineffectual against early seizures but effective in preventing spontaneous seizures in the end-stage disorder. This latter observation parallels experience with manic-depressive patients. Lithium tends to be most effective when a patient has had three or fewer episodes of mania. Thereafter, antiepileptic drugs, such as Tegretol, are more likely to work.

The kindling model has led researchers to fear that, in progressive manic depression, drugs appropriate to the early stages of illness become ineffective as the illness worsens, because of structural changes in the sufferer's brain. Most researchers now recommend medicating manic depression early and keeping patients for extended periods of time on the drugs that treat the initial stages of the disorder. Increasing evidence that depression alone, in the absence of mania, can have the form of a progressive, kindled illness is causing psychiatrists to apply these same rules broadly to all mood disorders. The goal is to prevent the hard-to-reverse deterioration that occurs as the illness progresses.

If we accept the analogy between mood disorders and kindled epilepsy, this is how we will see manic depression, and perhaps all depression: It is a progressive, probably lifelong disorder. It can be induced in normals. The induction can take place through a series of small stimuli, none of which at first causes overt symptoms. The latency to fully expressed illness can be long, and the absence of overt symptoms is no guarantee that the underlying process is not under way. Illness, once expressed, can become responsive to ever smaller stimuli and, in time, independent of stimuli altogether. The expression of the disorder becomes more complex over time. Even the early stimuli are translated into anatomical, difficult-to-reverse changes in the brain. Different treatments are appropriate to different stages of the illness. Early and prolonged intervention is crucial.

•   •   •

Kindling mimics the time course of mood disorders, but the stress to which animals are subjected, electrical current, is not the same as the stress that depresses humans. Researchers have tried to bridge the gap through experiments in which rats are exposed instead to various forms of physical and psychosocial stress.

Biochemical responses to stress have been of interest to researchers for decades. By the middle of this century, scientists were focused on the functions of the adrenal glands, small organs sitting atop the kidneys (therefore ad-renal). The adrenals were known to produce hormones that set the body's tone in response to stress. One such hormone is adrenaline, a fight-or-flight substance named after the gland that produces it in greatest quantity. "Adrenalin" is actually a proprietary name for the chemical that scientists, using Greek rather than Latin roots, call "epinephrine." Parsimoniously, nature often uses the same substance as a hormone in the body and a transmitter in the brain. It was the role of epinephrine or adrenalin in the body's handling of stress that led scientists studying depression to look at epinephrine and its close relative, norepinephrine, in their role as brain neurotransmitters.

For an equally long time, psychiatric researchers have been interested in another hormone produced by the adrenal gland, cortisol. Cortisol is the hormone that is abnormal in Addison's disease and Cushing's disease. Its effects on healing and inflammation are taken advantage of in creams, pills, and inhalants containing synthetic analogues of cortisol, such as hydrocortisone. The body's own cortisol, when released into the bloodstream, affects mood, food intake, the sleep-wake cycle, and level of locomotor activity—all factors altered in depression—and cortisol is known to be released in response to stress; so close is the connection that cortisol and related substances are sometimes called "stress hormones." Scientists have long wondered whether cortisol will turn out to be the biochemical factor that connects stress to resultant depression.

A host of observations associate depression with abnormalities in stress hormones. Many depressed patients, if given a substance that ordinarily causes the body to decrease its output of cortisol, fail to suppress—that is, the system is so revved up that it no longer responds to ordinary forms of regulation. Cortisol levels (the amount of hormone in the blood) are high in many acutely depressed adults. Autopsies often show the adrenal gland to be enlarged in adults who have died by suicide. The gland is also enlarged, according to imaging studies, in about a third of depressed patients. Put briefly, elevated, nonsuppressible cortisol levels can be a marker of depression. Elevated cortisol may even account for certain symptoms of depression.

The adrenals are far from the brain, and most of what interests researchers is not so much cortisol produced by the adrenals as the substances in the brain that stimulate the adrenals. There is a cascade of such hormones; one brain center stimulates another, and so on down the line until a hormone is released that causes the adrenals to produce and release cortisol. At the top of the cascade is a substance produced in the brain called corticotropin-releasing factor (CRF). Elevated CRF levels can be measured in the brains of rats subjected to stress—and here is where a more homologous model of stress and depression emerges.

Rats can be stressed in a variety of ways—through pain (such as electric shock to the foot pads or pinching of the tail), through exposure to cold, through switching of cage-mates, or through close confinement in a small cage. There are also more complex forms of stress, one of which, "learned helplessness," is the basis for a variety of research. In the learned-helplessness model, a rat may be trained to avoid a foot shock by pressing a lever; later, shocks are administered randomly. The rats from whom control has been withdrawn evince symptoms, such as social isolation and passivity, that look like depression. As in humans who commit suicide, chronically stressed rats have enlarged adrenal glands. Moreover, stressed rats produce excess CRF in regions of the brain that parallel those known to affect mood in humans.

As in the case of kindling, repeated stress "sensitizes" rats to produce ever higher levels of CRF. The mediating substances within the receptor cells look very similar in stressed and in kindled rats; that is, the same sorts of substances lead to the changes in what the cell's genetic material, the DNA and RNA, produces. Like electrical current, stress can cause cell death and changes in the neural architecture—the hard wiring—of the brain. For instance, one study has shown that rats restrained in small cages for part of each day will experience localized brain-cell death within three weeks. As in kindling, medications (in fact, antidepressants) can prevent neural damage in stressed rats. The anticonvulsant Dilantin blocks cell loss in stressed rats, just as it blocks kindling.

It is harder to work with stress than with kindling (for instance, it is easy to measure the number and frequency of seizures in rats, but harder to assess the time course of depression), so researchers know less about the cellular effects of stress than they do about the results of electrical stimulation. But the parallels between rats' responses to electrical current and to psychic stress make it tempting to combine the two models conceptually. Together, they give weight to the conclusion that psychosocial stressors like pain, isolation, confinement, and lack of control can lead to structural changes in the brain and can kindle progressively more autonomous acute symptoms.

Lest the stressors to which rats are subjected seem too simple to relate to the influences that might cause depression or behavioral inhibition in humans, we should note that researchers have found that a variety of psychological "stressors" can cause cell death in the nerves affected by the cortisol system. Entirely nonpsychological stressors can have the same effect: chronically diminished blood flow to the brain causes comparable brain-cell death, and so does normal aging. The "stress-hormone" system seems vulnerable to a variety of noxious influences.

One psychological stress that has been looked at in humans is sexual abuse. An important study in progress appears to be pointing to a marked effect of childhood sexual abuse on the stress-hormone system. The National Institute of Mental Health has been following

160 girls, aged six to fifteen when the research began, who had in the prior six months been subjected to legally documented sexual abuse by a family member. Over a four-to-five-year follow-up period, these girls (as opposed to a group of girls matched for age, social class, presence of one or two parents in the home, and other factors) were found to have consistently higher-than-normal cortisol levels, disruption of the normal daily pattern of the rise and fall of cortisol levels, and exaggerated cortisol responses to stimulation. These disruptions of the stress-hormone system were correlated with high levels of depression in the abused girls, generally some years after the episodes of abuse. Early results indicate that abuse may even affect physical maturational changes in the abused girls.

This and other studies seem to make the rat model of "stress-hormone" dysfunction relevant to our understanding of human mood regulation. Taken together, the rat studies indicate that a variety of stressors can cause chemical and anatomical changes whose behavioral effects may not be apparent for some time.

●   ●   ●

The credibility of the kindling model has been further strengthened by studies of nonhuman primates, such as rhesus monkeys. Rhesus monkeys are of particular interest because they are our near neighbors genetically and they bond socially. Underappreciated for many years, research on mood in rhesus monkeys has attracted widespread attention recently, not least because monkeys manifest disturbances parallel to those that in humans respond to antidepressants.

The rhesus monkey (a type of macaque) shares over 90 percent —perhaps as high as 94 percent—of its unique segments of DNA with humans. Rhesus monkeys are, after humans, the most successful of the primates, in terms of their numbers, their distribution over the globe, and their ability to thrive in a host of settings from the jungle to the city. Highly social, rhesus monkeys travel in troops of twenty to one hundred or more members. Monkeys identify and interact on an individual basis with all other members of the troop. Infants are tied closely to their mothers in the first year, and they also rapidly become attached to their peers.

In the wild, rhesus monkeys are seasonal breeders who court and mate intensively over the same two-month period each year, so that babies are born in clusters; for the same reason, young monkeys are routinely deserted by their mothers at seven months, when breeding females again focus on courtship. The young monkeys respond to this separation with increased activity (perhaps searching for the mother) and what are called "coo" vocalizations. Some temporarily abandoned monkeys are "adopted" by older siblings. Others go on to display signs of distress, withdrawing and clasping themselves. No one looking at a photograph of such a monkey can miss the blank, defeated, hopeless look around the eyes. It seems rhesus monkeys are a species in which a particular stressor, separation, routinely, and in the natural setting, causes something very much like depression.

The best-known study of the effects of separation on monkey social development is an experiment by the pioneer animal ethologist Harry Harlow involving monkey infants separated from their mothers and exposed to wire-and-cloth "mother surrogates." Harlow demonstrated that warmth—a soft place to cling—is more crucial even than feeding in determining what an infant monkey will treat as a mother. In subsequent years, researchers have taken advantage of the social nature of rhesus monkeys to devise ever more complex observations of the effects of separation. Harlow's student and colleague, the psychologist Stephen J. Suomi, now director of the Laboratory of Comparative Ethology of the National Institute of Child Health and Human Development in Bethesda, Maryland, has extended Harlow's work in ways that bear directly on contemporary models of human depression.

It has long been known that rhesus infants reared apart from other monkeys for six months ("isolation-reared") will later exhibit pathological behavior, such as failure to explore or to affiliate socially when returned to the troop. As adults, isolation-reared monkeys may be inappropriately aggressive toward other monkeys; if they bear children, the females are likely to be neglectful or even abusive mothers, especially toward their firstborn. (To a psychiatrist who has seen a number of abused or neglected firstborn children, these findings have an eerie resonance.) It is clear that severe stress in infancy and childhood can produce major changes in monkeys' adult social behavior. But isolation-reared monkeys may seem too grossly disturbed to illuminate the more common minor disorders we see in humans.

Suomi has studied ever more subtle forms of separation stress. In particular, he has observed monkeys who were "hand-reared" (reared by humans, in the presence of inanimate surrogate "mothers") for the first thirty days of life. The hand-reared monkeys are then united with age-mates and later with a larger mixed troop. Such "peer-reared" monkeys look behaviorally normal throughout. Except for thumb-sucking, they show none of the abnormal behavior of infants raised in isolation. Peer-reared monkeys engage in normal social activities at every age, except that they cling to their peers longer than mother-reared monkeys cling to their mothers. The peer-reared monkeys are also somewhat more timid and slow to explore than are mother-reared monkeys. None of these differences is dramatic. Compared with isolation-reared monkeys, peer-reared monkeys have been only relatively deprived, and their behavior overlaps generously with the behavior of normals. Such aberrant behavior as exists tends to disappear with time. Peer-reared monkeys are, in effect, near-normal monkeys with a history of moderate trauma.

In Suomi's critical experiments, both peer-reared and mother-reared monkeys are subjected yearly to repeated social separation—housing in individual cages for four four-day periods—at a variety of ages (six, eighteen, and thirty months, and so on). When peer- and mother-reared monkeys who have lived in the same social group are separated from that group, they behave differently, the peer-reared monkeys showing more signs of distress and withdrawal. These include signs generally assumed to be related to depression (passivity, distress vocalizations, and such self-directed behaviors as huddling and rocking) and signs more related to compulsiveness or anxiety (self-directed behaviors such as excessive grooming and picking, as well as other repetitive stereotyped behaviors). Even though peer-reared monkeys act normal between separations, each subsequent separation elicits a greater variety and intensity of depression-related behavior.

The monkeys' biochemical reactions also show progressive deterioration over time. At the age of six months, the peer-reared monkeys, on separation, show higher levels of cortisol and more abnormal indicators of norepinephrine activity than do monkeys reared by their own mothers. At eighteen months, the biochemical distress indicators are more pronounced, and now markers for serotonin activity, which had previously been the same between the two groups, are abnormal in the peer-reared monkeys. "Moreover, the same basic pattern of more extreme behavioral and physiological response to separation in peer-reared monkeys was continued during subsequent annual separations," Suomi writes, though "there were few, if any, significant rearing condition differences during periods of stable group housing as the monkeys passed through puberty and into early adulthood."

Suomi's experiment produces in young rhesus monkeys a phenomenon that has a good deal in common with rejection sensitivity, kindling, and the stress model of depression. Suomi's peer-raised monkeys are, under ordinary circumstances, not depressed. They may at first appear a bit more timid and clinging than mother-reared monkeys, but even that behavior is within the normal range and short-lived. However, upon subsequent separation, these monkeys are more likely than mother-raised troop-mates to show behavioral signs of mood disorder and biological changes in the relevant hormone and neurotransmitter systems. Moreover, as in Post's rapid-cycling patients and kindled rats, each "depressive" episode is more complex, both behaviorally and biologically, than the preceding one. This kindled rejection-sensitivity occurs in response not to externally applied electric current but, rather, to the sort of stressor we know affects humans—disruption of important social bonds.

What happens to monkeys who are stressed early and then not restressed for a substantial time? It turns out that discrete trauma can sensitize animals for long periods, even in the absence of repeated challenges: A brief separation from the mother early in life—one or two six-day periods at thirty to thirty-two weeks of age—followed by a reunion and normal parenting predisposes young monkeys to an enhanced response to separation *two to three years later,* even in the absence of intervening abnormal stressors. Like the repeatedly separated monkeys, monkeys who have been subjected only to a brief separation from their mothers look largely normal in subsequent months, except for subtle evidence of social inhibition. (Though they are as ready as other monkeys to approach strange objects in a familiar environment, they will approach strange objects less readily in a strange environment.) But their protest and despair responses to later separation are heightened. What would appear to be a modest social stress, albeit at a critical period, produces a minor but long-standing change in personality style, and a vulnerability to separation that is highly reminiscent of rejection-sensitivity in humans.

The three models we have discussed interconnect. The kindling model implies that at least one sort of depression is a progressive condition, biologically encoded long before it manifests itself in the form of overt episodes. The stress research in rats implies that a variety of psychosocial stressors can serve as triggers for this insidious encoding. And the monkey-separation studies show what animals look like early in the course of stress-induced kindling: except for transient, minor social inhibition (anxiety in the face of novelty), they appear normal in ordinary social circumstances; but they have a heightened sensitivity to loss.

●   ●   ●

It is possible to argue that animal models should not influence the way we see mood patterns in humans, but there is no denying that the response of monkeys to early trauma bears a striking resemblance to patterns of behavior in certain patients we have met. The patients are normal in their everyday behavior and feeling states. They are, however, prone to extreme discomfort—minor variants of depression, anxiety, and compulsiveness—in response to social stressors. These patients may also be socially inhibited (just as the monkeys are timid or anxious in the face of novelty), perhaps not in an extreme fashion that is obvious to others, but enough so that their private social dealings are affected. Some of these patients have experienced social disruption early in life; others have not. Certainly the notion of functional autonomy—of a biologically sustained disorder of mood reactivity—in people who have suffered dramatic losses early in life gains credibility from analogous animal models that extend from the level of social behavior to that of chemical functioning within the individual brain cell.

The animal models seem to say that pain has its price, even for those in whom trauma does not produce major depression. The victim carries his scars. Indeed, the vagaries of life being what they are, we all bear scars. We should not expect any clear line of division, then, between health and the early stages of illness. Very likely, a good many of us are in the early stages of kindled depression. The only question is whether good fortune or ongoing processes of protection or repair will save us from suffering a full-blown course of illness.

What distinguishes this view of depression from, say, traditional psychoanalytic models is the recognition that the scars are not, or not only, in cognitive memory. It is not merely a question of inner conflict or of "growing up": "Stop fussing over what your parents did to you!" as skeptics command patients in therapy. The scar consists of changed anatomy and chemistry within the brain. Some of that brain change *is* memory: presumably recollected thought and emotion are encoded in ways that bear resemblance to the kindling model. But another part of that change is "functionally autonomous" emotional sensitivity, even vulnerability to quite serious emotional disorder.

Psychological theories have long held that personality is largely the expression of "defenses"—that is, characteristic ways of avoiding awareness of inner conflict. By adding the concept of functional autonomy, we are saying that defenses, and therefore the whole array of character armor, are not mobilized only against inner conflict but also against the likelihood of further pain from injury in the social world, a type of pain to which certain people have been biologically sensitized. And part of what we consider personality—the part corresponding to traumatized monkeys' reluctance to explore—may be directly encoded by trauma.

A parsimonious, though not entirely comfortable, way of describing these events is to expand our concept of memory. We readily accept the notion of cognitive and emotional, or at least emotion-laden, memory. But perhaps sensitivity is memory as well—"the memory of the body," as we might say "the wisdom of the body." In this sense, social inhibition and rejection-sensitivity are both memory. That is, they do not *stem from* a (cognitive, emotion-laden, conflicted) memory of trauma; they represent or just *are* memories of trauma. According to this way of thinking, much of who Lucy is— her neural pathways, her social needs—constitutes a biological memory of her mother's murder, just as Tess's social style is a memory of her precociously responsible childhood.

The separation, stress, and kindling models have pronounced implications for treatment of a variety of psychological conditions. If minor depression is an early stage of a kindled disorder—the period of latency between a sensitizing injury and overt illness—then continued depression, not to mention further stress or loss, will be dangerous to mental health. It is possible that minor depression can lead to mood disorders, like recurrent depression, manic depression, and even rapid cycling, that are difficult to influence. People to whom medication has been prescribed often express concern over unknown side effects, and this concern is understandable. There are instances in which taking medication has had terrible unanticipated consequences. What is less appreciated, especially in the case of mental health, are the unanticipatable consequences of failure to treat. Living with rejection-sensitivity and inevitably sustaining a series of perceived losses may lead to continued and worsening injury, further enhanced sensitivity, and even severe depression. Living with the sort of personality style that leads to repeated social failure may, beyond the pain caused to self and others, entail health risks.

Kindling studies have already affected the way some psychiatrists treat recurrent depression. Rather than take patients off medication as each episode of depression or mania ends, psychiatrists tend more and more to maintain patients on medication, sometimes indefinitely, once they have experienced a certain number of episodes within a brief period of time. This new method of treating recurrent depression is becoming widespread even in the face of evidence that antidepressants can set off episodes of mania in vulnerable people. The kindling model of recurrent depression as a dangerous progressive illness is coming to dominate within the profession.

•   •   •

Our interest here is in chronic low-level unhappiness or recurrent minor periods of demoralization, rather than in major depression. Just how the kindling, stress, and separation models ought to influence treatment of these near-normal conditions is not yet clear. No one advocates long-term antidepressant treatment for people who have had a single episode of major depression. But the question of how vigorously to treat low-level depression has suddenly been made more pertinent with the availability of new medicine that has more tolerable side effects.

A small body of evidence indicates that selective serotonin-reuptake inhibitors such as Prozac may be particularly effective for mild chronic and recurrent depression—the sort of depression that looks like the early stages of a kindled disorder. SSRIs may even be to depression what Valium is to kindled epilepsy, a specific treatment for the early stage of a kindled disorder.

Some of the evidence is indirect: SSRIs look just about as effective as tricyclics, like imipramine, in treating mildly depressed patients, primarily outpatients; but studies of severe depression—for instance, a large series of patients treated at a consortium of universities in Denmark—show that for *hospitalized* depressed patients SSRIs are substantially *less* effective than tricyclics.

It is difficult to show medication effect in minor mental illness, because so many subjects will improve spontaneously over the course of any study. A group at Indiana University has approached this problem by looking beyond response rates to the *pattern* of recovery of mildly depressed patients given either Prozac or a placebo. A sizable number of patients given placebo improved, as did a larger number of patients given Prozac. What distinguished the groups was the quality of response. The Prozac-treated group included many more patients who got *very substantially better* and *maintained* their improvement. The researchers concluded that, even if mildly depressed patients improve early in treatment (say, with psychotherapy), those whose improvement is not dramatic or does not persist should be considered for medication with an SSRI.

Finally, there is evidence that the type of depression being treated makes a difference. Psychiatrists at the University of Utah looked at a series of moderately depressed patients treated with antidepressants. The groups treated with imipramine and Prozac did about equally well. But those in the imipramine group who recovered tended to be patients with a clear-cut first episode of major depression. Those who did well in the Prozac-treated group were people with a chronic low-level course of depression or with "mixed chronic and episodic histories."

Taken together, these studies suggest that, whereas drugs like imipramine are more effective in major depression, drugs like Prozac have a special role in the treatment of minor depressive illness. If this sort of research holds up, we may find that SSRIs can help prevent the progression of early mood disorder into florid illness. It is at least possible that we will some day advocate early detection of depression the way we now advocate early detection of cancer or hypertension, and that treatment of nearly normal conditions will become standard preventive medicine.

•   •   •

Of course, the appropriate treatment for these normal or near-normal depressive states might be psychotherapy. Perhaps what is learned one way can be relearned another, and the memories created by psychotherapy will affect neural structure as well.

There is only a small literature on animal recovery from injury, most of it involving medication. Antidepressants or anticonvulsants can block the deleterious effects of the various sorts of stress we have discussed, from electric shock to separation, but whether they can induce or permit healing is not known.

The most influential animal study of social healing concerns separation-reared monkeys, the monkeys raised apart from troop and mother for six months, who typically grow into aggressive, abusive, socially isolative adults. The effects of separation from the mother can be lessened by exposing separation-reared young monkeys to other young monkeys, in a variety of formats. For instance, if separation-reared young monkeys are exposed to "therapists"—younger (because the isolated monkeys would fight with age-mates), troop-reared monkeys—they will within weeks accept invitations to play, then initiate play, and subsequently engage in normal social behavior whether or not the "therapist" monkeys are present. Indeed, the "rehabilitated" monkeys will display normal behavior through adolescence and adulthood, except when stressed. When stressed, the rehabilitated monkeys will briefly show abnormal self-directed behavior (for instance, clasping or sucking themselves), even if they have not shown such behavior for months—a sign of residual effects of early deprivation in these otherwise behaviorally normal adults.

These various animal studies depict mood disorder as a direct consequence of trauma. The precise nature of the trauma seems unimportant. In rats, a variety of stressors will reliably raise cortisol levels. In rhesus monkeys, separation, especially early in life, is a special stressor, regardless of the details of the separation experience. The resultant disorder presumably does not arise from unconscious conflict between incompatible ideas; it is a straightforward biological injury, one that can be made to reappear, in ever more severe form, by subsequent stress. In order for (partial) recovery to take place, what the animal needs is a certain sort of restabilizing—remothering, a chance to model social skills, and a return to social integration.

If we turn to psychotherapy with humans, evidence from animal studies casts a favorable light on certain sorts of reparative work. For instance, throughout the middle decades of this century, the great hypnotist Milton Erickson practiced a psychotherapy in which he specifically avoided helping patients understand why they were neurotically stuck. Instead, he devised cunning strategies to catapult patients into age-appropriate successful social behavior. (When he encountered a vigorous young patient who claimed he was Jesus Christ, Erickson put him to work as a carpenter; the point was never to understand the delusion but, rather, to help the young person fit in socially.) This therapy-without-insight can be seen as a series of techniques for reuniting a traumatized and socially self-defeating person with the peer group.

Cognitive therapy, lately much in vogue, helps patients reframe environmental stimuli—redefining what is to be perceived as rejection, expanding the definition of "home"—so that sensitive or anxious patients avert their characteristic "functionally autonomous" responses. The cognition that the therapy reshapes is not unconscious inner conflict, but the definition of the trigger for demoralization.

Within psychotherapy, the variants that best take into account animal models of attachment and separation are those that emphasize empathy, more than insight, as the crucial tool in treatment, in effect giving patients the kind of careful, attentive parenting they lacked in early life. Such therapies assume that patients will always remain dependent on social supports.

By contrast, in classical psychoanalysis the goal of treatment is independence, and the method of cure is understanding of the details of individual development. There is nothing in the animal models that speaks directly against the tenets of classical psychoanalysis. Indeed, Freudian analysis can be seen as a therapy obsessed with a particular memory of separation, namely the Oedipus conflict, in which the five-year-old boy buries his sexual desire for his mother out of fear of his punitive father. But infantile sexuality, so crucial to Freud's view of the Oedipal stage, is unimportant in the animal models. And even if one sees the Oedipus conflict as a struggle over separation—the son's realization that he can no longer cleave to the mother—fear of the father seems irrelevant. (For monkeys, separation from the mother is traumatic, but it occurs in the absence of any significant relationship between offspring and father.) The whole notion of inner conflict—in this case, of desire thwarted by fear—is alien to the animal models. Mere repeated separation, followed by social stress later in life, is sufficient to produce not only indecisiveness and compulsiveness (which *look* in the adult human like products of inner conflict) but also anxiety and depression. And the notion that interpretation of conflict is curative finds no equivalent in the animal literature.

Much of this reasoning is, of course, circular. If you look to monkeys as a model for human psychotherapy, you will necessarily end in attending to issues of social integration and reparenting while devaluing the role of insight. Monkeys do travel in troops, and they don't respond to dream interpretation. Here is a distant form of listening to drugs: the success of medication makes animal models more attractive, and then the animal models shape our view of human behavior in a way that makes our uniquely human functions, such as symbolic reasoning, seem less important.

Beyond psychotherapy, animal research throws into question the validity of specific diagnoses for minor mental disorder. Traits of depression, anxiety, compulsiveness, and social inhibition are thoroughly mixed in the repeatedly separated monkeys. These monkeys are vulnerable to depression, but they are also abnormally anxious in the face of certain challenges. They engage in stereotyped behavior, such as insistent self-grooming, reminiscent of compulsive human behavior, like hand-washing. And, in other studies, they prove themselves, more than their untraumatized peers, prone to repeated alcohol consumption in response to stress. Like neurotics, these monkeys have "not specialized" in terms of their psychic vulnerability; depending on circumstance, they are liable to symptoms associated with a variety of illnesses that the current diagnostic system considers discrete. And the neural-transmitter pathways that are out of kilter in each of these symptom complexes appear to be similar, whether the illness is depression or compulsivity or addiction, and whether the animal under study is rat, rhesus, or man.

This welter of animal observations has colored the way I see certain patients who respond to Prozac. The animal models imply that a number of environmental factors, including stress, and perhaps especially the stress of social separation, can give rise to changes in the brain that then predispose the animal to ever more poorly modulated responses to subsequent stress. These changes can take place in animals, and presumably people, whose mood and behavior seem normal under ordinary circumstances. Such near-normal conditions may constitute the early stage of a progressive deteriorating condition; and the subtle collection of abnormalities may persist in a stable way over substantial periods of time, even in the absence of renewed gross trauma. Further deterioration may be lessened by certain forms of social contact. The animal models do not tell us whether medication can reverse injury, but they imply it can confer a protective effect against the consequences of further trauma. The animal models give "functional autonomy" a good name and make medication for "neurosis," and even for quite normal forms of chronic unhappiness, seem a reasonable option, perhaps a highly compassionate one.

• • •

It would be interesting to know how low-level, chronic disturbances of mood relate to abnormalities in serotonin. The animal studies give no consistent answer. Scientific understanding of the connection between affect and the biogenic amines—norepinephrine and serotonin—is in particular disarray just now, because Prozac has scuttled a very appealing theory that promised to connect events at the level of cell-to-cell communication to the chronic mood states of stressed mammals.

The biogenic-amine theory—the hypothesis that depression results from a deficiency of norepinephrine and serotonin—has had a series of differing incarnations. In the mid-1960s, it was thought that low norepinephrine levels cause depression. By the mid-1970s, the prevailing theory held that there are two kinds of depression: one related to abnormalities in norepinephrine, the other to abnormalities in serotonin.

But inadequacies in these theories—for instance, the observation that depressions that look as though they relate to serotonin sometimes respond to medicines, like desipramine, that work via norepinephrine—caused researchers in the 1980s to take a new slant on the amine hypothesis. They began to focus less on cells that *transmit* signals—the neurons thought to be depleted of serotonin or norepinephrine—and more on the downstream cells that *receive* signals. These cells are called postsynaptic neurons, because they sit on the far side of the synapse, or gap between cells, into which the transmitting cell releases neurotransmitter. According to the new theory, the common abnormality in depressions is an alteration in the sensitivity of the postsynaptic (receiving) neuron. In depressed patients and stressed animals, the theory held, these postsynaptic neurons have sprouted too many norepinephrine receptors. (The receptor is a molecular-level structure on the cell membrane to which the norepinephrine temporarily attaches, thus producing its effect on the cell.) The hypersensitive postsynaptic neuron overreacts to normal levels of neurotransmitter. This is a chronic abnormality; the receiving cell remains hypersensitive whether the animal is depressed or not.

The postsynaptic-hypersensitivity model meshes well with the animal studies we have discussed. The animal models say that stress affects the anatomy of the brain—and the new amine theory points to structural changes in the receiving cell. The receiving cells' chronic hypersensitivity to norepinephrine corresponds nicely to traumatized animals' chronic sensitivity to stress, even between episodes of depression.

The theory also explained patients' sometimes confusing responses to the "wrong" antidepressant. Pharmacologic studies demonstrate that tricyclic antidepressants—whether they block the reuptake of serotonin or of norepinephrine—"downregulate" the postsynaptic neuron in terms of response to norepinephrine.

The postsynaptic-hypersensitivity model is dynamic: mood is set by the relationship between the amount of neurotransmitter present in the transmitting cell and the number of receptors available on the receiving cell. In simplified terms, the working model goes like this: Acute stress causes such an outpouring of neurotransmitters that in time the transmitting cell is depleted. The receiving cell then becomes starved of transmitter, so it sprouts excessive numbers of norepinephrine receptors (in order to soak up every last bit of the scarce neurotransmitter). The animal or person now has too many norepinephrine receptors. Transmitter levels may rise and fall depending on stress, but the receiving cells remain chronically overexcitable. In the resting state, the level of transmitter is low, because the brain compensates for the hypersensitive receiving cells by diminishing amine production; but because of the postsynaptic hypersensitivity, the compensation may be imperfect to the point where the animal or person is always a little depressed or anxious, as well as vulnerable to catastrophic inner responses to stress.

The postsynaptic-hypersensitivity model explained the action of tricyclic antidepressants. Antidepressants make more amine available in the synapse, and they do so in a sustained way. At first, the patient receiving the antidepressant may feel a bit jumpy, as if on amphetamine—because the receptor-rich receiving cells have been revved up by newly increased levels of stimulus. But as the increased neurotransmitter level in the synapse persists (under the constant drive of the medication), the receiving cell is bombarded into submission. The chronic, constant, reliable presence of high levels of neurotransmitter causes the cell to "downregulate"—reducing the number of receptors, by drawing them back into the cell membrane, where they become inactive, or by otherwise uncoupling them from further events.

But, like the other versions of the amine theory before it, the postsynaptic-hypersensitivity model proved to be wrong. Many flaws have been found with the theory; the strongest in political terms is that Prozac does not downregulate norepinephrine receptors. It is hard to hold to a model of depression that does not fit one of the most widespread contemporary forms of treatment. If there is a final common pathway to depression, it is almost certainly downstream from the receptor—perhaps inside the receiving cell, in the sites where the biological concomitants of learning take place.

But the postsynaptic-hypersensitivity model remains influential in one way: it has focused attention on the chronic changes in state that persist in patients who have been traumatized or who have suffered discrete depressions. Henceforth, any interesting account of depression will need to say something about how the brains of injured people look between acute episodes, when they appear to be functioning well but remain exceedingly vulnerable to stress.

No single theory is able to encompass the vast and complicated body of experiments regarding the cellular basis of depression. As one of the pharmacologists who developed Prozac said to me, given the limits of our current stage of scientific knowledge, "If the human brain were simple enough for us to understand, we would be too simple to understand it."

•   •   •

At the cellular level, there is a kind of standoff. We have a number of inadequate models, most centered on norepinephrine, and we have a highly successful medication, Prozac, that works via the serotonin system. Not long ago, I attended a state-of-the-art conference on chemical correlates of animal models of depression. At the end of the first day of meetings, there was a cocktail party to honor the participants, and I had a chance to speak informally with a man who has worked for decades in this area. I asked him if he has an image of serotonin that guides his research.

The meeting was held in a medical school that sits uneasily within a tough urban area. The researcher waved his drink at me and said something like this:

"Maybe serotonin is the police. The police aren't in one place—they're not in the police station. They are a presence everywhere. They are cruising the city—they are right here. Their potential presence makes you feel secure. It allows you to do many things that also make you feel secure. If you don't have enough police, all sorts of things can happen. You may have riots. The absence of police does not cause riots. But if you do have a riot, and you don't have police, there is nothing to stop the riot from spreading."

Although it fails to explain much of what is known about the biochemistry of mood, I like the model of serotonin-as-police. Yes, serotonin is known to affect sleep, appetite, and the like. But, most dramatically, raising the level of serotonin seems to enhance security, courage, assertiveness, self-worth, calm, flexibility, resilience. Serotonin sets tone. As the researcher at the cocktail party implied, serotonin may not have much to do with depression at all, even though in its absence depression is more likely, and in its presence depression can disappear. Serotonin-as-police goes a way toward explaining why Prozac should be so effective in minor depression, and relatively less effective in major depression. In minor depression, a feeling of security goes a long way; in major depression, a more specific cure is called for. Serotonin-as-police also addresses Prozac's effectiveness in so many different disorders. Panic anxiety, for instance, may be caused by dysregulation of nerves that work via norepinephrine—but a sense of security, induced by adequate serotonin levels, may prevent panic anxiety from ever emerging. More generally, many things will go right when an animal, including a human animal, feels safe.

•   •   •

However promising the research, it is hard to leave a conference on the neurobiology of depression with a feeling of optimism. It seems that the neural pathways are like the joints in the musculoskeletal system. They are worn down over the years by inevitable trauma. If you injure your knee when young, you can perhaps compensate—stabilize the joint—by increasing the strength of the thigh muscles. But repeated injury, and even ordinary wear and tear, or age alone, may weaken the quadriceps to the point where compensation for the old injury is no longer possible.

Age alone seems a trauma in the cortisol model; the system deteriorates over time. The implication seems to be that if we live long enough we will all become depressed, just as we lose resilience in our skin, muscle, and bones. Perhaps we all wage a lifelong struggle against depression, even though those who are blessed with happy childhoods, peppy serotonin systems, and stable adult lives may never feel the effects of the growing dysfunction in their neural connections. There may be mechanisms of repair in these neural systems, ways to learn or relearn resilience. Then again, there is no good biochemical model of repair, only of injury prevention and of compensation. A good many of us may live in compensated states of depression, like the recovered patients on Prozac or MAOI who have become depressed within hours of having their serotonin depleted, perhaps not because their depression is "serotonergic" but because without the police the interrupted riot resumes.

Certainly the rate of suicide increases with age. Compulsiveness, worry, emotional rigidity, a tendency toward catastrophic reactions to stress—these are popularly understood to increase as well. But there is one disputed clinical phenomenon that seems to me to mesh especially well with the view that depression can be a condition of insidious chronic deterioration. I have in mind "late-onset depression," the distinctive mood disorder of those who first experience depression after age sixty.

People who have been healthy all their lives, if they fall prey to depression in old age, tend to be more anxious, hypochondriacal, apathetic, self-reproachful, and suicidal than elderly patients whose first episode of depression occurred early. Like other elderly people who become depressed, late-onset depressives are likely to be more severely depressed, and more often psychotic, than younger adults with depression. But, unlike other elderly depressives, those with late-onset depression stand out in terms of the normality of their background and even their current functioning. Compared with early-onset elderly depressives, late-onset patients are more likely to have normal personality traits, healthy interpersonal relationships, psychologically healthy relatives, and lower levels of recent loss or trauma. The picture of late-onset depression is of a person with no distinctive previous signs of mental illness who suddenly and inexplicably experiences severe depression in which worrisome features, such as the urge to commit suicide, are prominent.

Though the idea of late-onset depression is compatible with the theory that mood-stabilizing systems deteriorate over time, it seems to conflict with the notion of kindling. We might imagine that first episodes of depression, whenever in life they occur, should on average be mild. Yet here is a previously healthy group of people under an ordinary amount of stress who in their first episode of mental disorder suffer the most terrible sort of melancholy. Serotonin-as-police appeals to me as a way of understanding the severity of late-onset depression. Perhaps what we are seeing is a person whose depression-related neural systems (involving, maybe, cortisol or norepinephrine) have deteriorated over time, but whose resilience-related systems (involving, say, serotonin) have been so effective that quite extensive damage has been effectively masked. When the ordinary losses of old age arrive, a final straw—perhaps a very minor stressor, perhaps further age-related erosion of one or another neural network—causes the protective effects of the resilience system to falter, and extensive silent damage is revealed in a sudden and frightening alteration of mood and behavior.

I want to introduce a patient whose first depression occurred late in life, to show how animal and cellular models of mental illness can color the way we see the person in front of us—and the way we see the long near-normal period that precedes overt deterioration.

Daniel is a distinguished scholar who, in his middle sixties, retired from his university post in order to pursue research in fields beyond the narrow boundaries of his academic discipline. His wife, also a scholar, retired in the same year, and at first they both were happy in what seemed an ideal life, spending more time at their vacation house, attending national and international conferences in their professions, and moving ahead on long-postponed writing projects. Daniel, however, suffered from a debilitating flutter of the heart that proved so difficult to treat that he intermittently required brief hospitalizations. Only after much experimentation with combinations of cardiac drugs was the abnormal rhythm contained. Then, suddenly, he became depressed. Anxiety overcame him frequently and left in its wake a sense of depletion of spirit. His mind was filled with foreboding, he felt pangs of guilt that attached themselves to a variety of past events, and he wished for death, spending hours wondering how he could make it come about and not hurt his wife.

This depression did not abate, and in time Daniel was referred to me. He spoke with me for some time before mentioning the events of his adolescence. Born to a German Jewish father and a French Catholic mother, he had spent months early in World War II in a concentration camp—his family was able to buy him out—and later in hiding, and finally in a Swiss internment center. He had many terrible memories. But he had been young and resourceful. In the postwar period, he met an American relief worker, whom he adored, and moved to this country with her. She was assertive and dominant. He had always been rather shy. Despite his successful career, he spent the marriage in his wife's shadow. He had no history of depression —nor had anyone in his family—but he had sometimes felt vulnerable in a hard-to-define way, and he had restricted or circumscribed his life in response. He had chosen to have no children, partly out of a sense that children bring unmanageable disorder, but also because of his wartime experiences and his and his wife's careers. These inhibited aspects of the self were, he felt, minor. He had formed many friend-ships, was well liked by students, and was seen as an approachable and nurturant teacher, a productive and original scholar.

Daniel was crushed by the onset of palpitations. They seemed to him a constant reminder of death, and he had too many horrifying memories of deaths. In the face of the threat of death, he felt infinitely vulnerable, even though other illnesses earlier in life had not elicited this reaction. The recent hospitalizations, too, were traumatic, car-rying overtones, as they did, of previous confinements. In this sense, Daniel's deterioration was understandable, and one could imagine other fruitful lines of inquiry as well. How had retirement affected him? Had extra hours with his still-dominant wife aroused resentment that conflicted with his belief that he owed her a debt of gratitude? And so forth.

Sitting with Daniel, I was struck most by the sense of depletion.

He seemed hollow, a man utterly without resources. His accomplishments, his family, his friends meant nothing. He had been emptied out, and what was left was exquisitely fragile. I had no sense of a struggle within, only of terror and exhaustion.

My first thoughts concerned medicine: perhaps a change in the cardiac regimen would reveal that one of the heart drugs had caused or contributed to the depression. But the balance here was so delicate that the cardiologist was reluctant to consider any change, nor was Daniel willing to risk the least chance that the arrhythmia might return. As an alternative, I suggested antidepressant medication, but this choice also was unacceptable. Daniel was unwilling to take any medication that would affect his mind, and, despite a cautious green light from the cardiologist, Daniel developed an almost delusional fear that antidepressants would make his heartbeat impossible to control. The antidepressant pills became an object for phobic and obsessional concern; he would carry a small number in his pocket and spend hours debating whether to take them, and then he would blame himself for his cowardice. Alternatives in these circumstances are electroconvulsive shock—it presents little risk to the heart, and sometimes it obviates the need for antidepressant medication—or hospitalization. I was reluctant even to raise these possibilities with my patient, and when at last I did, I discovered why. Daniel almost did not return to my office; the mere mention of these procedures made him see me as a sadist and a jailer.

One might imagine that this stalemate would resolve itself, but it did not. Daniel remained on the verge of suicide, unwilling to change his cardiac regimen, unwilling to risk a biological approach to his depression. And so we talked. I tried to create a setting in which this gentle, perceptive scholar could feel safe, in which he could discuss memories, fears, anger, grief. (The emphasis on safety before insight, in my therapy with Daniel, may already reveal my acceptance of a psychobiological model of damage and cure.) This approach was of some use. The relentless depression lifted and was replaced by a waxing and waning condition in which Daniel had days and sometimes weeks in which he felt normal. These good periods never lasted long, nor did Daniel seem to me entirely free of depression even at his best. He had a warm, lively, impish quality that now and then, pentimento-style, showed through the dense depression— a glimpse of how he would appear if well. Nothing we did restored him entirely, though in time he was able, as before, to write and publish, attend meetings, and travel.

Having seen other instances of late-onset depression (for I believe the category represents a useful distinction and that Daniel was suffering a representative case), I was not surprised by this chain of events. My image of the patient's inner state had disappointingly little to do with cognition and memory. I saw these terrible late years in an exemplary life as a consequence of the long-acting poison of trauma. That is to say, my sense of the patient was dominated by the animal and cellular models of depression. Here was a man whose hormone and neurotransmitter systems were battered by terrible inescapable stress early in life. Various compensatory mechanisms—and now I am alluding to biological compensation as well as defenses like repression, sublimation, reaction formation, and intellectualization —allowed him to lead a rather normal life throughout middle adulthood. But the covert progressive deterioration continued.

Although I am talking in highly speculative terms, my version of events corresponds to the consensus view of deterioration and overt disease held by scientists who work on the stress and kindling models in animals. Differing sources of damage can cause deleterious changes that may remain hidden, or only intermittently apparent, as long as they can be compensated for in a variety of ways. But there comes a day when compensation fails, and catastrophic changes in mood and behavior suddenly appear. (Indeed, we might guess that the stronger the individual is—and the more adept, biologically and psychologically, at compensation—the greater will be the extent of previously masked injury when the break finally occurs.) There are many examples in medicine of biological systems that can suffer major damage that remains inapparent. We survive easily with one kidney or the smallest fraction of working liver. But finally the balance is tipped, and the overwhelming damage is revealed all at once.

Certainly for Daniel the palpitations represented a new stressor, as did the brief hospitalizations. The immediate experience was traumatic, and it revived painful memories. We are symbol-centered creatures, and some of our worst stresses are symbolic. But to my mind these final causes were like the pebbles that finally turn a tenuously balanced collection of rocks into an avalanche. I had only a weak faith that repositioning the pebbles would cause the boulders to roll back up the mountain.

Daniel's own preference was to discuss his memories, a choice I would ordinarily welcome: what better way to treat depression than to explore its sources in repressed images of terror and suffering? But I found myself, in terms of my loyalty to the precepts of psychotherapy, something of an agnostic priest. Now that I had been exposed to the concept of progressive damage to transmitter systems, it no longer seemed as likely to me that re-examination of the events of half a century ago would reverse Daniel's catastrophic depression. I did try treating Daniel with psychotherapy. But as I sat with him, I was mostly struck by a sense that the biological underpinnings for mood had been badly weakened, and that what we were dealing with went so far beyond cognition that the patient's preference for psychological cures—for courage, for fortitude, perhaps for the very qualities that had permitted him to survive in earlier years—was now serving him ill.

I present this case as an example of the way in which the availability of medication, and the medication-supported predominance of biological models, influences the way we are likely to frame a human predicament. How extraordinary it is to see the depression of a concentration-camp survivor as finally a physiological event. It is conventional to call such an approach "reductionist," as if seeing mood and behavior in psychobiological terms diminished the person's humanity, and seeing them in purely psychological terms aggrandized or at least properly acknowledged that humanity. But I wonder if this dichotomy is always apt.

I am thinking of the late-life suicide of another concentration-camp survivor, the peerless writer Primo Levi. After his incarceration in Auschwitz, Levi, a paint chemist, returned to his native Italy and began writing essays, short stories, and novels of the Holocaust and its moral conundrums, all in an unerringly humane voice. Though he recognized the randomness of survival, he stood, through his person as well as his writerly persona, for hope, perseverance, and survival. It therefore came as a shock—even a personal injury—to his friends and his readers when, in 1987, he killed himself at the age of sixty-seven. So unwilling was a distant friend of Levi's—a British cardiologist who had met and corresponded with him—to acknowledge the suicide that he wrote an article propounding a theory by which the death could be seen as accidental. Levi's family declined to comment on his death, but certain facts are widely accepted. Levi was being treated for depression; his antidepressant regimen had recently been changed; his mother, to whom he remained close, had become ill; and he had recovered from minor surgery not long before his death.

Levi's suicide is hard to accept because it seems a failure of will. It disappoints us to think that human beings, especially those who have become icons, are not infinitely resilient—that they should change their minds and turn pessimistic and hopeless. To me, there is a sense in which the animal models, and the concept of late-onset depression, make Levi's suicide less shocking, less unexpected, more human; they may even enhance our appreciation of Levi's hardiness, in the face of the physiological forces tending to pull him toward dysfunction. The concentration camp attacks not just the soul but the animal part of man—attacks the soul largely through the animal. In this case, and in many others, we might want to say that biological models are not reductionistic but humanizing, in the sense that they restore scale and perspective and take into account the vast part of us that is not intellect.

The kindling model has the power to influence the way we see a range of mood states rooted in trauma, from Levi's suicidal depression to Lucy's sensitivity and Tess's seriousness. But how are we to understand the quite similar emotional difficulties of people—Sam, Gail, Julia—whose lives are devoid of dramatic losses and whose personality traits can be traced back to their earliest years? Here, too, medication response—especially that most puzzling phenomenon, the reshaping of personality traits by medication—may lead us to attend to a series of experiments and hypotheses it might otherwise have been easy to ignore.

CHAPTER
6

Risk

Two of my patients entered into marriages while taking Prozac. The first, a constitutionally sunny woman who found herself increasingly withdrawn in the years following her divorce from an erratic husband, rediscovered on medication the vigor and confidence she needed to rejoin the life of her community. This result, though gratifying, was perhaps unremarkable. But the second patient was a woman who had since early childhood stood at the periphery of the social universe. For her, marriage was an extraordinary achievement, a sign of victory over a crippling aspect of the self.

Sally had been temperamentally shy for as long as she could remember. As a young child, she never left her mother's side. She needed to be coaxed to talk even to family members, and she was always uncomfortable in conversation. Except for walking to school, she spent little time with girlfriends, and she avoided boys entirely. Throughout grade school, she was afraid of her teachers and would vomit breakfast every morning. At night, she was prone to fears of darkness, witches, and death.

Sally's parents, who were themselves quiet and inward-looking —prone to depression and a variety of physical ailments—did not find her behavior remarkable. They were easily overwhelmed and

144

intolerant of upset or intrusions. They expected Sally, from an early age, to care for her youngest sister, to behave while listening to adult conversation, and to socialize only at church and family functions.

This limited social circle did not protect Sally from trauma. Entering puberty, she was for a number of months sexually violated by an uncle who had heretofore treated her as a favorite niece. When Sally was twelve, her family suffered financial reverses. They moved into cramped quarters, where Sally was exposed to her parents' sexual behavior, an experience that left her troubled about her mother's submissiveness. Sally worried that the family would have another baby for her to tend.

By junior high school, Sally had come to feel that other children were more sophisticated than she, although she now was able to participate in group activities with girls. Sally's social inhibition did not prevent certain boys from telephoning her in high school, but the family discouraged dating and forbade makeup. Though she loved dancing, in all of high school Sally was allowed to attend only two dances, on chaperoned double dates.

After high school, Sally took an entry-level job at a large bank. At first she received promotions, but she remained afraid of entering a management position and soon was taken for granted and passed over by her superiors. She never had conflicts with her co-workers, but they kept their distance, because Sally seemed not to know how to act, have fun, or judge social limits. She stayed at the same job in the same department for eighteen years and began to worry more about losing her job than about progressing. She counted as friends a few women she had known since childhood; her contacts with men were infrequent and disappointing. Her home life remained remarkably unchanged—when her sisters moved out, Sally began caring for her parents—except that Sally's resentment broke through to the surface and she became openly desperate.

Before she came to the office, Sally wrote me a note. It began, "I am forty-one years old. I feel angry and hurt most of the time. I feel like my spirit has been shattered and fragmented with each piece having been trampled on and bruised. I am very, very anxious. I am afraid of everything, even centipedes and roaches. I keep thinking something very, very bad is going to happen to me, some great misfortune, or that I'll become handicapped and have to depend on people to take care of me. I don't know who I am, because that person stopped growing at the age of four, and it makes me very sad."

That Sally could formulate such a statement was a tribute to the psychotherapy she had engaged in over the course of many years with two talented social workers. The most recent therapy, however, had only made her more aware of her limitations and frustrations. At our first meeting, Sally had symptoms of depression: exhaustion, tearfulness, and poor concentration.

This story resembles others we have heard with one significant difference, the important role of inhibited temperament. Sally's shyness seems to have "been there from the start." Her mother, her mother's mother, her father, and her sisters all, to a greater or lesser degree, shared this trait. Because of Sally's entrenched timidity and social discomfort, there is a sameness to her life, a terrible monotony. In childhood, Sally's story has some of the lows but none of the highs we expect in a life history; in adult life, there are altogether too few ups and downs. Though before midlife Sally had never thought of herself as depressed, her social isolation and lack of confidence, combined with difficult circumstances, resulted in a life of intolerable bleakness.

Social introversion, when well established in adult life, is a difficult trait to change. I prescribed Prozac for Sally with an eye mainly toward her depressive symptoms but also with some hope of making a more profound difference.

Sally had been anxious in my presence at our first meeting, but she showed a touch of stubbornness, too—she was going to see treatment through, despite her fears. And though she looked younger than forty, there was nothing cloying or falsely naïve about Sally; she was going to work with whatever I could give her. After two months, she felt less depressed and much more angry. Indeed, Sally's anger was cause for concern, because irritability can be an early sign of mania, and mania is an infrequent bad outcome of antidepressant treatment. I lowered Sally's Prozac dose to half a capsule per day (ten milligrams), but I did not discontinue the medicine. Part of me was pleased to see Sally get angry: if we had been using only psychotherapy and not medication, I would have expected Sally's progress to include a period of anger—at her parents, at her superiors, at everyone who took advantage of her timidity.

In the third month, Sally remained angry and a bit too wired and bubbly. But after four months on Prozac, she looked brighter, calmer, self-assured, in firm control of herself. The most important effect of the medication, Sally felt, was that it cleared her head—made her more awake and aware, more confident of her perceptions. She said, "The medicine helps me to clarify problems. It takes me less time to find positive solutions. I don't panic. I don't feel my 'brain hurts' under stress, and I do not obsess."

After ten months on medication—her highest dose was one (twenty-milligram) capsule six days per week—Sally was decidedly more assertive at work. She negotiated a small promotion and pay raise at a time when the bank was cutting back staff, and she trained others to do some of the routine parts of her job.

More remarkable was the change in her private life. She started going to dances, making up for lost time. She even asked men to dance, and she dated a number of them. One she dropped because he drank; another because he bored her. After a year, she was dating two men steadily, without worrying how things would turn out and without letting either one pressure her into a premature choice. She was able to forgive men's faults: "They may be a little rough around the edges, but they can be fun." She was not afraid of men, or self-conscious around them.

I felt concern that Sally may have "overshot," that this new personality was too different from her old one. She demurred. She said the Prozac had let her personality emerge at last—she had not been alive before taking an antidepressant. Sally insisted I not stop the medication, but I tapered the dose slightly.

After a year and a half on a low dose of Prozac, Sally came in to tell me she was engaged. She was confident the man was the right one. He was divorced, with grown children, a successful businessman whose cultural background was similar to her own. She had been very strong in her dealings with him, negotiating her role in relation to finances, the children's visits, and other issues that arise in marriages later in life. "I never understood what people meant when they said things felt right. This is a big step, but I feel good about it. I am moving along fast, but not too fast. I love him, and he loves me. Before, I only felt closed in; now I feel happy."

● ● ●

Though Sally was abused in adolescence, her story—especially the persistence from early childhood of her shyness and timidity—raises questions about inborn predisposition to social behavior. We are talking, of course, about temperament, and, since inexactness is easy in this area, before going further I should say something about the words used to describe aspects of individual identity.

"Temperament" usually refers to an inborn, genetically determined and chemically mediated, predisposition to a cluster of responses and behaviors. Psychiatrists use the term sometimes to refer only to very basic functions, such as rhythmicity (is a person or an animal regular in its sleep-wake cycle, feeding and hunger schedule, etc.?), and sometimes to denote a cluster of functions, such as the optimism, heartiness, and energy of the sanguine temperament.

"Temperament" is generally contrasted to "character," which refers to stable, repeated behavior patterns arising from life experience. "Character" is also used to refer to a person's idiosyncratic traits or, more particularly, to a person's moral fiber; alternatively, it can refer to the defenses developed in response to different fears—a person's "character armor." "Character" describes acquired traits; it is environmental where temperament is inborn, psychological where temperament is biological.

"Personality" refers to the whole picture of habitual or characteristic social behavior and response to challenge, an amalgam of temperament and character. So permeated is our language by ancient scientific and philosophical theories that we can hardly discuss personality without falling back on words—"habitual," "characteristic," "typical"—that take sides in a centuries-old controversy.

Today, the dividing line between temperament and character is difficult to maintain. If trauma alters our biology, it changes our— what? Though the new traits are "acquired," and therefore constitute character, they arise from rewired neural circuitry, so we might want to say that what has changed is our temperament. And what about the effects of medication? The changed propensities that result, though surely they are acquired and not inborn, are due to altered brain chemistry. Therefore, we might want to say medication acts on temperament, except that, when it makes Tess less self-sacrificing, we want to say it has altered her (moral) character. For the sake of clarity, in this chapter I will use "temperament" to refer to the biological underpinnings of personality, even if the biology has been shaped or altered by circumstance or chemicals. In this sense, an adult's medicated temperament will differ from his or her "inborn temperament." It must—the neural chemistry with which we arrive in the world is inevitably modified by development, environment, life events, and now by discrete medicine. What we now know about the interaction of biology and experience tells us that the distinction between temperament and character will always be arbitrary and artificial.

●　●　●

For years, temperament in humans was the tar pit of psychological research. Whole careers disappeared into it. Every study that correlated childhood temperament with adult personality style was immediately followed by two or three refuting the same hypothesis. Worse, studies of temperament were sociologically suspect. The field was rooted in Carl Jung's concept of "attitudes"—introversion and extraversion—and was felt on a historical and also what might be called an aesthetic basis to be connected to Nazism, racism, and a denial of human equality and free will. In recent years, as much because of a change in zeitgeist as because of any dramatic shift in the evidence, temperament is once again fair ground for exploration. Indeed, when we try in today's climate to make sense of Sally's life, it is difficult to avoid consideration of a heritable predisposition to timidity—so difficult that we can perhaps scarcely imagine what a comparable discussion, omitting any such consideration, would have been like ten years ago.

The new research into inborn temperament has been both pioneered and popularized by the Harvard child psychologist Jerome Kagan. There are many components to temperament and personality. Kagan's genius lies in having focused on just one, inhibition. His work has been enormously influential.

Kagan began with three hundred twenty-one-month-old infants, a group from which he selected the 10 percent who were at each extreme—those who were most consistently shy, quiet, and timid, and those who were most consistently sociable, talkative, and emotionally spontaneous. The twenty-one-month-olds were tested by having their mothers bring them to an unfamiliar playroom with unfamiliar women and toys. In videotapes, the infants were rated for clinging to the mother, diminution of vocalization, and reluctance to approach objects or strangers. Later, thirty-one-month-olds (all of those tested ten months earlier and some others) were rated according to the time elapsed before they would interact, speak, or play with an unfamiliar child. Although the shy, timid children, for the most part, had experienced no serious trauma, their social responses paralleled those of the temperamentally normal but environmentally stressed young monkeys in Suomi's research—the ones who, after mild forms of separation from their mothers, showed inhibited behaviors, ranging from withdrawal in the face of strange objects to a diminished tendency to explore or affiliate.

The children in Kagan's study were retested in age-appropriate ways at two, three and a half, five and a half, and seven and a half years. For instance, by age seven and a half, a single unfamiliar child is not sufficiently stressful; the test condition involves introduction into a group of seven to ten children.

Kagan found that social inhibition tended to persist over time. In descriptive terms, he wrote of the seven-and-a-half-year-olds: "A frequent scene during the play sessions was a cluster of three or four children playing close to each other, often talking, and one or two children standing or playing alone one to several meters from the center of social activity. These isolated, quiet children were typically those who had been classified as inhibited 5 or 6 years earlier."

Children did not always remain "true to type." Supportive and assertive parents could sometimes move children out of the inhibited group, and there was a great deal of variability in the uninhibited group. Indeed, it looked as if *lack* of inhibition was not a special category—it existed on a spectrum with normal, and there were fluid changes in and out of the category. Nor did more minor degrees of inhibition make children special. But extreme inhibition appeared to be a distinct and relatively stable phenomenon.

These findings alone were not dramatic. Kagan believes that 15 percent of children are born inhibited. (In his study, however, Kagan did not identify nearly this many inhibited twenty-one-month-olds; he had an especially difficult time identifying inhibited boys.) Although as a group the severely inhibited children remain distinctive, a third to perhaps half of them are normally uninhibited by age seven. Kagan has estimated that, "for every ten children who are extremely shy in the second year of life, only five will be very shy in kindergarten and first grade; by adolescence, only three. By their twenties, only one or two will still be very shy. . . ." In other words, only 10 or

20 percent of the original cohort of 15 percent will remain shy. This amounts to 1.5 to 3 percent of adults. But not all shy adults will have been inhibited infants; some people—perhaps one in a hundred?—become inhibited on the basis of environmental trauma. The Kagan experiment, seen objectively, involves observing a group of, say, one hundred healthy toddlers and saying, "I will choose fifteen of the toddlers and predict that in this group are one or two who, in adulthood, will be among the two or three shyest of the original one hundred." This is not a very astounding achievement— and we do not yet know whether Kagan has pulled the trick off.

What has made the Kagan study more interesting is the extension of the inquiry into the realm of physiology. Kagan and his colleagues looked mainly at correlates of norepinephrine and the stress hormones. For instance, at age five and a half, children's urine was tested for breakdown products of norepinephrine, and their saliva for a form of cortisol. The neurotransmitter ratings correlated modestly with the children's current level of inhibition, and the hormone ratings correlated modestly with the children's original behavioral ratings as infants. In other words, both acutely and chronically, the inhibited children seemed to have the physiology of an animal under stress.

The strongest and most consistent findings, however, had to do with heart rate. Kagan looked at two measures: how fast the heart was beating and how much variability there was in the interval between heartbeats. Ordinarily, our heart rate rises and falls slightly as we breathe, and of course heart rate speeds when we are stressed. The two measures are related: the faster the heart rate, the less the beat-to-beat variability. From infancy, the inhibited children—who were selected according to behavior, not heart function—showed a high and invariant heart rate. They showed this pattern even when asleep. The children with the highest heart rates in infancy were those most likely to remain inhibited through age seven and a half. Children with intense fears at age five and a half or seven and a half (for instance, fear of kidnappers, of going to bed alone, of violence on television) were in the group with high heart rates; the group with low heart rates contained no fearful children. These and other measures (such as tightness of the vocal cords, as measured by analysis of quavering in tapes of children's speech) seemed to indicate that severely inhibited children are biologically different: they are in a state of constant arousal from infancy, and many of them remain in that state throughout childhood.

Having conducted these initial studies, Kagan speculated that "most of the children we call inhibited belong to a qualitatively distinct category of infants who were born with a lower threshold for limbic-hypothalamic [that is, norepinephrine- and stress-hormone-mediated] arousal to unexpected changes in the environment or novel events that cannot be assimilated easily." He made this statement, however, before having studied the physiology of inhibited newborns. Kagan had demonstrated that children who are socially inhibited around age two tend to have high and invariant heart rates. These children account for a high percentage of those who are socially inhibited as five- to eight-year-olds; and by that age inhibited children show the rapid turnover of norepinephrine and the high levels of cortisol typical of chronic physiological arousal.

Kagan also speculated that the translation of inhibited temperament into inhibited behavior requires environmental trauma—in other words, he propounded what is called a stress/risk model of inhibition, one in which the condition arises in children at risk only if they are also stressed. He predicted that inhibition as a behavioral trait would emerge primarily in children who had been stressed by such events as "prolonged hospitalization, death of a parent, marital quarreling, or mental illness in a family member," but the inhibited children in his sample had, in fact, experienced few such events. Kagan then looked elsewhere for stressors. Two-thirds of Kagan's uninhibited children were firstborn, as against only one-third of the inhibited. Kagan speculates, "An older sibling who unexpectedly seizes a toy, teases, or yells at an infant who has a low threshold for limbic arousal might provide the chronic stress necessary to transform the temperamental quality into the profile we call behavioral inhibition."

Kagan's more fundamental conclusion, that inhibition is largely grounded in inborn temperament, was modestly supported by his early experiments. The evidence was not overwhelming. Inhibition was a stable trait, but only to a degree: most inhibited infants blended with the average population in time, and a substantial number even came to overlap on test results with the children selected for lack of inhibition. Tests were not conducted over a long enough period to demonstrate a correlation with adult personality. There was no proof that the inhibition shown by the twenty-one- and thirty-one-month-old infants was inborn temperament rather than a result of yet earlier trauma. Nonetheless, the appearance, in *Science* magazine in 1988, of Kagan's overview of his research had a dramatic effect in legitimizing the discussion of inborn temperament, the part of personality that is innate.

Some of the impact had to do with who Kagan is and what he stands for. In the 1960s, Kagan was a leader in opposing the contention that intelligence is largely heritable. The debate over IQ—whether it measures intelligence, whether it measures the same thing in blacks and whites, and whether it is heritable—was especially heated. Those who concluded that IQ is heritable were branded as racists and sometimes banned from or shouted down at campus lecture halls. The assertion in the eighties that personality is partly heritable had greater effect coming from a thoughtful, eloquent Harvard professor who had in the sixties opposed an arguably more limited proposition of behavioral genetics.

Kagan's work on shyness was careful and comprehensive, and, relative to other sets of studies of inborn temperament, its results were strong. Kagan and others were also able, in the few years after the influential

monograph in *Science,* to bolster the hypothesis that observed differences were due to nature rather than nurture.

For instance, Kagan's group had found inhibited children to differ
in a genetic trait. Among white children, more inhibited children
and their parents, brothers, and sisters had blue eyes, whereas more
uninhibited children and their first degree relatives had brown eyes.
There also turned out to be an excess of allergies among relatives of
inhibited infants, so that the constellation of blue eyes, hay fever,
and temperamental shyness may be a distinct syndrome.

These findings were followed up by further laboratory studies. A
group at Brown University gave a novel stimulus to newborns by
suddenly changing the content of what they were sucking from water
to sugar water. All newborns increase their rate of sucking in response
to the sugar water. But some infants change their rate of sucking
dramatically; they are said to be more "avid." Avidity is thought to
be a measure of arousal, vigilance, and awareness of novelty—traits
that relate to later inhibition. And, indeed, those infants who are
most avid on the first or second day of life were found to be most
inhibited at a year and a half.

Kagan's group tested four-month-olds and found that those who
had more motor movements (such as flexing and extending arms or
legs, arching the back, and sticking out the tongue) and more fretful
crying in response to unusual toys and sounds were more often inhibited at later ages. Kagan's work-in-progress, aimed at examining
possible antenatal precursors of inhibition, is extending this inquiry
into the womb, correlating high and invariant heart rates in fetuses
with childhood temperament.

Researchers are also extending inhibited-temperament research in the
other direction. Not enough time has elapsed for researchers to follow
inhibited infants into adulthood, but adult relatives of inhibited
infants seem unusually prone to conditions such as panic anxiety; and
there is suggestive evidence that among these relatives is a greater-

than-average number of inhibited adults. The result of inhibition may not be limited to anxiety; one study has found that among mildly depressed adults a disproportionate number had experienced extreme shyness in childhood compared to the general population.

This field of study, inhibited temperament, consists of a large body of modest, tentative experimental results. But the scope of the field is remarkable—from the fetus to the adult—and by and large the quality of the studies is excellent. As a result, something like a consensus has arisen in psychology and psychiatry that certain children are born different—different in terms of the reactivity of their stress-hormone systems, and therefore different in their response to novelty—and that this difference can lead to later social inhibition and probably to various disturbances of mood. People don't have to be made vulnerable by trauma: they can be born vulnerable.

•　　•　　•

We have seen that in rhesus monkeys early separation can produce a sensitivity to subsequent separations. The animals tested in those studies are either unselected or bred for genetic uniformity. That is, they are normal animals, and the chronic disturbances they suffer, including inhibition in the face of novel stimuli, can presumably be produced in any member of the species. But it looks as if monkeys can also be born sensitive, and work with those monkeys has lent strong support to Kagan's research on innate temperament.

In his observation of a breeding colony of rhesus monkeys, Stephen Suomi was able to identify individuals—20 percent of rhesus young—who appeared anxious and shy. Suomi called these monkeys "uptight" and contrasted them to the other 80 percent, who responded more flexibly to challenge, the "laid-back" macaques. Even more than in humans, Suomi found that in monkeys "differences in response to novelty and challenge show up very early in life and are stable over the life span." Differences are observable from the time infants first "stray from their mother and explore the environment."

Using four-month-old monkeys, Suomi replicated Kagan's research, starting with the sorts of challenges to which Kagan exposed twenty-one-month-old children. As with the human infants, the uptight monkeys were slower to explore a playroom, and they tended to have high and invariant heart rates and elevated levels of stress hormones. On subsequent exposures to the playroom, this contrast faded; differences in quickness to explore showed themselves only in response to novelty.

Kagan's and Suomi's models were influenced by earlier monkey studies looking at heart rate and behavior. Fifteen years ago, it was observed that reactive monkey infants—those who at age one month have a pronounced change in heart rate in anticipation of irritating noise— develop, by age two and one half years, a heightened behavioral disturbance in response to handling by humans. The study was remarkable for its findings regarding the origins of this variability. The monkey infants were "nursery-reared" together, so all had received the same environmental "mothering." Some of the monkeys were also similar genetically: though they had different biological mothers, groups of two to three shared a biological father and were thus half-siblings. In terms of heart rate—and, later, sensitivity to handling —monkeys grouped very closely according to their paternity. The two monkeys with the greatest agitation when handled had the same biological father. Three of the four monkeys with the least agitation in response to handling had the same biological father. For a behavioral trait to sort out cleanly among *half*-siblings so far into the middle of childhood implies the presence of a genetic factor with a very robust influence.

A simple recent test using the Kagan/Suomi paradigm again demonstrates the strong impact of genetics on reactivity. Researchers looked at monkey pairs who on first mating produced an uptight infant. These parents were mated again, and the second offspring were immediately given to adoptive mothers. These adoptive mothers had been selected to be either uptight or laid-back. Whatever the adoptive mothers' degree of reactivity, these infants biologically at risk for inhibition emerged uptight.

In another study, monkey infants tested to be either uptight or laid-back were given to adoptive mothers who were more complexly selected. As in the last study, the adoptive mothers were chosen because they were either uptight or laid-back. In addition, they were selected according to whether they had been highly nurturant and protective or more punitive and rejecting in their maternal style with earlier offspring. Whether reared by laid-back or uptight new mothers—and whether reared by nurturant or demanding mothers —the infants tended to remain true to heritable type. The reactivity or nurturance of the adoptive monkey mother had no effect on the way her adopted infant reacted to novel challenges. Suomi concluded, "Clearly, for these infants the only significant predictor of scores on the neonatal measures was the infants' pedigree."

High reactivity or "uptightness" in rhesus monkeys looks a good deal like the minor disturbances of mood we have seen in human patients. Uptight monkeys behave normally when well supported. When separated from mother or peer group, initially they look more anxious than do their laid-back age-mates; upon longer separation, the uptight monkeys become withdrawn or depressed. The constant pattern throughout life is anxiety in the face of acute challenge and depression in the face of chronic stress. In adolescence, the monkeys who were uptight in infancy tend when stressed to fiddle in front of their cages or engage in other repetitive, stereotypic behavior. These tendencies—to anxiety, depression, and compulsiveness—increase with age and repeated challenge, as do parallel abnormalities in neurotransmitters.

Like traumatized monkeys, monkeys who are "born reactive" are nonspecifically "neurotic." Throughout life, they are especially prone to both anxious responses to novelty and depressive reactions to separation. When allowed to self-administer alcohol, they drink more when under stress than do low-reactive monkeys. Like "inhibited" humans, reactive monkeys are more likely to show allergic reactions starting in infancy.

What researchers have hypothesized about innate temperament in humans has been conclusively demonstrated by Suomi in rhesus monkeys. Monkeys do not need to be subjected to traumatic stress to become sensitive: they can be born uptight.

•   •   •

Seeing the monkey and human observations juxtaposed, the reality of inborn temperament may seem irrefutable. Some people are just born with a liability to grow up shy, quiet, timid, and vulnerable to stress or challenge, whereas others are likely to become, in Kagan's words, "consistently sociable, affectively spontaneous, and minimally fearful in the same unfamiliar situations." But it is worthwhile, I think, to remind ourselves that only a few years ago this same evidence might have been viewed differently—that for decades rather similar evidence was routinely dismissed. Studies showing high and invariant heart rates in inhibited dogs, for example, go back to the 1940s, as do reports regarding similarities in the degree of shyness in identical twins. And studies of reactivity among half-sibling monkeys were already quite advanced fifteen years ago.

Even before the era of formal studies of temperament, Carl Jung described "those reserved, inscrutable, rather shy people who form the strongest possible contrast to the open, sociable, jovial or at least friendly and approachable characters. . . ." Jung argued that these differences could not be accounted for by Freud's theory of sexual dynamism. Jung wrote, "The fact that children exhibit a typical attitude quite unmistakably even in their earliest years forces us to assume it cannot be a struggle for existence in the ordinary sense that determines a particular attitude." Citing the common occurrence of different personality "types" among children of the same mother, he concluded that, unless the mother's attitude is extreme, "Ultimately, it must be the individual disposition which decides whether the child will belong to this or that type despite the constancy of external conditions." Jung speculated that the cause of both extraversion and introversion is biological and based on evolutionary adaptation for the benefit of the species. "The one [extraversion] consists in a high rate of fertility, with low powers of defence and short duration of life for the single individual; the other consists in equipping the individual with numerous means of self-preservation plus a low fertility rate."

The extent of Jung's application of his beliefs regarding human "types" to contemporary racist dogma, and of his cooperation with the Nazis, is the subject of heated historical controversy. Certainly, late in World War II and afterward, Jung was horrified by the Nazis. But before the war, in 1934, Jung had accepted the editorship of the newly Nazified and Jew-free *Zentralblatt für Psychotherapie;* and he had opened the journal with an attack on Freudianism in which he argued, "The Aryan unconscious has a higher potential than the Jewish. . . . In my opinion it has been a great mistake of all previous medical psychology to apply Jewish categories which are not binding even to Jews, indiscriminately to Christians, Germans, or Slavs." It is fair to say that his views could be and were used to bolster the (already prevalent) concept of breeds within the human species, and to develop the Nazi depiction of Jews as the culturally destructive "antitype."

Because of the relationship of Jung's "types" to Nazi racism, and also because of the use of twisted biological determinism to bolster racism in the United States, the concept of temperament was culturally taboo throughout the forties and later, during the civil-rights struggles in the fifties, sixties, and seventies. Instead, the prevailing attitude was that enunciated by Margaret Mead in her studies in the 1930s of "primitive societies" in which women displayed personality traits associated in Western culture with maleness—namely, that "human nature is almost unbelievably malleable, responding accurately and contrastingly to contrasting cultural conditions." The concept of near-total malleability is especially appealing in an egalitarian society, and the idea of genetic determinism is especially alien. Carl N. Degler, a sociologist who has written an exhaustive study of the rise (and current descent) of cultural determinism in America, makes it clear that the role of scientific findings in the decline of biological determinism was limited: "The main impetus came from the wish to establish a social order in which innate and immutable forces of biology played no role in accounting for the behavior of social groups. . . . To the proponents of culture the goal was the elimination of nativity, race, and sex, and any other biologically based characteristic that might serve as an obstacle to an individual's self-realization."

Kagan has speculated that America was receptive to Freud precisely because of Freud's belief that experience determines personality. In introducing one of his recent studies, Kagan refers to "The return of the idea of temperament to discussions of personality after half a century of exile. . . ."

Forceful arguments are still made against the use of animal models in the study of human behavior. In a recent polemic against biological determinism, the evolutionary geneticist Richard C. Lewontin and colleagues repeatedly refer to the dissimilarity of human and animal brains. And, because human social behavior has never been linked successfully to particular genes, Lewontin contends that "all statements about the genetic basis of human social traits are necessarily purely speculative, no matter how positive they seem to be." But Lewontin's assertion sounds merely tendentious in today's scientific and cultural environment.

Without the related animal studies, we might conclude that Kagan's evidence for inhibited temperament is not overwhelming. Part of what makes Kagan's results convincing is that they confirm "what every parent knows"—namely, that infants are different, and that often parents do not so much influence personality as watch it develop. My sense is that, throughout our culture, the current assumption is that humans differ temperamentally, not just as regards inhibition, but in almost every aspect of personality.

•   •   •

Certainly hearing Sally's story makes it hard not to think about social inhibition, both as a matter of inborn predisposition and as an outcome of early stressors. Social inhibition, rather than depression or any distinct anxiety disorder, is the single quality most responsible for Sally's social and professional stagnation and for her unhappiness. Some psychiatrists and psychologists, however, would have difficulty with this point of view—not least because, if we attribute Sally's woes to personality rather than illness, when she recovers we must conclude that personality is what medication has altered. These clinicians have a different understanding of temperament: they believe it is less related to social qualities, such as shyness, than to chronic mood states.

In Sally's case, this alternative view would suggest that she becomes socially successful on Prozac because she is revved up. Patients prone to mania, the extreme and often psychotic state in which the brain is racing, sometimes enjoy a less extreme state of euphoria and energy, called "hypomania." "The goal is controlled hypomania," a pharmacologist once said to me. The relevant factor, according to this theory, is not what Kagan calls "inhibition" (and what Suomi calls "reactivity") but some broad measure of depression—whether Sally is sufficiently energetic, quick-thinking, sexually driven, optimistic, and sparkling.

The notion that people differ in affective, as opposed to social, temperament goes back to the beginnings of medicine, to the theory of the humors. The belief that both health and characteristic mood are governed by substances that flow through the body predates the earliest Greek medical texts available to us, from the fifth century B.C., and prevails in the medical literature almost to the present day. The classic humors are phlegm, blood, yellow bile (choler), and black bile, giving rise to the phlegmatic, sanguine, choleric, and melancholic temperaments. "Melan-cholia" is simply Greek for "black bile."

Hippocrates' *Nature of Man* is a treatise on the humors. Aristotle assumed that affective tone was set by the humors; like modern researchers who have found an association between mood disorder and creativity, Aristotle asked, "Why is it that all those who have become eminent in philosophy or politics or poetry or the arts are clearly of an atrabilious [that is, melancholic] temperament, and some of them to such an extent as to be affected by diseases caused by black bile?" The Greek concept of melancholic temperament is repeated in medical texts in astonishingly unaltered form throughout Western history—during the Middle Ages and the Renaissance and well into the eighteenth and even nineteenth centuries. Of Jung's "introversion" and "extraversion" we have already spoken; Freud's contemporary Kraepelin also recognized a depressive disposition. It is really only in the heyday of hidebound, theory-burdened post-Freudian psychoanalysis that the melancholic temperament drops from view and personality is assumed to be rooted mostly in experience. Today, in the era of the "neurohumors" (norepinephrine, serotonin), affective temperament has made a comeback, most notably in the work of Hagop Akiskal, a psychiatrist now at the National Institute of Mental Health who conducted most of his research at the University of Tennessee. Akiskal has devoted his career to the understanding and classification of minor affective disorders.

Akiskal believes that a good deal of what looks like personality, or personality disorder, is a *forme fruste,* or incompletely expressed version, of overt mental illness. Akiskal worked with a large number of patients in a private outpatient clinic in Memphis; he also collaborated with researchers who replicated his work in Europe. In these patient populations, he identified a variety of common personality types, including the depressive personality.

Before the advent of Prozac, Akiskal distinguished two forms of depressive personality. In both groups, patients reported having always felt depressed—since early childhood or adolescence. One group had a history of stress or loss; they tended to have had either a parent who was alcoholic or one who died while they were young. Akiskal assumed these patients' problems lay in the realm of character. Another group of patients with depressive personality reported a family history of overt depressive illness, especially manic depression. Even though they themselves were for the most part not acutely depressed, these patients tended not only to respond to antidepressants but also frequently to "overshoot" and become manic. Akiskal considered these people to have an "attenuated or 'subaffective dysthymic' disorder"—that is, to suffer a low-level chronic depression on a temperamental basis. Akiskal's subaffective dysthymia—a modern version of the melancholic humor—sounds like an alternative understanding not only of Sally, with her marked social inhibition, but also of certain other patients, such as Gail or Tess:

> These individuals, who are introverted, obsessional, self-sacrificing, brooding, guilt-ridden, gloomy, self-denigrating, anhedonic, lethargic, and who tend to oversleep, appear to be suffering from an attenuated but lifelong form of melancholia. . . . These dysthymic individuals were characterized by inability to enjoy leisure and overdedication to work that requires selfless devotion and much attention to detail. However, this stable adjustment in the vocational sphere was not paralleled in social adjustment. The somber personalities and intense attachment needs of these individuals may drive others away. Such interpersonal losses then cause them to sink into the lower depths of black humor.

Among the most enduring traits of depressive personality are introversion and social maladroitness, features reminiscent of inhibition in children.

Akiskal relies on a variety of evidence to argue that subaffective dysthymia is biological—that is, a result of temperament. In addition to family history and medication response, he has studied the sleep patterns of subaffective dysthymics. Depressed patients tend very early in the sleep cycle to enter the sort of dream sleep characterized by inactivity of the body except for rapid eye movements (REM). So characteristic is this pattern that "short REM latency" is considered a biological marker of depression. Even though they are not depressed, subaffective dysthymics have short REM latency.

For Akiskal, subaffective dysthymia sits on a spectrum of affective personalities. Elsewhere on the spectrum is the hyperthymic personality, understood to be an outgrowth of hyperthymic temperament. Many successful businesspeople and politicians are hyperthymics. These people are described by Akiskal with a series of adjectives, not all of which apply to any one person but the listing of which creates the image of a recognizable "type": hyperthymics are habitually "irritable," "cheerful," "overoptimistic," "exuberant," "overconfident," "self-assured," "boastful," "bombastic," "grandiose," "full of plans," "improvident," "impulsive," "overtalkative," "warm," "people-seeking," "extraverted," "overinvolved," "meddlesome," "uninhibited," "stimulus-seeking," and/or "promiscuous." They are habitual short sleepers, even on weekends. The traits are evident from early in life.

On first consideration, dysthymics and hyperthymics seem to stand at the extremes in terms of temperament. But there are similarities on a variety of levels. For instance, dysthymics are also driven in their careers. Throughout history, it has been known that melancholics, though they have little energy, use their energy well; they tend to work hard in a focused area, do great things, and derive little pleasure from their accomplishments. Much of the insight and creative achievement of the human race is due to the discontent, guilt, and critical eye of dysthymics.

Like hyperthymics, dysthymics can become extraverted and driven for brief periods of time. In symmetrical fashion, hyperthymics are liable to brief depressions. Both dysthymics and hyperthymics are prone to becoming revved up on medication. Like dysthymics, hyperthymics come from families with an excess of mood disorder and have a sleep cycle characterized by short REM latency. Both dysthymics and hyperthymics are at increased risk over time to suffer overt episodes of recurrent major depression. Thus, according to Akiskal's model, both depressive introverts and euphoric extraverts may owe their personality styles to a related biological instability in modulation of affect. Akiskal's writings suggest that both temperaments relate to manic-depressive illness rather than to depression alone—that there is a spectrum that runs from subaffective dysthymia (or melancholic temperament) through hyperthymia (or sanguine temperament) all the way out to rapid cycling.

Akiskal is a representative of the most ancient tradition in psychiatry, the humoral theory that links illness and personality. His signal contribution is the introduction into modern psychiatry of a new category of mental disorder, dysthymia (ill spirit—essentially, disordered humor), lying at the periphery of depression. The boundaries of dysthymia are hard to specify, but the term refers to a chronic condition in which a person has periodic intervals of depressed mood that are briefer or less severe, or involve fewer deranged functions, than episodes of major depression. Dysthymia sits in the penumbra of depression, and subaffective dysthymia sits in the penumbra of the penumbra.

Akiskal has reminded clinicians of what was understood from Greek times until the nineteenth century—namely, that dysthymia is not a matter of episodes alone. Dysthymics tend to have a gloomy and inhibited style between episodes, and there are those who have the style without the episodes but probably have the same underlying disorder. This view of the realm of disordered or variant personality raises a series of interesting issues regarding the patients we have encountered and their response to medication.

• • •

So far, it has appeared that changes in neurotransmission may have the ability to affect *social* temperament directly, turning a shy and conservative member of a human troop into an gregarious risk-taker. The concept of *affective* temperament raises another possibility. When Sally took Prozac, she at first became angry, wired, and bubbly. Perhaps medication "merely" transformed dysthymic into hyperthymic temperament.

Psychiatrists who are skeptical about the transformative powers of Prozac believe that what makes the drug popular is its ability to rev people up, to induce mild hypomania. The implication is that Prozac makes people silly, impairs their judgment, substitutes false euphoria for mild depression. Even if the skeptics are right, to turn dysthymia into hyperthymia is no minor achievement. A medication that can cause such a change in a stable, lasting way will alter personality. Specifically, it will take a person with a temperament that has led to loneliness and give him or her the equivalent of a temperament that, in moderation, often leads to social satisfaction.

My belief is different: I see hypomania as an infrequent but noteworthy side effect of Prozac, separate from its more common main effects. When Sally manages to date men, what the medicine helps her to overcome is decades of social inhibition. But is her interval of excessive energy mere coincidence? In the abstract, Akiskal's concept of temperament—at base, a chronic mood state—differs from Kagan's formulation, in which social inhibition is primary. But in particular patients, the distinction fades: Sally is both depressed and inhibited, and it is hard to say which is primary.

One of the most interesting understandings of the relationship between inhibited temperament and dysthymia comes from a novel perspective, that of sociobiology. The prime mover in this work is Michael T. McGuire, a California psychiatrist with a background in animal ethology. He is known for his work with monkeys, but he has done one fascinating study with humans. McGuire wanted to know what function dysthymia has played in the evolution of human behavior: Is it an illness, or a personality style? Did it confer evolutionary advantages? How has it persisted as a pattern of interrelating with the world?

To answer questions of this sort, McGuire and his colleagues created a center at which they could study dysthymic women not for a brief interview but for an average of 250 hours over an average of eighteen months each—an unheard-of degree of contact with experimental subjects, particularly outpatients. The testing and observations took place at a drop-in center. The atmosphere was such that the women got to know one another and the investigators; they began to function like a small society.

McGuire is still analyzing his data, but he gave a preview at a psychiatric meeting a few years ago. McGuire studied forty-six dysthymic women, ages twenty to forty, and forty-one age-matched controls who had no psychiatric diagnosis. Despite the use of very extensive test batteries, the researchers could not differentiate the groups in terms of cognitive function, such as intelligence or memory. But when they observed the women in social settings, the researchers found the dysthymics had a distinctive pattern of behavior. In contrast to the control subjects, the dysthymic women more often avoided social intercourse and were less likely to initiate social contact; they displayed more atypical social behaviors (such as decreased eye contact and atypical gesturing); they were more likely to express fear of negative evaluation by others; and they had "significantly limited capacities to develop novel behavior and interpretive strategies" and "significantly limited behavior capacities, including reduced capacities for: social maintenance, understanding social rules, self-maintenance, and communication efficacy." Interviews with both subjects and their relatives revealed that these tendencies were lifelong and had preceded the emergence of depressed mood. In other words, the dysthymic women had been *socially inhibited* but not depressed from an early age.

Accompanying the social inhibition were indications of chronic physiologic arousal. For example, the dysthymic women showed heightened responses to certain stimuli, such as anticipating a balloon burst. Behaviorally, these women—who were selected because of chronic minor depression, and not on the basis of social inhibition or anxiety—showed many of the traits we associate with Kagan's shy children or Suomi's uptight monkeys.

For these women, inhibition had social consequences. The dysthymic women differed from the control women in terms of access to life's bounty: "Experimental subjects had significantly fewer friends, social contacts, and living offspring. They had significantly smaller incomes, and significantly less living space per household." It seems dysthymic women's chronic temperamental characteristics —their social discomfort and their lack of flexibility—result in a restricted life with few social rewards.

McGuire was moved by his findings to apply to dysthymic women the sort of evolutionary theory that is more frequently, and perhaps more comfortably, applied to lower animals. The assumption of this theory is that animals, including humans, are "predisposed to achieve certain biological goals, such as acquiring resources, acquiring mates, developing social support networks, having offspring, remaining healthy, communicating efficiently, living in an optimally dense environment, and so on." Failures in these tasks, according to the theory, are the mediating circumstances that lead to chronic and recurrent depression. Inability to achieve goals or find access to resources—space, friends, mates—has direct adverse psychological and physiological consequences. The negative feelings may at first have adaptive value. For instance, anxiety may serve as a feedback signal—a warning—to the individual that goal achievement is suboptimal. The outward signs of depression may at first serve to elicit care-giving from companions. Later, the mechanisms for discontinuing anxiety and depression may be lost, and the conditions can become syndromic and almost wholly dysfunctional.

According to this evolutionary view, dysthymic women do not at base have an illness, depression. What they have is a characteristic strategy or mode of behavior that is not rewarded in contemporary society. People whom society does not reward—who do not find appreciation, love, career success, or a sense of competency—tend to become depressed; presumably this is a universal human vulnerability. But the fundamental problem is a mismatch between the women's coping style and the requisites for finding reward in this culture.

For example, McGuire's dysthymic subjects typically persevered at tasks beyond the point to which perseverance is rewarded in today's complexly demanding world. McGuire's staff made this observation after hearing the women, if they were scheduled at the center for morning and afternoon sessions, repeatedly complain that they had gotten little done during the lunch hour. Curious about what was going on, McGuire's staff followed the women as they took their lunch break.

A subject would leave at midday with a variety of goals—withdraw money from the bank, buy dinner supplies at the grocer's, pick up laundry at the dry cleaner's, and so forth. But, typically, if she arrived at the bank and found a long line, the woman would stand at the end rather than choosing to move on to the next task. She might make a commitment to the bank task, stand behind twenty people, advance, say, to the fourth spot from the front, and then abandon the line when she notices that it's almost time for her afternoon testing session. She would then return to the center without having accomplished any of what she had set out to do. So often did this phenomenon repeat itself that the researchers hypothesized half-seriously that the odds are that the last three people in any long line are chronically depressed.

This tendency to persist inflexibly at hopeless tasks was observed whether or not the women were acutely depressed: it seemed a "trait" as opposed to a "state" characteristic. Even at their best, the dysthymic women lacked the necessary quality—adaptability, optimism, aggression, sense of self-worth—to move on from a present, visible task that is likely to fail to other, imagined, unseen tasks that might possibly succeed. In terms of the virtues of an earlier generation, these women were single-minded, steadfast, loyal, and capable of remarkable perseverance. (This observation may lead us to wonder

whether certain women's tendency to remain stuck in abusive relationships relates not, as much contemporary belief has it, to masochism or self-defeating tendencies, but, rather, to a specific quality
of temperament having to do with persistence.)

McGuire's observations resonate suggestively with Kagan's and, more
particularly, Suomi's work on social inhibition. The sequence seems
to be that uptightness leads to social isolation, which leads to failure
to achieve goals or acquire resources and then to depression. McGuire
sees dysthymia as a secondary consequence of a "trait distribution
phenomenon"—a normal human temperament that happens not to
be rewarded in the modern world. McGuire's view combines se-
quentially the risk (inherited vulnerability, as in "children at risk")
and stress (trauma) approaches to mood disorder: inhibited temperament (risk) leads to social deprivation (stress) which then produces
dysthymia. The anthropological model resembles Jung's understanding of the sociobiological function of introversion: like introverts,
the dysthymic women are evolutionarily adapted to take few chances
and settle for few social contacts. But the social environment has
changed, so that what was once a successful reproductive "strategy"
is now the variant human trait underlying chronic and recurrent
depression.

McGuire's hypothesis meshes with a larger body of work concerning conservative, as opposed to adventurous, social choices. Evolutionary biologists have developed computer models testing different
behavioral strategies against different environmental conditions. For
example, a simple mathematical strategy, using game playing or
betting as the behavior, might be to make whatever choice you made
the last time until you fail twice in a row; then make a different
choice and continue with that one until it fails twice. It turns out
that there are many computer "environments" in which conservative
strategies lead to long-range survival for the individual. Moreover,
inhibited temperament contributes to social stability. Again, consider
the phenomenon of inhibited men and women who remain in abusive

marriages; though painful to behold, relationships between domineering and dysthymic spouses are often remarkable for their longevity. More broadly, we can see how the survival of the tribe, or gene pool, might be enhanced by the presence of some dogged, methodical members.

This evolutionary reasoning implies that inhibited temperament may have been biologically adaptive throughout the hunter-gatherer stage of man's existence. It may even have been more adaptive in the Middle Ages or during the Industrial Revolution than it is now. The problem is that our modern technological society demands the ability to face outward, expend high degrees of energy, take risks, and respond rapidly to multiple competing stimuli. In our society, tribal and familial means of assigning mates and sharing resources have been superseded by demands for individual assertiveness. The environment no longer rewards the full range of temperaments that were necessary for human survival in prior settings.

Writing about Julia's fastidiousness, I said that certain personality styles are no longer socially favored or fashionable. If McGuire's formulation is right, the problem is not simply that extreme caution is no longer admired but that, in the ordinary course of modern life, it does not garner social rewards. It is not only that contemporary social convention demands that women be more assertive (here meaning aggressive, outgoing, and flexible—not firm in defense of the right to be passive and perseverative), but that social circumstances tend to frustrate women who use too cautious a strategy. If Julia is to be happy in a two-career marriage, she will need to tolerate disorder. For Sally to avert depression, it is required that she ask men to dance—that she have a more extraverted temperament. A degree of introversion that might have been rewarded in a different social climate here leads only to deprivation, disappointment, and depression.

●   ●   ●

Not long ago, I treated a patient whose story illustrates the social injuries that can arise from even a mildly inhibited temperament. Jerry was a surgeon who came to see me as he finished his residency training and set out to enter practice. He was quiet, reserved, and self-effacing, and had been so since early childhood. He had always wanted to be a surgeon, and he had achieved his goal, but not without difficulty. A solid student, Jerry had excelled in high school, but was then rejected by the college he most hoped to enter. He went instead to a less prestigious school, and again did well. However, to his surprise and disappointment, he was rejected by all the medical schools to which he applied.

Jerry went on with his life. He married his childhood sweetheart, took jobs in research laboratories, and continued to apply to medical schools. For three years running, he was refused entry. When at last he confronted the college office in charge of organizing his application, Jerry discovered that the summary letter of recommendation in his folder implied he was plodding—a word that did not relate to his achievements, which were substantial, but to his self-presentation. His conduct during interviews, where he tended to be retiring and tentative, had probably amplified this misimpression. The omission of certain offending phrases improved the application, and on his fourth try Jerry was admitted to a top-flight program.

There he excelled at first, but as the pressures mounted he became prone to such anxiety that he could barely function. Although he spent day and night in the library, self-doubt prevented him from translating his learning into academic success. A therapist at school identified the problem as overfastidiousness the need to exercise more control than was possible in a complex program—and encouraged Jerry to study less. Jerry followed this advice and thrived.

When Jerry came to me, he was once again anxious, with an element of depression now added in. He was suddenly irritable, lashing out at nurses and colleagues in the operating room. He did not know whether he would be able to function in the "real world" outside residency. Just before coming to see me, he had put himself on Prozac.

What ensued was one of the simplest therapies I have ever conducted. I encouraged Jerry to review his history with me. It emerged that at every transition in his education his inhibition had been interpreted as incompetence—so he had been penalized for a particular personality style. This style had its productive side. It made him persistent in pursuit of his goals, allowed him to enter into a successful marriage without fuss, and made him a steady student and a clear-thinking, unimpulsive physician. Jerry's sense of self-worth and competency had been injured by the numerous rejections he suffered, rejections that had little to do with his ability and everything to do with various institutions' prejudice in favor of extraversion and "assertiveness." Toward the end of the therapy, one additional factor emerged. It seemed that in recent months Jerry had been seeing his son penalized—teased or excluded by peers—for the same quiet, retiring traits. Merely identifying this connection was empowering.

And it seemed that the Prozac did its job, too. Jerry found himself less frazzled by the complexity of the operating and recovery rooms, firmer in the outward expression of his opinions and decisions, at once more even-tempered and more commanding. I suspect the Prozac also helped quiet his reaction to "novelty"—that is, to the stress of leaving residency and entering practice.

The combination of therapy and medication in this brief treatment seemed to me especially effective. As Jerry reviewed his own history, he saw how he had been unfairly judged, and he changed the way he valued himself. This cognitive change was amplified by the Prozac directly, through visceral feelings of self-worth, and indirectly, through the good response of Jerry's colleagues to his new, more assertive behavior.

Jerry was not especially shy or affectively vulnerable; he might not have met Kagan's criteria for social inhibition, and he definitely would not have been studied by Akiskal or McGuire. But even in this mild case of social inhibition, Jerry's temperament interacted with an unfavorable environment to produce symptoms, and the sociobiological view of temperament and mood disorder was of use to Jerry in reshaping his sense of self.

•   •   •

Studies from a variety of perspectives—child development, animal ethology, descriptive psychiatry, and sociobiology—point to temperament as a crucial factor influencing personality and overall psychological well-being in a large and recognizable slice of humanity: the inhibited, the vulnerable, the highly reactive, the mildly depressed. What the different models have in common is an understanding that not only depression but also temperament rests on and is sustained by levels of neurotransmitters and stress hormones. One conclusion we might draw from this understanding is that medications that alter levels of, or transmission by, these substances *ought* to affect temperament. Indeed, we should be surprised if a medicine that resets the norepinephrine and serotonin systems does *not* directly alter temperament.

Psychiatrists have long recognized indirect effects of medication on temperament. If you give a child with attention deficits a stimulant, and if that child then succeeds academically and socially, you will—through the feedback from the external environment—produce a more confident child. The direct effect of medication on temperament is different. If you can alter serotonin and norepinephrine, you should be able, merely by virtue of that change in the biological interior milieu, to produce a more socially comfortable individual.

The medicines I have talked most about—imipramine, desipramine, the MAOIs, the SSRIs—are conventionally called antidepressants. But this label was applied as a matter of circumstance, because these medications were, historically, first found to ameliorate or end depressive episodes. The same medications are effective against panic anxiety, and they could as appropriately have been called anxiolytics. The term "antidepressant" encourages us to attend arbitrarily to one use to which these drugs can be put. Perhaps preferable is the old word "thymoleptic." A thymoleptic is a substance that acts on the "thymus"—Greek for the soul or spirit or seat of the emotions. ("Neuroleptic," a word in more common usage by psychiatrists, refers to antipsychotics, like Thorazine.) "Thymoleptic" comes close to expressing our understanding that medications act on the neurohumors, and that the medications' effects on anxiety, depression, and personality are particular manifestations of that deeper alteration.

Thymoleptic action is apparent in Sally's transformation in response to Prozac. On a chemical level, she is enhancing the activity of her serotonergic neurons; perhaps on a psychophysiological level she is altering her reactivity to challenge. But on the level we most readily observe, what is new about Sally is her reduced degree of social inhibition—a change in one of the most salient aspects of her personality. This change is more striking even than any decrease in depressed mood. There is, perhaps, no need to weigh these two consequences against each other: since both mood disorder and "reactivity" appear to be regulated by the same neurotransmitters and stress hormones, whenever a patient takes an antidepressant we will be uncertain whether what changes is illness or temperament.

Sally looks like one of the small percentage of people who remain shy into adulthood. Kagan believes 15 percent of young children are inhibited. Suomi sees similar tendencies in 20 percent of rhesus monkeys. The rhesus monkeys remain different—more "reactive"—into adulthood. If only 2 or 3 percent of adult humans remain inhibited, what has happened to the temperament of the other 12 or 13 percent of inhibited infants?

One possibility is that people "grow out of" childhood inhibition, so that their neurobiology becomes indistinguishable from that of their age-mates. This seems not to occur in monkeys, but monkeys may be less plastic than we are; monkey parents may expend a less focused effort on social education, may be more willing to write off a few unhappy offspring. If we are not very different from monkeys, however, a substantial percentage of human adults, though not outright shy, are walking around with highly reactive temperaments. Behaviorally, they may do fine under favorable circumstances; but they will become anxious and then depressed when confronted by novelty or social disruption. Indeed, we may wonder whether some of the patients we have met who enjoyed apparently tranquil childhoods came to their rejection-sensitivity by inheriting some element of the inhibited temperament.

Beyond Kagan's initial 15 percent, additional people may achieve a neural substrate similar to that of inborn inhibition through exposure to psychological or even physical trauma. If inhibited temperament and its inevitable variants are widespread, then a medication that affects the biological substrate of inhibition will be capable of altering personality in a substantial proportion of the adult population.

The vast majority of these people, including those who are outright inhibited socially, will be "normal" in psychological terms. Most of them will be highly functional in their careers and private lives. No one has ever called people with inhibited personalities mentally ill. The brief conclusion to this line of reasoning is that in patients like Sally, and in many others with less dramatic stories and perhaps with no history of depression at all, what we are changing with medication is the infrastructure of personality. That is, Sally is able to marry on Prozac because she has achieved chemically the interior milieu of someone born with a different genome and exposed to a more benign world in childhood.

I have talked often about the way medication colors our view of human nature, but there is also influence in the other direction. Once we believe that the state of biogenic amines determines aspects of temperament, we will expect amine-altering medications to influence personality. Indeed, we may wonder why antidepressants do not alter personality more often, or, if they do, why this effect was not noted in the past.

If altered serotonin levels change personality, this effect should have been seen in patients taking imipramine, as many as thirty years ago. There were, in fact, occasional mentions of the influence of imipramine on personality in the early literature. And after the reification of dysthymia as a diagnosis, even before the general use of Prozac, a few research reports appeared in the professional literature noting personality changes in depressed patients given conventional antidepressants. But for the most part, personality was the arena of psychotherapy. Indeed, what was called a "character disorder"—later "personality disorder"—was for many years a contraindication for treatment with medication.

Hagop Akiskal took this distinction into account when discussing depressive personality. Akiskal reserved the category of affective temperament ("subaffective dysthymia") for people with persistent biological markers of depression, a tendency to overshoot on medication, and a family history of manic depression. He distinguished these patients from people (the "characterologically depressed") who had come to their depressive personalities through trauma, such as growing up with alcoholic or absent parents. Akiskal for many years believed that characterologic depression did not respond to antidepressants—and, indeed, many of his patients did not improve on tricyclics.

According to Akiskal's early model, how you came to your personality mattered. Those who were born with a depressive temperament were considered likely to respond to medication, whereas those who were made depressive were not. This distinction corresponds well to the psychoanalytic view that problems of character require nonpharmacologic treatment, but it is curious. It corresponds poorly to the common observation that acute, major depression responds to medication whether or not an environmental cause is apparent. The idea that "characterologic" or environment-based depression does not respond to medication also flies in the face of animal research demonstrating that antidepressants can make genetically normal but behaviorally traumatized animals less vulnerable to stress.

———

Staking out a position more "biological" than Akiskal's, Donald Klein, the researcher known for his work on hysteroid dysphoria and phobic anxiety, weighed in on the side of medication treatment for characterologic depression. Klein holds that much chronic maladaptive behavior of all stripes arises from underlying physiological vulnerability.

The patients whom doctors most often diagnosed as characterologically depressed were those who had difficulty in social functioning—relations with others, job tenure, and the like. There was a derogatory cast to this distinction, as if to say that people with strong characters work whether they are depressed or not, and that characterologic depressives were complainers or "losers." Researchers never made such statements outright, but at worst character pathology carried the sort of stigma we have already seen attached to hysteria, and at best there was a sense that these patients were hard to help, not fully cooperative, perhaps two steps shy of malingering.

To test the relationship between medication responsiveness and character pathology, Klein's group looked at about two hundred chronically depressed adults almost all of whom scored as impaired on a scale rating social functioning, a measure of success in work and intimate relationships. After six weeks of treatment with imipramine or an MAOI, patients who responded in terms of mood (sadness, sleep, appetite, ruminations, etc.) also showed improvements in social functioning. Indeed, over 28 percent of those who responded to medication after six weeks showed social-adjustment scores as high as or higher than a general community sample—a remarkable phenomenon for a brief trial of medication. The greater improvement was in patients who had been given, and had responded to, the MAOI.

In strict terms, Klein had proved nothing. His study shows only that chronically depressed people who respond to antidepressants also show a rapid improvement in social functioning. But the ease with which "characterologic" handicaps disappeared on medication threw the utility of the concept "characterologic depression" into doubt.

Prozac settled this dispute. Once Prozac was available, Akiskal found that virtually all of his dysthymics and patients with depressive personality, whatever the origin of their pathology, responded to medication. Not all responded to Prozac, though responses to Prozac when they occurred were especially complete or dramatic. Some patients responded to imipramine or related antidepressants, some to lithium, some to a combination of lithium and antidepressant, some to anticonvulsants, but, one way or another, it was possible to get nearly every dysthymic patient to improve. In his research, Akiskal no longer divides patients with chronic low-level depression into the categories "subaffective dysthymia" and "characterologic depression." The distinction is of no clinical utility. There are no more "characterologic depressives," only dysthymics for whom the right biological treatment has not yet been discovered.

So strong is the influence of medication on the way we think about personality that a number of the psychiatrists charged with updating the standard diagnostic manual have suggested doing away altogether with the distinction between mental illness and personality disorder. Their assumption is that personality disorder and discrete mental illness are thoroughly intermixed—that much of what has been called personality disorder is the final, behavioral expression of a variant state of the biogenic amines. In the case of depression, this view holds that discrete bouts of depression are part of a recurrent illness which, between episodes, expresses itself as depressive personality. This illness has its more and less severe forms, and manifests itself differently in different people, just as atherosclerotic heart disease admits of different degrees, stages, and symptoms; but the distinction between recurrent depression, depressive personality, and dysthymia becomes superfluous. My own sense is that it is premature to lump all derangements of personality with acute illness. But I do think it is reasonable to use the word "dysthymia" to refer to depressive personality or chronic minor depression, whether the presumed cause is nature or (traumatic) nurture.

———

180

The conceptual leap Akiskal and others have made in recent years—all depressive personality is responsive to biological influence—raises the possibility that there is something special about Prozac. Perhaps "characterologic depression" did not in the past respond to medication because the medication available was ill-suited to the task.

Prozac is distinctive in a variety of ways. It may selectively treat atypical depression, thus filling a gap missed by tricyclic antidepressants like imipramine. It may be especially effective in minor depression. It can reduce compulsiveness. And it has a favorable side-effect profile, so it is acceptable to a wider range of people—certainly much more acceptable than MAOIs, which also seem to work through enhancement of serotonin. As for serotonin, it may have a broader effect on the stabilization of affect ("serotonin-as-police") than do the neurotransmitters altered by other medications; in particular, a serotonergic antidepressant might be more multipurpose than a medicine that acts on norepinephrine.

Certain researchers have speculated privately that Prozac may be especially effective in the full range of dysthymia because of quirks in the Prozac molecule. Prozac is particularly narrow in its locus of action. Most antidepressants influence multiple sites on the same neuron; they may, for example, increase serotonin production at one end of the neuron, but also diminish norepinephrine or serotonin production through ordinarily less marked effects at receptors elsewhere on the same cell. Perhaps Prozac's extreme specificity is overwhelming to the neuron; the cell responds at one site, in one direction, and cannot, through mechanisms that otherwise allow neurons to "compensate" for changes in state, return to a prior level of functioning.

Also, Prozac is especially long-acting. Its extended half-life in the body can be a pharmacologic disadvantage; if a patient experiences a side effect of Prozac, such as nausea or headache, the medication will not wash out for many days, and the side effect may persist for the whole of that time, even though the patient has stopped taking medicine. But long action may also have positive consequences. With short-acting drugs, the level of the chemical in the brain rises as the drug is absorbed and falls as the drug is excreted or digested. In contrast, the brain levels of Prozac are extremely steady. This lack of fluctuation may have peculiar neurochemical efficacy, or the invariance of the brain's chemical status may have psychological ramifications. In terms of sensitivity to disappointment, a very steady cushion against decompensation may translate into a new continuous sense of self—that is, the change may be experienced as altered temperament rather than temporarily altered circumstance. These speculations are untested—they are scientific table talk—but they suggest a willingness in the research community to consider the idea that our ability to influence temperament in pharmacologic terms is new and growing.

Or perhaps our ability to influence temperament with antidepressants is old and overlooked. In an era when personality was understood to be the summation of psychological defenses, and the defenses were understood as responses to trauma during development, it was threatening to see personality as responding to medication. It may be that Prozac is special in its effect on temperament, or that Prozac arrived at a propitious moment and as a result—because the time was ripe and also because the drug had few side effects and was given to many people—Prozac has allowed us to see an effect of medications that we should have attended to long ago.

● ● ●

The effect of medication on personality makes research on biological temperament look more interesting, and that research in turn makes plausible the idea that "antidepressants" are really "thymoleptics." In the midst of this reverberation between changed views of personality and of medication, it is impossible that our view of mental illness should remain constant. After all, what does it mean that the same medications can treat depression and anxiety? Antidepressants, or thymoleptics, are used in the management of eating disorders, especially anorexia. They can ameliorate attention-deficit disorder, compulsive behaviors, and a host of other syndromes and individual symptoms. Inevitably, this plethora of indications has made doctors wonder what it is they are treating when they prescribe these drugs.

A viewpoint that is gaining currency in psychiatry, under the rubric "the functional theory of psychopathology," is that mental states are best understood first through the consideration of particular mental *functions,* such as mood, cognition, and perception—and that multifaceted entities such as mental illness or personality should be considered secondary. An assumption of the theory is that variation in functions will turn out to arise from a particular state of one or another neurotransmitter.

The thrust of the theory is most easily understood through example. Herman van Praag, the psychiatrist most associated with this method of analysis, suggests that serotonin may regulate such functions as anxiety and aggression, whereas norepinephrine relates to pleasure or, more specifically, "reward coupling"—the ability to anticipate future pleasure in activities that have been pleasurable in the past. This theory accounts for the success of the antidepressant desipramine, which changes norepinephrine-based transmission, in treating both depression and anorexia, since a central element of both disorders is reward uncoupling (loss of the ability to experience pleasure in the case of depression, loss of appetite in the case of anorexia). Likewise, panic anxiety, chronic depression, and social inhibition, all responsive to serotonergic medications, can be seen as turning on issues of proper levels of assertiveness and inner comfort. Van Praag is quick to state that such formulations are premature.

The details are less significant than the perspective. Van Praag is asking us to look past complex diagnoses (such as depression and anorexia, each of which has many symptoms) to behavioral building blocks of illness and personality (such as aggression or "reward coupling") which are presumably influenced by particular neurotransmitter states.

A virtue of the functional theory of illness and cure is that it explains an apparent paradox of Prozac, a medication that is at once specific in its biochemical action and useful in a wide variety of disorders. The functional theory predicts precisely this relationship: "The greater the biochemical specificity of a drug, the greater is the chance it will be nosologically [that is, diagnostically] nonspecific . . ." Since the same functions are deranged in a variety of illnesses, a medicine that affects only one neurotransmitter, and therefore only a few functions, will have broad applicability.

The availability of increasingly specific medicines should open the possibility of increasingly specific modifications to temperament. There are at least five, and very likely more, subtypes of the molecule that binds serotonin at the cell membrane. Researchers have begun to identify drugs that are specific for particular serotonin-receptor subtypes. Perhaps the future will bring drugs that can influence narrower functions than "anxiety and aggression." These drugs might be applicable to a very wide range of problems (mental illnesses, personality traits, individual symptoms), but the function they address within those problems might be quite specific. You might get the confidence Prozac instills without getting the quickness of thought.

The research that yields these results will not be targeted at changing personality. But once we believe that temperament is ruled by the neurohumors, there is no separating progress in treating mental illness from progress in altering temperament. Necessarily, research on the treatment of major illness will also be research into cosmetic psychopharmacology. The better we are at changing specific transmission patterns in the brain, the better we will be at recasting the foundations of normal variants in personality. New drugs should be able both to modify inborn predisposition and to repair traumatic damage to personality that has become functionally autonomous on a physiological basis.

● ● ●

My speculations, though based on research into social reactivity and the affective temperament, are far ahead of the evidence. They are not, however, ahead of the field. An increasing number of psychiatrists believe the genetic set of the neurohumors governs personality in ways that go far beyond anything we have discussed.

One who has spoken out boldly is C. Robert Cloninger, a member of the department of genetics and head of the department of psychiatry at Washington University in St. Louis, the nation's most biologically oriented psychiatry program. In the mid-1980s, Cloninger published two widely read, and widely criticized, scientific papers outlining a "unified biosocial theory of personality." In Cloninger's monographs, theory has outstripped experimental results. Still, there is pleasure to be had in observing a fertile imagination at work, and Cloninger gives us a sense of where biological psychiatry wishes it were now and where it hopes soon to be.

Fully elaborated, Cloninger's theory is immensely complex. But at its heart is a straightforward set of tenets we can understand in light of concepts we have already discussed. Cloninger believes there are three biologically determined axes of temperament, corresponding to the three neurohumors: norepinephrine, serotonin, and dopamine.

The axis governed by norepinephrine Cloninger calls "reward dependence." A person who is "severely high" on this axis will be, in Cloninger's words, "Highly dependent on emotional supports and intimacy with others; highly sensitive to social cues and responsive to social pressures; highly sentimental, crying very easily; [an] industrious, ambitious overachiever who pushes [him- or her-] self to exhaustion; extremely sensitive to rejection from even minor slights, leading to reward-seeking behaviors such as overeating; [and] highly persistent in craving for gratification even when frustrated in attempts to obtain expected recognition or benefits." This constellation is none other than rejection-sensitivity. At the severely low end of the axis are people who are insensitive to rejection. In Cloninger's words, people with low "reward dependence" are "Socially detached, never sharing intimate feelings with others, content to be alone . . . insensitive to social cues and pressures." Such a person might be an alienated nonconformist, unmotivated by ambition to please.

There are less extreme positions on this spectrum. A mildly high "reward-dependent" individual prefers intimacy to privacy, usually conforms to social pressures, is usually helpful and industrious, and is sensitive to major rejections. Someone mildly low for this trait will have social contacts but few intimate ones, will for the most part resist social pressure, and will experience only a transient upset in response to rejection or frustration. In other words, the whole range of possible positions on this axis of temperament is seen as being governed by norepinephrine. We are no longer talking, as Kagan was, about 15 percent of infants or 3 percent of adults who are extreme in a particular personality trait. Every person's level of reward dependence (or social reactivity) is influenced by and encoded in the state of his or her norepinephrine-related neurons.

In the same way, the other neurohumors determine the whole spectrum of hues in their respective affective and temperamental colorations. To serotonin, Cloninger ascribes a trait he calls "harm avoidance." Harm avoidance resembles the uptightness and separation-induced fearfulness we have seen in rhesus monkeys. "Severely high" harm avoidance entails: inhibition in the face of unfamiliar people or situations, fear and anticipation of harm even in the presence of reassurance and support, pessimism, and easy fatigability. Those with very low harm avoidance are laid-back—confident, carefree, optimistic, energetic, quick to recuperate, and calm in the face of unfamiliar or threatening circumstances.

Dopamine, another biogenic amine that acts as a neurotransmitter, is the chemical that is thought to be too high in schizophrenia and too low in Parkinson's disease. Thorazine, the first modern psychotherapeutic drug, *blocks* dopamine in the brain, the presumed mechanism by which the medicine ameliorates the symptoms of schizophrenia. L-dopa, the drug around which the book and movie *Awakenings* revolve, effectively *increases* brain dopamine and is useful in ameliorating the symptoms of Parkinsonism. In the past fifteen years, many biological psychiatrists have speculated about dopamine's role in the temperament of normal people.

In Cloninger's model, dopamine levels set the degree of a trait he calls "novelty seeking." In similar theories, such as those of Monte Buchsbaum at the University of California, Irvine, the same trait is called "stimulus seeking" or "impulsivity." At one extreme is the person who "Consistently seeks thrilling adventures and exploration [and is] intolerant of structure and monotony." Such people make decisions intuitively, act and spend impulsively, and engage in a rapidly shifting series of interests and social relationships. They often take self-destructive risks. At the other extreme are people with low levels of dopamine transmission. Orderly, organized people wedded to routine and enamored of structure, they are controlled, analytical, frugal, loyal, stoical, and slow to change interests or attachments.

To relate Cloninger's axes to concepts we have already discussed: high reward dependence (posited to be a function of the norepinephrine system) corresponds loosely to sensitivity; high harm avoidance (serotonin), to inhibition; and low novelty seeking (dopamine), to fastidiousness or inflexibility.

These three axes—reward dependence, harm avoidance, and novelty seeking—allow Cloninger to cover a vast territory. Looking only at reward dependence and harm avoidance, we can imagine a person who is highly reward-dependent (signified by the capital letter R) and highly harm-avoidant (H). Such a person would crave reward but be afraid to seek it openly. Cloninger describes the RH personality with these adjectives: "passive avoidance; submissive/deferential; indirectly manipulative; dependently demanding." Given more courage (low harm avoidance, or h) we have the person (Rh) who is "heroic, persuasive/pushy, perseverant, and gullible."

Extremes on three dimensions correspond to personality structures that begin to look like psychiatric deviance. Nhr is psychopathy or antisocial personality, the profile of a man or woman who always needs a stimulus "high," ignores risk, and has little need for the rewards of social intimacy or acceptance; criminals and cool, manipulative salespeople may be Nhr; nHr is the obsessional, nhr the imperturbable, socially isolative schizoid. Some of the Prozac-responders we have met might be classed as nHR (avoidant of novelty, cautious, and sensitive), though none is at the extreme of the three axes.

Cloninger's is a true spectrum theory of personality. We are all brothers under the skin, the sociopath, the hero, and the working drone. What distinguishes us is the state of our neurohumors. Where normal personality ends and personality disorder begins is only a matter of convention—of how far along each axis we set the cutoff points. Every human being has a biological temperament parsimoniously described by three numbers—the values for reward dependence, harm avoidance, and novelty seeking.

For all that this spectrum aspect of Cloninger's work has humane implications—the sociopath is not of a different species, he is like many of us but more so—the model, taken as a whole, embodies a humanist's nightmare. Many people, even some who know a good deal about psychiatry, enter the consulting room with the fear, which is also a sort of hope, that the doctor will be able to classify them with great scientific specificity—"Oh, he's a 231010-XW." This fantasy is a complicated one. At its heart, I think, is the wish to be cared for, but not on account of one's idiosyncratic self. Implicit is the sense that one's intimate self is not lovable, and that the patient will do better to count on professional objectivity to ensure appropriate care. Implicit also is a degree of passivity or even masochism, a willingness to put oneself at the mercy of a medical Svengali. The certainty that they are known scientifically makes many patients feel safe, although that safety hides seeds of rage that may sprout rapidly when a patient discovers, to his or her disappointment and relief, the limitations of the care-giver. Cloninger's system indicates that this hope or fear of objective omniscience is a fantasy shared by the profession as well.

Speaking of disappointment and relief, we may feel both in the face of this oversimple model. No theory so mechanistic could possibly capture our essence: we have escaped again! No one, I suspect not even Cloninger, imagines this schematic formulation is "right." In the study of personality, even more than in the study of major depression, there is too much contradictory information to allow us to embrace simple answers. Cloninger's effort—and I have not done justice to the volume of supportive information he adduces, from genetics, neurochemistry, and drug trials—serves most importantly as a vision or an ideal, an example of the form biological psychiatrists might like our understanding of personality to take. His model does resonate with certain of our earlier discussions. For example, the multiaxial approach gives support to the notion of non-hysteroid rejection-sensitivity, the concept I attached to patients who are vulnerable to loss but who have not developed a style that caricatures femininity. Rejection-sensitivity will produce hysteroid traits only in the presence of high stimulus seeking and low harm avoidance (NhR). But rejection-sensitivity (high reward dependence, or R) in combination with other tendencies—for example, caution (H) and fear of novelty (n)—will produce very different pictures. The multiaxial model serves to remind us that the way any one attribute manifests itself will depend on the other attributes that accompany it.

The model serves also to underline the implications of the biological drift in our understanding of personality. It is not just "sensitivity" or "inhibition" but a wide variety of temperamental traits that we may come to see as reified, especially if advances in psychopharmacology continue to play a role. If someone develops a pill that makes people less gullible, we will see gullibility as a biological predisposition—shake our heads sadly behind the backs of parents of gullible children, express annoyance at gullible adults who fail to seek treatment, and wonder in a different way about ourselves if now and then in our social dealings we find ourselves taken in.

But when it comes to the specifics of Cloninger's model, even a modest background in the neurochemistry of personality induces doubts. Cloninger attributes harm avoidance to serotonin, but Suomi's monkey studies suggest that early in the traumatic process leading to inhibition it is norepinephrine levels that change; serotonin comes into play only after multiple traumas and challenges. Post's kindling model, with its evidence that first one neurotransmitter system and then another becomes disordered as a disease progresses, makes any one-transmitter/one-trait model suspect. If different degrees of depression involve complex changes in a variety of transmitters, it seems likely that different degrees of any one personality trait will as well.

Cloninger associates norepinephrine with reward dependence, but rejection-sensitive patients respond less often to medications like desipramine that affect norepinephrine, and frequently to medications like MAOIs and SSRIs that very likely work through raising serotonin levels. Moreover, in Prozac-responsive patients, it seems that this serotonergic medication has simultaneous effects on a variety of axes—decreasing inhibition and harm avoidance while increasing assertiveness and energy—casting doubt on the assertion that Cloninger's three axes are independent. In Cloninger's terms, Prozac decreases reward dependence, increases novelty seeking, and decreases harm avoidance. In summary, it takes a passive-dependent person (nHR) and makes her more of a sociopath (Nhr)—an observation that may make us wonder what it takes to get along in this society.

The truth is, scientists have a slender grasp of possible biological substrates for a few aspects of personality, prominent among them social inhibition and depressive personality. But we are a species of theory builders. Once we begin to believe that personality has biological underpinnings, we act as if the future were already at hand. This speculation then drifts into the general culture, often in overstated form. I am thinking for instance, of the "Ideas" story in *Newsweek* that helped shape my awareness that we "listen to drugs." The article says genes "are estimated to account for . . . 30 percent of personality differences." A geneticist would deem this statement meaningless: the degree to which a trait is heritable varies according to the range of environments over which it is studied. Are we talking about a heterogeneous culture, or the culture within a single family? What is "personality," globally taken, and what measures it? The proportion of personality one finds to be heritable will depend to a great extent on how one defines and quantifies personality.

The *Newsweek* article is about why siblings differ. The writer says, "A child who is shy by nature will react very differently to having a social butterfly for a mother than does his outgoing sister." Hidden in the phrase "shy by nature" is a full acceptance, perhaps even an overvaluation, of the Kagan research. We have only modest evidence that even a small proportion of children are constitutionally shy; for the most part, the role of temperament remains a mystery.

The sentence about the social-butterfly mother and the shy-by-nature child made me think of *The Glass Menagerie*. I recently saw a performance in which the mother, played by Olympia Dukakis, seemed so sympathetic that the family conflict was drained of its tension. It is hard to remember how Tennessee Williams played a few years back, but part of the tragedy has always involved the mother's having destroyed her daughter. Today, I think we might just say it is difficult to raise a child who is shy by nature, and all the more difficult for a mother who is social by nature. Here is an example of how a reductionistic view of human nature at once takes something away, namely the force of the drama, and gives something back, by making the once-demonized mother a character with whose plight we can identify.

•   •   •

When Suomi studies monkeys separated from their mothers, he is investigating a stress or trauma model of mood regulation. Studies focused on inborn, heritable influences are called "risk" models; they concern subjects believed to be at risk on a genetic basis for various disorders or differences. Both trauma and risk seem capable of producing all the phenomena we have considered. Early separation leads to reactivity to novelty, but inborn temperament can have much the same effect. The prevailing developmental model of depressed or inhibited temperament combines these two factors into what is called a trauma/temperament or stress/risk model. According to this model, most manifestations of, say, dysthymia can be understood as resulting from different influences in combination—traumatic events in the life history of someone with a vulnerable temperamental predisposition.

The two factors can be interactive. To a "reactive" person, what might seem to others quite minor stress will be experienced as trauma. There may also be some clustering of stress and risk. For instance, when the California psychiatrist-sociobiologist Michael McGuire took careful histories of his dysthymic women, many of them reported having been (like Sally) abused as children; the dysthymic women were four times as likely to have been abused as the matched control subjects. For a variety of reasons, McGuire believes these women's social inhibition preceded the abuse. As girls, these women may have signaled their vulnerability in a way that made them more liable to be chosen as a target of abuse; this is a matter not of blaming the victim but of understanding the process of victimization. It is also possible that the relatives of dysthymic women are (biologically) predisposed to act dysfunctionally and thus to create harmful family environments; in the case of dysthymic mothers, through both their choice of mates and their behavior in the marriage. Even the penalties society attaches to depressive temperament—small living space, low income, social isolation—correlate with likelihood of abuse.

The work of all of the researchers we have discussed would lead us to believe that it is possible to come to dysthymia through stress, temperament, or both in combination. The type of stress may make a difference in humans, as it seems to in monkeys. For example, a recent genetic study of white twin girls and women showed that those who in childhood had lived through parental separation, generally through divorce, were more likely as adults to suffer major depression and generalized anxiety disorder—even though *death* of a parent did *not* have this effect. Death of a parent may well be a different stressor from parental divorce. The freedom to grieve death may be an important factor, as may be the sense that the parent did not choose to leave. And if a widow or widower remarries, a child may be freer to identify with the stepparent in cases of death than of divorce. As for separation, it is rarely a onetime event but, rather, a complex stressor over time, including perhaps family conflict before a divorce, social and economic disruption after, and prolonged pressures on the child from both parents.

Stress and risk commonly interact. A child born with depressive temperament may have a parent who suffered similarly. That parent, because of social handicaps or self-doubt, may have chosen a spouse poorly or may function poorly in marriage. The child at risk will therefore be a stressed child as well, and if the child is rejection-sensitive, whatever stressors he or she encounters will be psychologically and physiologically amplified. The child's growing dysfunction then affects the family, not least the temperamentally vulnerable parent.

The stresses the child suffers are encoded physiologically, as altered neurotransmitter systems. They are also encoded psychologically, as characteristic defenses, defenses that will be all the more necessary as the child's psychophysiologic vulnerability increases. The "highly defended" adult who emerges from these difficult circumstances will tell a story that makes sense in strict psychoanalytic terms—that is, a story of trauma, self-blame, loss, and so forth; but part of what maintains his or her dysfunctional status can also be understood as functionally autonomous, biologically maintained patterns of response to stress or novelty.

The stress/risk model admits of complexity. It attends to the mind, and to the broader social setting, as well as to the neurons. It illuminates the stories of patients we have met. And it corresponds to the commonsense belief that there should be biological as well as environmental components to personality and that they should interact in intricate ways.

But the psychological element in the stress/risk model is often overlooked. Implicit in the model is an openness to the sort of statement often made to psychiatrists at the initiation of treatment: "That's just who I am." As recently as ten or twenty years ago, the therapist would likely have responded that who a person habitually is, is largely a matter of defensiveness—that is, of characteristic ways of avoiding disorganizing thought and emotion. This point of view—in truth, not alien to the risk/stress model—demanded that patients take responsibility for broad areas of personality and try to reshape them through self-understanding and courage. Today a patient who protests, "But that's just who I am," is in line with the prevailing wisdom, and it may be harder to convince the patient to see the role that experience plays in the formation even of behaviors and traits that feel automatic, visceral, and unchangeable.

In light of the rapid efficacy of medication, psychiatrists and, increasingly, the public lean toward the belief that personality is "biological." In both Julia, the fastidious housewife and nurse, and Jerry, the self-effacing surgeon, it seems that inborn temperament played a major role in personality formation; Lucy, the student whose mother was murdered, seems shaped by trauma; Sally, both inhibited and abused, is most clearly a mixed case. But medication was transformative for all these patients, suggesting that, before treatment, temperament had a large role in shaping their personalities.

"Temperament," in the risk/stress model, is a biological substrate for adult personality that has inevitably been modified by life events such as profound trauma. But it is easy—seeing the effects of medicine, reading about differences between monkeys bred for laid-back or uptight temperament—to ignore the role of experience and focus only on the role of inborn "type." This point of view—a pure "risk" model—is one our society has resisted for decades, on grounds that it is antidemocratic or racist or sexist. Such a psychology raises questions about human malleability, about free will, about models of child-rearing and education, and about the degree of responsibility and level of effort we should expect of people vis-à-vis their personality traits. Even if we understand the complexity of temperament, to the extent that we believe personality is largely a matter of biology, we experience ourselves differently, and we may be less curious about psychological avenues of change.

Our view of psychotherapeutic drugs has changed already. Earlier, I said in passing that through medication Sally may have been given the interior milieu of someone born with a different genome and exposed to a more benign world in childhood. Is it not remarkable that such an assertion can now be made "by the way"? The capacity of modern medication to allow a person to experience, on a stable and continuous basis, the feelings of someone with a different temperament and history is among the most extraordinary accomplishments of modern science.

Part of what makes medicine seem so powerful is an ambiguity in the word "personality." On the one hand, it means what the researchers are able to measure—gross traits such as shyness, aggression, impulsivity, and the like. On the other hand, it refers to the many small and consequential features that make each person unique. When Sally took Prozac, she was able to change the most socially handicapping aspect of her personality. But after the transformation, she was still Sally. Most of what we would call her personality persisted in a recognizable way. Though no longer inhibited, she is the same woman, with the same determination, the same opinions, aspirations, bêtes noires, mannerisms, and memories—although each of these might be changed a bit, too, by medicine, and she would still be recognizably the same.

Tess's reaction to the return of her symptoms when she was off Prozac was: "I'm not myself." But many patients stress a continuity of self on and off drugs. "I am myself without the lead boots," "myself without swimming through Jell-O," "myself on a good day, although I never had days this good," "myself without fears"—these are words inhibited and dysthymic people use to describe the effect of thymoleptics. Their reactions acknowledge aspects of the personhood that medication does not alter.

Some months before her wedding, Sally said, "I am myself, but no longer shut out of everything. I am more comfortable in myself —not empty inside." She seems very much this way: liberated, filled out, at once grounded and lightened, but still very much Sally. Self and personality turn out to be greater than the sum of their parts. They are gestalts, hard to tease into factors, hard to pin down. Here is an additional effect of medication: When we see how essentially unchanged a shy person is without her shyness, we will want to say that personality extends far beyond the limited traits or axes researchers are able to study.

We may even ask: Is Sally's fiancé truly marrying the shy woman with the difficult history? The past self is not hidden from her fiancé, but neither is she fully present. However Sally experiences it, we may feel that her self contains a discontinuity. And if we sense this discontinuity, we are also saying something about the extent to which a person "just is" her stable, continuous biological inner self.

Still, we should be proud to dance at Sally's wedding because of the pleasure this sign of her liberation brings her. The wedding may stand also as an icon for another union in progress, that between biological and psychological views of personality, and therefore of self. Though it is not free of ominous portents—is it a match between equals, or will biology dominate?—after half a century in which physiologically based temperament had been banished from society, this marriage should be welcome.

7

Formes Frustes:

Low Self-Esteem

A reviewer of a recent book about antidepressants complains; she wishes that the author's "argument did not extend to such a huge and varied list of ailments." Recalling the syndromes we have seen Prozac treat, ranging from minor degrees of depression, anxiety, and compulsiveness to melancholic temperament and social inhibition, we may express a similar wish. It seems that any human frailty whatsoever is likely to be caught in our net. Worse, each of these conditions is itself composed of a list of symptoms, from alterations in bodily functions, such as sleep and appetite, to disturbances of mental functioning, such as memory and concentration, to distortions of self-assessment, including body image and global self-worth. But multifaceted syndromes can appear in incomplete forms—what Freud, in his discussion of anxiety neurosis, called "rudimentary" or "larval" presentations of the illness, or illness-equivalents, and what are now most often called *formes frustes.* The same underlying biological condition that in some people is expressed as the full picture of dysthymia will appear, in other people, as a single symptom.

Insomnia, for instance, may be the solitary symptom of what, in biological terms, is chronic minor depression. Sometimes a person with a long-standing sleep disorder and no depressed mood will find, on being given an antidepressant for an incidental indication (of which there are many—including prevention of migraine headaches), that the sleep problem disappears. This may occur even in response to a "stimulating" antidepressant whose side effects include arousal rather than sedation. Biologically, the insomnia was an isolated symptom of dysregulation of the biogenic amines. What is only mildly remarkable regarding sleep disturbance is more noteworthy in the case of such complex human functions as the assessment of self-worth or the ability to experience pleasure. These functions may be altered in depression, but they are also highly personal aspects of the self, linked closely to the individual's sense of who he is and how life events have shaped him.

• • •

Self-esteem is the most autobiographical of traits. A person's private assessment of his or her history, it contains, in integrated form, the victories and failures he or she has achieved and the cruelties and kindnesses with which he or she has met. Self-esteem is largely thought of as an intellectual function—the opposite, for example, of self-doubt, thinking ill of oneself, or undervaluing one's own capacities.

Self-esteem is hot as a defining and explanatory concept in today's culture. The goal of all modern parents is to give their children high self-esteem. Popular magazine articles debate what best fosters self-esteem in children: support or challenge, implicit trust or firm boundaries, room to grow or encouragement to excel. Every private organization that serves children, from preschools to summer camps, advertises itself as nurturing self-esteem, in the way that schools and camps of an earlier era stressed building character.

Alcoholics and adult children of alcoholics strive to reassess themselves in terms of past injuries to self-esteem. Low self-esteem is understood as a common impediment in women's social and professional struggles. Motivational tapes for businessmen purport to bolster self-worth. In myriad ways, American culture promotes self-esteem as the key to success and happiness, usually expressed as self-fulfillment, with the implication that self-esteem can be achieved through the experience of success or through the retraining of habitual patterns of thought.

This popular focus on the importance of self-esteem follows an evolution in the assumptions of psychotherapy. Self-esteem entered the psychiatric agenda through the rather odd theories of Alfred Adler. Though Freud later dismissed him as a dissident, Adler was part of Freud's inner circle in the first years of this century. Adler believed that many people suffer from defects, largely hereditary, in their bodily organs—he was especially interested in the bladder and kidneys. He maintained that people with "inferior" organs tend also to have defective nervous systems, and the already compromised nervous tracts become more strained as they try to compensate for the bodily defects. This "organic inferiority" is ultimately experienced by the person as a "feeling of inferiority" or insecurity. From insecurity comes neurosis—the result of a person's varied attempts to deny or compensate for the feeling of inferiority, perhaps through false bravado, perhaps through meekness and timidity. Though obscure and difficult to read, Adler's work had enormous popular influence in the 1920s, when the term "inferiority complex" became a near-synonym for neurosis.

Though Adler's ideas about the origins of low self-esteem were odd, his account of the effects of low self-esteem was prescient, presaging modern work on inhibition, reaction to novelty, and the role of self-image in family life. But to Freud, Adler's work was heretical: Adler grounded neurosis (albeit circuitously) in biological constitution; and Adler ignored unconscious inner conflict—the struggle of desire and guilt—in favor of the central role of the feeling of inferiority. Freud responded by arguing that low self-esteem was an incidental phenomenon, essentially a variant form of guilt. According to Freudian psychoanalysis, a person with low self-esteem typically had an overly strong conscience (in the language of psychoanalysis, the superego), which he attributed to an inner image of the exigent father. When psychoanalysis was employed to confront the sense of inferiority, its goal was to temper the power of the superego by making the (male) patient aware of his exaggerated sense of his father's power. (The less-developed theory regarding women centers on fear of loss of the mother's love.)

But Adler's concept of inferiority left its mark, and in time even faithful Freudians became interested in low self-esteem. In recent years, analysts have focused less on guilt as a source of low self-esteem and more on the role of childhood deprivation, or of misunderstandings between parent and child. Over the past twenty years, a consensus has formed that self-esteem arises, intact or damaged, from a person's experience of being recognized and appreciated at critical junctures in childhood.

The new guiding metaphor for the source of self-esteem is the gleam in the mother's eye. (Research on nurturance as a factor in the development of self-esteem shows attachment to the mother as of primary importance, with the father's role, in most cases, as surprisingly inconsequential, though that may change as fathers take on more of a nurturing role.) "What a lovely drawing!" the empathic mother says. In this, she is authentic; she does not praise what she does not see. She takes genuine pleasure in the child's stage-appropriate accomplishment, and she communicates her pleasure in a way that is neither overwhelming nor secretly demanding. She is aware of the child's needs more than of her own. And if she manages to gleam most of the time, she will be a "good-enough mother," providing sufficient security so that her occasional failures in empathy do not damage her child's sense of self. What a "good-enough mother" induces in her child is "appropriate grandiosity," the ability to imagine great things, without the need to scurry compulsively after superficial indicators of success. The values instilled by the rule-giving parent, traditionally the father, are still believed to influence self-worth, though, again, they are accorded relatively less importance.

Self-worth is a product of family experience and the family culture as they are absorbed by the growing child. Most developmental theories also recognize the role of later environmental influences outside the family. Children encounter success and failure in friendships, studies, sports, and their private play and exploration; adults succeed or fail at love and work. Self-esteem can grow, in response to achievements and the experience of competency, and it can be damaged by disappointments, humiliations, and losses.

But the effect of experience on self-worth in adult life is limited by the self-esteem with which a person enters adulthood. People with low self-esteem seemingly "do not know their own worth" and habitually discount successes. Typically, they are most aware of failures that confirm their negative self-image.

All the different maladaptive personality types that make life difficult and unhappy, ranging from the overscrupulous to the sociopathic, from the socially avoidant to the exhibitionistic, can be seen as outcomes of early failures in parental empathy interacting with painful life experiences. From this point of view, the diverse personality types represent responses to differing needs to shield the self from awareness of its own vulnerability, and then to conceal the imperfect, fragile, devalued self from the world. Psychotherapy allows change by helping a person reassess threats to integrity of the self, and by providing a person with a reparative relationship in which he or she is understood empathically, or empathically enough.

What is missing from this account is any appreciation of the factor Adler began with—the effect of biology on mood and temperament. To be sure, psychotherapists have begun to think about the issue of mismatched temperaments—the "swan raised by ducks" or a "bad fit" between child and parents. (Again, consider mother and daughter in *The Glass Menagerie*.) Certain parents have more trouble understanding certain children. But even this perspective may not be "biological" enough. Theories of parent-child mismatches may not explain a person's level of self-esteem. Temperament—sanguine or melancholic, for example—interacts with the environment both in childhood and in adult life. Positive mood leads to behaviors that are rewarded in the world and to full appreciation of those rewards —thus further enhancing self-regard and reinforcing the sanguine temperament. In the complementary sequence, melancholic temperament leads to maladaptive behaviors, which lead to disappointments, and thus to ever lower self-worth and ever more melancholy. The dysthymic women studied by Michael McGuire—the ones always at the end of long lines—suffered this constant sequence of maladaptive behavior, injury, and demoralization.

Some biologically oriented psychiatrists believe that self-esteem is directly related to mood—in the extreme, that low self-worth can be little more than a *forme fruste* of chronic minor depression. A happy, expansive, optimistic, energetic temperament includes positive self-regard as one of its elements; a more passive and pessimistic temperament includes low self-esteem. There are patients whose sense of self-worth seems to rise and fall in immediate response to the state of the biogenic amines—without any change in the degree of empathy they receive from others.

Donald Klein has written about such a person, a successful lawyer in his forties who, despite "a reasonably happy marriage, well-adjusted and successful children, and a career of moderate accomplishments and continuing upward social mobility," suffered persistent low self-esteem. The lawyer, whom the authors call William M., came to know himself better through psychotherapy, but without diminution of his sense of inadequacy or intermittent depressions. After six months of increasing feelings of groundless free-floating anxiety, the lawyer was referred for medication treatment.

Expecting an awkward and socially inept patient, the consulting psychiatrist was surprised to find William M. "good-looking, urbane, witty, intelligent and psychologically sensitive"—far from dysthymic or socially inhibited. William M.'s only chronic problem was low self-esteem. The psychiatrist prescribed an antidepressant. First the acute anxiety and depression faded. Then:

The patient's low self-esteem, which had been present since his earliest childhood, began to disappear. He began to re-evaluate his aptitudes and assets in a thoroughly realistic manner. The insights gained in psychotherapy, which heretofore had had no emotional impact, were now accompanied by a different attitude toward himself. It was as if William M. had been subtly depressed throughout his life and as if his low self-esteem had been a superficial manifestation of the depression.

On medication, William M. experienced a sense of self-worth superior to any he had felt before. What is more remarkable is that each time the medication was tapered—in the hope that William M. would be able to do without the antidepressant—the low self esteem returned. When medication was reinstituted, his self-esteem improved.

The case of William M. has a number of implications. For him, medication—an impersonal, ahistorical intervention, far from the realm of empathy or revised autobiography—affected self-esteem dramatically and decisively. The success of medication suggests that in some people levels of self-esteem may be largely a matter of neurobiology, related more to inborn temperament than to life experience.

Most important, beyond the question of how self-esteem arises, this case makes plausible a new understanding of what self-esteem is. For William M., psychotherapy was useful only when he was on medication; off antidepressants, he was unable to use insight. The beliefs that accompany low-self esteem—I am a failure, what I have achieved is of no importance—appeared and disappeared, or gained and lost potency, in conjunction with the changed feeling regarding the self. Neurologists use the term "proprioception" to refer to perceptions that monitor the self; proprioceptive pathways tell us where our hands and feet are, so we know where we are in the world. In the story of William M., low self-esteem seems a matter of altered emotional proprioception—a neurological distortion in self-awareness.

•   •   •

I have treated a number of patients like William M., people plagued by low self-esteem for whom medication works. The story of one such patient, Allison, reinforces this metaphor of proprioception—low self-esteem as an almost neurological inability to locate the self.

Allison wavered for over a year before coming to me. Her psychotherapy with a social worker had focused on issues of self-esteem; she had made slow, steady progress and then plateaued. The social worker had seen other such patients improve on Prozac but could not convince Allison to seek a consultation. Allison feared that an antidepressant might cause her to gain weight, and she believed she would be even more worthless and intolerable to others if she were not thin and unobtrusive. The more Allison obsessed about whether to make an appointment, the more the psychologist believed she was right in urging her on. At last, while trying in psychotherapy to face her feelings toward her mother, Allison hit a period of paralysis and found herself spending whole weekend days in bed, consumed with self-pity and vague fears. It was at this point that she wrote me an autobiographical letter in preparation for an appointment.

Allison began by describing her persistent feelings of sadness and fear. "It's like woe-is-me and doom-and-gloom are my partners," she wrote. "I want to be happy but can't give up the negatives, and can't get to that point of feeling self-worth."

Allison, an only child, saw her self-valuation as grounded in family life. Her father, she wrote, lacked the ability to assert himself. Instead, like Zelig, Woody Allen's chameleonlike film protagonist, he took on the personality of whomever he was with. To his daughter, the father was confusing, consistent only in his unhappiness, his focus on money issues, and his rejection of almost all members of the extended family. "He never knew me," Allison said, "and I never knew him."

Allison's mother was disappointed in her husband and lived through their daughter, dressing her like a doll but also comparing her with her cousins in ways that made Allison feel stupid. As a child, Allison was frail. She spent many hours alone—her favorite form of play was dressing paper dolls—but she had little sense of privacy, because her mother, who demanded that Allison confide in her, divulged Allison's secrets to cousins, aunts, and uncles. Allison's mother seemed content to have an ill daughter. The mother was gentle, but she used the excuse of Allison's infirmity to make all the decisions for her daughter and acted wounded if Allison tried to make any choice independently.

In adult life, Allison felt physically weak, intellectually second-rate, and socially awkward, although there were intervals when she was healthy and had friends. With the help of a supportive husband, she achieved many of her dreams. She raised three reasonably well-adjusted children and rose to a responsible position in her work as a fashion designer. But Allison never felt connected to her successes. She took no credit for the children's progress, doubted even that they had felt the effect of her love for them. And she behaved as if her design work had been done by someone else; she could not look at the clothes and see them as her own.

Her family complained that Allison repeated herself in conversation. She could not help it—she never believed that anyone ever listened to her. Even her body felt alien. She found herself occasionally staring at her own face or hands, or looking at photographs, to remember what she looked like. What she was searching for included and went beyond the physical self. She remembered in fifth grade having seen her image in the mirror and thinking, "There is a person there," but being unable to connect that person with Allison. The month before she to wrote me, Allison's husband bought her a sports car for a special birthday. She found she would adjust the side-view mirror so she could see the car, or adjust the interior mirror so she could see herself in the car, so difficult did she find it to accept the gift as real or connected to her.

When she showed up in the office, Allison's low self-esteem was written all over her. Though attractive and well dressed, she maintained a self-conscious posture for much of the interview and then apologized for her unease. Her conversation gave no indication of the slowed thoughts or impaired concentration typical of depression, but when I tried to check these functions by asking her to do simple mental tasks—recalling four phrases after five minutes, counting down by sevens from one hundred—self-doubt impeded her performance.

In the realm of pleasure, Allison's problem was her inability to believe that anything good would, or should, befall her. She lacked any certainty of her right to live and be. She said she was not outright depressed but, rather, "always on the verge of tears."

Because of her apprehensions and her acute sensitivity to any changes in her body, I started Allison on half the usual dose of Prozac. Even so, she felt side effects: excessive energy at first, and a sense of spaciness or difficulty concentrating. These diminished rapidly, and within a month Allison declared herself better.

The feeling of impending tearfulness had disappeared. With this change came a profound alteration in self-regard. "I am convinced my husband loves me," Allison said. She was able to experience the sports car as her own, able to appreciate and enjoy the fact that her husband had meant to give it to her in particular. And she found she no longer needed to repeat herself, no longer feared being overlooked.

A problem had arisen at work, and her first thought was "I can get over this hurdle," something she was not aware of ever having thought before. She threw herself into the fray. "I was always a watcher," she tried to explain. "I did not want to make waves. I was constantly afraid I would make people angry. Now I am more forward, and at the same time I feel I am a more gentle person, a more loving person. My staff has noticed it."

After three months on Prozac, Allison developed a rash, and we interrupted treatment. Off the drug, she again felt devastated, unworthy, and physically clumsy. The rash turned out to have had an unrelated cause, and when we restarted the Prozac, the sensation of confidence and connectedness returned. Allison's self-esteem, like William M.'s, was exquisitely medication-sensitive.

A few weeks after she resumed taking Prozac, Allison related a telling story. She had just been to visit a cousin she adored. She had always wanted red hair and green eyes like this cousin; Allison had blond hair and blue eyes, but somehow the family had made her feel this coloring was second best. As a grade-schooler, Allison ate carrots and beets in the hopes that her hair would turn red. She made over her dolls in the cousin's image. Over the years, everything about this cousin had been better: her native intelligence, the college she went to, her field of study, the man she married, the part of the country she lived in. And, of course, the cousin was taller and thinner.

But this time when she visited the cousin, Allison no longer felt like the dumb one: "So she went to a better college. What does she do with it? She sits home and reads women's magazines. I would never trade my children for her children." The two went grocery shopping, and the cousin tried to convince Allison that sea scallops were better than bay scallops. "I almost believed her—any other time I would have believed anything she said. This time I said, 'Whatever do you mean?' What I meant was, 'I am not an ugly idiot.' And then I noticed I was taller than she was—and I had been for thirty years."

Two things struck me as remarkable about Allison. Before she responded to medicine, she impressed me with the variety of ways in which she described low self-esteem as a perceptual experience. It was hard not to listen to her accounts with the ear of a literary critic in search of a subtext, underlining the frequency with which she referred to an inability to find the self. She was virtually invisible to herself, except for her faults.

After the Prozac "kicked in," I was impressed with her instantaneous change in self-image. Though I suspect that the medicine would have been less effective without the prior and concomitant psychotherapy, when the change occurred, it seemed a matter of changed self-valuation leading to changed self-understanding, rather than the reverse: the medication allowed her to locate herself. Before seeing Prozac work in this way, I would have said that to alter your self-image you have either to understand yourself differently or to live through a relationship in which you experience being valued differently. Surely a pill cannot reshape the inner representations you carry of your disconnected father and narcissistic mother. But Allison's self-image had indeed changed, on Prozac. And prior to her change in proprioception, Allison's marriage and her psychotherapy, both of which offered new forms of self-understanding and appreciation, seemed powerless to improve her self-esteem.

Other patients we have met, Tess and Julia prominent among them, responded to medication with rapid changes in self-image. The story of Jerry, the self-effacing surgeon, could be retold making self-image the central theme. What distinguishes these stories is the immediacy of the metamorphosis. We think of self-image as something accreted over time, acquired through living, subject mostly to incremental change. But in my practice I have seen case after case in which self-image changes overnight.

Patients who do well on medication quickly take on positive beliefs about the self. The new valuation of self seems to come from nowhere. The visceral sense of self-worth, positive or negative, appears to have an enormous effect on self-image, social efficacy, and overall well-being. And, as in the cases of William M. and Allison, medication works like a switch. When the patient is taking medication, self-esteem is high; when medication is interrupted, self-esteem is absent. There is nothing incremental about this change. The switch flips, and the whole package of self-valuation changes: beliefs about the self, assessment of personal history, sense of place in the world. The response to medication is independent of self-understanding.

Psychotherapeutic drugs have the power to remap the mental landscape—lithium makes manic depression seem ubiquitous, Xanax does the same for panic anxiety. But pharmacotherapy is not the only technology that has this effect; psychotherapy is a technology as well, and it has shaped the modern vision just as surely. In the half-century before the development of antidepressants, the facilitation of self-understanding was the most reliable way to alter low self-worth. Reasoning by inverses, and starting from the observation that improved self-understanding results in improved self-esteem, we have come to believe that a disorder of self-understanding causes low self-esteem, or even that low self-esteem is simply a disorder of self-understanding.

This belief is reasonable on other grounds. People with low self-esteem often say or believe bad things about themselves. And, historically, we find that many people with low self-esteem were taught in childhood that they are inferior to others. In Allison's case, we could conclude that her mother undermined her by criticizing, while her father injured her sense of self-importance through his emotional unavailability. Allison came to see herself as unworthy among women and unlovable among men. This view appeals to our sense of man as a creature of reason even as regards his unreason.

The way that negative belief about the self tends to accompany feelings of low self-esteem, and the way that effective psychotherapy fosters self-esteem, encouraged the belief that self-valuation is primarily a matter of self-understanding—that is, of cognition. In retrospect, however, there have always been reasons to question this idea. For one thing, self-esteem often does not respond to changes in cognition. There have always been patients like Allison and William M. who progress intellectually in psychotherapy without benefiting in terms of self-worth. Indeed, the distinguishing feature of the damaged sense of self is its poor responsiveness to evidence, even to evidence that is cognitively appreciated.

If we had looked at drug abuse as carefully as we now look at the licit use of medications, we would long have been aware that self-worth can respond to biological interventions. One reason amphetamine is popular as a drug of abuse is that people feel good about themselves on it. Uppers enhance users' sense of their place in the world. They feel big, important, worthy of attention. The classic experience of college students writing papers while on amphetamines is to overvalue the composition while the drug is active—even to imagine they are great writers and have dashed off a masterpiece— and then, as the drug wears off and they "crash," to undervalue their work and themselves. The problem with amphetamine as a treatment for disorders in self-image is precisely that it exposes the user to dramatic ups and downs. But its ability temporarily to alter self-valuation might have told us something about the physiological nature of self-esteem.

Even without referring to drugs, we know that self-worth has a distinct visceral component. Think about being overcome by a sudden failure of nerve. Like an attack of shyness or an urgent desire to gain the attention or approval of an admired person, this sensation is gripping and poorly responsive to reason. Accompanying it are profound bodily sensations: butterflies, flushing, weakness, and dizziness. The physical aspect of self-esteem is encapsulated in the common statement "I just don't feel good about myself." Feeling bad about oneself is an affective, not a cognitive, state, although feeling bad about oneself and thinking poorly of oneself are clearly related.

If psychiatry has ignored the physical aspect of self-image, it is in part because the autobiographical model of self-image has been so predominant and in part because there have been no alternate models around which to organize discrepant evidence. This is changing. First, there has been a re-emergence of the James-Lange theory of emotion, known in America through the writings of the nineteenth-century philosopher and psychologist William James, brother of the novelist Henry James. William James argued that the bodily elements of emotion, the parts we usually think of as secondary phenomena, are its core: the rapid heartbeat *is* fear, and we come to think "I am afraid" only after we sense palpitations. James was largely forgotten in the psychoanalytic era. But Donald Klein's explanation of panic anxiety has made James's psychology more appealing. As we have seen, the new dominant theory holds that the bodily sensations of anxiety, including the sense of dread that is so characteristic of panic attacks, can arise spontaneously and then accrete around them a series of explanations that are the mind's way of integrating this overwhelming emotion into a coherent experience. In a similar way, the cognitive element of self esteem, far from being primary, might be a response to negative feelings about the self. Just as, when parents divorce, a child will make the world coherent by taking on the belief that he or she is bad, a person with a visceral sense of low self-worth will take on negative beliefs about the self, in order to make sense of the bad feelings.

Once again, the animal world provides an analogy for the problem of high and low self-esteem. Human experiences of self-worth seem to bear a relationship to pecking orders in the animal kingdom.

Much mammalian social behavior revolves around what is formally called "dominance hierarchy." We think of hierarchy as a reproductive strategy. The strongest lion is able to impregnate a group of females and then defend enough territory to guarantee that his lionesses are well fed and rival males kept at a distance. But hierarchy is also a way of organizing social behavior, of introducing an element of order into the pride to prevent what otherwise would degenerate into a war of all against all.

Those who watch natural-history specials on television will be familiar with the dominant-submissive rituals of a variety of animals. How are these encoded? Consider the alpha-beta hierarchy of pack animals like wolves, in which certain males lead and others follow. How does a wolf know he is the alpha wolf? Yes, the experience of success in combat must have something to do with it, but surely we do not believe that the feeling of being the alpha wolf is maintained in the wolf's mind by cognition. To be the alpha wolf must be a pervasive experience, a feeling that informs every action, a state of the neurons that differs every minute of the day from that of the low-status "babysitter" wolf. And this visceral superiority probably exists in the absence of anything we would recognize as autobiographical memory. Rather than say a wolf learns to feel worthy of leadership, we might say that, on achieving alpha status, a wolf has become, neurochemically, a leader. This analogue of self-esteem pervades the wolf's physiology. He grows bold and voracious.

A research team—including Michael McGuire, the sociobiologist who studied dysthymic women—observed dominance hierarchy in multimale, mixed-sex troops of captive vervet monkeys. They noted that in each troop there was one male monkey in whose bloodstream there was a distinctly elevated level of serotonin, the mood-setting amine whose reuptake is blocked by Prozac. The level of serotonin in this male was about one and a half times that in other males, and in every instance the high-serotonin male was the dominant male in the troop.

The researchers first looked at groups that experienced a spontaneous change in leadership. Barring a change in status, blood-serotonin levels over time are remarkably stable in individual monkeys, as they are in man. But when a monkey changed status, his serotonin level changed dramatically. The serotonin level in newly dominant monkeys rose almost 40 percent, whereas the level in newly subordinate (formerly dominant) males fell almost 50 percent, to a level below that of the average subordinate male.

Dominance hierarchy can be manipulated in captive monkeys. Researchers remove the dominant male from the troop, and a new male takes on the dominant role. If the original leader is returned to the troop within ten weeks, he will resume the dominant role, and the interim dominant male will again become submissive. Here the changes are even more dramatic. Serotonin levels in the submissive monkey rise over 60 percent when he becomes the interim dominant male, and then fall to below their original level when the old leader returns. The old leader's blood serotonin falls to the levels of a subordinate monkey during the period of isolation, and returns to its usual elevated level on restoration to the troop and his former status. Subordinate males' blood serotonin is unaltered by social isolation. The factor that affects and sustains a high serotonin level is active dominance within the troop. Even removing a dominant male from a multimale group and housing him with three females causes his serotonin level to drop.

This research leads to the conclusion that, at least in vervet monkeys, serotonin levels are influenced by social status. In particular, receiving submissive behavior from other males elevates serotonin levels. Conversely, do serotonin levels influence social status?

To investigate this issue, the same researchers influenced vervet monkeys with drugs (including Prozac) that raise serotonin levels, as well as with drugs that lower them. The researchers looked at twelve social groups, each consisting of three males, three females, and their offspring. There were two experimental conditions.

In the first, the dominant male was removed from the group and one of the two remaining males was given a drug that increases serotonin levels; the other male was given a drug that lowers serotonin levels. The monkeys were observed for eight or more weeks, and then the dominant male was returned to the group, and all medicines were withdrawn.

After the group was given eight weeks to restabilize, the dominant male was removed again. This time, the monkey that had been given the serotonin-elevating drug was given a serotonin-depleting drug, and the monkey who in the first trial had been given the serotonin-depleting drug was given a serotonin-elevating drug. This is called a crossover design.

The results were dramatic. In every instance, after three or four weeks, the male monkey given a serotonin-elevating drug achieved dominance over the monkey given the serotonin-depleting drug. Dominance was complete and stable—the dominant monkey always won over 85 percent, usually 95 to 100 percent, of aggressive encounters. Because of the crossover design, it is clear that the effect had nothing to do with inherent traits in the monkeys selected. Whichever monkey got Prozac, or a drug with similar effect, dominated.

When the originally dominant monkey returns to the group, he assumes dominance once again, even if a formerly subordinate male is kept on a serotonin-enhancing drug. Mostly this is a function of the extreme stability of dominance hierarchy in vervet monkeys; monkeys instinctively remain loyal to old leaders even after relatively protracted absences, a trait that must provide continuity to troop life. But perhaps it is also an indicator that serotonin status is not the whole story: dominant males have other features, beyond high serotonin levels, that make them leaders. When coexisting in a group with a naturally dominant male, a Prozac-treated male achieves intermediate rank. The researchers have concluded that "serotonergic mechanisms seem to promote dominance acquisition only when hierarchical relationships are in flux."

There is suggestive evidence that serotonin levels in both humans and monkeys are under genetic influence. In juvenile rhesus monkeys, a breakdown product of serotonin has been shown to correlate with their fathers' levels of the same metabolite, even though the fathers do not raise the children. The vervet monkey researchers hypothesize that, in nature, certain male monkeys are endowed with high levels of serotonin. This endowment causes them to engage in successful behaviors—affiliation with female monkeys seems particularly important—which in times of flux can lead to the assumption of the dominant role. This status then leads to yet higher levels of serotonin, as well as to stable behaviors that reinforce dominance status.

Comparable studies of serotonin levels in man have not been carried out; it is difficult to vary status hierarchy experimentally in humans. But the monkey studies suggest that self-esteem, or the tendency toward assertiveness, is maintained by the serotonin system, and that the setting of the serotonin system is important in predisposing to levels of both self-esteem and certain kinds of social success. The vervet-monkey studies also suggest that self-esteem is a function of social reward, whether or not mediated by complex cognition. Perhaps in some people low self-esteem may be less a result of biography than of genetics: a low serotonin setting in a sense *is* low self-esteem—a feeling of unworthiness or submissiveness—and leads to low self-esteem by engendering unassertive behavior and an acceptance of low social status. Perhaps there are even people with a serotonin system so unresponsive that they do not experience high self-esteem whatever their social good fortune. Other people may come to low self-esteem by experiencing social deprivation, but even their self-image may be encoded less in cognitive memory than in the condition of their neurons. However low self-worth is acquired, a medication that raises serotonin levels might move a person biochemically from the feelings of subordinate status toward the feelings and even the behaviors of dominant status.

Low self-esteem is so closely related to other concepts we have considered—depressed mood, social inhibition, reactivity to novelty—that it can be conceptualized in terms of a now familiar model. Though it is a far stretch from dominance hierarchy in lower primates to self-esteem in humans, it is possible to imagine that for us low self-worth is either "biological" on a primary basis (that is, inborn, perhaps through serotonin levels) or else biological on a basis that is mediated by social status and in which self-understanding is a secondary, compensatory process.

Still, no one is likely to abandon the idea that self-esteem can be autobiographical. Constantly critical parents do often destroy the confidence of their children. Much research attests to the role of parenting in the formation of self-esteem. For instance, an often cited study of children in Connecticut concludes that self-esteem in ten-to-twelve-year-olds correlates with measures of "parental warmth, acceptance, respect, and clearly defined limit setting."

But after acknowledging the role of autobiographical memory in self-esteem, we will likely end by saying that much of the autobiography is stored in transmission patterns of mood-setting neurons. I can imagine a "kindling" model of low self-esteem parallel to that for depression: Over the years it may take less and less humiliation to set off—neurochemically—the same feeling of low status. As such feelings become endemic, low self-worth may become relatively insulated from the reparative powers of success. I can also imagine a sort of "failure-sensitivity," an analogue to rejection-sensitivity, in which minor humiliations strongly reinforce feelings of worthlessness. As in the case of kindled depression, such models would presumably entail progressive change in a number of neurotransmitters, not just serotonin. The concept of kindled low self-esteem implies that idiosyncratic, autobiographical experience does shape a person's sense of self-worth, but in the context of biological constraints. Those constraints may be inborn or may arise from trauma, or persistent low social status—perhaps enforced by insensitive, domineering parents.

We understand Allison's biography differently once she has responded to medication. We see her father's role as partly biological; perhaps his chameleonlike social behavior was a response to his own (neurochemically determined) inability to locate the self, a handicap he has passed on genetically to his daughter. The father's low self-worth has led him to attract and marry a woman who is dominant enough to lead but sufficiently inhibited to confine her expression of power to family matters. A child with a temperamental vulnerability to low self-esteem experiences the father's absence and the mother's stifling presence as neglect and abuse. With the extended family defined as the troop, Allison finds herself at the bottom of the pecking order. Her sense of self diminishes progressively to the point where she disappears from view, an absence that is encoded as a hard-to-influence, functionally autonomous trait, perhaps one maintained by anatomical changes in serotonin-responsive neurons. Later in life, not even marked social success can reverse the process. Medication restores to Allison the neurochemical substrate that appropriately corresponds to her adult social status, and she reappears to herself at last.

•   •   •

I perceived a complex interaction of medication and self-understanding in another patient with low self-esteem. Paul consulted me for what he called "problems arising from a crummy childhood." He had not thought about his own childhood until his struggle to be a proper father to his own son exacerbated feelings of inadequacy he had experienced for years.

Paul was a sensitive youngest child born into a family of noisy, volatile, and controlling go-getters. His parents were constantly annoyed at him. "They tried to break me," Paul said, as he recalled the parents' draconian methods of curing him of thumb-sucking and other minor bad habits. Throughout Paul's childhood, his father, who prided himself on his rugged masculinity, called Paul a sissy and tormented him over his lack of interest or ability in sports, an area where the older boys excelled. Paul's mother seemed overwhelmed by the number of sons her husband had, as she saw it, foisted on her. She was constantly yelling, something the other children seemed to tolerate. Paul recalled going to bed every night in tears. To Paul, childhood was a series of overwhelming family fights punctuated by teasing directed especially at him. He emerged into adulthood feeling inferior, unmanly, misunderstood, and cheated of love.

Paul dealt with his discomfort by burying himself in his studies. With the encouragement of teachers, he pursued an academic career and went on to teach and write about Renaissance history at the university level, a calling his family considered inferior to the practical professions favored by his brothers. Paul managed to hook up with an equally sensitive and accomplished young woman, and in time they had their first child, a son.

As the boy grew, Paul became aware of keen feelings of inadequacy as a father. One day, a college student came to Paul's office, seeking not so much help with his studies as moral support. Feeling he had nothing to offer, Paul broke into tears in front of the student. From that moment, a sense of inadequacy became foremost in his consciousness, and after some weeks he decided to consult me.

Once Paul had poured forth stories about his childhood, he saw how his identity as a father related to his feelings of inferiority. He had become paralyzed with his son, whom Paul saw as sensitive and unathletic, the way he had been as a child. Paul was afraid to get angry with the son, for fear of replicating his own father's behavior, and equally afraid of hugging and kissing him, for fear of turning the boy into a sissy. After Paul had verbalized these concerns, they seemed foolish. He understood that, even if he expressed anger, it would not be in the relentless, destructive way his father had. And he knew that a boy would not become a sissy because a parent was too affectionate; on a conscious level, Paul believed the opposite was the case, that sensitive children do best if they feel secure and loved.

This new self-understanding gave Paul substantial relief, and after five sessions he pronounced himself cured. I wondered whether this early end to therapy arose from Paul's need not to be weak: psychotherapy was an activity his father would have derided. But I was happy to see him take charge and move on with his life.

Eight months later, Paul returned. The hiatus had been an occasion for intense self-examination. He had puzzled over his relationship to his father, whom he now considered openly abusive, and he had immersed himself in reading about family relations. Paul believed that he had come a long way toward handling the consequences of his father's rage; but now he was troubled by insistent, highly emotional memories of rejection by his mother. He feared that these feelings were damaging his marriage. He saw himself as a constant disappointment to his wife, and he felt wounded by any hint of disapproval from her. Just as his father had needed him to be strongly masculine, his mother, surrounded by men, had badly wanted her last child to be a girl. Paul saw how he had been caught between his parents' contradictory wishes and subjected to anger rooted in their ambivalence and discord. Talking to me, he focused on his struggle to distinguish his wife's reasonable demands from his mother's impossible ones. Again, after a few sessions Paul disappeared.

Paul did not return until a year later, after the birth of his second son. Again he felt overwhelmed and worthless. This return of the sensation of low self-esteem was accompanied by signs of depression. We discussed parenting, but I did not feel my words or even his own reached him. I suggested Prozac, saying it might help with the depression, expecting it to do more as well.

Three weeks after he began the medication, Paul felt back in control. And, as I had hoped, the drug worked on the chronic issue of self-worth. Paul reported he no longer felt globally inadequate and inferior. He realized he had long been somewhat afraid of his wife, for no discernible reason; now he felt her equal. He was even able to stand up to his father, who until then had continued to dominate any one-on-one interactions.

Paul tried to describe his new state: "I just feel strong. I feel resilient. I feel confident. I can get bombarded and still feel in one piece. I no longer lack resolve when it comes to the children. This is who I am." He felt masculine enough to be a father of boys, and still sensitive and gentle enough to avoid becoming the type of father his own father had been. This feeling was a necessary complement to the insights that had reassured him about his capacities as a father.

Paul noted another remarkable difference. In the past, he said, he had been able to recall certain painful experiences and to *imagine* how he must have felt as a child. Now, when he remembered such incidents, he *felt* what he had felt as a child. He could not tell whether this striking change in the affective quality of his memory—just the connection between thought and deep feeling that psychotherapists hope to inspire—was due to a direct action of medication or, as he believed more likely, an increase in his tolerance for strong, disturbing emotions. The medicine, he said, gave him the will and the means to continue to face himself, and he soon left psychotherapeutic treatment again, to continue his private exploration, returning to see me only for brief, infrequent meetings to discuss medication management. This statement of independence, Paul felt, differed from the others. In the past, he had wanted therapy but denied himself; now he just felt beyond the need for psychotherapy. He did consider Prozac a "crutch" but said, "What the hell. Some people need a crutch to walk."

I find this case telling, because it speaks to an interaction between insight and medication in reversing a focused problem regarding self-worth. Psychotherapists talk about insight's not having impact until it is connected to the relevant affect: reattaching "split-off" memories to the feelings that accompanied them is a central task, for example, of psychoanalysis. For Paul, medication provided that link. In addition, the medicine seemed to give Paul a feeling of dominance that was helpful in dealing with his father and his sons, as well as his mother and his wife.

Paul's sense of low worth had been relatively circumscribed: he managed fairly well except around the birth of his sons. Medication gave him a sense of strength, with regard both to the people he faced and to his memories. Paul's feelings of low self-esteem could hardly be called meaningless; they related to his childhood experiences. Yet they seemed to have a physiological component—the neurochemistry of membership in a family that valued only leadership—that was dealt with most parsimoniously through drug treatment.

The question of medication as a crutch is interesting here. Ordinarily, we understand confidence to be a response to accomplishment, to overcoming obstacles through sustained effort; we might therefore imagine that taking medication would lower self-esteem. Here, and in most cases I have seen, the reverse was true: medication allowed Paul to experience what had heretofore meant little to him —namely, the truth that he had already perdured many difficult trials. Medication allowed him to reinterpret history—although this phrasing perhaps understates the role of the antidepressant. It might be more honest to say, "Medication rewrites history." Medication is like a revolution overthrowing a totalitarian editor and allowing the news to emerge in perspective.

As medication helped Allison locate her self, it helped Paul give his history flesh and blood. One of the functions of a psychotherapist addressing the abused is to say, "Yes, it was as bad as you imagine it must have been." Medication played that role for Paul: it made his injuries more real, his response to them more comprehensible. Paul's is a case in which, rather than say self-understanding promoted self-esteem, we might argue that chemically restored self-esteem catalyzed self-understanding. This new self-understanding then reshaped self-valuation. The medicine also worked directly, combating both a biological predisposition and the effects of family life that had assigned Paul the lowest position in the dominance hierarchy.

Alfred Adler identified low self-esteem as an organic handicap. Traditional psychoanalysis emphasized fear of the domineering father in fostering inferiority. More recently, psychoanalysts have deemed low self-esteem to result from failures in parental empathy. The ability of Prozac—in both humans and low-status monkeys—to alter self-valuation now adds a new dimension to the understanding of self-esteem.

From the viewpoint of biological psychiatry, it is possible to conceptualize low self-esteem as one of many possible expressions of low serotonergic transmission. Like the melancholic temperament, a predisposition to low self-esteem can be inborn, or can be induced or exacerbated by trauma. Perhaps there are particular sorts of trauma that lead more often to low self-esteem than, say, to compulsiveness or inhibition to novelty. Certainly humiliation by domineering parents, or by competitive siblings or classmates, might be as much a factor in low self-esteem as empathic failures by otherwise nurturant parents.

Low self-esteem may be grounded in unconscious conflict or cognitive self-doubt, but the efficacy of medication is evidence that low self-esteem exists as a state of the neurons and neurotransmitters. If insecure humans are like low-status monkeys, to have low self-esteem is a particular neurochemical state, one responsive both to the experience of social dominance and to the effects of serotonergic drugs. Self-esteem is not primarily a set of thoughts about the self; it is an aid or an impediment to locating the self, and a lens through which the self's history is viewed.

The various models of self-esteem remain to be integrated. But with the belief that self-esteem is as much physiological as psychological, we have moved a long distance toward ending the hegemony of mind over brain in our concept of the self. The change in paradigm to a perspective that is highly aware of the bodily aspect of mental functioning is sometimes called psychiatry's "loss of mind." And it is true, if we were to deny the obvious—namely, that ordinary life experience influences self-esteem—we would have lost our minds. But it can equally be said that by recognizing the visceral or perceptual aspect of the self we will save the concept of mind by making it more complete. As regards such issues as self-esteem, the contemporary mind is like a stroke victim who had lost both recognition of the physical self and memory of its own past but is now, with the help of medication, regaining both proprioception and an awareness of its history.

Formes Frustes:

Inhibition of Pleasure,
Sluggishness of Thought

*A*nnie Hall, Woody Allen's film about a man who on neurotic grounds can enjoy the pleasures of neither intimacy nor Los Angeles, was made with the working title *Anhedonia.* Anhedonia, the illness, is a quaint Victorian variant of neurasthenia in which a person cannot experience pleasure. Freud redefined the inhibition of pleasure as psychological. A girl who is forced, through fear of loss of her mother's love, to forsake her desire for her father may in adulthood suffer a global muting of desire, a numbing of the hedonic senses; she is then "repressed," which is to say she has repressed her capacity to enjoy. The ability to experience pleasure is a trait that has now for many years has been understood in purely psychological, as opposed to neurological, terms. Repressed people are "too hard on themselves" or, more deeply, afraid of pleasure. Anhedonia has disappeared as an illness; it persists in the language as a social or political metaphor, a sign of discord with contemporary culture, like "anomie," "ennui," and "alienation."

But anhedonia exists. It is another element of depression that can stand by itself, so that a patient may come to the consulting room complaining that there is nothing particular wrong with her except that the salt has lost its savor. I don't believe I have ever seen a case of pure anhedonia—in the absence of other signs of depression—but I worked for almost two years with a patient whose most persistent complaint was that she did not experience pleasure.

Hillary had tried a number of cures for her ailment. She had been in psychotherapy on and off throughout adolescence. Her last therapist became so intrigued or frustrated that, after many months of a failed traditional psychotherapy, he took to massaging her, according to the precepts of a fringe therapy called Rolfing. By the time she came to me, early in adult life, Hillary's problem had been labeled depression. But the gist of it was that she had no passion, no enthusiasm, no drive, no initiative, just a sort of lazy passivity grounded in her indifference to the pleasures of life. This take-it-or-leave-it attitude was so pronounced that, although she was funny and attractive and had the ability to consider situations with great originality, Hillary had few close friends and no boyfriends; men invariably developed the impression that she was bored with them. An admittedly overly sensual image of Hillary might be Marlene Dietrich in Alfred Hitchcock's film *Stage Fright*, where she sings the Cole Porter song "The Laziest Gal in Town." I have a pronounced memory of Hillary smiling languorously in a way that makes a therapist imagine his insights are less than compelling.

Hillary complained that she was bored, lonely, and underscheduled. She never had the willpower to bring order to her life. Nothing touched her or meant much to her, which was strange, because she came from a family of achievers, and on an intellectual level she shared their values. She loved her parents and wanted to please them, and she wanted to please herself, but without enthusiasm it was hard to sustain projects. She had limped through college and professional school, doing adequate work; she had been offered an interview with a respected firm on graduation, but she had not bothered to go to the interview, and now she was unemployed, paying her rent through odd jobs. She felt isolated because, as she put it, "The whole world seems to be in on something I just don't get."

Hillary had some of the traits of dysthymia or atypical depression:

sad mood, poor concentration, and constant sleepiness. (One doctor I consulted in her behalf suggested she suffered not from a mood disorder but from idiopathic central-nervous-system hypersomnia, a rare neurological condition in which patients sleep too much. Certainly Hillary yawned a lot.) Other than the sleepiness, most of Hillary's depressive symptoms seemed secondary or intermittent. The problem Hillary had early in life, and the one that persisted month after month, was an inability to understand what the fuss was all about.

Hillary combated her anhedonia in various ways. For instance, she learned how to hang-glide—and felt little thrill. (Her efforts made me think of the writer Graham Greene, who in his youth felt such ennui that he went to a dentist and feigned the symptoms that would lead the doctor to pull a tooth—to provide momentary respite from boredom.) She went to art galleries and concerts, but complained, "I don't see anything; I don't hear anything." Her isolation, low productivity, and lack of progress in a career all led to self-doubts.

Hillary's history with antidepressants was unusual. She responded to Prozac with a burst of activity that soon faded and did not return even with higher doses. Hillary would read her diary from the brief good period and ask, "Where did all the ideas come from? How did I manage to make so many plans?" She was angry at the medicine, because it had given her a taste of normal life, and now her emptiness was all the more poignant.

Though her last psychopharmacologist thought Hillary had suffered a major depression, he believed many of her problems were related to character and would respond best to extended psychotherapy. He wrote me: "She is a talented, creative individual who is stymied in her own mire of conflicts; I sincerely hope that she can allow herself to engage in the kind of treatment she would need in order to genuinely become unstuck." Hillary did enter psychotherapy with me for many months, but she found the process frustrating and considered me not a little foolish in my efforts to make connections between her affect and her life story. She herself could produce many plausible theories: "Being out of touch keeps me from being loved. Am I so afraid that I anesthetize myself?" But one hypothesis sounded as empty as another, and none of them helped her.

Because it had worked, if only briefly, I tried Hillary on Prozac again; with each increased dose, she got a slight effect which then faded. I added another drug (lithium) that sometimes acts synergistically with Prozac, but to no effect. At last, Hillary found a full-time job, one that demanded so many hours she could not find time to see me. Using the supply of Prozac she still had in the medicine cabinet, she resumed the medication in the hope that it would give her a little energy. On this third trial, the Prozac worked dramatically, and the effect was sustained.

"Now I understand what people were talking about," Hillary said. There were a hundred things to enjoy in life. She had no need to hang-glide: exhibits, concerts, films, and theater all spoke to her. She laughed about her relations with men. "They no longer intimidate me. I get a lot of attention from men these days, and frankly most of them are disappointing and unconvincing." She was able to enjoy dates even though she had her doubts about each man. She moved into and out of relationships with surprising ease. "I am in good control of my emotions," she said. "I don't get hurt. When I break up with a man, I have no bad feelings whatsoever, and I don't worry about whether I'm hurting him. Sometimes I wonder whether I haven't suffered a loss of moral sensibility." As for work, she was openly enthusiastic: "This is the perfect job for me." And it seemed her skills at work were enhanced; she loved what she was doing and could do it well.

I should emphasize that Hillary was not in the least manic, or even hyperthymic. Her social behavior seemed appropriate; her reasons for starting and ending liaisons sounded plausible, and if she was getting some of her own back with men, who could blame her?

I have no explanation for Hillary's initial failure and subsequent transformation on Prozac. Patients do occasionally improve on an antidepressant that previously did nothing for them. Sometimes I think the effect has to do with a synergy between the medicine and circumstances in the person's life that catalyze the cure—in this case, the job. I also wonder about the role of psychotherapy, as if some patients, through insight and a nurturant relationship, can be made psychobiologically "ready" to recover from a dysthymic syndrome. (If Prozac works best for lesser degrees of depression, perhaps in some patients it will only "kick in" when they are already psychologically and neurochemically on the mend.) It would be most honest to say that I do not know what factors allow medications to work where once they failed. But I have no doubt that what I saw in Hillary was a response to Prozac.

Here again, the medication seemed to flip a switch, to turn black and white into Technicolor. Prozac did things we have seen it do before—reduce rejection-sensitivity and increase liveliness—but it also seemed to provide access to a vital capacity that had heretofore been stunted or absent. Hillary's story made me appreciate how crippling the disregulation of "hedonic capacity" can be. The inability to experience pleasure as others do not only interferes with the motivation necessary to ambition or affiliation, it also leaves a person subtly uncomprehending of social behavior, and therefore utterly isolated.

Researchers have given a good deal of thought to the neurobiology of pleasure. Pleasure is essential to most social activity. In the form of reward, it influences attachment and learning, particularly social learning, and willingness to participate in groups and obey rules. It regulates appetite, for food and other substances. And it reaches broadly into every aspect of personality through enthusiasms, passion, aesthetic sensibility, and feelings of self-satisfaction. A host of disorders have been related to abnormalities of pleasure or reinforcement. Autism, schizophrenia, learning disabilities, delinquency and psychopathy, anorexia and bulimia, drug abuse, and depression have all been hypothesized to relate to dysfunction in the experiencing of pleasure in response to ordinary stimuli.

A variety of neurochemical systems and brain centers have been implicated in disorders of pleasure. Different neurotransmitters and different forms of injury are thought to be involved in, say, an autistic toddler's failure to respond to his parents' warmth and an anorexic adolescent's stubborn resistance to sustaining her body. Pleasure is so important to the establishment and maintenance of social and self-preservative behavior that its encoding in the brain is likely to be extensive and complex.

Though researchers have not elucidated the cellular biology of pleasure, theoreticians have given a good deal of thought to anhedonia. The modern reformulation of the concept began in the middle 1970s, when Paul Meehl, a psychologist at the University of Minnesota, published a critique of the prevailing psychoanalytic understanding of hedonic capacity. Meehl stepped back and looked from a distance at the Freudian view of psychological aberration. Freud assumed that all people strive for pleasure, and what distinguishes people are the forces that impede the striving. (To be fair, Freud also thought people differed in the strength of their drives, but that aspect of his thinking was never well elaborated.) The essence of psychoanalysis is the remove of defenses and resistances—various impediments to effective behavior and a full emotional life.

Meehl considered the impedance of drives to be only half a theory. Yes, people might come to mental illness through fear of various negative consequences; but why should they equally not come to it through the absence of positive reinforcers? His own observations led him to believe that, "just as there are some organisms impeded by fear, so there are other organisms whose fears are insufficiently softened, attenuated, or, I may even say, impeded by adequate pleasure."

In the normal population, there are, Meehl asserted, some children who are observably less capable of experiencing pleasure than others, just as there are adults who appear to have been "born three drinks behind." He suggested that, when a person reports he has just never gotten the same kick out of life that others do, therapists might consider, besides searching for impedances to pleasure, taking the patient's statement at face value. Just as McGuire saw the inflexibility in his dysthymic women as a an aspect of temperament that exists on a continuum, Meehl saw "cerebral 'joy-juice' " as a spectrum trait. Some people can take pleasure from almost any situation. Meehl wrote: "I conjecture that these people are the lucky ones at the high end of the hedonic capacity continuum, i.e., they were 'born three drinks' ahead." Both high and low levels of joy-juice are normal variants, not illness.

Anhedonia, however, can produce illness. Life at the low end of the continuum is difficult. People with little hedonic capacity must tolerate the same stresses as others, but without many of the rewards, and depression may result. Arming such patients with insight or even strategies for success is of little use. Their problem is precisely that success does not serve as a reward, because they do not experience the pleasure that ordinarily accompanies success. Meehl admitted that his formulation was speculative, but he conjectured that low hedonic capacity (hypohedonia), of the sort that leads to depression, can be a genetically heritable trait. Meehl might well say that a patient like Hillary is primarily hypohedonic; any depression she feels arises secondarily, from her inability to attain or appreciate life's bounty.

For the moment, Meehl wrote, the best treatment for (or prevention of) the depression that results from low hedonic capacity is a diminution of secondary guilt: the person who is socially limited because of hypohedonia ought not to blame himself for his social isolation; not everybody gets the same pleasure from affiliation. Meehl was not impressed, though, with strategies designed to encourage patients to "learn to live with a 'scarcity economy of pleasure' "; people just cannot maintain their mood or self-esteem without pleasure. Meehl believed that the best approach to hypohedonia would ultimately be psychopharmacologic.

———

Meehl's rejection of the "impedance" model of anhedonia was as challenging to the prevailing view of human nature as Klein's concept of rejection-sensitivity, and it suffered a similar fate. That is, in the absence of effective medication, it remained an interesting idea but one that was addressed by only a smattering of research. Much of that research is the work of a Chicago-based psychiatrist, Jan Fawcett, and his psychologist colleague, David Clark. In the early 1980s, Fawcett and Clark looked at hospitalized depressed patients and found that 12 percent complained of anhedonia. On a variety of psychological tests, the anhedonic group looked different from the other depressed patients. In particular, they showed fewer signs of neurotic conflict—that is, they seemed to have come to their ailment directly through a deficit in hedonic capacity, and not through guilt or anxiety. Anhedonic patients tended to recover faster than did other depressed patients, but even upon recovery they remained unable to experience pleasure. These results lend support to Meehl's conjectures. Fawcett and Clark's findings argue that hypohedonia is a chronic trait, that it is not especially associated with neurotic conflict, and that it results in a distinct subtype of depression.

Research regarding hypohedonia in normal populations has been more confusing. There are hints that low capacity for pleasure is a chronic trait, persistent throughout the life cycle, and that it correlates with difficulty in establishing or maintaining intimate relationships. These studies do not show that anhedonia results in depression, but the research has focused on very high-functioning populations—medical students, medical interns, and senior executives of Fortune 500 companies—in which anhedonic traits would likely have been compensated for in some way. And, of course, Meehl's assumption is precisely that, although low responsivity to reward can result in depression, for the most part it exists as a variant trait and is expressed differently depending on life circumstances and the additional temperamental traits that accompany it. One adaptation to low hedonic capacity is overachievement, in hopes of maximizing what little pleasure one can attain. Like Akiskal's dysthymics, the hypohedonic people Meehl describes can be driven in their careers.

When Meehl's monograph appeared, Donald Klein had just published an article that contained a different approach to anhedonia. Like Meehl, Klein was critiquing a basic tenet of psychoanalysis, but instead of impedance, Klein focused on Freud's claim—long since rejected even by most psychoanalysts—that there is only one sort of pleasure: excitation reduction. (According to Freud, pleasure is the replacement of irritating excitation, such as hunger, by satiation.) As usual, Klein's work rested on pharmacologic dissection.

Before studying imipramine, Klein had worked with drug addicts, and he noticed that addicts had distinct preferences. Those who favored morphine could generally be distinguished from those who favored cocaine or amphetamine. And though both types of drugs give a rush of pleasure, the eventual effects are different. Opiates satiate an addict, at least while they remain effective. Cocaine and amphetamine do not satiate but, rather, excite further desire; stimulant addicts will tend to "go on a run" and rapidly use all the drug at their disposal.

To Klein, these varieties of pharmacologic pleasure-seeking corresponded to varieties of ordinary enjoyment. Some pleasures, like eating a big meal or sexual orgasm, are satiating and do accord with Freud's concept of excitation reduction. But others, like "foraging, hunting, searching, and socializing," or sexual foreplay, are excitatory. Klein labeled these two sorts of pleasure "consummatory" and "appetitive."

Klein later looked to imipramine for clarification of this distinction. He pointed in particular to certain depressed patients who respond only partially to imipramine. These patients recover in terms of sleep and appetite, but they remain uninterested in work and other activities; adding amphetamine to the imipramine revives their interest and energy. Klein described such recovery as a two-step process.

Imipramine restores patients' responsiveness to the consummatory pleasures, but only on the second drug do they rediscover the pleasures of the hunt.

In his work with depression, Klein tried to distinguish those patients who were best treated with imipramine from those best treated with MAOIs (monoamine-oxidase inhibitors). Klein found that imipramine was most useful in the treatment of severe depressive episodes with a definite and rapid onset. Patients who looked less depressed, had arrived at depression more gradually, and complained mostly of boredom and apathy did not respond to imipramine but might respond to MAOIs. This second group could sometimes be interrupted by distractions or amusements; in the midst of a hospitalization for depression, they might be seen on the ward chatting happily. Yes, they were impaired. But the impairment extended only to appetitive pleasures. Though they had lost the capacity to forage, if pleasure landed on their plate, they consumed it.

Klein's theory holds that the pleasures of the hunt are neurobiologically distinct from the pleasures of the feast. The normal process of desire and satiation would go something like this: Encountering an appetitive stimulus (say, some mouth-watering prey), the organism experiences "hopeful expectancies and images." These lead in an excitatory fashion to heightened drive and heightened anticipatory pleasure. As the organism pursues the consumable object, it receives feedback from a "central comparator"—some part of the brain that mediates between desire and action—indicating it is doing well and encouraging further pursuit; in the case of impending failure, the comparator produces demoralization and energy conservation.

Atypical depression—the type in which patients eat and sleep too much—is nicely modeled by this theory; atypical depressives do not forage, but they do consume. They have appetitive, but not consummatory, anhedonia. Typical depression, in which appetite and sleep are lost, relates to consummatory anhedonia, which includes and supposes appetitive inaction: if you have no interest in eating, there is, *ipso facto,* no point in hunting.

Klein's account of anhedonia is often contrasted to Meehl's. But if we understand Meehl's "low hedonic capacity" to overlap with Klein's "appetitive anhedonia," Klein's work adds a nice refinement. Meehl's account is useful in underscoring the probability that responsiveness to pleasure is a spectrum phenomenon, and that unresponsiveness may be either a matter of defensiveness (impedance) or a deficit state (a low ability to experience pleasure) that exists as a normal variant. Klein's account helps explain a contradiction between what we see and what patients tell us. A patient may be perfectly charming in conversation and yet complain that she cannot function socially. The problem is that she can enjoy pleasures that happen to come her way, but she does not anticipate pleasure, and she is not moved to pursue it.

Hillary's case does not fit Klein's categories in any neat way. Like an appetitive anhedonic, she is lethargic and indifferent to anticipated pleasure; she also finds no (consummatory) thrill in art, music, or hang-gliding. But Klein's idea of an imperfectly inclusive anhedonic condition does go some way toward accounting for Hillary's ability to stumble through professional school as well as many of her pleasant traits, including her sense of humor. Both of these similar models help to make us comfortable with a biological approach to Hillary's frustration. If she is born with too little joy-juice, we should supply her with more; if her "central comparator" is misfunctioning, we should recalibrate it. And once Prozac works, it thoroughly undermines the Freudian hypothesis that "inhibition" of pleasure is merely a matter of defensiveness, guilt, and sexual shame.

The treatment of anhedonia with Prozac helps to clarify the distinction between drug use and drug abuse. Prozac does not provide pleasure; it restores the capacity for pleasure. It is neither excitatory like cocaine nor satiating like heroin. The drug taker does not crave Prozac and does not feel relief when it enters the system. The desired effect, a change in responsiveness to ordinary pleasures, occurs gradually and is unrelated to the daily act of consuming the drug.

But this is not to say that the use of medicine to alter the capacity for pleasure is without its accompanying questions, call them ethical or sociological, according to your taste. If we accept the proposition that hedonic capacity exists along a continuum, then in treating hypohedonia we are shifting a normal person from one part of that continuum to another. As long as we move from the extreme toward the middle—from atypical depression toward appetitive wellness—that exercise is unexceptionable. But should we aim for the precise center? Surely patients would prefer to be rendered a little hyper-hedonic, to have an enhanced enjoyment of the ordinary. And then there is the question of people who are not patients—who begin with hedonic capacities close to the norm. If the drug is developed that will, with minimal side effects, make the ordinary taste richer—psychopharmacologic MSG—will we accept its use by people whose hedonic capacity is average and who have reasonable self-esteem and social skills? What is reasonable? Certainly Meehl sees the whole range of hedonic capacities as normal. Most decisions regarding continua are arbitrary: Who can say that this much hedonic capacity is standard and that much is above standard? Where does treatment end and—to use the word—hedonism begin?

These questions are not solely hypothetical. Often patients say they feel all right if they take one Prozac capsule four days a week, but they feel better still if they take the medicine more frequently. And there are patients who, once successfully weaned from Prozac, want to restart it, not because they are depressed, but because life seemed brighter when they were medicated. If we believe that hypohedonia is a chronic trait intermittently expressed as depression, we will expect exactly this difficulty. Forced to decide what level of hypohedonia bears treating, we may *tell* ourselves we are making the determination on quite different grounds, that we are weighing the possible risks of exposure to Prozac against the countervailing risks of recurrent depression. But in truth the deciding issue, which is largely aesthetic, or related to a modern tribal standard, is just how much zest a person ought to have.

To look again at drug abuse: An untested but widely accepted hypothesis regarding drug abuse is that it is in large measure a form of self-regulation by people whose high rejection-sensitivity, low self-esteem, and low hedonic capacity leave them vulnerable to painful emotional states for which there is little counterbalancing pleasure. According to the "self-medication hypothesis of addictive disorders," a formulation of the Harvard psychiatrist Edward Khantzian, addicts use cocaine to treat affective states very similar to those I have discussed in relation to dysthymia; opiates, in contrast, may be used to mute the disorganizing effects of rage. In other words, drug abuse, particularly stimulant abuse, is not merely the pursuit of pleasure or, as was once thought, an attempt at regression, but, rather, a complex behavior aimed at coping with intolerable feelings in a person who, without medication, may experience little enjoyment. Indeed, the self-medication hypothesis has led to the treatment of certain drug abusers with antidepressants in the hope that antidepressants will at once increase addicts' hedonic capacity in their daily lives and decrease their vulnerability to loss or rejection. These projects generally meet with mixed success—so much in the addict's culture determines whether he gives up street drugs. But many addicts do kick the street-drug habit once on antidepressants; and many report that the prescribed medication makes them feel less empty and better able to enjoy ordinary pleasures.

The difference between use and abuse rests on such issues as legality, excitation, the characteristics of the drugs employed, and the relationship of drug procurement and use to the rest of the person's life—but not on the underlying purpose for which the medication is taken. Both the anhedonic on Prozac and the drug abuser on cocaine are trying to compensate for diminished hedonic capacities. In terms of treatment, for both the neurotic and the drug abuser, the goal is to adjust the capacity to experience pleasure in response to ordinary events. Psychiatrists have always worked on this goal with the "repressed" neurotic, by questioning his or her unconscious need for self-denial. For the addict, the hope is to enhance the ability to "postpone gratification," something antidepressants may do by increasing the ability to imagine future pleasure. In both cases, the problem may best be seen as anhedonia, and we may prefer to approach it pharmacologically, in the hope that, if the comparator is reset— if ordinary pleasure becomes appealing—self-understanding and self-control will follow.

● ● ●

Prozac alters an additional aspect of dysthymia that has been the subject of little research but that stands out prominently in case after case. Starting with the first patient we discussed, Sam, the architect who on Prozac found himself quicker of thought and more fluent in his presentations, we have met a series of people who, however else they responded to Prozac, also became more mentally adept. Tess, Julia, Gail, Jerry, and Hillary all responded to Prozac with a new fluency of thought. Most "good responders" to Prozac say that they think faster and function better at work when they are on the medication.

Perhaps this response should not surprise us. Impaired memory and concentration are characteristic symptoms of depression. And though dysthymics are generally normal in their mental functioning—McGuire's depressives were not distinctive on traditional tests of memory and concentration—"sluggishness of thought" has for centuries been recognized as a constituent of the melancholic temperament.

It follows, according to the principle we have been discussing—any single aspect of depression can stand for the whole— that there should be people who, despite the absence of other symptoms, can use antidepressants as a mental tonic. I do not imagine that otherwise contented people are flocking to psychiatrists to have their minds sharpened, nor do I know how psy-

236

chiatrists would respond to such requests. But I recently worked with a patient who in her own way made this issue real.

Sonia is a talented graphic artist referred to me by a social worker for medication consultation concerning her minor depression. My first impression, on meeting Sonia, was of what might once have been called an ethereal young woman. She had that vague, hesitant habit of speech sometimes characteristic of artists and often affected by members of the British aristocracy. For Sonia, even mild depression carried some urgency, because other members of her family had suffered serious mood disorders. I started her on Prozac, and the depression lifted. But she changed in other ways that will now sound familiar: she became more energetic and more assertive socially than she had been even in the years before the onset of her depressive symptoms.

In Sonia's case, an additional change was especially striking. She became more fluent of speech, more articulate, and better focused. Depression can cause "paucity of speech" and "psychomotor retardation"—a tendency to produce few utterances, and those slowly. But Sonia said she had never enjoyed such clarity of thought. This was not about recovering from a depression; it was something new.

I was able in time to withdraw the medication. In the ensuing months, Sonia reported that she was not quite so sharp, so energized, as she had been on Prozac, but she considered herself cured—back to normal.

Case closed.

And then, after another few months, Sonia called for an appointment. She was not certain she needed to see me. But she was still in psychotherapy with the referring social worker, and the social worker thought Sonia was again becoming "disorganized." Sure enough, the stumbling speech pattern had returned. Though it had once seemed appropriate to Sonia—in accord with some ideal of the tongue-tied artist whose true expression occurs on the canvas—now it was disturbing, even painful, to hear. Having experienced this young woman as articulate, I now considered her halting speech a symptom.

But a symptom of what? Sonia and I reviewed the indicators of depression, and we found she had few of them. Some early-morning wakening, yes, but early rising had been a lifelong pattern. Social withdrawal? Only to the degree that had characterized her throughout her adult life, and she had, after all, a husband and numerous family friends. No tearfulness, no guilt, no ruminations beyond the ordinary. She was not even sad, unless a tinge of *Weltschmerz* constitutes sadness. And even to mention these patterns is to exaggerate.

Sonia was not depressed. She was herself. But her fumbling speech now sounded pathological, and it was accompanied by a certain lack of precision in her ideas. I doubt she or I would have remarked on this mental vagueness had we not the hope of altering it with medication. What we were considering treating was a lifelong manner of thought and expression about which a friend might lovingly remark, "Oh, that's Sonia all over!"

Sonia had just finished a major exhibit, and she would be able to relax for a while. Since she was in reasonable spirits, I was somewhat reluctant to restart the medication. Whether from pharmacologic prudence or prudery, I suggested we hold off, and Sonia readily concurred. At the same time, we agreed that, if we saw any further deterioration, any indication that her fumbling speech was the prodrome of depression, she would resume medication.

The grace period was two days. By then, both the social worker and Sonia had called back. They had decided Sonia's mental disorganization—difficulty planning, difficulty following through—was too pronounced to go untreated. Sonia was having difficulty showing up on time for scheduled events, she seemed to lack the interest or ability to manage her finances, her husband had remarked on her murkiness of thought. And, contrary to what I had believed, her upcoming calendar included a number of difficult transitions. I called in the prescription—Prozac to treat ethereal temperament.

Sonia responded again, and at a very modest dose. Her focus was clearer, her speech crisper. Her characteristic pattern of thought, one that had not been remarked on in her schooling, one that she just considered a part of her makeup, was now a fit target for medication. In her husband's mind, and perhaps mine and her own, Sonia's habitual way of approaching problems, and her vague speech, are no longer delightful eccentricities but, rather, a biological handicap.

The question is: Which biological handicap? What is it in Sonia's thought that changes on medication? The answer is of scientific and, I would argue, philosophical interest. In medicating Sonia, am I curing an ailment or merely moving her along a continuum, in this case from lesser to greater mental quickness? The former use of medication is unexceptionable; the latter, perhaps problematic. We are justly suspicious of tonics for the normal brain.

One answer to what ails Sonia—the wrong one, I think, but worthy of a brief digression—involves the ability to pay steady attention to tasks. Attention deficit is both a legitimate arena of inquiry and something of a cult subject within the profession. Some psychiatrists believe that attention deficits are among the most poorly recognized and widespread of mental conditions, and whenever I write an essay about a patient like Sonia I hear from these partisans. At first blush, the suggestion that Sonia—and with her possibly Tess, Julia, Gail, Jerry, Paul, Tom, and Hillary—suffers from an attention deficit is an odd one, as a description of the concept should make clear.

Attention-deficit disorder is a condition that first manifests itself in childhood, where it is noticed by parents and teachers. Children with attention deficits are poor listeners. They are easily distracted, and fail to complete tasks, whether at schoolwork or in play. They are impulsive, a trait that tends to get them in trouble in school, where they fidget, have difficulty organizing work, speak without being called on, and require frequent special supervision. Many of these traits disappear in the face of challenge or novelty and reappear when routine reasserts itself.

Attention deficits in children often occur in conjunction with hyperactivity, the condition in which children are always on the go, as if driven by a motor. So common is this pairing that the standard term for marked attentional problems in children now is "attention-deficit hyperactivity disorder," or ADHD. In their play with peers, children with hyperactivity can be aggressive and domineering. They often have trouble falling asleep, and wake frequently at night. They have normal memory and produce no distinctive pattern on neuro-psychological tests. In the laboratory, children with ADHD display the skills to organize tasks, but in daily life, they do not use those skills. Although most of the children have otherwise normal developmental histories, studies of ADHD often find increased rates of intrauterine or birth complications, and minor neurological abnormalities can often be detected when these children are examined in detail. It is also believed that ADHD can be produced by certain environmental toxins, such as lead.

ADHD typically begins before age seven and is most evident during the school years. But it sometimes continues into adult life, where it may manifest itself in impulsive conduct. One would imagine that, on the basis of failure to gain rewards, ADHD would be associated with depression. But, although children with ADHD may show anxiety and sadness and may develop low self-esteem, as adults they do not suffer an excess of major depression. Other problems, however, such as criminal behavior and drug abuse, arise disproportionately in adults with residual attention disorders.

The dysthymic patients we have met seem to stand at the opposite pole from ADHD. Typically well organized, driven, and somewhat compulsive, they are extremely obedient and may overachieve in school, even in the face of disrupted home lives. They are good at following through on tasks, tend to sleep too much rather than too little, are rarely impulsive or domineering, and, indeed, tend to be timid and risk-averse. They do better in the face of routine and worse in the face of novelty. And they are prone to depression.

Why, then, would anyone say these patients have attention deficits? One reason rests in the history of the profession. It has been difficult to get ADHD recognized in children—so many children have social and school difficulties for so many different reasons—and even more difficult to accustom psychiatrists to look for the syndrome in adults. As a result, aficionados of ADHD tend to have in their sack a sheaf of histories of patients in whom the diagnosis was missed and for whom, once the diagnosis was made, the relevant drugs (usually stimulants, like amphetamine or Ritalin) were all but miraculous. They believe that symptoms of demoralization paired with a subtle disorganization of thought often represent ADHD.

But objective problems in memory and concentration are typical of ordinary depression. There is even a condition called "pseudodementia." People with pseudodementia look for all the world as if they were suffering a dementing biological illness, like Alzheimer's disease; but they recover with biological treatments for depression— antidepressants or electric-shock therapy. Their problem was precisely a *forme fruste* of depression. Most psychiatrists tend now to say that pseudodementia is not pseudo- at all; rather, major depression should be recognized as a reversible dementing condition. By analogy, minor depression in *forme fruste* can have as its primary symptom a minor impairment of mental agility.

Is disorganized thought in "neurotic depression" more like ADHD or more like melancholia? You might imagine that this dispute could be settled through pharmacologic dissection. The problem is that the treatments for ADHD overlap with those for depression. The drugs of choice for attention deficit are stimulants: Ritalin and the amphetamines. But stimulants are sometimes effective in depression. And the stimulants act on two neurotransmitter systems: dopamine, thought to be aberrant in ADHD, and norepinephrine, the neurotransmitter that is sometimes deficient in depression. So stimulants might help people with either disorder, perhaps through quite different mechanisms. The second-line drugs for ADHD are the antidepressants, including those, like Prozac, that act primarily on serotonin.

My own belief is that Hillary, Sonia, and the other patients we have discussed do not have ADHD. Quite the contrary. These are people who tend toward compulsiveness, social inhibition, and steadfastness. The disorganization of thought they suffer may have to do with a general mental slowing to the point where connections are not made rapidly enough for the system to function efficiently. One gets a different impression with attention-impaired, impulsive patients. They may make connections too rapidly, but the problem is not speed alone; it is that they occasionally skip certain intermediate steps that allow for continuity of thought processes, consideration of alternatives, and the application of mature judgment.

What is it, then, that improves in patients like Hillary, Sonia, and the many others who think more clearly and speak more fluently on Prozac? What they experience, and what we see, may entail a number of changes. The loss of social inhibition and increase in confidence they feel on medication leaves them less tongue-tied. The restored or enhanced sense of pleasurable anticipation makes them more present in the world, and thus more alert and responsive. But my impression is that these people also experience an alteration in a spectrum trait having to do with rapidity and agility of thought. Just as some people are less social, more risk-averse, or less responsive to pleasure than others, certain people think more slowly and are less intensely alert, whereas others think fast and are habitually highly focused and neurologically aroused. The features that typify hypomania or hyperthymia are "press of speech" and "flood of ideas"; dysthymia is characterized by a relative paucity of thought and speech. Antidepressants can reposition people along this continuum.

I believe that when Sonia speaks and thinks with her charming hesitancy, she is displaying a *forme fruste* of dysthymia; I have raised the issue of ADHD not because I think the diagnosis is right but because the contrast between the two explanations highlights the complexity of the ethical issues embedded in the treatment of patients like Sonia. Someone with ADHD presumably has a subtle neurological deficit; someone who is similarly handicapped on an "affective" basis is not neurologically damaged but, rather, comes to her condition by virtue of sitting toward one end of a normal continuum of speech and thought patterns.

Imagine the following. Into the office comes a patient who says she would never have consulted a psychiatrist but for the remarkable change she has seen in her identical-twin sister, who has responded to psychotherapeutic medication with a marked increase in productivity at work and a new crispness of thought in ordinary conversation. The as yet untreated twin has always felt ponderous in her thought, thick of tongue, a bit unfocused on the task at hand. Might the doctor recommend a medicine for her as well?

If the twins had been subtly injured in the birth process—if they both suffer from what used to be called "minimal brain dysfunction"—and as a result display a derangement of attention, then we will feel justified in applying any medical technology that might correct or help compensate for this damage. If we believe the twins have an attention deficit due to lead poisoning, we will rush to treat the problem. We will step in even if the attention deficit never causes the twins' performance to dip below the (low) normal range for every function we test.

But if the twins have suffered no birth deficit and no lead poisoning, if they just display a temperamentally based sluggishness of thought—if their deliberateness is a normal trait that has persisted, evolutionarily, because of the selective advantage it confers on the tribe—ought we to intervene? Let us say we diagnose Twin A with depression and notice that her thought becomes more agile on antidepressant medication; will we then treat Twin B, who has never been depressed?

Here is a peculiar situation. If the first twin had ADHD, we would not hesitate to treat the second mentally sluggish twin. In contrast, if the first twin experienced her improvement incidentally in the course of pharmacotherapy for depression, then we might have scruples about treating the second twin. But the two imagined twin pairs—one where the index twin has ADHD, one where she has depression—may have the same levels of concentration and agility of thought. There are circumstances in which we sanction the treatment of normal variant traits with medication, but we are more comfortable with the use of medication to treat illness.

Had she not experienced acute depression, no one would have medicated Sonia for vagueness of thought or speech. Having responded to medication with a sharpening of her thought processes, she became her own "twin." We now consider her mental disorganization and vague speech to be a handicap, not an eccentricity, but the handicap is not one of illness. Or, rather, if we do now label her ill, we will have redrawn our diagnostic map and once more allowed medication to tell us who is normal. What began as a consultation of a psychiatrist regarding medication will have become the consultation of a medication regarding psychiatry.

Sam, the architect whose personality lost some of its edge in response to Prozac, resumed taking the drug long after his depression had disappeared (as I learned when I ran into him at a social function). He found he drafted, thought, and talked more fluently when on medicine, so he "chipped" Prozac, taking a small dose daily, despite the misgivings of his wife. He had assumed that I, too, might disapprove of this use of medication, so he had asked his internist to arrange for an open prescription. And Sam had read me right. I would have been uneasy about prescribing Prozac to make him more mentally agile, although I might finally have done it.

The issue of using medication to improve mental acuity is not new. Jean-Paul Sartre wrote his last books while on amphetamines, fully believing he was hastening his death but preferring his version of Achilles' choice: the short, productive life. In the United States, we do not grant the individual this option. We know that many people feel more alert and productive on amphetamines, certainly in the short run. But amphetamines are addictive and cause paranoia—they are drugs of abuse—and for these reasons we allow them to be prescribed only for very narrow medical indications, chiefly ADHD. An American doctor would have to say to Sartre, "The choice is not yours: the book goes, you stay; we are caretakers for a whole society, not potentiators of your work."

The example of Sartre makes clear the arbitrary or contingent nature of our boundary-setting. Surely the moral calculus might change if the facts were to change. What if we knew that for certain people we had a nonaddicting, relatively safe drug that increases alertness, quickness of thought, and verbal and mechanical fluency? Should each person be permitted to weigh the risks and benefits and choose to take the drug, even in the absence of illness?

Perhaps traditional antidepressants can decrease mental sluggishness in people whose deliberateness of thought is set by their affective temperament. Until the advent of Prozac and other potent and specific medications, the prevalence of dangerous or even just troublesome side effects spared us from the need to make certain decisions about the socially acceptable use of medication. Now we have to ask the question: ought medicine to be used for self-enhancement? We might be quite pleased to find a pill that has few side effects and that speeds thought processes. But this option also gives rise to nightmare scenarios.

In his syndicated column, the management consultant Tom Peters recently wrote an essay, titled "The Quick and the Dead," whose central thesis is that executives who make decisions well tend to make them quickly, whereas those who make slow decisions tend to make poor ones. There are settings in which quickness of thought may be all but mandatory. We may well wonder whether the availability of licit mind-quickening drugs would lead to pressures on managers to use those drugs to become as quick of thought as possible. Think of the self-effacing surgeon, Jerry. Were he a junior executive in a fast-paced corporate atmosphere, might not a concerned superior suggest he go for a psychopharmacology consultation?

This nightmare view of the use of medication to increase mental agility—not to repair brain damage but to alter a spectrum trait—helped form the basis for my coining the term "cosmetic psychopharmacology" and speculating about the use of antidepressants as "steroids for the business Olympics." In the face of this vision—the all-but-coercive setting in which normal people must use drugs to keep up—the term may sound superficial and glib. If we put science fiction aside and think about the patients we have met who have responded to Prozac, the phrase may seem unfair in quite a different way: though the drug is altering spectrum traits, the help it provides is far from trivial.

When I first used the expression "cosmetic psychopharmacology," Edward Khantzian, the psychiatrist who proposed that drug abuse is often a form of self-regulation, wrote to ask whether his model might apply to the "cosmetic" use of Prozac. He suggested that the drug helps because it modifies "atypical or sub-clinical states of distress or suffering that are admittedly more subtle or less apparent." That objection applies well to some of the conditions for which we have seen Prozac used: the medication is treating subtle distress that is subclinical in the sense that it does not rise to the level of illness but exists on a continuum with illness.

There are a number of perspectives from which to see the Prozac-responsive minor conditions whose manifestations are limited to a single symptom, or a few of them. From one point of view, they are mild or early forms of illness—on the continuum with depression and even rapid cycling; this is the viewpoint that justifies treating Sonia. From another vantage, they are aspects of temperament that sit on a different sort of spectrum and relate to illness only insofar as the environment disfavors the traits that arise from that temperament; in this sense, Sonia needs treatment only because the contemporary world is so demanding. From a third point of view, to medicate these conditions is just to tamper with normal minds.

Categories aside, these minor and partial disorders entail a wide range of suffering. Hillary, unable to experience pleasure, is clearly in constant pain; Sam, if we believe his claim that he was taking medication only for the mental adeptness it offered, comes close to using Prozac "cosmetically"; Sonia falls in the middle. She was once comfortable enough but now sees herself as defective. And yet the responsiveness of all three to Prozac may be on a quite similar basis—a low-normal setting of a serotonin system in the brain.

When depressed patients respond well to Prozac, they often report that their mental processes run faster and more smoothly than they did before the onset of the depression. If we think about Sam and Sonia, it is easy to imagine that many people who have never suffered an episode of depression—and who do not routinely experience other symptoms of dysthymia—would discover an increase in mental agility or acuity in response to an antidepressant. We can say these are people whose hesitancy of thought is minor depression in *forme fruste*. Alternatively, we can say that they are normal people, and that if they ask for Prozac they are requesting, according to our point of view, legitimate enhancement, legalized cocaine, or a neurochemical nose job. If I am right, we are entering an era in which medication can be used to enhance the functioning of the normal mind. The complexities of that era await us.

They await us, and they are with us already. I do not want to give the impression that the ethical and aesthetic dilemmas around medication of long-standing traits exist only in some science-fiction future. I recently treated a patient who without knowing it used words similar to those I had written about Prozac. She was a social worker who suffered not dysthymia but the real thing, full-blown major depression. I had treated her for the acute episode, and on medication she seemed to me to have the increased acuity of thought we have been discussing, as well as a new verbal fluency that was noticed by her colleagues. Off medication and free of depression, she was again more fragile and vague—I might once have said sensitive and psy-

chologically attuned. When she was in the course of applying for a
new job, a terribly stressful undertaking for her, I asked if she might
not want to go back on medication, in the hopes that she would feel
and appear more focused. She objected, "Wouldn't that be like taking
steroids?"

Maybe I was acting toward this patient like an anxious or even
pushy parent. It is painful to see someone fail where she can succeed;
one wants to give all the help one can. I found it hard to contemplate
the possibility that my patient would stagnate in her career because
of a fuzzy style of thought that remained untreated. Having worked
with so many people who responded well to Prozac, I was now "out
ahead" of a patient, eager to give medicine in a circumstance that
seemed to her to call for a different approach. The social worker did
not take medication before her job interview, though she later resumed antidepressant use when it seemed her major depression was
beginning to recur.

Social definitions change through the accumulation of particular
instances. If other doctors are tempted to use medicines to treat
vagueness of thought in patients with *formes frustes* of dysthymia, then
in time as a society we will find ways to understand this practice as
acceptable. Perhaps we will expand the definition of disease, so that
patients like Sonia are considered ill, even in the absence of depression.
Alternatively, we may expand the indications for which medicine is
given, so that they encompass an increasing variety of characteristics
that are acknowledged not to be illness but that exist as normal
variants in healthy people. Either way, we are likely to see a variety
of traits associated with dysthymia as indications for pharmacologic
therapy.

We can now see that the possibilities of cosmetic psychopharmacology
extend far beyond the brightening of mood. Each of the *formes frustes*
of depressive temperament and personality should in principle be
reachable through medication: a variety of individual traits will be
treatable in people with otherwise unremarkable psychological his-

tories. We may not be quite at this point: Prozac seems to me most often to be transformative in a grand way, not merely influential of single functions. But as we have access to yet more specific drugs, our accuracy in targeting individual traits will improve.

We have talked about medication as altering personality, taking a person with dysthymia and making her temperamentally hyperthymic, sunny, and social. This potential has disturbing overtones; it may lead us to imagine a future in which the culture at large considers the depressive personality to be illness and the hyperthymic type to be optimal health. But perhaps the treatment of *formes frustes* is more disturbing yet. It raises the possibility of taking a normal individual and reaching into his or her personality to alter a particular trait—in the instances we have discussed, to reset self-esteem, or hedonic capacity, or mental agility. Here medication allows for tinkering with personality and particular mental styles. This possibility has worrisome implications, not only as regards the arrogance of doctors but as regards the subtly coercive power of convention.

At the same time, we should be aware of the moral tension in failing to tinker with particular traits. Returning to the thought experiment involving pairs of twins, it hardly seems right that equally handicapped people should be treated differently based on the category (dysfunction or normal variant) into which the hypothesized origin of their handicap is placed. Illness or spectrum trait, the vagueness of speech or hesitancy of thought is the same; whether the as yet untreated twin should be allowed the benefit of, say, an antidepressant ought not, in human terms, to depend on whether the co-twin had ADHD or dysthymia. We may want to rethink our reticence to treat normal variant traits with medication. The availability of potent and specific drugs is dislocating in many arenas. Once these medicines have colored our view of how the self is constituted, our understanding of related ethical issues inevitably will be affected.

The Message in
the Capsule

In *The Thanatos Syndrome,* the last novel by the Southern writer Walker Percy, a maverick doctor finds that plotters have introduced an insidious chemical, Heavy Sodium, into the water supply. On Heavy Sodium, shy and anxious women—the first example is "a housebound Emily Dickinson"—become erotic, bold, competitive, slim, un-self-conscious, and insensitive to the point of perfunctoriness. They shake off "old terrors, worries, rages, a shedding of guilt like last year's snakeskin."

Percy was writing before Prozac was marketed, but Heavy Sodium is like Prozac in so many respects that we must credit him with creating the art that life imitates. To Percy, the drug's effects are all to the bad. On Heavy Sodium, people are "not hurting, they are not worrying the same old bone, but there is something missing, not merely the old terrors but a sense in each of her—her what? her self?" Heavy Sodium reduces a person to his or her ignoble, animal being, a point Percy emphasizes by having the book's villains, overdosed on Heavy Sodium, take on the posture and behaviors of apes. By reducing human self-consciousness, the drug robs individuals of their souls. What links men and women to God is precisely their guilt, anxiety, and loneliness.

Percy's novel of ideas, written from a Catholic viewpoint, presages much of the controversy that followed the medical community's discovery of Prozac. Like Percy, medical ethicists asked: Is it a good thing?

Shortly after I saw my first patients respond to Prozac, I raised that question in a series of essays for psychiatrists. While I was struggling in print to put my finger on what was troubling about Prozac, colleagues had been doing much the same thing in private or in local hospital rounds. Those discussions gave rise to an interesting consideration of the ethical dilemmas raised by drugs like Prozac.

● ● ●

The debate about Prozac was catalyzed by a young Harvard psychiatrist, Robert Aranow, who challenged his colleagues to consider the ethical implications of "mood brighteners," a phrase he coined after seeing Prozac exert a dramatic effect on certain of his less ill patients. Aranow defined mood brightener as a medicine that can "brighten the episodically down moods of those who are not clinically depressed, without causing euphoria or the side effects that have accompanied the mood elevators of abuse," such as cocaine or amphetamine. Aranow stressed the lack of side effects in order to sharpen the discussion: once we set aside the argument that drugs are bad because they harm people physically, we are forced to focus on whether we really want to be able to use drugs to improve normal people's mood.

Until the advent of Prozac, most ethical questions involving psychotherapeutic drugs turned on clinical tradeoffs: For which indications may highly addictive medications be prescribed? Ought coercion to be permitted in the administration (to gravely disturbed or dangerous patients) of drugs that alleviate psychosis but can cause neurological damage? What constitutes informed consent regarding risks and benefits of medications given to the mentally ill? And so on.

Prozac made Aranow wonder about the ethical implications of a drug that demands no tradeoff. He further highlighted this issue by formulating a second concept, "conservation of mood." Amphetamine, cocaine, heroin, opium, alcohol, and other street drugs used to elevate mood all ultimately result in a "crash." Under conservation of mood, there are, Aranow notes, no shortcuts to happiness: "In effect, there has been an unspoken assumption that . . . any substance that induces an elevation of mood above an individual's long-term baseline will eventually result in an opposite equivalent or greater decline." What goes up must come down. What interested Aranow was the consequences of mood-elevating drugs that violate the principle of conservation of mood.

Aranow's inspiration was a familiar-sounding case. The patient was a forty-four-year-old woman who two days each week tended to feel apathetic and unable to complete her usual tasks. She met criteria for none of the depressive disorders, though she did appear to have a "personality disorder" characterized by dependency and passive aggression. One gets the impression that the patient may have struck her doctors as a whining complainer. She requested Prozac to give her energy on her down days. Her doctors suggested that psychotherapy would be more effective, but at the patient's insistence Prozac was prescribed. Six weeks later, she reported that she had much more energy, optimism, and self-confidence: "This is the way I have always wanted to feel." Twice she was weaned off Prozac, and each time she returned to her normal, unsatisfactory level of functioning. Back on the medication, she found her energy and optimism returned. She never became manic and never suffered a collapse in mood.

This case led Aranow to challenge his colleagues to think about the implications of a harmless drug that could "reduce the common experiences of drudgery such as going to work Monday mornings for those who, at present, are not seen as suffering from a mood disorder. . . ."

The first to respond to Aranow's speculations was his co-worker at McLean, Richard Schwartz. Although Schwartz had not read my essays, his stance was akin to the one I took upon seeing Sam and Tess respond to Prozac: he was disturbed, but he had some difficulty saying why.

In a paper published in 1991, Schwartz suggests that mood brighteners interfere with a person's relationship to reality in a way that traditional antidepressants do not. If depression entails a distortion of perception—the sufferer sees life as more bleak than it is—then antidepressants make a depressed person once again responsive to reality: "Recovery from a depressive illness therefore involves an act of connection, an act of integration." But when normal people experience pain, they are merely in touch with reality and their own human vulnerability. To use a pill to improve their mood is, Schwartz asserts, "an act of disconnection. You bring about a break, however small, between the individual and either his external reality or his humanity, by which I mean his tendency to react 'humanly' to external circumstance."

Schwartz acknowledges problems with his own line of argument. For one thing, studies show that depressed people tend to be more accurate in predicting probabilities than "normal" people, who are too optimistic; it is the "normal" whose view of reality is distorted, however adaptively. Giving an antidepressant to a depressed patient thus disconnects him or her from (bleak) reality. But no one faults that intervention—so to use a medicine to make a person more optimistic than strict realism allows must not be inherently unethical.

Nor is medication unique in tempering harsh reality. Psychotherapy sometimes helps a person confront unpleasant truths, but many psychotherapies entail support rather than confrontation. For example, a patient may feel strengthened because he comes to identify with an idealized, and therefore unrealistic, image of the therapist. If we value such therapies—and Schwartz does—it is because the result, not the means, of the treatment is reality-enhancing. But the result of a supportive psychotherapy is likely to be similar to the result of a mood-brightening medication—namely, improved mood.

Conceding the inadequacy of the argument that mood brighteners disconnect people from reality, Schwartz turns to his central idea, "affect tolerance," the ability to "stand to feel what you feel." Affect tolerance has its own history in psychiatry; it is the contribution of one of the most beloved and influential American psychoanalysts, the late Elizabeth Zetzel. Zetzel considered the capacity for emotional growth to be grounded in the capacity to bear anxiety and depression. To Schwartz, a mood brightener fails to induce the capacity to bear depression (it actually obviates the need to bear depression), and therefore it stunts emotional growth.

Schwartz's concern is not just at the level of the individual. He fears that mood brighteners have the capacity to reinforce oppressive cultural expectations. The issue he uses to make his argument is bereavement. Psychiatrists have reported success in using antidepressants in prolonged bereavement. But what is prolonged? Schwartz reports that American research psychiatrists prescribe antidepressants about one year after the death of the beloved. Schwartz contrasts this standard with that of rural Greece, where formal grieving, of a mother for a child or a wife for a deceased husband, lasts five years. Schwartz comments, "Here is a culture with impressive affect tolerance." When doctors pharmacologically mitigate the pain of bereavement after one year, they may be using medication to reinforce cultural norms and encourage conformity. The medication seems to justify the standard that is in place by labeling those who deviate from a cultural norm as ill and then "curing" them.

Schwartz's ethical arguments were immediately echoed from another quarter. Randolph Neese, a University of Michigan psychiatrist who has collaborated with Michael McGuire, criticized mood brighteners from the viewpoint of evolutionary biology.

Neese argues that bad feelings are useful. Pain, diarrhea, and nausea are distressing, but all carry information vital to the survival of the individual and the species. Unpleasant mood states are similarly adaptive. Anxiety reminds animals of circumstances in which they have encountered danger. In the modern world, anxiety protects humans from heedlessly attacking powerful leaders. More generally, anxiety and the internal threat of depression moderate primitive urges that would otherwise cause people to pursue ephemeral gain at the expense of stable social relationships. Sadness, Neese says, helps allocate energy resources: mild depression causes an animal that is failing to near its goals to slow down and return home. And a depressed mood helps people who are low on the totem pole to adjust to their social position.

Neese's argument seems to be careening toward quite ghastly conclusions, that the downtrodden should be glad of their depression and anxiety, and that people should tolerate every form of pain that is natural and was once adaptive, an argument that would ban analgesia and anesthesia as well as efforts to mitigate the feelings of low self-worth caused by low social status. Psychotherapy, which— beyond diminishing sadness and anxiety—aims directly, by analyzing Oedipal inhibitions, to allow people to be more assertive in the face of authority, would be as suspect as mood brighteners according to Neese's line of thought.

But Neese slams on the brakes and concludes mildly that psychiatrists should recognize that negative feelings may not be signs of family or developmental dysfunction but, rather, of adaptive mechanisms appropriate to a different environment, presumably mankind's hunter-gatherer phase. Neese believes awareness of this point of view can be a relief to patients: "The new perspective allows them to quit blaming themselves and others and to concentrate instead on making their lives better." Neese hopes the evolutionary perspective will convince sad-but-not-ill people to avoid mood brighteners and instead to welcome their own discomfort as useful.

As Schwartz and Neese see it, mood brighteners stand indicted on a number of grounds: they (unhelpfully) free the taker from struggling with reality and thus achieving affect tolerance; they act to reinforce dehumanizing social expectations; they interfere with adaptive mechanisms developed over eons of evolution; and they encourage people to understand as illness aspects of the self that are normal.

Aranow, in an article co-authored with Schwartz and Mark Sullivan, a psychiatrist and philosopher at the University of Washington in Seattle, adds to these philosophical objections a list of concrete issues that would follow from the availability of a harmless mood elevator. The concerns include the influence of mood brighteners on the role of the clinician, professional standards regarding use of medication for enhancement as opposed to treatment, and insurance coverage and general availability of drugs for such use. What drives these issues is an altered relationship of risk and benefit. With the hypothetical mood brightener there are no adverse effects, so there is no risk. And since the drug is used for people who are not ill, benefit is ambiguous. Doctors are adrift, without a yardstick against which to measure particular choices.

In his role as philosopher, Sullivan suggests "autonomy" as an ethical yardstick to replace the lost standard of risk and benefit. In judging whether the use of a medicine is for good or ill, Sullivan proposes we ask whether it promotes or retards a person's capacity to run his or her own life. An addicting drug may make a well person happier, but, by virtue of the compulsion inherent in addiction, it compromises autonomy. Illness also compromises autonomy, so an addicting drug might be used in the treatment of illness and on balance meet the ethical guideline. This standard of autonomy makes us rethink what our objections might be to a mood brightener, a drug that is by definition not addicting. In the end, Aranow and his colleagues return to Schwartz's concerns, that, even in the absence of the sorts of effects that normally give mood elevators (like cocaine) a bad name, mood brighteners might decrease true autonomy by distancing man from an aspect of his humanity—his legitimate despair—and by reinforcing dehumanizing cultural expectations, such as the requirement always to be happy and productive, even in the face of a world that deserves a more complex emotional response.

• • •

My impression, on listening to the medical ethicists and reading their essays, was that they had captured important concerns regarding the potential corrosive effects of mood brighteners on individuals and on society. Their arguments expressed in formal terms certain quiet worries I had felt on first working with Prozac. At the same time, I found the mood-brightener discussion unsatisfying.

After struggling to put my finger on what was lacking, I concluded that the problem had to do with the vast discrepancy between what the ethicists were imagining and what I was seeing in my office. The potential drug users in their model—the people whose level of distress did not rise to the level of illness—did not resemble the struggling, handicapped, often socially isolated patients I had seen respond to Prozac. And, more important (since I could imagine even healthier people taking medication), the effects they ascribed to a mood brightener bore only a vague resemblance to those of Prozac, the drug that had inspired the discussion. Much of the problem, I concluded, was inherent in the abstract concept "mood brightener," which fails to take into account the characteristics—the personality —of any actual drug that might affect an actual human brain. The mood-brightener discussion showed how elusive a target Prozac is, how quicksilverish in its resistance to being grasped.

For example, the argument that a mood brightener interferes with a person's development of affect tolerance might apply comfortably to a short-acting pill that gives people an hour or two of happiness (or relief from sadness, in the way anesthesia gives relief from pain) in the face of loss or humiliation. Given access to such a medicine, someone who is afraid of life might take it intermittently to avert sad moods, while failing to act in the world or face her or his own fears and weaknesses. But Prozac does something quite different: it lends people courage and allows them to choose life's ordinarily risky undertakings.

Schwartz is afraid that mood brighteners will rob life of the edifying potential for tragedy; but when Prozac works well—as it did for Sally, who chose to marry, or Julia, who took on pediatric nursing, or Gail, who simultaneously applied for an administrative post and re-engaged her husband—it catalyzes the precondition for tragedy, namely participation. Prozac both elevates mood and increases emotional resilience, perhaps because these two qualities are biologically represented by the same neurotransmitters. The example of Prozac thus raises the possibility that mood-brightening drugs necessarily, because of the way the brain is wired, will increase affect tolerance.

Of course, the phrase "affect tolerance" is ambiguous. The expression comes from psychotherapy; but when psychotherapy enhances affect tolerance, what exactly is it doing? Psychotherapy might make people more capable of bearing deep, disorganizing depression and anxiety in response to small, predictable losses. Alternatively, it might make people less likely to experience disruptive emotion in the face of ordinary loss. No doubt it does both—allows for more profundity of feeling and for more resilience—but which of the two is affect tolerance?

Turning to Elizabeth Zetzel, whose work sets the stage for this discussion, I have the impression that she, like most modern therapists, used psychotherapy as a means to make easily disorganized patients less disturbed by loss. (Secondarily, as they became less vulnerable to hard knocks, they would need fewer defenses against experiencing deep feelings.) If so, what happens to people in psychotherapy is similar to what happens when they take Prozac. The result is not so much that they are better at tolerating the most excruciating emotions—no one would do well with the sense of inner disorganization that the rejection-sensitive feel—but that they are more experience-tolerant.

In some patients, Prozac quite directly increases the ability to bear troubling emotions. On Prozac, Paul, the Renaissance history teacher, no longer just imagined but, for the first time, felt his childhood memories of trauma. His emotional palette expanded quite directly because of medication. In many patients, Prozac lets feelings emerge in new settings. Allison, the fashion designer, was able on Prozac to display her gentle and concerned side in the office, because she felt less anxious. Certainly people who become less obsessional on the drug are thereby made more open to emotion. Not only does Prozac increase resilience, in some people it increases the profundity of emotion available to them as well. Yes, there are some patients —Tess, perhaps, depending on how we value the muting of her intense concern for others—whom Prozac makes less "serious." But any theory of mood brighteners must take into account the many other people for whom medication produces an increase in depth and range of emotion. If we are uncomfortable with the use of mood brighteners in such people, it can hardly be on the grounds that the drugs decrease affect tolerance. Indeed, Prozac raises the opposite issue: how comfortable are we with a pill that *increases* affect tolerance?

Richard Schwartz anticipates a question of this sort when he writes of psychotherapy: ". . . a person grows by taking something human from another person, a process that I find more appealing than taking a pill. . . ." Schwartz's argument has the flavor of what has been called pharmacological Calvinism, the sense that there is something bad *per se* about taking pills. Cure by pill is seen as dehumanizing when compared with psychotherapy, even the parts of psychotherapy that provide support rather than insight. The problem is not that the medicine fails to confer affect tolerance or fails to move people toward an adaptive interaction with reality but, rather, that it succeeds. In doing just what psychotherapy aims to do, Prozac performs chemically what has heretofore been an intimate interpersonal function.

Both Schwartz and Neese worry about the capacity of medication to diminish a person's experience of sadness: Schwartz because sadness is morally and developmentally salutary; Neese because it is evolutionarily adaptive. Again, these concerns seem to apply to a different drug, a psychic anesthetic that makes people preternaturally invulnerable to grief or dismissive of danger. Exposure to the effects of Prozac raises an alternative possibility, a mood brightener that moves people from one common human state to another.

Prozac shifts people from dysthymia to hyperthymia, to use a shorthand for relative vulnerability and invulnerability to psychic pain. Dysthymia and hyperthymia are normal human states. Both have survived centuries of evolution. To say that a Prozac-style mood brightener is maladaptive, Neese would have to believe a normal variant condition like hyperthymia is maladaptive. Similarly, Schwartz can argue that Prozac diminishes people only if he simultaneously holds that hyperthymics are, by virtue of their temperament, immoral or inferior in their humanity. Melancholy is often engaging. And congenitally sunny people can be annoying; it is sometimes suggested that such people might be improved by the experience of suffering. Cynics might even favor the use of a pill to make bland and happy people more vulnerable. But I doubt that Schwartz and Neese would support this intervention by arguing that it favors the aims of morality or evolution.

Neese hopes that evolutionary theory will help us decide whether to continue to medicate a patient who requests a renewal of a prescription for Prozac. The patient Neese describes in his essay is one of our classic good responders. She says, "I used to be uncomfortable with strangers at parties, but now I can go up to anyone and say anything I want to. . . . I don't feel nervous or worried about what people think of me. Also I am more decisive, and people say I am more attractive. . . ." This quote is intended to make us worry that the woman now lacks an evolutionarily adaptive defense, social anxiety.

If the drug has made her manic or silly—if in effect it has made her ill—she is at a disadvantage in terms of self-protection. But if, despite her reduced anxiety and vigilance, she is nonetheless as self-protective as certain other normal people, we cannot worry about her from an evolutionary perspective. It may be bad for the species to have too many risk-takers and too few worriers in the population. But for the individual, every position on the dysthymic-to-hyperthymic spectrum has been adaptive over time, and the hyperthymic position is well rewarded today.

Evolutionary theory cannot tell us whether to refill that prescription. Nor would I want to be the one to tell that patient that the sadness and anxiety she experienced before she was medicated were normal adaptive states and that therefore she should accept them.

As a clinician, I will worry about Neese's patient if she too readily accepts the conclusion that her pain is a normal state, the result of her inborn temperament. Vulnerability to depressed and anxious feelings probably can be inborn, but it certainly can be caused by trauma. Adults who were abused in childhood are all too ready to hear that their pain is a random force of nature, and the therapist's challenge with these patients is precisely to give historical meaning to symptoms. An understanding of inborn temperament does not excuse the therapist from the obligation to approach each patient with an eye toward personal history.

It strikes me, in the end, that Neese has his worries backward. If the woman has anxiety or depression based on hidden wounds, we might conceivably worry about medication as a form of collusion with her traumatic history: we would want to help her gain awareness of her past. But if her pain—perhaps even a "normal" level of pain that she, as an individual, finds excessive—is a mere atavism, an evolutionary adaptation to a bygone environment, medication may be a particularly humane intervention—indeed, a singular accomplishment by a science that aims to free man of certain of his animal constraints.

Nor am I certain, as I once was, that the availability of mood brighteners would disrupt medical practice. Aranow has concerns about the effects of a mood brightener on various parts of the medical system:

Will it redefine the doctor's role? Will it present challenges to the Food and Drug Administration? These questions echo worries I have raised about the proper use of a drug that can increase mental agility or hedonic capacity. But, having worked with Prozac for some time now, I have the sense that, if mood brighteners are like Prozac, the disruption to current arrangements will be subtle.

For one thing, enhancement of normal functioning, as opposed to treatment of illness, is an established part of medicine. In the field of pharmacotherapy, the drug Rogaine is used to treat a normal condition, male pattern baldness. The concrete issues regarding Rogaine have not been especially complex: the FDA does regulate it, insurance does not reimburse for it, the rich can have it and the poor cannot. Much of office-practice medical dermatology, such as treatment of uncomplicated adolescent acne, can be seen as treatment of normality, or else as enhancement. And, of course, there is the example of plastic surgery, which is used both for treatment, such as repair of congenital defects and reconstruction after burn or trauma, and for enhancement of beauty and self-esteem. A mood brightener would presumably be handled similarly: it would be used both for treatment (of depression, in which case it would be covered by insurance) and enhancement (of normal people's mood, in which case it would not). Both uses, like both uses of plastic surgery, would be culturally sanctioned as "medical."

The treatment of undesired nonpathologic conditions is common in medicine. Estrogen used to combat the normal effects of menopause is controversial in terms of its risk and benefits, but not its morality. Treatment, with sedatives, of the normal decreased sleep in the elderly arouses technical objections (used chronically, sedatives do more harm than good), but no moral objections.

Closer to the point, psychiatrists use psychotherapy for an impossibly wide range of indications, from cure of illness to enhancement of "human potential." Psychotherapy defies conservation of mood— that is, no one believes that improving mood via psychotherapy leads inexorably to later deterioration of mood; on the contrary, psychotherapy's great selling point is that, in addition to being ameliorative, it is prophylactic. Psychiatrists who practice psychotherapy should be adept in managing the shaky boundary between health and illness and in applying judgment in using professional interventions— whether medication or talking and listening—for conditions on both sides of the line.

Perhaps most important, contemporary models of mental disorder—models Prozac has helped to legitimize—blur the line between illness and health. Minor depressive states—melancholic temperament—are normal variants, but they can also be seen, from the vantage of cellular biology, as early stages of kindled depression or, from the vantage of sociobiology, as risk factors, in a hostile culture, for the development of depression. New medicines create new challenges, but they do so in a context that is itself new.

● ● ●

In short, I think traditional medical ethics fails to pinpoint what it is about Prozac that makes us uneasy. Part of the problem lies in the phrase "mood brightener," which captures one aspect of Prozac's potential but at the same time mistakes the character of the drug. When we imagine a hypothetical mood brightener, we model the image on an actual drug, one that already exists. The tradition of medical ethics in the area of mood is to worry about heroin and cocaine; the antidepressants are different. The issue of mood enhancement really concerns hedonism—should we use drugs for pleasure? But the word "hedonism" contains the same ambiguity as the phrase "mood brightener." Stimulants, opiates, and antidepressants are all hedonic but in different ways.

Philosophers have long debated the nature of pleasure. Is it inherent in pleasurable acts, or is it a separable result of certain acts? The discovery ten years ago of endorphin receptors in the brain seemed to support the latter alternative, what the philosopher Dan Brock has called "the property-of-conscious-experience theory," of pleasure.

According to this theory (which I will call "separability"), we engage in actions for the pleasure they bring. Pleasure is a state of the brain neurons—satiety or excitation, for example—that is separable from the actions people undertake to make themselves happy. Opiates and amphetamines shortcut the hedonic process: they allow us to have the pleasure without the pleasurable acts, and thereby cut us off from the realities of the world. "Mood brightener" implies a substance that makes people happy when they haven't done anything to earn happiness.

Separability is the basis of the usual argument not only against psychotropic drugs but against hedonism altogether. The concern is that people will pursue pleasure directly—orgies are the usual sin of hedonists—rather than achieve pleasure through "distinctly human"—intellectual, altruistic, planful—efforts for which pleasure is the reward. This case against pleasure as the direct goal in life is sometimes called the "swine objection," from John Stuart Mill's contention that hedonism is a doctrine "fit only for swine."

Just as the endorphin receptor revived interest in the idea that pleasure is separable from pleasurable acts, I expect Prozac to refocus attention on an alternative theory: that pleasure is to be found throughout (and not separable from) certain activities such as reading a book. There is no receptor that corresponds to the pleasure of reading a book, and no single state of the neurons. By this understanding, pleasure is a matter of preference among experiences. Though generally not used in connection with illicit drugs, what Brock calls the preference theory of pleasure could well apply. For instance, marijuana not only gives pleasure directly (separability); it also may enhance, or allow an anhedonic uptight person to enjoy, the inherent pleasure of a walk through the countryside.

The swine objection to hedonic drugs seems irrelevant in the face of drugs that draw people *toward* ordinary and even noble human activities. My sense is that the preference theory of pleasure has received little attention because the usual experience-enhancing mood altering drugs, like marijuana or LSD, encourage self-absorption. The experience they enhance is most often autistic. Prozac is different. It induces pleasure in part by freeing people to enjoy activities that are social and productive. And, unlike marijuana or LSD or even alcohol, it does so without being experienced as pleasurable in itself and without inducing distortions of perception. Prozac simply gives anhedonic people access to pleasures identical to those enjoyed by other normal people in their ordinary social pursuits.

My impression is that Prozac, because it gives pleasure indirectly, by enhancing hedonic capacity and lowering barriers to ordinary social intercourse, generally increases personal autonomy. Aranow and his colleagues have argued to the contrary, using a fascinating example to make their point.

They describe a woman, Ms. B., prescribed Prozac for trichotillomania, a syndrome in which a person cannot resist the impulse to pull out her own hair. Hair-pulling in moderation is a sign of anxiety; but the need to pull hair relentlessly, to the point of disfigurement, is recognized as an illness, related to obsessive-compulsive disorder. Besides hair-pulling, Ms. B. has a second concern: she is unmarried at age thirty-six, despite her "appropriate, if somewhat strenuous efforts to meet eligible men." On Prozac, Ms. B.'s hair-pulling diminishes, but so does her feeling of urgency about meeting men. Ms. B. does not isolate herself: on the contrary, she now enjoys time spent with people, such as her parents, with whom she argued in the past. She is more content with life, more reconciled to the possibility of never marrying, and, though still interested in men, is no longer driven.

Regarding Ms. B.'s social behavior on Prozac, Aranow and his colleagues ask whether she has been opiated into a cocoon. Aranow puts forth drivenness as a desirable human quality that produces, if not happiness, certain admirable accomplishments on which the species thrives.

The notion that Prozac diminishes autonomy because it diminishes drive is an important one: it echoes Walker Percy's concern about "not worrying the same old bone." But Ms. B.'s case is unusual, and not only because she has a rare illness. Heretofore, we have seen nothing but examples in which Prozac moves people toward courtship activity. In this story, it moves someone away.

I think we can dismiss the concern that Prozac diminishes social intercourse: the usual complaint against Prozac is that it leaves people too social, too little in touch with their solitary core. Even Ms. B. seems to arrive at a more comfortable relationship with her social strengths and possibilities. The story as told implies that her drive produced strenuous social efforts that were ineffectual; her measured approach on medication might well work better.

Inner drive can lead to great accomplishments. But often "being driven" indicates compromised autonomy (as indicated by our use of the passive participle, "driven," as if by an alien force). To be opiated into a cocoon is one thing, but to be granted peace where once you were neurotically compelled is quite another: there are instances in which contentment contains more autonomy than drive.

It happens that the psychiatrist who treated Ms. B. has also given an account of her recovery. He is Ronald Winchel, who introduced the theory that an "aloneness affect" spurs primates to affiliate. Winchel describes himself as having been surprised when he learned that his hair-pulling patient, who had for so long engaged in "mildly agitated spouse-pursuit," socialized less on medication:

. . . For the first time in her memory she felt perfectly relaxed and happy sitting at home reading books or listening to music and felt less of the free-floating anxiety that was previously quelled by going out. She then mentioned, parenthetically, that for the first time in her adult life, she considered that maybe marriage wasn't in her future—but, she felt, that was not necessarily bad. She would make her life happy, she considered, in other ways.

Off Prozac, Ms. B. bar-hopped in search of men. Prozac moderated her sense of aloneness and allowed her to enjoy a variety of social settings. In Winchel's account, Ms. B. is not opiated, merely spared the pain of social desperation.

If Ms. B.'s story is disturbing, it is because she took medication to treat one problem, hair-pulling, and found a change in a quite separate area, courtship. For her, mood brightening is something like a side effect, one about which an ethically punctilious clinician might warn: We can diminish your hair pulling, but I must warn you, you may feel more contented.

If Ms. B. had taken Prozac as a mood brightener—more precisely, if she had taken it because she felt she was overanxious about men —we would see the drug as a useful tool toward a desired end. The vignette illustrates an important quality of Prozac—namely, that it often surprises us. Sometimes it will change only one trait in the person under treatment; but often it goes far beyond a single intended effect. You take it to treat a symptom, and it transforms your sense of self.

The medical ethicists approach Prozac as if it were a case of dull or bright, down or up. Unlike amphetamine, Prozac is not a case of down or up but of same or other. Prozac has the power to transform the whole person—illness and temperament, drive to pull hair and drive to affiliate, anxiety and hedonic capacity. When you take it, you risk widespread change.

The story of Ms. B. made me realize that the concept of mood brightener just will not do—it arises from the limited idea of an "antidepressant," when what we are dealing with is a thymoleptic, a drug that acts on personality. Instead of looking at mood and being surprised to discover that Prozac affects other areas, why not begin with the understanding that Prozac can induce the sort of widespread change ordinarily brought about by psychotherapy? There really is no way to assess Prozac without confronting transformation.

The idea of transformation leads us to address a new set of ethical issues. Who is Ms. B.? The change Prozac brings about in her is so profound that there are almost two different persons in the story, one discontented and driven, the other contented and complacent. Whose autonomy are we out to preserve?

Instinctively, we might want to say that the unmedicated woman has priority; this is the stance the ethicists take when they worry whether the patient has been opiated into a cocoon. But consider circumstances that might make us change our mind. If medication were not an issue, if Ms. B. had spontaneous mood swings, would we attend to her more closely in her driven or in her contented state? How would we see the matter if we considered her drivenness to be the result of a deficiency state—if we believed she "needed" more serotonin in the brain the way some people need vitamins or insulin or thyroid hormone? In that case, we would associate personhood with the medicated self. How would we understand Ms. B. if she were, like Sam, to "discover" on Prozac that her man-chasing had been compulsive? Or if she were, like Tess, to say she felt "like myself at last" on Prozac? Perhaps the most interesting case would arise if she reported she felt fully herself both on and off medication, so that the personality she chose would be purely a matter of preference.

There are many perspectives from which we might say that denial of medication would injure Ms. B.'s autonomy, precisely because we accept that Ms. B. as she is when medicated has the standing of personhood. If we believe that she is in fact transformed—one person when driven and one when contented—then we must determine how to choose between the autonomy of two distinct "persons," each fully human and deserving of autonomy. If Prozac has brought about a break between an individual and her humanity, the break may be so substantial that we are left asking, whose humanity is it?

My guess is that medical ethicists writing about Prozac have ignored the issue of personhood because they are hesitant to see in a medication this power to transform—and who can blame them? The idea is unlikely and uncomfortable.

Part of what may bother us is the nature of the changes that Prozac can accomplish. Michael McGuire hypothesized that low mood in dysthymic women results from a mismatch between the personality with which they enter adulthood and the one their culture rewards. It follows that a mood elevator for dysthymics, at least one that works through altering temperament, will necessarily be a drug that induces "conformity." I put "conformity" in quotation marks because here it means conformity to traits that society rewards, which might well be rebelliousness, egocentricity, radical self-confidence, or other qualities that lead to behaviors we ordinarily call nonconformist. (The evolutionary model entails certain paradoxes. It holds that in a given society an "antidepressant" is any chemical that leads to a rewarded personality—different cultures may have quite different antidepressants. In a culture that rewards caution, a compulsiveness-inducing drug might produce the temperament that leads to social rewards and thus brightened mood.) What are the implications of a drug that makes a person better loved, richer, and less constrained—because her personality conforms better to a societal ideal? These moral concerns seem at least as complex as those attending a drug that just inherently makes a person happy. In terms of its interaction with cultural norms, a transforming drug might be even more ethically troubling than a mood brightener.

•   •   •   •

Consider the Greek widow who over the course of five years is given a chance to allow her feelings to attenuate. She lives in an affect-tolerant culture, though she may be far from affect-tolerant: the widow may be rejection-sensitive and for that reason in need of an especially long time to recover after the death of a husband. Perhaps rural Greek society is organized precisely to allow widows with low affect tolerance to recover at their own pace. In an affect-tolerant traditional culture, rejection-sensitivity might be an adaptive trait. A more assertive widow, or one quicker to heal, would find the society stifling and infuriating: she might be happier in a less affect-tolerant culture, and indeed might find that rural Greek society makes impossible demands that she is temperamentally ill-equipped to meet.

To say that our society is less affect-tolerant is to say that it favors different temperaments. The Greek society is not preferable, just more comfortable for certain people. But it may be in our society that what doctors do when they treat mourning with medication goes far beyond elevating mood: they are asking a fragile widow to adopt a new temperament—to be someone she is not.

Prozac highlights our culture's preference for certain personality types. Vivacious women's attractiveness to men, the contemporary scorn of fastidiousness, men's discomfort with anhedonia in women, the business advantage conferred by mental quickness—all these examples point to a consistent social prejudice. The ways in which our culture favors one style over another go far beyond impatience with grief.

A certain sort of woman, socially favored in other eras, does poorly today. Victorian culture valued women who were emotionally sensitive, socially retiring, loyally devoted to one man, languorous and melancholic, fastidious in dress and sensibility, and histrionic in response to perceived neglect. We are less likely to reward such women today, nor are they proud of their traits.

We admire and reward a quite different sort of femininity, which, though it has its representations in heroines of novelists from Jane Austen to Fay Weldon, contains attributes traditionally considered masculine: resilience, energy, assertiveness, an enjoyment of give-and-take. Prozac does not just brighten mood; it allows a woman with the traits we now consider "overly feminine," in the sense of passivity and a tendency to histrionics, to opt, if she is a good responder, for a spunkier persona.

The Mexican poet and essayist Octavio Paz has put the issue of American expectations of women in the context of our form of economic organization: "Capitalism exalts the activities and behavior patterns traditionally called virile: aggressiveness, the spirit of competition and emulation, combativeness. American society made these values its own." Paz acknowledges that the position of women under American capitalism is legally and politically superior to that of women under Mexican traditionalism. But American social equality, Paz contends, comes in the context of a masculine society, in terms of values and expectations; Mexican society, though deplorable in the way it treats women, is more open to values Paz calls feminine.

Does Prozac's ability to transform temperament foster a certain sort of social conformity, one dominated in this case by "masculine" capitalist values? Thymoleptics are feminist drugs, in that they free women from the inhibiting consequences of trauma. But the argument can be made that, in "curing" women of traditional, passive feminine traits and instilling in good responders the attributes of a more robust feminine ideal, Prozac reinforces the cultural expectations of a particularly exigent form of economic organization.

This issue of conformity and psychotropic medication is an old and fascinating one. Consider opium. In the romantic imagination—I am thinking of Thomas De Quincey's *Confessions of an English Opium Eater*, and Coleridge's "Kubla Khan"—opium is an instrument of nonconformity, a source of sustenance for the individual imagination. But in Marx's metaphor for religion, "the opiate of the masses," opium is an instrument of conformity, a substance that deadens mind and body to pain or injustice against which one ought properly to rebel.

On the one hand, Prozac supports social stasis by allowing people to move toward a cultural ideal—the flexible, contented, energetic, pleasure-driven consumer. In the popular imagination, Prozac can serve as a modern opiate, seducing the citizenry into political conformity. The poet James Merrill writes of "The stick / Figures on Capitol Hill. Their rhetoric, / Gladly—no rapturously (on Prozac) suffered!" On the other hand, Prozac lends, or creates, confidence. It catalyzes the vitality and sense of self that allow people to leave abusive relationships or stand up to overbearing bosses. The impact of such a medicine remains unclear: perhaps the apparent liberation it offers is merely the freedom to be hyperthymic, that is, to embody a cultural ideal; or perhaps it allows formerly inhibited people to exercise power in social or political arenas that previously made them uncomfortable, where they may be disruptive of the status quo.

Early in this century, psychotherapy was criticized for inducing adaptation to the dominant culture; even if it contained a radical critique of that culture, psychotherapy was ultimately an agent of stasis. This argument applies well to Prozac. The counterargument is that Prozac, like psychotherapy, emboldens the inhibited and the injured. My own sense is that psychotherapy has been on balance a progressive force, and I suspect the same will prove true of Prozac.

The concern that Prozac raises regarding social coercion is that, once a transforming drug is available, people might be forced to take on new personalities. I am not thinking of drugs in the hands of a totalitarian state, though the interaction of psychotropic drugs and totalitarianism is always terrifying, but of the benign coercion that pervades all mass societies.

The ethics of drugs and social coercion have been most thoroughly addressed around the issue of steroids in competitive sports. We might say that a mentally competent adult athlete should be free to choose to take steroids even if they harm his body and mind; the drugs are not being used for mere pleasure but to increase excellence, a socially valued goal. But this choice has an impact on other athletes. Ethicists have argued against enhancing athletic performance with steroids because drugs diminish fairness in sport and because medical inventions ought not to be put to such a nonmedical use. But the strongest reason for banning steroids in competition has to do with coercion, or, more precisely, "free choice under pressure," as Thomas H. Murray puts it in his essay "Drugs, Sports, and Ethics." Once a few athletes take steroids, others remain free not to do so, but only at the cost of forsaking goals to which they have devoted many years of painful effort. The choice not to take drugs (with their attendant risks) has been diminished.

A parallel example is cosmetic surgery for breast enhancement among female fashion models. No one coerces women to have breast implants, but, according to media reports, only women with enlarged breasts receive the desirable and lucrative assignments in television and print advertising. For aspiring models, the decision whether to undergo surgery is free choice under pressure. What once was (arguably) a social good—allowing a woman to gain the appearance that gives her a sense of well-being—becomes a clear social ill, the requirement, putting it in the severest terms, that a woman undergo mutilating surgery in order to pursue her chosen career.

The possibility of chemical "enhancement" of a variety of psychological traits—social ease, flexibility, mental agility, affective stability—could be similarly coercive. In the science-fiction horror-story version of the interplay of drug and culture, a boss says, "Why such a long face? Can't you take a MoodStim before work?" A family doctor warns the widow, "If you won't try AntiGrief, we'll have to consider hospitalization." And a parent urges the pediatrician to put a socially anxious child on AntiWallflower Compound. (Parents tend to want their children to be leaders—but how does a troop of monkeys or a classroom of children function when every member has high levels of serotonin?) Only slightly less nightmarish is the prospect of free choice under pressure. There is always a Prozac-taking hyperthymic waiting to do your job, so, if you want to compete, you had better take Prozac, too. Either way, a socially desirable drug turns from boon to bane because it subjects healthy people to demands that they chemically alter their temperament.

Such an outcome would clearly be bad, but it also seems unlikely, not least because of our society's aversion to prescribed medication —our "pharmacological Calvinism." That phrase was coined over twenty years ago by the late Gerald Klerman, a pioneering researcher into the outcomes of both drug treatments and psychotherapy. Thinking about psychotropics in the late sixties and early seventies inevitably was influenced by the mushrooming use of street drugs in conjunction with a variety of forms of social ferment. Klerman characterized the contrasting reactions as psychotropic hedonism and pharmacological Calvinism. He defined the latter as "a general distrust of drugs used for nontherapeutic purposes and a conviction that if a drug 'makes you feel good, it must be morally bad.' "

Study after study has shown that, when it comes to prescribed drugs, Americans are conservative. Doctors tend to underprescribe (relative to the recommendations of academic psychiatrists) for mental conditions, and patients tend to take less medicine than doctors prescribe. This appears to have been true in the "mother's little helper" period, during which Klerman formulated his dialectic, and it is true today. Relative to the practice in other industrialized countries, prescribing in the United States is moderate.

Past experience suggests that we can count on our pharmacological Calvinism to save us from coercion. On the other hand, pharmacological Calvinism may be flimsy protection against the allure of medication. Do we feel secure in counting on our irrationality—our antiscientific prejudice—to save us from the ubiquitous cultural pressures for enhancement? Perhaps the widespread use of new medication will erode our "Calvinism," and then a myriad of private decisions, each appropriate for the individual making them, will result in our becoming a tribe in which each member has a serotonin level consonant with dominance.

But the pressure to engage in hyperthymic, high-serotonin behavior precedes the availability of the relevant drugs. The business world already favors the quick over the fastidious. In the social realm, an excess of timidity can lead to isolation. Those environmental pressures leave certain people difficult options: they can suffer, or they can change. Seen from this perspective, thymoleptics offer people an additional avenue of response to social imperatives whose origins have nothing to do with progress in pharmacology.

• • •

One aspect of pharmacological Calvinism is the belief that pain is a privileged state, a view inherent in the arguments concerning affect tolerance and the adaptive value of sadness. It is also at the heart of Walker Percy's concerns over Heavy Sodium. Better even than the ethicists who responded directly to Prozac, Percy both depicts and personifies the objection to technological attenuation of ordinary suffering.

Percy was a man to whom ailments proved precious. His father committed suicide when Percy was thirteen; his mother died in a traffic accident two years later. Percy, who had chosen medicine as a career, fell prey to tuberculosis during his internship year while performing autopsies at Bellevue Hospital. Calling tuberculosis "the best thing that ever happened to me," Percy spent two years recuperating at Saranac Lake, devoting this time to reading literature and philosophy. Upon his recovery, Percy traveled to the New Mexico desert for further self-exploration. He married and, after another year of self-examination, converted to Catholicism. For Percy, as for many of his protagonists, illness and solitude were transforming. Percy turned from medical pathology to a novelist's examination of the pathology of contemporary society. He found a central flaw to be precisely a lack of respect for symptoms: fear, pain, depression, anxiety. Had he been given Prozac (or iproniazid) along with the rest and exercise that were prescribed him, would Percy the seeker have emerged?

In his characterization of "a housebound Emily Dickinson," Percy implicitly alludes to the relationship between suffering (or neurosis) and art. This subject was best captured, to my mind, in a wonderful literary debate between Edmund Wilson and Lionel Trilling. Wilson, writing about Sophocles' *Philoctetes,* takes as his theme "the wound and the bow." Philoctetes is possessed of both a godly bow that never misses its mark and a suppurating, never-healing snakebite that causes him constant pain and makes him disgusting to others. Wilson traces the Philoctetes theme through contemporary drama, where wounds tend to be psychic, and he attributes to Sophocles "some special insight into morbid psychology." You cannot get Philoctetes the astonishing marksman without Philoctetes the loathsome invalid.

Lionel Trilling rebutted Wilson in an essay "Art and Neurosis." He concedes that numerous authors believed their wounds were what gave them insight: "Zola, in the interests of science, submitted himself to examination by fifteen psychiatrists and agreed with their conclusion that his genius had its source in the neurotic elements of his temperament." But Trilling argues that the wounds of most artists are mild—artists are ill only in the Freudian sense that "we are all ill"—and that art grows out of suffering no more than do all human activities, successful and unsuccessful. Trilling counters the Philoctetes myth with those of Pan, Dionysius, Apollo, and Hermes, in which art is associated with the antithesis of neurosis: superabundant energy and power. We might say, in the language of psychobiology, that there is hyperthymic as well as dysthymic art.

Surely Trilling is right. There are many founts of creativity; not all artists suffer. There is also the issue of whether an artist who does suffer denies the muse if he or she chooses relief from pain. The wound-and-bow argument applies equally to psychotherapy, a point made by the Peter Shaffer play *Equus,* in which a boy's unique visions succumb to psychoanalysis. Does relieving suffering amount to stifling art? Psychiatrists have claimed that manic depression is correlated with creativity, but there is no evidence that lithium or psychotherapy destroys creativity in manic-depressives. My own sense is that antidepressants improve artistic creativity in certain people. Indeed, it is a practice in certain segments of the artistic community to "chip" antidepressants, taking small doses in the hopes of treating low-level depression or creative inhibition.

Percy's concerns are not limited to art but extend to transcendence. His central metaphor is the quest. I suspect much of what draws me to Percy's work is my own predilection for quest in myself and in my patients—my agreement with Percy's definition of what gives man worth. The issue in judging Prozac or Heavy Sodium on Percy's terms concerns the role of discomfort as a stimulus to the quest that is man's proper pursuit.

To Percy, guilt and self-consciousness, as well as sadness, are important signals of what is wrong with us, signposts in the quest. Shame, Percy implies, links us to awareness of original sin. Anxiety is our visceral understanding of the ways in which the world is out of joint. Symptoms signify the human condition; they are mysteries to probe and savor. Percy's understanding of the quest is religious, but there is also an important secular tradition—the dominant tradition in psychology for a century—that considers anxiety and heightened self-consciousness to be intimate signs of inner disturbance, signs that ought not to be altered except through journeys of self-discovery.

According to psychoanalysis, to lose pain without quest or struggle is to lose self. Klerman mocked a simplistic form of this view: "Thus if a drug makes you feel good, it not only represents a secondary form of salvation but somehow it is morally wrong and the user is likely to suffer retribution with . . . medical-theological damnation." But the preciousness of suffering has always had a respectable place in intellectual life.

For Percy, the problem is not merely that the artist loses his art when he takes a pill, but that he loses his art because of the greater loss of what is distinctly human. Percy argued this case throughout his career, beginning as far back as the fifties. By attending to the biological, psychiatry becomes *"unable* to take account of the predicament of modern man." Percy favors Erich Fromm's formulation that anxiety among the affluent—that is, both the potential consumers of mother's little helpers and the heroes of Percy's novels—is the sign and symptom of alienation from the self, an appropriate reaction to the accurate feeling that life runs through our hands like sand. To Percy, the person who is anxious and confused is less pathological than the one who is complacent and tranquilized. Anxiety is "a summons to authentic existence, to be heeded at any cost."

Percy's argument successfully expresses the underpinnings of our unease with drugs. But I find that his case for transcendence becomes obscure in the face of actual patients and the research they call to mind. Here is Paul, the Renaissance historian who, off medication, could only imagine his feelings in childhood; on medication, he recaptures his past with all its richness of emotion, not least its pain. Here is Allison, the woman who, off medicine, continually checks the mirror to see who is in the driver's seat of the car she is driving; on medicine, she can see herself at last. In my experience, many patients, including some who may never have had a diagnosable mental illness, are better able to explore both their past and their current circumstances while they are taking Prozac. For these people, to whom medication constitutes help in recovery from childhood trauma or protection from the threat of terrible decompensation, the drug seems to aid rather than inhibit the struggle to locate the self.

There are cases that result in precisely what Percy fears: Julia stops struggling with her husband; Gail buys clothes with less guilt and fights for promotions; Tess distances herself from her needy mother; Hillary feels a loss of moral sensibility. These are affluent, or fairly affluent, consumers made more socially comfortable and less angst-ridden by medication. But are they really robbed of their life's meaning? Are they distanced from the existential dilemma?

Percy quotes approvingly Fromm's assertion that "there are no physiological substrata to the needs of relatedness and transcendence." Today, the first half of this statement seems false: lower animals have needs for relatedness (remember Winchel's serotonin-mediated "aloneness affect" in primates); and our own degree of inhibition or gregariousness seems to have biological underpinnings. To accept the second half of the statement, we must conclude that phenomena that respond to medication, from sensitivity to self-esteem, are not essential to transcendence.

In 1959, almost thirty years before he wrote *The Thanatos Syndrome*, Percy explored the connection between uncomfortable affect and quest in his celebrated essay "The Message in the Bottle." He begins by asking us to imagine a man, with no memory of where he came from, who finds himself cast upon the beach of an island with highly developed social institutions. The man becomes a member of the local community. But as he walks on the beach each morning, "he regularly comes upon bottles which have been washed up by the waves."

Initially, Percy uses this thought experiment to examine practical linguistics. He lists twenty-odd messages, such as "Lead melts at 330 degrees," "In 1943 the Russians murdered 10,000 Polish officers in the Katyn forest," "If water John brick is," and "There is fresh water in the next cove." Percy considers ways of grouping these messages. Some messages are sensible and some nonsensical. Some refer to repeatable events and some to unique historical events. But Percy is most interested in a division between *Wissenschaft* (professional knowledge, expressed perhaps in the language of physics, psychoanalysis, or literary criticism) and news (information, like the location of fresh water, that the islander can use now).

Whether a sentence is knowledge or news is not a function of anything a linguist can specify. It is not determined by the types of words the sentence contains or its grammatical structure. The posture of the reader makes a difference, as do the potential significance of the information and the reader's criteria for believing the truth of the message. What is news to one man will be a matter of indifference to another: "In summary, the hearer of news is a man who finds himself in a predicament. News is precisely that communication which has bearing on his predicament. . . ." If a man is searching for water, and another, seemingly reliable, man says, "Come! I know your need. I will take you to water," then the searcher will consider the speaker a bearer of news.

Percy next posits two commuters on a train. One is "fat, dumb, and happy." The other commuter "feels lost to himself: He knows that something is dreadfully wrong. More than that, he is in anxiety; he suffers acutely, yet he does not know why. What is wrong? Does he not have all the goods of life?" A stranger approaches each of the commuters and says, "My friend, I know your predicament; come with me; I have news of the utmost importance for you." To the happy commuter, the stranger's speech sounds nonsensical. But the lost and anxious commuter who needs help might well follow the stranger.

The preconditions for questing are the same as the preconditions for accepting a message as news: predicament, and hope or faith. What interests Percy is not the search for water (what Percy here calls "island news") but the search for transcendence. The news that matters to a castaway is not news of the island but news from across the seas—where he comes from and what he is to do. But the castaway can be ready for news from across the seas only if he faces the truth that he is a castaway: "To be a castaway is to be in a great predicament and this is not a happy state of affairs. But it is very much happier than being a castaway and pretending one is not." Forms of pretending, in response to our existential anxiety, are the resort to psychotherapy or to drugs. These alternatives may assuage anxiety or loneliness, but they allow the castaway to deceive himself as to the cause and meaning of his symptoms, so that, "even if his symptoms are better, he is worse off than he was." The proper response to symptoms is not to seek to allay them, but to use them as the stimulus for a search.

Percy's search leads him to apostolic Christianity—that is, the attempt to promulgate a particular call from across the seas. He groups drugs and psychotherapy as false friends. Less religious existential philosophers might allow psychotherapy as a proper form of quest—

here the news from across the seas is news from the repressed un-conscious. In either case, it is a grave error to understand symptoms as mere cries of the body. Percy, I think, would grant that there are instances of discrete mental illness for which drugs are appropriate. But in the case of the healthy person who feels out of touch or limited in some way—whether an anxious castaway or a housebound Emily Dickinson—medication is, to Percy, a soul-deadening distraction.

I suspect that the ways in which we see Percy's housebound Emily Dickinson and his anxious castaway have changed, over the course of a very few years. The issue is not whether man should strive for transcendence, but how often his disturbed affect is distinctively human, how often it is best seen as a stimulus for a quest. Here we return to the issue of personhood: Is the formerly inhibited and driven patient on Prozac pretending not to be a castaway? Or has she—beyond the need for pretense—found home?

If I were to rewrite Percy's thought experiment today, I would have us imagine a woman—one who finds herself a castaway, always feeling like an outsider, somewhat sad, compulsive in ways that seem alien to her, quirky in ways that are only partly comfortable, over-sensitive to slights, limited in her capacity to enjoy the fruits of the island, a bit vague in her thought, listless, doubtful of her worth. She has struggled to ascertain the roots of her unease and perhaps has come a certain distance toward that goal, having made herself aware of difficult experiences in her childhood. But her mood and social circumstances remain unchanged, and so her search continues. Now let us imagine that as she walks along the beach she finds a bottle containing not a slip of paper but a number of green-and-off-white capsules filled with a white powder. Questing and desperate, she decides to take the capsules, one each day, and in time she feels bolder and less troubled, more at ease with herself, keener of thought, energized, more open to ordinary pleasure. Is there a message after all, a message in the capsule?

———

Certainly patients draw conclusions from their responses to medication. We began with one such new understanding, Sam's inference that a valued idiosyncrasy was actually a biological compulsion. But the conclusions our discontented beachcomber draws might be broader. In discovering that self-esteem can be turned on and off like a switch, that without her seriousness she feels very much "like myself," that social inhibition can be laid down like a soldier's impedimenta, leaving the self light and unencumbered, she may arrive at a number of new understandings about what constitutes news and about the nature of her (human) nature.

Her startling transformation will make her seek out a fresh explanation for her old discomfort. Discarding her old beliefs—that she is self-undermining, defensive, and resistant to self-awareness—she may find herself attending to categories of analysis that might once have seemed quite foreign: rejection-sensitivity, social and affective temperament, hedonic capacity, kindled depression, and so forth. Given the physiological nature of her makeover, she may attend with more interest to a new range of inquiries, from cellular biology to animal ethology. What once seemed *Wissenschaft* may now seem news, and not just island news but news about the essence of the self.

Since she is inquisitive, our castaway may undergo a metamorphosis that reaches far beyond the mere effect of new chemicals on her neurons. Having pondered her response to the capsules from over the seas, our castaway may relate differently to her anxiety, guilt, shame, timidity, depression, and low self-worth, experiencing them no longer as uniquely human or preferentially responsive to insight and self-understanding. If so, she will attend to them in a new way, reading them not exclusively as signs of and stimuli to transcendence, but in part as scars of old injuries, in part as her family's physical heritage, burdens it would not be shameful to modify chemically. Or, noting a certain mismatch between her propensities and the demands of island culture, she may strive to create a culture that values her temperament. And if she spreads the news, a changed way

282

of understanding melancholy and angst may spread throughout the island.

Do we imagine that our castaway will be so contented that she no longer seeks a wider meaning in life? Does man's quest for transcendence rely for its motive force on anxiety and sadness? Perhaps, if she values self-understanding, the castaway will discover she has access to a richer store of memories, to long-suppressed feelings she is now unafraid to experience. Perhaps she will find the energy to pursue good works or to fulfill her creative potential. Or perhaps she will feel herself less morally driven, and then she will have to ask whether the pills have caused her to betray her self or to discover her self, whether her old drive—her tendency to worry the same old bone—was inspired, divinely or through wise forces of evolution, or only compelled, in a way that deprived her of autonomy.

The castaway, if she seeks out the professional knowledge, will discover that it is imperfect. Biologists do not know what depression is. The reigning model at the cellular and chemical level, the biogenic-amine hypothesis, is demonstrably false or incomplete. Understanding of minor mood disorders, or normal variants, is even more primitive. Though the kindling model of depression has its appeal, it constitutes argument by analogy. About affective and social temperament, the experts know least of all. Social inhibition may be a persistent trait in children, but how it relates to anxiety in adults is uncertain, its relevance to minor depression is wholly speculative, and its implications for other domains of personality theory are unknown. Animal studies remain a highly imperfect way to explore human behavior, especially such deeply human traits as valuation of the self. And about a most important issue, whether anatomically encoded injuries can be repaired or only compensated for, the professionals know nothing at all.

The biological study of the self is so primitive as to be laughable. And yet the experience of taking the pill will lead our castaway to look to biology for answers about the construction of personality and particular personality traits. The message in the capsule is "Dig here," in physiology, as well as there, where she had previously preferred to dig, in the territory of the mind.

Our castaway will avoid biological reductionism, because she thinks complexly. She will note that the experts whose work is of interest have been curious about social forces and social experiences, not just physiology. Jerome Kagan, in studying inborn temperament, wonders about the role of hostile siblings in a shy child's development. Michael McGuire leaves his monkey colonies to examine the way dysthymic women spend their lunch hours, at the end of a long line at the bank. Far from the laboratory bench, Robert Post sits with families of rapid cyclers, mapping out the history of his patients' illness in the manner of a turn-of-the-century German descriptive psychiatrist. Donald Klein asks about the inculcation of images of femininity in young girls. Even if certain aspects of mood and per- sonality now seem "biological" or "functionally autonomous," the mind maintains a role in assessing the environment: ultimately it is the imagination that defines the scope of "home" for the person with panic anxiety, of "loss" for the rejection-sensitive, of "novelty" for the socially reactive.

Our castaway may choose to dismiss the new perspectives on mind and brain. Conceding that her self has an animal aspect, she may argue that what makes her human is the way she applies her animal capabilities to higher purposes. A traumatized ape is uneasy when it feels far from the familiar; but only men and women can be alienated from the self. Only a person can say that the familiar—marriage, television shows, the political environment—is slightly askew and therefore "novel" or "not home." Only a person can feel lost in the cosmos.

This response is entirely reasonable: were he alive, Walker Percy might argue along these lines. But if our castaway is at all like the patients we have met, she will no longer experience her angst and melancholy as privileged, guiding, sentinel emotions. Even if she avoids reductionism, she will likely turn to new models to understand the formation of her personality and the meaning—or lack of meaning—of her emotional state. Those models will give biology, both cellular and evolutionary, a much-expanded role.

• • •

This change is not just a matter of "taking biology into account," as if one can maintain old ideas about behavior and personality and tack on a separate biological point of view. Medication has a pervasive influence, changing the way we see people and understand their predicaments. Its impact is especially apparent in the work of psychotherapists.

After I had seen a number of rejection sensitive patients respond to Prozac, I was consulted by a woman regarding unhappiness in her marriage. Susan had discussed the marriage in a psychotherapy that ended two years earlier, and she had concluded that she should leave her husband. He had disappointed her in different ways, and she believed that the constraints he placed on her stunted her growth. But something prevented her from separating.

Before Prozac, I might well have taken up where the former therapist had left off, exploring the possibility that unconscious wishes to remain in the marriage opposed Susan's expressed intention to leave. I would have begun with the assumption that clarifying the ambivalence—making her aware of unconscious conflict—would free her to act on whatever choice she made. Respecting a time-honored principle of psychotherapy called neutrality, I would have taken especial care not to side with Susan in her complaints about her husband.

But Susan seemed quite clear about the marriage—she had done her work in the previous therapy, understood her tendency to make certain sorts of bad choices. And she gave me abundant evidence of an extreme reactivity to loss. Since childhood, she had been sensitive to the disruption of even small attachments, as had her parents. In Susan, this pattern seemed relatively autonomous: it persisted despite her rather sophisticated self-understanding and her high degree of maturity in other aspects of her life.

I saw this woman differently than I would have before my exposure to Prozac. I did not perceive her as ambivalent, or at least I did not imagine that mixed feelings toward her husband were the main contributor to her current paralysis. I saw someone who wanted a divorce but could not make the move because of the overwhelming feelings of pain and disorganization she anticipated from separation.

Susan did not want to take medication, and I felt no need to press her to do so. But I did take her reactivity to loss—a mixture of rejection-sensitivity and separation anxiety—into account in the therapy. I supported her in her wish to leave her husband, something that in the past I would never have done so early in a therapy. And this choice worked out well for Susan. As she and I had both predicted, she became anxious and apathetic at each of the stages of separation, but once she had restabilized, she felt freer and happier, and she felt she had grown psychologically. My belief was that a relatively fixed trait of personality, one related to a biological reactivity to loss, had arbitrarily limited Susan's ability to carry out her own wishes, so that siding with her in her decision to divorce best supported her autonomy.

In the course of psychotherapy, Susan and I discussed both her personality structure—her difficulty letting go, her demands for admiration—and the reasons, based on her family history, that she had formed strong ties to the particular man she had married. But for the most part, in my role as psychotherapist, I acted like a medication—like Prozac—helping to mitigate my patient's sensitivity to loss. Soon we may be able to go further and say that the therapy mimicked medication more closely—that it altered Susan's serotonin levels—but that speculation is as yet a barely tested notion.

My brief account of this case serves as an example of an interaction of pharmacotherapy and psychotherapy that can take place even when no medication is prescribed. Taking biology into account entails attending to a new set of categories of analysis (such as reactivity to loss), and that new perspective leads to radical changes in the therapy—in this case, abandoning neutrality, de-emphasizing ambivalence, and giving the patient open support in her decision to divorce.

In traditional psychodynamic psychotherapy—my usual approach to patients—cure comes from within the patient through self-understanding. Here, in my work with a woman who was quite capable of self-examination, I opted instead to work through support for a concrete choice. I did so in part because I believed that Susan's reactivity—which I saw as a relatively fixed biological instability of mood in reaction to loss—would respond slowly, if at all, to psychotherapy; instead, I hoped a change in social circumstances would enhance her sense of her own status and her self-esteem.

My treatment of Susan was relatively simple, because she had already undertaken a course of self-examination that made her aware of her self-destructive impulses. A more complicated psychotherapy might address both ambivalence and reactivity. But in any case, seeing who people are, in the psychopharmacologic era, entails attending to their temperament and their functionally autonomous emotional responses.

Even at rather traditional institutions, psychoanalysis, the most conservative of psychotherapies, is changing in response to the perspective medication brings. A group of psychoanalysts at the Payne Whitney Clinic in New York, including a past president of the American Psychoanalytic Association, is constructing models for the treatment of panic disorder that integrate concepts drawn from biological psychiatry into psychoanalysis.

Though they do not accept Donald Klein's assertion that panic attacks "emerge 'out of the blue,' " the analysts' understanding of their patients has been influenced by the theories of Klein and other psychopharmacologists. The Payne Whitney analysts see panic as arising from a "bad fit" between a temperamentally inhibited or reactive child and a parent who cannot assuage the child's fear of novelty. (This new starting point is remarkable in itself: traditional psychoanalysis overlooks temperament in favor of a focus on the universal Oedipus complex.) The less empathic the parent is, the more dependent the child becomes. Rather than feel the humiliation of attributing the dependency to himself, the child projects dependency needs onto the parent, who is experienced as smothering. The parent is alternately experienced as overinvolved (smothering) and underinvolved (rejecting). In the words of the Payne Whitney group, "One result of this pattern can be heightened separation anxiety, in which the child clings to the parent in an attempt to ensure the child's and the parent's safety, and this clinging may in turn precipitate suffocation fears related to the parent's smothering presence."

What fascinates me is how brazenly this psychoanalytic model of panic borrows from psychopharmacology. The focus on smothering and rejection exactly parallels Klein's biological theories regarding the genesis of panic. Klein believes that the physiological problem in people prone to panic is either hypersensitivity of the carbon-dioxide receptor (the false-suffocation alarm) or a recrudescence in the adult of infantile separation anxiety (a failure of the adult brain to suppress a primitive, age-inappropriate, neurological function). In parallel fashion, the analysts trace panic anxiety to the patient's fears of suffocation and separation. Psychoanalysis, which in Freud's day leaned on physics for its metaphors—conservation of psychic energy, the hydraulic theory of repression—is now looking to psychopharmacology for its imagery.

Descriptive psychiatry—the diagnosis-centered discipline that traces its roots to Kraepelin's differentiation of schizophrenia from manic depression—is also undergoing changes in response to the observation that patients with widely differing conditions respond to the same medications.

Descriptive psychiatry today has two linked problems. On one hand, it is impossibly complex and overly specific. On the other, it contains no appropriate niche for a high percentage of patients who arrive at doctors' offices with serious psychological complaints. Perhaps 25 or even 35 percent of these patients are undiagnosable according to current criteria. Most of these undiagnosable patients have mixed forms of depression and anxiety. These figures do not include the much larger group of people, not disturbed enough to be counted "mentally ill but undiagnosable" in the studies, who also complain of depression, anxiety, and related symptoms.

The fact that a variety of people respond to medicines like Prozac—patients with specific diagnoses, patients without specific diagnoses, and nonpatients—presents a serious challenge to descriptive psychiatry. In the past, psychiatry has multiplied diagnoses—there are now over two hundred—in order to encompass new groups of distressed people. I believe that this strategy has failed, especially as regards minor disorders, prime evidence of this failure being the efficacy of both psychotherapy and Prozac (or other thymoleptics) for a wide range of these ostensibly distinct conditions. It is hard to know just how descriptive psychiatry will address the diverse syndromes that respond to new medications, but I think a good case can be made for the return of "neurosis," a catchall category for serious minor discomfort related to depression and anxiety.

The term will not mean what it meant in the 1950s. Neurosis then entailed trouble related to the "unanalyzed self," a self subject to the vicissitudes of castration anxiety, Oedipal conflict, and repressed sexuality. Neurosis of the twenty-first century will be a disorder that encompasses the effects of heredity and trauma—risk and stress—on a variety of neuropsychological functions encoded in neuroanatomy and the states of the neurotransmitters. The coalescing of diagnoses would then require descriptive psychiatrists to take into account the data of psychotherapy—parent-child interactions, significant losses, patterns of social relationships, quality of self-esteem. In other words, the success of medication is changing both mind-centered and biological psychiatry and moving them closer to each other.

The ideal modern psychiatrist will be one who can use drugs intimately and help patients to grow in self-understanding. Woody Allen has given us an image of such a healer: Dr. Yang, the all-knowing herbalist in Allen's fantasy *Alice*. The film tells the story of Alice Tait, a hypochondriacal, directionless wife and mother. Yang provides her with an herbal infusion that proves to be a sort of instant super-Prozac. Under its influence, the ordinarily shy and insecure heroine propositions a saxophonist in a dialogue that finds her mistress of both a seductive manner and an inexplicable fluency with jazz history and lingo. Like psychiatrists who have observed the effects of Prozac, Allen appreciates that a change in mood state can reveal hidden social skills.

Yang combines ever more fantastic potions with parsimonious interpretations, sending Alice on journeys of exploration that leave her "ten feet tall": confident, independent, able to sever ties with her husband and act with new moral decisiveness. Yang's herbs allow his patient to experience the world differently—to see husband, lovers, parents, siblings, and children in a new light—and then to bear the possibility of loss inherent in that fresh vision. Yang's magic is as much in his judgment as his pharmacopeia. His drugs only potentiate change; ultimately, it is Alice's quest that transforms.

The Dr. Yang fantasy is the fantasy of psychotherapy saved and redeemed by medication, where drugs do not cure patients but liberate them. Used properly, this new freedom can open people to insights that then shape the new self. Allen, so long inspired by psychoanalysis, creates in Dr. Yang a pharmacologist whose stock-in-trade is not science but wisdom. That is, Allen has imagined the ideal psychiatrist of the future, one who can use drugs, in the deepest sense, psychotherapeutically.

Dr. Yang stands in strong contrast to Walker Percy's selfish apes, who put Heavy Sodium in the water supply. These two fables, Allen's and Percy's, represent dialectical views of the potential of pharmacology: medication, in the wrong hands, as thief of the self; medication, in the right hands, as restorer of the self.

• • •

Our theme has been the significance of Prozac's transformative powers—its effects when it works well—for the modern view of the self. I have therefore had little occasion to discuss bad reactions to Prozac, a topic I broach in an appendix. But there is one negative response that has obvious bearing on whether Prozac is a good thing—on whether it is more like Heavy Sodium or more like Dr. Yang's herbs—and that is the feeling, reported by Hillary and Tess, of the numbing of moral sensibility.

I have treated other patients who, even if their depressed mood or social inhibition decreases on Prozac, complain that they feel uncomfortable, as if they have been deprived of a feeling state or a sense of urgency that is vital to them. In each case, I have tried to understand what this discomfort means.

I worked with an undergraduate whose constant complaint in psychotherapy was the series of humiliations he had suffered at the hands of his parents. Philip was moderately depressed and isolated from classmates, whom he scorned. But his moodiness and irritability were comfortable to him, because they represented his legitimate suffering and rage. Quite early in our time together, Philip's depression worsened to the point where he did not care whether he lived or died, and I suggested he take Prozac.

He was a "good responder." On Prozac, Philip felt better than well, and he hated it. He had been prematurely robbed of his disdain, his hatred, his alienation. His acute episode of depression had been frightening, and I urged him to stay on the Prozac for six months, in order to prevent a recurrence. He took my advice, but the six months of feeling fine were hell for Philip. He felt phony; he did not trust himself. He was truly relieved to stop the medicine and resume his bitterness, although in truth it did not return with its former vehemence.

———

The patients I medicate with Prozac tend first to have undergone extensive courses of psychotherapy. Philip had not, and one way to see his discomfort on Prozac is to say that he was not prepared to be well. I like this understanding of what occurred—the sense that there needs to be a readiness for Prozac, that Prozac works best in patients whose conflicts are resolved but whose biologically autonomous handicaps remain.

Philip's uncomfortable response to Prozac warns against a potentially unfortunate interaction between medication and another societal force: the focus on cost, rather than quality, in medicine. The patients we have met here almost all underwent treatments that entailed effort, time, and expense. If, at the start of those treatments, these patients had just been given Prozac, they would have felt some relief, and in some cases that intervention might have been enough; but I suspect it most often would not.

To my mind, psychotherapy remains the single most helpful technology for the treatment of minor depression and anxiety. Medication can speed treatment, and sometimes it can bring about remarkable transformation on its own. Certainly medication has had a profound influence on psychotherapy, and any psychotherapy today should include awareness of biological influences on mood and behavior. But the belief—espoused not infrequently by health-care cost-cutters in the "managed care" industry—that medication can obviate psychotherapy conceals, I believe, a cynical willingness to let people suffer. If medication does interfere with self-examination, it may be in this concrete and practical way—that it serves as a pretext for denying patients psychotherapy.

Philip's angry feelings were his problem to solve—his impetus to quest—and it was a hardship to be relieved of them prematurely. As regards Philip, Walker Percy is right: not worrying the same old bone is inherently self-alienating. For Hillary and Tess, the moral calculus seems different. Hillary—the laziest gal in town—wondered, when she recovered from anhedonia, whether she had lost a degree of moral urgency. On Prozac, Tess found herself less "serious"—less preoccupied with the needs of her mother, her siblings, and her boyfriends. But each patient went on to approach her dilemmas with new perspective and energy.

Moral urgency can be seen in clinical terms: Prozac tempered a compulsive trait in these women—affiliative neediness, or aloneness affect, or rejection-sensitivity, or the drive that forms part of the melancholic temperament. To the extent that biologically driven compulsion supported Hillary's and Tess's moral sensibility, Prozac diminished that sensibility. The dysthymic's critical appraisal of right and wrong has been replaced by the hyperthymic's easygoing acceptance of the world as it is.

Working with Prozac has heightened my awareness of the extent to which compulsion is a basis for moral action. Is it a sound basis? Surely one could make the case that what is compelled is inherently amoral; what characterizes moral action is choice. Still, in addressing this effect of Prozac, we face the least irrational, most cogent aspect of pharmacological Calvinism: perhaps diminishing pain can dull the soul.

In discussing evolutionary adaptation, I argued that, insofar as Prozac only makes Hillary and Tess as free of compulsiveness and aloneness as many other people, its effect on fitness is unexceptionable. We do not want to say that ordinarily flexible people are adaptively unfit. I am not sure whether the same approach answers the apprehensions apparent in Walker Percy's novels and essays. Perhaps Percy would see certain "good responders" to Prozac as happy, and therefore uninteresting, commuters; one gets the sense that he finds commuters who know something is dreadfully wrong to be more humanly complete. Presumably Percy's own quest, an enormously productive one, arose from his sense of unease, his feeling of being a castaway stranded in contemporary culture.

I find myself caught between paradigms. I agree with Percy that what distinguishes and dignifies humanity is the quest for transcendence, attentiveness to news from across the seas. But listening to Prozac has made me so attentive to the phylogenetic origins and biological underpinnings of free-floating anxiety and melancholy that I have trouble understanding them as special communications that make humans distinct from beasts. This posture arises from my observation of patients: I think of Allison, who had the most concrete form of alienation of self—an inability to find the self at all—and whose condition responded dramatically to medication. Her self-alienation added nothing to her life; medication freed her to pursue her quest.

One can hardly deny the cogency of Percy's observations about our culture—its lack of direction, its preference for stimulation over contemplation, its denigration of solitude. Percy was one of the keenest, most clear-eyed critics of American social mores. Still, what are we to make of patients who navigate that culture more effectively—and achieve self-realization—on medication? Once we see driven patients conduct their lives in free and complex ways on medication, and once we have looked at the evidence that emotional patterns much like the ones that handicapped them occur in lower animals in response to simple traumas, the connection between uncomfortable affect and transcendence becomes less self-evident. The question is not whether our culture undermines efforts at transcendence—surely it often does—but whether medication is a proper metaphor for those self-alienating social forces, and, more centrally, whether hurt, anxiety, melancholy, and inhibition—the whole range of affect states from which Prozac and Heavy Sodium free people—are privileged signals about man's condition.

The relationship between affective and moral sensibility is complex. When depressed, many people lose their interest in outside causes and become preoccupied with themselves; manics often seem sociopathic in their indifference to the consequences of their acts. In these patients, treatment of the mood disorder can turn a morally unattractive person into an admirable one. Other depressed patients are fascinating in their ethical ruminations or punctiliousness, and on recovery they may seem disappointingly ordinary in their moral focus.

Similar associations between mood and moral sensibility exist in the minor disorders, so that a movement along the spectrum from dysthymia to hyperthymia can be accompanied by a change in level of ethical sensitivity and profundity, although in different directions for different people. Some, who have been obsessed with moral concerns, may become less preoccupied; others, who have been self-centered, may find the emotional flexibility to attend to ethical concerns.

My own belief is that the moral sensibility can arise in the company of a variety of affect states. Perhaps even the fat, dumb, and happy commuter has his quest. The drive that results from inborn compulsiveness and pain experienced in childhood is only one reason to search for transcendence, and if lessening that drive ruins us morally, then our moral predicament is sad indeed. Still, the specter of Heavy Sodium is powerful. We cannot entirely escape the fear that a drug that makes people optimistic and confident will rob them of the morally beneficial effects of melancholy and angst.

• • •

We are, it seems to me, denizens of an island whose castaways have been receiving capsules rather than notes. What is most disturbing about those capsules is how they affect even those who never take medication. Castaway or not, in the psychopharmacologic era, when we look at our children, we will attend more to their constitution. At the same time, we will worry about losses children suffer, about our failures in empathy toward them, about the myriad of pains that can elevate stress hormones and stimulate dysfunctional neuronal sprouting.

Certain people we may tolerate better, or dismiss more readily, because their struggles are so transparently responses to functionally autonomous anxiety or depression, problems in regulation of mood that they ought really to get tended to, one way or another. Where once we might have sat with a friend, puzzling over her social dilemmas, now we will smile knowingly, wondering which subculture will best tolerate her quirks, or which medicine might enhance her appeal or her social skills.

We may become more aware of our own feelings of confidence or despondency, noting how they respond to our social circumstances—how applause is a tonic for us, how loss devastates. We will no doubt worry over our depressions as once we worried over carcinogens: are they causing covert damage? An unreliable lover enrages us—he is doing not just psychic but physical harm; we assume the two are much the same. Or we see our spouse as a sort of first neurotransmitter in a cascade of chemicals, one who keeps our serotonin levels high. We are keenly aware of our temperament, our psychic scars, our animal nature. Assessing both ourselves and others, we find ourselves attending to strange categories: reactivity, aloneness, risk and stress, spectrum traits, dysthymic and hyperthymic personality. We understand that our reliance on biological categories has run far ahead of the evidence, but we are scarcely able to help ourselves.

Or perhaps our transformation has been less thorough. Perhaps we are, like certain patients on Prozac, altered by our encounter with medication but still aware of the persons we were before. We stand between worlds, uneasy about the rapidity with which we have dropped old concerns.

Having seen people not unlike ourselves respond to medicine, we experience angst and melancholy differently—our own and others'. Perhaps what Camus's Stranger suffered—his anhedonia, his sense of anomie—was a disorder of serotonin. Kierkegaard's fear and trembling and sickness unto death are at once spiritually significant and phenomenologically unremarkable, quite ordinary spectrum traits of mammals, affects whose interpretation in metaphysical terms is wholly arbitrary.

This change in our sensibility may disconcert us. Yet we know

models of the relationship between affect and morality change in each
era. The romantic decadence that once swept Europe—the self-
absorption of Goethe's Werther and Chateaubriand's René—now
seems jejune. A few decades after he proposed it, Sartre's notion of
nausea as the most basic of human emotions is dismissed by most
psychologists and philosophers. It should not surprise us if today we
understand "existential anxiety" and even "self-alienation" to relate
not only to our loss of moral guideposts but also to our animal
heritage.

Perhaps it is best to imagine that we are in a transitional phase.
Our free-floating angst and melancholy feel less and less like signals
of our existential dilemma. But nothing we learn about our neuro-
physiology or our animal nature will deny the possibility of man's
transcendence. We remain cast away, perhaps more lost than ever,
precisely because we are less able to experience our affect as a guide
to our moral state. We must look elsewhere for signs. Despite our
sense of its limitations, we may turn more then ever to psychotherapy,
or introspection, or even spirituality.

Observing responses to Prozac, we learn not only about ourselves but
about our island's culture. Certain intellectuals at mid-century—
those who tried to combine the thoughts of Karl Marx and Freud,
such as Erich Fromm and the literary critic Norman O. Brown—
believed that industrial capitalist society instilled and rewarded the
"anal character," a style marked by dampened enthusiasms, compulsive control, and conformist rigidity. The success of Prozac says
that today's high-tech capitalism values a very different temperament.
Confidence, flexibility, quickness, and energy—the positive aspects
of hyperthymia—are at a premium.

Copernicus wrenched the earth from the center of the universe.
Darwin undercut the human race's uniqueness among God's creations.
Freud made the conscious mind less special. Modern biology attacks
the centrality of mind altogether, highlighting the roles of brain and
body. Psychiatrists used to concede that mind and brain were one,

where the concession entailed letting a little biology creep into a mind-dominated discussion. Today, an exclusively mind-centered psychology would have trouble finding a seat at the table. There is no privileged sphere of the mind, no set of problems that is the exclusive domain of self-understanding. We are not formed of experience alone, and those elements in us that have been shaped by experience are not infinitely plastic.

That there are limits to human malleability is disturbing to our political tenets. All men are created equal—at least in our political and moral ideal—but they are created biologically heterogeneous, in temperament, and in predisposition to a variety of specific traits that relate to temperament. By the time they reach adulthood, people also differ biologically according to their good or bad fortune in periods of critical development. Psychotherapeutic medication is both instructive and problematic for a liberal society. It leads us to focus on biological difference, whereas for years our culture has chosen to ignore biologically based characteristics that, in Carl Degler's words, "might serve as an obstacle to an individual's self-realization." Emphasis on temperament can be divisive and oppressive, if a culture too strongly favors one temperament over another—traditionally masculine over traditionally feminine traits, for example. Or awareness of temperament can be inspiring, leading perhaps to efforts to minimize psychological harm to children, or to foster a social environment welcoming to constitutionally diverse adults.

To the extent that medications are important agents of personal transformation, change becomes ever less a matter of self-understanding and ever more a matter of being understood by an expert. If what is wrong with us is explained on a physiological basis, it lies in a sphere with which we are unfamiliar and with whose manipulation we are inept. As modern men and women, we may already be uncomfortable with the extent to which our surroundings, in the form of complex equipment, are beyond our ken. Now we are faced with the likelihood that introspection alone will not explain us to ourselves.

The personality-altering pill is high technology, something unknowable, foreign, perhaps even hostile. Prozac arises from the science of twenty years ago; even that science is so complex it is beyond the reach not just of lay people but of most practicing doctors. Psychoanalysis was criticized for creating a cult of expertise, but analysis is at least a joint effort, a journey of self-exploration for the patient, with feeling, insight, and intuition as guides. In this context, pharmacology may be experienced as self-alienating even when, in particular instances, it restores people to themselves. Having diminished the power of psychoanalysis, we are all the more at the mercy of professional knowledge.

In this regard, we may recognize in ourselves a certain prejudice, in favor of humanism (narrowly taken) and against science. For centuries, people were comfortable with the belief that they were governed by humors whose workings were mysterious. Why should we be less comfortable with the neurohumors, substances about which, after all, our experts do know something?

None of the ethical concerns about Prozac—its influence on affect tolerance, autonomy and coercion, cultural expectations, evolutionary fitness, transcendence—has disappeared. But once we have lived with Prozac for a while, once we have taken the measure of the drug, and once it has worked on us, those worries may seem less urgent. Our worst fear—Walker Percy's fear, the fear of the medical ethicists and evolutionary biologists, my own fear when I first saw patients respond to Prozac—was that medication would rob us of what is uniquely human: anxiety, guilt, shame, grief, self-consciousness. Instead, medication may have convinced us that those affects are not uniquely human, although how we use or respond to them surely is.

In the end, I suspect that the moral implications of Prozac are difficult to specify not only because the drug is new but because we are new as well. Like so many of the "good responders" to Prozac, we are two persons, with two senses of self. What is threatening to the old self is already comfortable, perhaps eagerly sought after, by the new. Here, I think, is Prozac's most profound moral consequence, in changing the sort of evidence we attend to, in changing our sense of constraints on human behavior, in changing the observing self.

Is Prozac a good thing? By now, asking about the virtue of Prozac—and I am referring here not to its use in severely depressed patients but, rather, to its availability to alter personality—may seem like asking whether it was a good thing for Freud to have discovered the unconscious. Once we are aware of the unconscious, once we have witnessed the effects of Prozac, it is impossible to imagine the modern world without them. Like psychoanalysis, Prozac exerts influence not only in its interaction with individual patients, but through its effect on contemporary thought. In time, I suspect we will come to discover that modern psychopharmacology has become, like Freud in his day, a whole climate of opinion under which we conduct our different lives.

Appendix:

Violence

Though Prozac has been of remarkable help to millions of patients, a cloud hangs over the drug—accusations that its effects on a few patients have been devastating. These patients, or their families, believe that Prozac has caused them to attempt suicide or commit violent acts. The issue of dramatic negative effects—whether Prozac can arouse in certain people obsessional impulses to do terrible things that are otherwise alien to them—began as a scientific concern and rapidly became a media three-ring circus. The stories of many of the patients who appeared on television have been convincingly debunked, but the question of Prozac's dark side raises fascinating issues that relate to topics we have already discussed.

When it emerged in 1990, the allegation that Prozac could cause violent acts surprised scientists. To understand why, it is necessary to know something about studies of the relationship between serotonin and aggression, both in man and in monkeys.

The monkey research is of special interest. A variety of evidence—from blood serotonin levels in wild monkeys to medication responses of monkeys in captivity—points to a correlation between high serotonin levels and dominance. But dominance is quite different from aggression.

Dominant monkeys are almost never impulsively violent. On the contrary, they tend to be purposeful in their behavior; when challenged, they win the encounters they engage in, but they do not seek fights. Dominant, high-serotonin monkeys tend to be well integrated socially and to engage in a high level of affiliative activities, both with other males and with members of the opposite sex. Indeed, winning affiliation with females is part of the sequence that leads to and maintains dominance. Fighting with females is a sign of low hierarchy.

It is when they have low serotonin levels that monkeys become maladaptively aggressive and, at the same time, less socially competent. Low-serotonin monkeys tend to be socially deviant and ostracized; and socially deviant and ostracized monkeys tend to have low serotonin levels.

Drugs, like Prozac, that increase brain-serotonin transmission decrease aggression and impulsivity in low-serotonin animals. The most specific effect may be on what has been called "affective aggression"—that is, aggression against other members of the same species, marked by arousal and vocalization, as opposed to "predatory aggression," a more controlled form of aggression directed against other species. Affective aggression is thought to be a model for violence against the self or family members in humans.

The relationship between serotonin and aggression—as opposed to dominance—also has been studied in monkeys in their natural habitat. Because rhesus monkeys are naturally aggressive within the species, they were chosen for a large-scale correlational study. Scientists corralled small groups of free-ranging adolescent monkeys and rated them according to observed aggression, fight wounds, and old scars. The monkeys' spinal fluid was tested for levels of a serotonin-breakdown product, or metabolite. High aggressivity correlated with low levels of the metabolite, a sign of low brain-serotonin levels.

Studies indicate that humans are similar to monkeys in this regard. In human children and adolescents, low levels of a serotonin metabolite in the spinal fluid predict the severity of physical aggression on follow-up two and a half years later. Similarly, low levels of the same metabolite in spinal fluid correlate with highly planned suicide attempts—violence against the self—in hospitalized adults.

And research indicates that violent tendencies in aggressive and impulsive humans and other animals can be diminished with serotonin-enhancing drugs. Serotonin-elevating drugs, on the basis of this use, are sometimes called "serenics." BuSpar, a medication that acts on nerves that respond to a particular subtype of serotonin, has gained widespread use in the treatment of violence in retarded or brain-damaged patients; this usage qualifies BuSpar as a serenic. Prozac is also a serenic. In a study of depressed patients, some of whom were prone to impulsive anger, treatment with Prozac resulted in a marked decline in hostility and a decrease in the expression of anger.

Advocates of "assertiveness training" seem to be right when they say that assertiveness is different from aggression. Assertiveness gets you what you need, and it correlates with high brain-serotonin levels. Aggression—uncontrolled or rageful violence, whether against self or others—is unassertive, disruptive, and generally ineffectual, and it correlates with low brain-serotonin levels. Animal studies resulted in what might be called an ethological dissection between assertiveness and aggression, one that has had influence far beyond psychiatry, on the intellectual understanding of violence. Raising serotonin levels makes for assertiveness, not aggression. The notion of serotonin-enhancing drugs as serenity-inducing makes the purported association between Prozac and violence all the more puzzling.

Biochemically, suicide looks a good deal like aggression. A variety of postmortem studies have compared the brains of otherwise physically healthy people who died from suicide with those who died as accident victims. What distinguishes the suicides is low levels of brain serotonin. In other words, scientists had every reason to believe that a drug like Prozac, which enhances serotonergic transmission, would *decrease* aggression and suicidality.

The issue of Prozac and suicide—the beginning of wider concern about Prozac and violence—was first raised in a group of cases reported in the *American Journal of Psychiatry* in February 1990. Martin Teicher and two colleagues at McLean Hospital, part of the Harvard teaching system, had observed six depressed patients who developed "intense, violent suicidal preoccupations" after between two and seven weeks of treatment with Prozac. These patients were, by the authors' own description, "complex." Almost all had very extensive histories of depression and had failed to respond to a long series of prior drugs or even to electroshock treatment. Five had considered killing themselves in the past, and three had actually made prior attempts. Some were taking other psychotherapeutic medications along with Prozac; in one case, Prozac was the sixth medication in the regimen.

Still, in each of these patients, Teicher and his colleagues noted a distinct and surprising change: the emergence on Prozac of urgent, obsessional suicidal preoccupations. These preoccupations disappeared after discontinuation of Prozac, though often not for some weeks. Interestingly, two patients in whom a careful assessment was made (using standardized depression-rating scales) were found not to have gotten more depressed on Prozac, only more suicidal; and in some patients, when Prozac was withdrawn the self-destructive preoccupations diminished even though the depression did not. The suicidal thoughts seemed independent of the level of depression.

The Teicher report had certain flaws. Some of the studied patients were quite seriously depressed, and their deterioration and emerging suicidality might have represented the natural course of their depression, a failure of Prozac but not a side effect. Only one of the patients had the sort of minor disorder we have discussed here, and his story had a complication that makes the role of Prozac hard to interpret.

Mr. B was a successful professional who had been treated inter-mittently with psychotherapy over a twenty-one-year history of minor depression. His dysthymia deteriorated into depression after a divorce. What makes Mr. B's story distinctive is that he responded to a monoamine-oxidase inhibitor (MAOI), but then his depression re-emerged, while he was still taking the MAOI.

This phenomenon is called tolerance. When applied to antide-pressants, tolerance refers to cases in which a medicine at first sup-presses depression but then—while the patient is still on the same dose of the same medicine—the depression "breaks through" full-force. Tolerance has been most widely reported with MAOIs (it also occurs with lithium and, it now appears, Prozac), and tolerance to MAOIs is a difficult, disturbing phenomenon. Patients who become tolerant to MAOIs often suffer a quite vicious deteriorating course, one that does not respond to other medication treatment.

Mr. B was withdrawn from the MAOI. Two weeks later, he was placed on Prozac, and then Prozac and lithium, during which time he continued to deteriorate. In particular, his suicidal ideation, which had been present on the MAOI, became an alarming preoccupation. The worsening suicidality was, however, only one of many new symp-toms, and might not ordinarily have been considered remarkable following the development of tolerance to an MAOI. Over the next three months, Mr. B failed to respond to—and remained suicidal on—imipramine, a second tricyclic antidepressant (doxepin), and a stimulant. Only when placed back on an MAOI did he recover, as patients sometimes do upon re-exposure to a drug to which they were once "tolerant." It is not at all clear that what Mr. B suffered was Prozac-induced suicidality.

Whatever its shortcomings, the Teicher report aroused great in-terest. The emergence of suicidal thoughts in patients on Prozac was noteworthy because it flew in the face of what is known about the relationship between serotonin and suicide. Prozac increases serotonin levels, so it should decrease suicidality. Indeed, there is evidence from certain research centers that Prozac and related drugs act faster than other antidepressants in decreasing suicidality, and even that Prozac might be preferentially effective in patients with past histories of suicide attempts. And Prozac is known to decrease obsessionality. If what Teicher and his colleagues observed is real, it is, as they themselves put it, a paradoxical effect.

The Teicher report gave rise to a flurry of research regarding Prozac and suicide. These subsequent studies showed that Prozac is a remarkably safe drug, perhaps safer than other antidepressants in terms of any tendency to induce suicidality. Review after review found as few suicide attempts on Prozac as on other antidepressants, or fewer; in one study, it seemed there might also be less frequent emergence of suicidal ideas on Prozac.

However, survey research does not address the individual case. If the Teicher report is right—that Prozac has a special effect in eliciting suicidal ideation—what is happening may be this: Prozac induces suicidality in a few patients who would otherwise not have been suicidal; but because Prozac is simultaneously more effective than other antidepressants in treating suicidality, in survey data those few patients who deteriorate are swamped by the much larger number of patients who improve. As one group of researchers put it, "Examining large, placebo-controlled databases for treatment-emergent suicidal ideation is not likely to be instructive because the active treatment, even if it causes suicidal ideation in a subgroup, also *suppresses* it. As long as the treatment (fluoxetine) suppresses more suicidal ideation than it induces, it will compare favorably with the placebo group."

The reviews responding to the Teicher report serve as a reminder that suicidal ideas emerge frequently in depression and that they emerge on all antidepressants. The most extensive surveys estimated that a small but substantial number of depressed patients, under 5 percent and probably closer to 1 percent, experience a paradoxical worsening of suicidal thoughts on any antidepressant. The percentage is likely much lower for the healthier patients we have discussed here.

There are many reasons why patients worsen on medication: the drug may not be working, certain side effects may be intolerable, the energizing effects of the drugs may cause people to consider acting on fantasies they had earlier not expressed or formulated. But it is also possible that antidepressants, for unknown reasons, make certain people more depressed directly, through unintended changes for the worse in neurotransmission.

Teicher's group and others have raised the possibility that the induction of suicidality by Prozac, if and when it occurs, is due to an infrequent medication side effect. Prozac and many other psychotherapeutic medications can cause akathisia, a sense of physical restlessness that makes people pace or otherwise try to remain in constant motion. This side effect can be extremely unpleasant and disturbing. An alternative hypothesis posits an idiosyncratic response to Prozac that involves a lowering of serotonin levels. No one has measured such an effect, and no one knows whether it occurs.

The most extensive review article on antidepressants and worsening suicidality concludes: "Because patients seek treatment at different points during illness and a significant number do not respond to treatment, the appearance or worsening of suicidality in a small number of patients is not sufficient to implicate the medication as the cause. . . . If the association between an antidepressant drug and worsening suicidality is established, the question of the mechanism becomes relevant. Given the reported infrequency of this effect . . . it is likely that each case results from an interaction between a drug effect and a specific patient-related vulnerability."

The Teicher report, by respected clinician-researchers, remains the single most cogent piece of evidence linking Prozac to suicide, impulsivity, or violence. The association between Prozac and suicidal ideation is speculative, based on doctors' and nurses' observation of a few cases—like some of the conjecture I have engaged in elsewhere in this book.

I have had one patient attempt suicide while on Prozac. His chief complaint—the main reason he consulted me—was persistent, intrusive thoughts of suicide, and he had attempted suicide in the past. I had put him on Prozac in part because it seemed to me that he was becoming increasingly suicidal. His attempt, when he made it, was quite serious—he was discovered and rescued only by chance. Despite the differences between this case and those reported by the McLean group—though their patients had a history of suicidal thoughts, they were not suicidally obsessed when drug treatment began—I did consider the possibility that Prozac had made things worse. This patient ultimately did better on an MAOI.

My own impression is that the risk that Prozac will induce suicidal thoughts is small. On the basis of stories I have heard from colleagues and the report of the McLean group, whose observations I respect, I would say that Prozac may, in rare cases, stimulate or worsen suicidal thoughts and impulses, probably not just idiosyncratically but on some common basis, perhaps a paradoxical lowering of serotonin-based transmission. The public worry about this possibility is, however, so exaggerated as to be dangerous, because it tends to discourage people from taking Prozac even where it is very likely to do them good and very unlikely to cause harm.

Hard upon the Teicher article, there emerged a series of lawsuits involving Prozac. Soon there were claims that Prozac had caused not just suicide but violence against others. Two of these cases received national attention.

On September 14, 1989, a former employee named Joseph Wesbecker entered the Standard Gravure printing plant in Louisville, Kentucky, carrying several semi-automatic weapons. He killed eight workers, wounded twelve, and then killed himself. Wesbecker had taken Prozac for a short time—it had recently been discontinued by his physician. At autopsy, Wesbecker was found to have in his bloodstream therapeutic concentrations of Prozac and lithium and low concentrations of two or three other antidepressants and a sedative.

In the wake of Teicher's report, a lawyer named Leonard Finz filed suit against Prozac's manufacturer, on behalf of Wesbecker's family and victims. Two sons, Jim and Kevin Wesbecker, went on "Larry King Live." Jim Wesbecker said that none of his father's psychiatrists had noted "any kind of violent behavior, any kind of violent reactions of any kind in his behavior," before the father took

Prozac. Finz said he planned to file dozens of lawsuits based on the "300 to 400" reports he had received of violence, death, and suicide related to Prozac. One of Wesbecker's victims and former co-workers, again in the company of Leonard Finz, went on "Donahue" (the show was titled "Prozac—Medication That Makes You Kill"), where she said that, except for a single episode of suicidality, Wesbecker had never in the ten years she knew him shown any violent tendencies. "Everyone who know him, knew him to be just your average nice Joe." The impression given the public was that Prozac can turn average Joes into homicidal maniacs.

The local press in Louisville provided a different picture. They concluded that the slaughter in the Standard Gravure plant was the culmination of a "lifelong journey of disintegration" of a disturbed man with a substantial history of violence against himself and threats of violence against others.

Wesbecker's story appears to be one of chronic insecurity complicated by hypochondriasis, social awkwardness, a short temper, mood disorder, and finally paranoia. He was hospitalized for mental disorder in 1978, 1984, and 1987. The more serious deterioration began in 1984, after which Wesbecker tried to commit suicide three times and began threatening to kill himself with a gun; by the time of his 1987 hospitalization, he had attempted suicide twelve to fifteen times.

Four psychiatrists who treated Wesbecker over the years found him to have a variant of manic-depressive illness with paranoia. He had told one psychiatrist by 1987, and perhaps as early as 1984, that he might like to harm his foreman. He brought a gun to Standard Gravure and talked about killing a supervisor with it as early as 1986. A year before the actual shooting, Wesbecker told his ex-wife he would like to go to the plant and "shoot a bunch of people." He saved a January 1989 *Time* magazine with a cover story about a mass shooting. In May 1989, before he was prescribed Prozac, Wesbecker bought the AK-47. He was apparently prescribed Prozac late that summer.

Wesbecker was hardly your average Joe before the summer of 1989. He may have been made manic or agitated by Prozac; any antidepressant can "switch" depression to mania in a patient with pre-existing manic-depressive illness. There are other possibilities: Wesbecker may have been disinhibited by the sedative he took; the six drugs in his system may have had an idiosyncratic effect in combination; his illness may have progressed independent of medication. But one thing is clear: this was not an episode of Prozac's causing an obsession that had not previously existed. According to press reports, none of the doctors who treated Wesbecker believed that Prozac played a role in his behavior; certainly there is no indication that it played a special role related to the phenomenon described by Teicher and his colleagues.

The other highly publicized case—that of Rebecca McStoots— also involved a hidden history of prior difficulty. In March 1990, McStoots shot her doctor, John Tapp, in the neck. She was convicted by a jury and sentenced to ten years in prison for first-degree assault, but she turned around and sued Eli Lilly, Prozac's manufacturer, alleging that she had had no prior history of violence or depression. In March 1991, McStoots joined "Larry King Live" by phone from jail in Bowling Green, Kentucky. It appears she had taken Prozac some six months before the shooting and then on her own resumed taking it for a week before pulling the gun on Dr. Tapp. McStoots said she had been taking Prozac for back strain, although on further questioning she admitted to depression, past suicidal thoughts, and a suicide attempt. McStoots also appeared on "Prime Time Live" with a denial of past difficulties. In court, Eli Lilly introduced evidence that McStoots had been violent long before taking Prozac, saying she had told doctors she had shot a former husband in New Mexico and later stabbed a woman in California. A judge dismissed McStoots's suit, as well as her claim that Lilly had slandered her and interfered in her criminal trial.

Many other cases have been publicized in which people claim to have been made newly suicidal or violent on Prozac. I am not familiar with every episode, but those I have seen resemble the Wesbecker and McStoots stories. In general, the people who claim never to have been suicidal before taking Prozac turn out to have been suicidal in the past, and those who claim never to have been violent turn out to have histories of prior violent threats or acts. I have not seen a publicized case associated with Prozac that is convincing as an example of the new onset of violent obsessions. Much of the publicity regarding a link between Prozac and suicide or violence was fomented by the Citizens Commission on Human Rights, a group affiliated with the Church of Scientology, which opposes psychiatry in general.

The publicity attendant on stories of Prozac's violent dark side is intriguing. It represents, I think, our cultural conviction that there is no averting conservation of mood, that what goes up must come down. Because Prozac has done great good, we are ready to believe it can do great harm.

Prozac does have side effects, as do all drugs. It is not Heavy Sodium; you could not put it in the water supply without making some people sick. Prozac not uncommonly causes nausea, loss of appetite, nervousness, insomnia, drowsiness, fatigue, sweating, rash, dizziness, and headache. More rarely, it has been associated with damage of one sort or another to almost every body system and organ—from arrhythmia of the heart to inflammation of the liver to dysfunction of the thyroid gland. As antidepressants go, Prozac is relatively safe, but no drug is risk-free.

Part of what makes people uneasy about Prozac is precisely that it works so well and has so few side effects. Prozac is enormously seductive. It is not addictive—patients do not crave Prozac, and there is no known withdrawal syndrome—but people who have experienced a good response to it are often leery about coming off medication, out of fear that they will return to their old way of feeling and behaving. Since we continue to believe in conservation of mood, we are suspicious of a drug that is so pleasant to take.

This seduction is legitimately worrisome because we know that some drugs, especially those that are taken chronically, will have unknown or even late-appearing (tardive) side effects. Psychotherapeutic drugs can sometimes cause tardive neurological disorders, which may appear years after a drug is discontinued; and questions have already been raised whether Prozac can cause such syndromes. Recently a small, preliminary study in rats has raised concern—quite prematurely, according to oncologists—over whether antidepressants, Prozac among them, can promote tumor growth in patients with cancer. Concern over unforeseen or tardive effects is realistic, because Prozac has been around too briefly for anyone to know its long-term effects.

But the panic about Prozac and violence seems to me to have gone beyond rational fear—to be what psychoanalysts call "overdetermined," that is, welcome because of the way it corresponds to our fantasies. The reports about Prozac and violence made good television because they meshed with science-fiction images of chemicals that turn Jekyll into Hyde.

What does it mean that we are willing to believe that intent to commit suicide or homicide can be induced by a pill, perhaps (as in the McLean case studies) even in the absence of a change in mood? Thoughts about suicide—much less the killing of others—are intimate and complex. They encompass moral and religious tenets, beliefs about the value of life and about self-worth, and sentiments concerning friends and family. Yet the idea that medication can cause people to ruminate about suicide and homicide is commonly accepted.

The television talk show title, "Medication That Makes You Kill," says something not only about medication but about "You." Within you is evil: not the evil of the conflicted unconscious but the evil of an animal—an injured, ostracized, low-status, impulsive cur who turns against his own kind and then himself. You have a personality that is readily subject to biological influence. Medication can reshape you in quite particular ways.

If these fantasies are credible, it is because medication has shaped our beliefs about how the self is constituted. In the final analysis, the uproar about Prozac and violence represents further testimony to our focus on biologically determined feelings and behaviors. The scare about violence contains a backhanded tribute to Prozac, an acknowledgment, albeit in nightmare form, that Prozac can transform the self.

Notes

INTRODUCTION

ix   the antidepressant drug Prozac: The generic name for Prozac is fluoxetine. Regarding proprietary and generic names for drugs, I have used whichever I thought would cause least trouble for the reader. When discussing a series of related drugs (imipramine, desipramine, clomipramine), I use the generic names. But where the proprietary (trade) name is a household word, I take advantage of that familiarity—Valium, for example, rather than diazepam. All drugs are cross-referenced under both generic and the most common proprietary name in the index.

In referring to prescribed, licit substances, I have used the words "medication," "medicine," and "drug" interchangeably.

ix   I had occasion to treat an architect: This is a simplified account of a case I have described in detail elsewhere ("Metamorphosis," *Psychiatric Times,* May 1989, p. 3ff). Sam's illness was complex, as was his course of treatment; among other things, when he first fully responded to Prozac, Sam was also on an antianxiety medication, Xanax; later in the course of treatment, the Xanax became unnecessary. In general, I have not simplified other case vignettes in this book to this degree, but I have altered identifying details in order to protect privacy. One case (Philip, chapter 9) is a composite.

Freud noted the paradox "that it is far easier to divulge the patient's most intimate secrets than the most innocent and trivial facts about him; for, whereas the former would not throw any light on his identity, the latter, by which he is generally recognized, would make it obvious to everyone" ("Notes upon a

Case of Obsessional Neurosis (1909)," James Strachey, ed., *The Standard Edition of the Complete Psychological Works of Sigmund Freud*, vol X [London: Hogarth Press, 1955], p. 156). Since truth is in the details, this tension between the requirements of accuracy and privacy is an impossible one; to this difficulty are added the inevitable flaws in all communication. A colleague has phrased well what I believe is the proper disclaimer regarding case examples: "Any departure from 'real' events is in part intended, in part unintended: details are deliberately disguised to protect the privacy of patients; and the distortions of human perception and memory are unavoidable" (Byram T. Karasu, *Wisdom in the Practice of Psychotherapy* [New York: Basic Books, 1992], p. xix).

x   he enjoyed sex as much as ever: I mention this detail because a common side effect of Prozac is change in sexual function, usually difficulty achieving orgasm. (See note to p. 265, on p. 366.) Sam did not experience this side effect.

Subsequent to my treatment of Sam, preliminary objective evidence has emerged that Prozac can, indeed, diminish sexual obsessions and compulsions (Dan J. Stein, Eric Hollander, et al., "Serotonergic Medications for Sexual Obsessions, Sexual Addictions, and Paraphilias," *Journal of Clinical Psychiatry*, vol. 53 [1992], pp. 267–71). I believe Sam was right—the interest in pornography was something like an obsession or a compulsion—but even if the truth is different, what remains interesting is Sam's willingness to turn to the medication for definition of the self.

xii   like Kierkegaard and Heidegger: This issue is approached in the chapter "Philosophical Roots" of Robert Coles's book *Walker Percy: An American Search* (Boston: Atlantic-Little, Brown, 1978), especially pp. 22, 32. I return to the philosophical implications of a biological view of affect in chapter 9.

xii   assuming a patient's anxiety was meaningless: The concept of meaningless anxiety is not restricted to assumptions about patients on medication; it is central to the biological theory of panic anxiety. I take this matter up in some detail in chapter 4.

xiii   the genes for . . . asking directions: Since I wrote that sentence, a report of a serious study on this issue appeared in *The New York Times:* Sandra Blakeslee, "Why Don't Men Ask Directions? They Don't Feel Lost: Each Sex Has Its Own Way of Navigating, Study Finds," May 26, 1992, p. C1f.

xiii   "half the difference in individuals' IQs": *Newsweek*, October 29, 1990, p. 69.

xiv such disorders as manic-depressive illness: This disorder is now properly called "bipolar affective disorder," but it remains "manic depression" in popular speech. (For instance, the relevant patient advocacy group is the National Depressive and Manic-Depressive Association.) For the sake of readability, I have chosen for the most part to call various conditions by their popular names. As in the case of drug names, the popular and scientific names are cross-referenced in the index.

Also, I have not scrupled to employ "manic-depressive," "schizophrenic," and, for that matter, "obsessive" or "dysthymic" as substantives. Occasionally I receive letters saying this usage is pejorative (on the grounds that no one *is*, globally, schizophrenic, but that people can *have* an illness, schizophrenia) and is restricted to mental illnesses. Given the examples of "asthmatic" and "diabetic," and the long history of reference to consumptives, I find this assertion unconvincing. I hope it is clear that no disparagement is intended when I try to avoid awkward locutions by using such terms as "manic-depressive."

xiv the studies proved impossible to replicate: Richard C. Lewontin expresses a yet stronger opinion:

> The rage for genes reminds us of Tulipomania and the South Sea Bubble in McKay's *Great Popular Delusions of* [sic] *the Madness of Crowds*. Claims for the definitive location of a gene for schizophrenia and manic depressive syndrome using DNA markers have been followed repeatedly by retraction of the claims and contrary claims as a few more members of a family tree have been observed, or a different set of families examined. In one notorious case, a claimed gene for manic depression, for which there was strong statistical evidence, was nowhere to be found when two members of the same family group developed symptoms. The original claim and its retraction both were published in the international journal *Nature*, causing David Baltimore to cry out at a scientific meeting, "Setting myself up as an average reader of *Nature*, what am I to believe?" Nothing.

("The Dream of the Human Genome," *New York Review of Books*, May 28, 1992, pp. 31–40; quotation on p. 37.)

xiv Carl Degler: See Carl N. Degler, *In Search of Human Nature: The Decline and Revival of Darwinism in American Social Thought* (New York: Oxford University Press, 1991).

xvi "cosmetic psychopharmacology": The essay is "The New You," *Psychiatric Times*, March 1990, pp. 45–46.

xvi cover story in *Newsweek:* March 26, 1990. One of my favorite Prozac media pieces appeared in the French magazine *Santé* (April 1990, p. 56). Under a reproduction of the *Newsweek* cover run these story headers: "Pilule Anti-Cafard: La Folie Américaine. L'Amérique est tombée amoureuse d'une pilule. Ses fans l'ont surnommé BBB (Bye Bye Blues: adieu cafard). Tout un programme. Mais est-ce pour autant la panacée?"

xvi definitive contemporary article for physicians: William Z. Potter, Matthew V. Rudorfer, and Husseini Manji, "The Pharmacologic Treatment of Depression," *New England Journal of Medicine,* vol. 325 (1991), pp. 633–42.

xvi green-and-off-white capsule: Officially it is a "pulvule." I asked the public-relations officer for Prozac's manufacturer what a pulvule is. She said the word is a registered trademark that refers to a capsule one of whose ends is slightly tapered, a characteristic Prozac has in common with a few other drugs, such as Darvon, also manufactured by Eli Lilly. It is so like Prozac-the-media-phenomenon to have this special, and meaningless, word associated with it.

xvii an ominous report had appeared: Martin H. Teicher, Carol Glod, and Jonathan O. Cole, "Emergence of Intense Suicidal Preoccupation During Fluoxetine Treatment," *American Journal of Psychiatry,* vol. 147 (1990), pp. 207–10. The issue of suicide, other violence, and Prozac is discussed in the appendix.

xvii Geraldo . . . Donahue: The most inflammatory television program may have been the February 27, 1991, "Donahue": "Prozac—Medication That Makes You Kill." On that show, Leanne Westover, widow of Del Shannon, claimed that Prozac-induced agitation led to his suicide.

xvii *Newsweek* again: "Violence Goes Mainstream," April 1, 1991.

xviii cover exposé of the Scientologists: *Time,* May 6, 1991.

xviii "60 Minutes": October 27, 1991.

xviii clinician after clinician had written: For example, Theodore Nadelson, "The Use of Adjunctive Fluoxetine in Analytic Psychotherapy with High Functioning Outpatients," unpublished, 1991, 24 pp. Nadelson, a psychoanalyst and nationally renowned consultation-liaison psychiatrist based at Tufts University, found that the best Prozac responders were often patients who were also good candidates for psychoanalysis, including those who had formed a strong relationship to the therapist and who had achieved a degree of social and career success. The types of positive results Nadelson noted included "increased satisfaction [and] disappearance of sensitivity to social criticism" as well as elevation of mood and a decrease in pessimism.

CHAPTER 1: MAKEOVER

1   a woman I worked with only around issues of medication: The issue of what is often called "medication backup" is a complicated one for psychiatry. There are psychiatrists who believe that it is unprofessional to do less than the whole job—that psychiatrists should not medicate patients whom social workers and psychologists see in psychotherapy. I prefer to do both aspects of treatment, but I have come to trust a handful of psychologists and social workers in my community—and they me—with the result that we work comfortably with patients whose care we share. These nonphysician psychotherapists are all women, which helps explain something the reader will notice about this book—namely, that most of the patients are women.

Women have always been overrepresented in the taking of antidepressants, for at least two, and probably three, reasons. First, most depression occurs in women. The best current understanding of this gender difference is that it is partly "biological" (broadly speaking, genetic, and in some way related to the cyclicity of women's biological functions, hormonal differences, and perhaps a stronger innate propensity to bond and therefore to suffer losses more deeply) but more predominantly psychological, related to the stresses and losses in women's lives. We will consider a complex interactive model of the causes of mood disorder, in chapter 5 and elsewhere. Second, women seek help more often than men do, so doctors see depressed women out of proportion to their presence in the population. A third likelihood is that, all things being equal, doctors may prescribe antidepressants somewhat more often for women than they do for men.

Along with two women colleagues in public health, I once investigated these issues by analyzing a sample of ninety thousand visits to doctors (not just psychiatrists), representative of all visits to doctors' private offices in the United States in 1980–81. In that study, 60 percent of all office visits to a doctor, for any reason, were by women. Sixty-four percent of visits for a psychiatric diagnosis were by women. And 70 percent of visits in which therapeutic listening was employed were for women. Even so, we found that, controlling for diagnosis and many other factors, a female patient visiting her physician for mental-health care had a 28-percent chance of receiving a psychotherapeutic drug, compared with a 24-percent chance for a virtually identical male patient. My impression is that women are more likely to be listened to and more likely to be medicated—they are just more likely to be treated than are men, and this is on top of any increased vulnerability to depression. (Rachel A. Schurman, Peter D. Kramer, and Janet B. Mitchell, "The Hidden Mental Health Network: Treatment of Mental Illness by Nonpsychiatric Physicians," *Archives of General Psychiatry,* vol. 42 [1985], pp. 89–94; Rachel A. Schurman, Peter D. Kramer, and Janet B. Mitchell, "The Hidden Mental Health Network: Provision of Mental Health Services by Non-Psychiatrist Physicians," research report, supported by contract 232-81-0039 from Division of Health Professional Analysis, DHHS, 1983.)

However, the *minor* mood disorders we will discuss in this book may be different from major depression. There are some researchers who believe these conditions—particularly "dysthymia," a category we will turn to in chapter 6—are biologically most like manic-depressive illness, which occurs with *equal* frequency in men and women.

My sense is that the number of medicated women in my practice is influenced by "medication-backup" referrals from women therapists whose caseloads are predominantly women and who are sensitive to issues of biological treatment for minor depression. In terms of the patients I see for both psychotherapy and pharmacotherapy, a group that is more equally men and women, the gender distribution of patients on medication is fairly even.

8 "People on the sidewalk ask me for directions!": I have since heard this identical report from other people on Prozac. In all cases, the medicine must have stimulated the patient to display subtle cues of accessibility. None of these people was manic or exhibitionistic. The alteration was subtle but thorough.

16 mental condition called "hyperthymia": Even the term "hyperthymia" is sometimes used to refer to a rather extreme condition (see chapter 6). I am borrowing the word to indicate a characteristic exuberance and quickness without implying overexpansiveness.

19 But who had she been . . . if not herself: We do occasionally make such claims. Here is a snippet of dialogue from Anne Tyler's novel *The Accidental Tourist* (New York: Alfred A. Knopf, 1985), p. 249. The first speaker is the brother of a man who has been transformed by his interactions with a woman; the second speaker, Macon, is the man transformed:

> "You're not yourself these days. . . . Everybody says so."
> "I'm more myself than I've been my whole life long," Macon told him.
> "What kind of remark is that? It doesn't even make sense!"

CHAPTER 2: COMPULSION

22   a magazine article I had written about psychopharmacology: "Is Everybody Happy?," *Good Health Magazine*, supplement to Boston *Globe*, October 7, 1990, p. 15ff.

25   "for most of the day . . .": American Psychiatric Association, *Diagnostic and Statistical Manual of Mental Disorders*, 3rd ed., rev. (Washington, D.C.: American Psychiatric Association, 1987), p. 230 (DSM-III-R). (I turn to dysthymia in detail in chapter 6.) The definitions of "obsession" and "compulsion," as elements of OCD, are on p. 247; that of "obsessive compulsive personality disorder" (formerly "compulsive personality disorder") on p. 356. In the description of the personality disorder, I have chosen the language of DSM III (1980, pp. 326–28) because it is more expressive. The patient would equally fail to meet the criteria for DSM-III-R, which include certain other interesting considerations, such as "inability to discard worn-out or worthless objects" and "lack of generosity in giving time, money, or gifts when no personal gain is likely to result." There have been changes in the definition of compulsion, obsession, OCD, and the related personality disorder between DSM-III (1980) and DSM-III-R (1987), and changes are anticipated for DSM-IV (in progress). Some of the instability in diagnosis is due to a new focus on these disorders in light of their responsivity to medication.

28   I raised the dose: The majority of patients who respond do so on twenty milligrams per day. Prozac has a long half-life—it is degraded and excreted only slowly by the body. As a result, the patient taking twenty milligrams is, in effect, on a low dose for a number of days; it is often not for two weeks that the therapeutic level has been reached in the blood and brain, the result of the residual contributions of early doses added together. (With most other antidepressants, it is necessary to give a low dose for a few days, and then, when the body is acclimated, to add more. Someone taking imipramine may begin with twenty-five or fifty milligrams and end up needing two or three hundred milligrams daily.)

The manufacturer of Prozac made the brilliant marketing decision at first to manufacture only one form of Prozac, the twenty-milligram capsule. Then all doctors could be taught to dose their patients with one pill a day—so simple, as the pharmacists say, that even an internist can do it. This marketing decision was one factor in the enormous popularity of Prozac.

In fact, different patients do respond to different doses. For those prone to anxiety, twenty milligrams may be a high starting dose. Psychiatrists soon learned to have patients break open the capsule, dissolve it in water or juice, stir well, and drink half the solution to get a ten-milligram dose. Patients with panic anxiety are often started on a two-and-a-half-milligram dose, one ounce of the solution made from dissolving contents of the capsule in eight ounces of water.

Julia did well on forty milligrams—two pills in the morning—whereas Tess had been on the more usual dose of twenty milligrams. Eighty milligrams is the highest dose recommended by the manufacturer, but some patients with OCD do not respond until the dose reaches 160 milligrams.

32 Large numbers . . . are not "diagnosable": See Leon Eisenberg, "Treating Depression and Anxiety in Primary Care: Closing the Gap Between Knowledge and Practice," *New England Journal of Medicine*, vol. 326 (1992), pp. 1080–84; and James E. Barrett, Jane A. Barrett, et al., "The Prevalence of Psychiatric Disorders in a Primary Care Practice," *Archives of General Psychiatry*, vol. 45 (1988), pp. 1100–1106.

33 to encompass . . . personal idiosyncrasy: Not only the neat are obsessional. Clinicians recognize a category one might call the "sloppy obsessional." Behaviorally, the sloppy obsessional seems the opposite of Julia. He never cleans, and he scorns those who clean up for him; but his behavior is equally based on paralysis of choice, a strong superego (this is where some of the contempt for time wasted in cleaning arises), and a generally inflexible approach to life. Neat obsessives who fall into despair may also become slovenly in a decided, almost aggressive way.

33 I had described Tess: The full sentence is: "She was a hard-working executive so attentive to detail in her professional life that she found little time to socialize, and that she devoted to a hopeless attachment to a married man" ("Is Everybody Happy?," p. 15).

40 "Masochism is as unfashionable . . .": John Updike, "Falling Asleep Up North," *New Yorker*, May 6, 1991, pp. 36–39; quotation on p. 39.

41 an influential critique of capitalist society: See Daniel Burston, *The Legacy of Erich Fromm* (Cambridge, Mass.: Harvard University Press, 1991), pp. 33–34 and elsewhere.

41 like compulsiveness or . . . like depression: Before this century, this question would have been meaningless. Throughout most of history, obsessive-compulsive disorder was understood as a form or part of melancholia. For example, the early-seventeenth-century physician and clergyman Richard Napier described this typical picture in one of his melancholic patients:

Extreme melancholy, possessing her for a long time, with fear; and sorely tempted not to touch anything for fear that then she shall be tempted to wash her clothes, even upon her back. Is tortured until that she be forced to wash her clothes, be them never so good and new. Will not suffer her husband, child, nor any of the household to have any new clothes until they wash them for fear the dust of them will fall upon her. Dareth not to go to the church for treading on the ground, fearing any dust should fall upon them.

(Michael MacDonald, *Mystical Bedlam: Madness, Anxiety, and Healing in Seventeenth-Century England* [Cambridge: Cambridge University Press, 1981], quoted in Stanley W. Jackson, *Melancholia and Depression: From Hippocratic Times to Modern Times* [New Haven: Yale University Press, 1986], p. 106.)

From ancient times, a degree of compulsiveness was considered typical of minor depression. Melancholics were understood to be driven. They had little energy, but that little they could often channel effectively. (This point is emphasized by Hagop Akiskal, whose work we will consider in chapter 6.) It is only in recent decades that the minor disorders have been subdivided into many distinct categories.

42   Freud's contemporary Emil Kraepelin: For a clear and masterful discussion of Kraepelin's contribution, and of manic depression and schizophrenia, see "Objective-Descriptive Psychiatry: Emil Kraepelin," in Leston Havens, *Approaches to the Mind: Movement of the Psychiatric Schools from Sects to Science* (Cambridge, Mass.: Harvard University Press, 1973), pp. 13–34.

42   ". . . essentially the same in quality . . .": Karl Menninger, *The Vital Balance* (New York: Viking, 1963), p. 2.

42   "The predominant American psychiatric theory . . .": Donald F. Klein, "Anxiety Reconceptualized," in Donald F. Klein and Judith G. Rabkin, eds., *Anxiety: New Research and Changing Concepts* (New York: Raven Press, 1981), pp. 235–61; quotation on p. 235. This essay, one of the most important in modern biological psychiatry, appears also in Donald F. Klein, ed., *Anxiety* (Basel: Karger, 1987).

43   The landmark "U.S.-U.K. study": J. E. Cooper, R. E. Kendell, et al., *Psychiatric Diagnosis in New York and London: A Comparative Study of Mental Hospital Admissions* (London: Oxford University Press, 1972), p. 103.

44   "an unknown psychiatrist . . .": Quotation and accompanying history are from Cade's wonderful brief memoir, "The Story of Lithium," in Frank J. Ayd and Barry Blackwell, eds., *Discoveries in Biological Psychiatry* (Philadelphia:

J. B. Lippincott, 1970). The serendipity is discussed in Barry Blackwell's essay "The Process of Discovery," in ibid., pp. 11–29.

44 "pharmacological dissection": The phrase is in Klein, "Anxiety Reconceptualized," p. 235.

45 attempts to elucidate links between them: See the discussion of the functional theory of psychopathology, p. 182. One example of the backlash against splitting is a recent article by Michael Alan Taylor, "Are Schizophrenia and Affective Disorder Related? A Selective Literature Review," *American Journal of Psychiatry*, vol. 149 (1992), pp. 22–32. Its abstract begins: "Although most modern investigators accept the Kraepelinian view that schizophrenia and affective disorder are biologically distinct, others have suggested the psychoses are on a continuum of liability. This article is a selective review of evidence for the continuum model." (p. 22.) Affective disorder, of course, includes manic depression, so the monograph is a reconsideration of Kraepelin's seminal diagnostic distinction. A second, quite different example is an important study demonstrating common genetic factors in depression and an anxiety disorder in women: Kenneth S. Kendler, Michael C. Neale, et al., "Major Depression and Generalized Anxiety Disorder: Same Genes, (Partly) Different Environments?," *Archives of General Psychiatry*, vol. 49 (1992), pp. 716–22.

CHAPTER 3: ANTIDEPRESSANTS

47 Associated Press photograph of 1953: Mark Caldwell, *The Last Crusade: The War on Consumption, 1862–1954* (New York: Atheneum, 1988), opposite p. 245.

47 "psychic energizer": Nathan S. Kline, "Monoamine Oxidase Inhibitors: An Unfinished Picaresque Tale," in Frank J. Ayd and Barry Blackwell, eds., *Discoveries in Biological Psychiatry* (Philadelphia: J. B. Lippincott, 1970), pp. 194–204.

48 "The plethora of id energy . . .": Ibid., p. 197.

48 "Probably no drug in history . . .": Ibid., p. 202.

48 a more potent antidepressant coming to market: The newer antidepressant, isocarboxazid, carries a "less-than-effective" indication from the Food and Drug Administration.

49 the most effective drug treatment . . . opium: Ronald Kuhn, "The Imipramine Story," in Ayd and Blackwell, eds., *Discoveries*, pp. 205–17. It turns

out that medications that treat almost any mental condition can have a positive effect in depressed people. Today we criticize general practitioners for using anxiolytic (antianxiety) agents, like Valium, or neuroleptic (antipsychotic) agents, like Thorazine, or simple stimulants, like amphetamine, for depressed patients. There are good reasons to avoid these medications: the anxiolytics and stimulants can be habituating, and the neuroleptics can cause late-appearing and irreversible neurological damage. But studies show that all these classes of medication make depressed people feel better. One reason depressed patients improve on the "wrong" drugs is that depression results in, or comprises, a variety of symptoms—sadness, sleeplessness, feelings of guilt, loss of appetite, diminished concentration, listlessness—each of which can be terrible in itself. A medicine that, for example, allows a depressed patient to sleep better will be welcome, even if the underlying condition remains unaltered. But the individual brain is unique and complex; many brain pathways can become deranged in depression, and it seems now that some of these "wrong" drugs alleviate depression directly, through their effects on neurotransmitters other than norepinephrine and serotonin, in selected patients.

49 "to find a drug . . .": Ibid., p. 207.

50 "We have achieved a specific treatment . . .": Kuhn, "Imipramine Story," pp. 216–17.

50 "We knew that amphetamine . . .": Donald F. Klein, "Anxiety Reconceptualized," in Donald F. Klein and Judith G. Rabkin, eds., *Anxiety: New Research and Changing Concepts* (New York: Raven Press, 1981), pp. 235–61; quotation on p. 235.

52 the biogenic-amine theory of depression: A helpful review of both the strengths and flaws of this theory appears in Solomon H. Snyder, *The New Biology of Mood* (New York: Pfizer, 1988).

52 inactivated by "janitorial" enzymes: This metaphor was coined by Ross Baldessarini, a psychopharmacologist at Harvard Medical School and McLean Hospital.

A fuller account of iproniazid's effect is: Neurotransmitter cells release biogenic amines into the synapse in discrete packets. When the janitorial enzyme (monoamine oxidase; see p. 55) fails to digest excess biogenic amine, two consequences result. First, the transmitting cell stuffs more neurotransmitter into each packet; and, second, in subsequent firings, not only does the transmitting cell release the packaged amine, it also allows the undisposed-of loose amine to pass into the synapse. The cell whose enzyme has been inhibited thus provides more of the body's own excitatory neurotransmitters to the synapse and, therefore, to the receiving nerve cell.

52   This finding was taken as strong support: Of course, there was much other evidence for the biogenic-amine hypothesis, such as the fact that assays of the chemical content of the spinal fluid, blood, and urine of depressed people sometimes showed deficiencies in the breakdown products of biogenic amines. But some of these studies were contradictory, and all of them were equivocal. For instance, the biogenic amines are used *outside* the brain, and in much greater absolute amount than they are used within the brain; perhaps the low levels of breakdown products of biogenic amines in the urine of depressed patients is due to their lethargy and general lack of activity, not to a deficit of amines in the central nervous system. The strongest, most consistent evidence for the amine hypothesis remained the efficacy in treating depression of chemicals that increased the presence or effectiveness of biogenic amines.

53   a deficiency, depression: More precisely, depression relates to a deficiency in aminergic *transmission*. Scientists talk loosely about the "level" of biogenic amine as being high or low, or about a drug "acting on" or "raising" or "lowering" a given amine. It is hard to avoid falling into these locutions (and I will do so occasionally), but the issue is less the absolute amount of amine than the level of activity in the neural pathways in which amines are used as transmitters.

53   But it takes about four weeks: It generally takes two weeks to achieve an adequate blood (and brain) level of the antidepressant. Regarding the second two weeks, theories are now emerging, involving cellular regulation of amine production, that attempt to explain this time lag. One of the challenges in psychopharmacology remains the development of an antidepressant that does not take weeks to work.

53   only in about 20 percent: See Frederick K. Goodwin and William E. Bunney, Jr., "Depressions Following Reserpine: A Reevaluation," *Seminars in Psychiatry*, vol. 3 (1971), pp. 435–48.

54   drug development takes place by homology . . . analogy: I take these concepts from Ross Baldessarini, "Psychopharmacology for Psychosis and Affective Disorders: Receptors and Ligands," lecture, U.S. Psychiatric Congress, New York, November 1991.

54   70 percent . . . will improve on imipramine: However, they may not be free of depression. Many people classified in traditional studies as responders to drugs like imipramine are "better but not well." See Jerrold F. Rosenbaum,

"Depression and Polypharmacy," *Massachusetts General Hospital Clinical Psycho-pharmacology Unit Progress Notes*, vol. 3, no. 1 (1992).

56   MAOIs make blood pressure skyrocket: See Barry Blackwell, "The Process of Discovery," in Ayd and Blackwell, eds., *Discoveries*, pp. 11–29. Blackwell's reports appeared in 1964. The substance found in cheese is the amino acid tyramine. Other chemicals can also cause patients on MAOIs to develop hypertension. (In retrospect, perhaps physicians should have paid more heed to early reports of treated tubercular patients who suffered throbbing headaches and high blood pressure.)

56   American doctors remained wary of them: American psychiatrists, whose primary identity was often linked to psychotherapy, were traditionally highly concerned about physical side effects, relative to colleagues in countries where the identity of psychiatrists was clearly as physicians first and psychotherapists only secondarily. Even imipramine was very conservatively prescribed in the U.S. I do not want to leave the impression that MAOIs are impossibly dangerous drugs. They have a place today in the treatment of a variety of conditions and can be used safely by those who monitor their diet and avoid interacting medications. More selective MAOIs, including ones that do not cause the "cheese reaction," will likely be available here shortly.

57   *serotonin:* In the 1940s, a substance was identified in the blood serum that increased the constriction (tone) of blood vessels—hence, "serotonin." Serotonin was then found to be identical to an earlier-discovered substance known to be active in the gastrointestinal tract. Recognition of serotonin's role in the brain came only later.

57   came to be called "tricyclics": Some of the later-developed drugs had four carbon rings, so the class of drugs is more properly, but less commonly, called "heterocyclics."

60   the development of Prozac required serendipity: As Barry Blackwell pointed out when assessing Cade's work with lithium, "serendipity" originally referred not to blind luck but to deductions made by prepared minds. The fairy tale of the three princes of Serendip (an older name than Ceylon for Sri Lanka) told, for instance how one of them deduced "that a mule, blind in the right eye, had traveled the same road frequently because the grass was eaten only on the left side of the path." The word was apparently coined by Horace Walpole in 1754. (T. G. Remer, *Serendipity and the Three Princes* [Norman, Okla.: University of Oklahoma Press, 1965], cited in Blackwell, "Process of Discovery," pp. 14–15.)

60   The story begins in the 1960s: This history is based on a conversation with Ray W. Fuller, Brian B. Molloy, and David T. Wong at Eli Lilly's international headquarters in Indianapolis on December 9, 1991, and on a narrative provided me by Wong: David T. Wong, "History of Fluoxetine, a Selective Inhibitor of Serotonin Uptake and Antidepressant Drug (Prozac): My Recollection of the Formative Year," unpublished, 1991, 8 pp.

60   Fuller had worked with a method: Fuller's model was the chloroamphet-amine-treated rat. Ironically, the model bore little fruit; it led to the development of an irreversible nerve toxin, useful in some basic research, but not to pharmaceuticals.

60   minimize the acetylcholine-related side effects: No one knew whether such a substance would affect depression. All antidepressants discovered to that time were anticholinergic, and it was thought that this property might be essential to antidepressants.

61   A particular book had caught Wong's attention: H. Weil-Malherbe and S. I. Szara, *The Biochemistry of Functional and Experimental Psychosis* (Springfield, Ill.: Charles C. Thomas, 1971).

61   a role for serotonin: The evidence, developed in the 1960s, was equivocal, but it seemed to show that there were lower levels of serotonin and its breakdown products in the brains of suicides than in those of people dying from heart disease. There was also evidence of low serotonin turnover in depressed patients. Evidence was also emerging from Europe of brain tracts that used serotonin, as opposed to norepinephrine, as the primary neurotransmitter. And, of course, it was known that both imipramine and the MAO inhibitors, in addition to affecting norepinephrine, had various effects on the breakdown or efficient use of serotonin.

63   In June 1974: David T. Wong, Jong S. Horng, et al., "A Selective Inhibitor of Serotonin Uptake: Lilly 110140, 3-(p-Trifluoromethylphenoxy-)-N-Methyl-3-Phenylpropylamine," *Life Sciences,* vol. 15 (1974), pp. 471–79. In the understated way that is typical of scientific reporting, they wrote: "We believe the discovery of specific inhibitors of 5HT reuptake like 110140 will help in elucidating the function of 5HT in brain and the importance of reuptake as an inactivating mechanism in 5HT neurotransmission. In addition, such an agent may find clinical use as a therapeutic agent." ("5HT" is the usual abbreviation for serotonin, whose chemical name is "5-hydroxytryptamine.") LY 110140 (fluoxetine hydrochloride, or Prozac) was probably the first selective serotonin-reuptake inhibitor, although others were soon developed, using independent lines of research, in Sweden, Holland, and elsewhere.

64   Prozac is a designed drug: That is, it was selected on the basis of a sought neurochemical effect. Today, drugs are "designed" structurally—molecules are selected based on their three-dimensional geometry, to fit particular chemical receptors.

66   reduced likelihood of effects on the heart: At about the time Prozac was released here, I had occasion to talk with the chairman of the psychiatry department of the University of Amsterdam. He told me that as a group psychiatrists in the Netherlands had decided to make a selective serotonin-reuptake inhibitor (like Prozac—perhaps not coincidentally, the one chosen in Holland is made by a Dutch manufacturer) the drug of first use in depression; their decision was based almost solely on the drug's lack of cardiac effects, and he said that, after the policy was instituted, they had in fact observed a decrease in successful suicides with antidepressants.

The case of a woman who took approximately one hundred Prozac capsules (two thousand milligrams) without adverse effects beyond nausea and drowsiness is reported in Jeffrey L. Moore and Robert Rodriguez, "Toxicity of Fluoxetine in Overdose," *American Journal of Psychiatry*, vol. 147 (1990), p. 1089 (letter).

66   patients . . . for whom Prozac is most helpful: For suggestive evidence that Prozac is especially effective in treating those with atypical and minor depression, see pp. 86–89 and 125–27.

CHAPTER 4: SENSITIVITY

72   To Klein, a number of hospitalized patients: See Donald F. Klein, "Psychiatric Diagnosis and a Typology of Clinical Drug Effects," *Psychopharmacologia* (Berlin), vol. 13 (1968), pp. 359–86; and Donald F. Klein, "Who Should Not Be Treated with Neuroleptics, but Often Are," in Frank Ayd, ed., *Rational Psychopharmacotherapy and the Right to Treatment* (Baltimore, Md.: Ayd Medical Communications, 1974). The monographs by Klein referred to in the notes on page 330 are also relevant.

73   the renowned analyst Elizabeth Zetzel: "On the So-Called Good Hysteric," in Elizabeth R. Zetzel, *The Capacity for Emotional Growth* (New York: International Universities Press, 1970), pp. 229–45. Zetzel ended her essay with this cautionary ditty:

There are many little girls
Whose complaints are little pearls

Of the classical hysterical neurotic.
And when this is true
Analysis can and should ensue,
But when this is false
'Twill be chaotic.

74 "These patients are usually females . . .": Donald F. Klein, "Approaches to Measuring the Efficacy of Drug Treatment of Personality Disorders: An Analysis and Program," in *Principles and Problems in Establishing the Efficacy of Psychotropic Agents* (Washington, D.C.: U.S. Department of HEW, Public Health Service No. 2138, 1971), pp. 187–204; quotation on pp. 194–95. For a similar description, see also Donald F. Klein, "Psychopharmacological Treatment and Delineation of Borderline Disorders," in Peter Hartocollis, ed., *Borderline Personality Disorders: The Concept, the Syndrome, the Patient* (New York: International Universities Press, 1977), pp. 365–83, especially pp. 372–73; Donald F. Klein, Rachel Gittelman, et al., *Diagnosis and Drug Treatment of Psychiatric Disorders: Adults and Children,* 2nd ed. (Baltimore, Md.: Williams & Wilkins, 1980), pp. 243–45. See also Michael R. Liebowitz and Donald F. Klein, "Hysteroid Dysphoria," *Psychiatric Clinics of North America,* vol. 2 (1979), pp. 555–75; Michael R. Liebowitz and Donald F. Klein, "Interrelationship of Hysteroid Dysphoria and Borderline Personality Disorder," *Psychiatric Clinics of North America,* vol. 4 (1981), pp. 67–87.

75 "a cause engenders an adaptive response . . .": Donald F. Klein, "Cybernetics, Activation, and Drug Effects," in R. H. Van den Hoofdakker, ed., "Biological Measures: Their Theoretical and Diagnostic Value in Psychiatry," *Acta Psychiatrica Scandinavica,* vol. 77, suppl. 341 (1988), pp. 126–37.

76 ". . . no need for these hypotheses": Klein made this assertion in the context of a discussion of panic anxiety, but he seems to hold the same position regarding rejection-sensitivity (Donald F. Klein, "Anxiety Reconceptualized," in Donald F. Klein and Judith G. Rabkin, eds., *Anxiety: New Research and Changing Concepts* [New York: Raven Press, 1981], pp. 235–61; quotation on p. 260).

77 "A crucial consequence . . .": Donald F. Klein, "Psychopharmacological Treatment and Delineation of Borderline Disorders," in Hartocollis, ed., *Borderline Personality Disorders,* p. 375. See also Klein, Gittelman, et al., *Diagnosis and Drug Treatment,* p. 440.

78 In 1895: "On the Grounds for Detaching a Particular Syndrome from Neurasthenia Under the Description 'Anxiety Neurosis,' " in James Strachey, ed., *The Standard Edition of the Complete Psychological Works of Sigmund Freud,*

vol. III (London: Hogarth Press, 1962), pp. 85–115. See also Sigmund Freud, "A Reply to Criticisms of My Paper on Anxiety Neurosis," in ibid., pp. 119–39.

78 "does not originate . . .": Ibid., p. 97.

79 One of my favorite footnotes: Sigmund Freud, "Miss Lucy R., Age 30," in Josef Breuer and Sigmund Freud, *Studies on Hysteria,* in Strachey, ed., *Standard Edition of Freud,* vol II (1955), pp. 106–24; footnote on 112–14. The footnote is a wonderful example of the early Freud—condensed, compelling, and amusing.

79 "neurosis" even encompassed conditions: According to the manual that defined official American psychiatric diagnoses from the late sixties until 1980, "neurosis" included conditions in which anxiety was "controlled unconsciously and automatically by conversion, displacement, and various other psychological mechanisms"—that is, in which it was out of the sufferer's awareness (American Psychiatric Association, *Diagnostic and Statistical Manual of Mental Disorders,* 2nd ed. [Washington, D.C.: American Psychiatric Association, 1968], p. 39). The definition of anxiety neurosis does use the word "panic," but in practice the diagnosis was applied promiscuously.

80 his followers, came to see meaningful anxiety: I am here simplifying what is in fact a diverse literature. As early as 1941, the respected psychoanalyst Phyllis Greenacre argued for a return to acknowledgment of a substantial biological and genetic component to anxiety. She distinguished unanalyzable (basic, blind, or amorphous) anxiety (also called the "essential" neurosis) from experiential and secondary anxieties; she advocated a modified psychoanalysis for severely anxious patients, one that would take into account the irreducible nature of aspects of their ailment. In these regards, she anticipated contemporary models of etiology and treatment. (See "The Predisposition to Anxiety," in Phyllis Greenacre, *Trauma, Growth, and Personality* [New York: W. W. Norton, 1952], pp. 27–82.) I want to thank Donald Klein for pointing me in the direction of Greenacre's work.

80 "The predominant American psychiatric theory . . .": Klein, "Anxiety Reconceptualized," p. 235.

81 "By the third week . . .": Klein, "Anxiety Reconceptualized," p. 238.

82 Klein did hypothesize about the origin: Donald F. Klein and Hilary M. Klein, "The Definition and Psychopharmacology of Spontaneous Panic and Phobia," in P. J. Tyrer, ed., *Psychopharmacology of Anxiety* (London: Oxford University Press, 1989), pp. 135–62; Donald F. Klein and Hilary M. Klein,

"The Nosology, Genetics, and Theory of Spontaneous Panic and Phobia," in ibid., pp. 163–95; Rachel Gittelman and Donald F. Klein, "Relationship Between Separation Anxiety and Panic and Agoraphobic Disorder," *Psychopathology*, vol. 17, suppl. 1 (1984), pp. 56–65; Donald F. Klein and Michael R. Liebowitz, "Psychotherapeutic Attitudes in the Drug Treatment of Anxiety and Phobic Reactions," in Maurice H. Greenhill and Alexander Gralnick, eds., *Psychopharmacology and Psychotherapy* (New York: Free Press, 1982), pp. 145–63; Donald F. Klein, "False Suffocation Alarms and Spontaneous Panics: Subsuming the CO_2 Hypersensitivity Theory," unpublished, draft of August 7, 1991, 85 pp.

84 lecture by an eminent psychoanalyst: John Nemiah, "The Psychoanalytic View of Anxiety," in Klein and Rabkin, *Anxiety*, pp. 291–330. The Nemiah talk was gracious but unyielding and could have been written at any time in the prior fifty years. His core statement is: "Anxiety is the reaction of the individual's ego . . . to the threatened emergence into conscious awareness of unpleasant, forbidden, unwanted, frightening impulses, feelings, and thoughts" (p. 294).

86 Donald Klein's model of panic anxiety now prevails: A curious side effect of the carving out of panic anxiety from generalized anxiety was the reopening of a lacuna on the diagnostic map; now that the anxiety disorders had specific meanings and "anxiety neurosis" had disappeared, there was no category to deal with "nervous exhaustion." Into this gap stepped . . . neurasthenia, which is now making a comeback! An entire issue of *Psychiatric Annals* (vol. 22, no. 4 [April 1992]), guest-edited by Joe Yamamoto, is dedicated to "Neurasthenia Revisited."

87 converging evidence of diverse sorts: Here I am relying heavily on research reported at the Neurobiology of Affective Disorders conference at Yale University School of Medicine, New Haven, Conn., October 25–26, 1991. The dietary L-tryptophan deprivation studies are the work of a team headed by Pedro Delgado and Dennis Charney at Yale (see Pedro L. Delgado, Dennis S. Charney, et al., "Serotonin Function and the Mechanism of Antidepressant Action: Reversal of Antidepressant-Induced Remission by Rapid Depletion of Plasma Tryptophan," *Archives of General Psychiatry*, vol. 47 [1990], pp. 411–18). The cellular-level research results are from Claude de Montigny of McGill University; the anatomical research is by Alan Frazer of the University of Pennsylvania.

The preliminary report on Prozac's effectiveness in atypical depression was given by Atul C. Pande, of the University of Michigan, at the Annual Meeting of the American Psychiatric Association, May 2–7, 1992, in Washington, D.C.

The issues are, of course, more complex than I have so far indicated. Considering only the question of where in the brain these medications act, even within a drug class there is variability. That is, different MAOIs are most active in different parts of the brain. This result should not surprise us, since sometimes a patient will respond to one MAOI but not another.

Researchers have identified subtypes of the monoamine-oxidase enzyme, just as they have identified numerous distinct subtypes of the serotonin receptor. There are already experimental medications that are selective for one or another subtype of MAO, as well as medications that selectively affect uptake at cells with specific serotonin-receptor subtypes. These laboratory findings are rapidly being translated into marketed drugs, so the story I am presenting here will soon have complex subplots.

91   "the interpersonal tactics . . .": Klein, Gittelman, et al., *Diagnosis and Drug Treatment*, p. 245.

91   Klein did twice rename: See Donald F. Klein, "Endogenomorphic Depression: A Conceptual and Terminological Revision," *Archives of General Psychiatry,* vol. 31 (1974), pp. 447–54; Klein, "Psychopharmacological Treatment," pp. 372–75. Klein's descriptions of hysteroid dysphoria, chronic overreactive dysphoria, and rejection-sensitive dysphoria are for all purposes identical. I have corresponded with Klein on the question whether people who are not histrionic can, in his diagnostic system, be rejection-sensitive. They can, but Klein limits rejection-sensitivity to a fairly small group—those diagnosed with hysteroid dysphoria and those in its immediate penumbra. Rejection-sensitivity, for Klein, always entails both vulnerability to loss and a strong drive for positive attention; even nonhysteroid rejection-sensitivity is characterized by touchiness rather than clinging in relationships. My definition is broader: I have come to see rejection-sensitivity as applying to people who respond to loss with symptoms of atypical depression, whether or not applause hunger is a prominent feature. Klein would characterize some of these people as having separation anxiety, even though their symptoms entail depression rather than panic. I reserve separation anxiety for the infantile behavior that serves as a possible model for panic in adults.

96   "aloneness affect": Ronald M. Winchel, "Self-Mutilation and Aloneness," *Academy Forum* (of the American Academy of Psychoanalysis), vol. 35 (1991), pp. 10–12.

97   a particular element of personality: That element of personality, under differing names, has long been a focus of psychotherapy. Psychoanalysis pays great attention to the patient's reaction to brief interruptions in the relationship,

not least the analyst's famous August vacation. Brief separations test the patient's ability to tolerate loss. And the end of therapy—the termination phase—is the subject of an extensive literature. Some brief therapies, especially ones used for healthy college students, rely heavily on the stress of termination. Patient and therapist agree to meet for twelve sessions, and half of the therapy concerns the patient's inability to tolerate that agreement—that is, to experience the end of a relationship without the usual distortions that result from his or her customary style of avoiding the pain of separation. See James Mann, *Time-Limited Psychotherapy* (Cambridge, Mass.: Harvard University Press, 1973).

CHAPTER 5: STRESS

108 "rapid cycling": Much of this material is from Robert M. Post and James C. Ballenger, eds., *Neurobiology of Mood Disorders* (Baltimore, Md.: Williams & Wilkins, 1984), especially Post's own contributions to that book. I have also relied on a lecture, Robert M. Post, "Episode and Stress Sensitization in the Longitudinal Course of Affective Disorders: Role of Proto-Oncogenes and Other Transcription Factors," Neurobiology of Affective Disorders conference, Yale University School of Medicine, New Haven, Conn., October 25–26, 1991.

See also Robert M. Post, Keith G. Kramlinger, et al., "Treatment of Rapid Cycling Bipolar Illness," *Psychopharmacology Bulletin,* vol. 26 (1990), pp. 37–47; R. M. Post, "Sensitization and Kindling Perspectives for the Course of Affective Illness: Toward a New Treatment with the Anticonvulsant Carbamazepine," *Pharmacopsychiatry,* vol. 23 (1990), pp. 3–17; Robert M. Post, David R. Rubinow, and James C. Ballenger, "Conditioning and Sensitization in the Longitudinal Course of Affective Illness," *British Journal of Psychiatry,* vol. 149 (1986), pp. 191–201; Robert M. Post, "Transduction of Psychosocial Stress into the Neurobiology of Recurrent Affective Disorder," *American Journal of Psychiatry,* in press; Robert M. Post, "Prophylaxis of Bipolar Affective Disorders," *International Review of Psychiatry,* vol. 2 (1990), pp. 277–320; Robert M. Post, Gabriele S. Leverich, et al., "Carbamazepine Prophylaxis in Refractory Affective Disorders: A Focus on Long-Term Follow-Up," *Journal of Clinical Psychopharmacology,* vol. 10 (1990), pp. 318–27.

The trend toward increasing frequency and severity of episodes with recurrence is almost certainly not limited to manic-depressive illness but occurs in "unipolar" (i.e., without mania) depression as well. See, for example, Mario Maj, Franco Veltro, et al., "Pattern of Recurrence of Illness After Recovery from an Episode of Major Depression: A Prospective Study," *American Journal of Psychiatry,* vol. 149 (1992), pp. 795–800.

110 "negative feedback loop": More precisely, a negative feedback system is one in which output of a product inhibits further production of that product—for example, a rising level of thyroid hormone inhibits the production and release of thyroid hormone. This is the most common homeostatic mechanism in biology. See, for example, Peter C. Whybrow, Hagop S. Akiskal, and William T. McKinney, Jr., *Mood Disorder: Toward a New Psychobiology* (New York: Plenum Publishing, 1984), pp. 98–101.

110 Seizures are "kindled" in an experimental animal: The reader may be made uncomfortable or even outraged by some of the animal experiments I describe. My own less judgmental attitude arises from having spent many hours with seriously depressed patients in the search for whose cure I would willingly sacrifice any number of rats and mice, or separate monkey infants from their mothers. Though crucial to our understanding of human mental disorder, animal research can be cruel.

One of the oddities of research is that, though antidepressants are used mostly in depressed human females, they are tested mostly in healthy male rats: the estrus cycle in rats is four to five days, creating constant hormonal variability in females, which makes data analysis difficult and adds greatly to the complexity of experimental design and the number of animals needed. However, testing of female rats would be of interest, because they appear to differ from male rats in terms of stress responses and brain anatomy. (I thank Dr. Huda Akil of the University of Michigan for answering my inquiry on these points.) In earlier decades, "reserpinized" rats—ones whose biogenic amines had been depleted to produce "depression"—were widely used for drug testing; in recent years, this model has been dropped as unwieldy.

112 Some cells . . . change shape: Other animal models, using various sorts of stress to change brain-hormone levels, also show anatomical changes, including cell atrophy and death. There are, in fact, numerous models of stress that cause changes in cell shape, synapse numbers, and local synapse density. See in particular the work of Bruce S. McEwen, of Rockefeller University.

114 Thereafter, antiepileptic drugs, such as Tegretol: Depakote is another anticonvulsant, more recently studied, that may be especially effective in refractory, late-stage manic-depressive illness. It is interesting that antidepressants and anticonvulsants act in a stabilizing way at two levels: at the organismic level, they affect mood balance in response to stress; at the cellular level, they affect the cell's protein production in response to stress. It is not known whether this second effect is a result of the first.

116   Cortisol levels . . . high in many acutely depressed adults: But not in acutely depressed adolescents, a finding that reverberates with our theme of kindling: the human organism becomes less flexible—less able to recuperate— with aging and repeated injury.

116   according to imaging studies: See, for example, Charles B. Nemeroff, K. Ranga, R. Krishnan, et al., "Adrenal Gland Enlargement in Major Depression: A Computed Tomographic Study," *Archives of General Psychiatry*, vol. 49 (1992), pp. 384–87.

116   Rats can be stressed: I have taken much of this material from a lecture by Bruce S. McEwen, "Glucocorticoid Actions in the Hippocampus: Implications for Affective Disorders," Neurobiology of Affective Disorders conference, Yale University School of Medicine, New Haven, Conn., October 25– 26, 1991. See also Whybrow, Akiskal, and McKinney, *Mood Disorder*.

118   160 girls: This study, headed by Frank Putnam, was reported on in *Clinical Psychiatry News*, vol. 19, no. 12 (December 1991), p. 3ff.

118   research on mood in rhesus monkeys: I am here largely reviewing the work of Stephen J. Suomi. See especially Stephen J. Suomi, "Primate Separation Models of Affective Disorder," in John Madden IV, ed., *Neurobiology of Learning, Emotion, and Affect* (New York: Raven Press, 1991), pp. 195–214; Stephen J. Suomi, "Early Stress and Adult Emotional Reactivity in Rhesus Monkeys," in *The Childhood Environment and Adult Disease*, Ciba Foundation Symposium 156 (Chichester: Wiley, 1991), pp. 171–88. See also Stephen J. Suomi, "Uptight and Laid-Back Monkeys: Individual Differences in the Response to Social Challenges," in S. Branch, W. Hall, and E. Dooling, eds., *Plasticity of Development* (Cambridge, Mass.: M.I.T. Press, 1991), pp. 27–55; J. Dee Higley, Stephen J. Suomi, and Markuu Linnoila, "Developmental Influences on the Serotonergic System and Timidity in the Nonhuman Primate," in Emil F. Coccaro and Dennis L. Murphy, eds., *Serotonin in Major Psychiatric Disorders* (Washington, D.C.: American Psychiatric Press, 1990), pp. 29–46; Stephen J. Suomi, Harry F. Harlow, and Carol J. Domek, "Effect of Repetitive Infant-Infant Separation of Young Monkeys," *Journal of Abnormal Psychology*, vol. 76 (1970), pp. 161– 72; Stephen J. Suomi, Stephen F. Seaman, et al., "Effects of Imipramine Treatment of Separation-Induced Social Disorders in Rhesus Monkeys," *Archives of General Psychiatry*, vol. 35 (1978), pp. 321–25; J. D. Higley, S. J. Suomi, and M. Linnoila, "CSF Monoamine Metabolite Concentrations Vary According to Age, Rearing, and Sex, and Are Influenced by the Stressor of Social Separation in Rhesus Monkeys," *Psychopharmacology*, vol. 103 (1991), pp. 551–56.

119   rapidly become attached to their peers: At eleven weeks, a monkey infant will interact as often with other monkey infants as with his or her mother, and by the age of six months, young monkeys have four or five times as many contacts with age-mates as with their mothers. Except in unusual circumstances, fathering is much less important to young rhesus monkeys than are ties to mother and peers.

119   best-known study: Harry F. Harlow and Robert R. Zimmerman, "Affectional Responses in the Infant Monkey," *Science,* vol. 130 (1959), pp. 421–32.

121   "Moreover, the same basic pattern . . .": Suomi, "Early Stress and Adult Emotional Reactivity," p. 177. See also Higley, Suomi, and Linnoila, "Developmental Influences."

124   "the memory of the body": I think here of a passage from the Jane Smiley novella "Ordinary Love." To a brother who has witnessed suffering, a young man asks: "Would you prefer not to have seen it?" The affected brother replies: "I would prefer not to be shaped by experiences. I would like just to have them, not to incorporate them." (*Ordinary Love and Good Will* [New York: Ballantine, 1989], p. 80.) Our troubling experiences are not just known to us; they become us.

I think also of dialogue in Smiley's short story "Long Distance" (*The Age of Grief* [New York: Ballantine, 1987], pp. 61–79), in which a man who is hurting over a love affair says, "It seems so dramatic to say that I will never get over this." His sister-in-law replies, "Does it? To me it seems like saying that what people do is important." To say that loss is biologically encoded, perhaps irreversibly, is to say that what people do and experience is important.

125   This new method: The role of antidepressants in prevention of recurrence, while now widely accepted, remains controversial. Important contrary research, pioneered by Frederick K. Goodwin at the National Institute of Mental Health, shows that, in patients prone to recurrent depression, tricyclics—and perhaps all antidepressants—can *hasten* the onset of subsequent episodes and increase cyclicity. The field has not reconciled the two contradictory bodies of evidence.

126   universities in Denmark: Danish University Antidepressant Group, "Citralopram: Clinical Effect Profile in Comparison with Clomipramine: A Controlled Multicenter Study," *Psychopharmacology,* vol. 90 (1986), pp. 131–38; Danish University Antidepressant Group, "Paroxetine: A Selective Serotonin Reuptake Inhibitor Showing Better Tolerance, but Weaker Antidepressant Effect than Clomipramine in a Controlled Multicenter Study," *Journal of Affective Disorders,* vol. 18 (1990), pp. 289–99.

126 A group at Indiana University: Stephen R. Dunlop, Bruce E. Dornseif, et al., "Pattern Analysis Shows Beneficial Effect of Fluoxetine Treatment in Mild Depression," *Psychopharmacology Bulletin*, vol. 26 (1990), pp. 173–80.

126 Psychiátrists at the University of Utah: Fred W. Reimherr, David R. Wood, et al., "Characteristics of Responders to Fluoxetine," *Psychopharmacology Bulletin*, vol. 20 (1984), pp. 70–72. The Prozac responders also tended to meet Donald Klein's criteria for atypical depression.

126 Taken together, these studies: J. Craig Nelson, of Yale University, juxtaposed these four articles and brought them to my attention.

127 psychotherapy will affect neural structure: Biological technologies are only just beginning to be applied to the study of psychotherapy. An intriguing preliminary report, albeit still far from the level of cellular repair, is Lewis R. Baxter, Jr., Jeffrey M. Schwartz, et al., "Caudate Glucose Metabolic Rate Changes with Both Drug and Behavior Therapy for Obsessive-Compulsive Disorder," *Archives of General Psychiatry*, vol. 49 (1992), pp. 681–89. In this experiment, ten weeks of behavioral instruction, supplemented by cognitive therapy, was shown to resemble Prozac in its ability to change metabolism in a part of the brain thought to be affected by OCD.

127 exposed to "therapists": Suomi, "Early Stress and Adult Emotional Reactivity."

128 the great hypnotist Milton Erickson: See Jay Haley, *Uncommon Therapy: The Psychiatric Techniques of Milton Erickson* (New York: W. W. Norton, 1973).

128 those that emphasize empathy: I have in mind self psychology. The central image of healing in self psychology is "transmuting internalization": the patient takes in a function previously provided by the therapist, and this taking in, rather than insight, results in a changed structure of mind. A typical jibe at self psychology goes, "The couch is not a bassinet" (George Vaillant, "Managing Defense Mechanisms in Personality Disorders," lecture, U.S. Psychiatric Congress, New York, November 1991). That is, although self psychology does rely on interpretations and insight as techniques, its critics see it as fundamentally an attempt at reparenting and nothing more.

130 prone to repeated alcohol consumption: J. D. Higley, M. F. Hasert, et al., "Nonhuman Primate Model of Alcohol Abuse: Effects of Early Experience, Personality, and Stress on Alcohol Consumption," *Proceedings of the National Academy of Sciences, U.S.A.* (Psychology), vol. 88 (1991), pp. 7261–65. The "not specialized" quip is from Vaillant, "Managing Defense Mechanisms."

131   In the mid-1960s: See William E. Bunney and John M. Davis, "Nor-epinephrine in Depressive Reactions: A Review," *Archives of General Psychiatry*, vol. 13 (1965), pp. 483–94; Joseph J. Schildkraut, "The Catecholamine Hypothesis of Affective Disorders: A Review of Supporting Evidence," *American Journal of Psychiatry*, vol. 122 (1965), pp. 509–22. These were enormously influential publications.

131   By the mid-1970s: James W. Maas, "Biogenic Amines and Depression: Biochemical and Pharmacological Separation of Two Types of Depression," *Archives of General Psychiatry*, vol. 32 (1975), pp. 1357–61.

131   in the 1980s: Dennis S. Charney, David B. Menkes, and George R. Heninger, "Receptor Sensitivity and the Mechanisms of Action of Antidepressant Treatment: Implications for the Etiology and Therapy of Depression," *Archives of General Psychiatry*, vol. 38 (1981), pp. 1160–80; Dennis S. Charney, Pedro L. Delgado, et al., "The Receptor Sensitivity Hypothesis of Antidepressant Action: A Review of Antidepressant Effects on Serotonin Function," in Serena Lynn Brown and Herman M. van Praag, eds., *The Role of Serotonin in Psychiatric Disorders* (New York: Brunner/Mazel, 1991), pp. 27–56.

132   meshes well with the animal studies: I have presented the postsynaptic-receptor-sensitivity model in highly simplified form. But see Robert M. Cohen and Iain C. Campbell, "Receptor Adaptation in Animal Models of Mood Disorders: A State Change Approach to Psychiatric Illness," in Post and Ballenger, eds., *Neurobiology of Mood Disorders*, pp. 572–86.

133   Prozac does not downregulate norepinephrine receptors: In almost all experimental models in which tricyclics downregulate norepinephrine receptors, Prozac fails to do so, although, as always, there is an exception, and in one line of research Prozac *has* been shown to downregulate a receptor in one part of the brain. It does seem that, when the drugs are given in combination, Prozac quickens desipramine's downregulation of norepinephrine receptors; this may be due to an interesting pharmacologic synergy at the cellular level, or it may be an artefact related to Prozac's interference with the metabolism of desipramine.

134   "Maybe serotonin is the police . . .": There is a serious scientific model that in some regards corresponds to serotonin-as-police: the "permissive biogenic amine hypothesis" proposed by A. J. Prange. According to this theory, serotonin deficiency permits depression but is an insufficient cause; the emergence of overt depression depends on changes in norepinephrine or other transmitters. (That is, low serotonin + normal norepinephrine = normal affective state; low serotonin + low norepinephrine = depression; and low serotonin + high

norepinephrine = mania. But, again, this model is too simple to explain a variety of phenomena.) See Arthur J. Prange, Jr., Ian C. Wilson, et al., "L-Tryptophan in Mania: Contribution to a Permissive Hypothesis of Affective Disorders," *Archives of General Psychiatry*, vol. 30 (1974), pp. 56–62. What I have in mind when I refer to serotonin-as-police goes beyond the permissive hypothesis and implies that serotonin has a role in the maintenance of confidence, assertiveness, and overall social and emotional resilience.

136 "late-onset depression": An excellent summary, albeit by authors who doubt the validity of the late-onset/early-onset distinction, is Henry Brodaty, Karin Peters, et al., "Age and Depression," *Journal of Affective Disorders*, vol. 23 (1991), pp. 137–49.

142 So unwilling was a distant friend of Levi's: Esther B. Fein, "Book Notes: A British Doctor Casts Doubt on Primo Levi's Suicide . . . ," *New York Times*, December 11, 1991, p. C26. The background material is from an essay in *The New York Times Book Review* by Alexander Stille. For a relevant perspective on judgmental views of suicide, see Alexander Gralnick, "Is Suicide a Cause of Death?," *American Journal of Social Psychiatry*, vol. 5 (1985), pp. 24–28.

CHAPTER 6: RISK

147 mania is an infrequent bad outcome: Although there are scant data on the subject, many psychiatrists believe Prozac causes this side effect more frequently than do tricyclic antidepressants.

147 half a capsule per day (ten milligrams): Regarding dosage, see the note to p. 28, on pp. 321–22.

148 the words used to describe: Here I am relying mostly on the usage of Hagop Akiskal. See his chapter, "Validating Affective Personality Types," in Lee N. Robins and James E. Barrett, *The Validity of Psychiatric Diagnosis* (New York: Raven Press, 1989), pp. 217–27. I have added in concepts from Alexander Thomas and Stella Chess, *Temperament and Development* (New York: Brunner/ Mazel, 1977), and others. This particular usage of "temperament" (nature), "character" (nurture), and "personality" (both) was employed by David Riesman in *The Lonely Crowd* (New Haven, Conn.: Yale University Press, 1950), and before that in psychiatry by Erich Fromm. See Daniel Burston, *The Legacy of Erich Fromm* (Cambridge, Mass.: Harvard University Press, 1991).

149 temperament . . . the tar pit of psychological research: A notable exception is the acceptance, especially in the field of child development, of the

work of Alexander Thomas and Stella Chess. In addition to *Temperament and Development*, cited above, see Stella Chess and Alexander Thomas, *Temperament in Clinical Practice* (New York: Guilford Press, 1986). The authors have summarized their research in a book for a general audience, Stella Chess and Alexander Thomas, *Know Your Child: An Authoritative Guide for Today's Parents* (New York: Basic Books, 1987). Their key concept is the importance of "goodness of fit" between the child and the family in which he or she is raised.

150 Kagan began with three hundred: Jerome Kagan, J. Steven Reznick, and Nancy Snidman, "Biological Basis of Childhood Shyness," *Science*, vol. 240 (1988), pp. 167–71; Cynthia Garcia Coll, Jerome Kagan, and J. Steven Reznick, "Behavioral Inhibition in Young Children," *Child Development*, vol. 55 (1984), pp. 1005–19; Jerome Kagan, J. Steven Reznick, et al., "Behavioral Inhibition to the Unfamiliar," *Child Development*, vol. 55 (1984), pp. 2212–25.

151 "A frequent scene . . .": Kagan, Reznick, and Snidman, "Biological Basis," p. 168.

151 *lack* of inhibition was not a special category: In some of the studies, extreme lack of inhibition did look like a discontinuous, distinct category.

151 15 percent of children are born inhibited: Ruth M. Galvin, "The Nature of Shyness," *Harvard Magazine*, vol. 94 (1992), pp. 40–45; see especially p. 41. Just what this statement means is not perfectly clear. Kagan has observed that 10 to 15 percent of two- and three-year-olds are inhibited. Whether these come from a larger pool with predispositions to be inhibited, or from a smaller pool which is then supplemented by children who are traumatized, is unclear; a much smaller percentage of adults is openly shy.

151 In his study: Garcia Coll, Kagan, and Reznick, "Behavioral Inhibition," and Kagan, Reznick, et al., "Behavioral Inhibition."

151 "for every ten children . . .": Galvin, "The Nature of Shyness," p. 45. (Here Galvin is paraphrasing Kagan.)

152 even when asleep: Jerome Kagan, Grand Rounds, Bradley Hospital, Providence, R.I., December 1987.

153 "most of the children . . ." and subsequent quotations: Kagan, Reznick, and Snidman, "Biological Basis," p. 171.

153 before having studied: Kagan had shown some behavioral continuity in relation to inhibited play in infants as young as fourteen months—he could pick out a group half of whom still looked inhibited on retesting at age four years. Kagan, Reznick, and Snidman, "Biological Bases," p. 169.

154 In the 1960s, Kagan was a leader: Kagan was a figure to whom television anchors and other media reporters turned for comments in the IQ controversy. That debate was sparked by an article by the psychologist Arthur Jensen in a 1969 issue of the *Harvard Educational Review*, vol. 39, pp. 1–123. In reply, Kagan contended that the concept of intelligence is culturally defined and that IQ tests are culturally biased. He emphasized mother-child interaction as a key environmental contributor to intelligence. Kagan concluded that, although genetic constitution might set "a range of mental ability," the genetic contribution to IQ was unknown, and that this uncertainty applied even more strongly to the vague concept "intelligence." See Jerome S. Kagan, "Inadequate Evidence and Illogical Conclusions," *Harvard Educational Review*, vol. 39 (1969), pp. 274–77, a reply to the Jensen essay; Jerome Kagan, "IQ: Fair Science for Dark Deeds," *Radcliffe Quarterly*, vol. 56 (1972), pp. 3–5. For an overview of popular coverage and impact of the debate, see Mark Snyderman and Stanley Rothman, *The IQ Controversy, the Media and Public Policy* (New Brunswick, N.J.: Transaction Books, 1988).

155 Among white children: See Jerome Kagan and Nancy Snidman, "Infant Predictors of Inhibited and Uninhibited Profiles," *Psychological Science*, vol. 2 (1991), pp. 40–44. Most of the subjects in the early studies were middle-to-upper-class white children.

155 an excess of allergies: Jerome Kagan, Nancy Snidman, et al., "Temperament and Allergic Symptoms," *Psychosomatic Medicine*, vol. 53 (1991), pp. 332–40. There is suggestive evidence that, especially in women, migraine headaches and gastrointestinal symptoms are additional features associated with inhibition.

155 A group at Brown: L. La Gasse, C. Gruber, and L. P. Lipsett, "The Infantile Expression of Avidity in Relation to Later Assessments," in J. Steven Reznick, ed., *Perspectives on Behavioral Inhibition* (Chicago: University of Chicago Press, 1989), pp. 159–76.

155 Kagan's group tested four-month-olds: Kagan and Snidman, "Infant Predictors."

156 among mildly depressed adults: This result was reported by Radwan F. Haykal at the May 1992 Annual Meeting of the American Psychiatric Association in Washington, D.C., in conjunction with his presentation, "Is Early Onset Dysthymia More Treatable Today?" Haykal is a student and co-worker of Hagop Akiskal, whose research we will discuss later in this chapter.

156   Suomi . . . 20 percent: This and much of what follows is from Stephen J. Suomi, "Uptight and Laid-Back Monkeys: Individual Differences in the Response to Social Challenges," in S. Branch, W. Hall, and E. Dooling, eds., *Plasticity of Development* (Cambridge, Mass.: M.I.T. Press, 1991), pp. 27–55.

156   "differences in response to novelty . . .": Ibid., p. 38.

157   differences . . . only in response to novelty: The important role of novelty as a stimulus is crucial in humans, too. Kagan keeps pinned above his desk a note from a mother of one of the inhibited children he observed: "If something is new and different, his inclination is to be quiet and watch. . . . It's unfamiliarity that's the cause of his behavior. Not just new people, but *newness.*" (Quoted in Galvin, "Nature of Shyness," p. 41.) "Inhibition" in Kagan's usage is less social inhibition than inhibition to the unfamiliar, although in practice the two forms of inhibition seem linked.

157   earlier monkey studies: Summarized in Suomi, "Uptight and Laid-Back Monkeys," pp. 40–41.

157   in anticipation of irritating noise: In this model, infants are conditioned by being exposed to a steady tone followed by irritating white noise; in time, they show a conditioned response, a decrease in heart rate in response to the steady tone. Ibid. However, among unconditioned young monkeys, as in humans, those "who show extreme stress reactions typically have very high and stable heartrates relative to their less reactive counterparts faced with identical stressors, and these heartrate patterns are predictive of later extreme behavioral reactions with different kinds of stressors." Currents Interview, "In Our Wild: Studies from a Rhesus Colony" (interview with Stephen J. Suomi), *Currents in Affective Illness,* vol. 11 (1992), pp. 5–14, quotation p. 6.

157   among *half*-siblings: These studies have stood up to more recent replication. In addition, observations have found the fathers of reactive half-siblings themselves to be reactive on a variety of measures. (Stephen J. Suomi, "Primate Separation Models of Affective Disorders," in John Madden, ed., *Neurobiology of Learning, Emotion and Affect* [New York: Raven Press, 1991], pp. 195–214.)

157   second offspring . . . given to adoptive mothers: Merely being adopted out does not appear to increase reactivity in rhesus monkeys.

158   "Clearly, for these infants . . .": Suomi, "Uptight and Laid-Back Monkeys," p. 49. The style of the adoptive mothers did affect other traits and behaviors (particularly closeness to the mother when she was present) but not reactivity; as they grew, uptight infants appeared normal when with their mothers but more disturbed when separated.

More recent observations by Suomi suggest that nervous, shy infants foster-reared by unusually nurturant mothers grow up precocious and socially adept. In particular, when subjected to social stress these monkeys tend to recruit others to help—and this trait enhances their social status in the troop. (Currents Interview, "In Our Wild," p. 8.) It is interesting to speculate that the "reactive" trait may confer evolutionary fitness because it sometimes leads not to inhibition but to a particular coping skill: social collaboration. Perhaps social facilitation is the healthy version of reactivity and "people pleasing" is not so much a weakness as the characteristic strength of otherwise inhibited individuals.

158 become withdrawn or depressed: Suomi, "Uptight and Laid-Back Monkeys," p. 42.

158 parallel abnormalities in neurotransmitters: The uptight monkeys have higher-than-normal levels and turnover of stress hormones in their bloodstreams. In their spinal fluid, after separation they have lower levels of norepinephrine and higher levels of norepinephrine-breakdown products—preseumably a sign that they are exhausting the system—than do normally reactive monkeys. These abnormalities can be prevented with antidepressants, and the attenuation is most pronounced in the most uptight monkeys.

158 prone to both: Currents Interview, "In Our Wild," p. 6. Suomi believes the same individuals are at risk for both anxiety and depression, and the behavioral pattern elicited depends on which stressors the monkey encounters in life. Interestingly, both "reactivity" and the accompanying anxious and depressive patterns of behavior occur equally between the genders before puberty. But reactivity in males becomes blunted during adolescence, when for females it becomes more extreme. Ibid., pp. 7–8.

158 drink more when under stress: Ibid., p. 13.

159 to show allergic reactions: Ibid., p. 7.

159 they can be born uptight: In lower animals, there have been attempts to breed for temperament. For example, in mice the amount of activity displayed in a brightly lit open field is thought to be a marker for emotional reactivity. Mice were selectively bred to be high or low on this test trait. After thirty generations, the mice displayed a thirtyfold difference in terms of activity in this environment, with no overlap between the scores of the high and low line. (J. C. De Fries, J. C. Gervais, and E. A. Thomas, in *Behavioral Genetics,* vol. 8 [1978], p. 3, cited in Robert Plomin, "The Role of Inheritance in Behavior," *Science,* vol. 248 [1990], pp. 183–88.)

159 "consistently sociable . . .": Kagan and Snidman, "Infant Predictors."

159   "those reserved . . .": Carl Jung, *Psychological Types*, trans. R. F. C. Hull (Princeton, N.J.: Princeton University Press, 1971), p. 330. The subsequent quotes are from pp. 331–32.

160   in 1934: The complete quote is: "The Aryan unconscious has a higher potential than the Jewish; this is the advantage and the disadvantage of a youthfulness not yet fully escaped from barbarism. In my opinion it has been a great mistake of all previous medical psychology to apply Jewish categories which are not binding even to Jews, indiscriminately to Christians, Germans, or Slavs. In doing so, medical psychology has declared the most precious secret of the Germanic peoples—the creatively prophetic depths of soul—to be a childishly banal morass. . . ."

Whether Jung merely reflected the scientific racism of his times, or whether he contributed to it, is a difficult matter. My reading of *Psychological Types* is that it is dangerously, one might say irresponsibly, romantic. As for the editorship of the *Zentralblatt*, my sense is that Jung had a cultural contempt for the Nazis but was guilty of opportunism at Freud's and his colleagues' expense in a way that, because of what followed, reflects very badly on Jung. See my column, "Matters of Taste," *Psychiatric Times*, September 1988, p. 3ff; Vincent Brome, *Jung* (New York: Atheneum, 1978). However, many respected scholars consider Jung blameless and misunderstood; it appears he was helpful personally to certain Jewish physicians during the war. Those interested in the broader subject might consult Robert Jay Lifton's *The Nazi Doctors* (New York: Basic Books, 1986); and Geoffrey Cocks's eye-opening *Psychotherapy in the Third Reich* (Oxford: Oxford University Press, 1985).

160   her studies in the 1930s: Margaret Mead, *Sex and Temperament in Three Primitive Societies* (New York: William Morrow, 1963, orig. 1935), cited in Carl N. Degler, *In Search of Human Nature: The Decline and Revival of Darwinism in American Thought* (New York: Oxford University Press, 1991), p. 134.

161   "The main impetus . . .": Degler, *In Search*, p. viii. Degler points to many cultural and scientific factors that have led to the resurgence of interest in biology. One interesting minor detail (ibid., pp. 225, 232) is his tracing of the revival of interest among political scientists in biology to an article on ethology and psychopharmacology. Even though the author, Albert Somit, was not certain that antidepressants directly treated depression (he held open the possibility they might be facilitating psychotherapy), he believed that the effects of psychotherapeutic drugs in humans confirmed the relevance of animal ethology to human behavior. ("Toward a More Biologically-Oriented Political Science: Ethology and Pharmacology," *Midwest Journal of Political Science*, vol. 12 [1968], pp. 550–67.)

161   Kagan has speculated: Galvin, "Nature of Shyness," p. 44.

161   "The return of the idea of temperament . . .": Kagan and Snidman, "Infant Predictors," p. 332.

161   "all statements about the genetic basis . . .": R. C. Lewontin, Steven Rose, and Leon J. Kamin, *Not in Our Genes: Biology, Ideology, and Human Nature* (New York: Pantheon, 1984), p. 251. Lewontin's premise is slightly disingenuous; certainly major gene defects, like those producing phenylketonuria, Down's syndrome, and a number of other disorders associated with risk of mental retardation, have strong effects on human social behavior in ordinary, expectable environments. Still, it has been surprisingly difficult to link even major mental illness to specific genetic defects.

161   "what every parent knows": But we should remember that a previous generation of parents, certainly the educated middle class, knew differently. Degler, *In Search,* reminds us how recent is our new certainty about the power of temperament.

162   the theory of the humors: See Stanley Jackson, *Melancholia and Depression: From Hippocratic to Modern Times* (New Haven, Conn.: Yale University Press, 1986).

163   Aristotle asked: Jackson, *Melancholia and Depression,* p. 31. Regarding mood disorder and creativity, it is interesting to note, in light of our discussion in chapter 4, the observations of one of the great figures in public psychiatry, Philippe Pinel, at the close of the eighteenth century: "The excessive sensitivity that characterizes very talented people may become a cause for the loss of their reason. . . . Groups as diverse as investigators, artists, orators, poets, geometers, engineers, painters and sculptors pay an almost annual price to the hospice for the insane. . . . How many talents lost to society and what great efforts are needed to salvage them!" (Doris B. Weiner, "Philippe Pinel's 'Memoir on Madness' of December 11, 1794: A Fundamental Text of Modern Psychiatry," *American Journal of Psychiatry,* vol. 149 [1992], pp. 725–32; quotation on p. 728.)

163   the work of Hagop Akiskal: Hagop S. Akiskal, "Validating Affective Personality Types," in Lee N. Robins and James E. Barrett, eds., *The Validity of Psychiatric Diagnosis* (New York: Raven Press, 1989), pp. 217–27. See also Boghos I. Yerevanian and Hagop S. Akiskal, " 'Neurotic,' Characterological, and Dysthymic Depressions," *Psychiatric Clinics of North America,* vol. 2 (1979), pp. 595–617; Hagop S. Akiskal, Ted L. Rosenthal, et al., "Characterological Depressions: Clinical and Sleep EEG Findings Separating 'Subaffective Dys-

thymias' from 'Character Spectrum Disorders,' " *Archives of General Psychiatry*, vol. 37 (1980), pp. 777–83.

163 *forme fruste:* See note below, p. 352.

164 "These individuals . . .": Akiskal, "Validating Affective Personality Types," pp. 222–23.

164 Among the most enduring traits: Ibid., p. 221.

165 Elsewhere on the spectrum: "Euthymic" means "normal mood"; "hyperthymia" refers to a chronic elevation of mood that is less than hypomania, which is less than mania, the extreme perturbation of mood and level of energy in which a person may be so euphoric, irritable, impulsive, and fast-thinking as to be delusional. Theorists have argued about what a spectrum of these normal variants and disorders should look like. On first thought, it may seem that the proper ordering is depressed-dysthymic-euthymic-hyperthymic-hypomanic-manic. But there are those who believe that bipolar affective disorder is in effect a severe form of depression, so that depression lies between normality and mania. Others believe the sequence includes a number of distinct diseases, and that spectrum-ordering misrepresents reality: perhaps hyperthymic personality and recurrent depression are just different entities with distinct relations to mind and brain, in the way that asthma and tuberculosis are both lung diseases but do not sit on a spectrum.

165 hyperthymics are habitually "irritable": Akiskal, "Validating Affective Personality Types," p. 219.

166 both temperaments relate to manic-depressive illness: Akiskal refers to a "soft bipolar spectrum." See Hagop S. Akiskal, John Downs, et al., "Affective Disorders in Referred Children and Younger Siblings of Manic Depressives: Mode of Onset and Prospective Course," *Archives of General Psychiatry*, vol. 42 (1985), pp. 996–1003; Hagop S. Akiskal and Gopinath M. Mallya, "Criteria for the 'Soft' Bipolar Spectrum: Treatment Implications," *Psychopharmacology Bulletin*, vol. 23 (1987), pp. 68–73; Hagop S. Akiskal, "The Milder Spectrum of Bipolar Disorders: Diagnostic, Characterologic, and Pharmacologic Aspects," *Psychiatric Annals*, vol. 17 (1987), pp. 33–37.

166 subaffective dysthymia sits in the penumbra of the penumbra: Though some of the patients we have met are probably dysthymic or subaffectively dysthymic, my impression is that the patients Akiskal describes in his monographs tend chronically and recurrently to suffer more distinct periods of depressed mood than do the Prozac responders whose lives we have glimpsed in these pages. Perhaps this difference is due to the sorts of people who attend

the Mood Clinic in Memphis. Not just in Akiskal's reports but in general, although the words "dysthymia" and "depressive personality" appear in the research literature, little work has been done with people whose mood disorder or personality variant is chronic and mild. Most studies of dysthymia involve subjects who, at the time of the study, are suffering "double depression," major depression superimposed on chronic depressive symptoms. This tendency in the literature is easy to understand: people seek out doctors when they are in the midst of a depression, and it is in this state that patients are most willing to participate in drug trials.

Regarding the degree of illness of Akiskal's patients, a trade paper recently reported on a study of the use of Prozac in dysthymia conducted at Charter Lakeside Hospital in Memphis by Akiskal with Radwan Haykal ("Fluoxetine Found Effective for Dysthymia," *Clinical Psychiatry News,* vol. 20, no. 2 [February 1992], p. 4f. Of thirty-nine dysthymic outpatients under study, nineteen had been hospitalized previously for mental illness, and ten had made prior suicide attempts. This is greater past pathology than occurs in the typical history of patients with major depression—and much greater pathology than is reported by the patients we have discussed in this book. Of interest in Haykal and Akiskal's study is that a much higher percentage of dysthymic women than men responded to Prozac (fourteen of sixteen women responded to Prozac, versus six of fourteen men), whereas the ratio was more nearly equal for tricyclics.

167   Psychiatrists who are skeptical: William Z. Potter, Matthew V. Rudorfer, and Husseni Manji, "The Pharmacologic Treatment of Depression," *New England Journal of Medicine,* vol. 325 (1991), pp. 633–42. Potter and his colleagues express doubt about any special role for Prozac in treating dysthymia.

167   which is primary: Perhaps a unified concept of temperament would contain a more equal weighting of social and affective components, taking into account the ordinary social observation that few people are euphoric and inhibited, just as few are gloomy and gregarious. Arguing against a relationship between inhibition and dysthymia is the greater prevalence of anxiety, as opposed to depressive, disorders in relatives of inhibited infants. In favor of a relationship are: the overlap of traits related to both disorders in uptight monkeys, the apparent increased prevalence of inhibition in the history of dysthymics, the similarity in neurotransmitters and parts of the brain implicated, the prominence of social maladroitness in dysthymics between depressive episodes—and a fascinating theory, discussed next in the chapter, linking inhibition with subsequent dysthymia.

168   he gave a preview: Michael T. McGuire, "Can Evolutionary Theory Help Us Understand the Proximate Mechanism and Symptom Changes Characteristic

of Persons with Dysthymic Disorder?," American Psychiatric Association Annual Meeting in New York City, May 14, 1990. I thank Dr. McGuire for sharing his notes with me. It is interesting to see that in the pilot phase of this study the women were diagnosed as having "neurotic depression." The designations for minor and chronic depression are impossibly fluid.

168 the researchers could not differentiate: The lack of memory difference confirms that the experimental subjects were not deeply depressed, since memory and concentration are so often impaired in major depression. The dysthymic women had one interesting trait I do not mention in the text: they tended to attribute their frustration to chance or circumstance, and to engage in various forms of self-deception. This failure to organize experience in a usable way results in repetition of dysfunctional behavior. Internal locus of control—the belief that a person causes his own good or ill fortune—demands a constant re-examination of failed strategies; these women's external attribution of control caused them to persist in their maladaptive approaches. See also Michael T. McGuire and Alfonso Troisi, "Unrealistic Wishes and Physiological Change: An Overview," *Psychotherapy and Psychosomatics*, vol. 47 (1987), pp. 82–94.

175 Studies from a variety of perspectives: I should make it clear that this synthesis of the work of Kagan, Suomi, Akiskal, McGuire, and, in the background, Klein, Post, and others is my own, and that it brings together material the researchers themselves might consider incompatible. For example, Akiskal seems to see subaffective dysthymia as a discrete disorder in which social inhibition is a secondary feature; and Kagan implies that inhibited children will likely grow up to be anxious rather than depressed. Conventionally, social inhibition is thought to relate to the anxiety disorders, whereas dysthymia relates to the depressive disorders. But the prevalence of social inhibition as the (temporally) primary trait in McGuire's dysthymics points to the overlap of categories.

My own view is that the whole "affective spectrum" is tightly linked. The commonality of these prevalent minor conditions is supported not only by the common responsiveness of a range of anxiety and depressive disorders, from panic and OCD to dysthymia and depression, to the same drugs, but also by a growing body of basic research. See, for example, Kenneth S. Kendler, Michael C. Neale, et al., "Major Depression and Generalized Anxiety Disorder: Same Genes, (Partly) Different Environments?," *Archives of General Psychiatry*, vol. 49 (1992), pp. 716–22. This work meshes well with Suomi's speculation that a genetic predisposition to reactivity can give rise, depending on the nature of the stressors encountered, to either anxiety or depression.

179   Klein's group looked at about two hundred: Jonathan W. Stewart, Frederic M. Quitkin, et al., "Social Functioning in Chronic Depression: Effect of 6 Weeks of Antidepressant Treatment," *Psychiatry Research*, vol. 25 (1988), pp. 213–22. A good summary of the research on the relationship of dysthymia to personality disorder can be found in James H. Kocsis and Allen J. Frances, "A Critical Discussion of *DSM-III* Dysthymic Disorder," *American Journal of Psychiatry*, vol. 144 (1987), pp. 1534–42.

180   Akiskal no longer divides patients: This change in his point of view was apparent in a number of Akiskal's presentations at the 1992 Annual Meeting of the American Psychiatric Association, and Akiskal confirmed it in response to a question I asked him at that meeting. See also Haykal, "Early Onset Dysthymia."

183   "the functional theory of psychopathology": Herman M. van Praag, Serena-Lynn Brown, et al., "Beyond Serotonin: A Multiaminergic Perspective on Abnormal Behavior," in Herman M. van Praag and Serena-Lynn Brown, eds., *The Role of Serotonin in Psychiatric Disorders* (New York: Brunner/Mazel, 1991), pp. 302–32.

183   Likewise, panic anxiety: These examples are mine.

184   "The greater the biochemical specificity . . .": Van Praag, Brown, et al., "Beyond Serotonin," p. 325.

185   C. Robert Cloninger: "A Unified Biosocial Theory of Personality and Its Role in the Development of Anxiety States," *Psychiatric Developments*, vol. 3 (1986), pp. 167–226; "A Systematic Method for Clinical Description and Classification of Personality Variants: A Proposal," *Archives of General Psychiatry*, vol. 44 (1987), pp. 573–88.

185   "reward dependence" and related quotations: Cloninger, "Systematic Method," p. 578.

186   "harm avoidance": Ibid., p. 577.

187   "novelty seeking"; "Consistently . . .": Ibid., p. 576. This axis was the subject of the title essay of the popular book by the anthropologist-physician Melvin Konner, *Why the Reckless Survive: And Other Secrets of Human Nature* (New York: Viking, 1990), in which Konner argues that both risk-takers and risk-avoiders contribute to the survival of the species.

187   These three axes: Cloninger, "Unified Biosocial Theory," p. 185; Cloninger, "Systematic Method," p. 579.

As if three axes were not enough, other researchers have proposed a fourth, based on how people take in stimuli such as pain. Some people seem neurologically, when tested by means of brain-wave tests (electroencephalograms), to have exaggerated reactions to loud noises or flashes of light. They are called "augmenters"; the opposite end of the axis of "perceptual reactance" is "reducing." Theorists have especially discussed combinations of novelty seeking and perceptual reactance. High novelty seeking and augmenting seems a bad combination—the person is drawn to stimuli he or she cannot tolerate, and the result is an excess of mental illness. High stimulus-seeking and reducing leads to successful risk-taking, and so on. Cloninger argues that perceptual reactance is not a separate axis, and that he can cover the same territory more parsimoniously with his one-neurotransmitter/one-trait model.

Not only social ease, mood, and level of energy, but other qualities we have not mentioned, such as propensity toward anger and violence, have been shown in one or another experimental model to be influenced by transmitters and receptors.

187 "passive avoidance . . . gullible": Cloninger, "Systematic Method," p. 579.

191 the "Ideas" story in *Newsweek:* Sharon Begley, "Brother Sun, Sister Moon," *Newsweek,* October 29, 1990, p. 69, a discussion of Judy Dunn and Robert Plomin, *Separate Lives: Why Siblings Are So Different* (New York: Basic Books, 1990).

191 A geneticist would deem . . . meaningless: The reporting of the percent contribution of genes to behavioral traits is critiqued effectively by Richard Lewontin in his book *Human Diversity* (New York: Scientific American, 1982). Hidden in most twin studies, upon which percentage statements of this sort are often based, is the truth that most "adopted-out" twins are raised by aunts and uncles, not by people from vastly different cultural backgrounds.

191 *The Glass Menagerie:* Trinity Repertory Company, Providence, R.I., fall 1991.

193 a recent genetic study of white twin girls: Kenneth S. Kendler, Michael C. Neale, et al., "Childhood Parental Loss and Adult Psychopathology in Women: A Twin Study Perspective," *Archives of General Psychiatry,* vol. 49 (1992), pp. 109–16. This study is complex and has a number of interesting results. For instance, panic anxiety was found to be associated with both parental death and separation, but only if the separation was from the mother. This sort of result speaks against a nonspecific diagnosis such as neurosis, and indicates that panic anxiety and major depression may be distinct entities arising in response to differing social stressors. In aggregate, this twin study found a

variety of mental illnesses in the sample to correlate much more with genetic than environmental factors, though both sorts of effects were discernible.

196   personality extends far beyond: The effects of medication on inhibited people may also change our conception of "social skills" and social development. It is my observation that patients who say they have not grown since early childhood, and who in fact appear immature or socially stunted, often do quite well when properly medicated—and without the need for any social-skills training. Having observed people in the school or workplace, and watched television shows and read books that model social behavior, and dreamed of social competency, seems to be enough for them. Once they are less inhibited, they interact with surprising success. The limiting factor in their past failures was social anxiety or a missetting of the sensor for interpersonal distance, and not any failure to have matured.

196   Is Sally's fiancé truly marrying: There is an ethical aspect to this question: Are the psychiatrist and the patient colluding to deceive the prospective mate? Is the "real" Sally the woman off medication, as she was and may perhaps again be? Of course, similar issues are hidden in psychotherapy: a patient who is supported by therapy may appear socially more stable than he or she was in the past, or than he or she may be in the future.

My sense is that a good deal of marrying takes place around changes in affective state. One classic instance is marriage "on the rebound." Generally, a person may be more susceptible to marrying when depressed (and therefore needy) or when euphoric. The altered state may be helpful, in that it pushes a person past his or her inhibitions, or it may be a prelude to unhappiness. An empirically based assumption of marriage counseling is that both partners are probably in about the same state of maturity (more exactly, that they have the same level of "differentiation of self," or ability to resist regressive social and family forces). My sense is that many marital troubles arise when a depressed woman marries a man who is at her level of social competence at the time of her weakness; when she recovers from depression, she finds herself mismatched, but, afraid she may sink back into depression in response to a separation, unable to extricate herself.

CHAPTER 7: *FORMES FRUSTES:* LOW SELF-ESTEEM

197   A reviewer of a recent book: Elaine Showalter, "Ladies Sing the Blues," *New Republic,* vol. 206, no. 10 (March 9, 1992), pp. 44–45. The section cited

refers to Colette Dowling, *You Mean I Don't Have to Feel This Way?* (New York: Scribner's, 1992).

197   now most often called *formes frustes:* Regarding Freud's view of partial presentations of anxiety neurosis, see chapter 4. The classic example of a *forme fruste* is "migraine without migraine": migraine headaches are often accompanied or preceded by diverse symptoms, such as the illusion of flashing lights, queasiness in the stomach, numbness over one side of the face, and weakness or paralysis of one arm; people can suffer, on the same physiological basis as migraine, only the accompanying features without ever having a headache. For example, a patient may consult a gastroenterologist for recurrent queasiness when the problem is really "migraine without migraine." In discussing *formes frustes* of minor depression, I am saying that there is also "dysthymia without dysthymia."

   In medical school, I was told that a *forme fruste* was a "frustrated form" of an illness, and *Stedman's Medical Dictionary* supports this assertion, tracing *fruste* to the Latin *frustra,* "without effect" or "in vain." But a "frust," in the eighteenth-century English of *Tristram Shandy,* was a fragment; the *Oxford English Dictionary* relates the word to the Latin *frustum,* "a piece." In French, *fruste* refers specifically to something worn away by friction. A *forme fruste* is thus not a frustrated but a partial illness.

198   an earlier era stressed building character: My daughter for some years attended a girls' school based on Quaker principles one of whose mottoes was "lowliness," a thoroughly unmodern virtue and one that presupposes an unmodern mix of self-worth, self-doubt, and humility. The school stressed the inculcation of confidence, assertiveness, and leadership. I believe it is fair to say that the goal of instilling lowliness in girls was not especially talked up in the school's contacts with parents of prospective pupils.

   I think in this context of an Ed Koren cartoon that shows a mother, with an unhappy preschooler beside her standing in front of a school, addressing another mother with a child in a stroller: "Can you believe this is happening to me? Her scores are very low in self-esteem." (*New Yorker,* April 6, 1992, p. 35.)

   An interesting critique of self-esteem, and also of psychoanalysis as a clinical modality, is Christopher Lasch, "For Shame: Why Americans Should Be Wary of Self-Esteem," *New Republic,* August 10, 1992, pp. 29–34. Lasch's essay is in part a skeptical commentary on Gloria Steinem's *Revolution from Within: A Book of Self-Esteem* (Boston: Little, Brown, 1992), and the state of California's Task Force to Promote Self-Esteem, which Steinem praises (pp. 26–30). Regarding self-esteem as autobiographical, Steinem quotes psychiatrists to the effect that self-valuation in adults is "the inner child of the past" or "the child within" (pp. 34–39, 65–69, and throughout).

199   rather odd theories of Alfred Adler: Alfred Adler, *Study of Organ Inferiority and Its Psychical Compensation: A Contribution to Clinical Medicine* (1907), trans. Smith Ely Jelliffe (New York: Nervous and Mental Disease Publishing Co., 1917); Alfred Adler, *The Neurotic Constitution: Outlines of a Comparative Individualistic Psychology and Psychotherapy* (1912), trans. Bernard Glueck and John E. Lind (New York: Moffat, Yard and Co., 1917). In his early years, Adler was a major and beneficent figure in Viennese community medicine, taking an interest, for instance, in the ocular problems of tailors; in later years, he became a popularizer of psychology, focusing especially on people's innate social interest (not unlike the "aloneness affect" we have discussed) and their strivings for success.

199   a variant form of guilt: "But the major part of the sense of inferiority derives from the ego's relation to its super-ego. . . . Altogether, it is hard to separate the sense of inferiority from the sense of guilt." (Sigmund Freud, *New Introductory Lectures on Psycho-Analysis* [1933], in James Strachey, ed., *The Standard Edition of the Complete Psychological Works of Sigmund Freud,* vol. 22 [London: Hogarth Press, 1964], pp. 65–66. Although Freud emphasized the role of the superego, he also had a complex view of the development of self-worth, and a healthy respect for the role of maternal nurturance. And he had a modern understanding of the role of the cross-generational transmission of pathology, saying that, in the development of the superego, the child responded less to the parent than to the parent's superego—that is, the mother or father's recollection of the grandparents' (often severe) child-rearing practices.

200   The new guiding metaphor: In this and the following paragraph, I am relying on the theories of the modern school of psychoanalysis called "self psychology," whose emphasis on the self is evident in its very name.

202   Donald Klein has written: Paul H. Wender and Donald F. Klein, *Mind, Mood, and Medicine* (New York: Farrar, Straus & Giroux, 1981), especially pp. 39–66; the case of William M. is on pp. 46–48. Paul Wender is a psychiatrist best known for his work on attention-deficit hyperactivity disorder, a phenomenon we will encounter in chapter 9.

204   altered emotional proprioception—a neurological distortion: I find it hard to avoid words like "altered" or "distortion," but it may be more reasonable to think of self-esteem as a spectrum trait that differs among normal people. William M. may be not damaged but just different, with a sense of self that is logically defensible but socially maladaptive.

208   self-image changes overnight: Recent work on dysthymia indicates that not all responses are of this sort. An unpublished study from Cornell University finds that good antidepressant responders fall into two groups as regards personality. Some seem cured outright, like the patients we have met. Others also report dramatic change but find the change dislocating. In these patients, although the change in feeling about the self is strong, cognition (and organization of the defenses) lags; they generally need psychotherapy to deal with the success of medication. The study, by a group headed by James Kocsis, was cited in Arnold Cooper, "The Relevance of Psychotherapy to Clinical Practice Today," address, Rhode Island Psychiatric Society, Butler Hospital, Providence, R.I., March 2, 1992, 27 pp.

210   The classic experience of college students: This point is made by Wender and Klein, *Mind, Mood, and Medicine*, p. 202.

212   including Michael McGuire: Michael J. Raleigh and Michael T. McGuire, "Social and Environmental Influences on Blood Serotonin Concentrations in Monkeys," *Archives of General Psychiatry*, vol. 41 (1984), pp. 405–10. "Troop" is an inexact but convenient word for referring to groups of captive monkeys.

   Dominance and submission are not difficult to identify in vervets. A dominant male will win over 90 percent of his aggressive contacts (threatening, slapping and pushing, or "displaying"—bouncing, circling the tail, and swinging the penis) with other males, whereas no submissive male will win more than half of his encounters. Submissive behaviors are: avoiding or retreating from threat; signaling submission by squealing, hopping backward, and pawing the ground; and standing rigidly vigilant.

213   To investigate this issue: Michael J. Raleigh, Michael T. McGuire, et al., "Serotonergic Mechanisms Promote Dominance Acquisition in Adult Male Vervet Monkeys," *Brain Research*, vol. 559 (1991), pp. 181–90. It is important to note that the monkeys on serotonin-depleting or -elevating medication did not appear drugged; they engaged in all the normal behaviors of vervet males.

214   serotonic mechanisms . . . : Ibid., p. 188.

214   studies of serotonin levels in man: A political scientist at the University of Iowa has performed two preliminary experiments using blood serotonin levels to assess the influence of biology on power-seeking behavior in humans. Based on a study of male undergraduates placed in a stressful competitive situation, he concludes that serotonin levels correlate with self-assessed social rank and leadership qualities, albeit complexly. Among aggressive, ambitious, manipulative, and self-centered young men (the majority of the sample), high blood

serotonin correlated with high status; among deferential, nonaggressive, moralistic young men, high serotonin correlated with low status. Interestingly, serotonin levels, and social status, existed on a continuous spectrum in aggressive young men (as opposed to the discontinuous submissive-dominant dichotomy in vervets). Douglas Madsen, "Blood Serotonin and Social Rank Among Human Males," in Roger Masters and Michael McGuire, eds., *The Neurotransmitter Revolution* (unpublished).

Madsen had earlier found that very strong type A ("Machiavellian") behavior in young men—encompassing drive, aggressiveness, mistrust, and competitiveness—correlates with high blood serotonin levels. Madsen believes any relationship between hierarchy and serotonin levels in humans must necessarily be complex because humans achieve power through various means (money, inheritance, a group decision to compromise on a weak leader who won't rock the boat) that have little to do with biologically mediated leadership traits. Douglas Madsen, "A Biochemical Property Relating to Power Seeking in Humans," *American Political Science Review*, vol. 79 (1985), pp. 448–57.

215 **maintained by the serotonin system:** Serotonin is hardly likely to be the whole story. Researchers have also looked at stress hormones in relation to dominance hierarchy. To mention only two results: When male monkeys compete for dominance, their blood-norepinephrine and stress-hormone levels rise. Once the battle is decided, the stress-hormone levels in the newly dominant monkey fall; in the defeated monkey, they remain high. Likewise, aroused females have high stress-hormone levels that, however, "fall precipitously if they come under the protection of a dominant male" (Peter C. Whybrow, Hagop S. Akiskal, and William T. McKinney, Jr., *Mood Disorder: Toward a New Psychobiology* [New York: Plenum, 1984], p. 115). The norepinephrine and stress-hormone results are less impressive than the work on serotonin. Blood levels of norepinephrine and stress hormones vary widely in individuals over time—they are state variables. But serotonin levels are so stable that they appear to be trait variables, and to show that a trait variable changes according to social status is remarkable. Testosterone and other hormones almost certainly also play a role in dominance.

There was, by the way, an interesting article by Natalie Angier in *The New York Times* of November 12, 1991 (p. C1), referring to a study showing that a particular area of the brains of African cichlid fish increases in size when they achieve dominance. It is interesting to see dominance anatomically encoded, in any species.

215 **often cited study of children in Connecticut:** Stanley Coopersmith, *The Antecedents of Self-Esteem* (San Francisco: Freeman, 1967).

220 increase in his tolerance for strong, disturbing emotions: This increase, under the influence of pharmacotherapy, parallels a change certain theorists consider crucial in the psychotherapy of depression—namely, a replacement of the clinical syndrome of depression (which can include a deadening of affect, and is therefore called a "nonfeeling state") by the experiencing of sadness (a feeling state). See Irene Pierce Stiver and Jean Baker Miller, "From Depression to Sadness in Women's Psychotherapy," *Work in Progress* (The Stone Center, Wellesley College), vol. 36 (1988), pp. 1–12. Stiver and Miller consider a growing affective awareness of disappointment to be central to recovery from depression in women. The essay contains a useful review of social factors contributory to depression in women in our culture.

222 psychiatry's "loss of mind": Morton F. Reiser, "Are Psychiatric Educators 'Losing the Mind?,' " *American Journal of Psychiatry*, vol. 145 (1988), pp. 148–53.

CHAPTER 8: *FORMES FRUSTES:* INHIBITION OF PLEASURE, SLUGGISHNESS OF THOUGHT

223 *Annie Hall . . . Anhedonia:* Eric Lax, *Woody Allen: A Biography* (New York, Vintage, 1992), p. 284.

225 Graham Greene . . . felt such ennui: The following passage is from the autobiography of his early years, *A Sort of Life* (New York: Simon and Schuster, 1971), pp. 157–58:

> . . . the oppression of boredom soon began to descend. Once on my free day I walked over the hills to Chesterfield and found a dentist. I described to him the symptoms, which I knew well, of an abscess. He tapped a perfectly good tooth with his little mirror and I reacted in the correct way. "Better have it out," he advised.
> "Yes," I said, "but with ether."
> A few minutes' unconsciousness was like a holiday from the world. I had lost a good tooth, but the boredom was for the time being dispersed.

Greene is someone Jerome Kagan mentions as having come to social inhibition on an environmental basis, through having been hazed in school. But I wonder whether Greene did not suffer as well, or even primarily, from anhedonia, self-treated by means of extreme adventure and expressed in the remarkable laconic distance of his authorial voice. Kagan is quoted on Greene in Ruth M. Galvin, "The Nature of Shyness," *Harvard Magazine*, vol. 94 (1992), pp. 40–45.

228 A variety of neurochemical systems: Norepinephrine in particular has been proposed as key to "hedonic capacity," as, for example, in Herman van Praag's theory, referred to in chapter 6, of reward-coupling. Dopamine, through its relationship to schizophrenia, Parkinsonism, and the effects of amphetamine, has been proposed as a major factor in the regulation of pleasure. There is also interest in the endorphins, the internally produced substances whose effects heroin and morphine mimic. The encoding of pleasure in the brain probably extends far beyond the limbic system, where the biological correlates of depression are most often studied. See Nancy Andreason, "Affective Flattening: Evaluation and Diagnostic Significance," in David C. Clark and Jan Fawcett, eds., *Anhedonia and Affect Deficit States* (New York: PMA Publishing Corp., 1987), pp. 15–31.

228 Paul Meehl . . . published a critique: Paul E. Meehl, "Hedonic Capacity: Some Conjectures," *Bulletin of the Menninger Clinic*, vol. 39 (1975), pp. 295–307; reprinted in Clark and Fawcett, eds., *Anhedonia*, pp. 33–45. The various quotes from Meehl are all from this essay. Meehl quotes Sandor Rado in the phrase "scarcity economy of pleasure." See also Paul E. Meehl, " 'Hedonic Capacity' Ten Years Later: Some Clarifications," in ibid., pp. 47–50.

229 depression may result: Such depression is generally described, in a term favored by the behavioral psychologist B. F. Skinner, as "extinction depression." Michael McGuire's account of dysthymia as resulting from the effects of behavioral inflexibility—women who stand on long lines end up with few friends and cramped lodgings—is an extinction-depression model.

230 the work of . . . Jan Fawcett . . . and David Clark: See David Clark and Jan Fawcett, "Anhedonia, Hypohedonia and Pleasure Capacity in Major Depressive Disorders," in Clark and Fawcett, eds., *Anhedonia*, pp. 51–63.

230 fewer signs of neurotic conflict: The anhedonic subjects showed less indecision, pessimism, irritability, and hypochondriasis—the more neurotic depressive traits.

231 Klein had just published: Donald F. Klein, "Endogenomorphic Depression: A Conceptual and Terminological Revision," *Archives of General Psychiatry*, vol. 31 (1974), pp. 447–54. The ideas in that early monograph are expanded on and clarified in Donald F. Klein, "Depression and Anhedonia," in Clark and Fawcett, eds., *Anhedonia*, pp. 1–14. Much of what appears in the following paragraphs constitutes a condensation of that second monograph.

The reader will recognize the "central comparator" as conceptual kin to the "emotional thermostat" in Klein's theory of rejection-sensitivity, summarized in chapter 4.

232 consummatory anhedonia: Klein said consummatory anhedonia was mostly primary—perhaps the central problem in typical depression. More rarely, consummatory anhedonia might occur secondarily, as a result of severe and chronic appetitive anhedonia.

233 Klein's account . . . contrasted to Meehl's: If Meehl is right, anhedonia should be chronic and result primarily in "character pathology." If Klein is right, the most pervasive anhedonia (consummatory, which includes appetitive) should be a feature of the deepest major depressions. But this contrast is partly specious. When we talk about anhedonia, we tend to mean what Klein would call an appetitive disorder—boredom, lethargy, indifference to a variety of activities. And as regards appetitive dysfunction, Klein and Meehl are very largely in agreement.

Fawcett and Clark's research was in part an attempt to settle the apparent disagreement between Meehl and Klein. Fawcett and Clark's results shed doubt on Klein's account of comsummatory anhedonia. In their study, anhedonia is absent in the vast majority of depressed patients. The minority of patients who score high on Fawcett and Clark's measure of anhedonia appear to have a chronic trait that remains when depression subsides. Klein has argued that the researchers' scale measures appetitive anhedonia, because testing necessarily asks respondents to *imagine how they will feel*—and appetitive anhedonia is a disorder of *imagining* pleasure. Klein may well be right, but if consummatory anhedonia presupposes appetitive anhedonia, Fawcett and Clark's net ought to catch a more varied group of depressives—both pure appetitive anhedonics with atypical depression and those suffering from deep, acute, typical depression, of which appetitive anhedonia, as well as consummatory, is necessarily a feature.

233 And once Prozac works: Why Prozac? I have no good explanation. If anhedonia is a matter of problems with norepinephrine, dopamine, and the endorphins, Hillary should have responded to anything except Prozac. Hillary's initial short-lived success on Prozac sounds like a favorable reaction to the "amphetaminelike effect," except that it lasted weeks rather than days. That response, along with certain of Hillary's symptoms, including lethargy and a lack of follow-through that might be interpreted as a sign of attention-deficit disorder, would lead some biological psychiatrists to prescribe a stimulant, such as Ritalin or an amphetamine (which affects norepinephrine and dopamine). The noradrenergic drug desipramine would be a likely candidate on theoretical

grounds—except that Klein's clinical experience showed the tricyclics to be relatively ineffective for anhedonia.

My guess is that serotonin plays a role in anhedonia, perhaps through something like Klein's comparator or center for appetitive pleasure. To reverse the issue, any adequate theory of anhedonia will have to explain the efficacy of Prozac and the MAOIs in treating the condition, which is to say that any adequate model will have to say something about serotonin.

235 "self-medication hypothesis . . .": Edward Khantzian, "The Self-Medication Hypothesis of Addictive Disorders: Focus on Heroin and Cocaine Dependence," *American Journal of Psychiatry*, vol. 142 (1985), pp. 1259–64; Edward Khantzian, "Self-Regulation and Self-Medication Factors in Alcoholism and the Addictions: Similarities and Differences," in Marc Galanter, ed., *Recent Developments in Alcoholism*, vol. 8 (New York: Plenum Publishing, 1990).

237 graphic artist: I discussed this case in an essay, "Medication Consultation," in *Psychiatric Times*, June 1991, pp. 4–5.

239 Attention-deficit disorder: I have drawn on American Psychiatric Association, *Diagnostic and Statistical Manual of Mental Disorders*, 3rd ed. (Washington, D.C.: American Psychiatric Association, 1980). By 1987, attention-deficit disorder without hyperactivity was considered rare; the revised manual (DSM III-R) recognizes only attention-deficit hyperactivity disorder (ADHD) and adds a minor category (undifferentiated attention-deficit disorder) as a sop to those clinicians who still distinguish attention-deficit disorder from ADHD. The point is that the complete syndrome (ADHD) is more common, and the incomplete may be merely a *forme fruste*.

A more recent overview of the topic is Russell A. Barkley, "Attention Deficit Hyperactivity Disorder," *Psychiatric Annals*, vol. 21 (1991), pp. 725–33. A major longitudinal study of hyperactive children which finds they do not have an excess of depression in later life is: Salvatore Mannuzza, Rachel G. Klein, et al., "Hyperactive Boys Almost Grown Up: V. Replication of Psychiatric Status," *Archives of General Psychiatry*, vol. 48 (1992), pp. 77–83. My description of ADHD is far from exhaustive. I have included primarily traits related to (mostly contrasting with) characteristics of dysthymia that we have discussed.

ADHD is often confused with learning disabilities, such as the various reading or decoding disorders, the dyslexias. Children with ADHD often have learning disorders, perhaps on the basis of a broad minor impairment of neurological development. But it seems the learning disorders occur on a different biological basis, in different parts of the brain, from the attention deficits. As opposed to ADHD, learning disorders may be associated with depression, perhaps even because of a relationship between the biological substrates of learning and mood disorders. See, for example, Drake D. Duane, "Dyslexia: Neurobiological and Behavioral Correlates," *Psychiatric Annals*, vol. 21 (1991), pp. 703–8.

240   But it sometimes continues into adult life: See Paul H. Wender, *The Hyperactive Child, Adolescent, and Adult: Attention Deficit Disorder Through the Lifespan* (New York: Oxford University Press, 1987), especially chapter 6, "Attention Deficit Disorder in Adults," pp. 117–40.

241   demoralization paired with a subtle disorganization of thought: I have just said that hyperactive boys tend not to suffer depression in adulthood, so the reader may well wonder how it is possible to say that ADHD can be confused with dysthymia. The answer is twofold. First, what characterizes ADHD in adulthood is not depression as a diagnosable illness but, rather, mood swings. ADHD patients as adults are overexcited by success and bored or discontented when frustrated or understimulated. Even though the "down" moods may be on a quite different basis, the account an adult with ADHD gives of himself —easily bored, joyless, self-deprecating—may lead to confusion with the anhedonia or low self-worth of dysthymia. Those who favor ADHD as a diagnosis in depressed adults with poor concentration also argue that ADHD is so underdiagnosed that even research studies tend to miss quiet or withdrawn children who have the disorder. It is these patients, they say, who on reaching adulthood will present with stories like Sonia's or Hillary's—depression characterized by boredom, disorganization, and a sense of not "getting" some of what is obvious to others. See, for example John J. Ratey, "Paying Attention to Attention in Adults," *Chadder*, Fall–Winter 1991, pp. 13–14.

241   pharmacologic dissection: The area of most distinct difference is responsiveness to very low-dose antidepressants. Some ADHD patients feel much less blue and impulsive after a few days on ten to thirty milligrams of desipramine—whereas most depressed patients require 150 to 300 milligrams given for four weeks. But dysthymic patients of all stripes sometimes respond to low-dose antidepressants. ADHD and dysthymia are both poorly studied pharmacologically, and the area of possible overlap has barely been studied at all.

241   But stimulants are sometimes effective in depression: There are depressed patients who respond only to stimulants. The work of Jonathan Cole of Harvard University is of particular interest in this area. ADHD has been associated with disorders of dopamine; it is at least possible that ADHD patients benefit from stimulants' dopamine effects and depressed patients from their norepinephrine

effects. It is also possible that these disorders are more closely connected than the evidence I have adduced here would indicate. It is of particular interest that ADHD sometimes responds to SSRIs, which affect the "wrong" neurotransmitter system. One could imagine that ADHD and the concentration and memory deficits of depression are related, as mania may be to be depression, through an abnormality of a thermostat or comparator.

243 If the twins had been subtly injured: I do not mean to say that ADHD is always a result of traumatic or chemical damage to the brain. There is evidence that in some cases ADHD may be heritable. It is nonetheless generally understood as a dysfunction, more like illness than like a normal variant.

245 the management consultant Tom Peters: "The Quick and the Dead: Slow, Careful Decisions Aren't Always the Best," Providence *Business News*, March 2, 1992, p. 12. The essay refers to a study contrasting slow and fast decision-makers at microcomputer firms. The faster executives use more real-time information, consider more alternatives, thrive on conflict and uncertainty, and integrate strategy and tactics. Their decisions are more timely and, in part for that reason, better. The essay ends with a quote from one executive: "The '90s will be a . . . nanosecond culture. There'll be only two kinds of managers: the quick and the dead." See also Jay Bourgeois and Kathleen Eisenhardt, "Strategic Decision Processes in High-Velocity Environments: Four Cases in the Microcomputer Industry," *Management Science*, vol. 34 (1988), pp. 816–35.

246 This nightmare view: As a parent, I sometimes think I see these pressures in an area that is far from the pharmacologic arena, but near to the issue of mental achievement—in grade placement for elementary-school children, particularly in affluent school districts or private schools. First a few enlightened parents hold back their developmentally immature children from first grade; then normal, late-birthday children are held back; soon all the parents who want their children to be leaders decide the boys and girls should wait a year; and before you know it the whole first grade is filled with seven-year-olds, and a normal six-year-old is too immature to compete successfully. We are used to theories about the influence of technology on cultural norms but perhaps do not appreciate that in the modern, intelligence-driven economy such nonmechanical entities as school placement and medication are technologies.

246 Khantzian . . . wrote to ask: Personal correspondence, cited in Kramer, "Medication Consultation."

CHAPTER 9: THE MESSAGE IN THE CAPSULE

250 the last novel by . . . Walker Percy: *The Thanatos Syndrome* (New York: Farrar, Straus & Giroux, 1987). The quotes are from p. 6 (Dickinson) and 21.

251 I raised that question in . . . essays: The first two were "Metamorphosis," *Psychiatric Times*, May 1989, p. 3ff, and "The New You," *Psychiatric Times*, March 1990, pp. 45–46. I am, I say with a mixture of pride and amusement, the first doctor to have posed these questions in print—indeed, the first to write that Prozac's effect sometimes goes beyond treating depression to brightening mood or altering personality traits. This distinction is minor: I only reported what thousands of doctors had seen. My small claim to priority is testimony mostly to the profession's overreliance on experiment and its neglect of ordinary observation. The Prozac columns were part of a larger series I had written, stretching back to 1986, on the way medications, and antidepressants in particular, color psychiatrists' understanding of patients. (Some of the earlier thinking is summarized in the chapter "The Mind-Mind-Body-Problem Problem" in my book *Moments of Engagement: Intimate Psychotherapy in a Technological Age* [New York: W. W. Norton, 1989], pp. 43–65.)

Robert Aranow was working independently on similar ideas; just before my second essay appeared, he chaired a clinical case conference at McLean Hospital on "The Clinical and Ethical Issues Raised by the Possible Development of 'Mood Brighteners,' " based on two cases of patients on Prozac, indicating "that significant improvement in mood can be gained in individuals who do not meet criteria" for mood disorder. Richard Schwartz (see p. 253) spoke at that conference. In May 1991, I joined Aranow, Schwartz, and Mark Sullivan in a symposium on "Mood Brighteners: Clinical and Ethical Dilemmas" at the American Psychiatric Association's Annual Meeting in New Orleans. The level of activity Prozac immediately aroused within the field of medical ethics is remarkable. Within two or three years of Prozac's introduction, articles on its ethical implications began to appear in professional journals, testimony to the strong impression the drug made on doctors as soon as they saw patients respond to it.

251 "mood brighteners," a phrase he coined: The concept "mood brightener" has been wrongly attributed to me. See Randolph M. Neese, "What Good Is Feeling Bad? The Evolutionary Benefits of Psychic Pain," *The Sciences*, November–December 1990, pp. 30–37.

251 "brighten the episodically down moods . . .": Robert Aranow quoted in Richard S. Schwartz, "Mood Brighteners, Affect Tolerance, and the Blues,"

Psychiatry, vol. 54 (1991), pp. 397–403; quotation on p. 397. The essay is a written version of the talk Schwartz presented at the May 1991 symposium.

252 "conservation of mood": Robert B. Aranow, Richard S. Schwartz, and Mark D. Sullivan, "Mood Brighteners," *American Journal of Psychiatry,* in press, draft of March 19, 1992, 16 pp.

252 "In effect, there has been . . .": Ibid, p. 1.

252 violate the principle of conservation of mood: It must seem ironic that such issues should arise around a medicine alleged to trigger impulses to commit suicide or homicide. But those allegations had just been made when Prozac caught the attention of the ethics community, and they have never dominated doctors' view of Prozac.

252 forty-four-year-old woman: Aranow, Schwartz, and Sullivan, "Mood Brighteners."

252 "reduce the common experiences . . .": Aranow quoted in Schwartz, "Mood Brighteners," p. 397.

253 "Recovery from a depressive illness . . .": Ibid., p. 398.

253 "an act of disconnection . . .": Ibid.

253 it is the "normal": Schwartz recounts the Russian story of two mice who fell into a bucket of milk. "Unable to swim, one mouse recognized the hopelessness of the situation, gave up, and drowned. The other became enraged, flailed at the milk, churned it to butter, and walked off." (Ibid., p. 399.)

254 "stand to feel . . .": Ibid., p. 400.

254 the contribution of . . . Zetzel: Elizabeth R. Zetzel, *The Capacity for Emotional Growth* (London: Hogarth Press, 1970), especially "Anxiety and the Capacity to Bear It," pp. 33–52, and "On the Incapacity to Bear Depression," pp. 82–114. This is the same Elizabeth Zetzel whom we met in chapter 4, in connection with the observation that, as psychoanalytic patients, hysterics can be either good or horrid.

254 "Here is a culture . . ." Schwartz, "Mood Brighteners," p. 401.

254 Neese . . . has collaborated with Michael McGuire: Michael T. McGuire, Isaac Marks, et al., "Evolutionary Biology: A Basic Science for Psychiatry," *Acta Psychiatrica Scandinavica,* in press, draft of February 22, 1992, 21 pp. I thank Dr. McGuire for sharing this manuscript with me.

254   criticized . . . from the viewpoint of evolutionary biology: Neese, "What Good Is Feeling Bad?"

255   "The new perspective . . .": Ibid., p. 37.

256   Aranow . . . co-authored with Schwartz and Mark Sullivan: Aranow, Schwartz, and Sullivan, "Mood Brighteners."

256   Sullivan suggests "autonomy": Mark Sullivan, "Ethics and the Perfection of Psychopharmacology," unpublished, 10 pp.; Aranow, Schwartz, and Sullivan, "Mood Brighteners." Regarding "autonomy," Sullivan draws on the work of Eric Cassell and Gerald Dworkin.

259   ". . . a person grows . . ." Schwartz, "Mood Brighteners," p. 400.

259   pharmacological Calvinism: The phrase is Gerald Klerman's (Gerald L. Klerman, "Psychotropic Hedonism vs. Pharmacological Calvinism," *Hastings Center Report*, vol. 2, no. 4 [1972], pp. 1–3). This issue is discussed further on p. 274. In the 1980s, Klerman told me he wished he had instead used the phrase "pharmacologic puritanism," as more expressive of the judgmental and prohibitive quality of the objection to medication.

260   Prozac shifts people from dysthymia: I am here using "dysthymia" and "hyperthymia" to refer to spectrum traits. Akiskal sometimes uses the same words to refer to illnesses. Any such distinction is complicated by the possibility that normal temperament at either end of the spectrum can be an early stage of a kindled mood disorder. It is in any case explicit in the mood-brightener debate that such a drug moves people from one nonillness state to another.

260   "I used to be uncomfortable . . .": Neese, "What Good Is Feeling Bad?," p. 30. I do not mean to deny that it can sometimes be useful to share with patients the impression that their social handicaps arise from normal variant traits. This viewpoint was, for example, quite helpful to Jerry, the surgeon whose treatment I discussed in chapter 6.

261   I will worry about Neese's patient: I am not saying that Neese believes all chronic sadness is inherited, only that in a clinical setting such a belief regarding a particular patient must come late in the evaluation process.

262   the rich can have it and the poor cannot: It might well be argued that access to a drug that enhances mood must be treated differently from access to a drug that enhances hair growth. Beyond issues of mood brightening, this argument (for greater equality of access to "enhancement" in the arena of mental functioning) would apply all the more strongly to a drug that improves mental agility or self-esteem. It strikes me as a peculiarity of our culture that this need

for equal access seems more obvious when applied to medication than when applied to psychotherapy, even, or especially, when the therapy has similar goals.

262   enhancement (of normal people's mood, in which case it would not): Or perhaps medication for certain forms of normal depressed mood will come to be considered prevention of kindled mood disorder, and therefore not enhancement but prophylactic treatment.

262   Estrogen used: But see Ronni Sandroff, "Menopause: Is It a Medical Problem?," *Good Health*, suppl. to *New York Times*, April 26, 1992, p. 22ff. To treat menopause, must we define it as endocrinopathy, or are we free to enhance or transform normal functioning? Is medication an attack on normal women, at the behest of a youth-conscious society? The issues are parallel to those for mood brighteners. See also Robert Michels, "Doctors, Drugs, and the Medical Model," in Thomas H. Murray, Willard Gaylin, and Ruth Macklin, eds., *Feeling Good and Doing Better: Ethics and Nontherapeutic Drug Use* (Clifton, N.J.: Humana, 1984), pp. 175–85. This book came to my attention through Aranow, Schwartz, and Sullivan, "Mood Brighteners."

263   what . . . Brock has called: Dan W. Brock, "The Use of Drugs for Pleasure: Some Philosophical Issues," in Murray, Gaylin, and Macklin, eds., *Feeling Good*, pp. 83–106. Much of this section on hedonism is based on Brock's essay. Brock is of course not responsible for my application of his model to the case of Prozac.

264   drugs that draw people *toward:* This argument would be vastly complicated by a short-acting drug that allows people to take on sociability at will. The authors of a pharmacologic overview of drugs of abuse that act via serotonin report: "The unique behavioral properties of MDA, a popular recreational drug for about twenty years, and its more recently abused congeners MDMA (Ecstasy) and MDEA (Eve), do not involve profound sensory disruption, but instead produce powerful enhancement of emotions, empathy, and affiliative bonds with other persons" (Martin P. Paulus and Mark A. Geyer, "The Effects of MDMA and Other Methylenedioxy-Substituted Phenylalkylamines on the Structure of Rat Locomotor Activity," *Neuropsychopharmacology*, vol. 7 [1992], pp. 15–31; quotation on p. 16.

265   Prozac is different: As a side note to the discussion of hedonism: Prozac can cause difficulties in achieving orgasm, more noticeably in men but in women as well. Probably because it is underreported, this side effect is not listed in standard references as being frequent, but clinicians see it fairly often. I have never had a patient discontinue Prozac because of it. Colleagues I have asked,

including some who do much more prescribing than I do, have, with rare exception, said the same thing. Here is an odd circumstance: a drug prescribed for relatively well-put-together people, often for the complaint of anhedonia, but well tolerated by them even when it causes sexual dysfunction. Patients' willingness to tolerate anorgasmia says something about Prozac and its relationship to pleasure. Prozac does not feel good to take, and it can cause a discouraging, even embarrassing, form of impotence, and yet it is "hedonic" because it allows people to experience the vibrancy of pleasure in the ordinary course of life. The degree to which ejaculatory delay or anorgasmia is tolerated speaks both to the diversity of pleasures people value and to the relative invulnerability of biologically supported self-esteem to particular physical and social failures.

This observation finds support in the following remark by a psychiatrist who works with OCD patients: "Surprisingly, orgasmic difficulties that are common with clomipramine [Anafranil] and fluoxetine [Prozac] result in discontinuing treatment less commonly than one might suppose, presumably because patients strongly desire the beneficial effects of the drugs" (John S. March, "Pharmacotherapy Effective in Obsessive-Compulsive Disorder," *Psychiatric Times*, May 1992, pp. 44–46).

265   Ms. B.: Aranow, Schwartz, and Sullivan, "Mood Brighteners," p. 10.

266   He is Ronald Winchel: Aloneness affect was mentioned in chapter 4. The description of the woman with trichotillomania is in Ronald M. Winchel, "Self-Mutilation and Aloneness," *Academy Forum* (of the American Academy of Psychoanalysis), vol. 35 (1991), pp. 10–12; quotation on p. 11.

267   If Ms. B. had taken Prozac as a mood brightener: Actually, Winchel describes the woman as having been treated for both compulsive hair-pulling and dysthymia. This erases much of our unease about the outcome.

269   Consider the Greek widow: Schwartz takes the example of the Greek widow from Anthony Storr, *Solitude* (New York: Ballantine, 1989). Storr was referring to a lovely work of anthropology and photography, enhanced by the poetry of funeral laments: Loring M. Danforth, *The Death Rituals of Rural Greece*, photographs by Alexander Tsiaras (Princeton, N.J.: Princeton University Press, 1982). The degree of recovery of the bereaved Greek women is unclear, even after five years of formal mourning. Several years after a child's death, one surviving mother will not attend a daughter's wedding and becomes upset whenever a member of the household listens to music on the radio. She calls her pain the wound that never heals.

The five-year period of mourning is enforced, and is thus an imposition for some women. The prolonged rituals sometimes result in strife; for example, a daughter-in-law may not mourn adequately according to the standards of the widow. The restrictions placed on men are much less stringent and of shorter duration. In effect, prolonged mourning is an enforced duty of women, as well as an opportunity to experience profound affect and accept loss.

271 The Mexican poet and essayist: Octavio Paz, "Mexico and the United States," in Paz, *The Labyrinth of Solitude, The Other Mexico, Return to the Labyrinth of Solitude, Mexico and the United States, The Philanthropic Ogre,* trans. Lysander Kemp, Yara Milos, and Rachel Phillips Belash (New York: Grove, 1985), p. 366.

272 The poet James Merrill: As is evident in a fuller excerpt, Merrill uses Prozac as one of a series of indicators of the simultaneously amusing and deadening banality of modern communal life:

> Still, not to paint a picture wholly black,
> Some social highlights: Dead white males in malls.
> Prayer breakfasts. Pay-phone sex. "Ring up as meat."
> Oprah. The G.N.P. The contour sheet.
> The painless death of History. The stick
> Figures on Capitol Hill. Their rhetoric,
> Gladly—no rapturously (on Prozac) suffered!
> Gay studies. Right-to-Lifers. The laugh track.

("Self-Portrait in Tyvek™ Windbreaker," *New Yorker,* February 24, 1992, pp. 38–39.)

272 steroids in competitive sports: Much of what follows is influenced by Thomas H. Murray, "Drugs, Sports, and Ethics," in Murray, Gaylin, and Macklin, eds., *Feeling Good,* pp. 107–126; see also 197–200, a helpful discussion of Murray's essay by Ruth Macklin.

274 "a general distrust of drugs . . .": Klerman, "Psychotropic Hedonism," p. 3. I served under Klerman when Jimmy Carter was in the White House and Klerman was director of the Alcohol, Drug Abuse, and Mental Health Administration of the Department of Health and Human Services. It was then that I chaired a government work group investigating the issue of women's use of prescribed psychotherapeutic drugs. Among our findings were the conclusions expressed in the text here, about the moderate use of prescribed psychotropics by Americans. (Peter D. Kramer, Mitchell E. Balter, and Louise Richardson,

"Women and the Abuse of Prescribed Psychotropic Medication," signed and distributed by U.S. Surgeon General, April 1981.)

274 prescribing . . . is moderate: Ibid. This issue is most extensively researched with regard to antianxiety drugs. See Mitchell B. Balter, Jerome Levine, and Dean L. Manheimer, "Cross-National Study of the Extent of Anti-Anxiety/Sedative Drug Use," *New England Journal of Medicine*, vol. 290 (1974), pp. 769–74; M. B. Balter, D. L. Manheimer, G. D. Mellinger, et al., "A Cross-National Comparison of Anti-Anxiety/Sedative Drug Use," *Current Medical Research and Opinon*, vol. 8, supplement 4 (1984), pp. 5–30; and M. B. Balter and E. H. Uhlenhuth, "Benzodiazepine Use: 1990 Survey Data," symposium presentation, Fifth World Congress of Biological Psychiatry, Florence, Italy, June 1991. The trends are much the same for antidepressants: if anything, antidepressants appear to be underprescribed in the United States and elsewhere. See Ira D. Glick, Lorenzo Burti, Koji Suzuki, et al., "Effectiveness in Psychiatric Care: I. A Cross-National Study of the Process of Treatment and Outcomes of Major Depressive Disorder," *Journal of Nervous and Mental Disease*, vol. 179 (1991), pp. 55–63; Martin B. Keller, Philip W. Lavori, Gerald L. Klerman, et al., "Low Levels and Lack of Predictors of Somatotherapy and Psychotherapy Received by Depressed Patients," *Archives of General Psychiatry*, vol. 43 (1986), pp. 458–67; and Martin B. Keller, Gerald L. Klerman, Philip W. Lavori, et al., "Treatment Received by Depressed Patients," *JAMA*, vol. 248 (1982), pp. 1848–55.

274 erode our "Calvinism": Another issue is whether acceptance of licit drugs legitimizes the use of illicit drugs. Of course, the appropriate use of thymoleptics might diminish illicit drug use by treating the underlying states for which addicts self-medicate. (See the discussion of the self-medication hypothesis of drug abuse, in chapter 8.)

275 "the best thing . . .": Mary Deems Howland, *The Gift of the Other: Gabriel Marcel's Concept of Intersubjectivity in Walker Percy's Novels* (Pittsburgh: Duquesne University Press, 1990), p. 1. A slim volume that has been helpful to me in my thinking about Percy is Linda Whitney Hobson, *Understanding Walker Percy* (Columbia, S.C.: University of South Carolina, 1988). An extraordinarily deep and thorough appreciation of Percy, one that has influenced the discussion that follows, is Robert Coles's book, part biography, part literary criticism, and part original philosophical contribution, *Walker Percy: An American Search* (Boston: Atlantic–Little, Brown, 1978).

276 Edmund Wilson and Lionel Trilling: "Philoctetes: The Wound and the Bow," in Edmund Wilson, *The Wound and the Bow: Seven Studies in Literature*

(Cambridge, Mass.: Riverside Press [Houghton Mifflin], 1941), pp. 272–95; "Art and Neurosis," in Lionel Trilling, *The Liberal Imagination: Essays on Literature and Society* (New York: Viking, 1950), pp. 160–80. See also my column "Heartbreak House," *Psychiatric Times*, December 1987, p. 3ff.

277 "Thus if a drug . . .": Klerman, "Psychotropic Hedonism," p. 3. Klerman's concern was medical treatment of psychiatric illness. He made the point that mental-health professionals, most of whom were psychotherapists, opposed drugs on an arbitrary, often counterfactual, basis. The complete quote is: "Thus if a drug makes you feel good, it not only represents a secondary form of salvation but somehow it is morally wrong and the user is likely to suffer retribution with either dependence, liver damage, or chromosomal change, or some other form of medical-theological damnation. Implicit in this theory of therapeutic change is the philosophy of personal growth, basically a secular variant of the theological view of salvation through good works." We can see from this quote why Aranow formulated "mood brightener," in order to tease apart the issue of drug side effect from that of moral wrong; we have also seen, in our discussion of ethical objections to mood brighteners, how easy it is to slip into pharmacological Calvinism.

277 *"unable* to take account . . .": Walker Percy, "The Coming Crisis in Psychiatry" (1957), collected in his *Signposts in a Strange Land* (New York: Farrar, Straus & Giroux, 1991), pp. 251–62; quotations on pp. 252, 259. In the same volume, see also "The Fateful Rift: The San Andreas Fault in the Modern Mind" (1989), pp. 271–91.

279 "The Message in the Bottle": Collected in Walker Percy, *The Message in the Bottle* (New York: Farrar, Straus and Giroux, 1975), pp. 119–49.

279 "he regularly comes upon bottles . . .": Ibid., p. 120; the messages quoted are from pp. 120–23.

279 "In summary . . .": Ibid., p. 130.

280 "Come! I know your need . . .": Ibid., p. 134.

280 two commuters on a train: Ibid.

280 "To be a castaway . . .": Ibid., p. 144.

280 the resort to psychotherapy or to drugs: Ibid., p. 139.

280 "even if his symptoms": Ibid., p. 140.

285 principle of psychotherapy: Technically, neutrality applies to mental structures. The dynamic therapist should "sit equidistant" from the id, ego,

and superego. In practice, neutrality often entails avoiding assent to, and dissent from, the patient's criticism of people about whom the patient has ambivalent feelings. See my essay "Non-Neutrality," *Psychiatric Times*, September 1992, p. 4.

287   support for a concrete choice: Awareness of such categories as rejection-sensitivity tends to change the relationship between doctor and patient. In this case, I accepted my patient's stated wish to divorce and ignored any mixed feelings she might have had. At the most obvious level, this decision respects Susan's freedom of choice; but when compared with a treatment in which the doctor remains neutral and waits for the patient to initiate each action, this treatment moves the locus of control from the patient to the therapist.

The notion that a therapist is free to "take sides," in assessing a patient's choices in the world, raises profound ethical issues. For instance, we may worry that a therapist who supports a divorce is acting on his or her distorted beliefs about marriage or men or the rescue of vulnerable women. But psychotherapy, at its heart, is a matter of facing reality in good faith. A therapist who sees patients' handicaps partly in terms of relatively fixed aspects of personality—rejection-sensitivity, separation anxiety, inhibition to novelty—must use that perspective in his or her work, not just incidentally but integrally—because the therapist will hear patients' stories differently.

Of course, patients become aware of this change in the psychiatrist's focus. A patient of mine had the following dream: "I am going to a safe-deposit box. I am bringing jewels to deposit. When I open the box, all it contains is hundreds of capsules." I interpreted to her that she was bringing her precious emotions to this safe place, my office, but she feared all she would find was pills. She replied that she associated her growing dependence on me, and the safety of the office, with craziness, and that her engagement in therapy meant she would need many pills. It is natural that medication should become a metaphor in psychotherapies that are accompanied by pharmacotherapy. See also the chapter "The Mind-Mind-Body-Problem Problem," in my book *Moments of Engagement*.

287   psychoanalysts at the Payne Whitney Clinic: Fredric N. Busch, Arnold M. Cooper, et al., "Neurophysiological, Cognitive-Behavioral, and Psychoanalytic Approaches to Panic Disorder: Toward an Integration," *Psychoanalytic Inquiry*, vol. 11 (1991), pp. 316–30; Arnold M. Cooper, "The Relevance of Psychotherapy to Clinical Practice Today," address, Rhode Island Psychiatric Society, Butler Hospital, Providence, R.I., March 2, 1992, 27 pp. The quotations are from the text of Dr. Cooper's speech.

287   the analysts' understanding: I have not done justice to the complexities of the work of the Payne Whitney group. The analysts draw on the full ar-

mamentarium of psychoanalytic theory to integrate the biological findings. They speculate, for example, that the fearfully dependent and unsatisfied child becomes angry at the parent, and then, since the parent is also loved, guilt-ridden. "The child will therefore become fearful not only of loss, but of the arousal or expression of anger for fear of loss. Defenses are triggered, including denial and projection, the latter leading to a perception of the parent as even more rejecting." This perception makes the child feel even less supported, thus heightening the fearful dependency and separation anxiety, and reinforcing the cycle.

The Payne Whitney model makes predictions about the sorts of internal representation of others that adults with this disorder will have (controlling and rejecting) and the life events that will lead to periods of panic (threats to attachment). Such speculation, itself based on clinical observation, allows for further formal research, which can be confirming, disconfirming, or modifying of the original hypotheses—a wonderful event in psychoanalysis, and itself a sign of the predominance of the biological model.

288 impossibly complex and overly specific: Here, for example, is a diagnosis that merits two pages in the newest diagnostic manual, and which I hazard to predict will not stand the test of time: "Gender Identity Disorder of Adolescence or Adulthood, Nontranssexual Type (GIDAANT)." GIDAANT refers to people with anxiety about their masculine or feminine identity; they may cross-dress to lower their anxiety, but if they cross-dress to attain sexual excitation, they get a different diagnosis. (American Psychiatric Association, *Diagnostic and Statistical Manual of Mental Disorders*, 3rd ed., rev. [Washington, D.C.: American Psychiatric Association, 1987], pp. 76–77.)

288 no appropriate niche: James E. Barrett, Jane A. Barrett, et al., "The Prevalence of Psychiatric Disorders in a Primary Care Practice," *Archives of General Psychiatry*, vol. 45 (1988), pp. 1100–1106; Leon Eisenberg, "Treating Depression and Anxiety in Primary Care: Closing the Gap Between Knowledge and Practice," *New England Journal of Medicine*, vol. 326 (1992), pp. 1080–84.

289 a good case . . . for the return of "neurosis": Another possibility is the further expansion of "post-traumatic stress disorder" (PTSD), originally applied to people who had suffered recent trauma (like shell shock or railway spine), but now used also in reference to adults who suffered stresses at crucial developmental phases of childhood. The emergence of PTSD is, under a new name, and with more attention to biological damage, the rebirth of the traumatic theory of neurosis and personality disorder, a century after Freud first proposed it.

Apropos of neurosis, Arnold Cooper, the senior figure in the Payne Whitney group cited above, recently reminded colleagues: "British authors have suggested that the [American diagnostic] system inappropriately focuses on the symptom rather than the high degree of neuroticism out of which the symptom emerges" (Cooper, "Relevance of Psychotherapy," p. 16).

289   The coalescing of diagnoses: I have already mentioned, in connection with the concept of depressive temperament (chapter 6), a movement within descriptive psychiatry to do away with the concept of personality disorder and think only in terms of clinical syndromes, such as recurrent depression. The argument here is an extrapolation of Donald Klein's work with rejection-sensitivity, panic anxiety, and characterologic depression—the notion that much of what looks like disordered character is really a response to a chronic or recurrent mood disorder.

290   Allen's fantasy *Alice:* See my column "Wonderland," *Psychiatric Times,* April 1991, p. 4ff. The film's working title was *The Magical Herbs of Dr. Yang* (Eric Lax, *Woody Allen: A Biography* [New York: Vintage, 1992], p. 321).

292   Prozac works best: An unpublished study from Cornell University finds that good antidepressant responders fall into two groups as regards personality. Some seem cured outright, like many of the patients we have met. Others (like Philip) also report dramatic change, but find the change dislocating. In these patients, the change in feeling about the self is strong, but change in cognition (and organization of the defenses) lags; they generally need psychotherapy to deal with the success of medication. The study, by a group headed by James Kocsis, was described by Cooper in "Relevance of Psychotherapy."

296   spouse as a . . . neurotransmitter: ". . . the psychoanalyst actually *is* a neurotransmitter—a generator of signals, transduced by the receiver into neurochemical activity—initially just inhibiting 'aloneness affect,' but eventually helping to reset the homeostatic controls so that the system responds to a new level or frequency of input" (Winchel, "Self-Mutilation," p. 12). In this passage, Winchel is assuming the patient suffers from reversible damage and that psychoanalysis is equivalent to psychotherapeutic medication in its ability to alter transmitter levels.

297   the self-absorption of Goethe's Werther: Hans-Jurgen van Bose, a German composer, has written a new opera titled *The Sorrows of Young Werther,* but *The New York Times* reports: "The facts of Goethe's original have been reassembled to create something quite distant from it. The tenderness of grief, the sweet self-indulgence of despairing love have been bled away." (Bernard Holland, "New Setting of Goethe's Melancholy Love Story," *New York Times,* August

7, 1992, p. C3.) The review goes on to emphasize how the emotions in the modern opera do not parallel those of the eighteenth-century novel. The reviewer attributes this difference to opera's difficulty in addressing ambiguity, but I wonder whether the difference does not have also to do with a change over time in sensibility as regards affect.

297 Karl Marx and Freud: Daniel Burston, *The Legacy of Erich Fromm* (Cambridge, Mass.: Harvard University Press, 1991), pp. 30–52. The Freudo-Marxists misunderstood the modern trend. They were concerned that sexuality would be repressed. Walker Percy correctly understood it would instead be trivialized.

300 for Freud to have discovered the unconscious: This is, of course, shorthand. There was an unconscious before Freud. See Henri Ellenberger, *The Discovery of the Unconscious* (New York: Basic Books, 1970).

300 a whole climate of opinion: ". . . to us, he is no longer a person / now but a whole climate of opinion / under whom we conduct our different lives" (W. H. Auden, "In Memory of Sigmund Freud [d. Sept. 1939]," in W. H. Auden, *Collected Shorter Poems 1927–1957* [London: Faber & Faber, 1966], pp. 166–70.

APPENDIX: VIOLENCE

301 serotonin and aggression: There is a large literature on aggression and neurotransmitters in man and other animals. The discussion that follows is based largely on Michael J. Raleigh, Michael T. McGuire, et al., "Serotonergic Mechanisms Promote Dominance Acquisition in Adult Male Vervet Monkeys," *Brain Research,* vol. 559 (1991), pp. 181–90; and a series of articles in the *Archives of General Psychiatry,* vol. 49, no. 6 (June 1992). These include: J. Dee Higley, P. T. Mehlman, et al., "Cerebrospinal Fluid Monoamine and Adrenal Correlates of Aggression in Free-Ranging Rhesus Monkeys," pp. 436–41; Burr Eichelman, "Aggressive Behavior: From Laboratory to Clinic: Quo Vadit?," pp. 488–92; Markus J. P. Kruesi, Euthymia D. Hibbs, et al., "A 2-Year Prospective Follow-Up Study of Children and Adolescents with Disruptive Behavior Disorders: Prediction by Cerebrospinal Fluid 5-Hydroxyindolacetic Acid, Homovanillic Acid, and Autonomic Measures?," pp. 429–35; J. John Mann, Anne McBride, et al., "Relationship Between Central and Peripheral Serotonin Indexes in Depressed and Suicidal Psychiatric Inpatients," pp. 442–59. The studies involving serotonin-altering medication given to monkeys include work by Michael McGuire's group (on vervet monkeys);

the study of scarred wild rhesus monkeys is by Stephen Suomi's group. As in the case of depression, other neurotransmitters and hormones, not just serotonin, are implicated in aggression; the parts of the brain involved, although there is overlap, almost certainly differ between depression and aggression. Both are basic, widely and complexly encoded functions. The use of BuSpar for violent retarded patients is associated with John Ratey of Massachusetts General Hospital.

303 Prozac resulted in a marked decline: A study by Maurizio Fava, Jerrold Rosenbaum, and others at Harvard showed "a dramatic decline" in hostility and a decrease in "anger attacks" in eighty-four patients treated with Prozac. Interestingly, the presence of anger attacks predicted positive mood response to Prozac. ("Antidepressants Found to Prevent Depression-Related 'Anger Attacks,'" *Clinical Psychiatry News*, September 1992, p. 6.)

303 What distinguishes the suicides: Indeed, there is a "biological-catharsis" theory that "The act of attempting suicide may make a depressed individual feel better by increasing serotonin activity" (Kevin M. Malone, quoted in "Potential Clinical, Biological Predictors of Suicide Reattempts Identified," *Clinical Psychiatry News*, August 1992, p. 8). The supportive research (showing higher responsivity of serotonin systems in male suicide attempters whose attempts were recent than in those whose attempts occurred longer ago) was done at Western Psychiatric Institute, Pittsburgh, Pa., in conjuction with John J. Mann.

304 Teicher and two colleagues: Martin H. Teicher, Carol C. Glod, and Jonathan O. Cole, "Emergence of Intense Suicidal Preoccupation During Fluoxetine Treatment," *American Journal of Psychiatry*, vol. 147 (1990), pp. 207–10. See also Patricia Thomas, "Sad Attack: Prozac," *Harvard Health Letter*, vol. 16, no. 12 (1991), pp. 1–4.

305 the Teicher report aroused great interest: John J. Mann and Shitij Kapur, "The Emergence of Suicidal Ideation and Behavior During Antidepressant Therapy," *Archives of General Psychiatry*, vol. 48 (1991), pp. 1027–33; Cynthia E. Hoover, "Suicidal Ideation Not Associated with Fluoxetine" (letter), *American Journal of Psychiatry*, vol. 148 (1991), p. 543; Maurizio Fava and Jerrold F. Rosenbaum, "Suicidality and Fluoxetine: Is There a Relationship?," *Journal of Clinical Psychiatry*, vol. 52 (1991), pp. 108–11; Charles M. Beasley, Bruce E. Dornseif, et al., "Fluoxetine and Suicide: A Meta-Analysis of Controlled Trials of Treatment for Depression," *British Medical Journal*, vol. 303 (1991), pp. 685–92; William C. Wirshing, Theodore Van Putten, et al., "Fluoxetine,

Akathisia, and Suicidality: Is There a Causal Connection?" (letter), *Archives of General Psychiatry*, vol. 49 (1992), pp. 580–81.

306 "Examining large, placebo-controlled databases": Wirshing, Van Putten, et al., "Fluoxetine," p. 581.

307 akathisia: The theory is plausible, because the "pacing urge," most often seen as a side effect of antipsychotic medication, has been associated with homicidal and suicidal behavior in psychotic patients. See Teicher, Glod, and Cole, "Emergence of Suicidal Preoccupation," Mann and Kaplan, "Emergence of Suicidal Ideation," and Wirshing, Van Putten, et al., "Fluoxetine."

307 "Because patients seek treatment . . .": Mann and Kapur, "Emergence of Suicidal Ideation," p. 1031. In the elision, I have omitted a long discussion of further research required to clarify any association between Prozac and suicidality.

308 Wesbecker . . . on "Larry King Live": "Prozac: Painful Legacy?," September 26, 1990.

309 "Donahue": February 27, 1991.

309 "lifelong journey of disintegration": "And the horror that unfolded that Thursday morning was merely the final step of a lifelong journey of disintegration, an extreme reflection of the alienation, anger and sorrow with which Wesbecker had been wrestling all his life. The man who stepped off the elevator with the spitting AK-47 was Joe. Himself. Doing what he'd vowed to do." (John Filatreau, "A Life in Pieces" [also titled: "Little Boy Lost: The Emotional Life and Death of Joe Wesbecker"], *Louisville*, January 1990, pp. 26–41.) I have relied very largely on this essay, in conjunction with reporting in the Louisville *Courier-Journal* and other news reports, for the biographical sketch of Wesbecker. I have no knowledge of Wesbecker other than what appeared in the press and on television.

310 McStoots joined "Larry King Live": March 18, 1991. In my account of McStoots, I have relied also on the order dismissing the civil complaint by Judge J. David Francis, Warren [Kentucky] Circuit Court, November 6, 1991, and news stories in the Louisville *Courier-Journal*, Indianapolis *Star*, and the Bowling Green *Daily News*. I have no knowledge of McStoots other than what appeared in the court order, in the press, and on television. Prozac had been prescribed to McStoots not by Dr. Tapp but by another physician, Lawrence Green.

310   Many other cases have been publicized: On "60 Minutes," October 27, 1991, Lesley Stahl reported, "But what about the other 100 plus people they [the Scientologists] claim Prozac made suicidal? We decided to look into some of those cases and what we found were people who, like Wesbecker, had already shown signs of mental instability or suicidal behavior before they ever went on Prozac."

311   the Church of Scientology: See *Time* magazine's cover story of May 6, 1991 ("Scientology: The Cult of Greed," also titled "The Thriving Cult of Greed and Power," pp. 32–39), and the series of stories in the June, July, and September 1991 issues of the *Psychiatric Times* regarding the Scientologists' crusade against psychiatry.

311   people . . . are often leery: This issue is difficult for doctors, too. Deciding when to discontinue medication is complicated by our ignorance regarding the biological process of healing. We have some sense of how stress, under the kindling model, causes anatomical damage in the brain even before a person experiences serious illness. But we do not know whether what takes place when people improve—through psychotherapy, medication, or change in circumstance—is cure or adaptation to injury. In the absence of good models of healing, we need to answer the pharmacologic issue through empirical observation: when can we stop the Prozac?

What evidence we have concerns the use of tricyclic antidepressants for episodes of major depression. Here a number of studies show that, if a person has not been entirely free of symptoms for a substantial period of time, at least five months and perhaps a year, then stopping medication will result in a swift relapse. These studies might be understood to say a patient can safely stop medication if he or she has been well for five to twelve months. But other, more controversial studies show that, if there is any tendency toward relapse, it may be wise to continue medication, probably at a full dose, for a good deal longer, perhaps indefinitely. Even patients who are are past the point where they will relapse immediately may benefit, in terms of the length of time before the next episode, from "continuation" or "maintenance" pharmacotherapy.

It is hard to know just how to apply these findings to the care of people with minor variants of depressive disorders or with the sorts of personality traits—compulsivity, inhibition, low self-esteem—we have discussed. My practice with "good responders" is to taper and stop Prozac after six or eight months. Some patients, those whose symptoms turn on and off as if in response to an electric switch, relapse almost immediately. Others notice a small deterioration in functioning off medication. A good number—over a third—ask to resume medication in the course of the next two or three years, and others may suffer recurrences of some of their problems without requesting medication. But there are people who continue to do very well off all medication, perhaps because of a stable resetting of neuronal functioning, perhaps because of the continuing effect of changes in career, friendships, and self-image, or perhaps for other biological and social reasons.

312 whether antidepressants . . . promote tumor growth: A team from the University of Manitoba injected susceptible rats with either cancer cells or a cancer-causing chemical. They then injected the same rats with salt water, Prozac, or a tricyclic antidepressant, amitriptyline. At certain stages in the brief study (in one model, at day 5 but not day 8), the antidepressant-injected rats had more tumors than the control rats. The study raised questions as to whether antidepressants might be dangerous to patients who already have cancer or who have high exposure to carcinogens. (Lorne J. Brandes, Randi J. Arron, et al., "Stimulation of Malignant Growth in Rodents by Antidepressant Drugs at Clinically Relevant Doses," *Cancer Research,* vol. 52 [1992], pp. 3796–3800.)

The study has a number of problems. For example, the control rats got suspiciously few tumors—fewer than rats on the same regimens in other studies. The number of rats tested was unusually small. And the data presented were scanty. For these and other reasons, it is unclear whether this study is of relevance to humans. The standard assays for carcinogenesis follow rats or mice liable to tumor formation for two years or until death, in the presence of high doses of medication. In those studies, Prozac did not cause cancer and may even have prevented it. A large series of studies in humans shows no connection between antidepressant use and cancer formation or progression, although antidepressants (and probably depression alone, without medication) can under some conditions affect immune function.

It is obviously important to know whether antidepressants promote tumor growth in cancer patients, who often are candidates for these drugs, or in those exposed to carcinogens, such as smokers. It is unclear whether the Brandes study is of clinical significance—it flies in the face of a large number of more thorough studies that failed to show an association between antidepressants and tumor progression—but it serves as a reminder that, despite extensive testing before drugs are introduced, concerns can arise about medications many years (in amitriptyline's case, almost forty years) after their introduction.

Acknowledgments

I could not have written this book without the generous help of patients, colleagues, friends, and family.

In particular, I want to thank the following researchers who discussed their work with me, answered queries, or shared material, often including unpublished monographs: Drs. Huda Akil (University of Michigan), Hagop Akiskal (National Institute of Mental Health), Robert Aranow (Harvard), Frank Ayd (West Virginia University), Ross Baldessarini (Harvard), Mitchell Balter (Tufts), Walter Brown (Brown), Jonathan Cole (Harvard), Arnold Cooper (Cornell), George Heninger (Yale), Jerome Kagan (Harvard), Edward Khanzian (Harvard), Donald Klein (Columbia), Douglas Madsen (University of Iowa), Michael T. McGuire (UCLA), Theodore Nadelson (Tufts), J. Craig Nelson (Yale), Robert Post (National Institute of Mental Health), Mark D. Sullivan (University of Washington, Seattle), Stephen J. Suomi (National Institute of Child Health and Human Development), and Ronald Winchel (Columbia). In addition, the following colleagues offered comments when this book was in manuscript: Drs. Jeffrey Blum, Walter Brown, and Alan Gruenberg.

My collaborators in treating certain of the patients whose stories I have told include: Anita Berger, M.S.W., Elena Gonzales, Ph.D.,

Diana Elliott Lidofsky, Ph.D., and Judith H. Puleston, M.S.W. They, as much as Prozac, are instruments of transformation.

Regarding a book written largely about one proprietary medication, questions will inevitably arise concerning the relationship between the author and the drug's manufacturer. I have had only one contact with Eli Lilly. I spent much of December 9, 1991, at Lilly's international headquarters in Indianapolis, Indiana. I paid for my own plane flight, hotel, and meals. In the morning, I spent two hours discussing the development of Prozac with Drs. Brian Molloy, Ray Fuller, and David Wong, the researchers who created the chemical twenty years earlier. In the afternoon, Ed West, Lilly's director of corporate communications, and his then assistant, Gerianne Hap, kindly permitted me to look through Lilly's library of newspaper clippings and television videotapes. Before that trip, Mr. West had sent me the "Clinical Investigation Brochure" for Prozac (the technical information relied on by drug researchers); subsequently he forwarded scientific reprints and photocopies of news clippings I had specifically requested. I have no relationship to Eli Lilly, and I have no financial stake in the company.

John Schwartz, editor of the *Psychiatric Times*, has printed my monthly column "Practicing" since 1985; though the essays are often speculative or controversial, John has never offered the least hint of editorial interference.

Nan Graham, my editor at Viking, supplied the warmth, enthusiasm, and clarity of judgment that every author hopes for. Courtney Hodell, Nan's assistant, read acutely and managed a host of important details. Going beyond the limited role of literary agent, Chuck Verrill provided valuable advice at each stage of the writing of this book.

Judith Henriques helped in the production of printed drafts from my computer files. Ruthann Gildea of the Isaac Ray Medical Library at Butler Hospital went out of her way to provide prompt assistance in locating technical materials.

My deepest thanks are to my patients. I have tried to protect their privacy, but I hope the spirit of our work together, and of their often heroic lives, is discernible in these pages.

Finally, I could never have written this book without the encouragement and support of my wife, Rachel Schwartz, and the indulgence of our three children, Sarah, Jacob, and Matthew. The drug will never be invented that sustains the spirit the way a family can.

Index

Abuse, 2, 16, 17, 120, 192, 261
 see also Masochism, social; Sexual
  abuse
Academy Forum, 333*n*., 367*n*.
Accidental Tourist, The (Tyler), 320*n*.
Acetylcholine, 55, 57, 58, 60, 61, 65,
  66, 328
Acta Psychiatrica Scandinavica, 330*n*.,
  364*n*.
Adler, Alfred, 199, 221, 354*n*.
Adolescence, rejection-sensitivity in
  late, 100–101
Adoption, 157–58, 343*n*., 344*n*.
"Adrenal Gland Enlargement in Major
  Depression: A Computed Tomo-
  graphic Study," 336*n*.
Adrenal glands, 115, 116
Adrenaline, 115
"Affectional Responses in the Infant
  Monkey," 337*n*.
"Affective Disorders in Referred Chil-
  dren and Younger Siblings of
  Manic Depressives: Mode of On-
  set and Prospective Course,"
  347*n*.
"Affective Flattening: Evaluation and
  Diagnostic Significance," 358*n*.
Affective loading, 14
Affect tolerance, 254, 256, 257, 258,
  269–70

increase of, 259
"Age and Depression," 340*n*.
Aggression, 183, 271, 303, 355*n*.–
  356*n*., 374*n*.–75*n*.
 affective, 302
 predatory, 302
 serotonin and, 301–4, 374*n*.–75*n*.
"Aggressive Behavior: From Laboratory
  to Clinic: Quo Vadit?," 374*n*.
Aging, 135–36
 late-onset depression, 136–43, 340*n*.
Agoraphobia, 78, 79, 82, 84
Akathisia, 307
Akil, Dr. Huda, 335*n*.
Akiskal, Hagop S., 163–66, 167, 178,
  179–80, 323*n*., 335*n*., 336*n*.,
  340*n*., 346*n*., 347*n*.–48*n*.,
  349*n*., 350*n*., 356*n*., 365*n*.
Alcohol, 252, 265
Alcoholism, 1, 2, 13, 14, 158, 164,
  178
 depression in near relatives and, 14–
  15
 heredity and, xiv
 self-esteem and, 198
Alice, 290
Allen, Woody, 223, 290, 304
Allergies, 49, 155, 159
"Aloneness affect," 96, 278, 333*n*.,
  367*n*., 373*n*.

Alprozam, *see* Xanax
American Journal of Psychiatry, 304,
    318*n*., 324*n*., 329*n*., 334*n*.,
    339*n*., 346*n*., 350*n*., 357*n*.,
    360*n*., 364*n*., 375*n*.
American Journal of Social Psychiatry,
    340*n*.
American Political Science Review, 356*n*.
American Psychiatric Association,
    321*n*., 331*n*., 332*n*., 342*n*.,
    349*n*., 350*n*., 360*n*., 363*n*.,
    372*n*.
Amines, biogenic, 52, 55, 62, 133,
    198, 335*n*.
  theory of depression and deficiency
    of, 52–54, 131, 283, 325*n*.–
    326*n*.
  see also Dopamine; Norepinephrine;
    Postsynaptic-hypersensitivity
    model; Serotonin
Amino acids, 87–88
Amitriptyline, *see* Elavil
Amoxepine, *see* Asendin
Amphetamines, 14, 16, 39, 210, 231,
    252, 325*n*., 358*n*., 359*n*.
  for ADHD, 241, 245
  mental acuity and, 244–45
  side effects of, 245
Anafranil (clomipramine), 22, 64–65
  for OCD, 22, 65
  side effects of, 27, 367*n*.
"Anal character," 41, 297
Analogy, drug development by, 54,
    326*n*.
Andreason, Nancy, 358*n*.
Anger, 147, 303, 375*n*.
Angier, Natalie, 356*n*.
Anhedonia, *see* Pleasure, inhibition of
Anhedonia and Affect Deficit States (Clark
    and Fawcett), 358*n*.
"Anhedonia, Hypohedonia and Pleasure
    Capacity in Major Depressive
    Disorders," 358*n*.
Annie Hall, 223
Anorexia, 183, 228
Antecedents of Self-Esteem, The (Cooper-
    smith), 356*n*.
Antianxiety medications, *see* Anxiolytics
Anticholinergics, 328*n*.
Anticonvulsants, 112, 127, 335*n*.
  Dapakote, 335*n*.

Dilantin, 113–14, 116
Tegretol, 111–12, 114
Antidepressants, ix, 9, 14, 47–66,
    72, 87–88, 124–25, 127, 139,
    175–76, 182–83, 197, 198,
    253, 262, 263, 307, 344*n*.,
    345*n*., 355*n*., 378*n*.
  amphetaminelike effect of, 28, 133,
    359*n*.
  as anxiolytics, 82, 84, 175
  best responders to, 373*n*.
  chosen on the basis of side effects, 58
  "clean" versus "dirty," 57–58, 65–
    66
  creativity and, 276–77
  cultural norms and drugs considered,
    269
  discontinuing, 29, 377*n*.
  dosage, 321*n*.
  for drug abusers, 235–36
  as feminist drugs, 39, 40
  mental clarity, to improve, 236–37,
    242, 243
  panic anxiety treated with, 81–82,
    84–85, 86, 175
  personality change from, 178–80
  progressive improvement of symp-
    toms on, 28
  in prolonged bereavement, 254
  recurrent depression, new method of
    treatment of, 125, 337*n*.
  side effects of, 54–60, 125, 147,
    337*n*., 340*n*.
  similarities between MAOIs and Pro-
    zac, 87–89
  suicidality and, 307
  testing of, on animals, 335*n*.
  time necessary to work, 27, 53,
    326*n*.
  tolerance, 305
  tricyclics, 57, 58, 60, 65–66, 88,
    126, 132, 133, 327*n*., 360*n*.,
    377*n*.
  type of depression and specific drug
    effectiveness, 126–27
  as underprescribed, 369*n*.
  women taking, 319*n*., 335*n*.
  see also Ascendin; Anafranil; Desipra-
    mine; Desyrel; Doxepin; Elavil;
    Imipramine; Iproniazid; Isocar-
    boxazid; Lithium; Monoamine-

oxidate inhibitors; Nardil; Pamelor; Prozac; Selective serotonin-reuptake inhibitor; Zoloft
"Antidepressants Found to Prevent Depression-Related 'Anger Attacks,' " 375n.
Antiepileptics, *see* Anticonvulsants
Antihistamines, 49–50, 55, 60, 61, 63
Antipsychotic drugs, *see* Chlorpromazine; Neuroleptics
Anxiety, xi–xii, 42–43, 80–81, 137, 158, 183, 211, 277–78, 281, 292, 348n.
  capacity to bear, 254
  castration, xii
  castration anxiety, 80
  depression and, 158, 173, 344n., 349n.
  distinctions among types of, 83, 331n., 332n.
  evolutionary biology, role in, 253
  existential, 280, 297
  function of, 255
  genetic or biological component of, 324n., 331n.
  at the heart of psychoanalysis, xii, 82
  meaningless, xii, 316n.
  medication as cause of, xii–xiii
  Oedipal, xii
  as response to novelty, 158
  separation anxiety, 83, 286, 288, 333n.
  "signal," xii
  social, 260
  studies of separated monkeys, 121, 129, 130
  see also Anxiolytics; Panic anxiety
Anxiety (Klein), 323n.
"Anxiety and the Capacity to Bear It," 364n.
Anxiety neurosis, xii, 78–80, 197, 332n.
  see also Panic anxiety
Anxiety: New Research and Changing Concepts (Klein and Rabkin), 323n., 325n., 330n., 332n.
"Anxiety Reconceptualized," 323n., 324n., 325n., 330n., 331n.
Anxiolytics (antianxiety medications), 24–25, 39, 84, 85
  antidepressants and, 82, 84, 175

for depression, 325n.
  side effects of, 325n.
  as underprescribed, 369n.
  see also BuSpar; Miltown; Valium; Xanax
Apomorphine, 61, 64
Appetitive anhedonia, 232, 233, 359n.
Appetitive pleasure, 231, 232, 233, 360n.
"Approaches to Measuring the Efficacy of Drug Treatment of Personality Disorders: An Analysis and Program," 330n.
Approaches to the Mind: Movement of the Psychiatric Schools from Sects to Science (Havens), 323n.
Aranow, Robert, 156, 251–52, 261–262, 265, 363n., 364n., 365n., 366n., 367n., 370n.
Archives of General Psychiatry, 320n., 322n., 332n., 333n., 336n., 338n., 340n., 347n., 349n., 350n., 351n., 355n., 358n., 360n., 369n., 372n., 374n., 375n., 376n.
"Are Psychiatric Educators 'Losing the Mind?,' " 357n.
"Are Schizophrenia and Affective Disorder Related? A Selective Literature Review," 324n.
Aristotle, 163
Arron, Randi J., 378n.
Art and neurosis, 275–77
"Art and Neurosis," 276
Asendin (amoxepine), 12
Assertiveness, 172, 174, 215, 303
Attention, need for, 69–70, 74, 90, 91
Attention-deficit disorder, 45, 183, 239–40, 359n., 360n.
"Attention Deficit Hyperactivity Disorder," 360n.
Attention-deficit hyperactivity disorder (ADHD), 240–45, 360n.–62n.
Atypical depression, 72, 73, 89, 181, 224–25, 232, 332n., 333n.
  Prozac for, 89, 181
Auden, W. H., 374n.
"Augmenters," 351n.
Autism, 227

Autonomy:
  as ethical yardstick, 256
  Prozac's effect on, 265–66, 268
Awakenings, 186
Ayd, Frank J., 323*n.*, 324*n.*, 325*n.*,
    327*n.*, 329*n.*

Backlash against Prozac, xvii–xviii,
    308–11, 318*n.*
"Backlash Against Prozac," xvii
Bakker, Jim, xvi
Baldessarini, Ross, 325*n.*, 326*n.*
Ballenger, James C., 334*n.*, 339*n.*
Balter, Jerome Levine, 369*n.*
Balter, Mitchell E., 368*n.*
Baltimore, David, 317*n.*
Barbiturates, 39, 93
Barkley, Russell A., 360*n.*
Barrett, James E., 322*n.*, 340*n.*, 346*n.*
Barrett, Jane A., 322*n.*, 372*n.*
Baxter, Lewis R., Jr., 338*n.*
Beasley, Charles M., 375*n.*
Begley, Sharon, 351*n.*
Behavioral Genetics, 344*n.*
"Behavioral Inhibition in Young Chil-
    dren," 341*n.*
"Behavioral Inhibition to the Unfamil-
    iar," 341*n.*
Belash, Rachel Phillips, 368*n.*
Benadryl (diphenhydramine), 49, 50,
    61
Bereavement, 254, 269–70, 367*n.*–
    368*n.*
"Beyond Serotonin: A Multiaminergic
    Perspective on Abnormal Be-
    havior," 350*n.*
"Biochemical Property Relating to
    Power Seeking in Humans, A,"
    356*n.*
*Biochemistry of Functional and Experimen-
    tal Psychosis, The* (Weil-Malherbe
    and Szara), 328*n.*
Biogenic amines, *see* Amines, biogenic
"Biogenic Amines and Depression: Bio-
    chemical and Pharmacological
    Separation of Two Types of
    Depression," 339*n.*
"Biological Basis of Childhood Shy-
    ness," 341*n.*
Biological determinism, xv, 18, 105,
    154, 160, 161, 195

IQ and heredity, xiii, 154, 342*n.*
  of temperament, *see* Temperament
Biological materialism, xii–xiv, xv
"Biological Measures: Their Theoretical
    and Diagnostic Value in Psy-
    chiatry," 330*n.*
Bipolar affective disorder, *see* Manic-
    depression (bipolar affective
    disorder)
Blackwell, Barry, 56, 323*n.*, 324*n.*,
    325*n.*, 327*n.*
Blakeslee, Sandra, 316*n.*
Blood pressure, 55
  MAOIs and, 56, 327*n.*
"Blood Serotonin and Social Rank
    Among Human Males," 356*n.*
Bloomsbury group, 41
Bonding, 96
"Book Notes: A British Doctor Casts
    Doubt on Primo Levi's
    Suicide . . . ," 340*n.*
*Borderline Personality Disorders: The Con-
    cept, the Syndrome, the Patient*
    (Hartocollis), 330*n.*
Bourgeois, Jay, 362*n.*
Bowling Green *Daily News*, 376*n.*
Boy-craziness, 67, 68–69, 75, 102
Brain Research, 355*n.*, 374*n.*
Branch, S., 336*n.*, 343*n.*
Brandes, Lorne J., 378*n.*
Breuer, Josef, 331*n.*
Britain, 43
British Journal of Psychiatry, 334*n.*
British Medical Journal, 375*n.*
Brock, Dan W., 263–64, 366*n.*
Brodaty, Henry, 340*n.*
Brome, Vincent, 345*n.*
"Brother Sun, Sister Moon," 351*n.*
Brown, Norman O., 297
Brown, Serena-Lynn, 339*n.*, 350*n.*
Brown University, 155, 342*n.*
Bulimia, 228
Bulletin of the Menninger Clinic,
    358*n.*
Bunney, William E., Jr., 326*n.*, 339*n.*
Buproprion, *see* Wellbutrin
Burston, Daniel, 322*n.*, 340*n.*, 374*n.*
Burti, Lorenzo, 369*n.*
Busch, Fredric N., 371*n.*
BuSpar (buspirone), 93, 303
Buspirone, *see* BuSpar

Cade, John F. J., 44, 84, 323*n.*
Caldwell, Mark, 324*n.*
California Task Force to Promote Self-
    Esteem, 353*n.*
Campbell, Iain C., 339*n.*
Camus, Albert, 296
Cancer, 312, 378*n.*
Cancer Research, 378*n.*
"Can Evolutionary Theory Help Us Un-
    derstand the Proximate Mecha-
    nism and Symptom Changes
    Characteristic of Persons with
    Dysthmic Disorder?," 348*n.*–
    349*n.*
Capacity for Emotional Growth, The
    (Zetzel), 329*n.*, 364*n.*
Capitalism, 271, 297
Carbamazepine, *see* Tegretol
"Carbamazepine Prophylaxis in Refrac-
    tory Affective Disorders: A Fo-
    cus on Long-Term Follow-Up,"
    334*n.*
Case vignettes:
    Allison, 204–8, 216–17, 259, 278,
        295
    Daniel, 137–42
    Gail, 92–95, 258, 278
    Hillary, 224–27, 233, 247, 278,
        292–93, 359*n.*
    Jerry, 173–75, 194, 245–46,
        365*n.*
    Julia, 22–41, 92, 172, 194, 258,
        278
    Lucy, 67–70, 76, 89–90, 102–7,
        124, 194
    Mr. B., 304–5
    Ms. B., 265–67, 268
    Paul, 217–21, 259, 278
    Philip, 291–92, 373*n.*
    privacy issues, 315*n.*–16*n.*
    Sally, 144–48, 162, 172, 176, 194,
        195, 196, 258, 352*n.*
    Sam, ix–xi, xvi, 17, 244, 247, 282,
        315*n.*, 316*n.*
    Sonia, 237–39, 242–43, 244, 246,
        247
    Susan, 285–87, 371*n.*
    Tess, 1–21, 33–37, 92, 124, 259,
        278, 293
    William M., 202–4,
        354*n.*

Cassell, Eric, 365*n.*
Castration anxiety, xii, 80
"Catecholamine Hypothesis of Affective
    Disorders: A Review of Support-
    ing Evidence," 339*n.*
"Caudate Glucose Metabolic Rate
    Changes with Both Drug and
    Behavior Therapy for Obsessive-
    Compulsive Disorder," 338*n.*
"Cerebrospinal Fluid Monoamine and
    Adrenal Correlates of Aggression
    in Free-Ranging Rhesus Mon-
    keys," 374*n.*
Character:
    characteriologic depressives, 163–66,
        178–80, 181
    defined, 148–49, 340*n.*
    see also Personality; Temperament
"Characteristics of Responders to Fluox-
    etine," 338*n.*
"Characterological Depressions: Clinical
    and Sleep EEG 'Subaffective
    Dysthymias' from 'Character
    Spectrum Disorders,' " 346*n.*–
    347*n.*
Charisma, 21
Charney, Dennis S., 332*n.*, 339*n.*
Charter Lakeside Hospital, 348*n.*
Chateaubriand, François-Auguste-René
    de, 20, 297
Chess, Stella, 340*n.*, 341*n.*
Child Development, 341*n.*
Childhood Environment and Adult Disease,
    336*n.*
"Childhood Parental Loss and Adult
    Psychopathology in Women: A
    Twin Study Perspective," 351*n.*
Chlordiazepoxide, *see* Librium
Chloroamphetamine, 328*n.*
Chlorpromazine (Thorazine), 50, 80,
    186
Church of Scientology, *see* Scientologists
Citizens Commission on Human
    Rights, 311
"Citalopram: Clinical Effect Profile in
    Comparison with Clomipramine
    A Controlled Multicenter
    Study," 337*n.*
Clarity of thought, *see* Sluggishness of
    thought
Clark, David L., 230, 358*n.*, 359*n.*

"Clinical and Ethical Issues Raised by the Possible Development of 'Mood Brighteners,' " 363*n*.
Clinical Psychiatry News, 336*n*., 348*n*., 375*n*.
Clomipramine, *see* Anafranil
Cloninger, C. Robert, 185–90, 350*n*.–351*n*.
Cocaine, 16, 231, 235, 252, 256, 263
Coccarro, Emil F., 336*n*.
Cocks, Geoffrey, 345*n*.
Coercion in administration of drugs, 251
  social, 272–75
Cognitive therapy, 128
Coitus interruptus, 78
Cole, Jonathan O., 318*n*., 361*n*., 375*n*., 376*n*.
Coleridge, Samuel Taylor, 271
Coles, Robert, 316*n*., 369*n*.
Collected Shorter Poems 1927–1957 (Auden), 374*n*.
"Coming Crisis in Psychiatry, The," 370*n*.
Compulsive personality disorder, 26, 27, 33, 136, 158, 181, 183
  compulsions defined, 26
  depression along with, 35, 36, 41–42, 323*n*.
  Julia, 22–46
  reevaluation of male, 41
  studies of separated monkeys, compulsive behavior found in, 129, 130
Concentration, 206, 225, 241, 349*n*., 362*n*.
"Conditioning and Sensitization in the Longitudinal Course of Affective Illness," 334*n*.
Confessions of an English Opium Eater (De Quincey), 271
Confidence, 9, 10, 11, 21, 94, 220, 242, 258, 272, 297
  see also Self-esteem
Conservation of mood, 252, 262, 311
Consummatory anhedonia, 232, 233, 359*n*.
Consummatory pleasure, 231–32
Cooper, Arnold M., 355*n*., 371*n*., 373*n*.
Cooper, J. E, 323*n*.

Coopersmith, Stanley, 356*n*.
Copernicus, Nicolaus, 297
Cornell University, 355*n*., 373*n*.
Corticotropin-releasing factor (CRF), 116–17
Cortisol, 115–16, 117–18, 121, 128, 135
  inhibition and levels of, 152, 153
  levels of, in depressed adults, 116, 336*n*.
"Cosmetic psychopharmacology," x, xv, xvi, 15, 97, 184, 246–49, 317*n*.
Cosmetic surgery, 273
Courage, *see* Confidence
Creativity:
  melancholic temperament and, 163, 346*n*.
  suffering and, 275–77
"Criteria for the 'Soft' Bipolar Spectrum: Treatment Implications," 347*n*.
"Critical Discussion of *DSM-III* Dysthymic Disorder, A," 350*n*.
"Cross-National Comparison of Anti-Anxiety/Sedative Drug Use, A," 369*n*.
"Cross-National Study of the Extent of Anti-Anxiety/Sedative Drug Use," 369*n*.
Crossover design, 213, 214
"CSF Monamine Metabolite Concentrations Vary According to Age, Rearing, and Sex, and Are Influenced by the Stressor of Social Separation in Rhesus Monkeys," 336*n*.
Cultural determinism, 161
Cultural expectations, 297, 298
  influence on evidence scientists attend to, xiv
  medication used to meet, 41, 269
  mood brighteners to reinforce, 254, 256–57
  perfectionism and, 38, 39, 40
  Prozac and, 17, 20, 270–72
  of women, 38–41, 172, 270–71
Current Medical Research and Opinion, 369*n*.
Currents in Affective Illness, 343*n*., 344*n*.

"Cybernetics, Activation, and Drug Effects," 330n.

Dalmane (flurazepam), 85
Danforth, Loring M., 367n.
Danish University Antidepressant
    Group, 337n.
Darwin, Charles, 297
Davis, John M., 339n.
Death of a parent, 1, 67, 164, 193,
    351n.
Death Rituals of Rural Greece, The, 367n.
"Definition Psychopharmacology of
    Spontaneous Panic and Phobia,
    The," 331n.
De Fries, J. C., 344n.
Degler, Carl N., xiv, 161, 298, 317n.,
    345n., 346n.
Delgado, Pedro, 332n., 339n.
Delinquency, 227
De Montigny, Claude, 332n.
Denmark, 126, 337n.
Depakote (divalproex sodium), 335n.
Dependency, 252
Depression, ix–xi, 1–21, 45, 115,
    124–125, 133–34, 146, 255,
    296, 304, 361n.–62n., 375n.
  affiliative needs and, 96
  aging and, 135–36
  alcoholism in a near relative and,
    14–15
  amine deficiency theory, 52–54,
    131, 283, 325n.–26n.
  anatomical change related to, 123–24
  anxiety and, 158, 173, 344n., 349n.
  atypical, *see* Atypical depression
  capacity to bear, 254
  case vignettes, 1–7, 93–94, 137–42,
    304–5
  characteriologic depression, 163–66,
    178–80, 181
  compulsiveness along with, 35, 36,
    41–42, 322n.–23n.
  cortisol levels as marker for, 116,
    336n.
  distinction between depressive temperament and trauma-caused
    depression, 164–66, 178–80
  dysthymia, *see* Dysthymia
  evolutionary biology, role in, 255

"extinction," 358n.
failure to medicate, 125
formes frustes of, *see* Pleasure, inhibition of; Self-esteem, low; Sluggishness of thought
  as functionally autonomous, 123–24
  genetic factors in, 324n.
  inhibition and, 146, 156, 158
  inhibition of pleasure and, 228, 229
  late-onset, 136–43, 340n.
  learning disorders and, 360n.–61n.
  major, 25, 50–51, 96, 123, 125,
    166, 178, 247, 349n., 351n.,
    377n.
    Prozac for, 65, 135
  minor, 100, 124, 125, 180, 197,
    246, 247, 263, 292, 304–5,
    323n.
    low self-esteem as *forme fruste* of, *see*
      Self-esteem
    Prozac for, 26, 135, 181, 227
  moral sensibility and, 294–95
  postsynaptic-hypersensitivity model,
    131–33, 339n.
  prevalence of, 48
  as progressive, kindled illness, 114,
    122, 283
  Prozac for, *see* Prozac, for depression
  rapid cycling, 334n.
  recurrent, 5–6, 99, 100, 109, 124,
    125–26, 166, 234, 334n.,
    373n.
    new method for treating, 125–26,
      337n.
  remission, 5
  sense of reality and, 253
  soft signs of, 5
  stress hormones and, 115–16, 117–
    118, 121
  studies of separated monkeys, 120,
    121, 129, 130
  in successive generations, 1, 3, 5, 9–
    10, 14
  suicide and, *see* Suicidal patients;
    Suicide
  treatment before antidepressants, 48–
    49
  in women, 357n.
    reasons for proportionally higher
      incidence of, 319n.
  "wrong" drugs for, 132, 325n.

Depression (*cont.*)
see also Antidepressants
"Depression and Anhedonia," 358*n*.
"Depression and Polypharmacy," 327*n*.
"Depression Following Reserpine: A Reevaluation," 326*n*.
Depressive personality, 163–66, 180–181
Depressive temperament, see Temperament, depressive/melancholic
De Quincey, Thomas, 271
Descriptive psychiatry, 288–90, 372*n*.–373*n*.
Desipramine (Norpramin), 57, 58, 88, 131, 183, 339*n*., 359*n*.–60*n*., 361*n*.
Desyrel (trazodone), 59
"Developmental Influence on Serotonergic System and Timidity in the Nonhuman Primate," 336*n*., 337*n*.
Development of drugs, 54, 64
Development of Prozac, 60–64, 299, 327*n*., 328*n*.
Diagnosis and Drug Treatment of Psychiatric Disorders: Adults and Children (Klein, Gittelman, et al.), 330*n*.
Diagnosis of mental illness, 43–46, 321*n*., 323*n*., 373*n*.
   animal studies and specific, 129–30
   descriptive psychiatry, challenge to, 288–90
   limitations of diagnostic specificity, 46, 324*n*.
   medication response and, 15, 16, 35–36, 42, 44–45, 72, 97
   pharmacological dissection, 45, 241, 324*n*., 361*n*.
   obsessional-to-hysteric continuum, 37
   obsessive-compulsive disorder, 32–33, 36–37
   pharmacologic dissection, 84
   undiagnosable patients, 32–33, 288–89, 322*n*.
Diagnostic and Statistical Manual of Mental Disorders (American Psychiatric Association):
   2nd edition, 331*n*.
   3rd edition, 321*n*., 360*n*.

3rd revised edition, 321*n*., 360*n*., 372*n*.
Diazepam, see Valium
Dilantin, 113–14, 116
Diphenhydramine, see Benedryl; Sominex
Discontinuing Prozac, 10, 18–19, 29–30, 102, 311–12, 377*n*.–78*n*.
Discoveries in Biological Psychiatry (Ayd and Blackwell), 323*n*.–24*n*., 325*n*., 327*n*.
Discovery of the Unconscious, The (Ellenberger), 374*n*.
Disorganization of thought, see Sluggishness of thought
Diuretics, 25
Divalproex sodium, see Depakote
Division of Health Professional Analysis, Department of Health and Human Services, 320*n*.
Divorce, 193, 285–87
"Doctors, Drugs, and the Medical Model," 366*n*.
Domek, Carol J., 336*n*.
Dominance, 302
Dominance hierarchy, 211–15
"Donahue," xvii, 309, 318*n*.
Dooling, E., 336*n*., 343*n*.
Dopamine, 58, 186–87, 241, 358*n*., 359*n*., 361*n*.
Dornseif, Bruce E., 338*n*., 375*n*.
Dowling, Colette, 353*n*.
Downs, John, 347*n*.
Doxepin (Sinequan), 305
"Dream of the Human Genome, The," 317*n*.
Drug abuse, 45, 228, 231, 235–36, 245, 369*n*.
   boundary between licit and illicit drugs, 16
   self-medication hypothesis, 235, 369*n*.
   see also Alcoholism
Drug development, 54, 64, 326*n*.
   Prozac, 60–64, 299, 327*n*., 328*n*.
"Drugs, Sports, and Ethics," 273, 368*n*.
Duane, Drake D., 361*n*.
Dukakis, Olympia, 191
Dunlop, Stephen R., 338*n*.
Dunn, Judy, 351*n*.

Dworkin, Gerald, 365n.
"Dyslexia: Neurobiological and Behavioral Correlates," 361n.
Dysthymia, 25, 166, 167, 224–25, 242, 260, 269, 347n.–49n., 355n.
 ADHD confused with, 241, 361n.
 as diagnostic category, 25, 321n.
 equal frequency in men and women, 320n.
 formes frustes of, *see* Pleasure, inhibition of; Self-esteem, low; Sluggishness of thought
 inhibited temperament and, 167–71, 349n.
 McGuire's study of, 168–71, 192, 202, 269
 OCD and, 46
 Prozac for, 179–80, 181
 Prozac's effectiveness for women with, 348n.
 response to medication, 180
 subaffective, *see* Subaffective dysthymia
 type of stress and, 192–93
 see also Depression

"Early Onset Dysthymia," 350n.
"Early Stress and Adult Emotional Reactivity in Rhesus Monkeys," 336n., 337n., 338n.
Eating disorders, 45, 182–83, 228
"Effectiveness in Psychiatric Care: I. A Cross-National Study of the Process of Treatment and Outcomes of Major Depressive Disorder," 369n.
"Effect of Repetitive Infant-Infant Separation of Young Monkeys," 336n.
"Effects of Imipramine Treatment of Separation-Induced Social Disorders in Rhesus Monkeys," 336n.
"Effects of MDMA and Other Methylenedioxy-Substituted Phenylalkylamines on the Structure of Rat Locomotor Activity," 366n.
Eichelman, Burr, 374n.
Eisenberg, Leon, 322n., 372n.
Eisenhardt, Kathleen, 362n.
Elavil (amitriptyline), 57

Electra complex, 90
Electroconvulsive shock, 48, 139, 241
Eli Lilly, 60–62, 310, 318n., 328n., 380
Ellenberger, Henri, 374n.
"Emergence of Intense Suicidal Preoccupation During Fluoxetine Treatment," 318n., 375n., 376n.
"Emergence of Suicidal Ideation and Behavior During Antidepressant Therapy, The," 375n.
Empathy, 34, 128–29, 295, 338n.
"Endogenomorphic Depression: A Conceptual and Terminological Revision," 333n., 358n.
Endorphins, 358n., 359n.
 receptors in the brain, 263
Epilepsy, kindled, 110–14
Epinephrine, 115
"Episode and Stress Sensitization in the Longitudinal Course of Affective Disorders: Role of Proto-Oncogenes and Other Transcription Factors," 334n.
Equus, 276
Erickson, Milton, 128
Estrogen, 262
Ethical concerns, 21, 234, 243–45, 247–49, 250–85, 291–95, 299–300, 352n., 363n.–74n.
"Ethics and the Perfection of Psychopharmacology," 365n.
Evolutionary biology, 171–72, 269
 criticism of mood brighteners from viewpoint of, 254–55, 256, 260–61
"Evolutionary Biology: A Basic Science for Psychiatry?," 364n.
Excitation behavior, 231
Extraversion, 150, 160, 163, 166, 174
"Eye on America," xvii

"Falling Asleep Up North," 322n.
False-suffocation alarm hypothesis, 83, 288
"False Suffocation Alarms and Spontaneous Panics: Subsuming the CO_2 Hypersensitivity Theory," 332n.
"Fateful Rift: The San Andreas Fault in the Modern Mind, The," 370n.

Fava, Maurizio, 375*n.*
Fawcett, Jan, 230, 358*n.*, 359*n.*
Feeling Good and Doing Better: Ethics and Nontherapeutic Drug Use (Murray, Gaylin, and Macklin), 366*n.*, 368*n.*
Fein, Esther B., 340*n.*
Fifth World Congress of Biological Psychiatry, 369*n.*
Fight-or-flight response, 55, 115
Filatreau, John, 376*n.*
Finz, Leonard, 308, 309
Fiorinal, 93, 95
5-hydroxytryptamine, *see* Seratonin
Fluoxetine (Prozac), *see* Prozac
"Fluoxetine, Akathisia, and Suicidality: Is There a Causal Connection?," 375*n.*–76*n.*
"Fluoxetine and Suicide: A Meta-Analysis of Controlled Trials of Treatment for Depression," 375*n.*
"Fluoxetine Found Effective in Dysthymia," 348*n.*
Flurazepam, *see* Dalmane
Food and Drug Administration (FDA), 7, 85, 262, 324*n.*
  drug approval by, 65
Formes frustes (partial illness), 163, 197–249, 353*n.*, 360*n.*
  defined, 197, 353*n.*
  inhibition of pleasure, *see* Pleasure, inhibition of
  low self-esteem, *see* Self-esteem
  sluggishness of thought, *see* Sluggishness of thought
"For Shame: Why Americans Should Be Wary of Self-Esteem," 353*n.*
Frances, Allen J., 350*n.*
Francis, Judge J. David, 376*n.*
Frazer, Alan, 332*n.*
Freud, Sigmund, 72, 73, 84, 159, 161, 197, 228, 297, 300, 372*n.*, 374*n.*
  on accuracy and privacy requirements in case histories, 315*n.*–16*n.*
  on Adler's work, 199, 354*n.*
  anxiety neurosis, 78–80, 197
  excitation reduction, 231
  on repressed capacity to enjoy, 223
Freud, Sophie Lowenstein, 103, 104

"From Depression to Sadness in Women's Psychotherapy," 357*n.*
Fromm, Erich, 277–78, 297, 340*n.*
Fuller, Ray W., 60, 62–63, 64, 328*n.*
Functional autonomy, 75–76, 97, 101, 102, 107, 128, 193, 287
  animal model supporting, 123, 130
  biologic image of, 113
  depression and, 123–24
Functional theory of psychopathology, 183–84

Galanter, Marc, 360*n.*
Galvin, Ruth M., 341*n.*, 343*n.*, 346*n.*, 358*n.*
Garcia Coll, Cynthia, 341*n.*
Gastrointestinal symptoms, inhibition and, 342*n.*
Gaylin, Willard, 366*n.*, 368*n.*
Gender Identity Disorder of Adolescence or Adulthood, Nontranssexual Type (GIDAANT), 372*n.*
Gender-role conflict, 31
Gervais, J. C., 344*n.*
Geyer, Mark A., 366*n.*
Gift of the Other: Gabriel Marcel's Concept of Intersubjectivity in Walker Percy's Novels, The (Howland), 369*n.*
Gittelman, Rachel, 330*n.*, 332*n.*
Glass Menagerie, The, 191, 201, 351*n.*
Glick, Ira D., 369*n.*
Glod, Carol C., 318*n.*, 375*n.*, 376*n.*
"Glucocorticoid Actions in the Hippocampus: Implications for Affective Disorders," 336*n.*
Glueck, Bernard, 354*n.*
Goethe, Johann, 20, 297, 373*n.*
Good Health Magazine, 321*n.*
Goodwin, Frederick K., 326*n.*, 337*n.*
Gosse, Edmund, 41
Gralnick, Alexander, 332*n.*, 340*n.*
Green, Lawrence, 376*n.*
Greenacre, Phyllis, 331*n.*
Greene, Graham, 225, 357*n.*–58*n.*
Greenhill, Maurice H., 332*n.*
Gruber, C., 342*n.*

Hair-pulling, 265, 267, 367*n.*
Halcion (triazolam), 85
Haley, Jay, 338*n.*

Hall, W., 336*n.*, 343*n.*

Harlow, Harry F., 119, 336*n.*, 337*n.*

"Harm avoidance," 186, 187–88, 190

Hart, Gary, xvi

Hartocollis, Peter, 330*n.*

Harvard Educational Review, 342*n.*

Harvard Health Letter, 375*n.*

Harvard Magazine, 341*n.*, 358*n.*

Harvard University, 375*n.*

Hasert, M. F., 338*n.*

Hastings Center Report, 365*n.*

Havens, Leston, 323*n.*

Haykal, Radwan F., 342*n.*, 348*n.*, 350*n.*

"Heartbreak House," 370*n.*

Heart rate, inhibition and, 152–53, 157, 159, 343*n.*

Hedonic capacity, 227–30, 233, 234, 235, 262, 265, 358*n.*

"Hedonic Capacity: Some Conjectures," 358*n.*

" 'Hedonic Capacity' Ten Years Later: Some Clarifications," 358*n.*

Hedonism, 263–65, 366*n.*–67*n.*

Heidegger, Martin, xii, 316*n.*

Heninger, George R., 339*n.*

Heroin, 252, 263, 358*n.*

Hibbs, Euthymia D., 374*n.*

"Hidden Mental Health Network: Provision of Mental Health Services by Non-Psychiatrist Physicians," 320*n.*

"Hidden Mental Health Network: Treatment of Mental Illness by Nonpsychiatric Physicians," 320*n.*

Higley, J. D., 336*n.*, 337*n.*, 338*n.*, 374*n.*

Hippocrates, 163

Histamine, 57, 58, 61, 65

"History of Fluoxetine, a Selective Inhibitor of Serotonin Uptake and Antidepressant Drug (Prozac): My Recollection of the Formative Year," 328*n.*

Histrionic personality disorder, 89

Hobson, Linda Whitney, 369*n.*

Holland, Bernard, 373*n.*

Hollander, Eric, 316*n.*

Homology, drug development by, 54, 326*n.*

Hoover, Cynthia E., 375*n.*

Horng, Jong S., 328*n.*

Howland, Mary Deems, 369*n.*

Hull, R. F. C., 345*n.*

Human Diversity (Lewontin), 351*n.*

Humors, 162–63, 166, 299

"Hyperactive Boys Almost Grown Up: V. Replication of Psychiatric Status," 360*n.*

Hyperactive Child, Adolescent, and Adult: Attention Deficit Disorder Through the Lifespan, The (Wender), 361*n.*

Hypersomnia, idiopathic central-nervous-system, 225

Hypertension, *see* Blood pressure

Hyperthymic personality, 16–17, 165–166, 167, 242, 260, 261, 272, 320*n.*, 347*n.*

Hyperthymic temperament, 13, 16, 162, 165–66, 201–2, 260, 297

Hypohedonia, 229–31, 234, 235

Hypomania, 17, 162, 167, 242

Hysteria, 33, 37, 72–74, 91

  medication of, 73–74, 76–77, 86–87

  symptoms of, 72–73

Hysteroid dysphoria, 72, 76–77, 86–87, 89, 90–91, 96, 333*n.*

  characteristics of, 74–75, 102

  see also Rejection-sensitivity

"Hysteroid Dysphoria," 330*n.*

Illicit drug use, licit versus, 16

  see also Drug abuse

Imipramine (Tofranil), xvi, 4–5, 7, 19, 36, 56–57, 80, 126, 305, 326*n.*, 327*n.*, 328*n.*

  anxiety treated with, 81–82, 84–85, 86

  consummatory pleasure and, 232

  dosage, 321*n.*

  effect on biogenic amines, 52, 53

  improvement of classically depressed patients on, 54, 326*n.*

  introduction of, 50–51

  migraines helped by, 93

  personality affected by, 177–78

  side effects of, 4, 7, 54–55, 57, 84

  time necessary to work, 53

"Imipramine Story, The," 324*n.*, 325*n.*

Impedance model of anhedonia, 230
"Inadequate Evidence and Illogical Conclusions," 342*n*.
Inderal (propanolol), 93
Indianapolis *Star*, 376*n*.
Indiana University, 126, 338*n*.
"Infantile Expression of Avidity in Relation to Later Assessments, The," 342*n*.
"Infant Predictors," 344*n*., 346*n*.
Inferiority complex, 199
Inflexibility, 187
Informed consent, 251
Inhibition, 122, 123, 144–46, 150–156, 162, 167–96, 283
   abusive relationships and, 170–72, 192
   animal studies, 156–59, 161
   depression and, 146, 156, 158
   depressive personality, 164
   dysthymia and inhibited temperament, 167–71, 348*n*., 349*n*.
   of dysthymic women, 168, 169
   evolutionary biology and, 171–72
   inborn, 144, 146, 150–61, 343*n*., 344*n*.
   Kagan's studies of, 150–54, 155, 161, 341*n*., 342*n*., 343*n*.
   physiology and, 152–53, 157, 159, 343*n*.
   social consequences of, 169–70, 172–75
"In Memory of Sigmund Freud," 374*n*.
"In Our Wild Studies from a Rhesus Colony," 343*n*., 344*n*.
In Search of Human Nature: The Decline and Revival of Darwinism in American Social Thought (Degler), 317*n*., 345*n*., 346*n*.
Insomnia, 54, 197–98, 225
Insulin, 48
International Review of Psychiatry, 334*n*.
"Interrelationship of Hysteroid Dysphoria and Borderline Personality Disorder," 330*n*.
Introversion, 150, 160, 163, 164, 166, 171, 172
Iproniazid (Marsilid), 47–49, 51, 55
   biogenic amines and, 52, 325*n*.–26*n*.
IQ, 154, 316*n*.
   heredity and, xiii, 154, 342*n*.

IQ Controversy, the Media, and Public Policy, The (Snyderman and Rothman), 342*n*.
"IQ: Far Science for Dark Deeds," 342*n*.
"Is Early Onset Dysthymia More Treatable Today?," 342*n*.
"Is Everybody Happy," 321*n*., 322*n*.
Isocarboxazid (Marplan), 324*n*.
"Is Suicide a Cause of Death," 340*n*.

Jackson, Stanley W., 323*n*., 346*n*.
Jagger, Mick, 39
JAMA, 369*n*.
James, William, 211
Jelliffe, Smith Ely, 354*n*.
Jensen, Arthur, 342*n*.
Jews, 160, 345*n*.
Journal of Abnormal Psychology, 336*n*.
Journal of Affective Disorders, 337*n*., 340*n*.
Journal of Clinical Psychiatry, 316*n*., 375*n*.
Journal of Clinical Psychopharmacology, 334*n*.
Journal of Nervous and Mental Disease, 369*n*.
Jung, Carl, 150, 159–60, 163, 171, 345*n*.
Jung (Brome), 345*n*.

Kagan, Jerome, 150–55, 159, 161, 167, 176, 284, 341*n*., 342*n*., 343*n*., 344*n*., 346*n*., 349*n*., 357*n*.–58*n*.
Kamin, Leon J., 346*n*.
Kapur, Shitij, 375*n*.
Karasu, Byram T., 316*n*.
Keller, Martin B., 369*n*.
Kemp, Lysander, 368*n*.
Kendell, R. E., 323*n*.
Kendler, Kenneth S., 324*n*., 349*n*., 351*n*.
Khantzian, Edward, 235, 246, 360*n*.
Kierkegaard, Soren, xii, 296, 316*n*.
Kindling, 110–14, 116, 118, 121, 122, 123, 125, 190, 283, 336*n*.
King, Larry, xvii, 308
Klein, Donald F., 42, 50–51, 71–77, 179, 323*n*., 324*n*., 325*n*.,

349*n.*, 354*n.*, 355*n.*, 356*n.*,
  358*n.*–59*n.*, 360*n.*, 373*n.*
anhedonia study, 231–33
on panic anxiety, 80–84, 86, 211,
  287, 288, 331*n.*–32*n.*
on rejection-sensitivity and hysteroid
  dysphoria, 71–77, 90–91, 104,
  329*n.*, 330*n.*, 333*n.*
Klein, Hilary M., 331*n.*
Klein, Rachel G., 360*n.*
Klerman, Gerald L., 274, 365*n.*,
  368*n.*, 369*n.*, 370*n.*
Kline, Nathan S., 47–48, 324*n.*
*Know Your Child: An Authoritative Guide
  for Today's Parents* (Chess and
  Thomas), 341*n.*
Kocsis, James H., 350*n.*, 355*n.*, 373*n.*
Konner, Melvin, 350*n.*
Koren, Ed, 353*n.*
Kraepelin, Emil, 42, 43, 110, 163,
  323*n.*
Kramer, Peter D., 320*n.*, 362*n.*,
  368*n.*, 370*n.*, 371*n.*
Kramlinger, Keith G., 334*n.*
Krishnan, R., 336*n.*
Kruesi, Markus J. P., 374*n.*
"Kubla Khan," 271
Kuhn, Ronald, 49–50, 55, 324*n.*,
  325*n.*

*Labyrinth of Solitude, The Other Mexico,
  Return to the Labyrinth of Solitude,
  Mexico and the United States, The
  Philanthropic Ogre, The* (Paz),
  368*n.*
"Ladies Sing the Blues," 352*n.*
La Gasse, L., 342*n.*
Laplace, Pierre Simon de, 76
"Larry King Live," 310
Lasch, Christopher, 353*n.*
*Last Crusade: The War on Consumption,
  The* (Caldwell), 324*n.*
Late-onset depression, 136–43, 340*n.*
Lavori, Philip W., 369*n.*
Lax, Eric, 357*n.*, 373*n.*
L-dopa, 186–87
Learned-helplessness model, 116
Learning disabilities, 227, 360*n.*–61*n.*
Legacy of Erich Fromm, The (Burston),
  322*n.*, 340*n.*, 374*n.*
Leverich, Gabriele S., 334*n.*

Levi, Primo, 142–43, 340*n.*
Levine, Jerome, 369*n.*
Lewontin, Richard C., 161, 317*n.*,
  346*n.*, 351*n.*
*Liberal Imagination: Essays on Literature
  and Society* (Trilling), 370*n.*
Librium (chlordiazepoxide), xvii, 39, 85
Liebowitz, Michael R., 330*n.*, 332*n.*
"Life in Pieces, A," 376*n.*
Life Sciences, 328*n.*
Lifton, Robert Jay, 345*n.*
Lilly Co., Eli, 60–62, 310, 318*n.*,
  328*n.*, 380
Lind, John E., 354*n.*
Linnoila, Markku, 336*n.*, 337*n.*
Lipsett, L. P., 342*n.*
Listening to drugs, 51–52, 86, 129,
  191
  division of mental illnesses, 42, 46
  pharmacologic dissection, 84
Listening to Prozac, 36, 42, 51, 294
  explanation of, xv
Lithium, 43–45, 64, 84, 111, 114,
  209, 305, 308
"Little Boy Lost: The Emotional Life
  and Death of Joe Wesbecker,"
  376*n.*
Lonely Crowd, The (Riesman), 340*n.*
Long-acting effect of Prozac, 181–82
"Long Distance," 337*n.*
Louisville, 376*n.*
Louisville *Courier Journal,* 376*n.*
"Low Levels and Lack of Predictors of
  Somatotherapy and Psychother-
  apy Received by Depressed Pa-
  tients," 369*n.*
LSD, 265
L-tryptophan, 87, 332*n.*
"L-Tryptophan in Mania: Contribution
  to a Permissive Hypothesis of
  Affective Disorders," 340*n.*

McBride, Anne, 374*n.*
MacDonald, Michael, 323*n.*
McEwen, Bruce S., 335*n.*, 336*n.*
McGuire, Michael T., 167–71, 192,
  202, 212, 269, 284, 348*n.*,
  349*n.*, 355*n.*, 356*n.*, 358*n.*,
  364*n.*, 374*n.*
McKinney, William T., 335*n.*, 336*n.*
McKinney, William T., Jr., 356*n.*

Macklin, Ruth, 366*n.*, 368*n.*
McLean Hospital, 363*n.*
McStoots, Rebecca, 310
Madden, John, 343*n.*
Madden, John, IV, 336*n.*
Madsen, Douglas, 356*n.*
Maj, Mario, 334*n.*
"Major Depression and Generalized
    Anxiety Disorder; Same Genes,
    (Partly) Different Environ-
    ments?," 324*n.*, 349*n.*
Mallya, Gopinath M., 347*n.*
Malone, Kevin M., 375*n.*
Management Science, 362*n.*
"Managing Defense Mechanisms in Per-
    sonality Disorders," 338*n.*
Manheimer, Dean L., 369*n.*
Mania, 12, 17, 44, 53, 109, 110, 125,
    147, 294, 340, 362*n.*
Manic-depression (bipolar affective dis-
    order), 42, 109, 124, 164, 166,
    276, 309, 310, 323*n.*, 324*n.*
  claim of gene for, 317*n.*
  diagnosis of, 43–45
  heredity and, xiv
  lithium to treat, 44–45, 84
  rapid cycling, 109–14, 334*n.*
Manji, Husseini, 318*n.*, 348*n.*
Mann, James, 334*n.*
Mann, John J., 374*n.*, 375*n.*
Mannuzza, Salvatore, 360*n.*
MAOIs, *see* Monoamine-oxidase
    inhibitors
March, John S., 367*n.*
Marijuana, 264, 265
Marital problems, 352*n.*
  couples counseling, 24
  Gail, 92, 94–95
  gender-role conflict, 31
  Julia, 23–24, 25, 28, 31
  Susan, 285–87
  Tess, 1–2
Marks, Isaac, 364*n.*
Marlowe, Christopher, 10
Marplan, *see* Isocarboxazid
Marsilid, *see* Iproniazid
Marx, Karl, 271, 297, 374*n.*
Masochism, social, 4, 99, 171–72, 192
  Tess, 2, 8, 18, 40
Mass, James W., 339*n.*
Massachusetts General Hospital, 375*n.*

*Massachusetts General Hospital Clinical
    Psychopharmacology Unit Progress
    Notes*, 327*n.*
Masters, Roger, 356*n.*
"Matters of Taste," 345*n.*
MDA, 366*n.*
MDEA (Eve), 366*n.*
MDMA (Ecstasy), 366*n.*
Mead, Margaret, 160, 345*n.*
"Medicalization of personality," 37
"Medication backup," 1, 4, 319*n.*,
    320*n.*
"Medication Consultation," 360*n.*,
    362*n.*
Meehl, Paul, 228–31, 233, 358*n.*
Mehlman, P. T., 374*n.*
*Melancholia and Depression: From Hippo-
    cratic Times to Modern Times*
    (Jackson), 323*n.*, 346*n.*
Melancholic temperament, 12–13,
    162–63, 164, 165, 201–2,
    236, 263
Mellinger, G. D., 369*n.*
Memory, 123, 124, 241, 349*n.*, 362*n.*
  "of the body," 124, 337*n.*
Menkes, David B., 339*n.*
Menninger, Karl, 42, 43, 323*n.*
Menopause, 262, 366*n.*
Menopause: Is It a Medical Problem?,"
    366*n.*
Mental agility, *see* Sluggishness of
    thought
Mental illness:
  continuity or separateness of, 42–43,
    46, 324*n.*
  diagnosis of, *see* Diagnosis of mental
    illness
  genetic basis of, xiv, 32, 96, 317*n.*,
    324*n.*, 331*n.*, 346*n.*, 352*n.*
  personality disorder versus, 180
  spectrum theory of, 42–43, 46, 80,
    324*n.*
Meprobamate, *see* Miltown
Merrill, James, 272, 368*n.*
"Message in the Bottle, The," 279–81
Message in the Bottle, The, (Percy),
    370*n.*
"Metamorphosis," 315*n.*, 363*n.*
Methyiphenidate, *see* Ritalin
"Mexico and the United States," 368*n.*
Michels, Robert, 366*n.*

Midwest Journal of Political Science, 345*n*.
Migraine headaches, 93, 198, 342*n*.,
    353*n*.
"Milder Spectrum of Bipolar Disorders:
    Diagnostic, Characterologic, and
    Pharmacologic Aspects, The,"
    347*n*.
Mill, John Stuart, 264
Miller, Jean Baker, 357*n*.
Milos, Yara, 368*n*.
Miltown (meprobamate), xvii, 39
Mind, Mood, and Medicine (Klein and
    Wender), 354*n*., 355*n*.
Minoxidil, *see* Rogaine
Mitchell, Janet B., 320*n*.
Molloy, Brian B., 60–64, 328*n*.
*Moments of Engagement: Intimate Psycho-
    therapy in a Technological Age*
    (Kramer), 363*n*., 371*n*.
Monkeys, 301–2
    rhesus, *see* Rhesus monkeys
    vervet, 212–15, 355*n*., 374*n*.
Monoamine-oxidase inhibitors (MAOIs),
    55–56, 58, 66, 232, 305, 308,
    328*n*., 360*n*.
    blood pressure and, 327*n*.
    food interactions, 56, 66, 86–87,
        327*n*.
    hysterics and, 73–74, 76–77, 86–87
    and Prozac:
        similarities with, 332*n*.–33*n*.
        as substitute for, 96
        similarities with Prozac, 87–89
"Monoamine Oxidase Inhibitors: An
    Unfinished Picaresque Tale,"
    324*n*.
Mood:
    determination by biogenic amines,
        52–53
    medication as mood brightener, *see*
        Mood brighteners
    rapid cycling of, 108–14, 124,
        334*n*.
Mood brighteners, 251–67, 370*n*.
    affect tolerance and, *see* Affect
        tolerance
    autonomy and, 256
    clinician's role, effect on, 256, 261–
        263
    coining of the term, 251, 363*n*.
    equal access to, 262, 365*n*.–66*n*.

    ethical questions, 251–67, 363*n*.
    evolutionary biology's view of, 254–
        255, 256, 260–61
"Mood Brighteners," 364*n*., 365*n*.,
    366*n*., 367*n*.
"Mood Brighteners, Affect Tolerance,
    and the Blues," 363*n*.
"Mood Brighteners: Clinical and Ethical
    Dilemmas," 363*n*.
*Mood Disorder: Toward a New Psychobiol-
    ogy* (Whybrow, Akiskal, and
    McKinney), 335*n*., 336*n*.,
    356*n*.
Moore, Jeffrey L., 329*n*.
Moral sensibility:
    affective and, 294–95
    numbing of, 291–93, 373*n*.
Morphine, 231, 358*n*.
"Mother's little helpers," xvii, 39, 40,
    278
Mozart, Wolfgang, 20
Murphy, Dennis L., 336*n*.
Murray, Thomas H., 273, 366*n*.,
    368*n*.
*Mystical Bedlam: Madness, Anxiety, and
    Healing in Seventeenth-Century En-
    gland* (MacDonald), 323*n*.

Nadelson, Theodore, 318*n*.–19*n*.
Napier, Richard, 322*n*.–23*n*.
Nardil (phenelzine), xvi
National Depressive and Manic-
    Depressive Association, 317*n*.
National Institute of Mental Health,
    109, 117–18, 163, 337*n*.
Nature, 317*n*.
Nature of Man, The (Hippocrates), 163
"Nature of Shyness," 341*n*., 343*n*.,
    346*n*., 358*n*.
Nazi Doctors, The (Lifton), 345*n*.
Nazis, 160, 345*n*.
Neale, Michael C., 324*n*., 349*n*.,
    351*n*.
Neese, Randolph M., 254–55, 259–
    261, 363*n*., 365*n*.
Negative feedback system, 110, 335*n*.
Nelson, J. Craig, 338*n*.
Nemeroff, Charles B., 336*n*.
Nemiah, John, 332*n*.
Neurasthenia, 78, 332*n*.
"Neurasthenia Revisited," 332*n*.

Neurobiology of Affective Disorders
  Conference, 1991, 332*n*.,
  334*n*., 336*n*.
Neurobiology of Learning, Emotion, and Affect (Madden), 336*n*., 343*n*.
Neurobiology of Mood Disorders (Post and
  Ballenger), 334*n*., 339*n*.
Neuroleptics, 176
  depression treated with, 325*n*.
  "pacing urge" and, 307, 376*n*.
  side effects of, 325*n*.
"Neurophysiological, Cognitive-
  Behavorial, and Psychoanalytic
  Approaches to Pain Disorder:
  Toward and Integration," 371*n*.
Neuropsychopharmacology, 366*n*.
Neurosis, 37, 43, 46, 79, 289, 331*n*.,
  372*n*., 373*n*.
  Adler's ideas on, 199
  art and, 275–77
  medication for, 129–30
" 'Neurotic,' Characterological, and
  Dysthymic Depressions," 346*n*.
*Neurotic Constitution: Outlines of a Comparative Individualist Psychology
  and Psychotherapy, The* (Adler),
  354*n*.
Neurotransmitter Revolution, The (Masters
  and McGuire), 356*n*.
Neurotransmitters, 52, 54, 61, 64,
  130, 132, 158, 175, 190, 289,
  325*n*.–26*n*.
  aggression and, 374*n*.–75*n*.
  psychoanalysts as, 373*n*.
  see also Acetylcholine; Amines, biogenic; Dopamine; Histamine;
  Norepinephrine; Serotonin
Neutrality of the therapist, 286, 287,
  370*n*.–71*n*.
New Biology of Mood, The (Snyder),
  325*n*.
New England Journal of Medicine, xvi,
  318*n*., 322*n*., 348*n*., 369*n*.,
  372*n*.
*New Introductory Lectures on Psycho-
  Analysis* (Freud), 354*n*.
New Republic, 352*n*., 353*n*.
"New Setting of Goethe's Melancholy
  Love Story," 373*n*.–74*n*.
Newsweek, xiii, xvi, xvii, 191, 316*n*.,
  318*n*., 351*n*.

New York, xvi
New Yorker, The, 322*n*., 353*n*., 368*n*.
New York Review of Books, 317*n*.
New York Times, The, 48, 316*n*., 340*n*.,
  356*n*., 366*n*., 373*n*.–74*n*.
New York Times Book Review, The, 340*n*.
"New You, The," 317*n*., 363*n*.
"Nightline," xvii
"Nonhuman Primate Model of Alcohol
  Abuse: Effects of Early Experience, Personality, and Stress on
  Alcohol Consumption," 338*n*.
"Non-Neutrality," 371*n*.
Norepinephrine, 57, 59, 61, 62, 63,
  88, 115, 121, 131, 132, 190,
  241, 344*n*., 359*n*., 361*n*.
  biological axis of temperament governed by, 185–86, 187
  functions regulated by, 183
  inhibition and levels of, 152, 153
"Norepinephrine in Depressive Reactions: A Review," 339*n*.
Norpramin, *see* Desipramine
Nortriptyline, *see* Pamelor
"Nosology, Genetic, and Theory of
  Spontaneous Panic and Phobia,
  The," 332*n*.
"Notes upon a Case of Obsessional
  Neurosis," 315*n*.–316*n*.
*Not in Our Genes: Biology, Ideology, and
  Human Nature* (Lewontin, Rose,
  and Kamin), 346*n*.
Novelty, response to, 156, 157, 174,
  193, 343*n*.
"Novelty seeking," 187–88, 190,
  351*n*.

"Objective-Descriptive Psychiatry: Emil
  Kraepelin," 323*n*.
Obsessive-compulsive disorder (OCD),
  41–42, 45, 321*n*.
  Anafranil for, 22, 65
  compulsions defined, 26
  dysthymia and, 46
  as form or part of melancholia,
  322*n*.–23*n*.
  medication and diagnosis, relationship between, 32–33, 36–37
  obsessions defined, 26
  patients taking Prozac with, x–xi
  perfectionism and, 26

Prozac to treat, x–xi, 27–28, 45,
     181, 306
  dosage, 28, 29, 30, 322*n*.
  sexual obsessions and compulsions,
     316*n*.
  "sloppy obsessional," 322*n*.
  symptoms of, 26
Oedipus conflict, xii, 129, 255*n*., 288
"On the Grounds for Detaching a Par-
     ticular Syndrome from Neuras-
     thenia Under the Description
     'Anxiety Nervosa,' " 330*n*.
"On the Incapacity to Bear Depression,"
     364*n*.
"On the So-Called Good Hysteric,"
     329*n*.
Opiates, 231, 235, 263
Opium, 49, 50, 252, 271
"Ordinary Love," 337*n*.
Ordinary Love and Good Will, 337*n*.
Orgasm, 366*n*.–67*n*.
Overachievement, 230–31
Overdoses of Prozac, 66, 329*n*.
Oversensitivity, *see* Rejection-sensitivity

"Pacing urge," 307, 376*n*.
Pain as privileged state, 275–78, 280,
     293
Pamelor (nortriptyline), 12
Pande, Atul C., 332*n*.
Panic anxiety, 45, 77–85, 135, 155,
     183, 351*n*.
  antidepressants used to treat, 81–82,
     84–85, 86, 175
  changes in treatment of, 287–88
  dosage of Prozac for, 322*n*.
  false-suffocation alarm hypothesis,
     83, 288
  Freud's writings on, 78–80, 84
  imipramine to treat, 81–82, 84–85,
     86
  Klein's model of, 83–84, 86, 211,
     287, 288, 332*n*.
  Klein's study of, 80–84
  personal history as cause of, 79
  prevalence of, 77
  as psychodynamic, case for, 84,
     332*n*.
  as recent diagnosis, 77–78, 83
  separation anxiety and, 83, 288
  symptoms of, 78

Xanax and the diagnosis of, 85–86
Paranoia, 309
Parental children, 3
Parkinson's disease, 186, 187, 358*n*.
"Paroxetine: A Selective Serotonin
     Reuptake Inhibitor . . . ,"
     337*n*.
Passive aggression, 252
"Pattern Analysis Shows Beneficial Ef-
     fect of Fluoxetine Treatment in
     Mild Depression," 338*n*.
"Pattern of Recurrence of Illness After
     Recovery from an Episode of
     Major Depression: A Prospective
     Study," 334*n*.
Paulus, Martin P., 366*n*.
"Paying Attention to Attention in
     Adults," 361*n*.
Payne Whitney Clinic, 287–88, 371*n*.–
     72*n*., 373*n*.
Paz, Octavio, 271, 368*n*.
"Perceptual reactance," 351*n*.
Percy, Walker, 250–51, 275–81, 284,
     290, 293, 294, 299, 363*n*.,
     369*n*., 370*n*., 374*n*.
Perfectionism, 38–39
  cultural expectations and, 38,
     39
  Julia, 22, 24, 25–26, 30–31, 32
"Permissive biogenic amine hypothesis,"
     339*n*.–40*n*.
Persistence, 170–71
Personality, xiii, xviii, 124, 149, 161
  ambiguity of the word, 195
  as biological, 194, 195
  change in, *see* Personality change
  defined, 149, 340*n*.
  depressive, 163–66, 180–81
  hyperthymic, 16–17, 165–66, 167,
     242, 260, 261, 272
  medication of, 37
  spectrum theory of, 165, 188
  unified biosocial theory of,
     185–90
  see also Character; Temperament
Personality change:
  from medication, xiv–xv, 14, 17, 37,
     167, 177–80, 182, 184, 249
  from Prozac, *see* Personality change
     from Prozac
  from therapy, xiv–xv

Personality change from Prozac, x–xi,
xviii–xix, 10–11, 179–80,
182, 190, 313, 318n.–19n.
Allison, 208–9
"better than well," *see* "Cosmetic
psychopharmacology"
ethics of, 257–85, 291–95, 299–
300
Julia, 22–41
Sally, 47–48, 195
suicidal thoughts, xix, xvii, 102,
136, 301, 304–8, 311, 312
Tess, 1–21, 33–37, 38, 195
as unnatural, 13–14
violence, xix, 301–4, 308–10, 312–
313
without increased self-knowledge,
31–32, 292
Personality disorder, 26, 178, 252,
372n., 373n.
mental illness versus, 180
Personal traits:
medicating patients to reshape individual, 97
trait distribution, 171
Perspectives in Behavioral Inhibition (Reznick), 342n.
Peters, Karin, 340n.
Peters, Tom, 245
Pharmacotherapy, 6, 34, 80, 209
Pharmacological Calvinism, 274, 275,
365n., 370n.
Pharmacological dissection, 45, 84,
241, 324n., 361n.
"Pharmacologic Treatment of Depres-
sion, The," 318n., 348n.
Pharmacopsychiatry, 334n.
Pharmacotherapy, 262, 286, 371n.
see also Psychopharmacology
"Pharmacotherapy Effective in
Obsessive-Compulsive Disor-
der," 367n.
Phenelzine, *see* Nardil
"Philippe Pine's 'Memoir on Madness'
of December 11, 1794: A Fun-
damental Test of Modern Psy-
chiatry," 346n.
Philoctetes (Sophocles), 276
"Philoctetes: The Wound and the
Bow," 369n.
Pinel, Philippe, 346n.

Plasticity of Development (Branch, Hall,
and Dooling), 336n., 343n.
Plastic surgery, 262, 273
Play, capacity to, 21
Pleasing others, compulsive need for, 3
Pleasure, 263–65
inhibition of, *see* Pleasure, inhibition
of
preference theory of, 264–65
separability, 263–64
Pleasure, inhibition of (anhedonia),
223–36
disorders related to, 227–28,
229
ethical questions of medication for,
234
heredity and, 229
Hillary, 224–27, 233, 247, 292–93
Klein's study of, 231–33, 328n.–
359n.
Meehl's study of, 228–31, 233
overachievement and, 230–31
Prozac's effect on, 225–27, 233,
234, 265, 359n.
Plomin, Robert, 344n., 351n.
Pornography, ix, x, 316n.
Post, Robert M., 109–12, 190, 284,
334n., 339n., 349n.
Postsynaptic-hypersensitivity model,
131–33, 339n.
Post-traumatic stress disorder (PTSD),
372n.
"Potential Clinical, Biological Predic-
tors of Suicide Reattempts Iden-
tified," 375n.
Potter, William Z., 318n., 348n.
Prange, A. J., Jr., 339n.–40n.
"Predisposition to Anxiety, The," 331n.
Preference theory of pleasure, 264
Premenstrual syndrome, 25, 29–30,
45
"Prevalence of Psychiatric Disorders in a
Primary Care Practice, The,"
322n., 372n.
"Primate Separation Models of Affective
Disorders," 336n., 343n.
"Prime Time Live," xvii, 310
Primrose oil, 25
*Principles and Problems in Establishing the
Efficacy of Psychotropic Agents*,
330n.

Privacy issue in case vignettes, 315*n.*–316*n.*
Proceedings of the National Academy of Sciences, U.S.A., 338*n.*
"Process of Discovery, The," 324*n.*, 327*n.*
Propanolol, *see* Inderal
Property-of-conscious-experience theory, 263–64
"Prophylaxis of Bipolar Affective Disorders," 334*n.*
Proprioception, 203–4, 208
Providence *Business News*, 362*n.*
Prozac:
  acceptance of, xvii
  for ADHD, 242
  affect tolerance affected by, 258–59
  for attention-deficit disorder, 45
  for atypical depression, 89, 181
  autonomy, effect on, 265–66, 268
  backlash against, xvii–xviii, 308–11, 318*n.*
  best responders to, 292, 300, 318*n.*
  capsule, xvi, 318*n.*
  clinical usage of, 97–99, 144
    Allison, 206–9
    Gail, 94
    Hillary, 225, 226–27
    Jerry, 174
    Julia, 27–30
    Lucy, 102, 105
    Sally, 147–48
    Sam, x–xi
    Sonia, 237, 238–39
    Tess, 7–10
  confidence gained with, *see* Confidence
  "cosmetic psychopharmacology" and, x, xv, xvi, 246–49
  cultural expectations and, 17, 20, 270–72
  for depression, x, xviii, xix, 7–9
    major, 65, 135
    minor, 126, 135, 181, 227
    serotonin-as-police model, 134–135, 181, 339*n.*–40*n.*
  descriptive psychiatry, challenge to, 289
  as designed drug, 64, 329*n.*
  desipramine given with, 339*n.*
  development of, 60–64, 299, 327*n.*, 328*n.*
  discontinuing, 10, 18–19, 29–30, 102, 311–12, 377*n.*–78*n.*
  doctor's role and, 14, 285–87
  dominance hierarchy study, use in, 213, 214
  dosage, 28, 147, 321*n.*–22*n.*
  downregulation of norepinephrine receptors, 133, 339*n.*
  for drug abuse, 45
  for dysthymia, 179–80, 181
  for eating disorders, 45
  ethical issues, 250–52, 257–63, 265, 268–69, 270–75, 278, 281–85, 293–94, 299–300, 363*n.*
    see also Mood brighteners
  for inhibition, 147–48
  for inhibition of pleasure, 225–27, 233, 234, 265, 359*n.*
  introduction of, ix, 7
  "listening to," *see* Listening to Prozac
  long-acting effect of, 181–82, 321*n.*
  for low self-esteem, 206–8
  MAOIs and:
    similarities, 87–89, 332*n.*–33*n.*
    as substitute for, 96
  media attention, xvi–xviii, 310, 318*n.*
  moral sensibility, numbing of, 291–293
  of obsessive-compulsive disorder, x–xi, 27–28, 35, 45, 181, 306
    dosage, 28, 29, 30, 322*n.*
  overdoses, 66, 329*n.*
  for panic anxiety, 45
    dosage, 322*n.*
  personality change from, *see* Personality change from Prozac
  for PMS, 45
  popularity of, xvii, xix, 10, 11, 12
  for rejection-sensitivity, 66, 94–100, 102, 105, 182
  response of dysthymic women to, 348*n.*
  self-concept affected by, xi, xix, 13, 14, 18–20, 267, 296, 300, 316*n.*
  as serenic, 303

Prozac (*cont.*)
  sexual function, and, x, 316*n.*,
    366*n.*–67*n.*
  sexual obsessions and compulsions
    and, 316*n.*
  side effects of, xvii, xix, 65, 66,
    206, 207, 211–13, 311–12
    as minimal, xviii, 11, 89, 181
    sexual function, 316*n.*, 366*n.*–
      367*n.*
    suicidal thoughts, *see* Suicide
    violence, xix, 301–4, 308–
      310, 312–13, 364*n.*, 375*n.*
  for sluggishness of thought, 237,
    238–39
  social coercion and, 272–73
  social ease and, *see* Social relation-
    ships, dramatic change in
  specificity of, biochemical, 89, 96,
    181, 184
  suicidal thoughts on, *see* Suicide
  as thymoleptic, 267–68
  tolerance, 305
  transformation and, xviii, xix, 7–9,
    13–14, 17, 21, 27–28, 29,
    94–95, 147–48, 167, 208,
    226–27, 249, 267–68, 313,
    320*n.*
    see also Personality change from
      Prozac; Self-concept, Prozac's ef-
      fect on; Social relationships, dra-
      matic change in
  violence and, xix, 301–4, 308–10,
    312–13, 364*n.*, 375*n.*
  work performance, *see* Work, perfor-
    mance at
"Prozac—Medication That Makes You
  Kill," 309, 312, 318*n.*
Pseudodementia, 241
Psychiatric Annals, 332*n.*, 347*n.*, 360*n.*,
  361*n.*
Psychiatric Clinics of North America,
  330*n.*, 346*n.*
Psychiatric Developments, 350*n.*
"Psychiatric Diagnosis and a Typology
  of Clinical Drug Effects," 329*n.*
*Psychiatric Diagnosis in New York and
  London: A Comparative Study on
  Mental Hospital Admissions*
  (Cooper, Kendell, et al.), 323*n.*
Psychiatric Times, 315*n.*, 317*n.*, 345*n.*,

360*n.*, 363*n.*, 367*n.*, 370*n.*,
  371*n.*, 373*n.*, 377*n.*
Psychiatry, 364*n.*
Psychiatry Research, 350*n.*
Psychoanalysis, 47–48, 75, 104, 220,
  221, 290, 299, 318*n.*, 373*n.*
  animal models as alien to, 129
  anxiety at the heart of, xii, 82
  for anxious patients, 331*n.*
  changes in, 287–88, 371*n.*–72*n.*
  Freudian, 72–73, 129, 199–200
  goal of treatment, 129
  interruptions in patient-analyst rela-
    tionship, 333*n.*–34*n.*
  primacy of family trauma in, 91
  psychoanalyst as neurotransmitter,
    373*n.*
  removal of the cause of neurosis with,
    75–76
  termination phase, 334*n.*
  treatment of the "worried well," 15
Psychoanalytic Inquiry, 371*n.*
"Psychoanalytic View of Anxiety, The,"
  332*n.*
Psychodynamic psychotherapy,
  80
Psychological Types (Jung), 345*n.*
Psychopathology, 332*n.*
Psychopathy, 227–28
Psychopharmacologia, 329*n.*
"Psychopharmacological Treatment,"
  333*n.*
"Psychopharmocological Treatment and
  Delineation of Borderline Disor-
  ders," 330*n.*, 333*n.*
Psychopharmacology, 34, 35, 58, 97,
  229, 234, 290, 299, 300,
  326*n.*
  as an art, 6, 34
  mood brighteners' effect on role of
    clinician, 256
  psychoanalysis and, 288
  see also Pharmacotherapy
Psychopharmocology, 336*n.*, 337*n.*
Psychopharmocology and Psychotherapy
  (Greenhill and Gralnick), 332*n.*
Psychopharmacology Bulletin, 334*n.*,
  338*n.*, 347*n.*
"Psychopharmacology for Psychosis and
  Affective Disorders: Receptors
  and Ligands," 326*n.*

Psychopharmacology of Anxiety (Tyrer),
  331*n*., 332*n*.
Psychosis, 42
Psychosomatic Medicine, 342*n*.
"Psychotherapeutic Attitudes in the
  Drug Treatment of Anxiety and
  Phobic Reactions," 332*n*.
Psychotherapy, 2, 9–10, 17, 21, 22,
  68, 98, 103, 104, 146, 209,
  255, 289, 297, 357*n*.
 affect tolerance and, 258
 cognitive, 128
 confrontation of reality in, 253
 conservation of mood defied by, 262–
  263
 criticisms of, 40, 272
 to decrease anxiety, 43
 Ericksonian, 128
 for hysteria, 73
 for inhibition of pleasure, 224, 225–
  226
 medication-induced change and, 31–
  32, 97, 106, 208, 259, 286,
  292, 355*n*., 373*n*.
 neural structure, effect on, 127,
  338*n*.
 neutrality, 286, 287, 370*n*.–71*n*.
 Prozac's effect on therapist's role,
  285–87
 psychodynamic, 287
 Rolfing, 224
 self psychology, 338*n*., 354*n*.
 self-understanding to improve low
  self-esteem, 209–10
 short-term, 101
 successful only in conjunction with
  medication, 203
 supportive, 253–54
 "taking sides," 371*n*.
 treatment of the "worried well," 15
Psychotherapy and Psychosomatics, 349*n*.
Psychotherapy in the Third Reich (Cocks),
  345*n*.
"Psychotropic Hedonism vs. Pharmacological Calvinism," 365*n*.,
  368*n*., 370*n*.
Putnam, Frank, 336*n*.

"Quick and the Dead: Slow, Careful
  Decisions Aren't Always the
  Best," 362*n*.

"Quick and the Dead, The," 245
Quitkin, Frederic M., 350*n*.

Rabkin, Judith G., 323*n*., 325*n*.,
  330*n*., 332*n*.
Radcliffe Quarterly, 342*n*.
Rado, Sandor, 358*n*.
Raleigh, Michael J., 355*n*., 374*n*.
Ranga, K., 336*n*.
Rapid cycling, 108–14, 124, 334*n*.
Ratey, John J., 361*n*., 375*n*.
Rathbun, Robert, 60–61, 62, 63
*Rational Psychopharmacotherapy and the
  Right to Treatment* (Ayd), 329*n*.
Reactivity, 156–59, 162, 176, 192,
  286–87, 343*n*., 344*n*.
Recent Developments in Alcoholism, 360*n*.
"Receptor Adaptation in Animal Models
  of Mood Disorders: A State of
  Change Approach to Psychiatric
  Illness," 339*n*.
"Receptor Sensitivity and the Mecha-
  nisms of Action of Antidepres-
  sant Treatment: Implications for
  the Etiology and Therapy of
  Depression," 339*n*.
"Receptor Sensitivity Hypothesis of Antidepressant Action: A Review
  of Antidepressant Effects on Serotonin Function," 339*n*.
"Reducing," 351*n*.
Reimherr, Fred W., 338*n*.
Reiser, Morton, F., 357*n*.
Rejection-sensitivity, xv, 67–77, 87–
  107, 121, 189, 190, 269–70,
  286
 change in understanding of, 95–96
 as characteristic of hysteroid dysphoria, 74, 75
 described, 70–71, 333*n*.
 as functionally autonomous trait, 97,
  101, 102, 107
 Gail, 92–95
 in late adolescence, 100–101
 looking for and finding, 97–100, 101
 Lucy, 67–70, 89–90, 102–7
 MAOIs for, 73–74, 76–77, 86–87
 norepinephrine and, 185–86, 187
 as personal trait, 97
 Prozac for, 66, 94–100, 102, 105,
  182

Rejection-sensitivity (*cont.*)
  reducing perception of rejection,
    103–5
"Relationship Between Central and Peripheral Serotonin Indexes in Depressed and Suicidal Psychiatric Inpatients," 374*n.*
"Relationship Between Separation Anxiety and Panic Agoraphobic Disorder," 332*n.*
"Relevance of Psychotherapy to Clinical Practice Today, The," 355*n.*, 371*n.*, 373*n.*
Remer, T. G. 327*n.*
"Reply to Criticisms of My Paper on Anxiety Neurosis," 331*n.*
Reserpine, 55
Restoril, 93
Revolution from Within: A Book of Self-Esteem (Steinem), 353*n.*–54*n.*
"Reward coupling," 183, 358*n.*
"Reward dependence," 185–86, 187–188, 190
Reznick, J. Steven, 341*n.*, 342*n.*
Rhesus monkeys, 302, 336*n.*, 375*n.*
  inhibition observed in, 156–59, 343*n.*
  separation studies, 118–22, 129, 130, 337*n.*
  social healing study, 127–28
Richardson, Louise, 368*n.*
Riesman, David, 340*n.*
Risk models, 192, 195
Ritalin (methyiphenidate), 241, 359*n.*
Rivera, Geraldo, xvii
Robins, Lee N. 340*n.*, 346*n.*
Rodriguez, Robert, 329*n.*
Rogaine (minoxidil), 262
"Role of Inheritance in Behavior, The," 344*n.*
Role of Serotonin in Psychiatric Disorder, The (Brown and Van Praag), 339*n.*, 350*n.*
Rolfing, 24
Rose, Steven, 346*n.*
Rosenbaum, Jerrold F., 326*n.*, 375*n.*
Rosenthal, Ted L., 346*n.*
Rothman, Stanley, 342*n.*
Rounds, Grand, 341*n.*
Rubinow, David R., 334*n.*
Rudorfer, Matthew V., 318*n.*, 348*n.*

"Sad Attack: Prozac," 375*n.*
Sandroff, Ronni, 366*n.*
Sanguine temperament, *see* Temperament, sanguine/hyperthymic
Santé, 318*n.*
Sartre, Jean-Paul, 244, 245, 297
Schildkraut, Joseph J., 339*n.*
Schizophrenia, 42–43, 72, 186, 227, 323*n.*, 324*n.*, 358*n.*
  diagnosis of, 43
  medications for, 50, 80
School placement, 362*n.*
Schubert, Franz, 30
Schurman, Rachel A., 320*n.*
Schwartz, Jeffrey M., 338*n.*
Schwartz, Richard, 253–54, 256, 258, 259–60, 363*n.*, 364*n.*, 365*n.*, 366*n.*, 367*n.*
Science, 154, 155, 337*n.*, 341*n.*, 344*n.*
Sciences, The, 363*n.*
Scientologists, xviii, 311, 318*n.*, 377*n.*
"Scientology: The Cult of Greed," 377*n.*
Seaman, Stephen F., 336*n.*
Sea View Sanatorium, 47
Sedatives, 49–50, 85, 262, 308, 310
  see also Dalmane; Halcion; Restoril; Sominex
Seductiveness, 73, 74–75, 90
Seizures, kindling of, 110–11, 112–14
"Selective Inhibitor of Serotonini Uptake," 328*n.*
Selective serotonin-reuptake inhibitor (SSRI), 62–63, 88, 105, 106, 107, 125–27, 132, 328*n.*, 329, 362*n.*
Self-concept, 68
  medication affecting, 18–20, 195–196
  Prozac's effect on, xi, xix, 13, 14, 18–20, 267, 296, 300, 316*n.*
Self-esteem, xv, 198
  Allison, 204–8, 216–17
  childhood experiences and, 200–201, 209, 215–16, 220
  dominance hierarchy among animals, 211–15
  kindled low self-esteem, 216
  low, 8, 198–222, 353*n.*, 354*n.*
  medication providing, 32
  medication's effect on, 203–4, 207,

208–9, 210, 214, 217, 219–21
Paul, 217–21
physical aspect of, 210–11
Prozac for low self-esteem, 206–8
relationship to mood, 202–3
self-understanding's effect on, 209–
210, 218, 221
serotonin and, 220, 221
William M., 202–4
see also Confidence
"Self-Medication Hypothesis of Addic-
tive Disorders: Focus on Heroin
and Cocaine Dependence,"
360n.
"Self-Mutilation and Aloneness," 333n.,
367n., 373n.
"Self-Portrait in Tyvek ® Windbreaker," 368n.
Self psychology, 338n., 354n.
"Self-Regulation and Self-Medication
Factors in Alcoholism and the
Addictions: Similarities and Dif-
ferences," 360n.
Seminars in Psychiatry, 326n.
Sensitivity, *see* Rejection-sensitivity
"Sensitization and Kindling Perspectives
for the Course of Affective Ill-
ness," 334n.
Separability, 263
*Separate Lives: Why Siblings Are So Dif-
ferent* (Dunn and Plomin), 351n.
Separation anxiety, 83, 286, 288,
333n.
Separation-reared monkeys, 118–22,
129, 130, 337n.
social healing study, 127–28
Serendipity, 44, 60, 327n.
Serendipity and the Three Princes (Remer),
327n.
Serenics, 303
Seriousness, 9, 36, 37
"Serotonergic Mechanisms Promote
Dominance Acquisition in Adult
Male Vervet Monkeys," 355n.,
374n.
"Serotonergic Medications for Sexual
Obsessions, Sexual Addictions,
and Paraphilias," 316n.
Serotonin, 57, 58, 60, 62, 63, 87–88,
121, 131, 134–35, 181, 190,
366n.

ACHD and, 242
aggression and, 301–4, 374n.
-as-police, 134–35, 136, 137, 181,
339n.–40n.
biological axis of temperament governed by, 186, 187
in dominant animals, 355n.–56n.
functions regulated by, 183
history of, 327n.
inhibition of pleasure and, 360n.
levels of, in dominant animals, 212–
215, 355n.–56n.
mental agility improved by Prozac,
247
research into role in mood regulation,
61, 328n.
self-esteem and, 220, 221
suicidal thoughts and, 305–6, 307
suicide and brain levels of, 303–4,
328n.
suicide attempts and, 375n.
"Serotonin Function and the Mechanism
of Antidepressants Action: Reversal of Antidepressant-Induced
Remission by Repaid Depletion
of Plasma Tryptophan," 332n.
Serotonin in Major Psychiatric Disorders
(Coccaro and Murphy), 336n.
Sertraline, *see* Zoloft
*Sex and Temperament in Three Primitive
Societies* (Mead), 345n.
Sexual abuse, 1, 117–18, 145
Sexual function, x, 316n.
difficulties in achieving orgasm,
366n.–67n.
Shaffer, Peter, 276
Shannon, Del, xvii, 318n.
Short REM latency, 165, 166
Showalter, Elaine, 352n.
Shyness, *see* Inhibition; Temperament,
inhibited or shy
Side effects, 124–25
of amphetamines, 245
of Anafranil, 27
of antidepressants, *see* Antidepressants, side effects of; *specific
antidepressants*
of anxiolytics, 325n.
choosing antidepressants on the basis
of, 59
of Desyrel, 59

Side effects (*cont.*)
  of imipramine, 4, 7, 54–55, 57, 84
  of iproniazid, 55
  of neuroleptics, 325*n.*
  of Prozac, *see* Prozac, side effects of
  of Tegretol, 111
  of tricyclic antidepressants, 65–66
Signal anxiety, xii
Signposts in a Strange Land (Percy),
    370*n.*
Sinequan, *see* Doxepin
"60 Minutes," xviii, 318*n.*, 377*n.*
Skinner, B. F., 358*n.*
Sleep patterns:
  in atypical depression, 89
  hypersomnia, 225
  of hyperthymics, 165, 166
  hysteria and, 73
  insomnia, 54, 197–98, 255
  of subaffective dysthymics, 165
Sluggishness of thought, 206, 236–49,
    262
  ethical questions of medication for,
    243–45, 247–49
  Sonia, 237–39, 242–43, 244, 246,
    247
Smiley, Jane, 337*n.*
Snidman, Nancy, 341*n.*, 342*n.*, 344*n.*,
    346*n.*
Snyder, Solomon H., 61–62, 64, 325*n.*
Snyderman, Mark, 342*n.*
"Social and Environmental Influences on
    Blood Serotonin Concentrations
    in Monkeys," 355*n.*
Social coercion, 272–75
"Social Functioning in Chronic Depres-
    sion: Effect of 6 Weeks of Anti-
    depressant Treatment," 350*n.*
Social relationships, 4
  avoidance of, 99
  dramatic change in, 7–8, 10–11,
    18, 21, 36, 147–48, 226, 265,
    266
  extraversion, 150, 160, 163, 166,
    174
  inhibition, *see* Inhibition
  inhibition of pleasure, 224
  introversion, 144–46, 150, 160,
    163, 164, 166, 171, 172
  social collaboration, 344*n.*
  social healing studies, 127–28

Social skills, 352*n.*
Sociobiology, 167–71
  view of compulsiveness, 35
Solitude (Storr), 367*n.*
Sominex (diphenhydramine),
    49–50
Somit, Albert, 345*n.*
Sophocles, 276
Sorrows of Young Werther, The, 373*n.*–
    374*n.*
Sort of Life, A (Greene), 357*n.*
Specificity of Prozac, biochemical, 89,
    96, 181, 184
Spectrum theory:
  of mental illness: 42–43, 46, 80,
    324*n.*
  of personality, 165, 188
SSRI, *see* Selective serotonin-reuptake
    inhibitors
Stahl, Lesley, xviii, 377*n.*
*Standard Edition of the Complete Psycholog-
    ical Works of Sigmund Freud, The*
    (Strachey), 316*n.*, 330*n.*, 331*n.*,
    354*n.*
Stein, Dan J., 316*n.*
Steinem, Gloria, 353*n.*–54*n.*
Steroids, 272–73, 368*n.*
Stewart, Jonathan W., 350*n.*
Stille, Alexander, 340*n.*
Stimulants, 263, 325*n.*, 359*n.*,
    361*n.*
  see also Amphetamines; Ritalin
"Stimulation of Malignant Growth in
    Rodents by Antidepressant
    Drugs at Clinically Relevant
    Doses," 378*n.*
Stiver, Irene Pierce, 357*n.*
Stopping Prozac, effects of, 10, 18–19,
    29–30, 102, 311–12, 377*n.*–
    378*n.*
Storr, Anthony, 367*n.*
"Story of Lithium, The," 323*n.*
Strachey, James, 316*n.*, 330*n.*, 331*n.*,
    354*n.*
"Strategic Decision Processes in High-
    Velocity Environments: Four
    Cases in the Microcomputer In-
    dustry," 362*n.*
Stress, 115–43
  postsynaptic-hypersensitivity model,
    131–33, 339*n.*

stress-hormone system, 115–16, 117–18, 121

structural changes in the brain resulting from, 117, 118, 130, 132, 193

type of, and dysthymia, 192–93

Stress/risk model, 192–94

Studies in Hysteria (Freud and Breuer), 79, 331*n*.

Study of Organ Inferiority and Its Psychical Compensation: A Contribution to Clinical Medicine (Adler), 354*n*.

Subaffective dysthymia, 164–66, 178, 180, 347*n*.

Substance abuse, *see* Drug abuse

"Suicidal Ideation Not Associated with Fluoxetine," 375*n*.

"Suicidality and Fluoxetine: Is There a Relationship?," 375*n*.

Suicidal patients, 66, 137–42

Suicide, 116, 136, 142–43, 303–8, 340*n*., 375*n*.–11*n*.

attempted, 304, 305–6, 307, 375*n*.

serotonin levels in the brain and, 328*n*., 375*n*.

thoughts of, xix, xvii, 102, 136, 301, 304–8, 311, 312, 364*n*.

Sullivan, Mark, 256, 363*n*., 364*n*., 365*n*., 366*n*., 367*n*.

Suomi, Stephen J., 119, 120, 121, 156–59, 176, 190, 192, 336*n*., 337*n*., 338*n*., 343*n*.–44*n*., 349*n*., 375*n*.

Superego, 36, 200, 354*n*.

Suzuki, Koji, 369*n*.

"Swine objection," 264

Synaptosome, 62, 64

"Systematic Method for Clinical Description and Classification of Personality Variants: A Proposal, A," 350*n*.

Szara, S. I., 328*n*.

Tapp, John, 310

Taylor, Michael Alan, 324*n*.

Tegretol (carbamazepine), 111–12, 114

Teicher, Martin H., 318*n*., 375*n*., 376*n*.

Teicher report, 304–8

Temperament, xv, 13, 14, 148–50, 162, 191, 194–95, 246, 261, 270, 283, 287–88, 298, 340*n*.–41*n*.

affective, 167

beliefs about, historically, 159–61

breeding of animals for, 344*n*.

choleric, 162

defined, 148, 149, 340*n*.

depressive/melancholic, 12–13, 162–163, 164, 165, 178, 193, 201–2, 236, 260, 263

genetic traits linked to, 155

inhibited or shy, 144, 146, 150–61, 343*n*., 344*n*.

dysthymia and, 167 71, 348*n*.

see also Inhibition

medicated, 149

medication's effect on, 175–76, 182

mismatched, between parent and child, 201

phlegmatic, 162

sanguine/hyperthymic, 13, 16, 162, 165–66, 201–2, 260, 297

social versus affective, 166–70, 282

unified biosocial theory of personality, 185–90

see also Character; Personality

"Temperament and Allergy Symptoms," 342*n*.

Temperament and Development (Thomas and Chess), 340*n*., 341*n*.

Temperament in Clinical Practice (Chess and Thomas), 341*n*.

Thanatos Syndrome, The (Percy), 250–251, 363*n*.

Thomas, Alexander, 340*n*., 341*n*.

Thomas, E. A., 344*n*.

Thomas, Patricia, 375*n*.

Thorazine, *see* Chlorpromazine

Thought process, sluggishness of, *see* Sluggishness of thought

"Treating Depression and Anxiety in Primary Care: Closing the Gap Between Knowledge and Practice," 332*n.n*., 372*n*.

"Treatment of Rapid Cycling Bipolar Illness," 334*n*.

"Treatment Received by Depressed Patients," 369*n*.

Triazolam, *see* Halcion

Trichotillomania (hair-pulling), 265, 267, 367*n*.
Tricyclic antidepressants, 57, 58, 60, 65–66, 88, 132, 133, 327*n*., 360*n*., 377*n*.
Trilling, Lionel, 276, 370*n*.
Troisi, Alfonso, 349*n*.
Trump, Donald, xvi
Tsiaras, Alexander, 367*n*.
"2-Year Prospective Follow-Up Study of Children and Adolescents with Disruptive Behavior Disorders . . . ," 374*n*.
Tyler, Anne, 320*n*.
Tyrer, P. J., 331*n*.

Uhlenhuth, E. H., 369*n*.
"Thriving Cult of Greed and Power, The," 377*n*.
Thymoleptics, 182, 196, 267–68, 271, 275, 289, 369*n*.
   defined, 176
Time, xvii, xviii, 318*n.n.*, 377*n*.
Time-Limited Psychotherapy (Mann), 334*n*.
Timidity, *see* Inhibition
"Today," xvii
Tofranil, *see* Imipramine
Tolerance, 305
"Toward a More Biologically-Oriented Political Science: Ethology and Pharmacology," 345*n*.
"Toxicity of Fluoxetine in Overdose," 329*n*.
Traits, *see* Personal traits
Transcendence, quest for, 277–83, 293–94, 295, 297
"Transduction of Psychosocial Stress into the Neurobiology of Recurrent Affective Disorder," 334*n*.
Trauma, Growth, and Personality (Greenacre), 331*n*.
Trauma/temperament model, 192–94
Trazodone, *see* Desyrel

Uncommon Therapy: The Psychiatric Techniques of Milton Erickson (Haley), 338*n*.

Understanding Walker Percy (Hobson), 369*n*.
Unified biosocial theory of personality, 185–90
"Unified Biosocial Theory of Personality and Its Role in the Development of Anxiety States, A," 350*n*.
U.S. Surgeon General, 369*n*.
University of Iowa, 355*n*.
University of Manitoba, 378*n*.
University of Tennessee, 163
University of Utah, 126, 338*n*.
"Unrealistic Wishes and Physiological Change: An Overview," 349*n*.
Updike, John, 40, 322*n*.
"Uptight and Laid-Back Monkeys: Individual Differences in the Response to Social Challenges," 336*n*., 343*n*.
"Use of Adjunctive Fluoxetine in Analytic Psychotherapy with High Function Outpatients," 318*n*.–319*n*.
"Use of Drugs for Pleasure: Some Philosophical Issues, The," 366*n*.

Vaillant, George, 338*n*.
"Validating Affective Personality Types," 340*n*., 346*n*., 347*n*.
Validity of Psychiatric Diagnosis, The (Robins and Barrett), 340*n*., 346*n*.
Valium, 39, 95, 113
van Bose, Hans-Jurgen, 373*n*.–74*n*.
Van den Hoofdakker, R. H., 330*n*.
Van Praag, Herman M., 183, 339*n*., 350*n*., 358*n*.
Van Putten, Theodore, 375*n*., 376*n*.
Veltro, Franco, 334*n*.
Vervet monkeys, 374*n*.
   dominance hierarchy study, 212–15, 355*n*.
Violence, xix, 301–4, 308–10, 312–313, 364*n*., 375*n*.
   unnecessary exposure to risk of, 67, 68, 70
"Violence Goes Mainstream," xvii, 318*n*.
Vital Balance, The (Menninger), 323*n*.

Walker Percy: An American Search (Coles), 316*n*., 369*n*.

Walpole, Horace, 327*n*.
Weil-Malherbe, H., 328*n*.
Weiner, Doris B., 346*n*.
Wellbutrin (buproprion), xvi
Wender, Paul H., 354*n*., 355*n*., 361*n*.
Wesbecker, Joseph, 308–10, 376*n*.
Western Psychiatric Institute, 375*n*.
Westover, Leanne, 318*n*.
"Wht Good Is Feeling Bad? The Evolutionary Benefits of Psychic Pain," 363*n*., 365*n*.
"Who Should Not Be Treated with Neuroleptics, but Often Are," 329*n*.
Whybrow, Peter C., 335*n*., 336*n*., 356*n*.
"Why Don't Men Ask Directions? They Don't Feel Lost: Each Sex Has Its Own Way of Navigating, Study Finds," 316*n*.
Why the Reckless Survive: And Other Secrets of Human Nature (Konner), 350*n*.
Williams, Tennessee, 191
Wilson, Edmund, 276, 369*n*.
Wilson, Ian C., 340*n*.
Winchel, Ronald M., 96, 266–67, 278, 333*n*., 367*n*., 373*n*.
Wirshing, William C., 375*n*., 376*n*.
Wisdom in the Practice of Psychotherapy (Karasu), 316*n*.
Women, 368*n*.
  antidepressants, taking, 319*n*., 335*n*.
  antidepressants as feminist drugs, 40
  assertiveness, 172
  cultural expectations of, 38–41, 172, 270–71
  depression in, 357*n*.
  reasons for proportionally higher incidence of, 319*n*.
  with hysteroid dysphoria, 74–75, 90–91
  medication of, seeking mental health care, 319*n*.–20*n*.
  "mother's little helpers," xvii, 39, 40, 278
  psychoanalysist's view of, 75
  thymoleptics as feminist drugs, 271
"Women and the Abuse of Prescribed Psychotropic Medication," 369*n*.
"Wonderland," 373*n*.
Wong, David T., 61, 62, 64, 328*n*.
Wood, David R., 338*n*.
Woody Allen: A Biography (Lax), 357*n*., 373*n*.
Work, performance at, 145, 147
  altered, 8–9, 17, 28, 94, 236
Work in Progress, 357*n*.
Wound and the Bow: Seven Studies in Literature, The (Wilson), 369*n*.–70*n*.

Xanax (alprazolam), 85–86, 93, 209, 315*n*.

Yale University, 87–88, 332*n*., 338*n*.
Yamamoto, Joe, 332*n*.
Yerevanian, Boghos I., 346*n*.
You Mean I Don't Have to Feel This Way? (Dowling), 353*n*.

Zetzel, Elizabeth R., 73, 254, 258, 329*n*.–30*n*., 364*n*.
Zimmerman, Robert R., 337*n*.
Zola, Émile, 276
Zoloft (sertraline), 106–7

Danielle Steel has been ha.... .e of the world's most popular authors, with o... ...illion copies of her novels sold. Her many int.... ...ional bestsellers include *Loving, Star, Family Album, ...he Ring, Summer's End, Season of Passion* and other highly acclaimed novels.

Visit the Danielle Steel website at www.daniellesteel.com

By Danielle Steel

SISTERS	BUNGALOW 2
LIGHTNING	H.R.H.
WINGS	COMING OUT
THE GIFT	TOXIC BACHELORS
ACCIDENT	MIRACLE
VANISHED	IMPOSSIBLE
MIXED BLESSINGS	ECHOES
JEWELS	SECOND CHANCE
NO GREATER LOVE	RANSOM
HEARTBEAT	SAFE HARBOUR
MESSAGE FROM NAM	JOHNNY ANGEL
DADDY	DATING GAME
THE HOUSE	ANSWERED PRAYERS
ZOYA	SUNSET IN ST TROPEZ
KALEIDOSCOPE	THE COTTAGE
FINE THINGS	THE KISS
WANDERLUST	LEAP OF FAITH
SECRETS	LONE EAGLE
FAMILY ALBUM	JOURNEY
STAR	THE HOUSE ON HOPE STREET
FULL CIRCLE	THE WEDDING
CHANGES	IRRESISTIBLE FORCES
THURST ON HOUSE	GRANNY DAN
CROSSINGS	BITTERSWEET
ONCE IN A LIFETIME	MIRROR IMAGE
A PERFECT STRANGER	PALOMINO
REMEMBRANCE	LOVE: POEMS
HIS BRIGHT LIGHT: *THE STORY*	THE RING
OF MY SON, NICK TRAINA	LOVING
THE KLONE AND I	TO LOVE AGAIN
THE LONG ROAD HOME	SUMMER'S END
THE GHOST	SEASON OF PASSION
SPECIAL DELIVERY	THE PROMISE
THE RANCH	NOW AND FOREVER
SILENT HONOR	GOLDEN MOMENTS*
MALICE	GOING HOME
FIVE DAYS IN PARIS	

* published outside the UK under the title PASSION'S PROMISE

DANIELLE STEEL

The Promise

Based on a screenplay by Gary Michael White

SPHERE

First published in Great Britain by Sphere Books 1978
Reprinted 1978 (three times), 1979 (twice), 1980 (five times),
1981 (twice), 1982 (twice),1983 (four times), 1984 (three times),
1985 (twice), 1986 (three times), 1987, 1988, 1989, 1990, 1993
Reprinted by Warner Books 1994
Reprinted 1994, 1995, 1997, 1998, 1999, 2000
Reprinted by Time Warner Paperbacks in 2002
Reprinted 2004
Reprinted by Time Warner Books in 2005
Reprinted by Sphere in 2007, 2008
Reissued by Sphere in 2010
Reprinted 2012 (twice), 2013 (twice)

A CIP catalogue record for this book
is available from the British Library.

ISBN 978-0-7515-4378-0

Typeset in New Baskerville by Hewer Text UK Ltd, Edinburgh
Printed and bound in Great Britain by
Clays Ltd, St Ives plc

Papers used by Sphere are from well-managed forests
and other responsible sources.

MIX
Paper from
responsible sources
FSC
www.fsc.org FSC® C104740

Sphere
An imprint of
Little, Brown Book Group
100 Victoria Embankment
London EC4Y 0DY

An Hachette UK Company
www.hachette.co.uk

www.littlebrown.co.uk

The early morning sun streamed across their backs as they unhooked their bicycles in front of Eliot House on the Harvard campus. They stopped for a moment to smile at each other. It was May and they were very young. Her short hair shone in the sunshine, and her eyes found his as she began to laugh.

'Well, Doctor of Architecture, how do you feel?'

'Ask me that in two weeks after I get my doctorate.' He smiled back at her, shaking a lock of blond hair off his forehead.

'To hell with your diploma, I meant after last night.' She grinned at him again, and he rapidly swatted her behind.

'Smartass. How do *you* feel, Miss McAllister? Can you still walk?'

They were hitching their legs over the bicycles now and she looked back at him teasingly in answer.

'Can you?' And with that, she was off, pulling ahead of him on the pretty little bike he had bought her for her birthday only a few months before. He was in love with her. He had always been in love with her. He had dreamed of her all his life. And he had known her for two years.

It had been a lonely time at Harvard before that, and well into his second year of graduate school he was resigned to more of the same. He didn't want what the others wanted. He didn't want Radcliffe or Vassar or Wellesley girls. He had known too many of them during his undergraduate days, and for Michael there was always something missing. He wanted something more. Texture, substance, soul.

Nancy was something very special. He had known from the first moment he had seen her in the Boston gallery that showed her paintings. There was a haunting loneliness about her landscapes, a solitary tenderness about her people that filled him with compassion and made him want to reach out to them and to the artist who painted them. She had been sitting there that day in a red beret and an old racoon coat, her delicate skin still glowing from her walk to the Charles Street gallery, her eyes shining, her face alive. He had never wanted any woman as he wanted her. He had bought two of her paintings, and taken her to dinner at Lockober's. But the rest had taken longer. Nancy McAllister wasn't quick to give her body or her heart. She had been too lonely for too long to give herself easily. At nineteen she was already wise and well versed in pain. The pain of being alone. The pain of being left. It had plagued her since she had been put in the orphanage as a child. She could no longer remember the day her mother had left her there shortly before she died. But she remembered the chill of the halls. The smells of the strange people. The sounds in the morning, as she lay in her bed fighting back tears. She would remember those things for the rest of her life. For a long time she thought nothing could fill the emptiness inside her. But now she had Michael.

Theirs wasn't always an easy relationship, but it was a strong one, built on love and respect; they had meshed her world and his, and come up with something beautiful and rare. And Michael was no fool either. He knew the dangers of falling in love with someone 'different', as his mother put it – when she got the chance. But there was nothing 'different' about Nancy. The only thing different was that she was an artist, not just a student. She wasn't still searching – she already *was* what she wanted to be. And unlike the other women he knew, she wasn't auditioning candidates, she had chosen the man she loved. In two years he had never let her down. She was certain he never would: they knew each other too well. What could there possibly be that she hadn't already learned? She knew it all. The funny stuff, the silly secrets, the childhood dreams, the desperate fears. And through him she had come to respect his family. Even his mother.

Michael had been born into a tradition, groomed since childhood to inherit a throne. It wasn't something he took lightly, or even joked about. Sometimes it actually frightened him. Would he live up to the legend? But Nancy knew he would. His grandfather, Richard Cotter, had been an architect, and his father as well. It was Michael's grandfather who had founded an empire. But it was the merging of the Cotter business with the Hillyard fortune, through the marriage of Michael's parents, that had created the Cotter-Hillyard of today. Richard Cotter had known how to make money, but it was the Hillyard money – *old* money – that had brought with it the rites and traditions of power. It was, at times, a heavy mantle to wear, but not one Michael disliked. And Nancy respected it too. She knew that one day Michael would be at the helm of Cotter-Hillyard. In the beginning they had talked about it incessantly, and then again later, when they realised how serious their relationship really was. But Michael knew that he had found a woman who could handle it, the family responsibilities as well as the business duties. The orphanage had done nothing to prepare Nancy for the role Michael knew she would fill, but the groundwork seemed to be laid in her very soul.

He watched her now with almost unbearable pride as she sped ahead of him, so sure of herself, so strong, the lithe legs pedalling deftly, her chin tucked over her shoulder now and then to look at him and laugh. He wanted to speed ahead and take her off the bike . . . there . . . on the grass . . . the way they had the night before . . . the way . . . He swept the thought from his mind and raced after her.

'Hey, wait for me, you idiot!' He was abreast of her in a few moments, and as they rode along more quietly now, he held out a hand across the narrow gap between them. 'You look beautiful today, Nancy.' His voice was a caress in the spring air, and around them the world was fresh and green. 'Do you know how much I love you?'

'Oh, maybe half as much as I love you, Mr Hillyard?'

'That shows what you know.' Michael always made her happy. He did wonderful things. She had thought so from the first moment he walked into the gallery and threatened to take off all his clothes if she didn't sell him all her paintings. 'I happen to love you at least seven times as much as you love me.'

'Nope.' She grinned at him again, put her nose in the air, and sped ahead again. 'I love you more, Michael.'

'How do you know?' He was pressing to catch up.

'Santa Claus told me.' And with that she sped ahead again, and this time he let her move out on the narrow path. They were in a festive mood and he liked watching her. The slim shape of her hips in jeans, the narrow waist, the trim shoulders with the red sweater loosely tied about them, and that wonderful swing of dark hair. He could watch her for years. In fact, he was planning to do just that. Which reminded him . . . he had been meaning to talk to her about that all morning. He narrowed the gap between them again, and tapped her gently on the shoulder.

'Excuse me, Mrs Hillyard.' She jumped a little at the words, and then smiled shyly at him as the sun shone across her face. He could see tiny freckles there, almost like gold dust left by elves on the creamy surface of her skin. 'I said . . . Mrs Hillyard . . .' He mouthed the words with infinite pleasure. He had waited for two years.

'Aren't you rushing things a little, Michael?' She sounded hesitant, almost afraid. He hadn't spoken to Marion yet. No matter what he and Nancy had agreed to between themselves.

'I don't think I'm rushing anything. And I was thinking about doing it two weeks from now. Right after graduation.' They had long since agreed on a small, intimate wedding. Nancy had no family, and Michael wanted to share the moment with Nancy, not a cast of thousands or an army of society photographers. 'In fact, I was planning to go down to New York to talk to Marion about it tonight.'

'Tonight?' There was an echo of fear in the word, and she let the bicycle come to a slow stop. He nodded in answer, and she grew pensive as she looked out at the lush hills around them. 'What do you think she'll say?' She was afraid to look at him. Afraid to hear.

5

'*Yes*, of course. Are you really worried about it?' But it was a stupid question and they both knew it. They had plenty to worry about. Marion was no flower girl. She was Michael's mother, and she had all the tenderness of the *Titanic*. She was a woman of power, of determination, of concrete and steel. She had carried on the family business after her father died, and again with renewed determination after her husband's death. Nothing stopped Marion Hillyard. Nothing. Certainly not a chit of a girl, or her only son. If she didn't want them to get married, nothing would make her grant that 'yes' Michael pretended to be so sure of. And Nancy knew exactly what Marion Hillyard thought of her.

Marion had never made any secret of her feelings, or at least, not from the moment she decided that Michael's 'fling' with 'that artist' might be for real. She had called Michael down to New York and cooed, soothed, and charmed, after which she had stormed, threatened, and baited. And then she had resigned herself or seemed to. Michael had taken it as an encouraging sign, but Nancy wasn't so sure. She had a feeling that Marion knew what she was doing; for the present she had clearly decided to ignore 'the situation'. Invitations were not extended, accusations were not made, apologies for things said to Michael in the past were never forthcoming, but no fresh problems had sprung up either. For her, Nancy simply did not exist. And oddly, Nancy was always surprised to find just how much that hurt. Having no family of her own, she had always had odd dreams about Marion. That they might be friends, that Marion would like her, that she and Marion would go shopping for Michael . . . that Marion

6

would be the mother she had never had or known. But Marion was not easily cast in that role. In two years, Nancy had had ample opportunity to understand that. Only Michael obstinately held to the position that his mother would come round, that, once she had accepted the inevitable, they would be great friends. But Nancy was never that sure. She had even forced Michael to discuss the possibility of Marion's never accepting her, never agreeing to the marriage. Then what? . . . 'Then we hop in the car and head for the nearest justice of the peace. We're both of age now, you know.' Nancy had smiled at the simplicity of his solution. She knew it would never be as easy as that. But what did it matter? After two years together, they felt married anyway.

They stood in silence for a long moment, looking at the view, and then Michael took Nancy's hand. 'I love you, babe.'

'I love you too.' She looked at him worriedly and he silenced her eyes with a kiss. But nothing could still the questions that either of them had. Nothing except the interview with Marion. Nancy let her bike fall, and with a sigh, slipped slowly into Michael's arms. 'I wish it were easier, Michael.'

'It will be. You'll see. Now come on. Are we going to ride, or just stand here all day?' She smiled as he picked up her bike for her. And in a moment they were off again, laughing and playing and singing, pretending that Marion didn't exist. But she did. She always would. Marion was more an institution than a woman. Marion would always be there. In Michael's life anyway. And now in Nancy's.

The sun rose higher in the sky as they pedalled through

7

the countryside, alternately riding ahead of each other, or side by side, at one moment raucously teasing, at the next growing silent and thoughtful. It was almost noon when they reached Revere Beach and saw the familiar face riding towards them. It was Ben Avery, with a new girl at his side. Another leggy blonde.

'Hi, you two. Going to the fair?' Ben grinned at them, and then with a vague wave of his hand introduced Jeannette. They all exchanged a round of hellos, and Nancy shielded her eyes to glance ahead at the fair. It was still several blocks away.

'Is it worth stopping for?'

'Well, yes. We won a pink dog' – he pointed at the ugly little creature in Jeannette's basket – 'a green turtle,' which somehow they had lost, 'and two cans of beer. Besides, they have corn on the cob and it's terrific.'

'You've convinced me!' Michael looked over at Nancy and smiled. 'Shall we?'

'Sure. You two going back already?' But she could see that they were. Ben had a recognisable gleam in his eyes, and Jeannette seemed to be in agreement. Nancy smiled to herself as she watched them.

'Yeah, we've been out since about six this morning. I'm beat. What are you doing for dinner tonight, by the way? Want to stop in for a pizza?' Ben's room was only a few doors down from Mike's.

'What are we doing for dinner, *Señor*?' Nancy looked at Michael with a broad smile, but he was shaking his head.

'I have some business to attend to tonight. Maybe another time.' It was a rapid reminder of the meeting with Marion.

8

'Okay. See ya.' Ben and Jeannette waved and were off, as Nancy stared at Michael.

'You're really going down to see her tonight?'

'Yes. And stop worrying about it. Everything is going to be just fine. By the way, Mother says he's got the job.'

'Ben?' Nancy looked up questioningly as they started pedalling towards the fair.

'Yes. We start at the same time. Different areas, but we start the same day.' Mike looked pleased. He had known Ben in prep school, and they were like brothers.

'Does Ben know yet?'

Michael shook his head with an expressive smile. 'I thought I'd give him the thrill of hearing the news officially. I didn't want to spoil it for him.'

Nancy smiled back at him. 'You're nice and I love you.'

'Thank you, Mrs H.'

'Stop that, Michael.' She wanted the name too much to hear it bandied about, even by Michael.

'I won't stop it. And you'd better get used to it.' He suddenly looked serious.

'I will. When the time is right. But until then, Miss McAllister will do just fine.'

'For about two more weeks, to be exact. Come on, I'll race you.'

They sped ahead, side by side, panting and laughing, and Michael reached the entrance to the fair a full thirty seconds before she did. But they both looked tanned and healthy and carefree.

'Well, sir, what's first?' But she had already guessed, and she was right.

'Corn, of course. Need you ask?'

'Not really.' They parked their bikes next to a tree, knowing that in that sleepy countryside, no one would steal them, and they walked off arm in arm. Ten minutes later, they stood happily dripping butter as they ate their corn, and then gobbled hot dogs and sipped ice-cold beer. Nancy followed it all up with a huge stick of candy-floss.

'How can you eat that stuff?'

'Easy. It's delicious.' The words were garbled through the sticky pink stuff she was eating. But she wore the happy face of a five-year-old girl.

'Have I told you lately how beautiful you are?' She grinned at him, wearing a faceful of pink candy, and he took out a handkerchief and wiped her chin. 'If you'd clean up a little we could have our picture taken.'

'Yeah? Where?' Her nose disappeared again, as she gobbled another pink cloud.

'You're impossible. Over there.' He pointed to a booth where they could stick their heads through round holes, and have their photographs taken over outlandish outfits. They wandered over and chose Rhett Butler and Scarlett O'Hara. And strangely enough, they didn't even look foolish in the picture. Nancy looked beautiful over the elaborately painted costume. The delicate beauty of her face and the precision of its features were perfect with the immensely feminine costume of the Southern belle. And Michael looked like a young rake. The photographer handed them their photograph and collected his dollar.

'I ought to keep that, you two look so good.'

'Thank you.' Nancy was touched by the compliment, but Mike only smiled. He was always so darn proud of her. Just another two weeks and . . . but Nancy's frantic tugging on his sleeve distracted him from his daydreams. 'Look, over there! A ring toss!' She had always wanted to play that at the fair when she was a little girl, but the nuns from the orphanage always said it was too expensive. 'Can we?'

'But of course, my dear.' He swept her a low bow, offered her his arm, and attempted to stroll towards the hoopla, but Nancy was far too excited to stroll. She was almost leaping like a child, and her excitement delighted him.

'Can we do it now?'

'Sure, sweetheart.' He put down a dollar and the man at the counter handed her four times the usual allotment of rings. Most customers only paid a quarter. But she was inexperienced at the game, and all her tries fell wide. Michael was watching her with amusement. 'Just exactly which prize are you trying for?'

'The beads.' Her eyes shone like a child's and her words were barely more than a whisper. 'I've never had a gaudy necklace before.' It was the one thing she had always wanted as a child. Something bright and shiny and frivolous.

'You're certainly easy to please, my love. You sure you wouldn't rather have the pink doggie?' It was just like the one Jeannette had had in her basket, but Nancy shook her head determinedly.

'The beads.'

'Your wish is my command.' And he landed all three tosses perfectly on target. With a smile, the man behind the counter handed him the beads, and Michael quickly put them around Nancy's neck. '*Voilà, mademoiselle.* All yours. Do you suppose we should insure them?'

'Will you stop making fun of my beads? I think they're gorgeous.' She touched them softly, enchanted to know they were sparkling at her neck.

'I think *you're* gorgeous. Anything else your heart desires?'

She grinned at him. 'More candyfloss.'

He bought her another stick of candyfloss, and they slowly wended their way back to the bikes. 'Tired?'

'Not really.'

'Want to go on a little further? There's a lovely spot up ahead. We could sit for a while and watch the surf.'

'It sounds perfect.'

They rode off again, but this time more quietly. The carnival atmosphere was gone, and they were both lost in their own thoughts, mostly of each other. They were nearing Nahant when she saw the spot he had chosen at the tip of a land split, under lovely old trees, and she was glad they had come this last leg of the trip.

'Oh Michael, it's beautiful.'

'It is, isn't it?' They sat down on a soft patch of grass, just before the narrow lip of sand began, and in the distance they watched long smooth waves break over a reef that lay just beneath the surface of the water. 'I've always wanted to bring you here.'

'I'm glad you did.' They sat silently, holding hands, and then Nancy suddenly stood up.

'What's up?'

'I want to do something.'

'Over there, behind the bushes.'

'No, you idiot. Not that.' She was already running towards a spot on the beach, and slowly he followed her, wondering what she had in mind. She stopped at a large rock and tried earnestly to move it, with no success.

'Here, silly, let me help you with that. What do you want to do with it?' He was puzzled.

'I just want to move it for a second . . . there.' It had given way under Michael's firm prodding, and it rolled back to show a damp indentation in the sand. Quickly, Nancy took off the bright blue beads, held them for a moment, her eyes closed, and dropped them into the sand beneath the rock. 'Okay, put it back.'

'On top of the beads?'

She nodded, her eyes never leaving the sparkle of blue glass. 'These beads will be our bond, a physical bond, buried fast for as long as this rock, and this beach, and these trees stand here. All right?'

'All right.' He smiled softly. 'We're being very romantic.'

'Why not? If you're lucky enough to have love, celebrate it! Give it a home!'

'You're right. You're absolutely right. Okay, here's its home.'

'Now let's make a promise. I promise never to forget what is here, or to forget what they stand for. Now you.' She touched his hand, and he smiled down at her again. He had never loved her more.

'And I promise . . . I promise never to say goodbye to you . . .' And then, for no reason in particular, they laughed. Because it felt good to be young, to be romantic, even to be corny. The whole day had felt good. 'Shall we go back now?' She nodded assent, and hand in hand they wandered back to where they had left the bikes. And two hours later, they were back at Nancy's tiny apartment on

Spark Street, near the campus. Mike looked around as he let himself fall sleepily on to the couch and realised once again how much he enjoyed her apartment, how much like home it was to him. The only real home he had ever known. His mother's mammoth apartment had never really felt like home, but this place did. It had all Nancy's wonderful warm touches in it. The paintings she had done over the years, the warm earth colours she had chosen for the place, a soft brown velvet couch, and a fur rug she had bought from a friend.

There were always flowers everywhere, and the plants she took such good care of. The spotless little white marble table where they ate, and the brass bed which creaked with pleasure when they made love.

'Do you know how much I love this place, Nancy?'

'Yeah, I know.' She looked around nostalgically.

'Me, too. What are we going to do when we get married?'

'Take all of these beautiful things to New York and find a cosy little home for them there.' And then something caught his eye. 'What's that? Something new?' He was looking at her easel, which held a painting still in its early stages but already with a haunting quality to it. It was a landscape of trees and fields, but as he walked towards it, he saw a small boy, hiding in a tree, dangling his legs. 'Will he still show once you put the leaves on the trees?'

'Probably. But we'll know he's there in any case. Do you like it?' Her eyes shone as she watched his approval. He had always understood her work, perfectly.

'I love it.'

'Then it'll be your wedding present – when it's finished.'

'You've got a deal. And speaking of wedding presents . . .' he looked at his watch. It was already five o'clock, and he wanted to be at the airport by six. 'I should get going.'

'Do you really have to go tonight?'

'Yes. It's important. I'll come back in a few hours. I should be at Marion's place by seven-thirty or eight, depending on the traffic in New York. I can catch the last shuttle back, at eleven, and be home by midnight. Okay?'

'Okay.' But she was hesitant. She was bothered by his going. She didn't want him to, and yet she didn't know why. 'I hope it goes all right.'

'I know it will.' But they both knew that Marion did only what she wanted to do, listened only to what she wanted to hear, and understood only what suited her. Somehow he knew they'd win her over, though. They had to. He had to have Nancy. No matter what. He took her in his arms one last time before slipping a tie around the collar of the sports shirt he was wearing and grabbing a light-weight jacket from the back of a chair. He had left it there that morning. He knew it would be hot in New York, but he knew too, that he had to appear at Marion's apartment in jacket and tie. That was essential. Marion had no toler-ance for 'hippies', or for nobodies . . . like Nancy. They both knew what he was facing when they kissed goodbye at the door.

'Good luck.'

'I love you.'

For a long time Nancy sat in the silent apartment looking at the photograph of them at the fair. Rhett and Scarlett, immortal lovers, in their silly wooden costumes, poking their faces through the holes. But they didn't look silly.

They looked happy. She wondered if Marion would understand that, if she knew the difference between happy and silly, between real and imaginary. She wondered if Marion would understand at all.

The dining-room table shone like the surface of a lake. Its sparkling perfection was disturbed only on the edge of the shore, where a single place setting of creamy Irish linen lay, adorned by delicate blue-and-gold china. There was a silver coffee service next to the plate, and an ornate little silver bell. Marion Hillyard sat back in her chair with a small sigh as she exhaled the smoke from the cigarette she had just lit. She was tired today. Sundays always tired her. Sometimes she thought she did more work at home than she did at the office. She always spent Sundays answering her personal correspondence, looking over the books kept by the cook and the housekeeper, making lists of what she had noticed needed to be repaired around the apartment and of items needed to complete her wardrobe, and planning the menus for the week. It was tedious work, but she had done it for years, even before she'd begun to run the business. And once she'd taken over from her husband, she had still spent her Sundays attending to the household and taking care of Michael on the nurse's day off. The memory made her smile, and for a moment she closed her eyes. Those Sundays had been precious, a few hours with him without anyone interfering, anyone taking him away. Her Sundays weren't like that anymore; they hadn't been in too many years. A tiny bright tear crept into her lashes as she sat very still in her chair, seeing him as he had been eighteen years before, a little boy of six, and all hers.

How she loved that child. She would have done anything for him. And she had. She had maintained an empire for him, carried the legacy from one generation to the next. It was her most valuable gift for Michael. Cotter-Hillyard. And she had come to love the business almost as much as she loved her son.

'You're looking beautiful, Mother.' Her eyes flew open in surprise as she saw him standing there in the arched doorway of the richly panelled dining-room. The sight of him now almost made her cry. She wanted to hug him as she had all those years ago, and instead she smiled slowly at her son.

'I didn't hear you come in.' There was no invitation to approach, no sign of what she'd been feeling. No one ever knew, with Marion, what went on inside.

'I used my key. May I come in?'

'Of course. Would you like some dessert?'

Michael walked slowly into the room, a small nervous smile playing over his mouth, and then like a small boy he peered at her plate. 'Hm . . . what was it? Looks like it must have been chocolate, huh?'

She chuckled and shook her head. He would never grow up. In some ways anyway. 'Profiteroles. Care for some? Mattie is still out there in the pantry.'

'Probably eating what's left.' They both laughed at what they knew was most likely true, but Marion reached for the bell.

Mattie appeared in an instant, black-uniformed and lace-trimmed, pale-faced and large-beamed. She had spent a lifetime running and fetching and doing for others, with only a brief Sunday here and there to call hcr own, and nothing to do with it once she had thc much coveted 'day'. 'Yes, madam?'

'Some coffee for Mr Hillyard, Mattie. And . . . darling, dessert?' He shook his head. 'Just coffee then.'

'Yes, ma'am.'

For a moment Michael wondered, as he often had, why his mother never said thank you to thc servants. As though they had been born to do her bidding. But he knew that was what his mother thought. She had always lived surrounded by servants and secretaries and every possible kind of help. She had had a lonely upbringing but a comfortable one. Her mother had died when she was three, in an accident with Marion's only brother, the heir to the Cotter architectural throne. The accident had left only Marion to become a substitute. She had done so very effectively.

'And how is college?'

'Almost over, thank God. Two more weeks.'

'I know. I'm very proud of you, you know. A doctorate is a wonderful thing to have, particularly in architecture.' For some reason the words made him want to say, 'Oh, Mother!' as he had when he was nine. 'We'll be contacting young Avery this week, about his job. You haven't said anything to him, have you?' She looked more curious than stern; she didn't really care. She had thought it a little childish that Michael thought it so important to surprise Ben.

'No, I haven't. He'll be very pleased.'

'As well he should be. It's an excellent job.'

'He deserves it.'

'I hope so.' She never gave an inch. 'And you? Ready for work? Your office will be finished next week.' His eyes shone at the thought. It was a beautiful office, wood-panelled the way his father's had been, with etchings that had belonged to her own father, an impressive leather couch and chairs, and a roomful of Georgian furniture. She had bought it all in London over the holidays. 'It really looks splendid, darling.'

'Good.' He smiled at his mother for a moment. 'I have some things I wanted to get framed, but I'll wait till I take a look at the décor.'

'You won't even need to do that. I have everything you'll need for the walls.'

So did he. Nancy's drawings. There was sudden fire in his eyes now, and an air of watchfulness in hers. She had seen something in his face.

'Mother—' He sat down next to her with a small sigh and stretched his legs as Mattie arrived with the coffee. 'Thank you, Mattie.'

'You're welcome, Mr Hillyard.' She smiled at him as warmly as she always did. He was always so pleasant to her, as though he hated to bother her, not like . . . 'Will there be anything else, madam?'

'No. As a matter of fact . . . Michael, do you want to take that into the library?'

'All right.' Maybe it would be easier to talk in there. His mother's dining-room had always reminded him of ballrooms he had seen in ancestral homes. It was not conducive to intimate conversation, and certainly not to gentle persuasion. He stood up and followed his mother out of the room, down three thickly carpeted steps, and into the library immediately to their left. There was a splendid view of Fifth Avenue and a comfortable chunk of

Central Park, but there was also a warm fireplace and two walls lined with books. The fourth wall was dominated by a portrait of Michael's father, but it was one he liked, one in which his father looked warm – like someone you'd want to know. As a small boy he had come to look at that portrait at times, and to 'talk' aloud to his father. His mother had found him that way once, and told him it was an absurd thing to do. But later he had seen her crying in that room, and staring at the portrait as he had.

His mother ensconced herself in her usual place, in a Louis XV chair covered in beige damask and facing the fireplace. Tonight her dress was almost the same colour, and for a moment, as the firelight glowed, Michael thought her almost beautiful. She had been once, and not so long ago. Now she was fifty-seven. Michael had been born when she was thirty-three. She hadn't had time for children before that. And she had been very beautiful then. She had had the same rich honey-blonde hair that Michael had, but now it was greying, and the life in her face had faded. It had been replaced by other things. Mostly the business. And the once cornflower-blue eyes looked almost grey now. As though winter had finally come.

'I have the feeling that you came down here tonight to speak to me about something important, Michael. Is anything the matter?' Had he got someone pregnant? Smashed up his car? Hurt someone? Nothing was irreparable, of course, as long as he told her. She was glad he had come down.

'No, nothing's the matter. But there is something I want to discuss with you.' Wrong. He cringed almost visibly at his own words. 'Discuss'. He should have said there was something he wanted to *tell* her, not *discuss* with her. Damn. 'I thought it was about time we were honest with each other.'

'You make it sound as though we usually aren't.'

'About some things we aren't.' His whole body was tense now, and he was leaning forward in his chair, conscious of his father looking over his shoulder. 'We aren't honest about Nancy, Mother.'

'Nancy?' She sounded blank, and suddenly he wanted to jump up and slap her. He hated the way she said her name. Like one of the servants.

'Nancy McAllister. My friend.'

'Oh, yes.' There was an interminable pause as she shifted the tiny vermeil and enamel spoon on the saucer of her demitasse cup. 'And in what way are we not honest about Nancy?' Her eyes were veiled by a sheet of grey ice.

'You try to pretend that she doesn't exist. And I try not to get you upset about it. But the fact is, Mother . . . I'm going to marry her.' He took another breath and sat back in his chair. 'In two weeks.'

'I see.' Marion Hillyard was perfectly still. Her eyes did not move, nor her hands, nor her face. Nothing. 'And may I ask why? Is she pregnant?'

'Of course not.'

'How fortunate. Then why, may I ask, are you marrying her? And why in two weeks?'

'Because I graduate then, because I'm moving to New York then, because I start work then. Because it makes sense.'

'To whom?' The ice was hardening, and one leg crossed carefully over the other with the slippery sound of silk.

Michael felt uncomfortable under the constancy of her gaze. She hadn't shifted her eyes once. As in business, she was ruthless. She could make any man squirm, and eventually break.

'It makes sense to us, Mother.'

'Well, not to me. We've been asked to build a medical centre in San Francisco, by the same group who were behind the Hartford Centre. You won't have time for a wife. I'm going to be counting on you very heavily for the next year or two. Frankly, darling, I wish you'd wait.' It was the first softening he'd seen, and it almost made him wonder if there was hope.

'Nancy will be an asset to both of us, Mother. Not a distraction to me, or a nuisance to you. She's a wonderful girl.'

'Maybe so, but as for being an asset . . . have you thought of the scandal?' There was victory in her eyes now. She was going in for the kill, and suddenly Michael held his breath, a helpless prey, not knowing where she would strike, or how.

'What scandal?'

'She's told you who she is, of course?'

Oh Jesus. Now what? 'What do you mean, *who* she is?'

'Precisely that. I'll be quite specific.' And in one smooth, feline gesture, she set down the demitasse and glided to her desk. From the bottom drawer she removed a file, and silently handed it to Michael. He held it for an instant, afraid to look inside.

'What is this?'

'A report. I had a private investigator look into your artistic little friend. I was not very pleased.' An

23

understatement. She had been livid. 'Please sit down and read it.' He did not sit down, but unwillingly he opened the folder and began to read. It told him in the first twelve lines that Nancy's father had been killed in prison when she was still a baby, and her mother had died an alcoholic two years later. It explained as well that her father had been serving a seven-year sentence for armed robbery. 'Charming people, aren't they, darling?' Her voice was lightly contemptuous, and suddenly Michael threw the folder on the desk, from which its contents slid rapidly to the floor.

'I won't read that garbage.'

'No, but you'll marry it.'

'What difference does it make who her parents were? Is that her goddamn fault?'

'No. Her misfortune. And yours, if you marry her. Michael, be sensible. You're going into a business where millions of dollars are involved in every deal. You can no longer afford the risk of scandal. You'll ruin us. Your grandfather founded this business over fifty years ago, and you're going to destroy it now for a love affair? Don't be insane. It's time you grew up, my boy. High time. Your salad days are over. In exactly two weeks.' She burned as she looked at him now. She was not going to lose this battle, no matter what she had to do. 'I won't discuss this with you, Michael. You have no choice.' She had always told him that. Goddamnit, she had always . . .

'The hell I don't!' It was a sudden roar as he paced across the room. 'I'm not going to bow and scrape before you and your rules for the rest of my life, Mother! I won't! What exactly do you think, that you're going to pull me into the business, groom me until you retire, and then run me as a puppet from a chaise-longue in your room? Well, to hell with that. I'm coming to work for you. But that's all. You don't own my life, now or ever, and I have a right to marry anybody I bloody well please!'

'Michael!'

They were interrupted by the sudden peal of the door-bell, and they stood eyeing each other like two jaguars in a cage. The old cat and the young one, each slightly afraid of the other, each hungry for victory, each fighting for survival. They were still standing at opposite ends of the room, trembling with rage, when George Calloway walked in, and instantly sensed that he had stepped into a scene of great passion. He was a gentle, elegant man in his late fifties who had been Marion's right-hand man for years. More than that, he was much of the power behind Cotter-Hillyard. But unlike Marion, he was seldom in the forefront; he preferred to wield his strength from the shadows. He had long since learned the merits of quiet strength. It had won him Marion's trust and admiration years ago, when she first took her husband's place in the business. She had been only a figurehead then, and it had been George who actually ran Cotter-Hillyard for the first year, while he determinedly and conscientiously taught her the ropes. And he had done his job well. Marion had learned all he had taught, and more. She was a power in her own right now, but she still relied on George on every major deal. That meant everything to him. Knowing that she still needed him after all these years. They were a team, silent, inseparable, each one stronger because of the other. He sometimes wondered if Michael knew just how close they were. He doubted it. Michael had always been the hub of his mother's life. Why would he ever have noticed just how much George cared? In some ways, even Marion didn't understand that. But George accepted that. He lavished his warmth and energies on the business. And perhaps, one day . . . George looked at Marion now with instant concern. He had learned to recognise the tightness around the mouth and the strange pallor beneath the carefully applied powder and rouge.

'Marion, are you all right?' He knew more about her health than anyone did. She had confided in him years before. Someone had to know, for the business. She had appallingly high blood-pressure, and a serious problem with her heart.

For a moment there was no answer, and then she pulled her eyes away from her son to look at her long-time associate and friend. 'Yes . . . yes, I'm fine. I'm sorry. Good evening, George. Come in.'

'I think I might have come at a bad time.'

'Not at all, George, I was just leaving.' Michael turned to look at him and couldn't even pretend a smile. Then he looked at his mother again, but made no move to approach her. 'Goodnight, Mother.'

'I'll call you tomorrow, Michael. We can discuss this over the phone.'

He wanted to say something hateful to her, to frighten her, but he couldn't, he didn't know how. And what was the point?

'Michael . . .'

He didn't answer her; he merely shook hands solemnly with George and walked out of the library without looking back. He never saw the look in his mother's eyes, or the concern in George's as she sank slowly back into her chair and brought her trembling hands to her face. There were tears in her eyes which she hid even from George.

'What on earth happened?'

'He's going to do something insane.'

'Maybe not. We all threaten mad things now and then.'

'At our age we threaten, at his age they do.' All her efforts for nothing. The investigators' reports, the phone calls, the . . . She sighed and slowly sat back against the delicate chair.

'Have you taken your medicine today?' She shook her head almost imperceptibly. 'Where is it?'

'In my bag. Behind the desk.' He walked to the desk, saying nothing of the pages of the report scattered there and on the floor, and found the black alligator handbag with the eighteen-carat-gold clasp. He knew it well; he had given it to her three Christmases before. He found the medicine and returned to her side, holding the two white pills in his hand. She heard the rattle of the demitasse cup and opened her eyes. This time she smiled at him. 'What would I do without you, George?'

'What would I do without you?' He couldn't even hear the thought. 'Shall I leave now? You should get some rest.'

'I'd just get upset thinking about Michael.'

'Is he still coming to work for the firm?'

'Yes, it was something else.'

The girl then. George knew about that too, but he didn't want to press Marion now. She was distressed enough, but at least the colour was coming back to her face and after swallowing the pills she took a cigarette out of her case.

He lit it for her as he watched her face. She was a beautiful woman. He had always thought so. Even now, as she grew tired and increasingly ill. He wondered if Michael knew how ill. He couldn't possibly or he wouldn't upset her like this.

What George did not know was that Michael was equally distressed at that moment. Hot tears burned his eyes as he sat in the back of a cab on his way to the airport.

He called Nancy as soon as he got to the terminal. His flight would leave in twenty minutes.

'How did it go?' She couldn't tell much from his voice when he said hello.

'Fine. Now I want you to get busy. I want you to pack a bag, get dressed, and be ready in an hour and a half when I get there.'

'Ready for what?' She was puzzled as she sat curled up on the couch, holding the phone.

He paused for a moment and then smiled. It was his first smile in two hours. 'An adventure, my love. You'll see.'

'You're crazy.' She was laughing her wonderful soft laugh.

'Yeah, crazy about you.' He felt like himself again, once more it was all beginning to make sense. He was back with Nancy. No one could ever take that away from him, not his mother, not a report, no one and nothing. He had vowed that day, on the beach where they had buried the beads, never to say goodbye to her, and he had meant it. 'Okay, Nancy, get moving. Oh, and wear something old, something new . . .' He wasn't just smiling now, he was grinning.

'You mean . . .' Her voice trailed off in astonishment.

'I mean we're getting married tonight. Okay with you?'

'Yes, but—'

'But nothing.'

'But why tonight?'

'Instinct. Trust me. Besides, it's a full moon.'

'It must be.' She was smiling now, too. She was going to be married. She and Michael were going to be married!

'I'll see you in an hour, babe. And . . . Nancy?'

'Yes?'

'I love you.' He hung up the phone and ran towards the gate. He was the last passenger to board the plane to Boston. Nothing could stop him now.

He had been pounding on the door for almost ten minutes, but he wasn't going to give up. He knew Ben was in there.

'Ben! Come on, you . . . Ben!! . . . For Chrissake, man . . .' Another rash of pounding and then at last the sound of footsteps and a sudden crash. The door opened to reveal a sleepy Ben, standing confusedly in his underwear and rubbing his shin. 'Christ, it's only eleven o'clock. What are you doing asleep at this hour?' But the grin on Ben's face told him with a second glance. 'Jesus. You're smashed.'

'To the very tips of my toes.' Ben looked down at his feet with an elfin smile, and an unsteady wobbling of the legs.

'Well, you're going to sober up real quick. I need you.'

'The hell you do. Six Beefeaters and tonic and you think I'm gonna waste it? Bullsh—'

'Never mind that. Get dressed.'

'I am dressed.' He squinted unhappily as Mike turned on the lights. 'Hey, what the hell are you doing?' But Mike only smiled as he headed towards the tiny dishevelled kitchen.

'What'd you do in here? Detonate a hand grenade?'

'Yeah. And I'm gonna shove one up your—'

'Now, now, this is a special occasion.' Mike turned to smile at him from the kitchen doorway, and for a moment there was hope in Ben's eyes.

'Can we drink to it?'

'All you want. But later.'

'Crap.' He let himself fall into a chair, and let his head loll back against the soft cushions.

'Don't you want to know what the occasion is?'

'Not if I can't drink to it. I'm graduating from graduate school. That I can drink to.'

'And I'm getting married.'

'That's nice.' And then he sat up straight, and the eyes came open. 'You're what?'

'You heard me. Nancy and I are getting married.' Mike said it with the quiet pride of a man who knows his mind.

'This is an engagement party?' Ben sat up with a look of delight. Hell, that was worth at least another six Beefeaters. Maybe even seven or eight.

'Not an engagement party, Avery. I told you. It's a wedding.'

'Now?' Confusion again. Hillyard was a real pain in the ass. 'Why now?'

'Because we want to. Besides, you're too loaded to understand anyway. Can you get it together enough to be our best man?'

'Sure. Son of a bitch, you're actually going to—' He leapt out of his chair, lurched horribly and stubbed his toe on the coffee table. 'Goddamn—'

'Go put some clothes on without killing yourself. I'll make you some coffee.'

'Yeah . . .' He was still muttering to himself when he disappeared into the bedroom, but he looked slightly more composed when he returned. He was even wearing a tie, with a blue and red striped T-shirt. Mike looked at him and shook his head with a grin.

'You could've at least picked a tie that went with the shirt.' The tie was a dark maroon with a beige and black design.

'Do I need a tie?' He suddenly looked worried. 'I couldn't find one that matched.'

'Just zip up your fly, and we're all set. You might want to find the other shoe, too.' Ben looked down to see only one loafer, and then he started to laugh.

'Okay, so I'm gassed. But did I know you'd need me tonight? You could've at least told me this morning.'

'I didn't know this morning.'

That brought a look of sudden seriousness to Ben's eyes. 'You didn't?'

'Nope.'

'Are you sure about this?'

'Very much so. And look, don't make any speeches. I've had enough of those tonight. Just get yourself decent so we can pick up Nancy.' He handed his friend a mug of steaming coffee, and Ben took a long hard swallow, then grimaced.

'What a waste of good gin.'

'We'll buy you another round after the wedding.'

'Where are you doing this, by the way?'

'You'll see. It's a beautiful little town I've been in love with for years. I spent a summer there once as a kid. It's only about an hour from here. It's the perfect place.'

'You've got a licence?'

'Don't need one. It's one of those crazy towns where you do it all in one shot. You ready?'

Ben downed the last of the coffee and nodded. 'I think so. Jesus, I'm getting nervous. Aren't you scared?'

He looked at Mike more soberly now, but Mike looked strangely calm.

'Not a bit.'

'Maybe you know what you're doing. I don't know . . . it's just that . . . marriage . . .' He shook his head again and stared at his feet. It reminded him that he had another loafer to find. 'Nancy's a hell of a nice girl though.'

'Better than that.' Mike spotted the other loafer under the couch and handed it to him. 'She's everything I've always wanted.'

'Then I hope the marriage brings you both everything you want, Mike. Always.' There was a bright glaze of tenderness in his eyes, and for a moment Mike held him by both arms.

'Thanks.' And then they both looked away, anxious to get going, to laugh again, to taste the moment with glee instead of solemnity.

'Do I look all right?' Ben checked his pants for his wallet, then searched for his keys.

'You look gorgeous.'

'Oh shove it . . . damn . . . where're my keys?' He looked around helplessly as Mike laughed at him. The keys were attached to one of the belt loops on his trousers.

'Come on, Avery. Let's get you out of here.' The two left, arm in arm and singing the beer hall songs of summers before. The entire building could hear them but no one really cared: the whole place was populated by students living off campus, and two weeks before the summer break everyone was raising hell.

They pulled up outside Nancy's place on Spark Street ten minutes later, and she waved nervously from the window as Mike honked. She felt as though she'd been ready for hours. A moment later she was standing beside the car, and for a few seconds both young men fell silent. It was Mike who spoke first.

'My God, Nance . . . you look beautiful. Where did you get that?'

'I had it.' They exchanged a long smile, and none of them moved. She suddenly felt every bit a bride, despite the late hour and the unorthodox circumstances. She was wearing a long white eyelet dress and there was a little blue satin cap on her shiny black hair. She had worn the dress at a friend's wedding three years before, but Mike had never seen it. She was wearing white sandals and carrying a very old, very beautiful lace handkerchief. 'See, something old, something new . . . the handkerchief was my grand-mother's.' And the cap was blue. She looked so beautiful that for a moment Mike didn't know what to say. Even Ben seemed totally sobered as he looked at her.

'You look like a princess, Nancy.'

'Thanks, Ben.'

'Hey, listen, you got something borrowed?'

'What do you mean?'

'You know . . . something old, something new . . . some-thing borrowed . . .' She laughed and shook her head. 'Okay, here.' He bent his head forward and began to fumble with something at his neck. A moment later he held out a narrow, handsome gold chain. 'Now, this is just a loan. My sister gave it to me for graduation, but I opened it early. You can borrow it for the wedding.' He leaned out of the car to fasten it around her throat and it fell just above the delicate neckline of the dress.

34

'It's perfect.'

'So are you.' Mike said it as he got out of the car and held the door for her. He had been so stunned by the way she looked that he hadn't been able to move. 'Get in the back, Avery. Darling, you sit in front.'

'Can't she sit on my lap?' Ben made a feeble protest as he scrambled towards the back, and Mike glared at him. 'Okay, man, okay, don't get excited. I just thought maybe since I was the best man, and—'

'You'll be the dead man if you don't watch it.' But the mood was strictly a teasing one as Nancy settled herself on the front seat and beamed at the man she was about to marry. She felt a moment's queasiness about Marion, but she pushed it from her mind. This was the time to think only of herself, and Michael.

'What a crazy night . . . but I love it.'

They alternately joked and fell silent on the road to the tiny town Mike had in mind, and at last none of them spoke. They had a lot on their minds. Michael was thinking back to his interview with his mother, and Nancy was thinking of all that this day meant to her.

'Is it much farther, love?' Nancy was getting fidgety and her grandmother's handkerchief was beginning to look crumpled as it passed through her hands.

'Only about five more miles. We're almost there.' Michael reached briefly for Nancy's hand. 'Just a few more minutes, babe, and we'll be married.'

'Then speed it up, mister, before I get cold feet,' Ben sang out from the back, and all three of them laughed. Mike put his foot on the gas and swerved around the next curve, but the laughter rapidly shrank to a gasp as

Michael veered helplessly to avoid a diesel truck occupying both lanes as it ploughed mercilessly towards them, going too fast, and almost out of control. The driver must have been half-asleep, and the only sounds Nancy remembered hearing were Ben's anguished 'Oh no!' and her own voice screaming in her ears. Then there was the endless shattering of glass . . . shattering . . . breaking . . . metal grinding, crunching, roaring, engines meeting and locking and arms flying and leather tearing and plastic cracking as everything was covered with a blanket of glass. And then at last everything stopped, and the world was black.

It seemed years later when Ben woke up, lying with his head jammed into the dashboard and a terrible pounding in his ears. Everything was dark around him and there seemed to be a handful of sand in his mouth. It felt like hours before he could open his eyes, and the effort it took made him feel sick. At first he couldn't understand what he saw. Nothing seemed to make sense, and then he realised that he was looking into Michael's right eye. He was in the front seat with him, but all he could see was Michael, and there was a thin river of blood trickling slowly down the side of Mike's face, on to his neck. It was strange to watch it, but for a while that was all Ben did . . . watch . . . Mike . . . bleeding . . . Jesus. It dawned on him what was happening. Accident . . . there had been an accident . . . and Mike had been driving and . . . he lifted his head from where it had lain and tried to look up but a blow as if from iron forced him back down. It was minutes before he caught his breath and could open his eyes again. Mike was still lying there, bleeding, but now

Ben could see that he was breathing, and this time when he stirred nothing happened. He could lift his head, and what he saw just beyond Mike was the truck that had hit them, lying flipped over the side of the road. What he did not see was the driver, lying dead beneath the cab of the truck. It would be a long time before anyone saw that. And then Ben realised something more . . . that he was seeing it all through open windows. There was no more glass left anywhere in the car, they were wearing it all, crushed into tiny particles all around them. And on Mike's side there was also no door. And then he remembered something more. Somebody else had been in the car . . . Nancy was . . . and where were they going? It was all so hard to hold on to, and his head hurt so badly, and as he moved a horrible pain shot through his leg, into his side. He moved to get away from the pain, and then he saw her. Nancy . . . Jesus . . . it was Nancy in some kind of red and white dress, lying face down on the hood . . . Nancy . . . she had to be dead . . . he didn't even care about the pain in his leg now, he dragged himself over the dashboard and to her side. He had to . . . turn her over . . . get to her . . . help her . . . Nancy . . . And then he saw the fine powder that dusted Nancy's hair. She was wearing the windshield all over her dress, all over the back of her head, all over . . . My God . . . With the last of his strength, he rolled her slowly to her side and then pitifully, like a terrified little boy, he began to whimper.

'Oh my God . . .' There was no face left beneath the blood-soaked blue satin cap. He couldn't tell if she were dead or alive, but for one horrible instant, he hoped she was dead, because there was simply no more Nancy. There

37

was no one there at all, not even a remnant of the once beautiful face. And then mercifully, in her blood and his tears, he passed out.

4

He looked so painfully pale as his mother sat there watching him. Marion Hillyard sat in a corner of the room with a bleak expression on her face. She had been there before, in that room, on that day, watching that face . . . not really that face, or that room, but she felt as though nothing had changed. It was just like when Frederick had the massive coronary that had killed him within hours. She had sat there, just as still, just as frightened, just as alone. And he had . . . Frederick . . . she felt a sob catch in her throat again and she took a deep, sharp breath. She couldn't cry. She couldn't let herself think those thoughts. Her husband was gone. Michael wasn't. Nothing was going to happen to Michael. She wouldn't let anything happen. She was holding on to him now with every ounce of strength she could give.

For a moment, she turned her gaze to the nurse's face. The woman was watching Michael intently, but with no sign of alarm. He had been in a coma all that day, since the accident the night before. Marion had got there at five in the morning. She had called a twenty-four-hour limousine service and been up from New York. But she would have walked if she'd had to. Nothing would have kept her from Michael's side; she had to be there to keep him alive. He was all she had now. Michael, and the business . . . and the business was for him. She had done it all for him . . . well, not all for him, but for the most part. It was the greatest gift she could give him. The gift of power, of success. He couldn't throw that away on that little bitch . . . he couldn't throw it away by *dying*. Jesus. It was all her fault, that damned girl. She had probably talked him into this. She had . . .

The nurse got up quickly and pulled at Michael's eyelids, as Marion went tense and forgot what she had been thinking. She stood up silently and quickly and walked to the nurse's side. Whatever there was to see, she wanted to see it. But there was nothing. No change. The expressionless woman in white held his wrist for a moment and then mouthed the same words again. 'No change.' She motioned towards the corridor then and Marion followed her outside. This time the woman's concern was not for Michael, but for his mother.

'Dr Wickfield told me to ask you to leave by five o'clock, Mrs Hillyard. And I'm afraid . . .' She looked menacingly at her watch, and then smiled apologetically. It was five fifteen. Marion had been at Michael's side for exactly twelve hours. She had sat there uninterrupted all day, with only two cups of coffee to keep her going. But she wasn't tired, she wasn't hungry, she wasn't anything. And she wasn't leaving.

'Thank you for the thought. I'll just walk down the hall for a moment and come back.' She wasn't leaving him. Not ever. She had left Frederick. Only for an hour to have dinner. They had insisted that she eat something, and it had happened then. He had died while she was gone. That wasn't going to happen this time. She knew that as long as she sat there, Michael wouldn't die. The damage was mostly internal, but even Wickfield felt he'd come out of the coma soon. Still, she wasn't taking any chances. They had thought Frederick would make it, too. There were tears in her eyes now as she stood staring blankly at the pale blue wall behind the nurse.

'Mrs Hillyard?' The woman gently touched her arm, and Marion started. 'You ought to get some rest. Dr Wickfield set aside a room for you on the third floor.'

'There's no need.' She smiled blankly at the nurse and walked away towards the far end of the hall. The sun was still bright in the window there, and she sat carefully on the ledge, to smoke her first cigarette in hours and watched the sun set over a little white church in the pretty New England town. Thank God the town only looked remote, and was actually less than an hour outside Boston. They had had no trouble bringing in the best doctors to consult, and as soon as he could stand it, Michael would be moved to a hospital in New York. But at least she knew that in the meantime he was in good hands. Medically, Michael had taken the worst of it. The Avery boy was pretty badly broken up, but he was awake and alive, and his father had had him taken to Boston by ambulance that afternoon. He had broken an arm, a thigh, a foot, and a collarbone, but he'd be all right. And the girl . . . well, it was her fault, there was no reason why she should . . . Marion stubbed out the cigarette with a quick crushing motion of her foot. The girl would be all right too. She'd live anyway. The only thing she had lost was her face. And maybe that was just as well. For a fraction of a second Marion wanted to fight the anger, wanted to make herself sorry for the girl – just in case all that stuff about Christian charity was true, just in case her feelings made some difference for Michael . . . just in case there was a God who would punish her by taking him. But she couldn't do it. She hated the girl with every ounce of her being.

'I thought I left orders for you to get some rest.' Marion turned towards the voice with a start, and then smiled tiredly when she saw her own Dr Wickfield. Wicky. 'Don't you ever listen to anyone, Marion?'

'Not if I can help it. How's Michael?' Her brow furrowed and she reached for another cigarette.

'I just looked in on him. He's stable. I told you, he'll come out of it. Give him time. His entire system received one hell of a shock.'

'So did mine when I got the news.' He nodded sympathetically. 'You're sure there won't be permanent damage from this?' She paused for a moment and then said the dread words. 'Brain damage?'

Wickfield patted her arm and sat next to her on the window ledge. Behind them the little town made a scene pretty enough for a postcard. 'I told you, Marion. As best we can tell, he'll be fine. A lot depends, of course, on how long he stays under. But I'm not frightened yet.'

'I am.' They were two tiny words in the mouth of a very strong woman, and they surprised her doctor, as he looked at her closely. There were sides to Marion Hillyard that no one even guessed at. 'What about the girl?' she went on. Now she was the Marion he knew again, eyes narrowed behind the smoke from her cigarette, face hardened, fear gone.

'Not much is going to change for her. Not for the time being anyway. She's been in stable condition all day, but there's not a damn thing we can do for her. For one thing, it's much too soon, and for another, there are only one or two men in the country who can cope with that kind of total reconstruction. There is simply nothing left of her face, not a single bone intact, not a nerve, not a muscle. The only thing not totally wiped out are her eyes.'

'The better to see herself with.' Dr Wickfield jumped at the tone of Marion's voice.

'Michael was driving, Marion. She wasn't.' But Marion only nodded in answer. There was no point in going over it with him. She knew whose fault it was. It was the girl's.

'What happens to someone like that if there's no repair work done? Will she live?'

'Unfortunately, yes. But she'll lead a tragic life. You can't take a twenty-two-year-old girl and turn her into a horror like that and expect her to adjust. No one could. Was she . . . was she pretty before?'

'I suppose so. I don't know. We'd never met.' Her tone was rock hard, and her eyes equally so.

'I see. In any case, she's in for some tough realities. They'll do what they can here at the hospital when she's a little more recovered, but it won't be much. Does she have money?'

'None.' Marion spoke the word like a death sentence. It was the worst thing she could say of anyone.

'Then she won't have many alternatives. I'm afraid the men who do this kind of thing don't do it for charity.'

'Do you have anyone particular in mind?'

'Well, I know some of the names. Two, actually. The best one is out in San Francisco.' A little fire kindled in

Dr Wickfield's heart. With all her money Marion Hillyard could . . . if only . . . 'His name is Peter Gregson. We met several years ago. He's really an amazing man.'

'Could he do this?'

Wickfield felt a rush of admiration for the woman. He almost wanted to hug her, but he didn't dare. 'He may well be the only man who could. Shall I . . . do you want me to call him?' He hesitated to say the words, and then she looked at him with those cold, calculating eyes and he wondered what she had in mind. The wave of admiration almost turned to fear.

'I'll let you know.'

'Fine.' He looked at his watch then, and stood up. 'I'd like you to go downstairs and rest now. I really mean that.'

'I know.' She favoured him with a wintry smile. 'But I'm not going to. You know that too. I have to be with Michael.'

'Even if you kill yourself doing it?'

'I won't. I'm too mean to die, Wicky. Besides, I still have a lot of work to do.'

'Is it worth it?' He looked at her curiously for a moment. If he had had one tenth of her ambition, he would have been a great surgeon, but he didn't and he wasn't. And he wasn't even sure that he envied her. 'Is it worth it?' He said it more softly the second time, and she nodded.

'Absolutely. Don't ever doubt it for a second. It's given me everything I want out of life.' Unless I lose Michael. She closed her eyes and pushed away the thought.

'Well, I'll give you another hour with him, and then I'm coming back up here. And I don't care if I have to shoot you with Nembutal and drag you away myself, you're going. Is that clear?'

'Very.' She stood up, dropped another cigarette to the floor where she crushed it, and patted his cheek. 'And Wicky . . .' She looked up at him from under long chestnut lashes, and for a moment she was all softness and elegant beauty, 'thank you.' He gently kissed her cheek, squeezed her arm, and stood back for a moment.

'He'll be all right, Marion, you'll see.' He didn't dare mention the girl again. They could talk about that later. He only smiled and walked away, as she stood there looking vulnerable and alone. He was glad he had called George Calloway a few hours before. Marion needed someone with her. He thought about her all the way down the corridor, as she stood watching him go. She hadn't moved from the spot where he had left her, and then slowly, she began the lonely walk up the hall, back towards Michael's room, past open doors and closed ones, heartbreaks to come and hopes never to be known again. And a few who would make it. This was a floor set aside for the critically ill, and there was no sound from any of the rooms as she walked slowly by, until she was halfway down the hall, where she heard little jerking sobs come from an open door. The sounds were so soft that at first she wasn't sure what she was hearing. And then she saw the room number, and she knew. She stopped as though she had come to a wall, staring at the door, and the darkness beyond.

She could see the bed dimly outlined in the corner, but the room was dark; all the blinds and curtains had been drawn, as though the patient could not be touched by light. Marion stood there for a long moment, afraid to go in, but knowing that she had to; and then slowly, one foot

45

after the other, softly, gliding, she walked a few feet into the room and stopped again. The sobs were a little louder now, and coming at quicker intervals, with little panicky gasps.

'Is someone there?' The girl's entire head was covered with bandages, and the voice was muffled and strange. 'Is someone . . .' She cried harder now. 'I can't see.'

'Your eyes are just covered with bandages. There's nothing wrong with your eyes.' But the words were met by fresh sobs. 'Why are you awake?' Marion spoke to her in a monotone. They were not words of reassurance. They were devoid of all feeling, and Marion herself felt as though she were standing in a dream. But she knew that she had to be there. Had to. For Michael's sake. 'Didn't they give you something to make you sleep?'

'It doesn't work. I keep waking up.'

'Is the pain very bad?'

'No, everything is numb. Who . . . who are you?'

She was afraid to tell her. Instead, she moved towards the bed and sat down in the narrow blue vinyl chair the nurse must have pulled up next to it. The girl's hands were wrapped in bandages, too, and lay useless at her sides. Marion remembered Wicky telling her that the girl had naturally used her hands to try to shield her face. The damage to them was almost as great as to her face, which would be devastating to her as an artist. In essence, her whole life was over. Her youth, her beauty, her work. And her romance. But now Marion knew what she had to say.

'Nancy.' It was the first time she had said the name, but now it didn't matter. She had no choice. 'Did they . . .' Her voice was smooth and silky as she sat next to the broken girl. 'Did they tell you about your face?' There was total silence in the room for an endless amount of time, and then a small broken sob freed itself from the bandages. 'Did they tell you how bad it was?' Her stomach turned over as she said the words, but she could not stop now. She had to free Michael. If she freed him, he would live. She felt that in her guts. 'Did they tell you how impossible it would be to put you back together?'

The sobs were angry now. 'They lied to me. They said . . .'

'There's only one man who can do it, Nancy, and it would cost hundreds of thousands of dollars. You can't afford it. And neither can Michael.'

'I'd never let him do that.' She was angry at the voice now, as well as at fate. 'I'd never let him . . .'

'Then what will you do?'

'I don't know.' And the sobs began again.

'Could you face him like that?' It took minutes for the stifled 'no' to emerge. 'Do you think he would love you like that? Even if he tried, because he felt some bond of loyalty, some obligation, how long could it last? How long could you bear knowing what you looked like and what you were doing to him?' The sounds Nancy made now were frightening. She sounded as though she were going to be sick, and Marion wondered if she herself would be as well. 'Nancy, there's nothing left of you. Nothing. There's nothing left of the life you had before today.' They sat in interminable silence, and Marion thought she would hear those sobs forever. But it had to be painful or it would never work. 'You've already lost him. You couldn't do this to him. And he . . . he deserves better than that. If you love him, you know that. And . . . and so do you. But you could have a new life, Nancy.' The girl didn't even bother to answer as her sobs went on. 'You *could* have a new life. A whole new world.' She waited until the sobs grew angrier again and then stopped. 'A whole new face.'

'How?'

'There's a man in San Francisco who could make you beautiful again. Who could make you able to paint again. It would take a long time, and a lot of money, but it would be worth it, Nancy . . . wouldn't it?' There was the tiniest of smiles at the corners of Marion's mouth. Now she was on familiar ground. It was just like making a multi-million-dollar deal. A *hundred*-million-dollar deal. They were all the same.

A small jagged sigh emerged from the faceless bandages. 'We can't afford it.' Marion almost shuddered at the 'we'. They were not a 'we' anymore. They never had been. She and Michael were the 'we'. Not this . . . this . . . She took a deep breath and composed herself. She had work to do. That was the only way she could think of it. She couldn't think of the girl. Only of Michael.

'You can't, Nancy. But I can. You do know who I am, don't you?'

'Yes.'

'You do understand that you've already lost Michael? That he could never survive the pressure and tragedy of what has happened to you, if he survives at all. You understand that, don't you?'

'Yes.'

'And you know that it would be a vicious thing to do,

48

to try and push him through it, to make him prove his loyalty to you?' She wouldn't say the word 'love'. The girl wasn't worthy of it. Marion had to believe that. 'Do you understand that, Nancy?' There was a silent pause. 'Do you?'

This time it was a very tired little word. She was sounding spent. 'Yes.'

'Then you've already lost everything you can lose, haven't you?'

'Yes.' The word had no tone, no life to it. It was as though life itself were seeping away from the girl.

'Nancy, I'd like to propose a little deal to you.' It was Marion Hillyard at her best. If her son had heard her, he would have wanted to kill her. 'I'd like you to think about that new face. About a new life, a new Nancy. Think about it. About what it would mean. You'd be beautiful again, you could have friends again, you could go places – to restaurants, to movies, to stores – you could wear pretty clothes and go out with men. The other way . . . people would shriek when you walked near them. You couldn't go anywhere, do anything, be anyone. Children would cry if they saw you. Can you imagine what that would be like? But you have a choice.' She let the words sink in.

'No, I don't.'

'Yes, you do. I want to give you that choice. I will give you that new life. A new face, a new world. An apartment in another city while the work is being done – anything you need, anything you want to do. There'll be no struggle, Nancy, and in a year or so, the nightmare will be over.'

'And then?'

'You're free. The new life is yours.' There was an endless pause as Marion prepared to lower the boom Nancy was waiting for. 'As long as you never contact Michael again. The new face is yours only if you give up Michael. But if you don't accept my . . . my gift, you'll know that you've already lost him, anyway. So why live the rest of your life as a freak if you don't have to?'

'What if Michael doesn't honour the agreement? What if I stay away from him, but he doesn't stay away from me?'

'All I want from you is the promise that you'll stay away from him. What Michael does is up to him.'

'And you'll honour that? If he wants me . . . anyway . . . if he comes after me, then it's up to him?'

'I'll honour that.'

Nancy felt victorious as she lay there. She knew Michael infinitely better than his mother did. Michael would never give up on her. He'd find her and want to help her through the ordeal, but by then she'd already be on her way to becoming herself again. His mother couldn't win this one, no matter how hard she tried. Accepting the deal would make Nancy a cheat, because she knew what the outcome would be. But she had to do it. She had to. There was no other way.

'Will you do it?' Marion almost held her breath as she waited for the one word she prayed for, the word that would free Michael, and at last it came.

But it would be a word of victory, not of defeat. It would be filled with all Nancy's faith in Michael. She remembered the words he had said to her at the rock where they'd hidden the beads the morning before. 'I promise never to say goodbye to you.' She knew he never would.

'Your answer, Nancy?' Marion couldn't wait any longer. Her heart wouldn't bear it.

'Yes.'

Marion Hillyard stood in the doorway of the hospital in a black wool dress and black Cardin coat watching them load the girl into an ambulance. It was six o'clock in the morning, and she had never spoken to her again. They had made their agreement the night before, and Marion had immediately asked Wicky to call the man he knew in San Francisco. Wickfield had been overjoyed. He had kissed Marion on the cheek and had got hold of Peter Gregson at his home. Gregson would do it. He wanted Nancy out west immediately, and Marion had arranged for a special compartment and two nurses in first class on a jet heading for San Francisco at eight o'clock that morning. She was sparing no expense.

'She's a lucky girl, Marion.' Wickfield looked at her in admiration as she crushed out another cigarette.

'I think so. And I don't want Michael to know, Wicky. Is that clear?' It was, and so was the 'or else' in her voice. 'If he finds out, if you mention any of this to him, I cancel the treatment.'

'But why? He has a right to know what you've done for the girl.'

'It's between the two of us. The four of us, including you and Gregson. Michael doesn't need to know anything. When he comes out of the coma, you're not to mention the girl to him at all. It will only agitate him.'

If he ever came out of the coma. Marion had dozed in

the chair at his side all night long despite Wicky's protests. But she had felt strangely revived after her talk with the girl. She had freed Michael at last. Now he could live. In a way, she had given them both life. She knew she had been right to do what she'd done. 'You won't say anything then, will you, Robert?' She never called him that, except to remind him what the Hillyard money had done for his hospital.

'Of course not, if that's what you want.'

'It is.'

There was the dull clank of the ambulance door closing, and the last of the blue blankets swathing the girl disappeared with the two nurses' backs. The nurses would be with her for the first six or eight months in San Francisco. After that, Gregson had said, she wouldn't need them. But for those six or eight months, she would spend much of her time with her eyes bandaged, as he worked on her lids and her nose, her brow and her cheekbones. He had a whole face to reconstruct. There would be other expenses involved too. Nancy would need almost constant care by a psychiatrist, as she underwent the emotional shock of becoming a new person. There was no way Gregson could give her back the self she had been. He had to create a whole new woman. And Marion liked that idea just fine. The girl would be that much more removed from Michael. It took away the possibility of an accident, a chance meeting in an airport five years later. Marion didn't want that to happen. Her mind ran over the list of arrangements she had made with Gregson on the phone at four o'clock that morning, one o'clock San Francisco time. He had sounded bright and alive and dynamic, a man in his forties with an extraordinary international reputation in his field. She was a damn lucky girl. He said he'd have his secretary work it all out. The apartment, the clothes. They had quickly run over the cost of eighteen months of surgery, and the additional expense of psychiatric help, constant nurses for a while, and even general support. They had settled on four hundred thousand dollars as a reasonable figure. Marion would call the bank at nine and have it transferred to Gregson's account on the coast. It would be there when his own bank opened at nine. Not that he was worried. He knew who Marion Hillyard was. Who didn't?

'Why don't you come inside and have some breakfast, Marion?' Wickfield was losing hope of having any influence on her at all, and Calloway had said that he couldn't leave New York until that morning. Wickfield didn't know that Marion had told him not to. She had wanted to be alone to work out her 'business' arrangements. And everything had worked out just perfectly. 'Marion?'

'Hm?'

'Breakfast?'

'Later, Wicky. Later. I want to see Michael.'

'I'll go up and take a look at him now.'

Marion stopped in the ladies' room for a moment, while Wickfield went ahead to see Michael. But he didn't expect any immediate change; he had checked him only an hour before.

But there was a strange stillness when Marion came into the room five minutes later. Wicky was standing back from the bed with a look of solemnity, and the nurse had left the room.

The New England sun was streaming across the bed, and from somewhere there was the steady sound of water dripping into a sink. Everything was much too still, and suddenly her heart flew to her mouth. It was like when Frederick . . . oh God . . . her hand went unwillingly to her heart and she stood frozen in the doorway looking from Wicky to the bed. And then she saw him . . . her boy. It wasn't like Frederick at all. A sob caught in her throat and she walked to the bed with trembling legs, and then she bent down and touched his face with her hands.

'Hi, Mom.' They were the most beautiful words she had ever heard, and the tears poured down her face as she smiled.

'I love you, Michael.'

'I love you, too.' Even Wickfield had tears in his eyes as he watched them. The boy, so young and handsome and alive again, and the woman who had given so much in the past two days. He slipped quietly from the room, and they never heard him go.

She held her son gently in her arms for a long moment as he ran a hand over her hair. 'Take it easy, Mom. Everything's okay. Christ, I'm hungry.' Marion laughed. He sounded so good. He was alive again. And all hers.

'We will get you the biggest, bestest, superest breakfast you've ever seen, if Wicky says it's all right.'

'To hell with Wicky. I'm starving.'

'Michael!' She couldn't be angry at him, though. She could only love him. But then as she looked at him, she saw his face cloud over as though he were suddenly remembering why he was there. Before that, he had

55

acted as if he had just awakened from having his tonsils out. All he wanted was ice cream and his mother. But now there was a great deal more in his face, and he tried to sit up. He didn't know how to say the words, but he had to ask. He searched her face, and she kept her eyes on his and his hand tightly held in hers. 'Take it easy, darling.'

'Mom . . . the others . . . the other night . . . I remember . . .'

'Ben has already gone back to Boston with his father. He's pretty badly banged up but he's all right. A lot more all right than you were.' She said it with a sigh and tightened her grip on his hand. She knew what was coming next. But she was prepared for it.

'And . . . Nancy?' His face was ivory white as he said her name. 'Nancy, Mom?' The tears already stood out in his eyes. He could see the answer in his mother's face as she sat down carefully in the chair next to him and ran a gentle hand along the outline of his face.

'She didn't make it, darling. They did all they could. But the damage was just too great.' She paused for only the slightest of seconds and then went on. 'She died early this morning.'

'Did you see her?' He was still searching her face for something more.

'I sat with her for a while last night.'

'Oh, God . . . and I wasn't there. Oh, Nancy . . .' He turned his head into the pillow and cried like a child as Marion held his shoulders. He said her name over and over and over again, until at last he could cry no more. And when he turned to look at his mother again, she saw something in his face that she had never seen there before.

56

It was as though he had lost something of himself in those moments when he said Nancy's name. As though part of him had bled away. Had just died.

Nancy heard the landing gear grind out of the plane's belly, and for the hundredth time since the flight began she reached out blindly for the hand that had been offered her before. It was strangely comforting to hold the nurse's hand, and it pleased her that she could already tell the difference between them. One woman had thin, delicate hands with long narrow fingers; her hands were always cold but there was great strength in the way she held on to Nancy. It made Nancy feel brave again just to touch her. The other nurse had warm, chubby, soft hands that made one feel safe and loved. She patted Nancy's arm a lot, and it was she who had given Nancy the two shots for the pain. She had a soft soothing voice. The first woman had a slight accent. Nancy had already come to like them both.

'It won't be much longer now, dear. We can see the bay now. We'll be there in no time at all.'

Actually, it would be another twenty minutes. And Peter Gregson was counting on that as he raced along the freeway in the black Porsche. The ambulance was meeting him there. He could have one of the girls from his office pick his car up later that morning. He wanted to ride into the city with the girl. He was intrigued by her. She had to be someone for Marion Hillyard to be so concerned about her. Four hundred thousand dollars was quite a sum, and only three of that was going to him. The other hundred was to keep the girl comfortable in the next year and a half. And she would be. He had promised Marion Hillyard. But he would have seen to that anyway. It was part of what he did. He would get to know the girl's very soul. They would become more than friends; he would mean everything to her and she to him. It had to be that way, because by the time that new face was born, she would be the person she looked like. Peter Gregson was going to give birth to Nancy McAllister, after a pregnancy of eighteen long months. She was going to have to be a very brave girl. But she would be. He would see to that. They would face it together. The very idea excited him. He loved what he did, and in an odd way he already loved Nancy. What he would make of her. What she would be. He would give her all that he had to give.

He looked at his watch and stepped on the gas. The car was one of his favourite releases. He also flew his own plane, went scuba diving whenever he had time, skied, and had climbed several mountains in Europe. He was a man who liked to scale heights. To defy the impossible and win. It was why he loved his work. People accused him of playing God. But it wasn't really that. It was the thrill of insuperable odds that stimulated him. And he had never yet been defeated. Not by women or mountains or sky, not even by a patient. At forty-seven, he had won at everything he touched, and he was going to win now. He and Nancy were going to win together. His dark hair blew softly in the breeze and his eyes almost crackled with life. He still had a tan from a recent week in Tahiti, and he was wearing grey slacks and a soft blue cashmere sweater that was just the colour of his eyes. He was always impeccably dressed, perfectly put together. He was an exceptionally

59

good-looking man, but there was more to him than that. It was his vitality, his electricity that caught one's attention even more than his looks did.

He pulled up at the airport precisely at the moment that Nancy's plane was touching down. He showed a special pass to a policeman, who nodded and promised to keep an eye on the car. Even the policeman smiled at Gregson. Peter was a man no one could ignore. He had an almost irresistible charm, and a strength that showed through everything he did. It made people want to be near him.

He picked his way expertly into the airport lobby and spoke rapidly to a ground supervisor. The man picked up a phone, and within moments Peter was ushered through a door, down a flight of stairs, and into a tiny airport vehicle, then rushed out to the runway, where he saw the ambulance standing by, the attendants waiting for the patient to be taken off the plane. He thanked his driver and hurried to the ambulance, where he quickly checked inside to see that his orders had been carried out. They had been, to the letter. Everything was there that he needed. It was hard to tell what kind of shape she might be in after the flight, but he had wanted her in San Francisco immediately, so he could keep a close eye on things. He had a lot of planning to do, and work would begin in just a few days.

The other passengers were held back a few more minutes while Nancy was carried out through the forward hatch. The stewardesses hung back, looking grave, averting their gazes from the bottles and transfusions that hung over the bandaged girl, but the nurses seemed to be speaking to her as she was carried out. He liked the look of the nurses, young but competent, and they seemed to work well as a team. That was what he wanted. They were all going to be part of a team for the next year and a half, and everyone was important. There was no room for reluctance or incompetence. Everyone had to be the very best they could be, including Nancy. But he would see to that. She was going to be the star of this show. He watched her being carried towards him and waited until the stretcher had been gently set down inside the ambulance. He smiled at the nurses but said nothing, and held up a hand gesturing them to wait as he eased in beside Nancy and sat down on a seat next to her. He reached for her hand and held it.

'Hello, Nancy. I'm Peter. How was the trip?' As though she was for real. As though she were still someone, not just a faceless blob. She could feel relief wash over her at the sound of his voice.

'It was okay. You're Dr Gregson?' She sounded tired but interested.

'Yes. But Peter sounds a little less formal between two people who're going to be working together.' She liked the way he said it, and if she could have, she would have smiled.

'You came out to meet me?'

'Wouldn't you have come out to meet me?'

'Yes.' She wanted to nod, but she couldn't. 'Thank you.'

'I'm glad I did. Have you ever been to San Francisco before, Nancy?'

'No.'

'You're going to love it. And we're going to find you an apartment you like so much you'll never want to leave here. Most people don't, you know. Once they dig in their heels, they want to stay here forever. I came from Chicago about fifteen years ago, and you couldn't get me back there on a bet.' She laughed at the way he said it, and he smiled down at her. 'Are you from Boston?' He was treating her as though they had been introduced by friends. But he wanted her to relax after the long flight. And a few minutes without movement would do her good. The nurses were also glad of the opportunity to stretch as they chatted with the two ambulance attendants. Now and then they glanced in to see Dr Gregson, still talking to Nancy, and they liked him already. He exuded warmth.

'No, I was from New Hampshire. That's where I grew up anyway. In an orphanage. I moved to Boston when I was eighteen.'

'It sounds very romantic. Or was the orphanage straight out of Dickens?' He gave everything a light touch, a happy note. Nancy laughed at the question about Dickens.

'Hardly. The nuns were wonderful. So much so that I wanted to be one.'

'Oh, God. Now listen you . . .' and she laughed at the tone of his voice. 'When we're through with our project, young lady, you're going to be ready for Hollywood. If you go hide in a convent somewhere I'll . . . I'll . . . why, I'll head off the bridge, damn it. You'd better promise me you won't go off and become a nun somewhere.' That was easy. She had Michael to get ready for. Her dreams of being Sister Agnes Marie had faded years ago, but she wanted to tease Gregson a little. She already liked him.

'Oh, all right.' She said it begrudgingly but with laughter in her voice.

'Is that a promise? Come on, say it . . . I promise.'

'I promise.'

'What do you promise?' They were both laughing now.

'I promise not to be a nun.'

'Whew. That's better.' He signalled to the two nurses to join them, and the attendants moved towards the front. She was ready to go now, and he didn't want to tire her with too much patter. 'Why don't you introduce me to your friends.'

'Well, let's see, the cold hands are Lily, and the warm ones are Gretchen.' All four of them laughed.

'Thanks a lot, Nancy.' Lily reached for her patient's hand and squeezed it gently as Nancy smiled to herself. She felt safe with her newfound friends, and all she could think of now was what she would look like for Michael after it was all over. She liked Peter Gregson, and suddenly she knew that he was going to make her someone very special, because he cared.

'Welcome to San Francisco, little one.' Lily's cool hands were replaced by his strong, graceful ones, and he held her hand all the way into the city. In an odd way, he made her feel as though she had come home.

The ambulance doors swung open and they carried the stretcher expertly into the hotel. The manager was waiting to greet them, and the entire penthouse suite had been reserved for their use. They were only planning to stay for a day or two, but the hotel would provide a breather between hospital and home. Marion had business meetings in Boston, and besides, Michael had for some reason, insisted on a few days in an hotel before going home. And his mother was ready to indulge his every whim.

The ambulance attendants set him down carefully on the bed, and he made a face. 'For Chrissake, there's nothing wrong with me, Mother. They all said I was fine.'

'But there's no need to push.'

'Push?' He looked around the suite and groaned as she tipped the ambulance attendants, who promptly vanished. The room was filled with flowers, and there was a huge basket of fruit on the table near the bed. His mother owned the hotel. She had bought it years before as an investment.

'Now relax, darling. Don't get over-excited. Do you want anything to eat?' She had wanted to keep the nurse, but even the doctor had said that was unnecessary, and it would have driven Michael crazy. All he had to do now was take it easy for another couple of weeks, and then he could go to work. But he had something else to do first. 'How about some lunch?' Marion asked.

'Sure. Escargots. Oysters Rockefeller. Champagne. Turtles' eggs and caviar.' He sat up in bed like a mischievous child.

'What a revolting combination, my love.' But she wasn't really listening to him. She was looking at her watch. 'But do order yourself something. George should be here any minute. Our meeting downtown is at one.' She walked out of the room distractedly, to look for her briefcase, and Mike heard the doorbell at the front of the suite. A moment later, George Calloway walked into his room.

'Well, Michael, how are you feeling?'

'After two weeks in the hospital, doing absolutely nothing, I feel most embarrassed.' He tried to make light of his situation, but there was still a broken look around his eyes. His mother saw it, too, but put it down to fatigue. She had shut out any alternative explanation from her mind, and she and Michael never discussed it. They talked about the business, and the plans for the medical centre in San Francisco. Never the accident.

'I stopped in at your office this morning. It looks very handsome indeed.' George smiled and sat down at the foot of the bed.

'I'm sure it does.' Michael watched his mother as she came into the room. She was wearing a light grey Chanel suit with a soft blue silk blouse, pearl earrings, and three strands of pearls around her neck. 'Mother has excellent taste.'

'Yes, she does.' George smiled at her warmly, but she waved nervously at them both.

'Stop throwing roses; we're going to be late. George, do you have the papers we need?'

'Of course.'

'Then let's go.' She walked quickly towards Michael's bed and bent down to kiss the top of his head. 'Rest, darling. And don't forget to order lunch.'

'Yes, ma'am. Good luck at the meeting.'

She raised her head and smiled with pure anticipation. 'Luck has nothing to do with it.' The two men laughed, and Michael watched them go. And then he sat up.

He sat patiently and quietly, waiting and thinking. He knew exactly what he was going to do. He had planned it for two weeks. He had lived for this moment. It had been all he could think of. It was why he had suggested the hotel, insisted on it in fact, and urged her to attend the meetings herself for the new Boston library building. He needed the afternoon to himself. He just didn't want to spoil anything by having them catch him. He wanted to be sure they were gone. So he sat exactly where he was for exactly half an hour. And then he was sure. He had rehearsed it a hundred times in his head. He went quickly to the suitcase on the rack at the foot of his bed and took out what he needed. Grey slacks, blue shirt, socks, underwear. It seemed a thousand years since he had worn clothes, and he was surprised at how wobbly he felt as he got dressed. He had to sit down three or four times to catch his breath. It was ridiculous to feel that weak, and he wouldn't give in to it. He wasn't going to wait another day. He was going there now. It took him nearly half an hour to dress and comb his hair, and then he called the desk and asked for a cab. He was pale on his way down in the lift, but the excitement of his plan made him feel better. Just the thought of it gave him life again, as nothing had done in two weeks. The cab was waiting for him at the kerb.

He gave the driver the address, and sat back with a feeling of great exhilaration. It was as though they had a date, as though she were expecting him, as though she knew. He smiled to himself all the way over, and gave the driver a large tip. He didn't ask the man to wait. He didn't want anyone waiting for him. He would stay there alone, for as long as he wanted. He had even toyed with the idea of continuing to pay rent on the place, so that he could come there whenever he liked. It was only an hour's flight from New York, and that way he would always have their apartment. Their apartment. He looked up at the building with a familiar glow of warmth, and almost in spite of himself, he heard himself say the words he'd been thinking. 'Hi, I'm home.' He had said the words a thousand times before as he walked in the door and found her sitting at her easel, with paint spattered all over her hands and arms and occasionally her face. If she was terribly involved in the work, she sometimes didn't hear him come in.

He walked slowly up the stairs, tired, but buoyed by the feeling of homecoming. He just wanted to go upstairs and sit down, near her, with her . . . with her things . . . All the same familiar smells pervaded the building, and there was the sound of running water, of a child, a cat meowing in a hallway below, and outside a horn honking. He could hear an Italian song on the radio, and for a strange moment he wondered if the radio was on in her studio. He had his key in his hand when he reached the landing, and stopped for a long, long moment. For the first time all day, he felt tears burn his eyes. He still knew the truth. She wouldn't be there. She was gone forever. She was dead. He tried the word out loud from time to time, just to make himself say it, to make himself know. He didn't want to be one of those crazy people who never faced the truth, who played games of pretend. She would have been scornful of that. But now and then he let the knowledge go, only to have it return with a slap. As it did now. He turned the key in the lock and waited, as though maybe someone would come to the door after all. But there was no one there. He opened the door slowly, and then he gasped.

'Oh, my God! Where is . . . where . . .' It was gone. All of it. Every table, every chair, the plants, the paintings, her easel, her paints. Her clothes, her . . . 'Jesus Christ, Nancy!' And then he heard himself crying as hot angry tears stung his face and he pulled open doors. Nothing. Even the refrigerator was gone. He stood there dumbly for a moment and then flew down the stairs two at a time until he reached the manager's apartment in the basement. He pounded on the door until the little old man opened it just the width of the protective chain and stared out with a look of fear in his eyes. But he recognised Michael and opened the door as he started to smile, until Michael grabbed him by the collar and began to shake him. 'Where is her stuff, Kawolski? Where the hell is it? What did you do with it? Did you take it? Who took it? Where are her things?'

'What things? Who . . . oh, my God . . . no, no, I didn't take anything. They came two weeks ago. They told me—' He was trembling with terror, and Michael with rage.

'Who the hell is "they"?'

'I don't know. Someone called me and said that the apartment would be vacant. That Miss McAllister was . . .

68

had . . .' He saw the tears still wet on Michael's face and was afraid to go on. 'You know. Well, they told me, and they said the apartment would be empty by the end of the week. Two nurses came and took a few things, and then the Goodwill truck came the next morning.'

'Nurses? What nurses?' Michael's mind was a blank. And Goodwill? Who had called them?

'I don't know who they were. They looked like nurses though – they were wearing white. They didn't take much. Just that little bag, and her paintings. Goodwill got the rest. I didn't take nothing. Honest. I wouldn't do that. Not to a nice girl like . . .' But Michael wasn't listening to him. He was already wandering up the stairs to the street, dazed, as the old man watched him, shaking his head. Poor guy. He had probably just heard. 'Hey . . . hey.' Michael turned around, and the old man lowered his voice. 'I'm sorry.' Michael only nodded and went out to the street. How did the nurses know? How could they have done it? They'd probably taken the little jewellery she had, a few trinkets, and the paintings. Maybe someone had said something to them at the hospital. Vultures, picking over what was left. God, if he'd seen them, he'd . . . his hands clenched at his side, and then his arm shot out to hail a cab. At least . . . maybe . . . it was worth a try. He slid into the cab, ignoring the ache that was beginning to pound at the back of his head. 'Where's the nearest Goodwill?'

'Goodwill what?' The driver was chewing a soggy cigar and was not particularly interested in Goodwill of any kind.

'Goodwill store. You know, used clothes, old furniture.'

'Oh yeah. Okay.' The kid didn't look like one of their customers, but a fare was a fare. It was a five-minute drive from Nancy's apartment, and the fresh air on his face helped revive Michael from the shock of the emptiness he had found. It was like looking for your pulse and finding that your heart had stopped beating. 'Okay, this is it.'

Michael thanked him absent-mindedly, paid twice the fare, and got out. He wasn't even sure he wanted to go inside. He had wanted to see her things in her apartment, where they belonged. Not in some stinking, musty old store, with price tags on them. And what would he do? Buy it all? And then what? He walked into the store feeling lonely and tired and confused. No one offered to help him, and he began to wander aimlessly up one aisle and down another, finding nothing he knew, seeing nothing familiar, and suddenly aching, not for the 'things' that had seemed so important to him that morning, but for the girl who had owned them. She was gone, and nothing he found or didn't find would ever make any difference. The tears began to stream down his face as he walked slowly back out to the street.

This time he didn't hail a cab. He just walked. Blindly and alone, in a direction his feet seemed to know, but his head didn't. His head didn't know anything any more. It felt like mush. His whole body felt like mush, but his heart was a stone. Suddenly, in that stinking old store, his life had come to an end. He understood now what it all meant, and as he stood at a red light, waiting for it to change, not giving a damn if it did, he passed out.

He woke up a few moments later, with a crowd around him as he lay on a small patch of grass where someone had carried him. There was a policeman standing over him, looking sharply into his eyes.

'You okay, son?' He was certain the kid was neither drunk nor stoned, but he looked a terrible grey colour. More likely he was sick. Or maybe just hungry or something. Looked like he had money though, couldn't have been a case of starvation.

'Yeah. I'm okay. I got out of the hospital this morning, and I guess I overdid it.' He smiled ruefully, but the faces around him did cartwheels when he tried to get up. The cop saw what was happening and urged the crowd to disperse. Then he looked back at Michael.

'I'll get a patrol car to give you a lift home.'

'No, really, I'm okay.'

'Never mind that. Would you rather go back to the hospital?'

'Hell, no!'

'All right, then we'll take you home.' He spoke into a small walkie-talkie and then squatted down near Michael. 'They'll be here in a minute. Been sick for a long time?'

Michael shook his head silently, and then looked down at his hands. 'Two weeks.' There was still a narrow scar near his temple, but too small for the policeman to notice.

'Well, you take it easy.' The patrol car slid up alongside them, and the policeman gave Michael a hand up. He was all right now. Pale, but steadier than he had been at first.

Michael looked over his shoulder and tried to smile at the cop. 'Thanks.' But the attempted smile only made the cop wonder what was wrong. There was a kind of despair in the kid's eyes.

He gave the men in the patrol car an address a block from the hotel, and thanked them when he got out. And then he walked the last block. The suite was still empty when he got there, and for a moment he thought about taking off his clothes and going back to bed, but there was no point in playing that game any more. He had done what he'd wanted to do. It had got him nowhere, but at least he'd gone through with it. What he'd been looking for was Nancy. He should have known that he wouldn't find her there, or anywhere else. He would only find her in the one place she still lived, in his heart.

The door to the suite opened as he stood looking out the window, and for a moment he didn't turn around. He didn't really want to see them, or hear about the meeting, or have to pretend that he was all right. He wasn't all right. And maybe he never would be again.

'What are you doing up, Michael?' His mother made it sound as though he were going to be seven in a few days, instead of twenty-five. He turned around slowly and said nothing at first, and then tiredly he smiled at George.

'It's time for me to get up, Mother. I can't stay in bed forever. In fact, I'm going to New York tonight.'

'You're what?'

'Going to New York.'

'But why? You wanted to stay here.' She looked totally confused.

'You had your meeting.' And I had mine. 'We have no reason to hang around here any more. And I want to be in the office tomorrow. Right, George?'

George looked at him nervously, frightened by the pain and grief he saw in the boy's eyes. Maybe it would do him good to get busy. He didn't look terribly strong yet, but lying about had to be difficult for him. It gave him too much time to think. 'You might be right, Michael. And you can always work half days at first.'

'I think you're both crazy. He only came out of the hospital this morning.'

'And you, of course, are famous for taking such good care of yourself. Right, Mother?' He cocked his head at her, and she sank down slowly on the couch.

'All right, all right,' she said with a slow smile.

'How was the meeting?' Michael sat down across from her and tried to look as though he cared. He was going to have to do a lot of that, because that afternoon he had made a decision. From now on he was going to live for one thing and one thing only. His work. There was nothing else left.

8

'Ready?'

'I guess so.' She couldn't feel anything above her shoulders, it was as though her head had been cut off. And the bright lights of the operating room made Nancy want to squint, but she couldn't even do that. All she could see clearly was Peter's face as he bent over her, his neatly trimmed beard covered by a blue surgical mask, and his eyes dancing. He had spent almost three weeks studying the X-rays, measuring, sketching, drawing, planning, preparing, and talking to her. The only photograph of Nancy he had was the one taken the day of the accident, at the fair. But her face had been partially obscured by the silly boardwalk façade she and Michael had stuck their heads through to have their picture taken. It gave him an idea though, a starting point, but he was going much farther than that. She was going to be a different girl when he was through, a person anyone would dream of being. He smiled down at her again as he saw her eyelids grow heavy.

'You're going to have to stay awake now, and keep talking to me. You can get drowsy but you can't go to sleep.' Otherwise she might choke on her own blood, but she didn't need to know that. Instead he kept her amused with stories and jokes, asked her questions, made her think of things, dig up answers, remember the names of all the nuns she knew when she was a child. 'And you're sure you don't still want to be Sister Agnes Marie?'

'Uh uh. I promised.' They teased back and forth during the whole three hours that the procedure took, and his hands never stopped moving. For Nancy it was like watching a ballet.

'And just think, in another couple of weeks we'll get you your own apartment, maybe something with a view, and then . . . Hey, sleepyhead, what do you think of the view? Do you want to see the bay from the bedroom?'

'Sure. Why not?'

'Just "sure"? You know, I think you're getting spoiled by the view from your room here at the hospital, Nancy.'

'That's not true. I love it.'

'Okay, then we'll go out together and find you something even better. All right?'

'Right.' Even with the sleepy voice, she sounded pleased. 'Can't I go to sleep yet?'

'You know what, Princess, you just about can. Just a few more minutes and we'll whisk you back to your room and you can sleep all you want.'

'Good.'

'Have I been boring you then?' She giggled at his mock hurt. 'There, love . . . all . . . set.' He looked up at his assistant with a nod, stood back for a moment, and a nurse gave Nancy a quick shot in the thigh. Then Peter stepped back to her side and smiled down at the eyes he already knew so well. He didn't even see the rest. Not yet. But he saw the eyes. And knew them intimately. Just as she knew his. 'Did you know that today is a special day?'

'Yes.'

'You did? How did you know?'

Because it was Michael's birthday, but she didn't want

to tell him that. He was going to be twenty-five years old today. She wondered what he was doing. 'I just knew, that's all.'

'Well, it's special to me because this is the beginning. Our first surgery together, our first step on a wonderful road towards a new you. How about that?' He smiled at her then, and she quietly closed her eyes and fell asleep. The shot had taken effect.

'Happy birthday, boss.'

'Don't call me that, you jerk. Christ, you look lousy, Ben.'

'Thanks a lot.' Ben looked over at his friend as he hobbled into the office with crutches and the assistance of a secretary. She eased him into a chair and withdrew from Michael's crammed and much panelled office. 'This is some place they fixed up for you. Is mine gonna look like this?'

'You can have this one. I hate it.'

'That's nice. So what's new?' The talk between them was still strained. They had seen each other twice since Ben arrived from Boston, but the effort of staying off the subject of Nancy was almost too much for them. It was all either of them could think of. 'The doctor says I can start work next week.'

Michael laughed and shook his head. 'You're stark staring crazy, Ben.'

'And you're not?'

A cloud passed over Mike's eyes. 'I didn't break anything.' Nothing you could see anyway. 'I told you, you've got a month. Two if you need it. Why don't you go to Europe with your sister?'

'And do what? Sit in a wheelchair and dream about bikinis? I want to come to work. How about two weeks?'

'We'll see.' There was a long silence and then suddenly Mike looked at his friend with an expression of bitterness Ben had never seen before. 'And then what?'

'What do you mean, Mike, "and then what?" '

'Just that. We work our asses off for the next fifty years, screw as many people as we can, make as much money as we can, and so what? So Goddamn what?'

'You're in a wonderful mood. What happened? Slam your finger in your desk this morning?'

'Oh for Chrissake, be serious for a change, will you? I mean it. Don't you ever think of that? What the hell does it all mean?' Ben knew what he meant, and there was no avoiding the questions now.

'I don't know, Mike. The accident made me think of that, too. It made me ask myself what's important in my life, what I believe in.'

'And what did you come up with?'

'I'm not sure. I think I'm just grateful to be here. Maybe it taught me how important life is, how good it is while you have it.' There were tears in his eyes as he spoke. 'I still don't understand why it happened the way it did. I wish . . . I wish . . .' His voice broke on the words. 'I wish it had been me.'

Mike closed his eyes on the tears in his own eyes and then came slowly around the desk to his friend. They stood there for a moment, the two of them, tears running slowly down their faces, holding tight to each other, and feeling the friendship of ten years comfort them as little else could. 'Thanks, Ben.'

'Hey, listen.' Ben wiped the tears from his cheeks with the sleeve of his jacket. 'You want to go out and get smashed? Hell, it's your birthday, why not?' For a minute Mike laughed, and then like a small boy drawn into a conspiracy, he nodded.

'Hell, it's almost five o'clock. I don't have any more meetings I'm supposed to be at. We'll go to the Oak Room.' He assisted Ben from the room, and then into a cab, and half an hour later they were well on their way to a major blow-out.

Mike didn't get back to his mother's apartment until after midnight, and when he did he required a considerable amount of help from the doorman to get upstairs. The next morning when the maid came in, she found him asleep on the floor of his room. But at least he had got through his birthday.

He could hardly see when he got to the breakfast table the next morning. His mother was already there, in a black dress, reading *The New York Times*. He wanted to throw up when he smelled the sweet rolls and coffee.

'You must have had an interesting time last night.' Her tone was glacial.

'I was out with Ben.'

'So your secretary told me. I hope you won't make a habit of this.'

Oh, Jesus. Why not? 'What? Getting smashed?'

'No. Leaving early. And actually, the other, too. You must have looked charming when you came home.'

'I can't remember.' He was trying desperately not to gag on his coffee.

'There's something else you didn't remember.' She

78

put the paper down on the table and glared at him. 'We had a dinner date last night, at Twenty One. I waited for you for two hours. With nine other people. Your birthday – remember?'

Christ. That would have been all he needed. 'You never told me about nine people. You just asked me to dinner. I thought it would have been just the two of us.' It was a moot point now, of course.

'And it was all right to stand up just me, is that it?'

'No, I just forgot, for Chrissake. This wasn't exactly my favourite birthday.'

'I'm sorry.' But she didn't sound as though she remembered why this birthday was different, or as though she really cared. She sounded miffed.

'And that brings up another point, Mother. I'm going to move out and get my own place.'

She looked up, surprised. 'Why?'

'Because I'm twenty-five years old. I work for you, Mother. I don't have to live with you, too.'

'You don't "have" to do anything.' She was beginning to wonder about the Avery boy and just what kind of influence he was. This sounded like his idea.

'Mother, let's not get into this now. I have an incredible headache.'

'Hangover.' She looked at her watch and stood up. 'I'll see you at the office in half an hour. Don't forget the meeting with the people from Houston. Are you up to it?'

'I will be. And Mom . . . I'm sorry about the apartment, but I think it's time.'

She looked at him sternly for a moment and then let out a small sigh. 'Maybe it is, Michael. Maybe it is. Happy birthday, by the way.' She bent down to kiss him, and he even smiled despite the terrible ache in his head. 'I left you a little present on your desk.'

'You shouldn't have.' There was no present that mattered any more. Ben had understood that. He had given him nothing.

'Birthdays are birthdays after all, Michael. See you at the office.'

After she left he sat for a long time in the dining-room, looking at the view. He knew just the apartment he wanted. Only it was in Boston. But he was going to do his damnedest to find one just like it in New York. In some ways he still hadn't given up the dream. Even though he knew he was crazy to cling to it.

'Hi, Sue. Is Mr Hillyard in?' Ben had the look of five o'clock as he arrived at Mike's office door: not quite dishevelled, but relieved that the day was almost over. He barely had time to sit down all day long, let alone relax.

'He is. Shall I let him know you're here?' She smiled at him, and he felt his eyes drawn to the carefully concealed figure. Marion Hillyard did not approve of sexy secretaries, even for her son . . . or was it especially for her son? Ben wondered as he shook his head.

'No, thanks. I'll announce myself.' He strode past her desk, carrying the files that had been his excuse, and knocked on the heavy oak door. 'Anybody home?' There was no answer so he knocked again. And still got no reply. He turned questioningly to the secretary. 'You're sure he's in there.'

'Positive.'

'Okay.' Ben tried again and this time a hoarse croak from the other side urged him in. Ben cautiously opened the door and looked around. 'You asleep or something?' Michael looked up and grinned at his friend.

'I wish I were. Look at this mess.' He sat surrounded by folders, mock-ups, drawings, designs, reports. It was enough to keep ten men busy for a year. 'Sit down, Ben.'

'Thanks, Boss.' Ben couldn't resist teasing him.

'Oh, shut up. What's in the files you brought me?' He ran a hand through his hair and sat back in the heavy leather desk chair he had grown accustomed to. He had even grown used to the impersonal prints on the walls. It didn't matter any more. He didn't give a damn. He never looked at the walls, or his office, or his secretary . . . or his life. He looked at the work on his desk and very little else. It had been four months. 'Please don't tell me you've brought me another set of problems with that damn shopping centre in Kansas City. They're driving me nuts.'

'And you love it. Tell me, Mike, what was the last movie you saw? *Bridge on the River Kwai,* or *Fantasia?* Don't you ever get the hell out of here?'

'When I get the chance.' Michael looked at some papers as he answered. 'So what about the files?'

'They're a decoy. I just wanted to come and talk to you.'

'And you can't do that without an excuse?' Michael grinned up at him. It was like being kids again, visiting each other's study halls with fake homework to consult on.

'I keep forgetting your mother isn't old Sanders up at St Jude's.'

'Thank God.' Actually they both knew she was worse, but neither of them could afford to admit it. She detested seeing people 'float around' the halls, as she put it, and she was usually quick to glance at whatever files they were carrying. 'So what's up, Ben? How were the Hamptons this summer?'

Ben sat very still for a moment, watching him, before he answered.

'Do you really care?'

'About you, or the Hamptons?' Michael's smile looked pasted on, and he had the ghostly pallor of December, not September. It was obvious he had gone nowhere all summer. 'I care a lot about you, Ben.'

'But not about yourself. Have you looked in the mirror lately? You'd scare Frankenstein's mother. We want you to come up to the Cape this weekend. They do. I do. We all do. And listen, if you say no, I'll come across that desk and drag you out of here. You need to get out of here, damn it.' Ben wasn't smiling any more. He was dead serious, and Mike knew it. But he shook his head.

'I'd love to, Ben. But I can't. I've got Kansas City to worry about, and forty-seven thousand problems with it that we just can't seem to solve. You know. You were in that meeting yesterday.'

'So were twenty-three other people. Let them handle it. For a weekend at least. Or is your ego such that you can't let anyone else touch your work?'

But they both knew it wasn't that. Work had become his drug. It numbed him to everything else. And he had been abusing the job since the day he walked into the office.

'Come on, Mike. Be good to yourself. Just this once.'

'I just can't, Ben.'

'Goddamn it, man, what do I have to say to you? Look at yourself. Don't you care? You're killing yourself, and for what?' His voice roared across the office and hit Michael with an almost physical force as he watched his friend's face convulse with emotion. 'What the hell's the use, Mike? If you kill yourself, it won't bring her back. You're alive, damn it. Twenty-five years old and alive – and wasting your life, driving yourself like your goddamn mother. Is that what you want? To be like her? To live, eat, sleep, drink, and die for this goddamn business? Is that it for you now? Is that who you are? Well, I don't believe it. I know someone else in that skin of yours, mister, and I love that other person. But you happen to be treating him like a dog, and I won't let you do it. You know what you should be doing? You should be out there, living. You should be out there, making it with that good-looking secretary who sits outside your office, or ten other broads you meet at the best parties in town. Get off your ass and get out of your coffin, Mike, before—'

But Mike cut him off before he could finish. He was leaning halfway across the desk at him, shaking, and even paler than he had been before. 'Get the hell out of my office, Ben, before I kill you. *Get out!!*' It was the roar of an injured lion, and for a moment the two men stood staring at each other, shaken and frightened by what they had felt and said. 'I'm sorry.' Mike sat down again and dropped his head into his hands. 'Why don't we just let this go for today?' He never looked up at Ben, who walked slowly across the room, squeezed his shoulder, and walked out, closing the door quietly behind him. There was nothing left to say.

Michael's secretary looked at Ben questioningly as he walked past, but said nothing. She had heard Mike's roar at the very end. The whole floor could have, if they'd been listening. Ben passed Marion in the hall on the way back to his office, but she was busy with something Calloway was showing her, and Ben wasn't in the mood for the usual pleasantries. He was sick of her, and what she was letting Mike do to himself. It served her purposes to have him work like that; it was good for the business, for the empire, for the dynasty . . . and it made Ben Avery sick.

He left the office at six-thirty that night, and when he

looked up from the street, he could still see the lights burning in Mike's office. He knew they would still be lit at eleven or twelve that night. And why not? What the hell did he have to go home to? The empty apartment he had rented three months before? He had found an attractive little apartment on Central Park South, and something about the layout had reminded Ben of Nancy's place in Boston. He was sure Mike had noticed that too. Maybe that was why he had taken it. But then something had happened. What little life had been left had gone out of him. He had begun this insane work thing, a marathon of madness. So he never bothered to do anything with the apartment. It just sat there, cold and empty and lonely. The only furniture he had put in it were two folding chairs, a bed, and an ugly old lamp which stayed on the floor. The whole place rang with empty echoes; it looked as though the tenant had been evicted that morning. Ben got depressed just thinking about coming home to such a place, and he could imagine what it did to Mike – if he even noticed his surroundings any more, which Ben was beginning to doubt. He had given him three plants for the place in early July, and all of them had been dead by the end of the month. Like the ugly lamp, they just sat there, unloved and forgotten.

Ben didn't like what was happening, but there was nothing anyone could do. No one except Nancy, and she was dead. Thinking about her still gave Ben an almost physical pang, like the twinge he felt in his ankle and his hip when he got tired. But the breaks had repaired quickly; youth had served him well. He only hoped it did the same for Mike. But Mike's breaks were compound fractures of parts of him that didn't even show. Except in his eyes. Or his face at the end of a day . . . or the set of his mouth in an unguarded moment as he sat at his desk and looked into the distance, at the endless stretch of the view.

10

'Well, young lady? Did I keep my promise? Do you have the most spectacular view in town?' Peter Gregson sat on the terrace with Nancy, and they exchanged a glowing look. Her face was still heavily bandaged, but her eyes danced through the bandages and her hands were free now. They looked different, but they were lovely as she made a sweeping gesture around her. From where they sat, they could see the entire bay, with the Golden Gate Bridge at their left, Alcatraz to their right, Marin County directly across from them, and from the other side of the terrace, an equally spectacular city view towards the south and east. The two-sided terrace also gave her an equal share of sunrises and sunsets, and boundless pleasure as she sat there all day. The weather had been glorious since she'd had the apartment. Peter had found the place for her, as promised.

'You know, I'm getting horribly spoiled.'

'You deserve to be. Which reminds me, I brought you something.'

She clapped her hands like a little girl. He always brought her something. A silly thought, a pile of magazines, a stack of books, a funny hat, a beautiful scarf to drape over the bandages, wonderful clattery bracelets to celebrate her new hands. It was a constant flow of gifts, but today's was the largest of all. With a mysterious look of pleasure, he left his seat on the terrace and went inside. The box he brought back was fairly large and looked as though it might be quite heavy. When he dropped it on her lap, she found her guess had been correct.

'What is it, Peter? It feels like a rock.' She smiled through the bandages and he laughed.

'Yes, the largest emerald I could find in the dime store.'

'Perfect!' But the gift was even more perfect than she suspected. The contents of the mysterious box proved to be a very expensive and highly elaborate camera. 'Peter! My God, what a gift! I can't—'

'You most certainly can. And I expect to see some serious work done with it.'

They both knew how disturbed she was that she didn't seem to want to paint any more. Now she no longer had the excuse of bandaged hands. But she couldn't. Something in her stopped every time she even thought of it. The paintings the nurses had brought from her Boston apartment were still enclosed in the large black artist's portfolio shoved to the back of a storage closet. She didn't want to see them, let alone work on them. But a camera might be different. Peter saw the spark in her eyes and prayed that he had opened a new door. She needed new doors. None of the old ones were going to reveal what she wanted them to. It would be better for her to start fresh.

'There is a fabulously complicated instruction booklet, which ten years of medical school never prepared me for. Maybe you can figure it out.'

'Hell, yes.' She glanced into the thick booklet and sat lost in concentration for a few moments, holding the camera and forgetting her friend, and then waved the booklet absently. 'It's fantastic, Peter. Look . . . this thing over here, if you flick that . . .'

She was gone, totally enthralled, and Peter sat back with a comfortable smile. It was half an hour later before she noticed him again. She looked up suddenly with delight in her eyes, and they told him how grateful she was. 'It's the most beautiful gift I've ever had.' Except for Michael's blue beads at the fair . . . but she forced them quickly from her mind. Peter was used to the sudden clouds which flitted across her eyes as old thoughts came to haunt her. He knew they would leave her in time.

'Did you bring film?'

'Of course.' He pulled another, smaller box out of the wrappings and plonked it in her lap. 'Would I forget film?'

'No. You never forget anything.' She was quick to load the camera and begin shooting photographs of him, and then of the view, and then a quick series of a bird as it flew past the terraces. 'They'll probably be awful, but it's a start.' He watched her silently for a long time, and then he put an arm around her shoulders and they went inside.

'You know, I have another gift for you today, Nancy.'

'A Mercedes. See, I always guess.'

'No. This one's serious.' He looked down at her with a gentle, cautious smile. 'I'm going to share a friend with you. A very special lady.' For an insane moment, Nancy felt a ripple of jealousy course down her spine, but something in Peter's face told her that she didn't need to feel that way. He sensed her watching him closely, though, as he went on. 'Her name is Faye Allison, and we went to medical school together. She is, without a doubt, one of the most competent psychiatrists in the West, maybe in the country, and she's a very good friend and a very special person. I think you're going to like her.'

'And?' Nancy waited, tense but curious.

'And . . . I think it might be a good idea for you to see her for a while. You know that. We've talked about it before.'

'You don't think I'm adjusting well?' She sounded hurt, and put the camera down to look at him more seriously.

'I think you're doing remarkably well, Nancy, but if nothing else, you need another person to talk to. You have Lily and Gretchen and me, and that's it. Don't you want someone else to talk to?'

Yes. Michael. He had been her best friend for so long. But for the moment, Peter was enough. 'I'm not sure.'

'I think you will be once you meet Faye. She is incredibly warm and kind. And she's been very sympathetic to your case from the beginning.'

'She knows about me?'

'From the first.' She had been there the night Marior Hillyard and Dr Wickfield had called, but Nancy didn't need to know that. He and Faye had been lovers on and off for years, more as a matter of companionship and convenience than as a result of any great passion. They were friends most of all. 'She's coming to join us for coffee this afternoon. All right with you?'

But she knew she had little choice. 'I suppose so.' She grew pensive as she settled herself in the living room. She wasn't at all sure she liked this addition to her scene, particularly a woman. She felt an instant sense of competition and distrust.

Until she met Faye Allison. Nothing Peter had said had prepared her for the warmth she felt from the other woman. She was tall, thin, blonde, and angular, but all the lines of her face were soft. Her eyes were warm and alert; there was an instant joke, an instant answer, an instant burst of laughter always ready in those eyes. Yet one sensed, too, that she was always ready to be serious and compassionate. Peter left them alone after the first hour, and Nancy was actually glad.

They talked about a thousand things, and none of them the accident. Boston, painting, San Francisco, children, people, medical school. Faye shared chunks of her life with Nancy, and Nancy gave her glimpses of herself that she hadn't given anyone for a long time, not since she had first got to know Michael. Views of the orphanage, real views, not the amusing ones she gave Peter. The loneliness of it, the questions about who she really was, why she had been left there, what it meant to be totally alone. And then for no reason she could think of, she told Faye about her arrangement with Marion Hillyard. There was no shock, no reproach, there was nothing but warmth and understanding in the way Faye Allison listened, and Nancy found herself sharing feelings which covered years, not just the past four months. But the relief of telling her about Marion Hillyard was enormous.

'I don't know, it sounds so strange to say it, but . . .' She hesitated, feeling foolish, and looking childlike as she glanced up at her new friend. 'But I . . . I had never had any kind of family, growing up in the orphanage. The mother superior was the closest I had to a mother, and she was more like a maiden aunt. But despite what I knew about Marion, from Michael, from his friend Ben, just from what I sensed – despite all that, I always had these crazy dreams, fantasies that she would like me, that we would be friends.' Her eyes filled with unexpected tears and she looked away.

'Did you think that maybe she'd become your mother?'

Nancy nodded silently and then blinked away the tears with a terse laugh. 'Isn't that insane?'

'Not at all. It was a normal assumption. You were in love with Michael. You have no family of your own. It's normal that you should want to adopt his. Is that why your deal with her hurt so much?' But she already knew the answer, as did Nancy.

'Yes. It was proof of just how much she hated me.'

'I wouldn't go that far, Nancy. From the look of things, she's done an awful lot for you. She did send you out to Peter for a new face.' Not to mention the extremely comfortable lifestyle she had provided during the process.

'As long as I give up Michael. She was rejecting me, for him – and for herself. I knew then that I had never had a chance with her. It was a horrible moment.' She sighed, and her voice became more gentle. 'But I guess I've lost before and survived it.'

'Do you remember losing your parents?'

'Not in any real way. I was too little to remember anything when my father died, and not much older when my mother left me at the home. I remember the day they told me she had died. I cried, but I'm not really even sure why I cried. I don't think I remembered her. Maybe I just felt abandoned.'

'The way you do now?' It was a guess, but a good one.

'Maybe. That bottomless feeling of "but who will take care of me now?" I think of that sometimes. But then I knew the home would take care of me until I grew up. Now

I know Peter will, and Marion's money will, until I'm all patched up. But then what?'

'What about Michael? Do you think he'll come back to you?'

'Sometimes I do. A lot of the time I do.' There was a long pause.

'And the rest of the time?'

'I'm beginning to wonder. At first I thought that maybe he was afraid of the way I'd look, the way that would make him feel about me. But by now he knows about the surgery, and he must figure there's some improvement. So how come he's not here yet?' She turned to face Faye squarely. 'That's what I wonder.'

'Do you come up with any answers to that question?'

'Nothing very pretty. Sometimes I think she's got at him, and convinced him that a girl from my "unsavoury background" will harm him professionally. Marion Hillyard has helped build an empire, and she's counting on Michael to carry on in the best family traditions. That doesn't include marrying a nameless nobody out of an orphanage, an artist. She wants him to marry some débutante heiress who can do him some good.'

'Do you think that matters to him?'

'It didn't used to matter, but now . . . I don't know.'

'What if you lose him?'

Nancy flinched but she didn't answer. Her eyes said everything though.

'What if he didn't feel able to cope with all that you're going through? That's possible, Nancy. Some men aren't as brave as we like to think they are.'

'I don't know. Maybe he's waiting till it's all over.'

'Wouldn't you resent him then? For not being here when you need him?'

Nancy let out a long sigh in answer. 'Maybe. I don't really know. I think about it all a lot, but I don't have many answers.'

'Only time has the answers. All you need to know is how you feel. That's all. How do you feel about you? The new you? Are you excited? Scared? Angry that you'll look different? Relieved?'

'All of the above.' They both laughed at her honesty. 'To tell you the truth, it terrifies me. Can you imagine looking in the mirror after twenty-two years and seeing someone else there? Christ, talk about freaking out!' She laughed, but there was real fear in the laughter.

'Are you freaked out?'

'Sometimes. A lot of the time I don't think about it.'

'What do you think about?'

'Honestly?'

'Sure.'

'Michael. Peter sometimes. But mostly Michael.'

'Are you falling in love with Peter?' There was no hesitation in the question. This was Dr Allison speaking now, not Faye. She was thinking only of Nancy.

'No, I couldn't fall in love with Peter. He's a nice man, a good friend. He's sort of like the wonderful father I never had. He brings me presents all the time. But . . . I'm in love with Michael.'

'Well, we'll just have to see what happens.' Faye Allison looked at her watch and was amazed. The two of them had been talking for almost three hours. It was after seven o'clock. 'Good lord, do you know what time it is?'

Nancy looked at her watch, too, and her eyes widened in surprise.

'Wow! How did we do that?' And then she smiled. 'Will you come back and see me again sometime, Faye? Peter was right. You're a very special lady.'

'Thank you. I'd love to. In fact . . . Peter was thinking that we might do it on a regular basis. What do you think?'

'I think it would be wonderful to have someone to talk to, like we did today.'

'I can't always promise you three hours.' They both laughed as Nancy walked her to the door. 'How about three times a week for an hour, professionally? And we can get together separately, as friends. Sound okay to you?'

'Sounds wonderful.'

They shook hands on it at the door, and Nancy was amazed to find herself already impatient for their first official session, only two days away.

11

Nancy settled herself comfortably in the easy chair near the fire and sighed as she leaned her head back. She was five minutes early today, and anxious to talk to Faye. She heard the click-clack of her high heels coming across the hall to the study she used for seeing patients, and Nancy smiled and sat up straight in her chair. She wanted to give Faye the full benefit.

'Good morning, early bird. Don't you look pretty in red today.' And then she stopped in the doorway and smiled. 'Never mind the red. Let me see the new chin.' Faye advanced on her slowly, looking at the lower part of Nancy's face, and at last, with a victorious smile, she found Nancy's eyes.

'Well, how do you like it?' But she could see the answer in Faye's face. Admiration for Peter's work, and pleasure for the girl.

'Nancy, you look beautiful. Just beautiful.' Now one could see the lovely young neck, arching gracefully away from the slim shoulders, the delicate chin and gentle, sensuous mouth. What one could see was exquisite and perfectly suited the girl's personality. Peter's endless sketches and sculptures had not been in vain. 'My God, I want one like that too!'

Nancy chortled with glee, and sat back in the chair, hiding the rest of her face, which was still concealed by bandages, behind the dark brown felt hat she had bought a few weeks before. It went well with the new brown wool coat and brown boots she was wearing with the red knit dress. Her figure had always been excellent, and with the striking new face, she was going to be a very dazzling girl. She was even beginning to feel beautiful, now that she could see something of what was to come. Peter was keeping his promises. 'It's embarrassing, Faye. I feel so good I could squeak. And the weird thing is, it doesn't even look like me, but I love it.'

'I'm glad. But what about it not looking like you? Does that bother you, Nancy?'

'Not as much as I thought it would. But maybe I still expect the rest to look like me. This is just one isolated part, and I never much liked my mouth before anyway. Maybe it'll seem stranger when the rest looks like someone else too. I don't know.'

'You know something, Nancy? Maybe you ought to just sit back and enjoy it. Maybe you ought to play with this a little. Go with it.'

'What do you mean?'

'Well, you're working on being Nancy, and we've been trying to adjust to giving up pieces of that Nancy as we go along. Maybe you ought to just stand back and look at the whole canvas. For instance, did you like your walk before?'

Nancy looked puzzled as she thought about it. This was a whole new idea, and something they had never discussed in the four months she'd been seeing Faye. 'I don't know, Faye. I never thought about my walk.'

'Well, let's think about it. What about your voice? Have you ever considered a voice coach? You have a marvellous voice, smooth, and soft. Maybe with a little coaching you could make more of it. Why don't we play with what you've got and really make the most of it? Peter is. Why don't you?'

Nancy's face lit up at the idea, and she began to catch some of Faye's excitement. 'I could develop all kinds of new sides to myself, couldn't I? Play the piano . . . a new walk . . . I could even change my name.'

'Well, let's not leap into any of this. You don't want to feel you've lost yourself. You want to feel you've added to yourself. But let's think about it. I have a feeling it's going to take us in some very interesting directions.'

'I want a new voice.' Nancy sat back and giggled.

'Like this.' She lowered her voice by several octaves, and Faye laughed.

'If you do enough of that, Peter may have to give you a beard.'

'Terrific.' They were suddenly in a holiday mood, and Nancy got up and began to prance around the room. At times like that, Faye remembered how young she really was. Twenty-three now. Her birthday had come and gone, and she was growing up in ways many people never had to. But beneath the surface, there was still a very young girl.

'You know, I do want you to be aware of one thing though, Nancy.' She sounded more serious now.

'And what's that?'

'I think you should understand why you're so willing to try out a new you. It's not unusual for orphans, as you were, to feel unsure of their identities. You're not certain what your parents were like, and as a result, you feel as though a piece of you is missing, a link to reality. So it's a lot easier for you to give up parts of the person you once were than it would be for someone who retained very clear images of her parents – and all the responsibilities that entails. In some ways it may make things simpler for you.'

Nancy was silent, and Faye smiled at her as she sank back into the cosy chair near the fire. It was a wonderful room to see patients in. It set everyone instantly at ease. She had put her grandmother's Persian carpets to good use in the room, which also boasted splendid panelling and old brass sconces. The fireplace was also trimmed in brass. The curtains were old and lacy, there were walls of books, tiny paintings tucked away in unexpected corners, and everywhere was a profusion of leafy ferns. It looked like the home of an interesting woman, and that was exactly the effect Faye wanted. 'Okay, it'll take you some time to think about that. For the moment, there's another serious subject we have to get into. What about the holidays?'

'What about them?' Nancy's eyes closed like two doors, and the laughter of moments before was now completely gone. Faye had known it would be this way, which was why the subject had to be broached.

'How do you feel about the holidays? Are you scared?'

'No.' Nancy's face was immobile, as Faye watched.

'Sad?'

'No.'

'Okay, no more guessing games, Nancy. Suppose you tell me. What do you feel?'

'You want to know what I feel?' Nancy suddenly looked straight back at her, dead in the eye. 'You want to know?' She stood up and strode across the room and then back again. 'I feel pissed off.'

'Pissed off?'

'Very pissed off. Super pissed off. Royally pissed off.'

'At whom?'

Nancy sank into the chair again and looked into the fire. This time when she spoke her voice was soft and sad. 'At Michael. I thought he'd have found me by now. It's been over seven months. I thought he'd have been here.' She closed her eyes to keep back the tears.

'Who else are you mad at? Yourself?'

'Yes.'

'Why?'

'For making the deal with Marion Hillyard in the first place. I hate her guts, but I hate mine worse. I sold out.'

'Did you?'

'I think so. And all for a new chin.' She spoke with contempt where moments before there had been pride. But they were delving deeper now.

'I don't agree with you, Nancy. You didn't do it for a new chin. You did it for a new life. Is that so wrong at your age? What would you think of someone else who did the same thing?'

'I don't know. Maybe I'd think they were stupid. Maybe I'd understand.'

'You know, a few minutes ago we were talking about a new life. New voice, new walk, new face, new name. Everything is new, except one thing.' Nancy waited, not wanting to hear her say it. 'Michael. What about thinking about a new life without him? Do you ever think about that?'

'No.' But her eyes filled with tears, and they both knew she was lying.

'Never?'

'I never think of other men. But sometimes I think about not having Michael.'

'And how do you feel?'

'I wish I were dead.' But she didn't fully mean that, and they both knew it.

'But you don't have Michael now. And it's not so bad, is it?' Nancy only shrugged in answer, and then Faye spoke again, her voice infinitely soft. 'Maybe you need to do some real thinking about all that, Nancy.'

'You don't think he's coming back to me, do you?' She was angry again. This time at Faye, because there was no one else to be angry at.

'I don't know, Nancy. No one knows the answer to that except Michael.'

'Yeah. The son of a bitch.' She got up and paced the room again, and then like a wind-up toy winding down, the fury of her pacing slowed, until she finally stood in front of the fire, with tears rolling down her face and her hands clenched on the screen in front of the fire. 'Oh Faye, I'm so scared.'

'Of what?' The voice was soft behind her.

'Of being alone. Of not being me any more. Of . . . I wonder if I've done a terrible thing that I'll be punished for. I gave up love for my face.'

'But you thought you'd already lost everything. You can't blame yourself for the choice you made, and in the end you may be glad.'

'Yeah . . . maybe . . .' There were fresh sobs from the fireplace, and Faye watched the slim shoulders shake. 'You know, I'm scared of the holidays too. It's worse than being back at the orphanage. This time there's no one. Lily and

Gretchen left last month, and you're going skiing. Peter's going to Europe for a week, and . . .' She couldn't stop the tears. But these were the realities of her life now. She had to face them. Faye shouldn't be made to feel guilty for leaving, nor should Peter. They had their own lives, as well as their time with her.

'Maybe it's time you got out and made some friends.'

'Like this?' She turned to face Faye again and pulled off the soft brown hat, revealing a great deal of bandaging. 'How can I go out and meet anyone like this? I'd scare them to death.'

'It isn't frightening looking, Nancy, and in time it'll be gone. It's not permanent. They're only bandages. People would understand.'

'Maybe so.' But she wasn't ready to believe that. 'Anyway, I don't need friends. I keep busy with my camera.' Peter's gift had been a godsend.

'I know. I saw your last batch of prints at Peter's the other day. He's so proud of them he shows them to everyone. It's beautiful work, Nancy.'

'Thank you.' Some of the anger drained out of her with the talk of her work. 'Oh Faye . . .' She sat back in the chair again and stretched her legs. 'What am I going to do with my life?'

'That's what we're working on figuring out, isn't it? And in the meantime, why don't you think about some of what we talked about today? The voice coach, music lessons – something to amuse you, and all part of the person you'll become.'

'Yeah, I guess I will give it some thought. When are you coming back from skiing, by the way?'

'In two weeks. But I'll leave a number where you can reach me in an emergency.' Faye was more worried about Nancy's getting through the holidays than she was willing to admit. Holidays were prime time for depression, even suicide, but Nancy seemed solid for the moment. She just didn't want her to become hysterical in her loneliness. It was rotten luck that she and Peter were both going away at the same time, but on the other hand she had to learn not to depend on them totally. 'Why don't we make an appointment for two weeks from today? And I want to see a mountain of beautiful prints you've made over the holidays.'

'That reminds me.' Nancy jumped up again and vanished into the hallway, where she had left a flat package wrapped in brown paper. She returned with it in a moment, and smilingly held it out to Faye. 'Merry Christmas.'

Faye opened it with a look of pleasure and then of awe when she tore away the brown paper. It was a photographic portrait of herself that looked as though she had sat for it for hours, to allow the photographer to capture just the right look, the right mood. It had a dreamy, impressionistic quality. She had been standing on Nancy's terrace, the wind in her hair, and the pale pink of her shirt reflected in the colours of the distant sunset. She remembered the day, but couldn't remember Nancy taking the picture. 'When did you take it?' She looked stunned.

'When you weren't looking.' Nancy was obviously pleased with herself; she had printed and enlarged the photograph herself, and then had it handsomely framed. It was as evocative as a painting.

'You're incredible, Nancy. What a beautiful, beautiful gift.'

'I had a good subject.'

The two women exchanged a hug, and Nancy regretfully shrugged back into her coat. 'Have a wonderful ski trip.'

'I will. I'll bring you some snow.'

'Idiot.' Nancy hugged her again and they wished each other a Merry Christmas as she left. There was a tug at Faye's heart after she was gone. Nancy was a beautiful girl. Inside. Where it mattered.

12

'Mr Calloway's on the line for you, Mr Hillyard.' The snow had been falling for five or six hours on the already slush-ridden streets of New York, but Michael had noticed nothing. He had been at his desk since six that morning, and it was after five o'clock now. He grabbed the phone while signing a stack of letters for his secretary to mail. At least the job in Kansas City was off his back. Now he had Houston to worry about, and in the spring he'd be getting ulcers over the medical centre in San Francisco. His job was a never-ending stream of headaches and demands, contracts and problems and meetings. Thank God.

'George? Mike. What's up?'

'Your mother's in a meeting, but she asked me to call and tell you that we'll be back from Boston tonight, if the snow lets up. Tomorrow if it doesn't.'

'Is it snowing there?' Michael sounded surprised, as though it were June and snow was preposterous.

'No.' George sounded momentarily confused. 'They said there was a blizzard in New York . . . isn't there?' Mike looked out his window and grinned. 'Yeah, there is. I just hadn't looked. Sorry.'

The boy was killing himself, just as his mother always had. George wondered for a moment what it was about the breed that made them so hard on themselves, and on the people who loved them. 'Anyway, now that we've settled that.' George chuckled for a moment. 'She wanted me to call you and make sure you're home for Christmas dinner tomorrow night. She has a few friends coming and of course she wants you there.'

Michael took a deep breath as he listened. 'A few friends'. That meant twenty or thirty, all of them people he either disliked or didn't know, and the inevitable single girl, from a good family, for him. It sounded like a stinking way to spend Christmas. Or any other day. 'I'm sorry, George. I'm afraid I owe Mother an apology. I've got a prior commitment.'

'You have?' He sounded stunned.

'I meant to tell her last week and I totally forgot. I was so busy with the Houston centre that I just never got to it. I'm sure she'll understand.' He'd been working miracles with the Houston client so she'd damn well better understand. Michael knew he had her on that one.

'Well, she'll be disappointed of course, but she'll be pleased to know that you have plans. Something . . . uh . . . something exciting, I hope.'

'Yeah, George. A real knockout.'

'Anything serious?' Now George sounded worried. Christ, there was no satisfying them.

'No, nothing to worry about. Just some good clean fun.'

'Excellent. Well, Merry Christmas and all that.'

'Same to you, and give Mother my love. I'll call her tomorrow.'

'I'll tell her.' George was wreathed in smiles when he hung up, pleased that the boy was finally recovering. Michael had been leading a very strange life for a while there. Marion would be relieved, too, though undoubtedly she'd be mad as hell for a few minutes that he wouldn't be home for dinner with her friends. But he was young after all. He had a right to a little fun. George grinned to himself as he took a sip of his Scotch and remembered a Christmas in Vienna twenty-five years before. And then, as always his thoughts wandered back to Michael's mother.

In Michael's office, the phone continued to ring. Ben wanted to be sure he had plans. Michael assured him that he would be at his mother's, boring but expected, and assorted clients called, alternately to complain, congratulate, and wish him a Merry Christmas. As he hung up after the last one he muttered to himself. 'Ah, go to hell,' and then looked up in astonishment when he heard unfamiliar laughter from the doorway. It was that new interior designer Ben had hired. A pretty girl, too, with rich auburn hair that fell in thick waves to her shoulders and set off creamy skin and blue eyes. Mike never noticed, of course. He never noticed anything any more, unless it was lying on his desk and needed a signature.

'Do you always wish people Merry Christmas that way?'

'Only the people I truly enjoy hearing from.' He smiled at her and wondered what she was doing there. He hadn't asked to see her, and she had no direct business with him, not that he knew of anyway. 'Is there anything I can do for you, Miss . . .' Damn. He couldn't remember her name. What the hell was it?

'Wendy Townsend. I just came to wish you a Merry Christmas.'

Ah. An apple polisher. Michael was amused and waved her to a chair.

'Didn't they tell you I'm the original Scrooge?'

'I gathered that when you didn't show up at either the office party or the Christmas dinner last night. They also say you work too hard.'

'It's good for my complexion.'

'So are other things.' She crossed one pretty leg over the other, and Michael checked it out. It did as little for him as anything else had since last May. 'I also wanted to thank you for the raise I just got.' She flashed a set of perfect teeth at him, and he returned the smile. He was beginning to wonder what she really wanted. A bonus? Another raise?

'You'll have to thank Ben Avery for that. I'm afraid I had nothing to do with it.'

'I see.' It was a pointless conversation, and she knew it. Regretfully, she stood up, and then glanced out the window. There were seven or eight inches of snow piled up on the window ledge. 'Looks like it's going to be a white Christmas after all. It's also going to be practically impossible to get home tonight.'

'I think you may be right. I probably won't even try.' He pointed to the leather couch with a grin. 'I think that's why they put that there, to keep me chained to my office.' No, mister, you do that to yourself. But she only smiled and wished him a Merry Christmas. Michael went back to signing letters, and true to his word, he spent the night on the couch. And the next night as well. It suited him perfectly. Christmas fell over a weekend this year, so no one knew where he was. Even the janitor and the maids had been given the holiday. Only the night watchman realised that Michael never left the office from Friday until late Sunday night, and by then

Christmas was over. And when he got back to his empty apartment, he had nothing more to fear. Christmas, with all its memories and ghosts, was already a thing of the past. There was a large, ostentatious poinsettia wilting outside his door, sent to him by his mother. He put it near the trash can.

In San Francisco, Nancy had spent the holiday more comfortably than Michael, but in equal solitude. She had cooked a small capon, sung Christmas carols alone on the terrace on Christmas Eve, after she came home from church, and slept late on Christmas Day. She'd hoped to keep the day from coming, but there was no escaping it. It was relentless with its tinsel and trees, its promises and lies. At least in San Francisco the weather reminded her less of Christmases she had known in the East. It was almost as though these people were pretending it was Christmas, when she knew it actually wasn't. The unfamiliarity made it a trifle easier to bear. And she had two presents this year, a beautiful Gucci handbag from Peter, and a funny book from Faye. She curled up in a chair with it in the afternoon after she had eaten her capon and stuffing and cranberry sauce. It was all rather like celebrating Christmas at Schrafft's, with all the old ladies, and all your life's hopes stashed in a shopping bag. She had always wondered what they carried in those bags. Old letters maybe, or photographs, trinkets or trophies or dreams.

It was after six o'clock when she finally put down the book, and stretched her legs. A walk would be nice; she needed to get some air. She slipped into her coat, reached for her hat and her camera, and smiled at herself in the mirror. She still liked the new smile. It was a great smile. It made her wonder what the rest of her face would look like when Peter was through. It was a little bit like becoming his dream woman. And once he had told her that he was making her his 'ideal'. It was an uncomfortable feeling, but still, she liked that smile. She slipped the camera over her shoulder and took the lift downstairs.

It was a crisp, breezy evening, with no fog – a good night for taking pictures – and she headed slowly down towards the wharf. The streets were mostly deserted. Everyone was recovering from Christmas dinner, recuperating in easy chairs and on couches, or snoring softly in front of the TV. The vision she created in her own head made Nancy smile, and then suddenly she tripped, making a little shrieking noise as she stumbled. Peter had warned her to be careful of falling. She couldn't indulge yet in any active sports because of that danger, and now she'd almost fallen on the street. Her arms had gone out to save her and she had regained her balance before hitting the pavement. And then she realised that she wasn't the only one who had shrieked. She had stumbled over a small shaggy dog, who looked greatly offended. Now he sat down, waved a paw at Nancy, and yipped. He was a tangled little fur ball of beige and brown. He stared at her and barked again.

'Okay, okay. I'm sorry. You scared me too, you know.' She bent to pet him and he wagged his tail and barked once more. He was a comical little dog, barely older than a puppy. She was sorry she had nothing to give him to eat. He looked hungry. She patted him again, smiled, and stood up, grateful that she hadn't dropped her camera. He barked at her again and she grinned. 'Okay. Bye-bye.' She started to walk away, but he immediately followed, trotting along at her side until she stopped and looked down at him again. 'Now listen you, go on home. Go on . . .' But each time she took a step, he did too, and when she stopped he sat down, waiting happily for her to go on. She stood there and laughed at him. He was really a ridiculous little dog, but such a cute one. She stooped down to pat him again and felt his neck for a collar, but there was none. A totally naked dog. And then suddenly, in amusement, she decided to snap some pictures of him. He proved to be a natural, prancing, posing, waving, and having a marvellous time. Nancy had made a new friend, and at the end of half an hour he still showed no sign of deserting her. 'All right, you, come on.' So off they went, to the wharf, where she shot pictures of crab stalls and shrimp vendors, tourists and drunken Santa Clauses, boats and birds and a few more of the dog. She had a good time, and never succeeded in losing her friend. He remained at her side until at last she stopped for coffee. She had become quite good at going into coffee shops and fast food places, lowering her head so she concealed most of her face beneath her hair, and ordering whatever she wanted. Now she even had a smile to go with the thank you, and it wasn't as hard to pull off as she had once thought. This time she ordered black coffee for herself, and a hamburger for the dog. She put the red paper plate on the sidewalk next to him, and he gobbled it up and then barked his thanks.

'Does that mean thank you, or more?' He barked again and she laughed, and someone stopped to pat him and ask his name. 'I don't know. He just adopted me.'

'Did you report him?'

'I guess I should.' The man told her how and she thanked him. She would call from her apartment if the dog stuck with her that far. And he did. He stopped at the door of her building as though he lived there, too. So she took him upstairs and called the Society for Prevention of Cruelty to Animals, but no one had reported losing a dog that looked like him, and they suggested she either resign herself to having a new dog, or drop him off at the shelter and have him put to sleep. She was outraged at the thought and put a protective arm around him as they sat side by side on the floor. 'You look a mess, you know kid. How about a bath?' He wagged tongue and tail simultaneously and she scooped him up in her arms and deposited him in the bathtub. She had to be careful not to get splashed, so as not to get her face bandages wet, but he submitted to the bath with no resistance. And as they progressed, she discovered that he was not beige and brown, but brown and white. His brown was the colour of milk chocolate, and his white was the colour of snow. He was really an adorable dog, and Nancy hoped no one called to report him missing. She had never had a dog before, and she had already fallen in love with this one. It hadn't been possible to have a dog at the orphanage, and pets weren't allowed at her apartment building in Boston. But this building's management had no objection to pets. Nancy sat back on her heels and rubbed him again with the towel as he rolled over on his back, waving all four feet. And then she thought of a name. It was the name of a dog Michael had told her about, the first puppy he'd had as a child, and somehow it seemed the perfect name for this independent little dog. 'How do you feel about Fred, little friend? Sound okay to you?' He barked twice, and Nancy took that to mean yes.

13

Nancy peeked her head around the door to grin at Faye, already cosily settled near the fire.

'And what do you have up your sleeve today, young lady?' Faye smiled at her, relieved that she looked so well.

'I brought a friend.'

'You did? I'm gone for two weeks and you already have a new friend? Well, how do you like that?' And with that, Fred bounced into the room, obviously proud of his new red collar and leash. No one had reported losing him, and as of that morning he officially belonged to Nancy. He had a licence, a bed, a bowl, and about seventeen toys. Nancy was lavishing him with love.

'Faye, I'd like you to meet Fred.' She smiled down at him with motherly pride, and Faye laughed.

'He's adorable, Nancy. Where'd you get him?'

'He adopted me on Christmas night. Actually, I should probably have called him Noel, but Fred seemed more appropriate.' For once, she was embarrassed to tell Faye why. She was beginning to feel like a fool for clinging to Michael. 'I also brought you a stack of work to look at.'

'My, haven't you been busy? Maybe I should go away more often.'

'Do me a favour – don't.' A glimpse into Nancy's eyes told Faye just how lonely she'd been. But at least she had made it through Christmas, and alone. That was no small accomplishment for anyone. 'And . . .' She drew the word out with pride . . . 'I've made arrangements for a voice coach. Peter says it's all part of the package. I start tomorrow at three. I can't do a dance class yet, because my face isn't finished, but I can do that next summer.'

'I'm proud of you, Nancy.'

'So am I.'

They had a good session that day, and for the first time in eight months, they didn't talk about Michael. Much to Faye's astonishment, it was spring again before Nancy mentioned his name. It was almost as though she were determined not to. All she talked about now was her plans. Her voice lessons. Her photography. The work she wanted to do with the photography when her techniques became more sophisticated. And in the spring she and Fred went for long walks in the park, through the rose gardens and along the remoter paths near the beach. She sometimes went on drives with Peter to out-of-the-way beaches where her bandages didn't matter. But little by little her face was emerging, and so was her personality. It was as though by remoulding her cheekbones and her forehead and her nose, he was also revealing more of the soul that had been hidden by youth. She had matured a great deal in the year since the accident.

'Has it already been a year?' Faye was astonished as she looked at Nancy one afternoon. Peter was working on the area around her eyes just then, and she was wearing huge dark glasses which hid her cheekbones as well as her eyes.

'Yes. It happened last May. And I've been seeing you for eight months, Faye. Do you really think I'm making progress?' She sounded discouraged. But she was tired from her last surgery three days before.

'Do you doubt your progress?'

'Sometimes. When I think of Michael too much.' It was a heavy confession for her to make. She was still clinging to the last shreds of hope – that he would finally find her, and the deal with his mother would be off. 'I don't know why I still do that to myself, but I do.'

'Wait till you get out in the world a little more, Nancy. You have nothing to do now but look back at things you remember, or ahead at things you don't yet know. It's natural that you spend a fair amount of time looking back. You have no other people in your life just now, but you will. In time. Be patient.'

Nancy sighed a long tired sigh. 'I'm so sick of being patient, Faye, and I feel like this work on my face will go on forever. Sometimes I hate Peter for it, and I know it's not his fault. He's doing it as fast as he can.'

'It'll be worth the time you invest in it. It already is.' She smiled, and Nancy smiled back. The delicate shape of the girl's face had already emerged, and each week there seemed to be changes. The voice coach had done her work well, too. Nancy's voice was pitched a little lower now, beautifully modulated, and she had far greater control over the smoothness of her voice than anyone without training could have. It gave Faye an idea. 'Have you ever thought of acting when this is all over? This experience might give you an incredible amount of insight.'

Nancy smiled at her and shook her head. 'Making films maybe, acting in them, no. It's so plastic. I'd rather be at my end of the camera.'

'Okay, it was just a thought. So what's on your agenda for this week?'

'I told Peter I'd take some pictures for him, and we're flying down to Santa Barbara for the day on Sunday. He wants to see some people there, and he offered to take me along for the ride.'

'I should lead such a life. Well . . .' She looked at her watch. 'See you on Wednesday.'

'Yes ma'am.' Nancy saluted with a smile, and Fred bounced out of the room with his leash in his mouth. He was used to the sessions in Faye's office. Nancy never left him behind.

When she left Faye's office, she decided to walk a few blocks towards a little park nearby, to see if there were any children to photograph in the playground. She hadn't taken any shots of kids in a while. When she got there, there was an ample supply of subjects climbing and pushing and shoving and running. Nancy sat down on a bench for a while to watch them and get a feeling for who they were and what they were up to. It was a beautiful day, and she felt good about life.

'Do you come here often?' Michael looked up in surprise from the bench where he sat. He had escaped to the park for an hour, just to get away from the office and see something green. There was always something magical about those first spring days, when New York turns from grey to lush green, bushes and trees and flowers exploding into life. But he had felt sure he would be alone in the secluded little spot where he had found an empty bench. The sudden voice surprised him. When he looked up he saw Wendy Townsend, the designer from his office.

'No . . . I . . . as a matter of fact, almost never. But I was having a rare case of spring fever today.'

'So was I.' She looked embarrassed as she held her dripping ice cream stick and then took a quick lick to keep from losing a big slice of chocolate.

'That looks delicious.' He smiled at her in the warm spring air.

'Want some?' She held it out like a friendly third-former, but he shook his head.

'But thanks for the offer. Would you like to sit down?' He felt a little silly being caught in the park, but it was such a nice day he didn't mind sharing it, and she was a pleasant girl. Their paths had crossed a number of times since she'd walked into his office five months before, to wish him a Merry Christmas. She sat down next to him and ate the last of her ice cream. 'What are you working on these days?' he asked.

'Houston and Kansas City. My work is always five or six months behind yours. It's kind of interesting to follow on your heels that way.'

'I'm not quite sure how to take that.' But he wasn't particularly worried about it.

'As a compliment.' She smiled at him from under long auburn lashes.

'Thank you. Is Ben treating you decently or is he the slave driver I tell him to be?'

'He wouldn't know how.'

'I know.' Michael smiled at the thought. 'We've known each other for half our lives. He's like my brother.'

'He's a hell of a nice man.'

Mike nodded silently, thinking how little he had seen of

Ben in the past year. He never had time. He never made time. He didn't even know what was happening in Ben's life. It had been months since he'd taken the time to find out. It made him feel guilty as he sat next to the girl, lost in his own thoughts. But a lot had changed for him in the past year. He had changed.

'You're a long way away, Mr Hillyard. Somewhere pleasant, I hope.'

He shrugged. 'Spring does strange things to me. It kind of makes me stop from year to year and take stock. I think that's what I was doing today.'

'That's a nice idea. For some reason, I always do that in September. I think the idea of the "school year" marked me forever. A lot of other people take stock in January. But spring makes the most sense. Everything is starting again, so why shouldn't we start our lives again each spring?' They exchanged a smile and Michael looked out over the little lake, still except for a few contented-looking ducks. There were no other people in sight. 'What were you doing last year at this time?' She went on. It was an innocent question, but it cut through him like a knife. A year ago on that day . . .

'Nothing very different from what I'm doing now.' He furrowed his brow, looked at his watch and stood up. 'I'm afraid I have a meeting in ten minutes. I'd better be getting back. But it was nice chatting with you.' He barely smiled at her before striding away, and she sat there wondering what she had said. She'd have to ask Ben sometime what was wrong with the man. You couldn't get within a thousand miles of him.

14

Much to Michael's surprise, Wendy was due at the same meeting he was, ten minutes later. Ben had wanted her there. They were going to discuss the very early plans for the San Francisco Medical Centre, and interior design would be a big factor. A lot of local art would be used to highlight the basic design. Ben was going to take care of finding that art himself, but Wendy would be doing a lot of the co-ordinating on the home front – more than usual, since Ben would be in San Francisco a lot of the time. The project was, of course, a long way away, but it was time to start working out the plans and the problems and the details.

It was a long, demanding, interesting meeting, run in great part by Marion, with George Calloway's assistance. But Michael took an almost equal part in the proceedings. This project was his; his mother had wanted it to be, from the first. Every major architectural firm in the country had been lusting after this job, and Marion intended to use it to establish Michael's name and reputation in the business.

It was almost six o'clock when the meeting ended, and Wendy was drained. She had presented her ideas well, stood up to Marion when she had to, and made a great deal of sense to Mike. Ben was proud of her and patted her on the shoulder as they left.

'Nice job, kid. Damn nice job.' He was called away by his

secretary then, and Wendy continued down the corridor alone. She was surprised when Mike stopped her, too.

'I was very impressed with your work, Wendy. I think that together we're going to pull off a beautiful job out there.'

'So do I.' She virtually glowed with the praise – and from him of all people. 'I . . . Michael, I . . . I'm really sorry if I said anything to offend you this afternoon. I really didn't mean to pry, and if it was an inappropriate question, I'm awfully . . .'

He felt a pang for her discomfort and put up a hand to stop her as he smiled gently down at her. 'I was rude and I apologise. I guess spring fever makes me crazy as well as dreamy. Can I make it up to you this evening with dinner?' He was as surprised as she was when the words tumbled out of his mouth. Dinner? He hadn't had dinner with a woman for a year. But she was a nice girl, she was doing a good job, and she meant well. And she was looking up at him, pink-cheeked and embarrassed.

'I . . . you don't have to . . .'

'I know, but I'd like to.' And this time he meant it. 'Are you free?'

'Yes. And I'd love to.'

'Fine. Then I'll pick you up at your place in an hour.' He jotted the address on the back of his notepad and smiled as he hurried back to his office. It was a crazy thing to do, but why the hell not?

He arrived punctually at her apartment an hour later, and he liked what he saw. It was a neat little brownstone with a shiny black door and a large brass knocker. The house was divided into four apartments, and Wendy had the smallest one, but hers boasted a perfectly kept little garden in the back. Her apartment was a wonderful mesh of old and new, antique shop, thrift shop, and good modern; it was all done in soft warm colours with soft lighting, plants, and candles. She seemed to have a great fondness for old silver, all of which she had polished to mirror perfection. He looked around him with pleasure, and sat down to enjoy the hors d'oeuvres she had made. They drank Bloody Marys and exchanged absurdities about the various projects they had worked on. An hour flew by in easy conversation, and Michael hated to break it up and move on to dinner, but he had made reservations at a French restaurant nearby, and they never held late-comers' tables for more than five minutes.

'I'm afraid we'll have to run if we want to make it. Or do we really care?' He was startled to hear her voice his own thoughts, and he wasn't quite sure what the mischief in her eyes meant. It had been so long since he'd been out with anyone that he was afraid to misinterpret and make the wrong move.

'Just exactly what are you thinking, Miss Townsend? Is the thought as outrageous as the look on your face?'

'Worse. I was thinking we could put together a picnic and go watch the boats on the East River.' She looked like a little kid with a naughty idea. There they both were, dressed for dinner, he in a dark suit and she in a black silk dress, and she was proposing a picnic on the East River.

'It sounds terrific. Do you have any peanut butter?'

'Certainly not.' She looked offended. 'But I make my own paté, Mr Hillyard. And I have sour-dough bread.' She looked very proud of herself, and Michael was suitably impressed.

'My God. I was thinking more in the line of peanut butter and jelly, or hot dogs.'

'Never.' With a grin, she disappeared into the kitchen, where in ten minutes she concocted the perfect picnic for two. Some leftover ratatouille, the promised paté, a loaf of sourdough bread, a healthy hunk of Brie, three very ripe pears, some grapes, and a small bottle of wine. 'Does that seem like enough?' She looked worried, and he laughed.

'Are you serious? I haven't eaten that well since I was twelve. I live mostly on leftover roast beef sandwiches and whatever my secretary feeds me when I'm not looking. Probably dog food, I never notice.'

'That's great. It's a wonder you don't die of starvation.' He wasn't starving, but he was certainly very thin. 'Are we all set?' She looked around the living room and picked up a delicate beige shawl, while Michael gathered up the picnic basket. Then they were off. They walked the few blocks to the East River, found a bench, and settled themselves happily to look at the boats. It was a beautiful warm night with a sky full of stars, even a few sailboats from time to time, out for an evening excursion. Mike and Wendy weren't the only ones with spring fever.

'Is this your first job, Wendy?' His mouth was half-full of paté, and he looked younger than he had in a year.

She nodded happily. 'Yes. First one I applied for, too. I was really glad I got it. As soon as I graduated from Parsons I came straight to you.'

'That's nice. It's my first job, too.' He was dying to ask her how she liked his mother, but he didn't dare. It wouldn't have been fair. Besides, if the girl had any sense at all, she must hate her. Marion Hillyard was a monster to work for; even Michael knew that.

'You should do well there, Michael.' She was teasing him again, and he laughed.

'What are you going to do after this? Get married and have kids?'

'I don't know. Maybe. But if I do, it won't be for a long time yet. I want a career first. I can always have kids later, in my thirties.'

'Boy, things sure have changed. Everyone used to be dying to get married.' He grinned at his new friend.

'Some girls still are.' She smiled at him and took a little piece of the Brie with a slice of pear. It had been an excellent dinner. 'You want to get married?' She glanced at him curiously, and he shook his head as he looked out at the boats. 'Never?' He turned to face her and shook his head again, and something in his eyes cried out to her. She wasn't sure if she should get off the question or not. She decided to ask him. 'Should I ask why, or should I let it be?'

'Maybe it doesn't matter any more. I've been running away from it for a whole year. I even ran away from you today at lunch. I can't run forever.' He paused for a moment, looked down at his hands, then back at her. 'I was supposed to get married last year, and on the way to the wedding, Ben Avery, and . . . and my fiancée and I . . . were in a car accident. The other driver was killed, and so was . . . She was, too.' He didn't cry, but he felt as though his insides had been shredded. Wendy was looking at him with wide, horrified eyes.

'Oh God, Michael, how awful. It sounds like a nightmare.'

'It was. I was in a coma for a couple of days and when I came to, she was already gone. I . . . I . . .' He almost couldn't say the words, but now he had to. He had to tell someone. He had never even told Ben. 'I went back to her apartment when I got out of the hospital two weeks later, but it was already empty. Someone had just called Goodwill, and her paintings had . . . had been stolen by a couple of nurses from the hospital. She was an artist . . .' They sat in silence for a long time, and then he said the words again, as though to understand them better himself. 'There was nothing left. Of me either, I guess.' When he looked up he saw tears running down Wendy's face.

'I'm so sorry, Michael.'

He nodded, and then for the first time in a year, he cried, too. The tears just slid slowly down his face as he took her into his arms.

15

'Mike, what do you think of that woman running the Kansas City office of . . .' She looked over at him, sprawled out on a deck chair in her garden. He wasn't listening. 'Mike.' He was staring at the Sunday paper as they sat in their bathing suits, in the hot New York sun, but Wendy knew he wasn't paying attention to the paper either. 'Mike.'

'Hm? What?'

'I was asking you about that woman in the Kansas City office.' But she had already lost him. She stared at him in irritation. 'Do you want another Bloody Mary?'

'Huh? Yeah. I think I'll go to the office in a while.' He gazed past her at an invisible spot just beyond her left shoulder.

'Wonderful.'

'What's that supposed to mean?' He was watching her now, and he wasn't quite sure what he read in her face. If he'd tried a little harder, he would have understood instantly. But he never tried.

'Nothing.'

'Look, the medical centre in San Francisco is going to have me working my ass off for the next two years. It's one of the biggest jobs in the country.'

'And if it weren't that it would be something else. You don't need an excuse. It's okay.'

'Then don't make it sound like I'm punching a time clock around here.' He shoved the paper away with his foot and glared at her as she started to steam.

'Time clock? You got here at twelve-thirty last night. We were supposed to have dinner with the Thompsons, and you didn't even call me until nine forty-five, Michael. I should have gone out with them anyway.'

'Then why didn't you? You don't have to sit around waiting for me.'

'No, but I happen to be in love with you, so I do it anyway. But you don't even try to be considerate. What the hell is up with you? Are you afraid to be anywhere but at your desk, afraid someone will get their hooks into you? Are you afraid that maybe you'll fall in love with me too? Would that be so awful?'

'Don't be ridiculous. You know what my work schedule is like. You should know better than anyone.'

'I do. Which is why I also know that half the hours you work aren't justified. You use your work as a place to hide, a way of life. You use it to avoid me. And yourself.' And Nancy. But she didn't say that.

'That's ridiculous.' He got up and strode around the narrow, well-tended garden, the flagstone walk warm under his feet. It was September, but still hot in New York. After the first few happy weeks of their romance, he and Wendy had had an erratic summer. He had spent most of it working, but they had managed one weekend away, on Long Island. 'Besides, what the hell do you expect from me? I thought we cleared all that up in the beginning. I told you I didn't want to get . . .'

'You told me you didn't want to get too involved. That you were afraid to be hurt. You weren't sure you'd ever want to get married. You never told me you were afraid to be alive for Chrissake, afraid to care at all, afraid to be a human being. Jesus, Michael, you spend more time with your dictaphone than you do with me. And you're probably nicer to it.'

'So?'

She felt a little shiver run up her spine as she watched his face. He really didn't care. She was crazy to stay with him. But there was something about him, a beauty, a strength, a wildness to him, a sorrow, that drew her like a magnet. And more than that, she sensed how great his pain was, his need. She wanted to reach out to him, show him he was loved. But he didn't really give a damn. She wasn't Nancy. And they both knew it.

Wendy got up silently and walked into the living-room so he wouldn't see the tears bright in her eyes. In the kitchen, she mixed herself a fresh Bloody Mary and stood there for a moment with her eyes closed, trembling, wishing she could reach out to him and find him there. But she was beginning to think he would never be 'there' for her. He wouldn't let himself be there for anyone.

She drained the drink with long steady gulps and set the empty glass down on the counter as she felt his hands float softly over her bronzed skin. She spent every weekend in her garden, getting a suntan, alone. She said nothing as he stood there now, just behind her. She could feel the heat from his body, and she wanted him desperately, but she was tired of his knowing that. It was time she made it harder for him.

'I want you, Wendy.' Her whole body ached for him at the words, but she wouldn't let herself. She kept her back to him, hating the gentleness of his hands as they travelled smoothly down her back.

'As you said earlier, "So?"'

'You know I can't deal with that kind of pressure.' His voice was as soft and smooth as her skin.

'It's not the pressure, Michael. It's love. The sad thing is you don't know the difference. Is that what it was like with her, too?' She felt the hands stop and the arms grow stiff. But she couldn't stop herself. She wanted to hurt him, too. 'Were you afraid to love her, too? Is it easier now that she's dead? Now you don't have to love anyone, and you can spend the rest of your life hiding behind the tragedy of how much you miss her. It certainly takes care of things, doesn't it?' She turned slowly to face him now, and there was hatred brewing in his eyes.

'How can you say a thing like that? How dare you?' For a moment he reminded her of his mother, almost as hard, almost as cold. But not quite. No one could equal Marion. 'How dare you twist the things I've told you.'

'I'm not twisting, I'm asking. If I'm wrong, I'm sorry. But I'm beginning to wonder if I am wrong.' She leaned against the counter, staring at him, and then he grabbed her by the shoulders and pulled her towards him. 'Michael . . .'

As they lay panting, ten minutes later, Wendy could hear the kitchen clock ticking in the silence. Michael said nothing. He only stared out at the garden, looking strangely sad.

'Are you all right?' He should have been asking her, but she was asking him. The whole affair was crazy, and she knew it, but she couldn't seem to stop herself. Sometimes she wondered what would happen when it was over. Maybe he'd have Ben Avery fire her. She almost expected it. 'Mike?'

'Hm? Yeah. I . . . I'm sorry, Wendy. Sometimes I'm really an incomparable ass.' There were tears glistening in his eyes.

'Well, I'm not sure I can argue with you on that one.' She looked up at him with a rueful smile and then kissed the tip of his chin. 'But I seem to love you anyway.'

'You could do a lot better, you know.' For the first time in months he looked down at her and really seemed to see her. 'Sometimes I hate myself for what I do to you. I just . . .' He couldn't go on, and she put her fingers over his lips.

'I know.' He nodded silently and stood up as she lay looking up at him from the kitchen floor.

'Michael?'

'Yeah?' His face was softer now than it had been half an hour before. She had done something for him after all.

'Do you still miss her all the time?'

He waited for a long moment, and then nodded, with a look of pain in his eyes. And then, without saying anything more, he went into the bedroom to dress. Wendy got up slowly. She perched on one of the stools at the kitchen counter and thought about what she'd seen in his eyes. When he came back to the kitchen a few moments later, he found her still sitting there, lost in her own thoughts. She looked up in surprise, and then regret as she saw him wearing jeans and a white shirt open at the neck. He had his briefcase in one hand and a sweater in the other. The briefcase told her that he was going to the office after all, in spite of the fact that it was Sunday, and the sweater told her that he would be staying late. None of it was good news to Wendy.

'Will I see you later?' She hated herself for the question. She was asking . . . begging. Damn him. And worse yet, he was shaking his head.

'I'll probably work till two or three and then go back to my place. I have to dress there in the morning anyway.' The brief gentleness of a few moments before was gone. He was Michael again, running away. She had already lost him in the ten or fifteen minutes since they'd made love. The situation was hopeless, yet she hated to give up. That kind of rejection just made her want to try harder and give more.

'I'll see you in the office tomorrow then.' She tried not to sound miserable, even to smile as she walked with him to the door, but she was glad when he left her quickly, with a vague peck on her forehead and without looking back, because when she closed the door she was already crying. Michael Hillyard was a lost cause.

16

The countryside flew past them as he floored the accelerator of the black Porsche. It was a delicious feeling, almost like flying, and there was no one else on the road. They took a drive almost every Sunday now. Peter picked her up around eleven, and they drove south as far as they wanted. Eventually they would stop somewhere for lunch, and then walk for a while hand in hand, laugh at each other's stories of the past, and eventually drift back towards home. It was a ritual she had come to love. And in an odd way, she was coming to love him. Peter was very special in her life now. He was giving her back all her dreams, along with some new ones.

Today they had stopped near Santa Cruz at a little country restaurant decorated like a French inn. They had had quiche and salad niçoise for lunch, with a very dry white wine. Nancy was getting used to meals like this. It was a long way from New England and county fairs and blue beads. Peter Gregson was a man of considerable sophistication. It was one of the things Nancy liked about him. He made her feel wonderfully worldly, even in her bandages and funny hats. But one could see more of her face now. The whole lower half of her face had been finished. Only the area around the eyes was still heavily taped, and the dark glasses covered most of it. Her forehead, too, was for the most part obscured. Yet from what one could see, he had not only wrought a miracle, he had done an exquisite job. Nancy herself was aware of it, and just knowing how she was beginning to look had given her an air of greater self-confidence. She wore her hats at a jauntier angle now, and bought more striking clothes, of a more sophisticated cut, than she had worn before. She had lost another five pounds and looked long and sleek, like a beautiful jungle cat. She even played with her new voice now. She liked the new person she was becoming.

'You know, Peter, I've been thinking of changing my name.' She said it with a sheepish little smile over the last of their wine. Somehow, it had sounded less foolish when she'd discussed it with Faye. Now she was sorry she'd brought it up. But Peter instantly put her at her ease.

'That doesn't surprise me. You're a whole new girl, Nancy. Why not a new name? Has anything special come to mind?' He looked at her fondly as he lit a Don Diego from Dunhill's. She had grown fond of their aroma, particularly after a good meal. Peter was introducing her to all the better things in life. It was a delightful way to grow up. 'So, who's my new friend? What's her name?'

'I'm not sure yet, but I've been thinking of Marie Adamson. How does it sound to you?'

He thought for a moment and then nodded. 'Not bad . . . in fact, I like it. I like it very much. How did you come to it?'

'My mother's maiden name, and my favourite nun.'

'My, what an exotic combination.' They both laughed and Nancy sat back with a small, satisfied smile. Marie Adamson. She liked it a lot. 'When were you thinking of changing it?' He watched her through the thin veil of blue smoke.

'I don't know. I hadn't decided.'

'Why not start using it right away? See how you like it. You know, you could use it on your work.' He looked excited at the idea. He was always excited when he spoke of her work or his. And much to her astonishment and pleasure, he viewed her work and his in the same light, as though they were equally important. He had come to respect her talent a great deal. 'Seriously, Nancy, why don't you?'

'What? Sign Marie Adamson on the prints I give you?' She was amused at how seriously he was taking her. He and Faye were the only ones who saw her work.

'You might broaden your horizons a little.'

This was not a new subject between them, and she put up a hand and shook her head with a firm little smile. 'Now don't start that again.'

'I'm going to keep at it until you get sensible on the subject, Nancy. You can't hide your light under a bushel forever. You're an artist, whether you work in paints or on film. It's a crime to hide your work the way you've been doing. You have to have a show.'

'No.' She took another swallow of wine and looked out at the view. 'I've had all the shows I want to have.'

'Wonderful. I put you back together so you can hide away for the rest of your life, taking photographs for me.'

'Is that such a terrible fate?'

'For me, no.' He smiled gently at her and took her hand in his. 'But for you, yes. You have so much talent, don't be stingy with it. Don't hide it. Don't do this to yourself. Why not have a show as Marie Adamson? There's anonymity in that. If you don't like the show or what it brings you, you scratch the name of Marie Adamson, and go back to taking pictures for me. But at least give it a try. Even Garbo was a success before she became a recluse. Give yourself a chance at least.' There was a pleading note in his voice that pulled at her, and he had a good point about the anonymity of her new name. Maybe that would make a difference. But she felt as though they'd been over this ground a thousand times before. Something froze in her at the thought of being a professional artist again. It made her feel vulnerable. It made her . . . think of Michael.

'I'll think about it.' It was the most positive response he'd ever had from her on the subject, and he was pleased.

'See that you do . . . Marie.' He looked at her with a broad smile, and she giggled.

'It feels funny to have a new name.'

'Why? You have a new face. Does that feel funny too?'

'Not really. Not any more. Thanks to Faye, and to you. I've got used to it.' Most women would have given their right arms to get used to that face, and she knew it.

'Should I start calling you Marie?' He was only teasing, until he saw a new light in her eyes. They were mischievous and wonderful and alive.

'As a matter of fact . . . yes. I think I'll try it on for size.'

'Perfect. Marie. If I slip, step on my foot.'

'No problem. I'll just hit you with my camera.'

He signalled for the bill and they exchanged a long, tender smile. After lunch they walked through the small beach town, peeking into shops, poking into narrow alleys, and wandering into galleries when something looked interesting. And everywhere they went, Fred ran along behind them, equally accustomed to his Sunday ritual. He always waited in the car when they had lunch, and then shared their walks with them afterwards.

'Tired?' He looked at her carefully after they had meandered for an hour. Although she was gradually building up her endurance, Peter, more than anyone, was aware of how easily she tired. But in the seventeen months since the accident, she had had fourteen operations. It would be another year before she felt fully her old self, although anyone who didn't know her well would never suspect her occasional fatigue. She always looked vivacious, but an hour's walk still required an effort. 'Ready to go back?'

'Much as I hate to admit it, yes.' She nodded ruefully, and he tucked her hand in his.

'A year from now, Marie, you'll outrun me in any race.'

She laughed at both the idea and his easy use of her new name. 'I'll accept that as a challenge.'

'I'm afraid you'll win. You have one great advantage on your side.'

'And what's that?'

'Youth.'

'So do you.' She said it earnestly, and he laughed with a shake of his handsome head.

'May you always see me through such kindly eyes, my dear.' But as he looked away there was a sad shadow lurking in his eyes. She caught only a glimpse of it, but she knew. There was no denying the age difference between them. No matter how much they enjoyed each other, how close they became, one could not deny the twenty-four-year gap. But she found that she didn't mind it; she liked it. She had told him that before, and sometimes he even believed her; it depended on his mood. But he never admitted just how much it bothered him. She was the first girl who had made him want to be young again, to throw away a decade or perhaps two, decades he had cherished but now found a burden in the face of her youth. 'Nancy . . .' The new name was suddenly forgotten as he looked at her with great seriousness, a question in his eyes.

'Yes?'

'Do you . . . do you still miss him?' There was such pain in Peter's eyes when he asked that she wanted to put her arms around him and tell him it was all right. But she couldn't lie to him either. She was surprised to find that the question brought tears to her eyes as she shrugged and then nodded.

'Sometimes. Not always.' It was an honest answer.

'Do you still love him?'

She looked very hard into his eyes before answering. 'I don't know. I remember him as he was, and us as we were, but none of that is real any more. I'm not the same person, and he can't be either. The accident must have left a mark on him. Maybe if we saw each other again we'd both find that we had nothing left together. Like this, it's hard to say. You're left with only dreams of the past. Sometimes I wish I could see him just to get it over with. But I . . . I've come to understand that I never will . . . see him again.' She said it with difficulty but finality. 'So I just have to put the dreams away.'

'That's not so easily done.' There was pain in his own eyes as he spoke to her. And suddenly she began to wonder if he had been through something similar. Perhaps that was why he always understood what she felt.

'Peter, how come you've never married?' They walked slowly towards the beach, with Fred at their heels, all but forgotten now. 'Or shouldn't I ask?'

'No, you can ask. A lot of sensible reasons, I suppose. I'm too selfish. I've been too busy. My work has swallowed up my life. All of that. Also, I move too fast, I'm not really the sort to settle down.'

'Somehow I don't believe that.' She looked at him closely, and he smiled.

'Neither do I. But there's some truth in all those reasons.' He seemed to pause for a long time, and then he sighed. 'There are other reasons too. I was in love with someone for twelve years. She was a patient when we met, and I was very taken with her, but I avoided getting involved. She never knew how I felt until . . . until much later. We seemed destined to be constantly thrown together. At every party, every dinner, every social or professional function. Her husband was a doctor, too. You see, she was married. I resisted "temptation", as it were, for a year. And then I couldn't any more. We fell in love, and we had a wonderful time together.

'We talked about getting married, running off together, having a child. But we never did. We simply went on as we were – for twelve years. I can't understand how we did it for so long, but I suppose things happen that way. They just go on and on and on, and one day you wake up and ten years have gone by, or eleven, or twelve. We kept finding reasons not to get married, for her not to get divorced – because of her husband, my career, her family. There were always reasons. Perhaps we preferred it the way it was, I don't know.' He had never admitted that before, and

Nancy watched him as he spoke. He was looking out at the horizon, and he seemed a thousand miles away, even as he talked to her.

'Why did you stop seeing each other?' Or maybe they hadn't. As the thought came to her, she blushed. Maybe she was prying. It was possible that there was a great deal about Peter's life that she didn't know, and had no right to know. She had never thought of that before. 'I'm sorry. I shouldn't have asked.'

'Don't be ridiculous.' His eyes and his thoughts came back to her with their usual gentleness. 'There's nothing you can't ask me. No, she died. Four years ago, of cancer. I was with her most of the time, except on the last day. I think . . . I think Richard knew at the end. It didn't matter any more. We had both lost her, and I think he was grateful that she didn't leave him in the years before. We mourned her together. She was an incredible woman. She was . . . very much like you.' There were tears in his eyes when he looked at her, and Nancy felt tears come to her own eyes. Without thinking, she reached up with a careful hand and wiped the tears softly from his cheeks, and then without taking her hand away from his cheek she moved gently towards him and kissed him, softly, on the lips. They stood there for a long, silent moment, very close, with their eyes closed, and then she felt Peter's arms go around her, and she felt more at peace than she had in over a year. She felt safe. He held her that way for what seemed like a very long time.

'Do you know that I love you?' He stepped back and looked down at her with a smile she had never seen before. It made her feel at once happy and sad, because she wasn't sure she was ready yet to give him all that he was giving her. She loved him, but not . . . not the way his eyes told her he loved her.

'I love you, too, Peter. In my own peculiar way.'

'That'll do for now.' Livia had told him that at first, too. It was frightening, sometimes, how much alike they were. 'You know, Faye helped me a great deal when she died. That was why I thought she'd be good for you.' She had also helped him in other ways, but that didn't matter, not now.

'You were right. She's been wonderful. You both have.' She took his hand then, and they began to walk back up the beach. 'Peter . . . I . . . I don't know how to say this, but . . . I don't want to hurt you. I do love you, but I'm still packing up my past. Piece by piece, bit by bit. I'm not sure of myself yet.'

'I'm in no hurry. I'm a man of great patience. Don't worry.' And the way he said it made her feel happy and warm. She wondered if perhaps she did love him more than she knew. And then as they walked along, she had a sudden thought. It frightened her and excited her, but she knew that she wanted to do it. He caught the sparkle in her eye when she looked up at him as they got back to the car. 'And just what exactly do you have up your sleeve?'

'Never mind.'

'Oh, God. Now what?' Several weeks before she had phoned him one morning at dawn, to tell him he had to get up to watch the sensational sunrise. 'Nancy . . . no, Marie. From now on, it's Marie, and only Marie. But tell me, is Marie as outrageous as Nancy?'

'More so. She has all kinds of new ideas.'

140

'Oh, no, spare me.' But he didn't look as though he wanted to be spared. Not for a moment. 'A little hint maybe? Just a small one?' But she was shaking her head and laughing at him as Fred hopped on to her lap and Peter started the car. 'Well, I have an idea for you myself. The work on your face will be done by the end of the year. How about starting the year with a show of the photographic artwork of Marie Adamson? Will you agree to that?'

'I might.' She was actually beginning to like the idea, and something had happened that afternoon to make her feel brave again. Maybe telling him how she felt about Michael, hearing about the woman he had loved. 'I'll think about the show.'

'No. Promise me. In fact,' he took the key out of the ignition, slipped it under him on the seat, and turned to smile at her. 'I won't take you home until you agree to a show, and I hope you're too much of a lady to wrestle me for the key.'

'Okay. You win.' She ruffled Fred's fur and laughed. 'I give up. I'll have a show.'

'As easy as that?' He was stunned.

'As easy as that. But just how do you propose I go about getting myself shown?'

'Leave that to me. Is that a deal?'

'Yes, sir, it is.' She trusted him with her work as much as she had with her face and her life.

'Darling, you won't regret it.' He gently took her face in his hands, kissed her, and started the car again. It had been a beautiful day.

They drove home slowly along the coast, and Peter

regretfully stopped the car in front of her house at six o'clock. He hated to see the day end. But he wanted her to rest.

'Okay, young lady. Get a good night's sleep. I want to see you in the office bright and early tomorrow.' He was removing more of the bandages the next day, and two more operations were scheduled for the next two months. But by December she would be through the surgery, and in January she would be 'unveiled'.

'Do you want to come up?' She wasn't really sure she wanted him to, and was slightly relieved when he said no.

'We'll have dinner some time this week. I'll have some news by then about the show.'

'I won't be disappointed if you don't.'

He smiled as she and Fred got out of the car, and she waved as she walked into the building. But she was already thinking of something else. She had thought of it on the beach as they walked back to the car, and now she knew it was something she had to do. Something she wanted to do. She walked straight to the closet without taking off her coat, and reached behind her clothes until she found it. She pulled it out into the hallway and looked at it for a long time before opening it. It was dusty, and she was almost afraid to open it, but she had to. Slowly, she pulled at the zipper, and the large black artist's portfolio opened at her feet, revealing sketches, a few paintings, and some unfinished work. But at the top of the pile was what she was looking for. She sank down on to the floor and looked at it thoughtfully. She had intended it to be Michael's wedding present, a year and a half ago. The landscape with the boy hidden in the tree. She sat there holding it, and slowly the tears slid down her face. It had taken eighteen months to face that again. But she had now, and she was going to finish it. For Peter.

It was a brisk, chilly day as Marie pulled down the brim of her white fedora, raised the collar of her bright red wool coat, and walked the last few blocks to Faye Allison's office. Fred was at her side, as always, and his collar and leash were exactly the same red as her coat. Marie smiled down at him as they turned the last corner. She was in high spirits, which even the fog couldn't dampen. She ran up the steps to Faye's office, and let herself in.

'Hello! I'm here!' Her voice sang out in the warm, cosy house, and a moment later there was a quick answer from upstairs. Marie slipped out of her coat. She was wearing a simple white wool dress with a gold pin Peter had given her a few months before. Almost absentmindedly, she glanced in the mirror and pulled her hat to a jauntier angle and then smiled at what she saw. The glasses were at last gone, and she could finally see eyes when she looked in the mirror. Only a few narrow bands of tape remained high on her forehead. And in a few weeks they would be gone, too. Finished. The job was done.

'Pleased with what you see, Nancy?' She suddenly noticed Faye standing behind her, an affectionate smile on her face and she nodded.

'Yes, I guess I am. I'm even used to myself now. But you're not!' There was mischief in her eyes as she turned and grinned impishly at her friend.

'What do you mean?'

'You keep calling me "Nancy". It's Marie now, remember? It's official.'

'I'm sorry.' Faye shook her head and led the way into the cosy room where they always talked. 'I keep slipping.'

'You certainly do.' But Marie didn't look upset as she slid into her favourite chair. 'I guess old habits are hard to break.' Her face grew sombre as she said the words, and Faye waited for the rest of her thoughts. 'I've been thinking of that a lot lately. But I think I'm finally over him.' She said it quietly, looking into the fire.

'Michael?' Marie only nodded and then finally looked up with great seriousness in her face. 'What makes you think you're over him?'

'I think I decided to be. I don't have much choice. The fact of it is, Faye, it's been almost two years since the accident. Nineteen months to be exact. He hasn't found me. He didn't tell his mother to go to hell, that he had to be with me no matter what. Instead he just let it go.' Her eyes found Faye's and held them fast. 'He let me go. Now I have to let him go.'

'That's not easy. You've expected a lot of him for a long time.'

'Too long. And he let me down.'

'How does that make you feel about yourself?'

'Okay, I guess. I'm mad at him, not at me.'

'You're not angry at yourself any more for your deal with his mother?' Faye was pressing a tender area and she knew it, but the ground had to be covered.

'I had no choice.' The voice was cool and hard.

'But you don't reproach yourself?'

'Why should I? Do you suppose Michael reproaches

himself that he let me down? That he never bothered to come to me after the accident? Do you think it's given him sleepless nights?'

'Is it still giving you sleepless nights, Nancy? That's what interests me.'

'Marie, damn it. And no, it's not. I decided to put the dreams away. I've lived with this nonsense for too long.' She sounded convincing, but Faye was still not entirely sure how the girl felt.

'So now what?' What would take Michael's place? Or who? Peter?

'Now I work. First, I take a vacation in the Southwest over the Christmas holiday. There are some beautiful areas I want to photograph. I've already made my plans. Arizona, New Mexico. I might fly into Mexico for a couple of days.' She looked pleased as she said it, but there was still something hard in her face, masking something sad. She had had another loss. She had finally let herself lose Michael. It had taken a very long time. 'I'll be gone for about three weeks. That ought to take care of the holidays pretty nicely.'

'And then what?'

'Work, work, and more work. That's all I care about right now. Peter's got the show all set up for me. It's going to be in January. And you'd better be there!'

Faye smiled. 'You don't think I'd miss it, do you?'

'I hope not. I've picked out some work that I really love. You haven't seen most of it, nor has Peter. I hope he likes it too.'

'He will. He loves everything you do. Which brings up a question, Nan . . . sorry, Marie. What about Peter? How do you feel about all that?'

Marie sighed and then looked back into the fire. 'I feel a lot of different things about Peter.'

'Do you love him?'

'In a way.'

'Could he ever replace Michael in your life?'

'Maybe. I keep trying to let him take Michael's place, but something stops me. I'm not ready. I don't know, Faye . . . I feel guilty not to be giving him more. He does so much for me. And . . . I know how much he cares.'

'He's a very patient man.'

'Maybe too patient. I'm afraid to hurt him.' She looked into Faye's eyes again, and her own were troubled. 'I care about him a great deal.'

'Then you'll just have to see what happens. Maybe you'll feel freer now that you've decided to let Michael go out of your life.' Faye saw the muscles tighten in the girl's neck as she heard the words 'Marie? You're not giving up on people, are you? Giving up on love?'

'No. Why should I?' But the answer was too quick and too glib.

'You shouldn't. Michael failed you. He's one man, not all men. Don't forget that. There's someone out there for you, maybe Peter, maybe someone else. But there's someone. You're a beautiful girl, and you're not quite twenty-five years old. You have a whole life ahead of you.'

'That's what Peter says too.' But she didn't look as though she really believed it. And then she looked up at Faye with a nervous little smile that masked both fear and sorrow. 'I made another decision, too.'

'And what's that?'

'About us. I think I've about done it, Faye. I've said all I

147

want to for a while. I'm ready to go out there, work my ass off, and beat the world.'

'Why not just enjoy it?' There was something about the girl that still worried her. She had given up on something. There was something she no longer believed in. She had been betrayed, and in a sense she was opting out. She was ready to fight for her work, but not for herself. 'You've been given a wonderful gift, Marie. The gift of beauty. Don't just hide that behind a camera.'

But Marie was looking at her with marble-hard eyes. 'It wasn't a gift, Faye. I paid for it with everything I had.'

They exchanged Merry Christmases as she left, but there was a tinselly echo to the words, an emptiness that still bothered Faye as Marie Adamson pulled at her white fedora and walked off with a jaunty wave back at her friend of two years. It was almost as though she were saying goodbye to those two years and walking into a new life, leaving behind everything she had once loved.

18

When Marie left Faye's office she caught a cab and headed straight to Union Square. She had already made the reservation; all she had to do now was stop off and pay for the ticket. It would be the first trip she had taken in years, the first since the weekend she and Michael had spent in Bermuda. That had been Easter and . . . she forced the thought from her mind as the cab headed down Post Street. Fred sat on her lap staring at the cars passing by and occasionally turning to look at his mistress. He sensed something different; there was an electricity about her that even the little dog could feel as she pulled a cigarette out of her handbag and lit it.

'Right here, miss?' the driver had stopped next to the Saint Frances Hotel, and Marie quickly nodded.

'This will be fine.' She paid the fare, opened the door of the cab, and let Fred hop out on to the pavement. She followed quickly, stubbed out the cigarette, and looked around. The ticket office was only a few steps away, and she was soon inside. For once, there wasn't even a queue, but it was still early in the day. Her appointments with Faye were always at eight forty-five. Were . . . had been . . . She suddenly realised again that she was through now. Free. Finished. Done. She was no longer seeing a psychiatrist. The thought frightened her a little. She felt both liberated and lonely, like celebrating and crying all at once.

'May I help you?' The girl behind the counter looked at

her with a smile, and Marie smiled back. 'Are you picking up tickets?'

'Yes, I am. I made reservations last week. Adams... McAllister.' It was strange using the old name again; she hadn't in two months. But even the trip was symbolic. Legally, her name would be changed on January first. When she returned she would no longer be Nancy McAllister, she would be Marie Adamson, for good. But when she left she would still be Nancy. It was almost like a wedding trip, all by herself. It was the final step in the endless process that had taken almost two years. Marie Adamson was finally, officially, going to be born. And Nancy McAllister could be forgotten forever. Hell, Michael had forgotten her; now she could forget her too. There was no one left to remember. Peter had seen to that. No one who had ever known her before would recognise her now. The delicate, perfectly etched face was someone other women dreamed of being, but no one she had known for the past twenty-four years. She wasn't a stranger any more, but neither was she Nancy McAllister. And her voice was different, too, smoother, deeper, more controlled. It was a subtle voice with sexual overtones, and she liked the way people listened to her, as though she had more to say now that she had a different way of saying it. Her hands were graceful and delicate, her movements smoother and more mature after the ballet classes Peter had finally let her take once his work was far enough along. Yoga had added to the whole. And all of it completed the picture of Marie Adamson.

'That'll be a hundred and ninety-six dollars.' The girl glanced at the computer and then at the customer standing before her. She couldn't take her eyes off her

150

– the perfect features, dazzling smile, and grace when she moved that held everyone's attention. Everything about her made you want to ask, 'Who is she?' Marie wrote out her cheque, received her receipt, and walked back out into the December sunlight of Union Square. She held Fred in her arms so he couldn't get stepped on, and smiled to herself as she wandered across the square. It was a beautiful day and she had a beautiful life. She was going away over the holidays; she was through with all those endless operations; she was starting a new life, a new career; she had an apartment she loved, a man who loved her. She couldn't ask for much more. She strolled into a big department store with a smile on her face and a bounce in her step, and decided to buy herself something pretty. An early Christmas present for herself, or maybe for the trip. She wandered from floor to floor, trying on hats, bracelets, scarves, jackets, handbags, a pair of boots, and a funny pair of gold lamé shoes. She finally settled on a soft white cashmere sweater, which with her silken skin and rich, dark hair made her look almost like Snow White. The thought amused her. And Peter would like it. The sweater moulded her figure in a pleasing sort of way. Even her shape had changed in the last year, with the ballet and yoga; her body seemed to have hardened and stretched until she looked long and lean and wonderfully lithe.

She made her way to the main floor again, looking at the displays, watching the people, and finally she stopped to buy a box of chocolates for Faye. They were a suitably festive gift for the last day of therapy. She wrote on the card only, 'Thank you. Love, Marie.' What more could she say? Thank you for helping me forget Michael? Thank you for helping me survive? Thank you . . . As she played with the thoughts, she stopped suddenly. She looked as though she had seen a ghost, and when the saleswoman handed her back her credit card, she only continued to stare. Ben Avery stood just a few feet away, looking over some very expensive women's luggage. Marie remained where she was for what seemed like an eternity, and then edged closer. She had to see him, touch him, hear what he was saying. For an insane moment, she wondered if he would recognise her; she prayed that he would, and then she knew that he wouldn't and forced herself to be glad. This way she could watch him, stand near him, for as long as she wanted. She wondered how long it had been since he'd seen Michael, if he'd taken the job with the firm. She sidled up to him and began fingering the suede attaché cases next to the pieces he was examining. Her eyes never left his face, then suddenly he turned to look at her and smiled his old easy smile in her direction. But there wasn't even a glimmer of recognition; instead he looked her over admiringly and then reached out a hand to Fred.

'Hi there, little fellow.' The voice was so familiar that it made her feel almost weak, but she just stood, feeling the warmth of his hand near hers as he patted the dog. She never would have imagined that merely seeing Ben would do this to her. But this was the first link she'd had with Michael since . . . She blinked back the tears and looked at the bags Ben had been looking over. Without thinking, her hand went to the chain around her neck that he had given her on her wedding night. She still wore it.

'Buying Christmas gifts?' She felt foolish making chitchat

with him, but she wanted to talk to him, and once again wondered if he'd recognise her, this time by her voice. But even she knew how different she sounded now. And again he looked at her with the blank easy smile passed between two strangers.

'Yes, for a young lady, and I can't decide what to get.'

'What's she like?'

'Terrific.'

Marie laughed. It was so like Ben. She almost wanted to ask him if it was serious this time, but she couldn't.

'She's got sort of red hair, and she's . . . about your height.' He was looking Marie over again, and his eyes roamed over her figure almost hungrily. She didn't know whether to laugh or to be upset, it was all so typically Ben.

'Are you sure she wants luggage?' It seemed a dull gift to Marie. She was hoping for something more exciting from Peter. Like maybe a new lens.

'We're going to be taking a trip together, so I thought . . . And the trip is kind of a surprise. I want to hide the tickets in the luggage.'

Five hundred dollars on imported luggage to hide some tickets? Benjamin Avery, such extravagance! The last two years must have been good to him. 'She's a lucky girl.'

'No, I'm the lucky guy.'

'Is this a honeymoon?' Marie was embarrassed at her own nosiness, but it was wonderful getting all this news of him, and maybe . . . maybe he'd . . . She kept her smile cool, pleasant, and detached as he shook his head.

'No. Just a business trip. But she doesn't know about it yet. Well, what do you think? The brown suede, or the dark green?'

'The brown suede with the red stripe. I think it's gorgeous.'

'So do I.' He nodded happily at Marie's choice and signalled to the salesgirl. He was taking three pieces, and asked her to ship them airmail to New York. Then he did live there. She had wondered. 'Thank you for your help, er . . . uh . . . Miss . . .'

'Adamson. I thoroughly enjoyed it, and I apologise if I asked too many questions. The holidays always have a strange effect on me.'

'Me too. But it's such a nice time of year. Even in New York, and that's saying a lot.'

'Is that where you live?'

'When I'm home. I travel a great deal for my job.'

That still didn't tell her if he was working for Michael, but she knew she couldn't ask. And suddenly, it made her ache, just standing there, being so near him, wanting to know about someone who no longer existed for her anyway – or shouldn't have. And then he looked at her again, as though something about her had bothered him. For a moment she felt her heart stop, but his smile told her that he had no idea who she was. She pulled at her hat a little to assure that he couldn't see the last of the tape and held Fred a little closer in her arms as Ben continued to stare at her.

'I know this is a crazy thing to ask,' he said, 'but could I invite you somewhere for a drink? I'm leaving on a plane in a few hours, but we could hop over to the St Francis, if . . .'

She returned the smile, but she was already shaking her head. 'I'm afraid I have a plane to catch too. But thank you for the offer, Mr Avery.'

And then his smile faded slowly. 'How did you know my name?'

'I heard the salesgirl say it.'

She was quick with the response, and he shrugged and then looked at her with regret. She was an incredibly beautiful girl. And no matter how much he had come to love Wendy in the three months since their romance began, he could still have a drink with a pretty girl. It was too bad she was leaving town, too. And then he had a thought. 'Where's your plane to, Miss Adamson?'

'Santa Fe, New Mexico.'

He looked as disappointed as a schoolboy, and she laughed at the look on his face. 'Damn. I was hoping you were going to New York. We could at least have enjoyed the flight together.'

'I'm sure the young lady with the luggage would have appreciated that.' Her eyes scolded him, but only a little, and they both laughed this time.

'Touché. Well, maybe next time.'

'Do you come to San Francisco often?' She was intrigued again.

'No, but I will.' And then with a look at the luggage and a smile, he added, 'We will. My firm is doing a big project here. I'll probably be spending more time here than in New York.'

'Then perhaps we'll meet again.' But her voice sounded almost sad. It was only Ben after all. It didn't matter how often she saw him, he still wasn't Michael. The salesgirl broke into her reverie, and she realised it was time to go. She looked at him for a long moment as he wrote out the cheque for the amount the salesgirl had added up, and then silently she squeezed his arm. He looked up in surprise, and she barely whispered, 'Merry Christmas,' before disappearing from where they had stood chatting for almost half an hour. He looked around when he had finished the cheque and was disappointed to find her gone. She had left so abruptly. He looked round the store as best he could through the throngs of Christmas shoppers, but she was nowhere to be seen. She had left by the side entrance, and was just then hailing a cab. She felt tired and heavy-hearted. It had been a long morning.

She gave the driver the vet's address, dropped Fred off there, and jumped back in the cab to go home. She was already packed. All she had to do was pick up her bags and head for the airport. She felt a little unkind leaving Fred behind, but she didn't really want him with her this time, and she was making too many stops in the three weeks she'd be gone. It was a trip she had to make alone. Her last moments as Nancy McAllister, the end of an old life, the beginning of a new. She took a last look around her apartment before she left, as though she expected never again to see it in quite the same way; and as she closed the door softly behind her, she whispered one word. She said it to herself, and to Ben, and to Michael, and to all those she had once loved or known . . . goodbye. There were tears in her eyes as she walked swiftly down the stairs with her camera bag and her suitcase tightly held in one hand.

19

She wouldn't let Peter come to the airport. Just as she had left alone, now she wanted to return alone. There had been something magical about the trip. It was a time of peace and hard work. She had spoken to almost no one as she travelled; she had merely observed, and been lost in her own thoughts. But as the days went by, her thoughts were lighter than they had been on the day she left San Francisco. Seeing Ben Avery again had been a blow. It had revived too many memories. But that was over now. She knew it. She could live with it. Her new life had begun.

Christmas Day got lost among the others, as she took photographs in the snow around Taos. She was tempted to ski, but didn't. She had promised Peter to avoid the risk of an accident, or too much sun. And had kept her word. So had he. She had told him when she was getting in but asked him not to be there, and he wasn't. She looked around the airport with relief. She was alone in an army of strangers. It was comforting to be lost in the crowd. It made her feel invisible and safe. She had spent a lot of time learning to be invisible in the last year and a half. Heavily bandaged most of the time, she had felt it important not to be seen. Now she attracted more attention than she had swathed in bandages: the very way she moved, the clothes she wore, the black stetson she had bought on her trip to hide the last bandages on her forehead, the black Levis and sheepskin coat, all contributed to her visibility simply because it was difficult to hide the kind of looks that she had. But she was not yet aware of just how striking she was.

She got a cab just outside the terminal, gave the driver her address, and settled back, with a sigh, against the seat. She was tired. It was almost eleven o'clock, and she'd been up at five that morning to take pictures. She looked at her watch and promised herself to be in bed by twelve. She had to be. Tomorrow was another big day. She had stayed away right up to the last moment. At nine the next morning, Peter would remove the last of the tape. No one else had been aware that she was still wearing tape. But she knew. And now even that would be gone. She was going to spend the morning alone after she left his office, and then they were meeting again for a celebration lunch. No more operations, no more stitches, no more tape. She would be just like everyone else. Her new name had become legal. Marie Adamson had been born.

The driver let her out in front of her building, and she walked slowly up the stairs, as though expecting to find a different apartment from the one she had left. But it was the same, and she was surprised to feel a sense of anticlimax. Then she laughed at herself. What did she want? She had told Peter not to meet her. Did she expect a brass band hiding in her bedroom? Peter under the bed? Something. She wasn't sure what. She peeled off her clothes and stretched out on the bed, thinking of what she had come home to. She had a lot on her mind. What would it mean now that Peter's work on her face would be finished? What if she never saw him again? But that was crazy and she knew it. He had arranged the exhibition of her work, which opened the day after the final 'unveiling' of her face. He cared about her as a person, not just as a reconstruction job. She knew that. But she felt oddly insecure as she lay there in the dark, wanting someone to tell her that everything was all right, that she wasn't alone, that she'd make it as Marie Adamson.

'Oh damn. What does it matter if I'm alone?' She stood up briskly and stared at herself in the mirror as she said the words, and then in irritation she picked up her camera and almost caressed it. That was all she needed. She was just tired from the trip. It was stupid to worry about being lonely, about her future, about Peter . . . With a sharp sigh, she climbed into bed. She had better things to think about, like her work.

She woke up shortly after six in the morning and was dressed and out of the house by seven-thirty. When she arrived at Peter's office at nine, she had already been to the food market and then the flower market to take pictures. She had added another shot to her series on China-town. And she had picked up Fred at the vet.

'My, don't you look chipper this morning – and beautiful. That's a marvellous coat.' Peter looked admiringly at the full-length coyote she had bought at a bargain price on a reservation in New Mexico. She wore it over jeans with a black turtleneck sweater and boots. And she had worn the black stetson until she got to his office. Now she held it in her hand for a moment, smiled at him in a way he had never seen before, and then poised over the wastebasket for only a fraction of a second, before crushing the hat into the bottom.

'And that, Dr Gregson, is the last time I will ever wear a hat.'

He nodded. He understood just how important the gesture was. 'You won't ever have to again.'

'Thanks to you.' She wanted to kiss him, but her eyes told him what he needed to know, and as she looked at him she realized that she had missed him on her trip. He was someone different to her now. He would no longer be her doctor after that morning. He would be her friend, and whatever else she let him become. They had not yet resolved that, no matter how often he told her he loved her. She had not yet taken the last step, and he had never pushed her. 'I missed you, Peter.' She touched his arm softly as she sat down in the all too familiar chair, closed her eyes, and waited.

He watched her for a moment as he stood there, and then he took his usual seat on the little swivel stool in front of her. 'You're in a hurry this morning.'

'After twenty months, wouldn't you be too?'

'I know, darling, I know.' She heard the clink of the delicate instruments in the little metal pan, and she felt the the tape being pulled slowly from her forehead and her hairline. With every millimetre of skin it exposed, she felt that much freer, until at last she felt nothing more, and she heard the little stool whoosh softly away from her. 'You can open your eyes now, Marie. And go look in the mirror.' She had made that trip a thousand times. At first only to see a tiny glimpse, a hint, a promise, and then bigger pieces of the puzzle. But she had never seen Marie Adamson's face free of tape, or stitches, or some reminder of what was being done. She had not seen her face, completely bare, since it had been the face of Nancy McAllister nearly two years before. 'Go on. Take a look.'

It was crazy. She was almost afraid to. But silently, she stood up and walked slowly to the mirror, and then she stood there with a broad smile, and a narrow river of tears gleaming on her face. He stood behind her, at a good distance. He wanted to leave her alone. This was her moment.

'Oh God, Peter, it's beautiful.'

He laughed softly. 'Not *it's* beautiful, silly girl. *You're* beautiful. It *is* you, you know.'

She could only nod and then turn to look at him. It wasn't so much that her face had changed without the few strips of tape on her forehead, but that it was over. She was entirely Marie now.

'Oh Peter . . .' Without saying more, she walked into his arms and held him tight. They stood there that way in his office for a long time, and then he pulled away and gently wiped her tears. 'Look, I can even get wet and I don't melt.'

'And you can take the sun, though not excessively. And you can do anything you want to for the rest of your life. What's first on the agenda?'

'Work.' She chuckled and sat down on the little swivel stool he had abandoned, and with her legs tucked up under her chin she spun herself round.

'God, she's going to break a leg in my office. That's all I need.'

'If I do, I'm walking out of here anyway, love. I have a life to celebrate this morning.'

'I'm glad to hear it.' And apparently Fred was, too. He jumped up, wagged his tail, and barked, as though he had understood what she had said. They both laughed and Peter stooped to pat his head. 'Are we still having lunch?'

There was an anxious look in his eyes and she was touched. She understood what he was feeling, too. Abandonment. Anxiety. Would she still want him in her life when she didn't need him any more? He looked very vulnerable to her as he stood there, and she held out a hand to him. 'Of course we're having lunch, silly. Peter . . .' Her eyes held his fast. 'There will always be time in my life for you. Always. I hope you know that. You're the only reason I have a life.'

'No. Someone else is responsible for that.' Marion Hillyard. But he knew how much she hated to hear the older woman's name, so he didn't say it. He never understood why Marie reacted that way, but he humoured her on the point. 'I'm glad I was around to help. I always will be, if you need me . . . for . . . for other things.'

'Good. Then see that you feed me at twelve-thirty.' The conversation had been serious enough. She stood up and shrugged her way into the new coyote coat. 'Where shall we meet?'

He suggested a new restaurant down at the docks, where they could watch the tugboats and ferries and tankers cruising by on the bay, and the hills of Berkeley beyond. 'Does that sound all right to you?'

'It sounds perfect. I may just hang around down there all morning and do some shooting.'

'I'd be disappointed if you did anything else.' He swept open the examining-room door with a bow, and she winked as she left, but she did not go straight to the docks as she had said. Instead, she went downtown to shop. Suddenly, she wanted to buy something fabulous to wear to lunch with Peter. It was the most special day of her life, and she wanted to enjoy every bit of it. In the cab, she glanced at her chequebook and was grateful for the money she had made before Christmas on some of her work. It would allow her to be extravagant for herself, and to buy Peter something as well.

She found a pale fawn cashmere dress which moulded her figure breathtakingly beneath the fur coat, and she stopped at the hairdresser and let him do her hair. It was the first time for years that she had worn it back, revealing her whole face. She bought big wonderful gold earrings at the costume jewellery bar, and a beige satin rope with a gold seashell on it. Beige suéde shoes and a bag, and the perfume she had always loved best and she definitely looked ready for lunch with Dr Peter Gregson. Or just about anyone else. She was a woman who would have stopped any man's heart.

Her last stop was at Shreve's where as though by pre-arranged plan, she found precisely what she had wanted but hadn't known she would ever find. It was a little gold face made up as a watch fob, and she knew that Peter had a pocket watch he was fond of and occasionally wore. She would have the date engraved on it for him later, but for the moment this would have to do. She had it gift wrapped, hailed a cab and arrived at the restaurant just as he was sitting down. She thought she might explode with joy as she watched his face while she approached. There were a number of others in the restaurant who watched her appreciatively too, but none with the tenderness of Peter Gregson.

'Is it really you?'

'Cinderella at your service. Do you approve?'

'Approve? I'm overwhelmed. What did you do all morning? Run around shopping?'

'But of course. This is a special day.'

She did things to his feelings that he had thought couldn't be done. He wanted to kiss her there, in the restaurant. Instead he held tightly to her hand, and smiled a long happy smile. 'I'm so glad you're happy, darling.'

'I am. But not just because of the face. There's the show tomorrow, and . . . and my work, and my life . . . and . . . you.' She said the last word very softly.

The moment meant so much to him that he could only make light of it. 'I come after all those things, eh? What about Fred?'

They both laughed and he ordered Bloody Marys for the two of them, and then he thought better of it and changed the order to champagne.

'Champagne? Good heavens!'

'Why not? And I closed the office for the afternoon. I'm as free as can be – unless, of course,' he hadn't even thought of it, 'you have other plans.'

'Doing what for God's sake?'

'Working?' He felt sheepish for even asking.

'Don't be ridiculous. Let's go and have fun today.'

He laughed at her answer. 'What would you like to do most?'

She tried to think and couldn't come up with anything, and then she looked at him with a broad smile. 'Go to the beach.'

'In January?'

'Sure. This is California after all, not Vermont. We could drive over to Stinson, and go for a walk.'

'All right. You're certainly easy to please.' But beach walks with him had become special to her and she wanted a special place to give him her gift. She wasn't sure if she could hold out till then. But she did. She waited until late that afternoon, when they were walking hand in hand along the windswept beach. The fur coat protected her from the stiff breeze that was coming in from the fog.

'I have something for you, Peter.' He looked at her in surprise as she stopped walking, as though he didn't quite understand, and then she pulled out the little gift-wrapped box. 'I'll have it engraved, if you like it.'

'Marie, that's outrageous. You shouldn't . . . I didn't want . . .' He was touched and embarrassed as he opened the little box and delighted when he saw the beautiful fob. He put an arm tightly around her shoulders. 'Why did you do a thing like that?' he scolded slowly.

'Because you're such a silly and you never do anything for me.' He laughed at the mischievous look in her eyes and this time took her in his arms for a long, tender kiss that told her all that he felt. And this time, she kissed him too.

'Shall we . . . maybe we'd better go back,' he said after a few minutes.

She nodded quietly and followed him back to the car, but her expression wasn't as sombre as his, and when they reached her apartment, she turned and looked at him with a smile. 'I have something else for you, Peter. I'd like you to come upstairs if you have time.'

'Are you sure?'

'Absolutely.'

She walked up the stairs ahead of him in silence, and when she opened the door of the apartment, she didn't turn on the lights. She walked straight across the living room, turned her easel away from the window and then turned on the light. What he saw was her landscape with the boy sitting partially hidden in the foliage of a tree. She had finished it for him before she left on her vacation, but she had been saving it for this day, if not for this moment. He looked at her now as though he didn't understand.

'It's for you, Peter. I started it a long time ago. And I . . . I finished it for you.'

'Oh darling.' He walked towards it with bright eyes and a gentle look on his face, as though he couldn't believe what she'd done for him. It had been a day filled with emotion and surprises. For both of them. 'I can't take this. I already have so much of your work. You give it all to me, and then you have nothing to exhibit.'

'You have photographs, Peter. This is different. This is a sign of my rebirth. It's the first time I've painted again. And . . . this painting used to mean a great deal to me. I want you to have it. Please.' There were tears in her eyes now, and he walked towards her and took her into his arms.

'It's exquisite. Thank you. I don't know what to say. You've been so good to me.'

'You don't have to say anything,' she whispered in the soft light of twilight, with the music of the foghorns bleating softly in the distance.

20

'Darling, can you zip me up?' She turned her graceful ivory back to him.

'I would rather zip you down than up.'

'Now, now, Peter.' Marie looked at him warningly and they both laughed. He was wearing a dinner jacket and she had just put on a beautifully cut black dress with soft dolman sleeves and a narrow waist in a fabric that allowed one to see her silhouette but nothing more. It was a striking dress, and Peter was suitably dazzled.

'I hate to tell you this, but no one is going to be looking at your work. They're all going to be looking at you.'

'Oh yeah?' He laughed at her obvious disbelief and straightened the tie he wore with a soft blue shirt and his dinner jacket. Together they made a very striking couple.

'Did they hang everything the way you wanted them to? I never got time to ask you.' When he had woken up at eight that morning, she had gone already.

She smiled at him as she watched him finish dressing. 'Yes, they put everything up exactly the way I wanted. Thanks to you. I get the feeling you told them to do it my way "or else". You or Jacques.' The gallery owner was one of Peter's oldest and closest friends. 'I feel thoroughly spoiled. The complete "artiste".'

'That's how you should feel. Your work is going to be very important, darling. You'll see.'

And indeed she did. The reviews in the paper the next

day were spectacular. They sat around in her apartment over morning coffee, and grinned at what they read.

'Didn't I tell you?' He looked even more pleased with himself than she did. 'You're a star.'

'You're crazy.' She plonked herself on his lap with a grin and rumpled the paper.

'You wait. You'll have every photographer's agent in the country calling you by next week.'

'Darling, you are out of your mind.' But he wasn't too far off. She was getting calls from Los Angeles and Chicago by the following Monday. She couldn't get over it, but she was thoroughly enjoying the whole thing. And she was amused by every phone call she got. Until the call from Ben Avery. It came on a Thursday afternoon, when she was developing some film. She heard the phone ring, and she wiped her hands and walked into the kitchen to answer it. She assumed it was Peter. He had said he would call to let her know what time he could see her that evening. He had some kind of meeting fixed for late afternoon. But she had plenty of darkroom work to keep her busy; there was a veritable avalanche of orders coming in as a result of the show.

'Hello?'

'Miss Adamson?'

'Yes.' She didn't recognise the voice, and the smile she had been wearing for Peter rapidly faded.

'I don't know whether we've met or not, but I met a Miss Adamson the last time I was here. I was doing some Christmas shopping . . . I bought some luggage, and . . .' He felt like a total ass, and for what seemed like an eternity she said nothing.

So it was Ben. Damn. How had he found her? And why had he bothered to?

'I . . . was that you?'

She was tempted to say no, but why lie? 'I believe it might have been.'

'Good. Well, at least we've met. I'm actually calling you because I've just seen your work at the Montpelier Gallery on Post Street. I'm enormously impressed, as is my associate, Miss Townsend.'

Marie was suddenly curious. Was that the girl he had bought the luggage for? But she didn't feel she could ask. Instead she sighed and sat down. 'I'm glad you liked it, Mr Avery.'

'You remembered my name!'

Oh, Jesus. 'I have a memory for these things.'

'How fortunate for you. I have a memory like a sieve, and in my business that's no asset, believe me. In any case, I'd very much like to get together with you to discuss your work.'

'In what sense?' What the hell was there to discuss?

'We're doing a medical centre here in San Francisco, Miss Adamson. It's going to be an enormous project, and we'd like to use your work in every building as the central theme of the décor. We're not quite sure how, but we know we want your pictures. We'd like to work it out with you. This could be the assignment of your career.' He said it with tremendous pride, and he was obviously waiting for a gasp at the other end of the line, a shriek of enthusiasm, anything but what he heard.

'I see. And what firm are you representing?' She waited, holding her breath, but she already knew the answer before he said the words.

169

'Cotter-Hillyard, in New York.'

'Well, no thanks, Mr Avery, it's just not my scene.'

'Why not?' He sounded stunned. 'I don't understand.'

'I don't want to go into it with you, Mr Avery, but I'm not interested.'

'Can we get together and discuss this?'

'No.'

'But I've already spoken to . . . I—'

'The answer is no. Thank you for your call.' And then, very quietly, she replaced the receiver and walked back to the darkroom door. She wasn't going to do business with them. That was all she needed. She was through with Michael Hillyard. He didn't want her as his wife; she didn't want him as her employer. Or anything else.

The phone rang again before she had closed the darkroom door. She knew it would be Ben again, but she wanted to settle the matter once and for all. She strode back to the phone, picked it up, and almost shouted into it. 'The answer is no. I already told you that.' But the voice on the other end was not Ben's, it was Peter's.

'Good God, what have I done?' He was half laughing, half stunned, and Marie felt herself relax at the sound of his voice.

'Oh, Christ. I'm sorry. I just had someone call me with an annoying request.'

'As a result of the show?'

'More or less.'

'The gallery shouldn't be giving out your number to crackpots. Why don't they take the message there?' He sounded upset.

'I think I'll suggest that to Jacques.'

Peter was disturbed at the thought of some crazy calling her. 'Are you all right?'

'I'm fine.' But she sounded shaken, and he could hear it.

'Well, I'll be there in an hour. Don't answer the phone till I get there. I'll handle it if anyone calls after that.'

They exchanged a few more words and then hung up, and she found herself feeling guilty for not telling him the truth about the call. Ben Avery was no crackpot, he just worked for Michael Hillyard. But she didn't want to tell Peter that that was what had unnerved her. He didn't need to know how shaky she still was on the subject of Michael. But she was getting better every day. And fortunately Ben didn't call again that night. He waited until the next morning. And then surprised her again as she got ready to go to work.

'Hi, Miss Adamson. Ben Avery again.'

'Look. I thought we got this thing settled last night. I'm not interested.'

'But you don't even know what you're not interested in. Why not have lunch with my associate and me, and we'll talk? It can't hurt, can it?'

Oh yes it can, Ben, oh yes it can. 'I'm sorry, I'm busy.' She wasn't giving an inch, and sitting in his hotel room, Ben rolled his eyes at Wendy. It was hopeless. And he couldn't understand why. What the hell did she have against Cotter-Hillyard? It didn't make sense.

'How about tomorrow?'

'Look, Ben . . . Mr Avery . . . I won't do it. I'm not interested. And I don't want to discuss it with you, your associate, or anyone else. Is that quite clear?'

'Unfortunately, yes. But I think you're making a huge professional mistake. If you had an agent, he'd tell you just that.'

'Well, I don't. So I don't have to listen to anyone but myself.'

'That's your mistake, Miss Adamson. But we'll keep in touch.'

'It's nice of you to be interested, but really, don't bother.'

21

It was a freezing February day as Ben Avery huddled turtle-like in his coat, and ran all the way from the subway exit to his office in Park Avenue. There would be snow by the end of the day – he could feel it in the air – and it seemed as though daylight had barely emerged. It was not quite eight o'clock in the morning. But he had an enormous amount of work to do. This would be his first day back from the coast, and the big meeting with Marion was scheduled for ten-thirty that morning. He had mostly good news for her.

There were already a number of people in the lobby of the building, and the lift was almost full. Even at that hour, the business world was bustling. After the slower pace of San Francisco, and even Los Angeles, it was a shock to be back in the mainstream again. In Mecca, people started early. But at least there seemed to be no one else at work on his floor when he walked down the long, beige-carpeted, wood-panelled hall to the office Marion had given him when he'd joined the firm. It was smaller and far less handsome than Mike's office, but it was well put together. Marion spared no expense on the offices of Cotter-Hillyard.

Ben looked at his watch as he shrugged out of his coat and rubbed his hands together for a moment to get warm. There was no getting used to the freezing winds and damp cold of New York. Some winters he wondered if he'd ever get warm, and why he put up with it when there were cities like San Francisco, where people lived in a temperate dream world all year long. Even his office felt icy cold. But he had no time to waste. He emptied the contents of his briefcase on his desk, and began to sort through the papers and reports. Everything had gone splendidly. With one minor exception. And maybe something could still be done about that. He looked at his watch again after a few moments, grew pensive, and then decided to give it a try. It would be a major coup if he could come into the meeting with that one last piece of good news.

Ben had brought home a few samples of Marie Adamson's work; he had had to buy them at the gallery. But he had been sure they were worth the investment; once Marion and Michael got a look at her style, and saw just how good she was, Marion herself would probably get into the act, and talk the girl into signing. He smiled at the thought that would have sent shivers up Marie's spine.

He dialled her number and waited. It was an insane thing to do. In San Francisco, it was five fifteen in the morning, but maybe if he could get her half asleep . . .

'Hello?' She sounded groggy when she answered the phone.

'Uh . . . Miss . . . Miss Adamson, I'm terribly sorry to do this to you, but this is Ben Avery in New York. I'm going into a meeting this morning with the head of our firm, and I want more than anything to tell her that you'll work with us on the medical centre. I just thought that—' But he already knew he had done the wrong thing. He could sense it in the silence that overwhelmed him from the other end, and then suddenly she came alive.

'At five o'clock in the morning? You called to tell me

about your meeting with . . . for Chrissake, what kind of crazy business is this? I told you no, didn't I? What the hell do I have to do? Get an unlisted phone number?' As he listened to her, he closed his eyes, partially in embarrassment, and partially because of something else. The voice. It was strange. He didn't know why, but it sounded familiar. And it didn't sound like Marie Adamson. It was higher, younger, and different enough to strike a chord of memory that bothered him. Whom did she sound like? But he couldn't remember. 'Haven't you got the message yet, for Chrissake?'

Her angry words brought him back to the present and the reality that he was indeed speaking to Marie Adamson, and she was far from pleased with his phone call. 'I'm really sorry. I know this was an insane thing to do. I just hoped that—'

'I told you. No. I will not listen to, discuss, consider, ponder, or further speak to you about your lousy medical centre. Now leave me alone.' And with that she hung up on him again, and he sat there with the dead phone in his hand, smiling sheepishly.

'Okay, guys. I blew it.' He said the words to himself or thought he did. He hadn't seen Mike leaning easily in the doorway.

'Welcome home. What did you blow?' Mike didn't look particularly concerned. He looked very pleased to see his friend as he sauntered into the room and sat down in one of the large comfortable leather chairs. 'It's good to see you back, you know.'

'Nice to be back. But it's damn cold in this town. Jesus, after San Francisco, I may never readjust.'

'We'll be sure to keep you on the Southern route from now on, O delicate one.' He grinned at his friend. 'And what was that phone call about?'

'The one and only hair in my soup on this trip.' He ran a hand through his hair in irritation, and sat back in his chair. 'Absolutely everything went the way we wanted. Your mother is going to be in ecstasy over the reports. With one exception. Granted it's a minor problem, but I wanted everything to be perfect.'

'Should I start worrying?'

'No. I'm just pissed off. I found an artist. A girl. A marvellous photographer. I mean really a huge talent, Mike, not just some kid with a Brownie. She is brilliant. I saw her current show in San Francisco, and I wanted to sign her for the lobby décor in all the main buildings. You know, the photographic motif we all okayed at the last meeting before I left.'

'And?'

'And she told me to drop dead. She won't even discuss it.' He looked beaten as he said it.

'Why? Too commercial for her?' Mike looked unimpressed.

'I don't even know why. She went into a tailspin from the first time I called her. It just doesn't make any sense.'

But Mike was smiling at him with an expression of cynical amusement. 'Of course it makes sense, my naïve friend. She's holding out for big money. She knows who we are, so she figures she'll play hard to get and hit us up for a fat contract. Is she really that good?'

'The best. I brought you some samples of her work. You'll love them.'

'Then maybe she'll get what she wants. Show me later. First, there's something I want to ask you.' Mike looked momentarily serious. This was a subject he'd been meaning to bring up for weeks.

'Anything wrong?' Ben was quick to pick up on his mood.

'No, in fact I feel like a horse's ass even asking you. It shows how out of touch I've been. But . . . well . . . is there something between you and Wendy?'

Ben searched his face for a moment before answering. Mike looked curious, but not hurt. Of course, Ben had known about Wendy's affair with Mike. But it was no secret that Mike had never cared about her. Still, Ben found it a little odd picking up his old friend's castoff. This had been the first time it had happened, and he had never been quite sure how Mike would take it when he found out. And the truth was, he and Wendy were in love. They had spent an incredible month together on the business trip to the Coast. Wendy had teasingly called it their honeymoon.

'Well, Avery, what's up? You haven't answered my question.' But now there was a small smile playing around Mike's mouth. He already knew.

'I feel like a jerk for not telling you sooner. But the answer is yes. Does it bother you, Mike?'

'Why should it? I'm embarrassed to admit that I . . . well, I haven't exactly kept up with things. I'm sure Wendy told you how wonderfully attentive I was.' He sounded bitter at the last words, but Ben's tone was gentle in reply.

'She never said anything, except that she thought you weren't a very happy man. That doesn't exactly come as a shock to either of us, pal, does it?' Mike nodded silently.

'I didn't move in on your scene with her, Mike. I want you to know that. You two had stopped going out for a while. And to tell you the truth, I always did have a kind of a soft spot for her.'

'I suspected that when you hired her. She's a hell of a nice girl. Better than I deserved.' And then he smiled again. 'And probably better than you deserve too. Hey, wait a minute.' There was pure mischief in his eyes now. 'Is this serious by any chance?'

Ben grinned at his friend and then nodded. 'I think so.'

'Jesus. You mean it? You're thinking of getting married?' He was stunned. Where had he been? Why hadn't he noticed? Of course, Ben had been away for a month, but still . . . he hadn't paid attention to things like that in two years. 'I'll be goddamned. Married, Avery. Jesus. Are you sure?'

'I didn't say that. But we're thinking about it. I'd say the odds are all for it. Do you have any objections?' But they both knew he was only teasing. The awkward moment was already past.

'No objections whatsoever.' He sat there shaking his head, with a grin on his face. 'I feel like I missed a page here and there. Or have you been particularly discreet?'

'No, not at all. You've just been particularly busy. All work and no play will make you rich and celebrated in your field, but totally out of touch with office gossip.' Ben was only half teasing, and Mike knew it.

'You could have told me, you jerk.'

'You're right and I'm sorry, and when there's big news to report, I will. Speaking of which, will you be my—' And then he could have bitten off his tongue for what he had

178

started to ask. He had been acting as Mike's best man the night of the accident, and now he had almost asked Mike to be his. 'Never mind. There's plenty of time.' Mike stood up, nodded, and went to shake hands with his friend, but there was something dark and hidden in his eyes again. He knew only too well what Ben had been about to say.

'Congratulations, old man.' The smile was genuine, but so was the pain. 'And don't worry about the photographer in San Francisco. If she's really as good as you say we'll hit her with a fat contract and a good deal, and she'll give in. She's just playing games.'

'I hope you're right.'

'Trust me. I am.' Mike saluted smartly and then disappeared as Ben mused over what he had said. He felt better now that Mike knew. He was only sorry about his own stupid tactlessness. Even after all this time, any reference to Nancy caused explosions of agony in his friend's eyes. He hated himself for bringing it up, but it had seemed a natural question to ask and he hadn't thought first. He shook his head with regret and then went back to the work on his desk. He had barely an hour before the big meeting with Marion. And it seemed like only moments later when Wendy knocked on the open door and beckoned him with a smile.

'Come on, Ben. We have to be in Marion's office in five minutes.'

'Already?' He looked up nervously from his desk, and then smiled as he looked at her. She was just exactly what he had always wanted. 'By the way, I told Mike this morning.' He looked pleased with himself.

'Told him what?' Her mind was on the medical centre

in San Francisco and the meeting with Marion. Meetings with the great white goddess of architecture always scared the hell out of her.

'I told him about us, silly. I think he was actually pleased.'

'I'm glad.' She didn't really care, but she knew it meant something to Ben. She really didn't give a damn about Mike any more, one way or the other. He had been unkind and unfeeling, absent from every moment they had ever spent together. It was almost as though nothing had ever happened between them. 'Ready for the meeting?'

'More or less. I tried the Adamson girl again this morning. She told me to go to hell.'

'That's a shame.' They talked about it quietly as they walked down the hall to the private lift that led to Marion's ivory tower in the penthouse. Everything on the floor was the colour of sand, even the lift, which was entirely carpeted, floor, ceiling, and walls. It was like travelling upwards in a soundless, plush, creamy-beige womb, until suddenly you reached the floor which housed Marion's office with its spectacular view. Wendy could feel her palms grow moist on the file she was carrying. Marion Hillyard always made her feel like that, no matter how pleasant she was: Wendy had seen what lay beneath the poise and the charm.

'Nervous?' Ben whispered it softly as they walked around a bend to the chrome and glass door to Marion's conference room.

'You bet.' They laughed with each other and then quietly took their seats in the long, plant-filled room. There was a Mary Cassatt on one wall, and an early Picasso on another, and ahead of them lay all of New York, a magnificent view that always made Wendy feel almost dizzy as she sat there on the sixty-fifth floor. It was like taking off in a plane, except for the silence. Marion always seemed to move surrounded by a hush.

There were twenty-two people seated at the long smoked-glass conference table when Marion finally walked into the room flanked by George, Michael, and her secretary Ruth. Ruth carried an armful of files and George and Michael were engaged in an earnest conversation. Little by little he had been turning over the reins to Michael, and was surprised to find it a relief.

Only Marion seemed interested in the group, and she looked around at the faces, making sure everyone was there. She looked the same sandy colour as her décor today, but Wendy assumed it was simply New York pallor. She had grown so accustomed to seeing tanned faces on the West Coast that it was a bit of a shock to come back to New York and realise how pale everyone still was in the dead of the Eastern winter.

But Marion looked as chic as ever in a dress that appeared to be Givenchy or Dior, of simple heavy black wool, relieved by four rows of very large, perfectly matched pearls. Her nail polish was dark, and she seemed to be wearing very little make-up. Even Michael thought she looked unusually pale and was probably working too hard on this project, and ten other projects as well. His mother had her finger in every pie baked by the firm. That was just the way she was. And Michael was following in her footsteps. She admired the total dedication of his work for the past two years. That was how successful empires kept healthy, infused by the life's blood of those who nurtured him. Sacred guardians. Keepers of the holy grail.

Marion was the first to speak. She reached over for the first folder in front of Ruth, and began questioning the groups, department by department, discussing the various problems that had come up in the last meeting, and checking up on their solutions. All went well until she got to Ben, and even there she was immensely pleased with what he and Wendy had to say. They explained their progress in San Francisco, the results of their meetings, all the new developments, and she checked off a list in front of her and looked over at Michael with pleasure. The San Francisco job was taking shape splendidly.

'We only had one problem.' Ben said it a little too softly and her eyes were instantly on him again.

'Oh? And what was that?'

'A young photographer. We saw her work and liked it very much. We wanted to discuss the possibility of signing her for the lobby art in all the major buildings. But she wouldn't talk to us.'

'What does that mean?' Marion did not look pleased.

'Just that. When she found out why I called her, she almost hung up on me.' Marion raised an eyebrow in query.

'Did she know whom you represent?' As though that would change everything. Michael concealed a smile, as did Ben. Marion had such overwhelming pride in the firm, she expected everyone to want to do business with them.

'Yes. I'm afraid that didn't sway her. If anything, it seemed to anger her more.'

'Anger her?' For the first time all morning there was colour in Marion's face, but her expression was grim. Who did she think she was this young woman who turned up her nose at Cotter-Hillyard?

'Well, maybe anger is the wrong word. Maybe scared her off would be more appropriate.' It wouldn't, but it suited the need for the moment. To pacify Marion. The two bright red spots in her cheeks began to fade, to everyone's relief, especially Ben's.

'Is she worth pursuing?'

'I think so. And we brought back some samples of her work to show you. I hope you'll agree.'

'How did you get samples of her work if she wouldn't agree to discuss the job with you?'

'We bought them from her gallery. It was an extravagance, but if there's any problem with it, I'd be happy to buy them from the firm myself. She does beautiful work.' And with that, Wendy quietly went to a table near the back wall and came back with a good-sized portfolio, from which she took three very handsome colour photographs Marie had shot in San Francisco. One was a park scene, its composition simple; it showed an old man seated on a bench, watching some small children at play. The picture could have been sentimental, but it wasn't; it was compassionate. The second was a wharf scene, the vitality of its crowds not detracting from the grinning shrimp vender who dominated the foreground. And finally, a shimmering view of San Francisco at dusk – the city as tourists and residents alike loved to see it. Ben said nothing. He merely propped up the photographs and stood back. They were enlarged so that everyone could see clearly how fine the work was. Even Marion sat in silence for a long time, before finally nodding.

'You're right. She is worth pursuing.'

'I'm glad you agree.'

'Mike?' She turned to her son, but he seemed lost in thought as he looked at the work. There was something haunting and familiar about the quality of the art, the nature of the subjects. He wasn't sure what it was, but it instantly put him in a pensive mood that he fought to shake off. He wasn't sure why the photographs bothered him as they did, but even he had to agree that they were remarkably good work and would enhance any building with the Cotter-Hillyard name on it.

'Do you like them as much as I do?' Marion persisted. He looked at his mother with a silent, sober nod. 'Ben, how do we get her?' Marion wasted no time.

'I wish I knew.'

'Money, obviously. What sort of girl is she? Did you meet her at all?'

'Oddly enough, I met her the last time I was in San Francisco. She's a strikingly beautiful girl. In an almost unreal way. She's almost too perfect. All you can do is stare at her. She's poised, pleasant – when she wants to be – and obviously gifted. Used to be an artist, before she took up photography. She looked expensively dressed so I don't suppose she's starving. In fact, the gallery owner said that she has some sort of sponsor. An older man. A doctor I think he said, a famous plastic surgeon. At any rate, she doesn't need the money. And that's really all I know.'

'Then maybe money isn't the answer.' But suddenly Marion looked as pensive as her son. She had had a mad, unreasonable thought. It would be an outrageous coincidence, but what if . . . 'How old is this girl?'

'Hard to say. She was wearing kind of a big hat the first time I met her; it sort of hid her face. But I'd say she's . . .

I don't know, twenty-four, twenty-five maybe. At the most twenty-six. Why?' He didn't understand that question at all.

'I was just curious. I'll tell you what, Ben. I'm sure you and Wendy did your best, and it's quite possible that there's no getting through to this girl at all, but I'd like to give it a try. Leave me the information, and I'll get in touch with her myself. I have to be in San Francisco anyway, some time in the next few weeks. Maybe she'll feel more awkward turning down an old woman than a young man.'

Ben smiled at the reference to an 'old woman'. Marion Hillyard looked anything but the part. A tough middle-aged dynamo perhaps, but a withered grandmama she would never be. But his smile grew serious as he watched her face. She was growing paler by the moment, and he suddenly wondered if she were ill. But she never gave him or anyone else time to inquire. She stood up, expressed her satisfaction with the meeting, got the information she needed from Ben, and thanked everyone for coming upstairs. When she left the room, the meeting was over. The brass-bordered door to her office closed softly behind Ruth a moment later, and the rest of them flowed slowly towards the lift, commenting on the progress of the job. Everyone seemed pleased, and relieved that Marion had been too. Usually someone set her off, but today she had been almost uncharacteristically mellow, and once again Ben found himself wondering if she were ill. He was among the last to leave the conference room, and Wendy had already gone downstairs when Ruth came rushing out of the inner sanctum and signalled for Michael. She looked terribly frightened.

'Mr Hillyard! Your mother . . . she's . . .'

But it was George who reacted first, literally running to her office, with a thunderstruck Michael and Ben at his heels. And once there, it was again George who knew what to do. Where to find the pills, which he rapidly gave her with a small glass of water, supporting her with her son's help, from her desk chair to the couch. She was a pale greyish-green, and she seemed to be having a great deal of difficulty breathing. For a terrified moment, Mike found himself wondering if she was dying, and he felt tears spring to his eyes. He rushed to the phone to call Dr Wickfield, but she waved weakly from the couch, and then spoke in a barely audible whisper.

'No, Michael . . . don't call . . . Wicky. Happens . . . all . . . the time.' Michael looked instantly at George. This was news to him, but it couldn't be to George, or he wouldn't have known where to find the pills, what to do. Jesus. How much of the world around him had he grown totally oblivious of in recent months? As he looked at his mother, pale and trembling on the couch, he began to wonder just how sick she was. He knew that she saw rather a lot of Dr Wickfield, but he had always assumed that was to make sure she was fit, not because she had any major problems. And this certainly appeared to be major. And a glance at the little bottle of pills George had left on the desk confirmed Michael's fears. They were for heart trouble.

'Mother,' Michael sat down in a chair next to her, and took her hand. 'Does this happen often?' He was almost as pale as she. She opened her eyes and smiled at him, then at George. George knew.

'Don't worry about it.' The voice was still soft, but stronger now. 'I'm fine.'

'You're not fine. And I want to know more about this.' Michael spoke and Ben found himself wondering if he were intruding, but he didn't want to leave, either. He was too stunned by what he had seen. The great Marion Hillyard was human after all. And she looked terribly vulnerable and frail as she lay there in the expensive black dress which only made her look paler. She was the colour of very fine parchment as she talked to her son, but her eyes were more alive than they had been a moment before.

'Mother . . .' Michael was going to press her until she told him.

'All right, darling, all right.' She took a little breath and slowly sat up on the couch, swinging her feet back to the floor and looking straight into the eyes of her only child. 'It's my heart. You know I've had the problem for years.'

'But it was never serious.'

'Well, now it is.' She was matter of fact. 'I may live to be a very nasty old woman, or then again I may not. Only time will tell. In the meantime, the little pills keep me going, and I manage. That's all there is to say.'

'How long has this been going on?'

'A while. Wicky started worrying about it two years ago, but it's got quite a lot worse this year.'

'Then I want you to retire.' He looked like a stubborn child as he sat staring worriedly at his mother. 'Immediately.' She only laughed and smiled up at George. But this time her ally's face told her he was worried too.

'Not a chance, darling. I'll be here till I drop. There's too much to do. Besides, I'd go crazy at home. What would I do all day? Watch soap operas and read movie magazines?'

'It sounds perfect for you.' They all laughed. 'Or,' he looked at his mother and then at George. 'You could both retire, get married, and go enjoy yourselves for a change.' It was the first time Michael had openly acknowledged George's attentions of the past twenty years, and George blushed crimson. But he did not look displeased.

'Michael!' His mother almost sounded like herself again. 'You're embarrassing George.' But oddly enough, she, too, looked neither shocked nor appalled at the idea. 'In any case, my retirement is out. I'm too young, sick or not. You're stuck with me, I'm afraid, for the duration.'

Michael already knew he had lost the battle. But he was going to give up by inches. 'Then at least be sensible, for God's sake, and stop travelling. You don't have to go to San Francisco. I can do all that myself. Don't be such a busybody. Stay home and take care of yourself.'

She only laughed at him and got up and walked to her desk. She looked rattled and tired and pale as she sank into her desk chair while they all watched her with terrible concern in their faces.

'I do wish you'd go away and stop looking so maudlin. *All* of you. I have work to do. Even if you don't apparently.'

'Mother, I'm taking you home. Today at least.' Michael looked belligerent as he watched her, but she only shook her head.

'I'm not going. Now go away, Michael, or I'll have George throw you out.' George looked amused at the idea. 'I may leave early, but I'm not leaving now. So thank you for your concern and ta ta. Ruth.' She pointed to the door, which her secretary obediently opened, and one by one they helplessly filed out. She was stronger than all of them, and she knew it.

'Marion?' George stopped in the doorway with a worried look in his eyes.

'Yes?' Her face softened as she looked at him and he smiled.

'Won't you go home now?'

'In a little while.'

He nodded. 'I'll be back in half an hour.'

She smiled, but she could hardly wait for the door to close behind him. There was no doubt in her mind about what had caused the attack. She couldn't afford to get excited about anything any more. It was really becoming a terrible nuisance. She looked at her watch as she dialled the number Ben had given her, and listened to the phone ring three or four times. She didn't know why she was so certain, but she was. Had been from the moment Ben started to describe Marie Adamson. She would try to see the girl when she went to San Francisco; maybe then she'd know for sure. Or maybe not. Maybe the changes would be too great. She wondered if she'd really know. And then, as she wondered, the girl answered the phone. Marion took a breath, closed her eyes, and spoke smoothly into the receiver. No one would have known she'd had an attack half an hour before. Marion Hillyard was, as ever, totally in control.

'Miss Adamson. This is Marion Hillyard, in New York.'

The conversation was brief, cold, and awkward, and Marion knew nothing more when she hung up than she had when she dialled. But she would know. In exactly three weeks. They had an appointment at four o'clock on a Tuesday afternoon in three weeks. Marion marked it on her calendar, and then sat back and closed her eyes. The meeting might tell her nothing, and yet . . . there were some things she had to say. She only hoped she lived another three weeks.

22

The clock seemed to tick interminably as she sat in the living room of her suite at the Fairmont. It offered an impressive view of the bay and Marin County beyond, but Marion Hillyard was not interested in the view. She was thinking about the girl. What had become of her? What did she look like? Had Gregson really wrought the wonders he had promised two years before? Ben Avery had seen a stranger when he met Marie Adamson. But what about Michael – would he still recognise her? And was she in love with someone else now, or, like Michael, had she become bitter and withdrawn? It made Marion think of her son again as she waited for this stranger who might indeed turn out to be the girl Michael had once loved. But what if she wasn't? She could be just anyone, a local photographer who had caught Ben Avery's eye. Maybe her theory was all wrong. Maybe . . .

She crossed and uncrossed her legs, and then reached into her handbag again for her cigarette case. It was a new one. George had given it to her for Christmas, with her initials set in lovely sapphires along the side of the handsome gold case. She lay in her chair for a moment with her eyes closed. She was exhausted. It had been a long flight that morning, and she should have given herself a day to rest before seeing the girl. But she was too anxious to put the meeting off for another day. She had to know.

She looked up at the mantel clock again. It was

four-fifteen. Seven-fifteen in New York. Michael would still be at his desk. Avery would already be off gallivanting with that girl from the design department. Her mouth pursed as she thought of them. He wasn't a serious boy, like Michael. But then again . . . she sighed. He wasn't unhappy, like Michael, either. Had she done the wrong thing? Had she been totally mad two years before? Had she asked too much of the girl? No. Probably not. She had been the wrong girl for Michael. And in time, perhaps, he'd find someone. There was no reason why he shouldn't. He certainly had everything it took: looks, money, position. He was going to be president of one of the leading companies in America. He was a man with power and talent, gentleness and charm.

Her face softened again as she thought of him. How good and strong he was . . . and how lonely. She sensed that, too. He even maintained a certain distance from her. It was as though some part of him had never bounced back. At least the drinking and brooding had stopped, but only to be replaced by a bleak, jagged determination that showed in his eyes. Like a man who has struggled through the desert for too long, determined to make it, but no longer quite sure why. And yet he had so much to be happy about, such a good life to enjoy. But he never took time to enjoy anything. She wasn't even entirely sure he enjoyed his work, not the way she did. Not the way his father and grandfather had. She thought of her own husband with tenderness again, and then slowly her thoughts drifted to George. How good he had been to her in these recent years. It would have been impossible to continue her work without him. He took the burdens from her shoulders as

often as possible, and left her only the interesting decisions, the creative work, and the glory. She knew how often
he did that for her. He was a man of great strength, and
at the same time great humility. She wondered why she
hadn't paid closer attention to all his virtues a dozen or so
years before. But there had never been time. For him, or
anyone. Not since Michael's father.

Maybe the boy wasn't so unlike her after all. She
smiled to herself, and the buzzer at the door of the
suite suddenly interrupted her thoughts. She started, as
though for a moment she had forgotten where she was.
And then she remembered. The meeting with the girl. It
was four twenty-five now. The girl was twenty-five minutes
late. But secretly, she was glad of the time alone. She set
her face in a dignified mask and walked sedately to the
door. She knew her navy blue silk dress and four rows of
pearls suited her perfectly, as did the smooth coif, the
perfect manicure, the artful make-up that made her look
more like forty-five than sixty. She would still be a beautiful woman in twenty years. If she lived that long. But she
would see to it that she stayed looking the way she wanted
to. Nothing got the better of Marion Hillyard, not even
time. She congratulated herself on that as she opened
the door to the elegant young woman with the artist's
portfolio in her hand.

'Miss Adamson?'

'Yes.' Marie nodded with a small taut smile. 'Mrs
Hillyard?' But she knew. She had not actually seen Marion
Hillyard that night, because her eyes had been bandaged,
but she had seen photographs around Michael's apartment. She would have recognised his mother in a back

alley in Tokyo. This was the woman who had haunted her dreams for two years. This was the woman she had once wanted as her mother and friend. But no more.

'How do you do?' Marion extended a cool firm hand, and they shook hands ceremoniously just inside the door, before Marion made a gesture towards the suite. 'Won't you come in?'

'Thank you.'

The two women eyed each other with interest and caution, and Marion seated herself easily in a chair near the table. She had had room service set up tea and some soft drinks for her guest. It seemed a great deal of trouble to go to for a girl who had already cost her almost half a million dollars. *If* this was the girl. She eyed her carefully, but she could see nothing. There was no resemblance to any of the photographs she had seen over the years. This was not the same girl. At least she didn't seem to be. But Marion sat back to watch her, and listen. She would always remember that torn, broken voice as they had made their agreement.

'What may I offer you to drink? Tea? Soda? We can order a drink if you like.'

'No, thank you, Mrs Hillyard. I'd really just prefer to . . .' But her voice just trailed off as they watched each other, the pretext of their meeting almost forgotten as the older woman appraised the younger, watched her move, studied the shape and texture of her hair, and then glanced quickly at the overall picture again. She was a terribly pretty girl, in very expensive clothes. Marion found herself wondering if she were spending her living allowance on outfits like that one. Her wool dress bore the distinct mark

194

of Paris, her suede handbag and shoes were Gucci, and her unassuming beige trench coat was lined in a dark fur that looked to Marion like possum.

'That's a very attractive coat, by the way. Must be a marvellous weight for this city. I envy you the easy climate. I left New York in two feet of snow. Or rather,' she smiled winningly at the girl, 'two inches of snow, and twenty-two inches of slush. Do you know New York?'

It was a loaded question and Marie knew it, but she could answer it honestly. She had lived in New England, but spent little time in New York. Had she married Michael, she would have lived there. But she hadn't. Her face set and something hardened in her voice. 'No, I don't know it very well. I'm not really a big-city person.' She was pure Marie now, there wasn't a trace of Nancy.

'I find that hard to believe. You look extremely "big-city" to me.' Marion smiled at her again, but it was the smile of a barracuda eyeing a small and tender minnow.

'Thank you.' And then without further ado, Marie reached towards her portfolio, put it on her lap as Marion watched her, and unzipped the case. She smilingly handed Marion a thick black book with copies of her work. The book was large and unwieldy, and the older woman seemed to falter as she took it. It was then that Marie noticed the violent trembling of her hands, and how weak she was when she tried to hold the book. Time had not been kind to Marion Hillyard after all. Was it possible that some of her own ugly prayers had been answered? She watched the woman intently, but Marion seemed to regain her composure as she silently turned the pages.

'I can see why Ben Avery was so anxious to sign you for

our centre. This is extraordinarily fine work. You must have been at this for years.' For once it was an innocent question, and Marie shook her head.

'No, photography is new to me. I was a painter before.'

'Ah yes, Ben mentioned that.' Marion seemed surprised. She had actually forgotten this might be Nancy McAllister she was talking to, she was so engrossed in the beautiful work. 'Are you as good as this at painting?'

'I thought I was.' Marie smiled at the woman. An almost eerie exchange was going on. She felt as though she were watching Marion Hillyard through a trick mirror. She could see Marion plainly, yet the person Marion saw was actually someone else. Marie thought that she alone knew the secret. 'I like photography just as much now.'

'Why did you change?' Marion looked up, intrigued.

'Because everything in my life changed very suddenly, so much so that I became a new person. The painting was part of that old life, that old me. It hurt too much to bring it with me.' Marion almost winced at the words.

'I see. Well, the world hasn't suffered a loss, from what I can see anyway. You're a marvellous photographer. Who got you started? Undoubtedly one of the local greats. There are so many out here.'

But Marie only shook her head, with a small smile. It was strange. She had come here to hate this woman, and now she found that she couldn't. Not quite. She didn't like her. But she couldn't hate her either. She looked so tired and frail beneath the bravado and the pearls. She wore a death mask carefully concealed with good make-up, but beneath the veneer lurked the sorrows of autumn, with winter already clutching at her heels. Marie forced herself

196

back to the woman's question, trying to remember what that question was . . . Oh, yes.

'No, actually, it was a friend who got me started. My doctor, in fact. He's been responsible for getting me launched as a photographer. He knows everyone in town.'

'Peter Gregson.' The words were soft and dreamy on Marion Hillyard's lips, as though she hadn't meant to speak them, and then they were both shocked into silence.

'Do you know him?' Why had the woman said that? Did she know? But she couldn't. Had Peter . . . No, he'd never do that.

'I . . . yes . . .' Marion hesitated for a long moment and then looked at her squarely. 'Yes, Nancy, I do. He did a beautiful job on you.' It was a long shot. A wild guess. But she had to say it, even if she made a fool of herself. She had to know.

'There must be some misunderstanding. My name is Marie . . .' and then, like a rag doll, she crumpled. There were tears in her eyes as she stood up and walked away, to stand at the window with her back to the room. 'How did you know?' The voice was shattered and angry. The voice of two years before. Marion sat back in her chair, tired but relieved. Somehow it comforted her to know she had been right. She had not made this difficult trip for nothing. 'Did someone tell you?' Marie demanded.

'No. I guessed. I don't even know why. But I had a feeling the first time Ben mentioned you to us. The details fit.'

'Did—' Goddamn. She wanted to ask her about him. She wanted to . . . would this never leave her life? Would they never go away? 'Why did you come here? To reconfirm our little deal?' Marie turned on her heels at the window, to stare at the woman who tormented her. 'To make sure I'd stick by my promise?'

'You've already proved that.' Marion's voice was tired and gentle, and uncharacteristically old. 'No, I'm not even sure I understand it myself, but I came to see you. To talk to you. To find out how you are, if indeed it was you.'

'Why now? Why should I be so interesting after two years?' Suddenly there was venom in Marie's voice, and hatred in her eyes. The hatred she had dreamed of spewing for months. 'Why now, Mrs Hillyard, or were you just curious to take a look at Gregson's work? Was that it? Well, how do you like your four-hundred-thousand-dollar baby? Was it worth it? Why don't you answer that? Was it? Are you pleased?'

Marion hoped so. She suddenly desperately hoped so. They had all paid such a high price for that new face. It had been wrong. Suddenly she was sure of it. But it was too late. They were not the same people any more. She could see that in the girl as much as she could in Michael. It was far, far too late, for either of them. They would have to find their dreams somewhere else. 'You're a very beautiful girl now, Marie.'

'Thank you. Yes, I know Peter did a good job. But it was like making a deal with the devil. A face for a life.' With a rugged sigh Marie sank into a chair.

'And I'm the devil.' Marion's voice trembled as she looked at the girl. 'I suppose it's an obscene thing to say to you now, but at the time I thought I was doing the right thing.'

'And now?' Marie looked at her squarely. 'Is Michael

happy? Was it worth getting rid of me, Mrs Hillyard? Was the mission a success?' Christ, she wanted to hit her. Just haul off and demolish her, in her ladylike dress and her pearls.

'No, Marie, Michael isn't happy, any more than you are. I always thought he'd pick up his life again. I assumed you'd do the same. Something tells me, though, that you haven't. Not that I have any right to ask.'

'No, you don't. And Michael? He's not married?' She hated herself for it, but she prayed for a 'no'.

'Yes, he is.' Marie almost felt herself gasp and then catch her breath again. 'To his work. He lives, eats, sleeps, and breathes it. As though he hopes to get lost in it forever. I hardly ever see him.'

Good, you bitch. Good! 'Then would you say you'd been wrong? I loved him, you know. More than anything in life.' Except my face . . . oh, God . . . except . . .

'I know. But I thought it would pass.'

'Has it?'

'Perhaps. He never mentions you.'

'Did he ever try to find me?'

Marion slowly shook her head. 'No.' But she did not tell her the reason why. She did not tell Marie that Michael thought she was dead. The lie weighed on her even as she said the word, and she saw the girl's face set in a fresh mask of hatred.

'All right then, why am I here? Just to satisfy your curiosity? To show you my work? Why?'

'I'm not sure, Nancy. I'm sorry . . . Marie. I simply had to see you. To know how it had gone with you. I . . . I suppose it's maudlin to say it, but I'm dying, you know.' She looked faintly sorry for herself as she faced the girl, and then she was annoyed for having told her. But Marie did not appear moved. She stared at the woman for a very long time and then in soft, broken voice she spoke to her again.

'I'm sorry to hear it, Mrs Hillyard. But I died two years ago. And it sounds to me as though your son did too. That's two of us. On your hands, Mrs Hillyard. To be honest with you, it's hard for me to feel a great deal of sympathy for you. I suppose I should be grateful to you. I suppose I should thank you from the bottom of my heart that men turn and stare at me every day, instead of running from me in horror. I suppose I should feel a lot of things, but I don't. I don't feel anything for you now, except sorry for you, because you've ruined Michael's life, and you know it. Not to mention what you did to mine.'

Marion nodded silently, feeling the full weight of the girl's reproach. She knew it all herself. Secretly, she had known it for two years. About Michael anyway. She hadn't known about the girl. Maybe that was why she had had to come. 'I don't know what to say.'

'Goodbye will be fine.' Marie picked up her coat and her portfolio and walked to the door of the suite. She stopped for a moment at the door, her hand on the knob, her head bowed, and tears beginning to creep down her face. She turned slowly then, and saw tears running down Marion's face as well. The older woman was speechless with her private agony, but the young girl managed to catch her breath and speak again. 'Goodbye, Mrs Hillyard. Give . . . give Michael . . . my love.' She closed the door softly behind her, but Marion Hillyard didn't move. She felt her heart rip through her lungs with long searing pains. Gasping for air, she stumbled towards the buzzer that would summon a maid. She managed to press it once before passing out.

23

His heels rapped hollowly in the hospital corridor as he almost ran to her room. Why had she insisted on coming out alone? Why did she always have to be so damned independent, still, after all these years? He knocked softly on the door, and a nurse opened it with a pointed look of inquisition.

'Is this Mrs Hillyard's room? I'm George Calloway.' He looked nervous and tired and old, and he felt that way, too. He had really had enough of this nonsense. And he was going to tell her so as soon as he saw her. He had said as much to Michael before leaving New York.

The nurse smiled at the sound of his name. 'Yes, Mr Calloway, we've been expecting you.' Marion had only been in the hospital since six o'clock that evening. George had managed to arrive in San Francisco by eleven o'clock local time. It was now just after midnight. That was about as fast as anyone could make the trip. Marion's smile acknowledged that when the nurse opened the door to let George step inside, and slipped quietly past him into the hall.

'Hello, George.'

'Hello, Marion. How do you feel?'

'Tired, but I'll live. At least that's what they tell me. It was only a small seizure.'

'This time. But what about next time?' He looked leonine as he paced the room, glaring at her. He hadn't even stopped to kiss her, as he usually did. He had too much to say.

'We'll worry about next time when it gets here. Now sit down and relax, you're making me nervous. Do you want something to eat? I had the nurses save you a sandwich.'

'I couldn't eat.'

'Now stop that. I've never seen you like this, George. It wasn't serious, for heaven's sake. Don't be like that.'

'Don't tell me how to be, Marion Hillyard. I've been watching you destroy yourself for far too long, and I'm not going to tolerate it any more.'

'You're quitting?' She grinned at him from the bed. 'Why don't you just retire?' She was suddenly amused at the whole scene, but she was less amused in a moment when he turned to face her with something immovable in his face.

'That's exactly what I'm going to do, Marion. Retire.'

She could see that he was serious. This was all she needed. 'Don't be ridiculous.' But she wasn't so sure she could jolly him out of this one. She sat up in bed with a nervous smile.

'I'm not. It's the first intelligent decision I've made in twenty years. And do you know who else is retiring, Marion? You are. We're both retiring. With no notice at all. I discussed it with Michael on the way to the airport. He was good enough to drive me out, and he said to tell you that he's sorry he couldn't come but he's just too tied up at the moment. He thinks our retiring is a fine idea. And so do I. In fact, no one is interested in what you think of it, Marion. The decision is made.'

'Are you crazy?' She sat up in bed and glared at him in

the dim room. 'And just exactly what do you think I'll do with myself if I retire? Knit?'

'I think that's a fine idea. But the first thing you'll do is marry me. After that, you may do anything you like. Except,' his voice rose menacingly on the word, 'work. Is that clear, Mrs Hillyard?'

'Aren't you at least going to ask me to marry you? Or are you just telling me? Or is this an order from Michael, too?' But she wasn't angry. She was touched. And relieved. She'd had enough. She'd done enough, in the best and worst senses of the word. And she knew it, too. The meeting with Marie had driven the point home that afternoon.

'We have Michael's blessing, if that makes any difference.' And then his voice softened as he approached her bed and reached for her hand, which he held gently in his. 'Will you marry me, Marion?' He was almost afraid to ask after all this time, but he had finally spoken to Michael about it in the anxious moments before his flight, and Michael had said something strange to him about 'celebrating their love'. George had not really understood, but he had been grateful for the encouragement. 'Will you?' He held her hand a little tighter as he waited.

She nodded slowly, with a warm, tired smile, and a look of near regret. 'We should have thought of this years ago, George.' But she wanted to say something else too . . . that she wasn't sure if she had the right . . . not after . . .

'I thought of it years ago, but I never thought you'd accept.'

'I probably wouldn't have. Fool that I am. Oh George.' She sighed and fell back against the pillows. 'I've done such stupid things in my life.' Her face suddenly showed the agony of the afternoon, and he watched her, puzzled by the torment he saw mixed with the fatigue.

'What a silly thing to say. I can't think of a single foolish thing you've done in all the years I've known you.' He kept a gentle hold of her hand and stroked it lovingly. He had wanted to do that for years, in just that way. 'Don't torment yourself with nonsense from the past.'

But Marion was sitting up very straight, and she looked at him from the bed, her hand cold and taut in his.

'What if the "nonsense", as you call it, destroyed people's lives? Do I have a right to forget that, George?'

'Why, Marion, what could you have done to destroy someone's life?' He suddenly wondered if the doctor had given her some powerful drug. Or perhaps this last attack had affected her mentally. She wasn't making sense.

But she settled back among her pillows and closed her eyes. 'You don't understand.'

'Should I?' His voice was gentle in the dimly lit room.

'Perhaps. Maybe, if you knew, you wouldn't be so anxious to marry me.'

'Don't be absurd. But if that's how you feel, then I think I have a right to know what's bothering you. What is it?' He never let go of her hand, and at last she opened her eyes. She stared at him for a long time before she spoke.

'I don't know if I can tell you.'

'Why not? I can't think of anything that would shock me. And I can't imagine anything about you that I don't know.' They had had no secrets from each other for years. 'I'm beginning to think the seizure this afternoon rocked you just a bit.'

'The truth I had to face did that.' Her tone was one

he had never heard from her, and when he looked at her again there were tears in her eyes. He wanted to put his arms round her and make it all better, but he understood now that she really did have something very important to tell him. Could she have been having an affair with someone all these years? The idea suddenly shocked him. But he could even have accepted that. He loved her. He had always loved her. He had waited too long for this moment to let anything spoil it.

'Did something special happen this afternoon?' He watched her very closely, waiting for the answer, but her eyes only closed as the tears poured silently down her cheeks, and at last she nodded and whispered 'Yes.'

'I see. Well, relax now. Let's not get all excited about it.' She was beginning to worry him. He didn't want her to have another seizure.

'I saw the girl.'

'What girl?' What in God's name was she talking about?

'The girl Michael was in love with.' The tears stopped for a moment, and she sat up very straight and looked at him. 'Do you remember the night of Michael's accident, when he came down to the city to see me? You came in, and he stalked out. He was furious. He had come down to tell me that he was going to marry that girl. And I showed him that . . . that report I'd had done on her . . .'

Her voice drifted off for a moment as she remembered, and George's brow furrowed deeper. She must be confused by some drug. That was the only explanation. That girl had *died* in the accident.

'Marion, dear, you couldn't have seen the girl. As I recall, she . . . she uh . . . passed on in the . . .'

But Marion shook her head, her eyes never leaving his. 'No, George. She didn't. I said she did, and Wicky kept his mouth shut, but the girl lived. Her face was destroyed, though. Everything but her eyes.' George watched her silently but he was listening. This was a distraught Marion, an agonised Marion, but it wasn't a crazy Marion. He knew she was telling the truth. 'I went into her room that night and offered her a deal.' He waited, silently. She closed her eyes as though in pain, and he squeezed her hand tighter.

'Are you all right?'

She nodded quietly and opened her eyes again. 'Yes. Maybe I'll feel better once I tell you. I offered her a deal. Her face in exchange for Michael. There was a lot of prettier ways to say it, but that's what it boils down to. Wicky said he knew of one man in the country who could restore her face. It would cost a fortune, but he could do it. I told her about it, offered to pay for it and anything else she needed until all the operations were over. I offered her a whole new life, a life she'd never had, as long as she agreed not to seek out Michael again.'

'And she agreed?'

'Yes.' It was a small, rock-like word.

'Then she couldn't have loved him very much anyway. And you did a damn nice thing offering to pay for the surgery. Hell, if they'd loved each other so much, neither of them would have accepted that.'

'You don't understand, George.' Her tone was icy now. But her anger was against herself, not George. 'I wasn't honest with either of them. I told Michael she was dead, for God's sake, and I knew damn well that she never expected Michael to honour the agreement. That's probably why she agreed to it. That and the fact that she had no choice. She had nothing left. Except me – offering her a deal with the devil, as she herself put it today. George, you know Michael never would have accepted that agreement either, if he'd known the truth. He'd have gone back to her in a moment.'

'He hasn't suffered in the interim. He's recovered. Maybe they wouldn't even like each other now.' He was desperately looking for balm for her wounds, but he had to admit that it was a pretty nasty wound, and it must have been damned hard to live with. He knew Marion had thought she was acting in Michael's best interests, but she had played a very serious game with his life. 'That's true, you know, they've probably grown to be quite different. They might not even want each other now.'

'I realise that.' She leaned back with a sigh. 'Michael is obsessed with his work. He has no love, no gentleness, no time, nothing. There's nothing left, and I knew it better than anyone. And she . . .' She thought back painfully to that afternoon. 'She's exquisite. Elegant. Beautiful. And bitter, angry, filled with hate. They'd make a charming couple.'

'And you think you did all that?'

'Knowing what you know now, don't you agree?' In spite of herself, her eyes filled with tears again. 'I was wrong to come between them, George, I know that now.'

'Maybe the damage can be repaired. And in the meantime, you've given the girl her life back. A better life, in some ways.'

'And she hates me for it.'

'Then she's a fool.'

Marion shook her head. 'No. She's right. I had no right to do what I did. And if I had any courage at all, I'd tell Michael.' But in spite of himself, George hoped she would not do that. Michael's anger would destroy her. Her son would never feel the same about her.

'Don't tell him, darling. There's no point now.'

Marion saw the fear in his eyes, and she smiled.

'Don't worry. I'm not that brave. But he'll find out. In time. I'll see to that. He has a right to know. But I hope he'll hear it from her, if she takes him back. Maybe then he'll forgive me.'

'Do you think there's a chance of that? That she'll take him back, I mean?'

'Not really. But I must do what I can.'

'Oh, God—'

'I started this. Now I owe it to both of them to do something. Maybe nothing will come of it, but I can try.'

'And you've kept in touch with her during all this time?'

'No. I saw her again for the first time today.'

'Now I understand. And how did that happen?'

'I arranged a meeting. I wasn't even sure it was her, but I suspected. And I was right.' She sounded pleased with herself, and he smiled for the first time in half an hour.

'It must have been quite a meeting.' Now he understood the fresh seizure. It was a wonder it hadn't killed her.

'It could have been worse.' Her voice grew gentle, and her eyes filled with tears again. 'It could have been much worse. All it really did was show me how wrong I'd been, that I'd destroyed her life as well as his.'

'Stop that. You didn't destroy either one of them. You've

given Michael a career any man would give his life for, and you've given her something no one else could have.'

'What? Heartbreak? Disillusionment? Despair?'

'If that's how she feels then she's very ungrateful. What about a new face? A new life? A new world?'

'I suspect it's a very empty world, except for her work. In that sense, she's very much like Michael.'

'Then maybe they'll build something together again. But in the meantime, what's done is done. You can't punish yourself forever over this. You did what you must have thought right at the time. And they're young, darling. They have full lives ahead of them. If they waste them, it's their own doing. What we mustn't do is waste ours.' He wanted to say 'we have so little time left', but he didn't. He leaned closer to her as she lay in the bed, and she raised her arms to him. He held her very tight and felt the warmth of her body in his arms. 'I love you, darling. I'm sorry you went through all that alone, without telling me. You should have told me two years ago.'

'You'd have hated me for it.' Her voice was muffled by his shoulder and her sobs.

'Never. Not then and not now. I could never do anything but love you. And I respect you for telling me about this now. You didn't have to. You could have hidden it. I would never have known.'

'No, but I would. And I had to know what you thought.'

'I think the whole thing has been an agony for everyone. Now, do what you can about it, and then let it go. Drop it from your thoughts, your heart, your conscience. It's over. And we have a new life to begin. We have a right to that life. You've paid dearly for everything you've had. You don't have to punish yourself for anything. We're going to get married, and go away, and live our life. Let them work out their own.'

'Do I really have a right to that?' She looked younger again when he looked into her face.

'Yes, my love, you do.' And then he kissed her, gently. To hell with Michael and the girl and all of it. He wanted Marion, with her good and her bad, her genius and her outrageousness, all of it. 'And now, you are going to forget about all this, and go to sleep, and tomorrow we are going to sit down and plan the wedding. Start thinking about sensible things like what kind of dress to order and who's to do the flowers. Is that clear?'

She looked up at him and laughed.

'George Calloway, I love you.'

'It's a good thing, because if you don't, I'd marry you anyway. Nothing would stop me now. Is that clear?'

'Yes, sir.' They were beaming at each other when the nurse finally stuck her head into the room. It was one in the morning. And special instructions from the doctor or no, he had to leave. George nodded that he understood, and with a gentle kiss, a touch on the hand, and a smile that nothing could have dimmed, he reluctantly left the room. And in her bed, Marion felt enormously relieved. He loved her anyway. And George had restored a little of her own faith in herself. And then with a look at the clock, she decided to give Michael a call. Maybe she could do something about all that right now. To hell with the time difference. She didn't have a moment to waste. None of them did. She turned to the phone in the darkened room and dialled his apartment in New York. It took him four rings to find the phone and answer groggily with a muffled 'llo?'

'Darling, it's me.'

'Mother? Are you all right?' He quickly switched on the light and tried to force himself awake.

'I'm fine. I have something to tell you.'

'I know. I know. George told me.' He yawned and smiled at the phone and then blinked at the clock. Jesus. It was five o'clock in the morning in New York. Two in San Francisco. What the hell was she doing up, and where was her nurse? 'Did you accept?'

'Of course. Both his proposals. I'm even going to retire. More or less.' Michael laughed at her last words. That sounded like her. George was going to have his hands full but he was pleased for the two of them. 'But I'm calling about something else.' She sounded very businesslike and firm, and he groaned. He knew the tone.

'The girl.'

'What girl?' His mind was a blank. It had been an incredible day. Three meetings, five appointments, and the news that his mother had had another seizure, alone in San Francisco.

'The photographer, Michael. Wake up.'

'Oh. Her. So?'

'We want her.'

'We do?'

'Absolutely. I can't pursue it now. George would have my head. But you can.'

'You must be kidding. I have too much to do. Let Ben handle it.'

'She already turned him down. And she's a young

212

woman with style, intelligence, and character. She is not going to deal with underlings.'

'She sounds like a pain in the ass to me.'

'That's how you sound to me. Now listen. I don't care what you have to do to sign her, but do it. Woo her, win her, fly out to see her, take her to dinner. Be your best charming self. She's worth it. And I want her work in the centre. Do it for me.' She was actually wheedling. She smiled to herself. This was new.

'You're crazy, and I don't have time.' He was lying in bed, grinning to himself. His mother was going nuts. 'You do it.'

'I won't. And if you don't, I'll come back to the office full time and drive you round the bend.' She sounded as though she meant it, and he had to laugh.

'I'll do it, I'll do it.'

'I'll hold you to that.'

'Jesus. All right. Are you satisfied? Can I go back to sleep now?'

'Yes. But I want you to follow this up right away.'

'What's her name again?'

'Adamson. Marie Adamson.'

'Fine. I'll take care of it tomorrow.'

'Good, darling. And . . . thank you.'

'Good night, you crazy old bat. And by the way, congratulations. Can I give away the bride?'

'Of course. I wouldn't dream of having anyone else. Goodnight, darling.'

They each hung up, and at her end Marion Hillyard was finally at peace. Maybe it wouldn't work. Maybe it was too late. The two years had taken a hard toll on both of them. But it was all she could do. No, that wasn't true. She could have told him the truth. But with a small sigh, as she drifted off to sleep, she admitted to herself that she wasn't quite that ready for sainthood yet. She'd help them along a little. But she wouldn't do more than that. She wouldn't tell Michael what she had done. He would probably find out eventually, but perhaps by then there would be enough happiness to cushion the blow.

24

George kissed her tenderly on the mouth and the soft music began again. Marion had hired three musicians to play at the wedding in her apartment. There were roughly seventy guests, and the dining room had been cleared as a ballroom. The buffet had been set up in the library. And it was a perfect day. The very last day in February and a clear, cold, magnificent New York day. Marion was completely recovered from her little mishap in San Francisco, and George looked jubilant. Michael kissed her on both cheeks, and she posed between her husband and her son for the photographer from the *Times*. She was wearing champagne lace to the floor and both George and Michael were wearing morning dress. George wore a white carnation as his boutonniere, Michael a red one, and the bride carried delicate beige orchids, especially flown in from California along with the lavish show of flowers around the apartment. Her decorator had seen to it himself.

'Mrs Calloway?' It was Michael offering her his arm to the buffet as she laughed girlishly at the new name and then smiled at George. 'Celebrate it,' as Nancy had said, and that was what they had done. Michael was pleased for them both. They deserved it. And they were going to spend two months in Europe to relax. He couldn't get over how sensible she had been about stepping out of the business. Maybe she had been ready to retire after all, or maybe her heart was finally frightening her after all this time, but she and George had been wonderful to work with as they transferred the power from their hands to his. He was the president of Cotter-Hillyard now, and he had to admit that he didn't mind the way it felt. President . . . at his age! He had made the cover of *Time*. And that had felt good too. He supposed his mother and George would make *People* with the wedding.

'You look very elegant, darling.' His mother beamed at him as they swept into the library. It was filled with flower trees and tables laden with food. And the walls seemed to be lined with additional servants.

'You look pretty snazzy yourself. And the house doesn't look bad either.'

'It's pretty, isn't it?' She seemed amazingly young as she flitted away from him to talk to some of the guests and give last minute instructions to the servants. She was totally in her element, and as excited as a girl. His mother, the bride. He smiled to himself again at the thought.

'You're looking very pleased with yourself, Mr Hillyard.' The voice was soft and familiar, and when he turned to find Wendy right at his elbow, he was no longer embarrassed to see her. She was wearing the diamond solitaire Ben had given her for Valentine's Day when they got engaged. They were getting married the following summer. And he was to be best man.

'She looks lovely, doesn't she?'

Wendy nodded and smiled at him again. For once he looked happy too. She had never really figured him out, but at least it didn't bother her any more, now that she had Ben. Ben made her happier than any other man ever had.

'But I'm sure you'll look lovely next summer too. I have

a weakness for brides.' It seemed very unlike him and Wendy smiled again. She liked him much better, now that she shared his friendship with Ben.

'Trying to chase after my fiancée, old man?' It was Ben at their elbow, juggling three glasses of champagne. 'Here, these are for you two. And by the way, Mike, I'm in love with your mother.'

'Too late. I gave her away this morning.' Ben snapped his fingers as though at a loss and all three laughed as the music began in the dining room. 'Oops, I think that means me. The son gets the first dance, and then George cuts in on me. Emily Post says . . .' Ben laughed at him and gave him a shove as he disappeared towards the door to do his duties.

'He looks happy today,' Wendy said softly after Mike had left.

'I think he is, for once.' Pensively, he sipped his champagne, and a moment later smiled at Wendy again. 'You look happy today, too.'

'I'm always happy, thanks to you. By the way, did you follow up on that girl in San Francisco, the photographer? I keep meaning to ask you, and I never have time.'

But Ben was shaking his head. 'No, Mike said he'd take care of it.'

'Does he have time?' Wendy looked surprised.

'No. But he'll probably manage anyway. You know Mike. He's going out there next week, for that and four thousand other reasons.'

No, Wendy thought to herself, I don't know Mike. No one does. Except maybe Ben. But sometimes she even wondered if Ben knew him as well as he liked to think he did. Used to maybe. But did he still?

'Care to dance?' He set down his glass and put an arm around her to guide her to the next room.

'Love to.'

But they'd only been dancing for a moment, it seemed, when Michael cut in on them. 'My turn.'

'The hell it is. We just got started. I thought you were dancing with your mother.'

'She ditched me for George.'

'Sensible of her.' The three of them had been shuffling around together on the dance floor and Wendy was starting to laugh. Seeing the two of them together this way was like getting a glimpse of the Ben and Michael of years gone by. This was the kind of occasion they had once thrived on. A good healthy dose of champagne, an occasion worth celebrating, and they were off.

'Listen, Avery, are you going to get lost, or aren't you? I want to dance with your fiancée.'

'And what if I don't want you to?'

'Then I dance with both of you, and my mother throws us out?'

Wendy was grinning again. They were like two kids, dying to raise hell at a birthday party. They were just breaking into a song about 'a girl in Rhode Island' that was beginning to worry her.

'Listen you two, this is supposed to be twice as much fun. Instead, I'm getting both my feet walked on at once. Why don't we all go have some wedding cake?'

'Shall we?' Ben and Michael eyed each other, nodded in unison, and each obligingly took one of Wendy's arms and led her off the floor, as Michael looked over her head and winked at Ben.

'Cute, but I think she's crocked. Did you notice the way she danced? My shoes are practically ruined.'

'You should see mine.' Ben spoke in a stage whisper, over her left shoulder, and Wendy sharply elbowed them both.

'Listen, you two, has anyone seen my shoes? Not to mention my poor aching feet, dancing with you two drunken louts.'

'Louts?' Ben looked at her, horrified, and Michael started to laugh as he accepted three plates of wedding cake from a uniformed maid, and then proceeded to juggle the plates, almost dropping two.

'Never mind her. The cake looks terrific. Here.' Michael handed a plate to each of the other two, and the three leaned against a convenient column and watched the action as they ate, eyeing dowagers in grey lace, young girls in pink chiffon, cascades of pearls, and a river of assorted gems.

'Jesus, just think what we could make if we held them up.' Michael looked enchanted with his idea.

'I never thought of that. We should have done it years ago. Up at school, when we were broke.' They nodded sagely at each other, as Wendy looked at them with a suspicious grin.

'I'm not sure I should trust you two alone while I go to powder my nose.'

'Not to worry. I'll keep an eye on him, Wendy.' Michael winked broadly and polished off another glass of champagne. Wendy had never seen him like this, but he amused her. Ben had been right. He was human after all. Seeing him that way, giddy and all, was like meeting him five years before, or even two.

'I don't think either of you could uncross your eyes long enough to keep an eye on anything, let alone each other.'

'Bull . . . I mean . . . we're in great shape.' He accepted two more glasses of champagne, handed one to Michael, and waved his fiancée off in the direction of the ladies' room. 'She's a hell of a girl, Mike. I'm glad you didn't get mad when I told you about . . . about us.'

'How could I get mad? She's just right for you. Besides, I'm too busy for that stuff.'

'One of these days you won't be.'

'Maybe so. In the meantime, the rest of you can run off and get married. Me, I have a business to run.' But for once he didn't look grim when he said it. He looked over his glass of champagne with a grin, and toasted his friend. 'To us.'

25

The plane set down gently in San Francisco as Michael snapped shut his briefcase. He had a thousand things to do in the week to come. Doctors to see, meetings to attend, building sites to visit, architects to organise, and people, and plans and demands and conferences, and . . . damn . . . that photographer, too. He wondered how he'd find time for it all. But he would. He always did. He'd give up sleeping or eating or something. He took his raincoat out of the overhead rack where he had folded it, put it over his arm, and followed the other passengers out of first class. He felt the stewardesses' eyes on him. He always did. He ignored them. They didn't interest him. Besides, he didn't have time. He looked at his watch. He knew there would be a car waiting for him at the terminal. It was two-twenty in the afternoon. He had done a full day's work in half a day at the office in New York, and now he had time for at least four or five hours of meetings here. Tomorrow morning he had a breakfast conference scheduled for seven. That was the way he ran his life. That was the way he liked it. All he cared about was his work. That and a handful of people. Two of whom were happily off in Majorca by now, at the house of friends, and the other of whom was in Wendy's good hands in New York. They were all taken care of. And so was he. He had the medical centre to pull together. And it was coming along beautifully. He smiled to himself as he walked into the terminal. This baby was his.

'Mr Hillyard?' The driver recognised him immediately, and he nodded. 'The car is over here.'

Michael settled back in the car while the driver retrieved his luggage from the chaos inside. It was certainly pleasant to be in San Francisco again. It had been a freezing cold March day when he left New York, and it was sixty-five in San Francisco that afternoon. All around him, the world was already green and lovely and lush. In New York, the trees were still barren and brittle and grey, and green would be a forgotten colour for another month. It was hard waiting for spring in New York. It always seemed as though it would never come. And just when you gave up, and decided that nothing would ever be green again, the first buds would appear, bringing back hope. Michael had forgotten how pleasant spring was. He never noticed. He didn't have time.

The driver took him straight to his hotel, where some minor employee of the company had already checked him in, and seen to it that his suite was in order for the first meeting. He had reserved two suites, one in which he could stay, the other for meetings. And if necessary there could be conferences held simultaneously in both. It was nine o'clock that night before he was through with his work, and tiredly he called room service and asked for a steak. It was midnight in New York, and he was beat. But it had been a fruitful few hours, and he was pleased. He settled back on the couch, pulled off his tie, threw his feet up on the coffee table, and closed his eyes. And then it was as though he heard his mother's voice in the room. 'Did you call that girl?' Oh, Christ. The words sounded loud in the suddenly quiet room, which still reeked of cigarette smoke, and the round of Scotches they'd ordered at the end. But the girl . . . well, why not? He had the time, while he waited for his steak. It might keep him from falling asleep. He reached for his briefcase, found the number in a file, and dialled from where he sat. The phone rang three or four times before she answered.

'Hello?'

'Good evening, Miss Adamson, this is Michael Hillyard.'

She felt herself almost gasp and had to sharply control her breathing. 'I see. Are you in San Francisco, Mr Hillyard?' Her voice was clipped and brusque; she sounded almost angry. Maybe he had got her at a bad time, or maybe she didn't like to be called at home. He didn't really care.

'Yes, I am, Miss Adamson. And I was wondering if we might get together. We have a few things to discuss.'

'No. We have absolutely nothing to discuss. I thought I made that very clear to your mother.' She was trembling all over and clutching the phone.

'Then perhaps she forgot to relay the message.' He was beginning to sound as uptight as she. 'She had a mild heart attack just after her meeting with you. I'm sure it had nothing to do with the meeting, but she didn't tell me a great deal about what either of you said. Understandably, given the circumstances.'

'Yes.' Marie seemed to pause. 'I'm sorry to hear it. Is she all right now?'

'Very much so.' Michael smiled. 'She got married last week. Right now she's in Majorca.'

How sweet. The bitch . . . she ruins my life and goes on a honeymoon. Marie wanted to grit her teeth, or slam down the phone.

'But that's neither here nor there. When can we meet?'

'I've already told you. We can't.' She almost spat the words through the phone, and he closed his eyes again. He was really too tired to be bothered.

'All right. I concede. For now. I'm at the Fairmont. If you change your mind, call.'

'I won't.'

'Fine.'

'Goodnight, Mr Hillyard.'

'Goodnight, Miss Adamson.'

She was surprised at how quickly he ended the conversation. And he hadn't really sounded like Michael. He sounded worn out, as though he didn't really give a damn. Just what had happened to him in the last two years? She sat wondering for a long time after she hung up the phone.

26

'Darling, you're so solemn-looking. Is anything wrong?' Peter looked at her across the lunch table, and she shook her head, toying with her glass of wine.

'No. I'm just thinking of some new work. I want to start a new project tomorrow. That always keeps me preoccupied.' But she was lying and they both knew it. Ever since Michael had called the night before, she had been catapulted back into the past. All she could think of was that last day. The bicycling, the fair, the gaudy blue beads, burying them at the beach, and then dressing in the white eyelet dress and blue satin cap to run off and marry Michael . . . and then his mother's voice as she lay bandaged and unseeing in her hospital bed. It was like having a movie shown constantly before her eyes. She couldn't get away from it.

'Darling, are you all right?'

'Fine. Really. I'm sorry I'm such bad company today. Maybe I'm just tired.' But he had seen the haunted look, and there was a troubled little frown between her eyes.

'Have you seen Faye lately?'

'No, I keep meaning to call her for lunch, and I never have time. Ever since the show,' she smiled gratefully at him, 'I've spent half my time in the darkroom and the other half racing around town with my camera.'

'I didn't mean socially. Have you seen her professionally?'

'Of course not. I told you, we finished before Christmas.'

'You never told me if that was her decision or yours, to finish the sessions.'

'Mine, but she didn't disagree.' Marie was hurt that he seemed to think she needed more work with the psychiatrist. 'I'm just tired, Peter. That's all.'

'I'm not so sure. Sometimes I think you're still haunted by . . . well, by events of two years ago.' He said it carefully, watching her face. And he was dismayed when he saw her almost visibly cringe.

'Don't be ridiculous.'

'It's perfectly normal, Marie. People have been tormented by things like that for ten or twenty years. That's a very traumatic thing to live through, and even if you were unconscious after the accident, some part of you deep down will always remember what happened. If you can put it to rest, you'll be free of it.'

'I have and I am.'

'Only you can judge that. But I want you to be sure. Otherwise, subtly, it'll affect you for the rest of your life. It will limit your abilities, cripple your life . . . anyway, there's no need to go on. Just think about it carefully. You may want to see Faye for a while longer. It wouldn't do any harm.' He looked worried.

'I don't need to.' Her mouth was set in a firm line, and he patted her hand. But he didn't apologise for bringing it up. He didn't like the way she looked.

'All right. Shall we go then?' He smiled at her more gently and she tried to return the smile, but he was right, of course. She was obsessed with having talked to Michael.

Peter paid the bill and helped her into the navy blue velvet blazer she had worn with the white Cacherel skirt, and delicate silk blouse. She was always impeccably dressed, and Peter loved being seen with her. 'Shall I take you home?'

'No. I thought I'd stop at the gallery. I want to discuss some things with Jacques. I want to change around some of the pieces. Some of my earlier work is getting more play now than the recent work. I want to switch that round.'

'That makes sense.' He put an arm round her shoulders as they walked out into the spring sunshine. The morning fog had burned off and it was a beautiful warm day. The attendant brought round the black Porsche in a few moments, and Peter held open the door as Marie slipped inside. She smoothed down her skirt and smiled at him as he took his place behind the wheel. She knew now just how much she mattered to him. Sometimes she wondered, though, if he loved her because he had created her, or perhaps because she remained somewhat unattainable. Often it made her feel guilty that she wasn't freer with him. But despite the affection she felt for him, there was always a shadow of reserve between them. It was her fault, she knew it. And maybe he was right. Maybe she would always be haunted and crippled by the accident. Maybe she should go back and see Faye.

'You're not very talkative today, my love. Still thinking of the new project?'

She nodded with an embarrassed smile and then ran a delicate hand over the back of his neck.

'Sometimes I wonder why you put up with me.'

'Because you're very special to me, Marie. I hope you truly know that.'

But why? Sometimes she wondered. Was she like the

other woman he had loved? Had he *made* her that way? It was an eerie thought.

She settled back in her seat for a moment and closed her eyes, trying to relax, but they flew open again as she felt Peter swerve in the bullet-like little car. As she opened her eyes, all she could see was a sleek red Jaguar hurtling towards her side of the car, head on, as its driver swooped around a double-parked truck. For some reason the driver of the Jaguar had overshot his mark, and was well into the opposite lane, until he was almost nose to nose with Marie. She stared wide-eyed in horror, too terrified to make a sound. But in an instant, the incident was over. Peter had avoided the car, and the delinquent Jaguar had sped off in the opposite direction, running a red light. But Marie sat frozen and terrified in her seat, clutching the dashboard, her eyes staring straight ahead, her jaw trembling, her eyes filled with unshed tears, her mind rooted to something it had seen twenty-two months before. Peter realised instantly what was happening, stopped the car, and reached out to take her in his arms, but she was too stiff to move, and as he touched her, the car was suddenly filled with her screams. She howled from the very bottom of her soul, and he had to shake her and pull her into his arms to subdue her.

'Shhh . . . it's all right, darling. It's all right. Ssshhhh. It's all over now. Nothing like that will ever happen again. It's all over.' She subsided into terrified sobs, the tears streaming down her face, her whole body trembling as she let herself fall against him while he held her. It was almost half an hour before she stopped, and lay back exhausted in her seat. He watched her silently for a time, stroking her face and her hair, holding her hand and letting her feel that she was indeed safe. But he was deeply troubled by what he had seen. It proved what he had thought all along. When at last she had stopped shaking and rested quietly, next to him, he spoke to her softly but firmly and she closed her eyes. 'You have to go back to Faye. It isn't over for you yet. And it won't be until you face it and heal it.'

But how much more could she face? And what was there to heal? Her love for Michael? How could she heal that? How could she tell Peter that she had spoken to him on the phone; and that it had made her want to hold him and kiss him and feel his hands on her again? How could she tell Peter that? Instead she looked at him with tired eyes and silently nodded.

'I'll give it some thought.'

'Good. Shall I take you home?' His voice was very soft, and she nodded. She didn't have the strength to go to the gallery now. And they didn't speak again until they reached her house. 'Do you want me to take you up?' But she only shook her head and kissed him on the cheek.

The only words she said to him as she got out of the car were, 'thank you'. And she didn't look back when she got out. She slowly climbed up the stairs, the burden of twenty-two lonely months heavy on her shoulders. If only Michael hadn't called. It had brought back all the pain. And for what? What was the point? He probably didn't give a damn anyway. He just wanted her photographs. Well, let him buy someone else's work, the bastard. Why the hell couldn't he leave her alone?

She let herself into her apartment and went straight to

the bed. Fred was leaping and jumping at her feet, and instantly joined her on the bed, but she wasn't in the mood. She pushed him to the floor, and lay there for a long time, staring at the ceiling, wondering if she should call Faye, or if there was any point in that either. She was just beginning to doze in fitful exhaustion when the phone rang and she jumped up with a start. She didn't really want to answer it, but it was probably Peter wanting to know if she was all right, and she didn't have the right to worry him any more than she already had that afternoon. Slowly, she reached for the phone.

'Hello.' It was a soft broken word from her lips.

'Miss Adamson?' Oh Jesus, it wasn't Peter, it was . . . a sigh shook her entire body. 'For God's sake, Michael, leave me alone.' She hung up the phone, and at the other end Michael stared at the receiver in total confusion. What the hell was this all about? And why had she called him Michael?

27

Marie looked tired and drawn the next morning when she walked into the gallery with Fred. She was wearing a black trouser suit with a brilliant green sweater that set off her colouring to perfection. But she looked unusually pale after a long, sleepless night, in which, at least ten thousand times, she had relived her last day with Michael and the accident that followed. She felt as though she would never get away from it if she lived to be a thousand years old. And she felt at least a hundred that morning.

'You look as though you've been working too hard, my love.' Jacques smiled at her from behind the desk in his office. He was wearing his standard uniform. Impeccably tailored French blue jeans grafted to his body, black turtle-neck sweater, and suede St Laurent jacket. On him the combination looked perfect. 'Or are you staying up too late with our favourite doctor?' He was an old friend of Peter's and he had already grown fond of Marie.

She smiled in answer and sipped the coffee he had poured. It was strong and dark, a café filtre, the only kind he ever served. He brought it over from France, along with countless other precious items without which he could not survive. She loved to tease him about his chauvinism and his expensive tastes. She had bought him toilet paper imprinted with the Gucci logo for his birthday. That and a briefcase which was slightly more his style. But he had liked the joke too.

'No, I haven't been partying. Maybe too much time in the darkroom.'

'Crazy girl. A woman like you should be out dancing.'

'Later. After I do some more work.' She started describing her new idea for a series on San Francisco street life, and he nodded in satisfaction.

'*Ça me plait*, Marie. I like it. Okay. Do it as soon as you can.' He was about to go into the details with her when there was a knock on his office door. It was his secretary, making hushing gestures. 'Aha! Probably one of your girls.' Marie loved to tease him, and he grinned and shrugged 'helplessly' as he walked around the desk to confer with the secretary just beyond the door. He listened to her whispered words, and then nodded, looking exceedingly pleased. He gave one final affirmative sign, and then walked back in and sat down, looking at Marie as though he were about to bestow a wonderful gift.

'I have a surprise for you, Marie.' And with that, she heard another knock on the door. 'Someone very important is interested in your work.' The door swung open before she fully had time to understand the meaning of his words, or their implication, and suddenly she found herself turning around to face Michael. She almost gasped, and felt the cup of steaming dark coffee tremble in her hand. He was very handsome in a dark blue suit, white shirt, and dark tie, and he looked every bit the magnate he was.

Marie set down the coffee cup to take his outstretched hand, and he was impressed with how poised she looked in Jacques' office. It hardly seemed possible that this was the girl who had answered the phone the night before, with agony in her voice, begging him to leave her alone.

Maybe she had other problems, with men perhaps. Maybe she'd been drunk. You never knew with artists. But none of his thoughts showed on his face, nor did her discomfort show on hers.

'I'm awfully glad to meet you at last. You've led me a merry chase, Miss Adamson. But then, as talented as you are, I suppose you have that right.' He gave her a benevolent smile, and she looked at Jacques, who was standing behind his desk extending a hand towards Michael. He was extremely impressed by Cotter-Hillyard's interest in Marie's work. Michael had made it quite clear to the secretary that his interest was professional, not for his own collection or even for his office. He wanted her work for one of the largest projects the company had ever done, and Jacques was overwhelmed. He could hardly wait until Marie heard. Even her cool reserve would be shattered over this. But she looked as unruffled as ever, at least for the moment. She sat very still in her chair, avoiding Michael's gaze, and with an icy little smile on her lips. 'May I get right to the point and explain to you both what I have in mind?'

'But of course.' Jacques waved at the secretary to pour Michael some coffee, and sat back to listen as Michael went on to explain in full detail what he wanted to do with Marie's work. It was a project any artist would have fought for, but at the end of the discussion Marie seemed unmoved. She nodded very quietly and then turned to look at Michael.

'I'm afraid my answer is still the same, Mr Hillyard.'

'You've discussed this before?' Jacques looked confused, and Michael was quick to explain.

'One of my associates, my mother, and I myself have all

233

contacted Miss Adamson at her home. We've mentioned this project to her, though only briefly, and her answer has been a firm no. I was hoping to change her mind.'

Jacques looked at her in stupefaction. Marie was shaking her head.

'I'm sorry but I can't do it.'

'But why not?' cried Jacques. He was almost frantic.

'Because I don't want to.'

'May we at least know your reasons?' Michael's voice was very smooth, and it held something new, the knowledge of his own power. Marie was irritated to find she liked this side of him. But it did nothing to change her mind.

'Call me a temperamental artist if you like. Whatever. The answer is still no. And it will stay no.' She put down her cup, looked at the two men, and stood up. She held out a hand to Michael and sombrely shook his hand. 'Thank you, though, for your interest. I'm sure you'll find the right person for your project. Maybe Jacques can recommend someone. There are several wonderful artists and photographers associated with this gallery.'

'But I'm afraid we only want you.' He sounded stubborn now, and Jacques looked apologetic, but Marie was not going to lose this battle. She had already lost too much.

'That's unreasonable of you, Mr Hillyard. And childish. You're going to have to find someone else. I won't work with you. It's as simple as that.'

'Will you work with someone else in the firm?'

She shook her head again and walked to the doorway.

'Will you at least give it some thought?'

Her back was to Michael as she paused for an instant in the doorway, but once again she only shook her head

234

and then they heard the word 'no' as she disappeared with her little dog. Michael did not waste a moment with the stunned gallery owner, who remained seated at his desk. He ran out into the street after her, shouting 'Wait!' He wasn't even sure why he was doing it, but he felt he had to. He got to her side as she began to walk hurriedly away. 'May I walk with you for a moment?'

'If you'd like, but there isn't much point.' She was looking straight ahead, avoiding his eyes as he strode doggedly beside her.

'Why are you doing this? It just doesn't make any sense. Is it personal? Something you know about our firm? A bad experience you've had? Something about me?'

'It doesn't make any difference.'

'Yes it does, damn it. It does.' He stopped her and held fast to her arm. 'I have a right to know.'

'Do you?' They both seemed to stand there for an eternity, and finally she softened. 'All right. It's personal.'

'At least I know you're not crazy.'

She laughed and looked at him in amusement. '*How* do you know? Maybe I am.'

'Unfortunately, I don't think so. I just think you hate Cotter-Hillyard. Or me.' It was ridiculous though. Neither he nor the firm had had any bad press. They weren't involved in controversial projects, or with dubious governments. There was no reason for her to act like this. Maybe she'd had an affair with someone in the local office and had a grudge against him. It had to be something like that. Nothing else made sense.

'I don't hate you, Mr Hillyard.' She had waited a long time to say it as they walked along.

'You sure do a good act.' He smiled, and for the first time he looked like a boy again. Like the kid who used to tease with Ben in her apartment. That glimpse of the past tore at her heart and she looked away. 'Can I invite you out somewhere for a cup of coffee?' She was going to refuse, but maybe it would be better to get it over with once and for all. Maybe then he'd leave her alone.

'All right.' She suggested a place across the street, and they walked there with Fred at their heels. They both ordered espressos, and without thinking she handed him the sugar. She knew he took two, but he only thanked her, helped himself, and set the bowl down. It didn't seem unusual to him that she had known.

'You know, I can't explain it, but there's something odd about your work. It haunts me. As though I've seen it before, as though I already know it, as though I understand what you meant and what you saw when you took the pictures. Does that make any sense?'

Yes. A great deal of sense. He had always had a wonderful understanding of her paintings.

She sighed and nodded. 'Yes, I guess it does. They're supposed to do something like that to you.'

'But they do something more. I can't explain it. It's as though I already know . . . well, your work. I don't know. It sounds crazy when I say it.'

But don't you know me? Don't you know these eyes? She found herself wanting to ask him those questions as they quietly drank their coffee and discussed her work.

'I get the terrible feeling you're not going to give in. You won't, will you?' Sadly, she shook her head. 'Is it money?'

'Of course not.'

'I didn't think so.' He didn't even mention the enormous contract he had in his pocket. He knew it would do him no good, and perhaps make things worse. 'I wish I knew what it was.'

'Just my eccentricities. My way of lashing out at the past.' She was shocked at her own honesty but he didn't seem to be.

'I thought it was something like that.' They were both at peace now as they sat in the little Italian restaurant. There was a sadness to the meeting too, a bitter-sweet quality Michael couldn't understand. 'My mother was very taken with your work. And she's not easy to please.' Marie smiled at his choice of words.

'No, she isn't. Or so I've heard. She drives a very hard bargain.'

'Yes, but she made the business what it is today. It's a pleasure to take over from her. Like a perfectly run ship.'

'How fortunate for you.' She sounded bitter again, and once more Michael didn't understand. In a little nervous gesture he ran his hand across a tiny scar on his temple, and abruptly Marie set down her coffee cup and glanced at him.

'What's that?'

'What?'

'That scar.' She couldn't take her eyes from it. She knew exactly what it was. It had to be from . . .

'It's nothing. I've had it for a while.'

'It doesn't look very old.'

'A couple of years.' He looked embarrassed. 'Really. It was nothing. A minor accident with some friends.' He tried to brush it off, and Marie wanted to throw her coffee in his face. Son of a bitch. A minor accident. Thanks, baby.

Now I know everything I need to know. She picked up her handbag, looked down at him icily for a moment, and held out her hand.

'Thanks for a lovely time, Mr Hillyard. I hope you enjoy your stay.'

'You're leaving? Did I say something wrong?' Jesus. She was impossible. What the hell was wrong with her now? What had he said? And then he found himself shocked at the look in her eyes.

'As a matter of fact, you did.' She in turn was shocked at her own words. 'I read about that accident of yours, and I don't think it was what anyone would call minor. Those two friends of yours were pretty well banged up, from what I understand. Don't you give a damn about anything, Michael? Don't you care any more about anything but your bloody business?'

'What the hell is wrong with you? And what business is it of yours?'

'I'm a human being, and you're not. That's what I hate about you.'

'You are crazy.'

'No, mister. Not any more.' And with that, she turned on her heel and walked out, leaving Michael to stare at her. And then, as though pushed by an invisible force, he found himself on his feet and running after her. He had dropped a five-dollar bill on the little marble table and fled in her wake. He had to tell her. He had to . . . No, it hadn't been a minor accident. The woman he loved had been killed. But what right did she have to know that? He didn't get a chance to tell her, though, because when he reached the street, she was just slipping into a cab.

28

She had just got to the beach and was setting up her tripod when she suddenly saw the figure approach. His determined step puzzled her until she realised who it was. Michael, damn it. He walked down the beach and over the small dune, until he stood in front of her, blocking her view.

'I have something to say to you.'

'I don't want to hear it.'

'That's tough. Because I'm going to tell you anyway. You have no right to pry into my private life and tell me what kind of human being I am. You don't even know me.' Her words had tormented him all through the night. And he had found out from her answering service where she was. He wasn't even sure why he had come here, but he had known he had to. 'What right do you have to make judgements about me, damn you?'

'None at all. But I don't like what I see.' She was cool and removed as she changed lenses.

'And just exactly what do you see?'

'An empty shell. A man who cares about nothing but his work. A man who cares about no one, loves nothing, gives nothing, is nothing.'

'You bitch, what the hell do you know about what I am and do and feel? What makes you think you're so together?' She stepped around him and focused on the next dune. 'Damn you, listen to me!' He reached for her camera and she dodged him, turning on him in fury.

'Why don't you get the hell out of my life?' Like you have for the last two years, you bastard . . .

'I'm not in your life. I'm trying to buy some work from you. That's all I want. I don't want your pronouncements about my personality, or my life, or anything else. I just want to buy some stinking photographs.' He was almost trembling, he was so angry, and all she did was walk past him to the portfolio that lay on a blanket on the beach. She unzipped it, looked into a file, and pulled out a photograph. Then she stood up and handed it to him.

'Here. It's yours. Do whatever the hell you want with it. Then leave me alone.'

Without saying a word he turned on his heel and walked back to the car he'd left parked in the road.

She never turned to look at him, but went back to work until the light began to dim and she could work no longer. Then she drove back to her apartment, scrambled some eggs, heated some coffee, and headed for the darkroom. She went to bed at two in the morning, and when the phone rang, she didn't answer it. Even if it was Peter, she didn't care. She didn't want to speak to anyone. And she was going back to the beach at nine the next morning. She set her alarm for eight, and fell asleep the moment she hit the bed. She had freed herself of something back there on the beach. And she had to be honest with herself. Even if she hated him, at least she had seen him. In an odd way, it was a relief.

She showered and dressed in less than half an hour the next morning. She was wearing wellworn work clothes, and she sipped her coffee as she read the paper. She left the apartment on schedule, a few minutes before nine, and she was already thinking of her work as she hurried down the steps with Fred. It was only when she reached the foot of the steps that she looked up and gasped. Across the street was an enormous billboard mounted on a truck, driven by Michael Hillyard. He was smiling as he watched her, and she sat down on the last step and started to laugh. He was really crazy. He had taken the photograph she had given him, had it blown up and mounted, and then driven it to her door. He was grinning as he left the truck and walked towards her. And she was still laughing when he sat down next to her on the step.

'How do you like it?'

'I think you're a scream.'

'Yeah, but doesn't it look good? Just think how your other stuff would look blown up and mounted in the medical centre buildings. Wouldn't that be a thrill?' He was a thrill, but she couldn't tell him that. 'Come on, let's go have breakfast and talk.' This morning he wasn't taking no for an answer. He had cleared his morning schedule just for her. And she found his determination touching, as well as amusing. She just wasn't in the mood for another fight.

'I should say no, but I won't.'

'That's better. Can I give you a ride?'

'In that?' She pointed to the truck and started laughing again.

'Sure. Why not?'

So they hopped into the cab of the truck and headed down to Fisherman's Wharf for breakfast. Trucks were a familiar sight there, and no one was going to walk off with a photograph that size.

Surprisingly, it was a very pleasant breakfast. They both put aside the war, at least until the coffee.

'Well, have I convinced you?' He looked very sure of himself as he smiled at her over his cup.

'No. But I've had a very nice time.'

'I suppose I should be grateful for small favours, but that's not my style.'

'What is your style? In your own words.'

'You mean you're giving me a chance to explain myself, instead of your telling me what I am?' He was teasing, but there was an edge to his voice. She had come too close to home with some of her comments the day before. 'All right, I'll tell you. In some ways you're right. I live for my work.'

'Why? Don't you have anything else in your life?'

'Not really. Most successful people probably don't. There just isn't room.'

'That's stupid. You don't have to exchange your life for success. Some people have both.'

'Do you?'

'Not entirely. But maybe one day I will. I know it's possible anyway.'

'Maybe it is. Maybe my incentive isn't what it used to be.' Her eyes grew soft at the words. 'My life has changed a great deal in the last few years. I didn't wind up doing any of the things I once planned to. But . . . I've had some damn nice compensations.' Like becoming president of Cotter-Hillyard, but he was embarrassed to say it.

'I see. I take it you're not married.'

'Nope. No time. No interest.' How lovely. Then it was probably just as well they hadn't married after all.

'You make it sound very cut-and-dried.'

'For the moment it is. And you?'

'I'm not married either.'

'You know, for all your condemnation of my way of life, I can't see that yours is all that different from mine. You're just as obsessed with your work as I am with mine, just as lonely, just as locked away in your own little world. So why are you so hard on me? It's not very fair.' His voice was soft but reproachful.

'I'm sorry. Maybe you're right.' It was hard to argue the point. And then, as she thought over what he had said, she felt his hand on hers, and it was like a knife in her heart. She pulled it away with a stricken look in her eyes. And he looked unhappy again.

'You're a very difficult woman to understand.'

'I suppose I am. There's a lot that would be impossible to explain.'

'You ought to try me some time. I'm not the monster you seem to think I am.'

'I'm sure you aren't.' As she looked at him, all she wanted to do was cry. This was like saying goodbye to him. It was knowing, all over again, what she could never have. But maybe she would understand it better now. Maybe she would finally be able to let go. With a small sigh she looked at her watch. 'I really should get to work.'

'Have I come any closer to a yes in answer to our proposal?'

'I'm afraid not.'

He hated to admit it, but he would have to give up. He knew now that she would never change her mind. All his efforts had been for nothing. She was one very tough woman. But he liked her. He was surprised just how much, when she let down her guard. There was a softness and a kindness that drew him to her in a way that he hadn't been drawn to anyone in years. 'Do you suppose that I could talk you into having dinner with me, Marie? Sort of a consolation prize, since I don't get my deal?' She laughed softly at the look on his face and patted his hand.

'I'd like that some time. But not just now. I'm afraid I'll be going out of town.' Damn. He had really lost this one, round after round.

'Where are you going?'

'Back east. To take care of some personal business.' She had made the decision in the last half hour. But now she knew what she had to do. It was not a question of burying the past, but unburying it. In a way, Peter had been right. And now she was sure. She had to 'heal it' as he had said.

'I'll call the next time I'm in San Francisco. I hope I'll have better luck.'

Maybe. And maybe by then I'll be Mrs Peter Gregson. Maybe by then I'll be healed. And it won't matter any more. Not at all.

They walked quietly back to the truck, and he dropped her off at her apartment. She said very little when she left him. She thanked him for breakfast, shook his hand, and walked back up the steps. He had lost. And as he watched her go, he felt an overwhelming sadness. It was as though he had lost something very special. He wasn't quite sure what. A business deal, a woman, a friend? Something. For the first time in a long time, he felt unbearably alone. He shoved the truck into gear, and drove grimly through Pacific Heights and up the hill back to his hotel.

Marie was already on the phone to Peter Gregson.

'Tonight? Darling, I have a meeting.' He sounded flustered, and he was in a hurry between patients.

'Then come after the meeting. It's important. I'm leaving tomorrow.'

'For where? For how long?' He sounded worried.

'I'll tell you when I see you. Tonight?'

'All right, all right. Around eleven. But that's really foolish, Marie. Can't this thing wait?'

'No.' It had waited two years, and she had been crazy to let it sit for that long.

'All right. I'll see you tonight.' He had hung up in a hurry, and she called the airline to make a reservation, and the vet to make arrangements for Fred.

29

Marie had been lucky. There had been a cancellation that afternoon, so now she found herself sitting in the familiar, comfortable room she had not visited in months. She sat back against the couch and stretched her legs towards the unlit fireplace, as though by habit, staring absently at her feet in delicate sandals. Her thoughts were so far away that she didn't hear Faye come in.

'Are you meditating or just falling asleep?'

Marie looked up with a smile as Faye sat down in the seat across from her. 'Just thinking. It's good to see you.' Actually, she was surprised how good it felt to be back. There was a feeling of homecoming in just being there, an ease about fitting back into an old and happy groove. She had had some good moments in that room, as well as some difficult ones.

'Should I tell you that you look marvellous, or are you already tired of hearing it?' Faye beamed at the girl, and Marie laughed.

'I never get tired of hearing it.' Only with Faye would she dare to be that honest. 'I guess you want to know why I'm here.' Her face sobered as she looked into the other woman's eyes.

'The question certainly crossed my mind.' They exchanged another rapid smile, and then Marie seemed to get lost in her own thoughts again.

'I've seen Michael.'

'He found you?' Faye sounded stunned, and more than a little impressed.

'Yes, and no. He found Marie Adamson. That's all he knows. One of his underlings has been hounding me about my work. Cotter-Hillyard is doing a medical centre out here, and they seem to want my photographs blown up to enormous proportions as part of the decor.'

'That's very flattering, Marie.'

'Who gives a damn, Faye? What do I care what he thinks of my work?' But that wasn't entirely true either. She had always basked in the warmth of his praise, and even now there was a certain satisfaction in knowing that she had caught his attention again, with her work. 'Anyway, his mother was out here a while back, and I told her the same thing I'd been telling them. No. I'm not interested. I won't sell to them. I won't work with them. Period.'

'And they've pursued it?'

'Ardently.'

'That must feel good. Do any of them realise who you are?'

'Ben didn't. But Michael's mother did. I think that's why she set up the meeting.' Marie fell silent and stared at her feet. She was a long way away, back in that hotel room, the day she had seen Marion.

'What did it feel like when you saw her?'

'Terrible. It reminded me of everything she'd done to me. I hated her.' But there was more in her voice, and Faye heard it.

'And?'

'All right.' Marie looked up with sigh. 'It made everything hurt all over again. It reminded me of how much I

247

had once wanted her to like me, to love me even, to accept me as Michael's wife.'

'And she still rejected you?'

'I'm not sure. I guess so. She's sick now. She seems different. She seemed almost sorry about what she'd done. I gather Michael hasn't been particularly happy in the last two years.'

'And how did you feel about that?'

'Relieved.' She said it with a soft, tired sigh. 'And then I realised that it doesn't make any difference how he's been. It's all over for us, Faye. All of that was years ago. We're different people now. And the fact is that he never came back to me. He probably wouldn't even be running after me for my work now, if he knew who I really was – who I used to be. But I'm not Nancy McAllister any more, Faye. And he's not the Michael I knew.'

'How do you know that?'

'I saw him. He's callous, hard, driven, cold. Oh I don't know, maybe there's something there. But there's a lot of new stuff too.'

'How about pain? Loss? Disappointment? Grief?'

'No, Faye, how about betrayal, abandonment, desertion, cowardice? Those are the real issues, aren't they?'

'I don't know. Are they? Is that how you still feel when you see him?'

'Yes.' Her voice was hard again now. 'I hate him.'

'Then you must still care for him a great deal.' Marie started to deny it, but then she shook her head as tears sprang to her eyes. She looked at Faye for a long time without speaking. 'Nancy, do you still love him?' She had purposely used the old name.

The girl sighed deeply and let her head fall back against the couch before answering, and when she did, she looked at the ceiling and spoke in a monotone. 'Maybe Nancy still loves him, what little bit of her is left. But Marie doesn't. I have a new life now. I can't afford to love him any more.' She looked up at Fay with sorrow.

'Why not?'

'Because he doesn't love me. Because that's not real. I have to let it go now. Totally, completely. I know that. That isn't why I came here today, to cry on your shoulder about still being in love with Michael. But I needed to tell someone how I feel. I can't really talk to Peter about it; it would upset him too much, and I needed to get some of this off my chest.'

'I'm glad you did come, Marie. But I'm not sure you can just decide to let something go as simply as that, and have it fall away from you from one moment to another.'

'In truth, it fell away from me two years ago, I just didn't let it go until now. I told myself I had, but I hadn't. So . . .' She sat up straight again and looked squarely at Faye. 'I'm leaving for Boston tomorrow to attend to some business.'

'What kind of business.'

'Letting-go business.' She smiled for the first time in an hour. 'There are some things I left unfinished back there, some things that Michael and I shared. I've let them stand as a monument to us, because I always thought he'd be back. Now I have to go back there and take care of it.'

'Do you really think you're ready to handle that?'

'Yes.' She sounded sure of herself, even to Faye.

'Is that what you really want to do?'

'Yes.'

'You don't want to tell Michael who you are, or rather who you were, and see what happens?'

Marie almost shuddered. 'Never. That's over. Forever. And besides,' she sighed again, and looked down at her hands, 'that wouldn't be fair to Peter.'

'You have to think about being fair to Marie.'

'That's why I'm going to Boston tomorrow. But I keep thinking, too, that maybe after this I'll be free to make some kind of real commitment to Peter. He's such a nice man, Faye. He's done so much for me.'

'But you don't love him.'

It was frightening to hear someone else say the words, and Marie instantly shook her head. 'No, no, I do!'

'Then why the problem making a commitment?'

'Michael always stood between us.'

'That's too easy, Marie. That's a cop out.'

'I don't know.' She paused for a long time. 'Something always stopped me. Something isn't . . . there. I guess I haven't really let myself be there. In some ways I was waiting for Michael, and in some ways it just hasn't felt . . . I don't know, it just doesn't feel right, Faye. Maybe it's me.'

'Why do you think it doesn't feel right?'

'Well, I'm not sure, but sometimes I get the feeling that he doesn't know me. He knows me, Marie Adamson, because that's the person he helped create. He doesn't know the person I was or the things I cared about before the accident.'

'Could you teach him about that, Marie?'

'Maybe. But I'm not sure he wants to know. He makes me feel loved, but not for myself.'

'Well, there are a lot of other fish out there, you know.'

'Yes, but he's a good man, and there's no reason why it shouldn't work.'

'No. Unless you don't love him.'

'But I *do* love him.' She was getting agitated as they spoke.

'Then relax, and let that problem take care of itself. You can come back here and discuss it with me, if you like. First, let's deal with your feelings about Michael.'

'I just want to get this trip east over with. Then I'll be free.'

'All right, then do that, but come and see me when you get back. Sound okay to you?'

'Very okay.' In a way, she was glad to be back. It was a relief.

With that, Faye looked at her watch regretfully and stood up. It had already been an hour and a half, and she had to teach at the university in an hour. 'Will you call for an appointment when you get back?'

'The minute I do.'

'All right then, and be good to yourself when you go back there. Don't torment yourself about the past. And if you have any problems, call me.'

It was comforting to know that she could do that, and as she left her mood felt lighter than it had all afternoon. Their conversation was going to make it easier for her to explain her decision to Peter.

30

'Boston? But why, Marie? I don't understand.' Peter looked tired and irritable, which was rare. But it had been a long day and a tiresome meeting. All this nonsense about the new medical centre. And he had to meet with the architects in the morning. Why did he have to be on the committee? He had better things to do with his time. 'I think you're crazy to make this trip.'

'No, I'm not. I have to. And I'm ready. The past is over for me. Completely.'

'So completely over that when we almost had an accident in the car the other day you had hysterics for an hour. It's not over.'

'You have to trust me. I'm going to do the only thing I've left unfinished, and then I'll be free. I'll be back the day after tomorrow.'

'It's insane.'

'No. It's not.' Her voice was so quiet and firm that it stopped him, and he sat back on the couch with a tired sigh. Maybe she knew what she was doing after all.

'All right. I don't understand. But I have to hope that you know what you're doing. Will you be okay back there?'

'I'll be fine. Trust me.'

'I do, darling. It's not that I don't trust you. It's that . . . oh, I don't know. I don't want you to get hurt. May I ask you a totally crazy question?'

Oh Jesus. She hoped it wasn't that one. Not yet. But that

wasn't what he had on his mind as he watched her carefully from the couch. 'Go ahead.' She waited, as though
for surgery.

'Do you know that Michael Hillyard is in town?'

'I do.' She was strangely calm.

'Have you seen him?'

'Yes. He came to the gallery. He wants me to do some
work for a new project of his out here. I turned him down.'

'Did he know who you were?'

'No.'

'Why didn't you tell him?'

Now was the time for her to tell him about the deal with
Michael's mother, but it was too late. It didn't matter any
more. 'It didn't make any difference. The past is over.'

'Are you sure?'

'Yes. That's why I'm going to Boston.'

'Then I'm glad.' And then he looked momentarily
worried. 'Does the trip have anything to do with Hillyard?'
But he knew it couldn't. He was seeing Michael Hillyard
in the morning.

Marie firmly shook her head. 'No. Not the way you mean.
It has to do with my past, Peter. And it has to do with only
me. I don't want to say any more about it than that.'

'Then I'll respect that.'

'Thank you.'

He left quietly, with a gentle kiss. He sensed that she
needed to be alone.

It was a peaceful night, and she still felt that way when
she dropped off Fred at the vet the next morning. She
knew exactly what she was doing, and why, and she knew
it was right.

She caught the plane with plenty of time to spare, and she arrived in Boston at nine p.m. local time. She thought about driving out that night, but that was asking too much of lady luck. So she put it off until the following morning. She had already rented the car. All she had to do was drive there, and then drive back. She was taking the last plane home.

She felt like a woman with a sacred mission as she went to bed in the motel that night. She had no desire to see the city, to call anyone, or go anywhere. She wasn't really there. It was all like a dream, a two-year-old dream, and she would relive it only one last time.

31

'Dr Gregson?'

'Yes?' He was still distracted when his secretary came into the room. He had just spoken to Marie at the airport. He still had a queasy feeling about the trip, but he had to respect her feelings about something as personal as this. Still, he would feel better when she got back the next day. He looked up and tried to pay attention to his nurse 'Yes?'

'A Mr Hillyard here to see you. He say's you're expecting him. And there are three of his associates with him.'

'Fine. Send him in.' Christ. That was all he needed now. But why not? At least he'd get a look at the boy. He was actually young enough to be his son. What a miserable thought. He wondered if Marie ever thought of that.

The four men came in and shook hands with the doctor, and the meeting got underway. They wanted to enlist his support to make their new medical centre a success. They already had fifteen of the more illustrious doctors on their 'team', and there was no doubt that the buildings would be ideally located, and magnificently appointed. It was an easy choice to make. Gregson agreed to take new offices there, and was willing to talk to some of his colleagues. But even though his responses were mechanical, he watched Michael with fascination throughout the meeting. So this was Michael Hillyard. He didn't look like a formidable opponent. But he looked young, and handsome, and very sure of himself. And in an unsettling way, Peter began to realise how much like Marie he was. There was a similarity of energy, of determination, and even of humour. The realisation made Peter feel shut out, and suddenly, too, he understood. He sat very quietly for a long time, watching Michael and saying nothing at all. He wasn't even listening to the meeting any more; he was adjusting to the reality he had avoided for so long. It made him wonder, too, exactly why Marie had gone east that morning. Was it really to destroy the last shreds of the past, or to honour them?

For the first time, Peter wondered if he had a right to interfere. Just watching Michael, he felt as though he were seeing another side of Marie, a side he had no knowledge of. This man represented a part of her life that he didn't even understand, a part he had never wanted to know. He had wanted her to be Marie Adamson. She had never been Nancy to him. She had been someone new, someone who had been born in his hands. But now he recognised there was someone else. All the pieces of the puzzle began to fit, and he felt a sense of resignation as well as loss. He had been fighting an unfightable war, and he had been trying to recapture his own past. Marie was indeed someone new, but there were glimpses in her of the woman he had once loved, the woman who had died . . . he had cherished those glimpses of Livia as well as the reality of the girl he had brought to life. Maybe he had no right to do that. He had never before had such free rein with a patient, because Marie had had no one to rely on but him. It allowed him to be everything to her . . . everything except what he wanted to be now. Watching Michael, he realised that his own role in Marie's life had been very like a father's. She didn't realise it yet, but one day she would.

The meeting was over when they stood up to shake hands, and Michael's three associates were already out of the office, waiting for him in the anteroom beyond. Gregson and Michael were exchanging pleasantries, when suddenly everything stopped, and Michael stared fixedly at something over the older man's shoulder. It was the painting she had been doing two years before . . . it was to have been his wedding present . . . it had been stolen from her apartment by those nurses after she died. And now it was in this man's office, and it was finished. Mesmerised, Michael walked towards it before Gregson could stop him. But nothing would have stopped him. He stood there, staring, looking for the signature, as though he already knew what he would see. There, in tiny letters in the corner, were the words. Marie Adamson.

'Oh, my God . . . oh, my God . . .' It was all he could say as Gregson watched him. 'But how? It isn't . . . oh, Jesus . . . God . . . why didn't someone tell me? What in . . .' But he understood now. They had lied to him. She was alive. Different. But alive. No wonder she had hated him. He hadn't even suspected. But he had been haunted by something in her, in her photographs, all that time. There were tears in his eyes as he turned to look at Gregson.

Peter looked at him sorrowfully, afraid of what would come. 'Leave her alone, Hillyard. It's all over for her now. She's been through enough.' But even as he said it, the words lacked conviction. Just looking at Michael that morning, he wasn't sure that Michael should stay away from her at all. And something deep inside him wanted to tell him where she was.

But Michael was still staring at him with a look of

astonishment. 'They lied to me, Gregson. Did you know that? They lied to me. They told me she was dead.' His eyes were brimming with tears. 'I've spent two years like a dead man, working like a robot, wishing I had died instead of her, and all this time . . .' For a moment he couldn't go on, and Gregson looked away. 'And when I saw her this week, I never knew. I . . . it must have killed her . . . no wonder she hates me. She does, doesn't she?' Michael sank into a chair, staring at the painting.

'No. She doesn't hate you. She just wants to put it behind her. She has a right to do that.' And I have a right to her. He wanted to say the words, but he couldn't bring himself to. But suddenly it was as though Michael had heard his thoughts. Michael had just remembered what he'd heard about Marie having a sponsor, a plastic surgeon. The words suddenly rang in his ears, and just as suddenly the anger and pain of two years was upon him. He jumped to his feet and grabbed Gregson's lapels.

'Wait a minute, damn it. What right do you have to tell me that she wants to "put it behind her"? How the hell do you know? How can you even begin to understand what we had together? How can you know what any of that meant to her, or to me? If I get out of her life without saying a word, then you have it all your way, is that it, Gregson? Is that what you want? Well to hell with you! This is my life you're playing with, mister, and it seems to me that enough people have played with it already. The only person who can tell me she wants this thing finished is Nancy.'

'She already told you to leave her alone.' His voice was quiet, as he looked into Michael's eyes.

Michael backed away from him now, but there was hope

mixed in with the anger and confusion in his face. For the first time in two years there was something alive there. 'No, Gregson. Marie Adamson told me to leave her alone Nancy McAllister hasn't said a word to me in two years. And she's going to have a lot of explaining to do. Why didn't she call me? Why didn't she write? Why didn't she let me know she was alive? And why did they tell me she was dead? Was that her doing, or . . . or someone else's? And as a matter of fact,' he hated to ask the question because he already knew what he would hear, 'who paid for her surgery?' His eyes never left Gregson's face.

'I don't know the answers to some of your questions, Mr Hillyard.'

'And the ones you do have answers to?'

'I'm not at liberty to—'

'Don't give me that—' Michael advanced on him again, and Peter put up a hand.

'Your mother has paid for all of Marie's surgery, and for her living expenses since the accident. It was a very hand-some gift.' It was what Michael had feared, but it didn't really come as a shock. It fitted the rest of the picture he saw now, and maybe in some insane, misguided way his mother had thought she was doing it for him. At least she had led him back to Nancy now. He looked at Gregson again, and nodded.

'And what about you? Just exactly what is your relation-ship with Nancy?' Now he wanted to know it all.

'I don't know that that concerns you.'

'Look, damn it . . .' His hands were at the other man's coat again, and Peter held up a hand in defeat.

'Why don't we stop this now? The answers are all in

259

Marie's hands. What she wants, who she wants. She may not want either one of us, you know. For whatever reasons, you haven't contacted her in two years, nor has she contacted you. And as for me, I'm almost twice her age, and for all I know, suffering from a Pygmalion complex.' He sat down heavily in his desk chair and smiled ruefully. 'I almost think she could do better than either one of us.'

'Maybe, but this time I want to hear it from her myself.' He looked at his watch. 'I'm going over to her place right now.'

'It won't do you much good.' Peter watched him and stroked his beard. He almost wished the boy luck. Almost. 'She called me from the airport just before you got here this morning.'

Once again Michael looked shocked. 'Now what? Where was she going?'

For a long moment Peter Gregson hesitated. He didn't have to tell him anything. He didn't have to . . . 'She was going to Boston.'

Michael looked at him for one moment, and a shadow of a smile flitted through his eyes as he dashed for the door. He stopped, glanced back, and saluted Peter with a full-blown smile. 'Thank you.'

32

She was up at dawn. Awake, alive. She felt better than she had in years. She was almost free now. In a few hours she would be. As though that childish promise had held her all this time. And only because she had let it. Its only power had been the power she had given it.

She didn't even bother with breakfast. She only drank two cups of coffee, and got into the rented car. She could be there in two hours, by ten o'clock. Back at the hotel at noon. She could catch a plane back to San Francisco and be home by late afternoon. She might even be able to pick up Peter at the office and surprise him. Poor man, he had been so patient about the trip.

She found herself thinking about him as she drove along, wishing she had given him more, wishing she had been able to. Maybe after today that would change too. Or was it that . . . She didn't even let herself finish the question. Of course she loved him. That wasn't the point.

She drove through the New England countryside, barely noticing anything she passed. The landscape was still grey and dark; the new leaves had not yet emerged. It was as though the countryside too had lain buried for two years. It was nine-thirty when she passed Revere Beach, where the fair had been, and she felt a little jolt in her heart when she recognised the place. She followed an old road which wandered along the coast, and then she came to a stop, and got out of the car. She was stiff, but not tired.

She was exhilarated, and nervous. She had to do this . . . had to . . . she could already see the tree from where she stood. She stood staring at it for a long time, as though it held all the secrets, knew her story too well, as though it had waited for her return. She walked slowly towards it, as though going to meet an old friend. But it was no longer a friend. Like everything and everyone she had once loved, it was a stranger. It was just another marker on Nancy McAllister's grave.

She stopped when she reached it, and then walked the last steps across the sand to the rock. It was still there. It hadn't moved. Nothing had. Only she and Michael had moved, in opposite directions and to different worlds. She stood there for a very long time, as though trying to summon the strength and the courage to do it. And at last she bent down and began to push. The rock moved after a few moments, and quickly, with a stick, she dug under it for what she sought. But there was nothing there. She dropped the rock, breathless, and then with fresh strength, she pushed it again, until this time she could see that they were gone. Someone had already taken the beads. She let the rock slip back into place just as she heard his voice.

'You can't have them. They belong to someone else. To someone I loved. To someone I never forgot.' There were tears in Michael's eyes as he spoke to her. He had waited half the night for her to come. It had taken a chartered jet to get him here before she arrived. But he would have flown on his own wings if he had had to. He held out a hand now, and she saw the beads, still caked with the sand from under the rock. Her own eyes filled with tears when she saw them. 'I promised never to say goodbye. I never did.' His eyes never left hers as he stood there.

'You never tried to find me.'

'They told me you were dead.'

'I promised never to see you again if . . . if they gave me a new face. I promised because I knew you'd find me. And then . . . you didn't.'

'I would have, if I'd known. Do you remember your promise to me?'

She closed her eyes and spoke solemnly, like a child, and for the first time in a long time, it was the voice of Nancy McAllister, the voice he had loved, not the smooth new one she had learned. 'I promise never to forget what lies buried here. Or what it stands for.'

'Did you forget?' The tears were sliding slowly from his eyes now. He was thinking of Gregson, and of the two years that had passed.

But she shook her head. 'No. But I tried very hard to.'

'Are you willing to remember now? Nancy, will you . . .' But then he couldn't speak. He only walked towards her and took her very tightly into his arms. 'Oh God, Nancy, I love you. I always have. I thought I would die when you died . . . when I thought you had. I died the moment they told me.'

But she was crying too hard to speak, remembering the endless days and months and years of waiting for him, and then giving up hope. She held him tightly, like a child holds a doll, as though she would never let go. And at last she caught her breath and smiled. 'Darling, I love you, too. I always thought you'd find me.'

'Nancy . . . Marie . . . whatever the hell your name is!'

They both laughed like children through their tears. 'Will you please do me the honour of becoming my wife? This time like civilised people, at a wedding, with everyone there, and music and . . .' He was thinking of his mother's wedding only a few weeks before. It was odd how totally free of anger he was. He should have hated his mother for what she had done. Instead, he wanted to forgive. He had Nancy back now. That was all he cared about. He smiled down at her in his arms, thinking of their wedding. But she was shaking her head, and he thought his heart would stop.

'Do we really have to wait that long? Do all that stuff about music and people and—'

'Yes. Why not? Now. I don't want to wait again. I couldn't bear it. Every moment I'd be afraid that something would happen again. Maybe this time to you.'

He nodded silently and held her tight as the surf roared in softly and the pale eastern sun peeked through the clouds. He understood.

FAMILY ALBUM

Danielle Steel

Families are held together by blood, by obligation, by desire and sometimes, if you are very lucky, by love.

Everything happened so quickly for shipping heir Ward Thayer and screen star Faye Price. Within days they were in love and within weeks they were married. But how was Faye to choose between her Hollywood career and motherhood? How could she decide between fame and family? Faye's choice would not only change her life; it would shape the lives of generations to come.

From the uncertain post-war days when fortunes were swiftly made and as swiftly lost, through Hollywood in the storm-torn political years and the turmoil of the Vietnam era, right up to the present, *Family Album* follows the Thayer dynasty through generations of love and hope, strife and passion.

978-0-7515-4070-3

KALEIDOSCOPE

Danielle Steel

When Sam Walker returned from the front lines of World War Two, bringing with him his exquisite French bride, no one could have imagined that their fairytale love would end in such shattering tragedy . . .

Nine-year-old Hilary, the eldest of the orphaned Walker children, clung desperately to her two sisters – five-year-old Alexandra and baby Megan. However, before the year was out they would be painfully wrenched from her young arms. Cut off from love and security, Hilary swore she would one day track down the man who had destroyed her family, and find her beloved sisters again. But would they risk everything to confront a dark, forgotten past?

John Chapman – lawyer, prestigious private investigator – chosen to find the Walker sisters, embarks on a labyrinthine trail which leads him to Paris, New York and Boston. John knows that, at some point in their lives, the three sisters must face each other and the final, most devastating secret of all . . .

978-0-7515-4248-6

PALOMINO

Danielle Steel

From shattered dreams to lasting love . . .

Every time Samantha went back to the flat, John's words rang through her head – 'I can't live with you any more – I've got to get out.' He'd been seeing another woman, and now she was promising him the one thing Sam couldn't give: a child. The man she had shared her life with, her love and laughter, had lied to her.

When the agency gave her four months on a ranch she thought they were crazy. Did they think a holiday would change her? She knew she was wild and untameable, a lone free Palomino – until she met the man who could break any horse on the range and entered a world of endless and enduring love . . .

978-0-7515-4239-4

Other bestselling Danielle Steel titles available by mail:

☐ Kaleidoscope	Danielle Steel	£6.99
☐ Palomino	Danielle Steel	£6.99
☐ Family Album	Danielle Steel	£6.99
☐ Zoya	Danielle Steel	£6.99
☐ Going Home	Danielle Steel	£6.99
☐ Now and Forever	Danielle Steel	£6.99
☐ Loving	Danielle Steel	£6.99
☐ The Ring	Danielle Steel	£6.99
☐ Remembrance	Danielle Steel	£6.99

The prices shown above are correct at time of going to press. However, the publishers reserve the right to increase prices on covers from those previously advertised, without further notice.

-- sphere --

Please allow for postage and packing: **Free UK delivery.**
Europe; add 25% of retail price; Rest of World; 45% of retail price.

To order any of the above or any other Sphere titles, please call our credit card orderline or fill in this coupon and send/fax it to:

Sphere, P.O. Box 121, Kettering, Northants NN14 4ZQ
Fax: 01832 733076   Tel: 01832 737526
Email: aspenhouse@FSBDial.co.uk

☐ I enclose a UK bank cheque made payable to Sphere for £ . . . .
☐ Please charge £ . . . . . . to my Visa, Delta, Maestro.

☐☐☐☐☐☐☐☐☐☐☐☐☐☐☐☐☐

Expiry Date ☐☐☐☐   Maestro Issue No. ☐☐

NAME (BLOCK LETTERS please) . . . .
ADDRESS . . . .
. . . .
. . . .
Postcode . . . . Telephone . . . .
Signature . . . .

Please allow 28 days for delivery within the UK. Offer subject to price and availability.